S0-BSQ-823

BAEN BOOKS by KEITH LAUMER

Retief!
Odyssey (forthcoming)

KEITH LAUMER

RETIEF!

edited & compiled by
ERIC FLINT

RETIEF!

This is a work of fiction. All the characters and events portrayed in this book are fictional, and any resemblance to real people or incidents is purely coincidental.

Copyright © 2001 by the estate of Keith Laumer
"Aide Memoire" was first published in *IF*, July, 1962. "The Brass God" (aka "Retief, God-Speaker") was first published in *IF*, January, 1965. "The Castle of Light" was first published in *IF*, October, 1964. "Courier" (aka "The Frozen Planet") was first published in *IF*, September, 1961. "Cultural Exchange" was first published in *IF*, September, 1962. "Diplomat-at-Arms" was first published in *Fantastic*, January, 1960. "Native Intelligence" (aka "The Governor of Glave") was first published in *IF*, November, 1963. "Palace Revolution" (aka "Gambler's World") was first published in *IF*, November, 1961. "Policy" (aka "The Madman From Earth") was first published in *IF*, March, 1962. "The Prince and the Pirate" was first published in *IF*, August, 1964. "Protest Note" (aka "The Desert and the Stars") was first published in *IF*, November, 1962. "Protocol" (aka "The Yllian Way") was first published in *IF*, January, 1962. *Retief's War* was first serialized in *IF*, October–December, 1965, and published in novel form by Doubleday in 1966. "Saline Solution" was first published in *IF*, March, 1963. "Sealed Orders" (aka "Retief of Red-Tape Mountain") was first published in *IF*, February, 1962. "Ultimatum" (aka "Mightiest Qorn") was first published in *IF*, November, 1961. "Wicker Wonderland" (aka "The City That Grew in the Sea") was first published in *IF*, March, 1964.

All rights reserved, including the right to reproduce this book or portions thereof in any form.

A Baen Books Original

Baen Publishing Enterprises
P.O. Box 1403
Riverdale, NY 10471

ISBN: 978-0-7394-8740-2

Distributed by Simon & Schuster
1230 Avenue of the Americas
New York, NY 10020

Production by Windhaven Press, Auburn, NH
Printed in the United States of America

TABLE OF CONTENTS

———

PART V: MAGNAN MAKES GOOD!

EXTRAORDINARY DIPLOMATS

by David Drake

Keith Laumer was a perfectionist who lived on a two-acre island in the middle of an eighteen-acre Florida lake. He had what is almost certainly the world's largest collection of original bodystyle (that is, 1967–68) Mercury Cougars. (The picture in *The Faces of Science Fiction* shows him sitting in #44, but he reached that number many years before his death.)

Keep those independently verifiable facts in mind, in case something strikes you as improbable as you read on.

Keith wrote in most of the sub-genres within science fiction. Picking a few off the top of my head, there's alien invasion (*The House in November*), military SF (the Bolo series), parallel worlds (*Worlds of the Imperium*), space opera (*Galactic Odyssey*, one of my all-time favorite SF novels, and one of the very few to have a black hero)—

—And the Retief series, the most remarkable of the lot, because the stories are funny besides being . . . but we'll come to the "besides" later.

The main thing all of Keith's work has in common is its aura of realism. A writer ought to know what he's describing. There are plenty of writers who've seen and done things, but they can't make those things vivid to the reader. You feel the reality of a Laumer story.

And of course, he did have the knowledge. For example, the Bolo series so perfectly captures the awesome power of a tank that I figured the author had served in an armored unit at some point in his varied career. Nope. But part of Keith's World War II training (in what was then the US Army Air Corps) involved lying down in a slit trench while tanks drove over him. Which, when you think about it, is an even better way to come to appreciate tanks than riding inside one.

He also came by the diplomatic background of the Retief stories honestly, having served in the US Foreign Service in the late '50s as vice consul in Burma.

Burma was—and is—a fragment of British imperialism rather than a nation state. The area which the British administered from Rangoon included three major tribal groups, all of whom hated each other even more than they hated the British (after all, they'd known each other longer).

When the British left Burma in 1948, they handed the administration over to the tribe which happened to live in the neighborhood of Rangoon—thereby spawning national resistance movements in both the north and south of the country which continue active to this day. What passes for a Burmese central government is intensely xenophobic and handles internal protest by (for example) machinegunning crowds who are waiting outside hospitals for word on relatives machinegunned during earlier peaceful protests.

It was the practice of the diplomatic community of the time to pretend that Burma was a normal country, civilized according to Western standards. As a matter of fact, the Secretary General of the United Nations then was Burmese. (A similar process goes on today in regard to Iran. About the only people who publicly deny that Iran is civilized are the theocrats who lead Iran.)

The pretense would have been difficult to maintain for those diplomats stationed in Burma who went beyond the social whirl and actually learned something about the country. Of course, most of them didn't get out into the country. The US presence in Burma was just as remarkable as Burma itself.

The United State Foreign Service had gone through reorganizations both before and after World War II, leaving several different types of diplomats coexisting rather uncomfortably. The older and greater in the status, the less awareness of the realities of the modern international community and the greater scorn for pragmatists like Captain Keith Laumer, who'd transferred into the diplomatic service from the Air Force.

What I'm trying to imply with all this is that the incredible byzantine backgrounds of the Retief stories owe as much to Keith's memory as to his imagination.

The humor (sometimes pretty black humor, granted) and realism which pervade the Retief stories are both pretty obvious. Besides those things, the stories are sometimes constructed with very, very sneaky cleverness. I'll give one example (but I won't tell you what the story was).

Analog was always a squeaky-clean magazine (even before it became a deadly dull magazine). But back in the '70s, *Analog* ran a Retief story in which the native names were what appeared at first glance to be collections of unpronounceable consonants—a science fiction cliché for suggesting alien sounds.

If you looked very carefully, though (and to be quite honest, I didn't, until a linguist friend pointed it out to me) and noted the ways the natives mispronounced English words, it turned out that all those native names were scatological. John Campbell must have been spinning in his grave.

So what you have in your hands are some of the funniest, cleverest, and most (unfortunately) realistic stories ever written about life at the sharp end of international relations. You're about to have fun.

And who knows? You may also learn something that'll make the international news a little easier to understand.

David Drake
david-drake.com

Note: This essay is closely based on one I did for Keith in 1990. I had to change references to Keith to past tense. Nothing about international diplomacy has changed. Unfortunately.

D.A.D.

———◆———

David Drake is a sweet and lovable man who has dogs, cats, a wife, and one son. Among his published works are the Hammer's Slammers series of military science fiction and a number of novels using his background in the classics and his interest in ancient Rome. He has been a fan of Keith Laumer's work since 1959.

PART I:
IN THE END

Editor's Note: "Diplomat-at-Arms" is the very first Retief story that Laumer ever wrote, and depicts Retief as an old man toward the end of his career. It has a very different tone and feel from any of the other Retief stories. It's a matter of taste, of course, but this is my personal favorite of all of them.

DIPLOMAT-AT-ARMS

The cold white sun of Northroyal glared on pale dust and vivid colors in the narrow raucous street. Retief rode slowly, unconscious of the huckster's shouts, the kaleidoscope of smells, the noisy milling crowd. His thoughts were on events of long ago on distant worlds; thoughts that set his features in narrow-eyed grimness. His bony, powerful horse, unguided, picked his way carefully, with flaring nostrils, wary eyes alert in the turmoil.

The mount sidestepped a darting gamin and Retief leaned forward, patted the sleek neck. The job had some compensations, he thought; it was good to sit on a fine horse again, to shed the gray business suit—

A dirty-faced man pushed a fruit cart almost under the animal's head; the horse shied, knocked over the cart. At once a muttering crowd began to gather around the heavy-shouldered gray-haired man. He reined in and sat scowling, an ancient brown cape over his shoulders, a covered buckler slung at the side of the worn saddle, a scarred silver-worked claymore strapped across his back in the old cavalier fashion.

Retief hadn't liked this job when he had first learned of it. He had gone alone on madman's errands before, but that had been long ago—a phase of his career that should

7

have been finished. And the information he had turned up in his background research had broken his professional detachment. Now the locals were trying an old tourist game on him; ease the outlander into a spot, then demand money . . .

Well, Retief thought, this was as good a time as any to start playing the role; there was a hell of a lot here in the quaint city of Fragonard that needed straightening out.

"Make way, you rabble!" he roared suddenly. "Or by the chains of the sea-god I'll make a path through you!" He spurred the horse; neck arching, the mount stepped daintily forward.

The crowd made way reluctantly before him. "Pay for the merchandise you've destroyed," called a voice.

"Let peddlers keep a wary eye for their betters," snorted the man loudly, his eye roving over the faces before him. A tall fellow with long yellow hair stepped squarely into his path.

"There are no rabble or peddlers here," he said angrily. "Only true cavaliers of the Clan Imperial . . ."

The mounted man leaned from his saddle to stare into the eyes of the other. His seamed brown face radiated scorn. "When did a true Cavalier turn to commerce? If you were trained to the Code you'd know a gentleman doesn't soil his hands with penny-grubbing, and that the Emperor's highroad belongs to the mounted knight. So clear your rubbish out of my path, if you'd save it."

"Climb down off that nag," shouted the tall young man, reaching for the bridle. "I'll show you some practical knowledge of the Code. I challenge you to stand and defend yourself."

In an instant the thick barrel of an antique Imperial Guards power gun was in the gray-haired man's hand. He leaned negligently on the high pommel of his saddle with his left elbow, the pistol laid across his forearm pointing unwaveringly at the man before him.

The hard old face smiled grimly. "I don't soil my hands in street brawling with new-hatched nobodies," he said. He nodded toward the arch spanning the street ahead. "Follow me through the arch, if you call yourself a man and a Cavalier." He moved on then; no one hindered him. He rode in silence through the crowd, pulled up at the gate barring the street. This would be the first real test of his cover identity. The papers which had gotten him through Customs and Immigration at Fragonard Spaceport the day before had been burned along with the civilian clothes. From here on he'd be getting by on the uniform and a cast-iron nerve.

A purse-mouthed fellow wearing the uniform of a Lieutenant-Ensign in the Household Escort Regiment looked him over, squinted his eyes, smiled sourly.

"What can I do for you, Uncle?" He spoke carelessly, leaning against the engraved buttress mounting the wrought-iron gate. Yellow and green sunlight filtered down through the leaves of the giant linden trees bordering the cobbled street.

The gray-haired man stared down at him. "The first thing you can do, Lieutenant-Ensign," he said in a voice of cold steel, "is come to a position of attention."

The thin man straightened, frowning. "What's that?" His expression hardened. "Get down off that beast and let's have a look at your papers—if you've got any."

The mounted man didn't move. "I'm making allowances for the fact that your regiment is made up of idlers who've never learned to solider," he said quietly. "But having had your attention called to it, even you should recognize the insignia of a Battle Commander."

The officer stared, glancing over the drab figure of the old man. Then he saw the tarnished gold thread worked into the design of a dragon rampant, almost invisible against the faded color of the heavy velvet cape.

He licked his lips, cleared his throat, hesitated. What in the name of the Tormented One would a top-ranking battle officer be doing on this thin old horse, dressed in plain worn clothing? "Let me see your papers— Commander," he said.

The Commander flipped back the cape to expose the ornate butt of the power pistol.

"Here are my credentials," he said. "Open the gate."

"Here," the Ensign spluttered. "What's this . . ."

"For a man who's taken the Emperor's commission," the

old man said, "you're criminally ignorant of the courtesies due a general officer. Open the gate or I'll blow it open. You'll not deny the way to an Imperial battle officer." He drew the pistol.

The Ensign gulped, thought fleetingly of sounding the alarm signal, of insisting on seeing papers . . . then as the pistol came up, he closed the switch, and the gate swung open. The heavy hooves of the gaunt horse clattered past him; he caught a glimpse of a small brand on the lean flank. Then he was staring after the retreating back of the terrible old man. Battle Commander indeed! The old fool was wearing a fortune in valuable antiques, and the animal bore the brand of a thoroughbred battle-horse. He'd better report this. . . . He picked up the communicator, as a tall young man with an angry face came up to the gate.

Retief rode slowly down the narrow street lined with the stalls of suttlers, metalsmiths, weapons technicians, free-lance squires. The first obstacle was behind him. He hadn't played it very suavely, but he had been in no mood for bandying words. He had been angry ever since he had started this job; and that, he told himself, wouldn't do. He was beginning to regret his high-handedness with the crowd outside the gate. He should save the temper for those responsible, not the bystanders; and in any event, an agent of the Corps should stay cool at all times. That was essentially the same criticism that Magnan had handed him along with the assignment, three months ago.

"The trouble with you, Retief," Magnan had said, "is that you are unwilling to accept the traditional restraints of the Service; you conduct yourself too haughtily, too much in the manner of a free agent . . ."

His reaction, he knew, had only proved the accuracy of his superior's complaint. He should have nodded penitent agreement, indicated that improvement would be striven for earnestly; instead, he had sat expressionless, in a silence which inevitably appeared antagonistic.

He remembered how Magnan had moved uncomfortably, cleared his throat, and frowned at the papers before him. "Now, in the matter of your next assignment," he said, "we have a serious situation to deal with in an area that could be critical."

Retief almost smiled at the recollection. The man had placed himself in an amusing dilemma. It was necessary to emphasize the great importance of the job at hand, and simultaneously to avoid letting Retief have the satisfaction of feeling that he was to be entrusted with anything vital; to express the lack of confidence the Corps felt in him while at the same time invoking his awareness of the great trust he was receiving. It was strange how Magnan could rationalize his personal dislike into a righteous concern for the best interests of the Corps.

Magnan had broached the nature of the assignment obliquely, mentioning his visit as a tourist to Northroyal, a charming, backward little planet settled by Cavaliers, refugees from the breakup of the Empire of the Lily.

Retief knew the history behind Northroyal's tidy, proud, tradition-bound society. When the Old Confederation broke up, dozens of smaller governments had grown up among the civilized worlds. For a time, the Lily Empire had been among the most vigorous of them, comprising twenty-one worlds, and supporting an excellent military force under the protection of which the Lilyan merchant fleet had carried trade to a thousand far-flung worlds.

When the Concordiat had come along, organizing the previously sovereign states into a new Galactic jurisdiction, the Empire of the Lily had resisted, and had for a time held the massive Concordiat fleets at bay. In the end, of course, the gallant but outnumbered Lilyan forces had been driven back to the gates of the home world. The planet of Lily had been saved catastrophic bombardment only by a belated truce which guaranteed self-determination to Lily on the cessation of hostilities, disbandment of the Lilyan fleet, and the exile of the entire membership of the Imperial Suite, which, under the Lilyan clan tradition, had numbered over ten thousand individuals. Every man, woman, and child who could claim even the most distant blood relationship to the Emperor, together with their servants, dependents, retainers, and protégés, were included. The move took weeks to complete, but at the end of it the Cavaliers, as they were known, had been transported to an uninhabited, cold sea-world, which they named Northroyal. A popular bit of lore in connection with the exodus had it that the ship bearing the Emperor himself had slipped away en route to exile, and that the ruler had sworn that he would not return until the day he could come with an army of liberation. He had never been heard from again.

The land area of the new world, made up of innumerable islands, totaled half a million square miles. Well stocked with basic supplies and equipment, the Cavaliers had set to work and turned their rocky fief into a snug, well-integrated—if tradition-ridden—society, and today exported seafoods, fine machinery, and tourist literature.

It was in the last department that Northroyal was best known. Tales of the pomp and color, the quaint inns and good food, the beautiful girls, the brave display of royal cavalry, and the fabulous annual Tournament of the Lily attracted a goodly number of sightseers, and the Cavalier Line was now one of the planet's biggest foreign-exchange earners.

Magnan had spoken of Northroyal's high industrial potential, and her well-trained civilian corps of space navigators.

"The job of the Corps," Retief interrupted, "is to seek out and eliminate threats to the peace of the Galaxy. How does a little story-book world like Northroyal get into the act?"

"More easily than you might imagine," Magnan said. "Here you have a close-knit society, proud, conscious of a tradition of military power, empire. A clever rabble-rouser using the right appeal would step into a ready-made situation there. It would take only an order on the part of the planetary government to turn the factories to war production, and convert the merchant fleet into a war fleet—and we'd be faced with a serious power imbalance—a storm center."

"I think you're talking nonsense, Mr. Minister," Retief said bluntly. "They've got more sense than that. They're not so far gone on tradition as to destroy themselves. They're a practical people."

Magnan drummed his fingers on the desk top. "There's one factor I haven't covered yet," he said. "There has been what amounts to a news blackout from Northroyal during the last six months. . . ."

Retief snorted. "What news?"

Magnan had been enjoying the suspense. "Tourists have been having great difficulty getting to Northroyal," he said. "Fragonard, the capital, is completely closed to outsiders. We managed, however, to get an agent in." He turned, gazing at Retief. "It seems," he went on, "that the rightful Emperor has turned up."

Retief narrowed his eyes. "What's that?" he said sharply.

Magnan drew back, intimidated by the power of Retief's tone, annoyed by his own reaction. In his own mind, Magnan was candid enough to know that this was the real basis for his intense dislike for his senior agent. It was an instinctive primitive fear of physical violence. Not that Retief had ever assaulted anyone; but he had an air of mastery that made Magnan feel trivial.

"The Emperor," Magnan repeated. "The traditional story is that he was lost on the voyage to Northroyal. There was a legend that he had slipped out of the hands of the Concordiat in order to gather new support for a counter-offensive, hurl back the invader, all that sort of thing."

"The Concordiat collapsed of its own weight within a century," Retief said. "There's no invader to hurl back. Northroyal is free and independent, like every other world."

"Of course, of course," Magnan said. "But you're missing the emotional angle, Retief. It's all very well to be independent; but what about the dreams of empire, the vanished glory, destiny, et cetera?"

"What about them?"

"That's all our agent heard; it's everywhere. The news strips are full of it. Video is playing it up; everybody's talking it. The returned Emperor seems to be a clever propagandist; the next step will be a full-scale mobilization. And we're not equipped to handle that."

"What am I supposed to do about all this?"

"Your orders are, and I quote, to proceed to Fragonard and there employ such measures as shall be appropriate to negate the present trend toward an expansionist sentiment

among the populace." Magnan passed a document across the
desk to Retief for his inspection.

The orders were brief, and wasted no wordage on details.
As an officer of the Corps with the rank of Counselor,
Retief enjoyed wide latitude, and broad powers—and cor-
responding responsibility in the event of failure. Retief
wondered how this assignment had devolved on him, among
the thousands of Corps agents scattered through the Galaxy.
Why was one man being handed a case which on the face
of it should call for a full mission?

"This looks like quite an undertaking for a single agent,
Mr. Minister," Retief said.

"Well, of course, if you don't feel you can handle it . . ."
Magnan looked solemn.

Retief looked at him, smiling faintly. Magnan's tactics
had been rather obvious. Here was one of those nasty jobs
which could easily pass in reports as routine if all went well;
but even a slight mistake could mean complete failure, and
failure meant war; and the agent who had let it happen
would be finished in the Corps.

There was danger in the scheme for Magnan, too. The
blame might reflect back on him. Probably he had plans
for averting disaster after Retief had given up. He was too
shrewd to leave himself out in the open. And for that
matter, Retief reflected, too good an agent to let the situation get out of hand.

No, it was merely an excellent opportunity to let Retief
discredit himself, with little risk of any great credit accruing
to him in the remote event of success.

Retief could, of course, refuse the assignment, but that
would be the end of his career. He would never be advanced
to the rank of Minister, and age limitations would force his
retirement in a year or two. That would be an easy victory
for Magnan.

Retief liked his work as an officer-agent of the Diplomatic
Corps, that ancient supranational organization dedicated to
the contravention of war. He had made his decision long ago,
and he had learned to accept his life as it was, with all its
imperfections. It was easy enough to complain about the
petty intrigues, the tyrannies of rank, the small inequities.

But these were merely a part of the game, another challenge to be met and dealt with. The overcoming of obstacles was Jame Retief's specialty. Some of the obstacles were out in the open, the recognized difficulties inherent in any tough assignment. Others were concealed behind a smoke-screen of personalities and efficiency reports; and both were equally important. You did your job in the field, and then you threaded your way through the maze of Corps politics. And if you couldn't handle the job—any part of it—you'd better find something else to do.

He had accepted the assignment, of course, after letting Magnan wonder for a few minutes; and then for two months he had buried himself in research, gathering every scrap of information, direct and indirect, that the massive files of the Corps would yield. He had soon found himself immersed in the task, warming to its challenge, fired with emotions ranging from grief to rage as he ferreted out the hidden pages in the history of the exiled Cavaliers.

He had made his plan, gathered a potent selection of ancient documents and curious objects; a broken chain of gold, a tiny key, a small silver box. And now he was here, inside the compound of the Grand Corrida.

Everything here in these ways surrounding and radiating from the Field of the Emerald Crown—the arena itself—was devoted to the servicing and supplying of the thousands of First Day contenders in the Tournament of the Lily, and the housing and tending of the dwindling number of winners who stayed on for the following days. There were tiny eating places, taverns, inns; all consciously antique in style, built in imitation of their counterparts left behind long ago on far-off Lily.

"Here you are, Pop, first-class squire," called a thin red-haired fellow.

"Double up and save credits," called a short dark man. "First Day contract . . ."

Shouts ran back and forth across the alleylike street as the stall keepers scented a customer. Retief ignored them, moved on toward the looming wall of the arena. Ahead, a slender youth stood with folded arms before his stall, looking toward the approaching figure on the black horse. He leaned forward, watching Retief intently, then straightened, turned and grabbed up a tall narrow body shield from behind him. He raised the shield over his head, and as Retief came abreast, called "Battle officer!"

Retief reined in the horse, looked down at the youth.

"At your service, sir," the young man said. He stood straight and looked Retief in the eye. Retief looked back. The horse minced, tossed his head.

"What is your name, boy?" Retief asked.

"Fitzraven, sir."

"Do you know the Code?"

"I know the Code, sir."

Retief stared at him, studying his face, his neatly cut uniform of traditional Imperial green, the old but well-oiled leather of his belt and boots.

"Lower your shield, Fitzraven," he said. "You're engaged." He swung down from his horse. "The first thing I want is care for my mount. His name is Danger-by-Night. And then I want an inn for myself."

"I'll care for the horse myself, Commander," Fitzraven said. "And the Commander will find good lodging at the sign of the Phoenix-in-Dexter-Chief; quarters are held ready for my client." The squire took the bridle, pointing toward the inn a few doors away.

Two hours later, Retief came back to the stall, a thirty-two-ounce steak and a bottle of Nouveau Beaujolais having satisfied a monumental appetite induced by the long ride down from the spaceport north of Fragonard. The plain banner he had carried in his saddlebag fluttered now from the staff above the stall. He moved through the narrow room to a courtyard behind, and stood in the doorway watching as Fitzraven curried the dusty hide of the lean black horse. The saddle and fittings were laid out on a heavy table, ready for cleaning. There was clean straw in the stall where the horse stood, and an empty grain bin and water bucked indicated the animal had been well fed and watered.

Retief nodded to the squire, and strolled around the courtyard staring up at the deep blue sky of early evening above the irregular line of roofs and chimneys, noting the other squires, the variegated mounts stabled here, listening to the hubbub of talk, the clatter of crockery from the kitchen of the inn. Fitzraven finished his work and came over to his new employer.

"Would the Commander like to sample the night life in the Grand Corrida?"

"Not tonight," Retief said. "Let's go up to my quarters; I want to learn a little more about what to expect."

Retief's room, close under the rafters on the fourth floor of the inn, was small but adequate, with a roomy wardrobe and a wide bed. The contents of his saddlebags were already in place in the room.

Retief looked around. "Who gave you permission to open my saddlebags?"

Fitzraven flushed slightly. "I thought the Commander would wish to have them unpacked," he said stiffly.

"I looked at the job the other squires were doing on their horses," Retief said. "You were the only one who was doing a proper job of tending the animal. Why the special service?"

"I was trained by my father," Fitzraven said. "I serve only true knights, and I perform my duties honorably. If the Commander is dissatisfied . . ."

"How do you know I'm a true knight?"

"The Commander wears the uniform and weapons of one of the oldest Imperial Guards Battle Units, the Iron Dragon," Fitzraven said. "And the Commander rides a battle horse, true-bred."

"How do you know I didn't steal them?"

Fitzraven grinned suddenly. "They fit the Commander too well."

Retief smiled. "All right, son, you'll do," he said. "Now brief me on the First Day. I don't want to miss anything. And you may employ the personal pronoun."

For an hour Fitzraven discussed the order of events for the elimination contests of the First Day of the Tournament of the Lily, the strategies that a clever contender could employ to husband his strength, the pitfalls into which the unwary might fall.

The tournament was the culmination of a year of smaller contests held throughout the equatorial chain of populated islands. The Northroyalans had substituted various forms of armed combat for the sports practiced on most worlds; a compensation for the lost empire, doubtless, a primitive harking-back to an earlier, more glorious day.

Out of a thousand First Day entrants, less than one in ten would come through to face the Second Day. Of course, the First Day events were less lethal than those to be encountered farther along in the three-day tourney, Retief learned; there would be few serious injuries in the course of the opening day, and those would be largely due to clumsiness or ineptitude on the part of the entrants.

There were no formal entrance requirements, Fitzraven said, other than proof of minimum age and status in the Empire. Not all the entrants were natives of Northroyal; many came from distant worlds, long-scattered descendants of the citizens of the shattered Lily Empire. But all competed for the same prizes; status in the Imperial peerage, the honors of the Field of the Emerald crown, and Imperial grants of land, wealth to the successful.

"Will you enter the First Day events, sir," Fitzraven asked, "or do you have a Second or Third Day certification?"

"Neither," Retief said. "We'll sit on the sidelines and watch."

Fitzraven looked surprised. It had somehow not occurred to him that the old man was not to be a combatant. And it was too late to get seats. . . .

"How . . ." Fitzraven began, after a pause.

"Don't worry," Retief said. "We'll have a place to sit."

Fitzraven fell silent, tilted his head to one side, listening. Loud voices, muffled by walls, the thump of heavy feet.

"Something is up," Fitzraven said. "Police." He looked at Retief.

"I wouldn't be surprised," Retief said, "if they were looking for me. Let's go find out."

"We need not meet them," the squire said. "There is another way . . ."

"Never mind," Retief said. "As well now as later." He winked at Fitzraven and turned to the door.

❖   ❖   ❖

Retief stepped off the lift into the crowded common room, Fitzraven at his heels. Half a dozen men in dark blue tunics and tall shakos moved among the patrons, staring at faces. By the door Retief saw the thin-mouthed Ensign he had overawed at the gate. The fellow saw him at the same moment and plucked at the sleeve of the nearest policeman, pointing.

The man dropped a hand to his belt, and at once the other policeman turned, followed his glance to Retief. They moved toward him with one accord. Retief stood waiting.

The first cop planted himself before Retief, looking him up and down. "Your papers!" he snapped.

Retief smiled easily. "I am a peer of the Lily and a battle officer of the Imperial forces," he said. "On what pretext are you demanding papers of me, Captain?"

The cop raised his eyebrows.

"Let's say you are charged with unauthorized entry into the controlled area of the Grand Corrida, and with impersonating an Imperial officer," he said. "You didn't expect to get away with it, did you, Grandpa?" The fellow smiled sardonically.

"Under the provisions of the Code," Retief said, "the status of a peer may not be questioned, nor his actions interfered with except by Imperial Warrant. Let me see yours, Captain. And I suggest you assume a more courteous tone when addressing your superior officer." Retief's voice hardened to a whip crack with the last words.

The policeman stiffened, scowled. His hand dropped to the nightstick at his belt.

"None of your insolence, old man," he snarled. "Papers! Now!"

Retief's hand shot out, gripped the officer's hand over the stick. "Raise that stick," he said quietly, "and I'll assuredly beat out your brains with it." He smiled calmly into the captain's bulging eyes. The captain was a strong man. He threw every ounce of his strength into the effort to bring up his arm, to pull free of the old man's grasp. The crowd of customers, the squad of police, stood silently, staring, uncertain of what was going on. Retief stood steady; the officer strained, reddened. The old man's arm was like cast steel.

"I see you are using your head, Captain," Retief said. "Your decision not to attempt to employ force against a peer was an intelligent one."

The cop understood. He was being offered an opportunity to save a little face. He relaxed slowly.

"Very well, uh, sir," he said stiffly. "I will assume you can establish your identity properly; kindly call at the commandant's office in the morning."

Retief released his hold and the officer hustled his men out, shoving the complaining Ensign ahead. Fitzraven caught Retief's eye and grinned.

"Empty pride is a blade with no hilt," he said. "A humble man would have yelled for help."

Retief turned to the barman. "Drinks for all," he called. A happy shout greeted this announcement. They had all enjoyed seeing the police outfaced.

"The cops don't seem to be popular here," the old man said.

Fitzraven sniffed. "A law-abiding subject parks illegally for five minutes, and they are on him like flies after dead meat; but let his car be stolen by lawless hoodlums—they are nowhere to be seen."

"That has a familiar sound," Retief said. He poured out a tumbler of vodka, looked at Fitzraven.

"Tomorrow," he said. "A big day."

A tall blond young man near the door looked after him with bitter eyes.

"All right, old man," he muttered. "We'll see then."

The noise of the crowd came to Retief's ears as a muted rumble through the massive pile of the amphitheater above. A dim light filtered from the low-ceilinged corridor into the cramped office of the assistant Master of the Games.

"If you know your charter," Retief said, "you will recall that a Battle Commander enjoys the right to observe the progress of the games from the official box. I claim that privilege."

"I know nothing of this," the cadaverous official replied impatiently. "You must obtain an order from the Master of the Games before I can listen to you." He turned to another flunkey, opened his mouth to speak. A hand seized him by the shoulder, lifted him bodily from his seat. The man's mouth remained open in shock.

Retief held the stricken man at arm's length, then drew him closer. His eyes blazed into the gaping eyes of the other. His face was white with fury.

"Little man," he said in a strange, harsh voice, "I go now with my groom to take my place in the official box. Read your Charter well before you interfere with me—and your Holy Book as well." He dropped the fellow with a crash, saw him slide under the desk. No one made a sound. Even Fitzraven looked pale. The force of the old man's rage had been like a lethal radiation crackling in the room.

The squire followed as Retief strode off down the corridor. He breathed deeply, wiping his forehead. This was some old man he had met this year, for sure!

Retief slowed, turning to wait for Fitzraven. He smiled ruefully. "I was rough on the old goat," he said. "But officious pipsqueaks sting me like deerflies."

They emerged from the gloom of the passage into a well-situated box, to the best seats in the front row. Retief stared at the white glare and roiled dust of the arena, the banked thousands of faces looming above, and a sky of palest blue with one tiny white cloud. The gladiators stood in little groups, waiting. A strange scene, Retief thought. A scene from dim antiquity, but real, complete with the odors of fear and excitement, the hot wind that ruffled his hair, the rumbling animal sound from the thousand throats of the many-headed monster. He wondered what it was they really wanted to see here today. A triumph of skill and courage, a reaffirmation of ancient virtues, the spectacle of men who laid life on the gaming table and played for a prize called glory—or was it merely blood and death they wanted?

It was strange that this archaic ritual of the blood tournament, combining the features of the Circus of Caesar, the joust of Medieval Terran Europe, the Olympic Games, a rodeo, and a six-day bicycle race should have come to hold such an important place in a modern culture, Retief thought. In its present form it was a much-distorted version of the traditional Tournament of the Lily, through whose gauntlet the nobility of the old Empire had come. It had been a device of harsh enlightenment to insure and guarantee to every man, once every year, the opportunity to prove himself against others whom society called his betters. Through its discipline, the humblest farm lad could rise by degrees to the highest levels in the Empire. For the original Games had tested every facet of a man, from his raw courage to his finesse in strategy, from his depths of endurance under mortal stress to the quickness of his intellect, from his instinct for truth to his wiliness in eluding a complex trap of violence.

In the two centuries since the fall of the Empire, the Games had gradually become a tourist spectacle, a free-for-all, a celebration—with the added spice of danger for those who did not shrink back, and fat prizes to a few determined finalists. The Imperial Charter was still invoked at the opening of the Games, the old Code reaffirmed; but there were few who knew or cared what the Charter and Code actually said, what terms existed there. The popular mind left such details to the regents of the tourney. And in recent months, with the once sought-after tourists suddenly and inexplicably turned away, it seemed the Games were being perverted to a purpose even less admirable . . .

Well, thought Retief, perhaps I'll bring some of the fine print into play, before I'm done.

Bugle blasts sounded beyond the high bronze gate. Then with a heavy clang it swung wide and a nervous official stepped out nodding jerkily to the front rank of today's contenders.

The column moved straight out across the field, came together with other columns to form a square before the Imperial box. High above, Retief saw banners fluttering, a splash of color from the uniforms of ranked honor guards. The Emperor himself was here briefly to open the Tournament.

Across the field the bugles rang out again; Retief recognized the Call to Arms and the Imperial Salute. Then an amplified voice began the ritual reading of the Terms of the Day.

" . . . by the clement dispensation of his Imperial Majesty, to be conducted under the convention of Fragonard, and there being none dissenting . . ." The voice droned on.

It finished at last, and referees moved to their positions. Retief looked at Fitzraven. "The excitement's about to begin."

Referees handed out heavy whips, gauntlets and face shields. The first event would be an unusual one.

Retief watched as the yellow-haired combatant just below the box drew on the heavy leather glove which covered and protected the left hand and forearm, accepted the fifteen-foot lash of braided oxhide. He flipped it tentatively, laying the length out along the ground and recalling it with an effortless turn of the wrist, the frayed tip snapping like a pistol shot. The thing was heavy, Retief noted, and clumsy; the leather had no life to it.

The box had filled now; no one bothered Retief and the squire. The noisy crowd laughed and chattered, called to acquaintances in the stands and on the field below.

A bugle blasted peremptorily nearby, and white-suited referees darted among the milling entrants, shaping them into groups of five. Retief watched the blond youth, a tall frowning man, and three others of undistinguished appearance.

Fitzraven leaned toward him. "The cleverest will hang back and let the others eliminate each other," he said in a low voice, "so that his first encounter will be for the set."

Retief nodded. A man's task here was to win his way as high as possible; every stratagem was important. He saw the blond fellow inconspicuously edge back as a hurrying referee paired off the other four, called to him to stand by, and led the others to rings marked off on the dusty turf. A whistle blew suddenly, and over the arena the roar of sound changed tone. The watching crowd leaned forward as the hundreds of keyed-up gladiators laid on their lashes in frenzied effort. Whips cracked, men howled, feet shuffled; here the crowd laughed as some clumsy fellow sprawled, yelping; there they gasped in excitement as two surly brutes flogged each other in all-out offense.

Retief saw the tip of one man's whip curl around his opponents' ankle, snatch him abruptly off his feet. The other pair circled warily, rippling their lashes uncertainly. One backed over the line unnoticing and was led away expostulating, no blow having been struck.

The number on the field dwindled away to half within moments. Only a few dogged pairs, now bleeding from cuts, still contested the issue. A minute longer and the whistle blew as the last was settled.

The two survivors of the group below paired off now, and as the whistle blasted again, the tall fellow, still frowning, brought the other to the ground with a single sharp flick of the lash. Retief looked him over. This was a man to watch.

More whistles, and a field now almost cleared; only two men left out of each original five; the blond moved out into the circle, stared across at the other. Retief recognized him suddenly as the fellow who had challenged him outside the gate, over the spilled fruit. So he had followed through the arch.

The final whistle sounded and a hush fell over the watchers. Now the shuffle of feet could be heard clearly, the hissing breath of the weary fighters, the creak and slap of leather.

The blond youth flipped his lash out lightly, saw it easily evaded, stepped aside from a sharp counterblow. He feinted, reversed the direction of his cast, and caught the other high on the chest as he dodged aside. A welt showed instantly. He saw a lightning-fast riposte on the way, sprang back. The gauntlet came up barely in time. The lash wrapped around the gauntlet, and the young fellow seized the leather, hauled sharply. The other stumbled forward. The blond brought his whip across the fellow's back in a tremendous slamming blow that sent a great fragment of torn shirt flying. Somehow the man stayed on his feet, backed off, circled. His opponent followed up, laying down one whistling whipcrack after another, trying to drive the other over the line. He had hurt the man with the cut across the back, and now was attempting to finish him easily.

He leaned away from a sluggish pass, and then Retief saw agony explode in his face as a vicious cut struck home. The blond youth reeled in a drunken circle, out on his feet.

Slow to follow up, the enemy's lash crashed across the circle; the youth, steadying quickly, slipped under it, struck at the other's stomach. The leather cannoned against the man, sent the remainder of his shirt fluttering in a spatter of blood. With a surge of shoulder and wrist that made the muscles creak, the blond reversed the stroke, brought the lash back in a vicious cut aimed at the same spot. It struck, smacking with a wet explosive crack. And he struck again, again, as the fellow tottered back, fell over the line.

The winner went limp suddenly, staring across at the man who lay in the dust, pale now, moving feebly for a moment, then slackly still. There was a great deal of blood, and more blood. Retief saw with sudden shock that the man was disemboweled. That boy, thought Retief, plays for keeps.

The next two events constituting the First Day trials were undistinguished exhibitions of a two-handed version of an old American Indian wrestling and a brief bout of fencing with blunt-tipped weapons. Eighty men were certified for the Second Day before noon, and Retief and Fitzraven were back in the inn room a few minutes later. "Take some time off now while I catch up on my rest," Retief said. "Have some solid food ready when I wake." Then he retired for the night.

With his master breathing heavily in a profound sleep, the squire went down to the common room and found a table at the back, ordered a mug of strong ale, and sat alone, thinking.

This was a strange one he had met this year. He had seen at once that he was no idler from some high-pressure world, trying to lose himself in a fantasy of the old days. And no more was he a Northroyalan; there was a grim force in him, a time-engraved stamp of power that was alien to the neat well-ordered little world. And yet there was no doubt that there was more in him of the true Cavalier than in a Fragonard-born courtier. He was like some ancient warrior noble from the days of the greatness of the Empire. By the two heads, the old man was strange, and terrible in anger!

Fitzraven listened to the talk around him.

"I was just above," a blacksmith at the next table was saying. "He gutted the fellow with the lash! It was monstrous! I'm glad I'm not one of the fools who want to play at warrior. Imagine having your insides drawn out by a rope of dirty leather!"

"The games have to be tougher now," said another. "We've lain dormant here for two centuries, waiting for something to come—some thing to set us on our way again to power and wealth. . . ."

"Thanks, I'd rather go on living quietly as a smith and enjoying a few of the simple pleasures—there was no glory in that fellow lying in the dirt with his belly torn open, you can be sure of that."

"There'll be more than torn bellies to think about, when we mount a battle fleet for Grimwold and Tania," said another.

"The Emperor has returned," snapped the warlike one. "Shall we hang back where he leads?"

The smith muttered. "His is a tortured genealogy, by my judgment. I myself trace my ancestry by three lines into the old Palace at Lily."

"So do we all. All the more reason we should support our Emperor."

"We live well here; we have no quarrel with other worlds. Why not leave the past to itself?"

"Our Emperor leads; we will follow. If you disapprove, enter the Lily Tournament next year and win a high place; then your advice will be respected."

"No thanks. I like my insides to stay on the inside."

Fitzraven thought of Retief. The old man had said that he held his rank in his own right, citing no genealogy. That was strange indeed. The Emperor had turned up only a year ago, presenting the Robe, the Ring, the Seal, the crown jewels, and the Imperial Book which traced his descent through five generations from the last reigning Emperor of the Old Empire.

How could it be that Retief held a commission in his own right, dated no more than thirty years ago? And the rank of Battle Commander. That was a special rank, Fitzraven remembered, a detached rank for a distinguished noble and officer of proven greatness, assigned to no one unit, but dictating his own activities.

Either Retief was a fraud . . . but Fitzraven pictured the

old man, his chiseled features that time had not disguised, his soldier's bearing, his fantastic strength, his undoubtedly authentic equipage. Whatever the explanation, he was a true knight. That was enough.

Retief awoke refreshed, and ravenous. A great rare steak and a giant tankard of autumn ale were ready on the table. He ate, ordered more and ate again. Then he stretched, shook himself, no trace of yesterday's fatigue remaining. His temper was better, too, he realized. He was getting too old to exhaust himself.

"It's getting late, Fitzraven," he said. "Let's be going."

They arrived at the arena and took their places in the official box in time to watch the first event, a cautious engagement with swords.

After four more events and three teams of determined but colorless competition, only a dozen men were left on the field awaiting the next event, including the tall blond youth whom Retief had been watching since he had recognized him. He himself, he reflected, was the reason for the man's presence here; and he had acquitted himself well.

Retief saw a burly warrior carrying a two-handed sword paired off now against the blond youth. The fellow grinned as he moved up to face the other.

This would be a little different, the agent thought, watching; this fellow was dangerous. Yellow-hair moved in, his weapon held level across his chest. The big man lashed out suddenly with the great sword, and the other jumped back, then struck backhanded at his opponent's shoulder, nicked him lightly, sliding back barely in time to avoid a return swing. The still grinning man moved in, the blade chopping the air before him in a whistling figure-eight. He pressed his man back, the blade never pausing.

There was no more room; the blond fellow jumped sideways, dropping the point of his sword in time to intercept a vicious cut. He backstepped; he couldn't let that happen again. The big man was very strong.

The blade was moving again now, the grin having faded a little. He'll have to keep away from him, keep circling, Retief thought. The big fellow's pattern is to push his man back to the edge, then pick him off as he tries to side-step. He'll have to keep space between them.

The fair-haired man backed, watching for an opening. He jumped to the right, and as the other shifted to face him, leaped back to the left and catching the big man at the end of his reach to the other side, slashed him across the ribs and kept moving. The man roared, twisting around in vicious cuts at the figure that darted sideways, just out of range. Then the blond brought his claymore across in a low swing that struck solidly across the back of the other's legs, with a noise like a butcher separating ribs with a cleaver.

Like a marionette with his strings cut, the man folded to his knees, sprawled. The other man stepped back, as surgeons' men swarmed up to tend the fallen fighter. There were plenty of them available now; so far the casualties had been twice normal. On the other mounds in view, men were falling. The faint-hearted had been eliminated; the men who were still on their feet were determined, or desperate. There would be no more push-overs.

"Only about six left," Fitzraven called.

"This has been a rather unusual tournament so far," Retief said. "That young fellow with the light hair seems to be playing rough, forcing the pace."

"I have never seen such a businesslike affair," Fitzraven said. "The weak-disposed have been frightened out, and the fighters cut down with record speed. At this rate there will be none left for the Third Day."

There was delay on the field, as referees and other officials hurried back and forth; then an announcement boomed out. The Second Day was officially concluded. The six survivors would be awarded Second Day certificates, and would be eligible for the Third and Last Day tomorrow.

Retief and Fitzraven left the box, made their way through the crowd back to the inn.

"See that Danger-by-Night is well fed and exercised," Retief said to the squire. "And check over all of my gear thoroughly. I wish to put on my best appearance tomorrow; it will doubtless be my last outing of the kind for some time."

Fitzraven hurried away to tend his chores, while Retief

ascended to his room to pore over the contents of his dispatch case far into the night.

The Third Day had dawned gray and chill, and an icy wind whipped across the arena. The weather had not discouraged the crowd, however. The stands were packed and the overflow of people stood in the aisles, perched high on the back walls, crowding every available space. Banners flying from the Imperial box indicated the presence of the royal party. This was the climactic day. The field, by contrast, was almost empty; two of the Second Day winners had not reentered for today's events, having apparently decided that they had had enough honor for one year. They would receive handsome prizes, and respectable titles; that was enough.

The four who had come to the arena today to stake their winning and their lives on their skill at arms would be worth watching, Retief thought. There was the blond young fellow, still unmarked; a great swarthy ruffian; a tall broad man of perhaps thirty; and a squat bowlegged fellow with enormous shoulders and long arms. They were here to win or die.

From the officials' box Retief and Fitzraven had an excellent view of the arena, where a large circle had been marked out. The officials seated nearby had given them cold glances as they entered, but no one had attempted to interfere. Apparently, they had accepted the situation. Possibly, Retief thought, they had actually studied the Charter. He hoped they had studied it carefully. It would make things easier.

Announcements boomed, officials moved about, fanfares blasted, while Retief sat absorbed in thought. The scene reminded him of things he had long forgotten, days long gone, of his youth, when he had studied the martial skills, serving a long apprenticeship under his world's greatest masters. It had been his father's conviction that nothing so trained the eye and mind and body as fencing, judo, savate, and the disciplines of the arts of offense, and defense.

He had abandoned a priceless education when he had left his home to seek his fortune in the mainstream of galactic culture, but it had stood him in good stead on more than one occasion. An agent of the Corps could not afford to let himself decline into physical helplessness, and Retief had maintained his skills as well as possible. He leaned forward now, adjusting his binoculars as the bugles rang out. Few in the crowd were better qualified than Retief to judge today's performance. It would be interesting to see how the champions handled themselves on the field.

The first event was about to begin, as the blond warrior was paired off with the bowlegged man. The two had been issued slender foils, and now faced each other, blades crossed. A final whistle blew, and blade clashed on blade. The squat man was fast on his feet, bounding around in a semicircle before his taller antagonist, probing his defense with great energy. The blond man backed away slowly, fending off the rain of blows with slight motions of his foil. He jumped back suddenly, and Retief saw a red spot grow on his thigh. The apelike fellow was more dangerous than he had appeared.

Now the blond man launched his attack, beating aside the weapon of the other and striking in for the throat, only to have his point deflected at the last instant. The short man backed now, giving ground reluctantly. Suddenly he dropped into a grotesque crouch, and lunged under the other's defense in a desperate try for a quick kill. It was a mistake; the taller man whirled aside; and his blade flicked delicately once. The bowlegged man slid out flat on his face.

"What happened?" Fitzraven said, puzzled. "I didn't see the stroke that nailed him."

"It was very pretty," Retief said thoughtfully, lowering the glasses. "Under the fifth rib and into the heart."

Now the big dark man and the tall broad fellow took their places. The bugles and whistles sounded, and the two launched a furious exchange, first one and then the other forcing his enemy back before losing ground in turn. The crowd roared its approval as the two stamped and thrust, parried and lunged.

"They can't keep up this pace forever," Fitzraven said. "They'll have to slow down."

"They're both good," Retief said. "And evenly matched."

Now the swarthy fellow leaped back, switched the foil to his left hand, then moved quickly in to the attack. Thrown off his pace, the other man faltered, let the blade nick him on the chest, again in the arm. Desperate, he backpedaled, fighting defensively now. The dark man followed up his advantage, pressing savagely, and a moment later Retief saw a foot of bright steel projecting startlingly from the tall man's back. He took two steps, then folded, as the foil was wrenched from the dark man's hand.

Wave upon wave of sound rolled across the packed stands. Never had they seen such an exhibition as this! It was like the legendary battle of the heroes of the Empire, the fighters who had carried the Lily banner half across the galaxy.

"I'm afraid that's all," Fitzraven said. "These two can elect either to share the victory of the Tourney now, or to contend for sole honors, and in the history of the Tournament on Northroyal, there have never been fewer than three to share the day."

"It looks as though this is going to be a first time, then," Retief said. "They're getting ready to square off."

Below on the field, a mass of officials surrounded the dark man and the fair one, while the crowd outdid itself. Then a bugle sounded in an elaborate salute.

"That's it," Fitzraven said excitedly. "Heroes' Salute. They're going to do it."

"You don't know how glad I am to hear that," Retief said.

"What will the weapon be?" the squire wondered aloud.

"My guess is, something less deadly than the foil," Retief replied.

Moments later the announcement came. The two champions of the day would settle the issue with bare hands. This, thought Retief, would be something to see.

The fanfares and whistles rang out again, and the two men moved cautiously together. The dark man swung an open-handed blow, which smacked harmlessly against the other's shoulder. An instant later the blond youth feinted a kick, instead drove a hard left to the dark man's chin, staggering him. He followed up, smashing two blows to the stomach, then another to the head. The dark man moved back, suddenly reached for the blond man's wrist as he missed a jab, whirled, and attempted to throw his opponent. The blond man slipped aside, and locked his right arm over the dark man's head, seizing his own right wrist with his left hand. The dark man twisted, fell heavily on the other man, reaching for a headlock of his own.

The two rolled in the dust, then broke apart and were on their feet again. The dark man moved in, swung an open-handed slap which popped loudly against the blond man's face. It was a device, Retief saw, to enrage the man, dull the edge of his skill.

The blond man refused to be rattled, however; he landed blows against the dark man's head, evaded another attempt to grapple. It was plain that he preferred to avoid the other's bearlike embrace. He boxed carefully, giving ground, landing a blow as the opportunity offered. The dark man followed doggedly, seemingly unaffected by the pounding. Suddenly he leaped, took two smashing blows full in the face, and crashed against the blond man, knocking him to the ground. There was a flying blur of flailing arms and legs as the two rolled across the turf, and as they came to rest, Retief saw that the dark man had gotten his break. Kneeling behind the other, he held him in a rigid stranglehold, his back and shoulder muscles bulging with the effort of holding his powerful adversary immobilized.

"It's all over," Fitzraven said tensely.

"Maybe not," Retief replied. "Not if he plays it right, and doesn't panic."

The blond man strained at the arm locked at his throat, twisting it fruitlessly. Instinct drove him to tear at the throttling grip, throw off the smothering weight. But the dark man's grip was solid, his position unshakable. Then the blond stopped struggling abruptly and the two seemed as still as an image in stone. The crowd fell silent, fascinated.

"He's given up," Fitzraven said.

"No; watch," Retief said. "He's starting to use his head."

The blond man's arms reached up now, his hands moving

over the other's head, seeking a grip. The dark man pulled his head in, pressing against his victim's back, trying to elude his grip. Then the hands found a hold, and the blond man bent suddenly forward, heaving with a tremendous surge. The dark man came up, flipped high, his grip slipping. The blond rose as the other went over his head, shifted his grip in midair, and as the dark man fell heavily in front of him, the snap of the spine could be heard loud in the stillness. The battle was over, and the blond victor rose to his feet amid a roar of applause.

Retief turned to Fitzraven. "Time for us to be going, Fitz," he said.

The squire jumped up. "As you command, sir; but the ceremony is quite interesting. . . ."

"Never mind that; let's go." Retief moved off, Fitzraven following, puzzled.

Retief descended the steps inside the stands, turned and started down the corridor.

"This way, sir," Fitzraven called. "That leads to the arena."

"I know it," Retief said. "That's where I'm headed."

Fitzraven hurried up alongside. What was the old man going to do now? "Sir," he said, "no one may enter the arena until the tourney has been closed, except the gladiators and the officials. I know this to be an unbreakable law."

"That's right, Fitz," Retief said. "You'll have to stop at the grooms' enclosure."

"But you, sir," Fitzraven gasped . . .

"Everything's under control," Retief said. "I'm going to challenge the champion."

In the Imperial box, the Emperor Rolan leaned forward, fixing his binoculars on a group of figures at the officials' gate. There seemed to be some sort of disturbance there. This was a piece of damned impudence, just as the moment had arrived for the Imperial presentation of the Honors of the Day. The Emperor turned to an aide.

"What the devil's going on down there?" he snapped.

The courtier murmured into a communicator, listened.

"A madman, Imperial Majesty," he said smoothly. "He wished to challenge the champion."

"A drunk, more likely," Rolan said sharply. "Let him be removed at once. And tell the Master of the Games to get on with the ceremony!"

The Emperor turned to the slim dark girl at his side. "Have you found the Games entertaining, Monica?"

"Yes, sire," she replied unemotionally.

"Don't call me that, Monica," he said testily. "Between us there is no need for formalities."

"Yes, Uncle," the girl said.

"Damn it, that's worse," he said. "To you I am simply Rolan." He placed his hand firmly on her silken knee. "And now if they'll get on with this tedious ceremony, I should like to be on the way. I'm looking forward with great pleasure to showing you my estates at Snowdahl."

The Emperor drummed his fingers, stared down at the field, raised the glasses only to see the commotion again.

"Get that fool off the field," he shouted, dropping the glasses. "Am I to wait while they haggle with this idiot? It's insufferable. . . ."

Courtiers scurried, while Rolan glared down from his seat.

Below, Retief faced a cluster of irate referees. One, who had attempted to haul Retief bodily backward, was slumped on a bench, attended by two surgeons.

"I claim the right to challenge, under the Charter," Retief repeated. "Nobody here will be so foolish, I hope, as to attempt to deprive me of that right, now that I have reminded you of the justice of my demand."

From the control cage directly below the Emperor's high box, a tall seam-faced man in black breeches and jacket emerged, followed by two armed men. The officials darted ahead, stringing out between the two, calling out. Behind Retief, on the other side of the barrier, Fitzraven watched anxiously. The old man was full of surprises, and had a way of getting what he wanted; but even if he had the right to challenge the Champion of the Games, what purpose could he have in doing so? He was as strong as a bull, but no man his age could be a match for the youthful power of the blond fighter. Fitzraven was worried; he was fond of this old warrior. He would hate to see him locked behind the steel walls of Fragonard Keep for thus disturbing the order of the Lily Tournament. He moved closer to the barrier, watching.

The tall man in black strode through the chattering officials, stopped before Retief, motioned his two guards forward.

He made a dismissing motion toward Retief. "Take him off the field," he said brusquely. The guards stepped up, laid hands on Retief's arms. He let them get a grip, then suddenly stepped back and brought his arms together. The two men cracked heads, stumbled back. Retief looked at the black-clad man.

"If you are the Master of the Games," he said clearly, "you are well aware that a decorated battle officer has the right of challenge, under the Imperial Charter. I invoke that prerogative now, to enter the lists against the man who holds the field."

"Get out, you fool," the official hissed, white with fury. "The Emperor himself has commanded—"

"Not even the Emperor can override the Charter, which predates his authority by four hundred years," Retief said coldly. "Now do your duty."

"There'll be no more babble of duties and citing of technicalities while the Emperor waits," the official snapped. He turned to one of the two guards, who hung back now, eyeing Retief. "You have a pistol; draw it. If I give the command, shoot him between the eyes."

Retief reached up and adjusted a tiny stud set in the stiff collar of his tunic. He tapped his finger lightly against the cloth. The sound boomed across the arena. A command microphone of the type authorized a Battle Commander was a very effective device.

"I have claimed the right to challenge the champion," he said slowly. The words rolled out like thunder. "This right is guaranteed under the Charter to any Imperial battle officer who wears the Silver Star."

The Master of the Games stared at him aghast. This was getting out of control. Where the devil had the old man gotten a microphone and a PA system? The crowd was roaring now like a gigantic surf. This was something new!

Far above in the Imperial box the tall gray-eyed man was rising, turning toward the exit. "The effrontery," he said in a voice choked with rage. "That I should sit awaiting the pleasure . . ."

The girl at his side hesitated, hearing the amplified voice booming across the arena.

"Wait, Rolan," she said. "Something is happening. . . ."

The man looked back. "A trifle late," he snapped.

"One of the contestants is disputing something," she said. "There was an announcement—something about an Imperial officer challenging the champion."

The Emperor Rolan turned to an aide hovering nearby. "What is this nonsense?"

The courtier bowed. "It is merely a technicality, Majesty. A formality lingering on from earlier times."

"Be specific," the Emperor snapped.

The aide lost some of his aplomb. "Why, it means, ah, that an officer of the Imperial forces holding a battle commission and certain high decorations may enter the lists at any point, without other qualifying conditions. A provision never invoked under modern . . ."

The Emperor turned to the girl. "It appears that someone seeks to turn the entire performance into a farcical affair, at my expense," he said bitterly. "We shall see just how far—"

"I call on you, Rolan," Retief's voice boomed, "to enforce the Code."

"What impertinence is this?" Rolan growled. "Who is the fool at the microphone?"

The aide spoke into his communicator, listened.

"An old man from the crowd, sire. He wears the insignia of a Battle Commander, and a number of decorations, including the Silver Star. According to the Archivist, he has the legal right to challenge."

"I won't have it," Rolan snapped. "A fine reflection on me that would be. Have them take the fellow away; he's doubtless crazed." He left the box, followed by his entourage.

"Rolan," the girl said, "wasn't that the way the Tourneys were, back in the days of the Empire?"

"*These* are the days of the Empire, Monica. And I am not interested in what used to be done. This is today. Am I to present the spectacle of a doddering old fool being hacked to bits, in my name? I don't want the timid to be shocked by butchery. It might have unfortunate results for my propaganda program. I'm currently emphasizing the glorious aspects of the coming war, not the sordid ones. There has already been too much bloodshed today; an inauspicious omen for my expansion plan."

On the field below, the Master of the Games stepped closer to Retief. He felt the cold eyes of the Emperor himself boring into his back. This old devil could bring about his ruin. . . .

"I know all about you," he snarled. "I've checked on you, since you forced your way into an official area; I interviewed two officers . . . you overawed them with glib talk and this threadbare finery you've decked yourself in. Now you attempt to ride rough-shod over me. Well, I'm not so easily thrust aside. If you resist arrest any further, I'll have you shot where you stand!"

Retief drew his sword.

"In the name of the Code you are sworn to serve," he said, his voice ringing across the arena. "I will defend my position." He reached up and flipped the stud at his throat to full pick-up.

"To the Pit with your infernal Code!" bellowed the Master, and blanched in horror as his words boomed sharp and clear across the field to the ears of a hundred thousand people. He stared around, then whirled back to Retief. "Fire," he screamed.

A pistol cracked, and the guard spun, dropped. Fitzraven held the tiny power gun leveled across the barrier at the other guard. "What next, sir?" he asked brightly.

The sound of the shot, amplified, smashed deafeningly across the arena, followed by a mob roar of excitement, bewilderment, shock. The group around Retief stood frozen, staring at the dead man. The Master of the Games made a croaking sound, eyes bulging. The remaining guard cast a glance at the pistol, then turned and ran.

There were calls from across the field; then a troop of brown-uniformed men emerged from an entry, trotted toward the group. The officer at their head carried a rapid-fire shock gun in his hand. He waved his squad to a halt as he reached the fringe of the group. He stared at Retief's drab uniform, glanced at the corpse. Retief saw that the officer was young, determined-looking, wearing the simple insignia of a Battle Ensign.

The Master of the Games found his voice. "Arrest this villain!" he screeched, pointing at Retief. "Shoot the murderer!"

The ensign drew himself to attention, saluted crisply. "Your orders, sir," he said.

"I've told you!" the Master howled. "Seize this malefactor!"

The ensign turned to the black-clad official. "Silence, sir, or I shall be forced to remove you," he said sharply. He looked at Retief. "I await the Commander's orders."

Retief smiled, returned the young officer's salute with a wave of his sword, then sheathed it. "I'm glad to see a little sense displayed here, at last, Battle Ensign," he said. "I was beginning to fear I'd fallen among Concordiatists."

The outraged Master began an harangue which was abruptly silenced by two riot police. He was led away, protesting. The other officials disappeared like a morning mist, carrying the dead guard.

"I've issued my challenge, Ensign," Retief said. "I wish it to be conveyed to the champion-apparent at once." He smiled. "And I'd like you to keep your men around to see that nothing interferes with the orderly progress of the Tourney in accordance with the Charter in its original form."

The ensign's eyes sparkled. Now here was a battle officer who sounded like a fighting man; not a windbag like the commandant of the Household Regiment from whom the ensign took his orders. He didn't know where the old man came from, but any battle officer outranked any civilian or flabby barracks soldier, and this was a Battle Commander, a general officer, and of the Dragon Corps!

Minutes later, a chastened Master of the Games announced that a challenge had been issued. It was the privilege of the champion to accept, or to refuse the challenge if he wished. In the latter event, the challenge would automatically be met the following year.

"I don't know what your boys said to the man," Retief remarked, as he walked out to the combat circle, the ensign at his left side and slightly to the rear, "but they seem to have educated him quickly."

"They can be very persuasive, sir," the young officer replied.

They reached the circle, stood waiting. Now, thought Retief, I've got myself in the position I've been working toward. The question now is whether I'm still man enough to put it over.

He looked up at the massed stands, listening to the mighty roar of the crowd. There would be no easy out for him now. Of course, the new champion might refuse to fight; he had every right to do so, feeling he had earned his year's rest and enjoyment of his winnings. But that would be a defeat for Retief as final as death on the dusty ground of the arena. He had come this far by bluff, threat, and surprise. He would never come this close again.

It was luck that he had clashed with this young man outside the gate, challenged him to enter the lists. That might give the challenge the personal quality that would elicit an angry acceptance.

The champion was walking toward Retief now, surrounded by referees. He stared at the old man, eyes narrowed. Retief returned the look calmly.

"Is this dodderer the challenger?" the blond youth asked scathingly. "It seems to me I have met his large mouth before?"

"Never mind my mouth, merchant," Retief said loudly. "It is not talk I offer you, but the bite of steel."

The yellow-haired man reddened, then laughed shortly. "Small glory I'd win out of skewering you, old graybeard."

"You'd get even less out of showing your heels," Retief said.

"You will not provoke me into satisfying your perverted ambition to die here," the other retorted.

"It's interesting to note," Retief said, "how a peasant peddler wags his tongue to avoid a fight. Such rabble should not be permitted on honorable ground." He studied the other's face to judge how this line of taunting was going on. It was distasteful to have to embarrass the young fellow; he seemed a decent sort. But he had to enrage him to the point that he would discard his wisdom and throw his new-won prize on the table for yet another cast of the dice. And his sore point seemed to be mention of commerce.

"Back to your cabbages, then, fellow," Retief said harshly, "before I whip you there with the flat of my sword."

The young fellow looked at him, studying him. His face was grim. "All right," he said quietly. "I'll meet you in the circle."

Another point gained, Retief thought, as he moved to his position at the edge of the circle. Now, if I can get him to agree to fight on horseback . . .

He turned to a referee. "I wish to suggest that this contest be conducted on horseback—if the peddler owns a horse and is not afraid."

The point was discussed between the referee and the champion's attendants, with many glances at Retief, and much waving of arms. The official returned. "The champion agrees to meet you by day or by night, in heat or cold, on foot or horseback."

"Good," said Retief. "Tell my groom to bring out my mount."

It was no idle impulse which prompted this move. Retief had no illusions as to what it would take to win a victory over the champion. He knew that his legs, while good enough for most of the business of daily life, were his weakest point. They were no longer the nimble tireless limbs that had once carried him up to meet the outlaw Mal de Di alone in Bifrost Pass. Nine hours later he had brought the bandit's two-hundred-and-ten-pound body down into the village on his back, his own arm broken. He had been a mere boy then, younger than this man he was now to meet. He had taken up Mal de Di's standing challenge to any unarmed man who would come alone to the high pass, to prove that he was not too young to play a man's part. Perhaps now he was trying to prove he was not too old. . . .

An official approached leading Danger-by-Night. It took an expert to appreciate the true worth of the great gaunt animal, Retief knew. To the uninitiated eye, he presented a sorry appearance, but Retief would rather have had this mount with the Imperial brand on his side than a paddock full of show horses.

A fat white charger was led out to the blond champion. It looked like a strong animal, Retief thought, but slow. His chances were looking better, things were going well.

A ringing blast of massed trumpets cut through the clamor of the crowd. Retief mounted, watching his opponent. A referee came to his side, handed up a heavy club, studded with long projecting spikes. "Your weapon, sir," he said.

Retief took the thing. It was massive, clumsy; he had never before handled such a weapon. He knew no subtleties of technique with this primitive bludgeon. The blond youth had surprised him, he admitted to himself, smiling slightly. As the challenged party, he had the choice of weapons, of course. He had picked an unusual one.

Retief glanced across at Fitzraven, standing behind the inner barrier, jaw set, a grim expression on his face. That boy, thought Retief, doesn't have much confidence in my old bones holding out.

The whistle blew. Retief moved toward the other man at a trot, the club level at his side. He had decided to handle it like a shortsword, so long as that seemed practical. He would have to learn by experience.

The white horse cantered past him swerving, and the blond fellow whirled his club at Retief's head. Automatically, Retief raised his club, fended off the blow, cut at the other's back, missed. This thing is too short, Retief thought, whirling his horse. I've got to get in closer. He charged at the champion as the white horse was still in midturn, slammed a heavy blow against his upraised club, rocking the boy; then he was past, turning again. He caught the white horse shorter this time, barely into his turn, and aimed a swing at the man, who first twisted to face him, then spurred, leaped away. Retief pursued him, yelping loudly. Get him rattled, he thought. Get him good and mad!

The champion veered suddenly, veered again, then reared his horse high, whirling, to bring both forefeet down in a chopping attack. Retief reined in, and Danger-by-Night sidestepped disdainfully, as the heavy horse crashed down facing him.

That was a pretty maneuver, Retief thought; but slow, too slow.

His club swung in an overhand cut; the white horse tossed his head suddenly, and the club smashed down across the animal's skull. With a shuddering exhalation, the beast collapsed, and the blond man sprang clear.

Retief reined back, dismayed. He hadn't wanted to kill the animal. He had the right, now, to ride the man down from the safety of the saddle. When gladiators met in mortal combat, there were no rules except those a man made for himself. If he dismounted, met his opponent on equal terms, the advantage his horse had given him would be lost. He looked at the man standing now, facing him, waiting, blood on his face from the fall. He thought of the job he had set himself, the plan that hinged on his victory here. He reminded himself that he was old, too old to meet youth on equal terms; but even as he did so, he was reining the lean black stallion back, swinging down from the saddle. There were some things a man had to do, whether logic was served or not. He couldn't club the man down like a mad dog from the saddle.

There was a strange expression on the champion's face. He sketched a salute with the club he held. "All honor to you, old man," he said. "Now I will kill you." He moved in confidently.

Retief stood his ground, raising his club to deflect a blow, shifting an instant ahead of the pattern of the blond man's assault. There was a hot exchange as the younger man pressed him, took a glancing blow on the temple, stepped back breathing heavily. This wasn't going as he had planned. The old man stood like a wall of stone, not giving an inch; and when their weapons met, it was like flailing at a granite boulder. The young fellow's shoulder ached from the shock. He moved sideways, circling cautiously.

Retief moved to face him. It was risky business, standing

up to the attack, but his legs were not up to any fancy footwork. He had no desire to show his opponent how stiff his movements were, or to tire himself with skipping about. His arms were still as good as any man's, or better. They would have to carry the battle.

The blond jumped in, swung a vicious cut; Retief leaned back, hit out in a one-handed blow, felt the club smack solidly against the other's jaw. He moved now, followed up, landed again on the shoulder. The younger man backed, shaking his head. Retief stopped, waited. It was too bad he couldn't follow up his advantage, but he couldn't chase the fellow all over the arena. He had to save his energy for an emergency. He lowered his club, leaned on it. The crowd noises waxed and waned, unnoticed. The sun beat down in unshielded whiteness, and fitful wind moved dust across the field.

"Come back, peddler," he called. "I want you to sample more of my wares." If he could keep the man angry, he would be careless; and Retief needed the advantage.

The yellow-haired man charged suddenly, whirling the club. Retief raised his, felt the shock of the other's weapon against his. He whirled as the blond darted around him, shifted the club to his left hand in time to ward off a wild swing. Then the fingers of his left hand exploded in fiery agony, and the club flew from his grasp. His head whirled, vision darkening, at the pain from his smashed fingers. He tottered, kept his feet, managed to blink away the faintness, to stare at his hand. Two fingers were missing, pulped, unrecognizable. He had lost his weapon; he was helpless now before the assault of the other.

His head hummed harshly, and his breath came like hot sand across an open wound. He could feel a tremor start and stop in his leg, and his whole left arm felt as though it had been stripped of flesh in a shredding machine. He had not thought it would be as bad as this. His ego, he realized, hadn't aged gracefully.

Now is the hour, old man, he thought. There's no help for you to call on, no easy way out. You'll have to look within yourself for some hidden reserve of strength and endurance and will; and you must think well now, wisely, with a keen eye and a quick hand, or lose your venture. With a movement stiffened by the racking pain-shock, he drew his ceremonial dagger, a jewel-encrusted blade ten inches long. At the least he would die with a weapon in his hand and his face to the enemy.

The blond youth moved closer, tossed the club aside. "Shall a peddler be less capable of the *beau geste* than the arrogant knight?" He laughed, drawing a knife from his belt. "Is your head clear, old man?" he asked. "Are you ready?"

"A gesture . . . you can . . . ill afford," Retief managed. Even breathing hurt. His nerves were shrieking their message of shock at the crushing of living flesh and bone. His forehead was pale, wet with cold sweat.

The young fellow closed, struck out, and Retief evaded the point by an inch, stepped back. His body couldn't stand pain as once it had, he was realizing. He had grown soft, sensitive. For too many years he had been a Diplomat, an operator by manipulation, by subtlety and finesse. Now, when it was man to man, brute strength against brute strength, he was failing.

But he had known when he started that strength was not enough, not without agility; it was subtlety he should be relying on now, his skill at trickery, his devious wit.

Retief caught a glimpse of staring faces at the edge of the field, heard for a moment the mob roar, and then he was again wholly concentrated on the business at hand.

He breathed deeply, struggling for clear-headedness. He had to inveigle the boy into a contest in which he stood a chance. If he could put him on his mettle, make him give up his advantage of tireless energy, quickness . . .

"Are you an honest peddler, or a dancing master?" Retief managed to growl. "Stand and meet me face to face."

The blond man said nothing, feinting rapidly, then striking out. Retief was ready, nicked the other's wrist.

"Gutter fighting is one thing," Retief said. "But you are afraid to face the old man's steel, right arm against right arm." If he went for that, Retief thought, he was even younger than he looked.

"I have heard of the practice," the blond man said, striking at Retief, moving aside from a return cut. "It was devised for old men who did not wish to be made ridiculous by more agile men. I understand that you think you can hoodwink me, but I can beat you at your own game. . . ."

"My point awaits your pleasure," Retief said.

The younger man moved closer, knife held before him. Just a little closer, Retief thought. Just a little closer.

The blond man's eyes were on Retief's. Without warning, Retief dropped his knife and in a lightning motion caught the other's wrist.

"Now struggle, little fish," he said. "I have you fast."

The two men stood chest to chest, staring into each other's eyes. Retief's breath came hard, his heart pounded almost painfully. His left arm was a great pulsating weight of pain. Sweat ran down his dusty face into his eyes. But his grip was locked solidly. The blond youth strained in vain.

With a twist of his wrist Retief turned the blade, then forced the youth's arm up. the fellow struggled to prevent it, throwing all his weight into his effort, fruitlessly. Retief smiled.

"I won't kill you," he said, "but I will have to break your arm. That way you cannot be expected to continue the fight."

"I want no favors from you, old man," the youth panted.

"You won't consider this a favor until the bones knit," Retief said. "Consider this a fair return for my hand."

He pushed the arm up, then suddenly turned it back, levered the upper arm over his forearm, and yanked the tortured member down behind the blond man's back. The bones snapped audibly, and the white-faced youth gasped, staggered as Retief released him.

There were minutes of confusion as referees rushed in, announcements rang out, medics hovered, and the crowd roared its satisfaction, after the fickle nature of crowds. They were satisfied.

An official pushed through to Retief. He wore the vivid colors of the Review regiment. Retief reached up and set the control on the command mike.

"I have the honor to advise you, sir, that you have won the field, and the honors of the day." He paused, startled at the booming echoes, then went on. The bystanders watched curiously, as Retief tried to hold his concentration on the man, to stand easily, while blackness threatened to move in over him. The pain from the crushed hand swelled and focused, then faded, came again. The great dry lungfuls of air he drew in failed to dispel the sensation of suffocation. He struggled to understand the words that seemed to echo from a great distance.

"And now in the name of the Emperor, for crimes against the peace and order of the Empire, I place you under arrest for trial before the High Court at Fragonard."

Retief drew a deep breath, gathered his thoughts to speak.

"Nothing," he said, "could possibly please me more."

The room was vast and ornate, and packed with dignitaries, high officials, peers of the Lily. Here in the great chamber known as the Blue Vault, the High Court sat in silent ranks, waiting.

The charges had been read, the evidence presented. The prisoner, impersonating a peer of the lily and an officer of an ancient and honored Corps, had flaunted the law of Northroyal and the authority of the Emperor, capping his audacity with murder, done by the hand of his servant sworn. Had the prisoner anything to say?

Retief, alone in the prisoner's box in the center of the room, his arm heavily bandaged and deadened with dope, faced the court. This would be the moment when all his preparations would be put to the ultimate test. He had laid long plans toward this hour. The archives of the Corps were beyond comparison in the galaxy, and he had spent weeks there, absorbing every detail of the facts that had been recorded on the world of Northroyal, and on the Old Empire which had preceded it. And to the lore of the archives, he had added facts known to himself, data from his own wide experience. But would those tenuous threads of tradition, hearsay, rumor, and archaic record hold true now? That was the gamble on which his mission was staked. The rabbits had better be in the hat.

He looked at the dignitaries arrayed before him. It had been a devious route, but so far he had succeeded; he had before him the highest officials of the world, the High Justices, the Imperial Archivist, the official keepers of the

Charter and the Code, and of the protocols and rituals of the tradition on which this society was based. He had risked everything on his assault on the sacred stasis of the Tournament, but how else could he have gained the ears of this select audience, with all Northroyal tuned in to hear the end of the drama that a hundred thousand had watched build to its shattering climax?

Now it was his turn to speak. It had better be good.

"Peers of the realm," Retief said, speaking clearly and slowly, "the basis of the charges laid against me is the assumption that I have falsified my identity. Throughout, I have done no more than exercise the traditional rights of a general officer and of a Lilyan peer, and, as befits a Cavalier, I have resisted all attempts to deprive me of those honored prerogatives. While it is regrettable that the low echelon of officials appears to be ignorant of the status of a Lilyan Battle Commander, it is my confident assumption that here, before the ranking nobles of the Northroyalan peerage, the justice of my position will be recognized."

As Retief paused, a dour graybeard spoke up from the Justices' bench.

"Your claims are incoherent to this court. You are known to none of us; and if by chance you claim descent from some renegade who deserted his fellow Cavaliers at the time of the Exile, you will find scant honor among honest men here. From this, it is obvious that you delude yourself in imagining that you can foist your masquerade on this court successfully."

"I am not native to Northroyal," Retief said, "nor do I claim to be. Nor am I a descendant of renegades. Are you gentlemen not overlooking the fact that there was one ship which did not accompany the Cavaliers into exile, but escaped Concordiat surveillance and retired to rally further opposition to the invasion?"

There was a flurry of muttered comment, putting together of heads, and shuffling of papers. The High Justice spoke.

"This would appear to be a reference to the vessel bearing the person of the Emperor Roquelle and his personal suite. . . ."

"That is correct," Retief said.

"You stray farther than ever from the credible," a justice snapped. "The entire royal household accompanied the Emperor Rolan on the happy occasion of his rejoining his subject here at Northroyal a year ago."

"About that event, I will have more to say later," Retief said coolly. "For the present, suffice it to say that I am a legitimate descendant—"

"It does indeed *not* suffice to say!" barked the High Justice. "Do you intend to instruct this court as to what evidence will be acceptable?"

"A figure of speech, Milord," Retief said. "I am quite able to prove my statement."

"Very well," said the High Justice. "Let us see your proof, though I confess I cannot conceive of a satisfactory one."

Retief reached down, unsnapped the flat dispatch case at his belt, drew out a document.

"This is my proof of my bona fides," he said. "I present it in evidence that I have committed no fraud. I am sure that you will recognize an authentic commission-in-patent of the Emperor Roquelle. Please note that the seals are unbroken." He passed the paper over.

A page took the heavy paper, looped with faded red ribbon and plastered with saucer-sized seals, trotted over to the Justices' bench and handed it up to the High Justice. He took it, gazed at it, turning it over, then broke the crumbling seals. The nearby Justices leaned over to see this strange exhibit. It was a heavily embossed document of the Old Empire type, setting forth genealogy and honors, and signed in sprawling letters with the name of an emperor two centuries dead, sealed with his tarnished golden seal. The Justices stared in amazement. The document was worth a fortune.

"I ask that the lowermost paragraph be read aloud," Retief said. "The amendment of thirty years ago."

The High Justice hesitated, then waved a page to him, handed down the document. "Read the lowermost paragraph aloud," he said.

The page read in a clear, well-trained voice.

"KNOW ALL MEN BY THESE PRESENTS THAT WHEREAS: THIS OUR LOYAL SUBJECT AND PEER OF THE IMPERIAL LILY JAME JARL FREELORD OF THE RETIEF; OFFICER IMPERIAL OF THE GUARD; OFFICER OF BATTLE; HEREDITARY LEGIONNAIRE OF HONOR; CAVALIER OF THE LILY; DEFENDER OF SALIENT WEST; BY IMPERIAL GRACE OFFICER OF THE SILVER STAR; HAS BY HIS GALLANTRY, FIDELITY AND SKILL BROUGHT HONOR TO THE IMPERIAL LILY: AND WHEREAS WE PLACE SPECIAL CONFIDENCE AND ESTEEM IN THIS SUBJECT AND PEER: WE DO THEREFORE APPOINT AND COMMAND THAT HE SHALL FORTHWITH ASSUME AND HENCEFORTH BEAR THE HONORABLE RANK OF BATTLE COMMANDER: AND THAT HE SHALL BEAR THE OBLIGATIONS AND ENJOY THE PRIVILEGES APPERTAINING THEREUNTO: AS SHALL HIS HEIRS FOREVER."

There was a silence in the chamber as the page finished reading. All eyes turned to Retief, who stood in the box, a strange expression on his face.

The page handed the paper back up to the High Justice, who resumed his perusal.

"I ask that my retinal patterns now be examined, and matched to those coded on the amendment," Retief said. The High Justice beckoned to a Messenger, and the court waited a restless five minutes until the arrival of an expert who quickly made the necessary check. He went to the Justice's bench, handed up a report form, and left the courtroom. The magistrate glanced at the form, turned again to the document. Below Roquelle's seal were a number of amendments, each in turn signed and sealed. The justices spelled out the unfamiliar names.

"Where did you get this?" the High Justice demanded uncertainly.

"It has been the property of my family for nine generations," Retief replied.

Heads nodded over the document, gray beards wagged.

"How is it," asked a Justice, that you offer in evidence a document bearing amendments validated by signatures and seals completely unknown to us? In order to impress this court, such a warrant might well bear the names of actual former emperors, rather than of fictitious ones. I note the lowermost amendment, purporting to be a certification of high military rank dated only thirty years ago, is signed 'Ronare.'"

"I was at that time attached to the Imperial Suite-in-Exile," Retief said. "I commanded the forces of the Emperor Ronare."

The High Justice and a number of other members of the court snorted openly.

"This impertinence will not further your case," the old magistrate said sharply. "Ronare, indeed. You cite a non-existent authority. At the alleged time of issue of this warrant, the father of our present monarch held the Imperial fief at Trallend."

"At the time of the issue of this document," Retief said in ringing tones, "the father of your present ruler held the bridle when the Emperor mounted!"

An uproar broke out from all sides. The Master-at-arms pounded in vain for silence. At length a measure of order was restored by a gangly official who rose and shouted for the floor. The roar died down, and the stringy fellow, clad in russet velvet with the gold chain of the Master of the Seal about his neck, called out, "Let the court find the traitor guilty summarily and put an end to this insupportable insolence. . . ."

"Northroyal has been the victim of fraud," Retief said loudly in the comparative lull. "But not on my part. The man Rolan is an imposter."

A tremendous pounding of gavels and staffs eventually brought the outraged dignitaries to grim silence. The Presiding Justice peered down at Retief with doom in his lensed eyes. "Your knowledge of the Lilyan tongue and of the forms of court practice as well as the identity of your retinal patterns with those of the warrant tend to substantiate your origin in the Empire. Accordingly, this court is now disposed to recognize in you that basest of offenders, a renegade of the peerage." He raised his voice. "Let it be recorded that one Jame Jarl, a freelord of the Imperial Lily and officer Imperial of the Guard has by his own words disavowed his oath and his lineage." The fiery old man glared around at his fellow jurists. "Now let the dog of a broken officer be sentenced!"

"I have proof of what I say," Retief called out. "Nothing has been proven against me. I have acted by the Code, and by the Code I demand my hearing!"

"You have spurned the Code," said a fat dignitary.

"I have told you that an usurper sits on the Lily throne," Retief said. "If I can't prove it, execute me."

There was an icy silence.

"Very well," said the High Justice. "Present your proof."

"When the man, Rolan, appeared," Retief said, "he presented the Imperial seal and ring, the ceremonial robe, the major portion of the crown jewels, and the Imperial Genealogy."

"That is correct."

"Was it noted, by any chance, that the seal was without its chain, that the robe was stained, that the most important of the jewels, the ancient Napoleon Emerald, was missing, that the ring bore deep scratches, and that the lock on the book had been forced?"

A murmur grew along the high benches of the court. Intent eyes glared down at Retief.

"And was it not considered strange that the Imperial signet was not presented by this would-be Emperor, when that signet alone constitutes the true symbol of the Empire?" Retief's voice had risen to a thunderous loudness.

The High Justice stared now with a different emotion in his eyes.

"What do you know of these matters?" he demanded, but without assurance.

Retief reached into a tiny leather bag at his side, drew out something which he held out for inspection.

"This is a broken chain," he said. "It was cut when the seal was stolen from its place in Suite-in-Exile." He placed the heavy links on the narrow wainscot before him. "This," he said, "is the Napoleon Emerald, once worn by the legendary Bonaparte in a ring. It is unique in the galaxy, and easily proved genuine." There was utter stillness now. Retief placed a small key beside the chain and the gem. "This key will open the forced lock of the Imperial Genealogical Record."

Retief brought out an ornately wrought small silver casket and held it in view.

"The stains on the robe are the blood of the Emperor Ronare, shed by the knife of a murderer. The ring is scratched by the same knife, used to sever the finger in order to remove the ring." A murmur of horrified comment ran around the room now. Retief waited, letting all eyes focus on the silver box in his hand. It contained a really superb copy of the Imperial Signet; like the chain, the key and the emerald, the best that the science of the Corps could produce, accurate even in its internal molecular structure. It had to be, if it were to have a chance of acceptance. It would be put to the test without delay, matched to an electronic matrix with which it would, if acceptable, resonate perfectly. The copy had been assembled on the basis of some excellent graphic records; the original signet, as Retief knew, had been lost irretrievably in a catastrophic palace fire, a century and a half ago.

He opened the box, showed the magnificent wine-red crystal set in platinum. Now was the moment. "This is the talisman which alone would prove the falseness of the impostor Rolan," Retief said. "I call upon the honorable High Court to match it to the matrix; and while that is being done, I ask that the honorable Justices study carefully the genealogy included in the Imperial patent which I have presented to the court."

A messenger was dispatched to bring in the matrix while the Justices adjusted the focus of their corrective lenses and clustered over the document. The chamber buzzed with tense excitement. This was a fantastic development indeed!

The High Justice looked up as the massive matrix device was wheeled into the room. He stared at Retief. "This genealogy—" he began.

A Justice plucked at his sleeve, indicated the machine, whispering something. The High Justice nodded.

Retief handed the silver box down carefully to a page,

watched as the chamber of the machine was opened, the great crystal placed in position. He held his breath as technicians twiddled controls, studied dials, then closed a switch. There was a sonorous musical tone from the machine.

The technician looked up. "The crystal," he said, "does match the matrix."

Amid a burst of exclamations which died as he faced the High Justice, Retief spoke.

"My lords, peers of the Imperial Lily," he said in a ringing voice, "know by this signet that we, Retief, by the grace of God Emperor, do now claim our rightful throne."

And just as quickly as the exclamations had died, they rose once more—a mixture of surprise and awe.

EPILOGUE

"A brilliant piece of work, Mr. Minister, and congratulations on your promotion," the Ambassador-at-large said warmly. "You've shown what individualism and the unorthodox approach can accomplish where the academic viewpoint would consider the situation hopeless."

"Thank you, Mr. Ambassador," Retief replied, smiling. "I was surprised myself when it was all over, that my gamble paid off. Frankly, I hope I won't ever be in a position again to be quite so inventive."

"I don't mind telling you now," the Ambassador said, "that when I saw Magnan's report of your solo assignment to the case, I seriously attempted to recall you, but it was too late. It was a nasty piece of business sending a single agent in on a job with the wide implications of this one. Mr. Magnan had been under a strain, I'm afraid. He is having a long rest now. . . ."

Retief understood perfectly. His former chief had gotten the axe, and he himself had emerged clothed in virtue. That was the one compensation of desperate ventures; if you won, they paid well. In his new rank, he had a long tenure ahead. He hoped the next job would be something complex and far removed from Northroyal. He thought back over the crowded weeks of his brief reign there as Emperor. It had been a stormy scene when the bitterly resisting Rolan had been brought to face the High Court. The man had been hanged an hour before sunrise on the following day, still protesting his authenticity. That, at least, was a lie. Retief was grateful that he had proof that Rolan was a fraud, because he would have sent him to the gallows on false evidence even had he been the true heir.

His first act after his formal enthronement had been the abolition in perpetuity of the rite of the tourney, and the formal cancellation of all genealogical requirements for appointments public or private. He had ordered the release and promotion of the Battle Ensign who had ignored Rolan's arrest order and had been himself imprisoned for his pains. Fitzraven he had seen appointed to the Imperial War College—his future assured.

Retief smiled as he remembered the embarrassment of the young fellow who had been his fellow-finalist in the tourney. He had offered him satisfaction on the field of honor as soon as his arm healed, and had been asked in return for forgetfulness of poor judgment. He had made him a Captain of the Guard and a peer of the realm. He had the spirit for it.

There had been much more to do, and Retief's days had been crowded with the fantastically complex details of disengaging a social structure from the crippling reactionary restraints of ossified custom and hallowed tradition. In the end, he had produced a fresh and workable new constitution for the kingdom which he hoped would set the world on an enlightened and dynamic path to a productive future.

The memory of Princess Monica lingered pleasantly; a true princess of the Lily, in the old tradition. Retief had abdicated in her favor; her genealogy had been studded with enough Imperial forebears to satisfy the crustiest of the Old Guard peerage; of course, it could not compare with the handsome document he had displayed showing his own descent in the direct line through seven—or was it eight—generations of Emperors-in-exile from the lost monarch of the beleaguered Lily Empire, but it was enough to justify his choice. Rolan's abortive usurpation had at least had the effect of making the Northroyalans appreciate an enlightened ruler.

At the last, it had not been easy to turn away forever from the seat of Empire which he so easily sat. It had not been lightly that he had said good-by to the lovely Monica, who had reminded him of another dark beauty of long ago.

A few weeks in a modern hospital had remedied the harsher after-effects of his short career as a gladiator, and he was ready now for the next episode that fate and the Corps might have in store. But he would not soon forget Northroyal. . . .

" . . . magnificent ingenuity," someone was saying. "You must have assimilated your indoctrination on the background unusually thoroughly to have been able to prepare in advance just those artifacts and documents which would prove most essential. And the technical skill in the production itself. Remarkable. To think that you were able to hoodwink the high priests of the cult in the very sanctum sanctorum."

"Merely the result of careful research," Retief said modestly. "I found all I needed on late developments, buried in our files. The making of the Signet was quite a piece of work; but credit for that goes to our own technicians."

"I was even more impressed by that document," a young counselor said. "What a knowledge of their psychology and of technical detail that required."

Retief smiled faintly. The others had all gone into the hall now, amid a babble of conversation. It was time to be going. He glanced at the eager junior agent.

"No," he said, "I can't claim much credit there. I've had that document for many years; it, at least, was perfectly genuine."

PART II:
A CAREER
BEGINS...BADLY

Editor's Note: The Retief stories were written over a period of many years, and Laumer does not seem to have had any overarching scheme guiding the development of his character. Still, some of the stories clearly belong toward the beginning of Retief's career—these three, in particular.

---

1) Cf. the original colorful language: "maintenance of a state of tension short of actual conflict." See CDT File 178/b/491, col. VII, spool 12: 745mm (code 2g)

" . . . into the chaotic Galactic political scene of the post-Concordiat era, the CDT emerged to carry forward the ancient diplomatic tradition as a great supranational organization dedicated to the contravention of war.[1] As mediators of disputes among Terrestrial-settled worlds and advocates of Terrestrial interests in contacts with alien cultures, Corps diplomats, trained in the chanceries of innumerable defunct bureaucracies, displayed an encyclopedic grasp of the nuances of Extra-Terrestrial mores as set against the labyrinthine socio-politico-economic Galactic context. Never was the virtuosity of a senior Corps diplomat more brilliantly displayed than in Ambassador Spradley's negotiation of the awkward Sirenian Question . . ."

—extract from the *Official History of the Corps Diplomatique*, Vol I, reel 2. Solarian Press, New York, 479 A. E. (AD 2940)

PROTOCOL

In the gloom of the squat, mud-colored reception building, the Counselor, two First Secretaries, and the senior Attachés gathered around the plump figure of Ambassador Spradley, their ornate diplomatic uniforms bright in the vast gloomy room. The ambassador glanced at his finger watch impatiently.

"Ben, are you quite certain our arrival time was made clear?"

Second Secretary Magnan nodded emphatically. "I stressed the point, Mr. Ambassador. I communicated with Mr. T'Cai-Cai just before the lighter broke orbit, and I specifically emphasized—"

"I hope you didn't appear truculent, Mr. Magnan," the Ambassador cut in sharply.

"No indeed, Mr. Ambassador. I merely—"

"You're sure there's no VIP room here?" The Ambassador glanced around the cavernous room. "Curious that not even chairs have been provided."

"If you'd care to sit on one of those crates, I'll use my hanky—"

"Certainly not." The Ambassador looked at his watch again and cleared his throat.

"I may as well make use of these few moments to outline our approach for the more junior members of the staff. It's vital that the entire mission work in harmony in the presentation of the image. We Terrestrials are a kindly, peace-loving race." The Ambassador smiled in a kindly, peace-loving way.

"We seek only reasonable division of spheres of influence with the Yill." He spread his hands, looking reasonable.

"We are a people of high culture, ethical, sincere."

The smile was replaced abruptly by pursed lips. "We'll start by asking for the entire Sirenian System, and settle for half. We'll establish a foothold on all the choicer worlds and, with shrewd handling, in a decade we'll be in a position to assert a wider claim." The Ambassador glanced around. "If there are no questions . . ."

Jame Retief, Vice-Consul and Third Secretary in the Corps Diplomatique and junior member of the Terrestrial Embassy to Yill, stepped forward.

"Since we hold the prior claim to the system, why don't we put all our cards on the table to start with? Perhaps if we dealt frankly with the Yill, it would pay us in the long run."

Ambassador Spradley blinked up at the younger man. Beside him, Magnan cleared his throat in the silence.

"Vice-Consul Retief merely means—"

"I'm capable of interpreting Mr. Retief's remark," Spradley snapped. He assumed a fatherly expression.

"Young man, you're new to the service. You haven't yet learned the team play, the give-and-take of diplomacy. I shall expect you to observe closely the work of the experienced negotiators of the mission, learn the importance of subtlety. Excessive reliance on direct methods might tend in time to attenuate the rôle of the professional diplomat. I shudder to contemplate the consequences."

Spradley turned back to his senior staff members. Retief strolled across to a glass-paneled door and glanced into the room beyond. Several dozen tall grey-skinned Yill lounged in deep couches, sipping lavender drinks from slender glass tubes. Black-tunicked servants moved about inconspicuously, offering trays. Retief watched as a party of brightly-dressed Yill moved toward a wide entrance door. One of the party, a tall male, made to step before another, who raised a hand languidly, fist clenched. The first Yill stepped back and placed his hands on top of his head with a nod. Both Yill continued to smile and chatter as they passed through the door.

Retief rejoined the Terrestrial delegation, grouped around a mound of rough crates stacked on the bare concrete floor, as a small leather-skinned Yill came up.

"I am P'Toi. Come thiss way . . ." He motioned. The Terrestrials moved off, Ambassador Spradley in the lead. As the portly diplomat reached the door, the Yill guide darted ahead, shouldering him aside, then hesitated, waiting. The Ambassador almost glared, then remembered the image. He smiled, beckoning the Yill ahead. The Yill muttered in the native language, stared about, then passed through the door. The Terran party followed.

"I'd like to know what that fellow was saying," Magnan said, overtaking the Ambassador. "The way he jostled your Excellency was disgraceful."

A number of Yill waited on the pavement outside the building. As Spradley approached the luxurious open car waiting at the curb, they closed ranks, blocking his way. He drew himself up, opened his mouth—then closed it with a snap.

"The very idea," Magnan said, trotting at Spradley's heels as he stalked back to rejoin the staff, now looking around

uncertainly. "One would think these persons weren't aware
of the courtesies due a Chief of Mission."

"They're not aware of the courtesies due an apprentice
sloat skinner!" Spradley snapped. Around the Terrestrials,
the Yill milled nervously, muttering in the native tongue.

"Where has our confounded interpreter betaken himself?" the Ambassador barked. "I daresay they're plotting
openly . . ."

"A pity we have to rely on a native interpreter."

"Had I known we'd meet this rather uncouth reception,"
the Ambassador said stiffly, "I would have audited the
language personally, of course, during the voyage out."

"Oh, no criticism intended, of course, Mr. Ambassador," Magnan said hastily. "Heavens, who would have
thought—"

Retief stepped up beside the Ambassador.

"Mr. Ambassador," he said. "I—"

"Later, young man," the Ambassador snapped. He beckoned to the Counselor, and the two moved off, heads
together.

A bluish sun gleamed in a dark sky. Retief watched his
breath form a frosty cloud in the chill air. A broad hard-
wheeled vehicle pulled up to the platform. The Yill gestured the Terran party to the gaping door at the rear, then
stood back, waiting.

Retief looked curiously at the grey-painted van. The
legend written on its side in alien symbols seemed to read
'egg nog'. Unfortunately he hadn't had time to learn the
script too, on the trip out. Perhaps later he would have a
chance to tell the Ambassador he could interpret for the
mission.

The Ambassador entered the vehicle, the other Terrestrials following. It was as bare of seats as the Terminal
building. What appeared to be a defunct electronic chassis lay in the center of the floor, amid a litter of paper and
a purple and yellow sock designed for a broad Yill foot.
Retief glanced back. The Yill were talking excitedly. None
of them entered the car. The door was closed, and the
Terrans braced themselves under the low roof as the engine
started up with a whine of worn turbos, and the van moved
off.

It was an uncomfortable ride. The unsprung wheels hammered uneven cobblestones. Retief put out an arm as the vehicle rounded a corner, caught the Ambassador as he staggered off-balance. The Ambassador glared at him, settled his heavy tri-corner hat, and stood stiffly until the car lurched again.

Retief stooped, trying to see out through the single dusty window. They seemed to be in a wide street lined with low buildings. They passed through a massive gate, up a ramp, and stopped. The door opened. Retief looked out at a blank grey facade, broken by tiny windows at irregular intervals. A scarlet vehicle was drawn up ahead, the Yill reception committee emerging from it. Through its wide windows Retief saw rich upholstery and caught a glimpse of glasses clamped to a tiny bar.

P'Toi, the Yill interpreter, came forward, gesturing to a small door in the grey wall. Magnan scurried ahead to open it and held it for the Ambassador. As he stepped to it a Yill thrust himself ahead and hesitated. Ambassador Spradley drew himself up, glaring. Then he twisted his mouth into a frozen smile and stepped aside. The Yill looked at each other, then filed through the door.

Retief was the last to enter. As he stepped inside a black-clad servant slipped past him, pulled the lid from a large box by the door and dropped in a paper tray heaped with refuse. There were alien symbols in flaking paint on the box. They seemed, Retief noticed, to spell 'egg nog'.

The shrill pipes and whining reeds had been warming up for an hour when Retief emerged from his cubicle and descended the stairs to the banquet hall. Standing by the open doors he lit a slender cigar and watched through narrowed eyes as obsequious servants in black flitted along the low wide corridor, carrying laden trays into the broad room, arranging settings on a great four-sided table forming a hollow square that almost filled the room. Rich brocades were spread across the center of the side nearest the door, flanked by heavily decorated white cloths. Beyond, plain white extended down the two sides to the far board, where metal dishes were arranged on the bare table top. A richly dressed Yill approached, stepped aside to allow a servant to pass and entered the room.

Retief turned at the sound of Terran voices behind him. The Ambassador came up, trailed by two diplomats. He glanced at Retief, adjusted his ruff and looked into the banquet hall.

"Apparently we're to be kept waiting again," he snapped. "After having been informed at the outset that the Yill have no intention of yielding an inch, one almost wonders . . ."

"Mr. Ambassador," Retief said. "Have you noticed—"

"However," Ambassador Spradley said, eyeing Retief, "a seasoned diplomat must take these little snubs in stride. In the end—ah there, Magnan . . ." He turned away, talking.

Somewhere a gong clanged. In a moment the corridor was filled with chattering Yill who moved past the group of Terrestrials into the banquet hall. P'Toi, the Yill interpreter, came up, raised a hand.

"Waitt heere . . ."

More Yill filed into the dining room, taking their places. A pair of helmeted guards approached and waved the Terrestrials back. An immense grey-jowled Yill waddled to the doors, ropes of jewels clashing softly, and passed through, followed by more guards.

"The Chief of State," Retief heard Magnan say. "The Admirable F'Kau-Kau-Kau."

"I have yet to present my credentials," Ambassador Spradley said. "One expects some latitude in the observances of protocol, but I confess . . ." He wagged his head.

The Yill interpreter spoke up.

"You now whill lhie on yourr intesstinss and creep to fesstive board there." He pointed across the room.

"Intestines?" Ambassador Spradley looked about wildly.

"Mr. P'Toi means our stomachs, I wouldn't wonder," Magnan said. "He just wants us to lie down and crawl to our seats, Mr. Ambassador."

"What the devil are you grinning at, you idiot?" the Ambassador snapped.

Magnan's face fell.

Spradley glanced down at the medals across his paunch. "This is . . . I've never . . ."

"Homage to godss," the interpreter said.

"Oh-oh—religion," someone said.

"Well, if it's a matter of religious beliefs . . ." The Ambassador looked around dubiously.

"Actually, it's only a couple of hundred feet," Magnan said.

Retief stepped up to P'Toi.

"His Excellency, the Terrestrial Ambassador will not crawl," he said clearly.

"Here, young man, I said nothing—"

"Not to crawl?" The interpreter wore an unreadable Yill expression.

"It is against our religion," Retief said.

"Againsst?"

"We are votaries of the Snake Goddess," Retief said. "It is a sacrilege to crawl." He brushed past the interpreter and marched toward the distant table. The others followed.

Puffing, the Ambassador came to Retief's side as they approached the dozen empty stools on the far side of the square opposite the brocaded position of the Admirable F'Kau-Kau-Kau.

"Mr. Retief, kindly see me after this affair," he hissed. "In the meantime, I hope you will restrain any further rash impulses. Let me remind you *I* am Chief of Mission here."

Magnan came up from behind.

"Let me add my congratulations, Retief," he said. "That was fast thinking."

"Are you out of your mind, Magnan?" the Ambassador barked. "I am extremely displeased."

"Why," Magnan stuttered, "I was speaking sarcastically, of course, Mr. Ambassador. Naturally I, too, was taken aback by his presumption."

The Terrestrials took their places, Retief at the end. The table before them was of bare green wood, with an array of shallow pewter dishes upon it.

The Yill at the table, some in plain grey, others in black, eyed them silently. There was a constant stir among them as one or another rose and disappeared and others sat down. The pipes and reeds of the orchestra were shrilling furiously and the susurration of Yillian conversation from the other tables rose ever higher in competition. A tall Yill in black was at the Ambassador's side now. The nearby Yill all fell silent as the servant ladled a whitish soup into the largest of the bowls before the Terrestrial envoy. The interpreter hovered, watching.

"That's quite enough," Ambassador Spradley said, as the bowl overflowed. The Yill servant dribbled more of the soup into the bowl. It welled out across the table top.

"Kindly serve the other members of my staff," the Ambassador commanded. The interpreter said something in a low voice. The servant moved hesitantly to the next stool and ladled more soup.

Retief watched, listening to the whispers around him. The Yill at the table were craning now to watch. The servant was ladling the soup rapidly, rolling his eyes sideways. He came to Retief and reached out with the full ladle for the bowl.

"No," Retief said.

The servant hesitated.

"None for me," Retief said.

The interpreter came up, motioned to the servant, who reached again, ladle brimming.

"I don't want any!" Retief said, his voice distinct in the sudden hush. He stared at the interpreter, who stared back for a moment, then waved the servant away and moved on.

"Mr. Retief," a voice hissed. Retief looked down the table. The Ambassador was leaning forward, glaring at him, his face a mottled crimson.

"I'm warning you, Mr. Retief," he said hoarsely. "I've eaten sheep's eyes in the Sudan, *ka swe* in Burma, hundred-year *cug* on Mars, and everything else that has been placed before me in the course of my diplomatic career, and by the holy relics of Saint Ignatz, you'll do the same!" He snatched up a spoon-like utensil and dipped it into his bowl.

"Don't eat that, Mr. Ambassador," Retief said.

The Ambassador stared, eyes wide. He opened his mouth, guiding the spoon toward it.

Retief stood, gripped the table under its edge, and heaved. The immense wooden slab rose and tilted; dishes crashed to the floor. The table followed with a ponderous slam. Milky soup splattered across the terrazzo; a couple of odd bowls rolled clattering across the room. Cries rang out from the Yill, mingling with a strangled yell from Ambassador Spradley.

Retief walked past the wild-eyed members of the mission to the sputtering chief. "Mr. Ambassador," he said. "I'd like—"

"You'd like! I'll break you, you young hoodlum! Do you realize—"

"Pleass . . ." The interpreter stood at Retief's side.

"My apologies," Ambassador Spradley said, mopping his forehead. "My profound—"

"Be quiet," Retief said.

"Wh—what?!"

"Don't apologize," Retief said.

P'Toi was beckoning. "Pleasse, arll come."

Retief turned and followed him.

The portion of the table they were ushered to was covered with an embroidered white cloth, set with thin porcelain dishes. The Yill already seated there rose, amid babbling and moved down to make room for the Terrestrials. The black-clad Yill at the end table closed ranks to fill the vacant seats. Retief sat down, finding Magnan at his side.

"What's going on here?" the Second Secretary said.

"They were giving us dog food," Retief said. "I overheard a Yill. They seated us at the servants' section of the table."

"You mean you understand the language?"

"I learned it on the way out—enough, at least—"

The music burst out with a clangorous fanfare, and a throng of jugglers, dancers, and acrobats poured into the center of the hollow square, frantically juggling, dancing, and back-flipping. Servants swarmed, heaping mounds of fragrant food on the plates of Yill and Terrestrials alike, pouring pale purple liquor into slender glasses. Retief sampled the Yill food. It was delicious. Conversation was impossible in the din. He watched the gaudy display and ate heartily.

Retief leaned back, grateful for the lull in the music. The last of the dishes were whisked away, and more glasses filled. The exhausted entertainers stopped to pick up the thick square coins the diners threw. Retief sighed. It had been a rare feast.

"Retief," Magnan said in the comparative quiet. "What were you saying about dog food as the music came up?"

Retief looked at him. "Haven't you noticed the pattern, Mr. Magnan? The series of deliberate affronts?"

"Deliberate affronts! Just a minute, Retief. They're uncouth, yes, crowding into doorways and that sort of thing. But . . ." He looked at Retief uncertainly.

"They herded us into a baggage warehouse at the terminal. Then they hauled us here in a garbage truck."

"Garbage truck!"

"Only symbolic, of course. They ushered us in the tradesmen's entrance, and assigned us cubicles in the servants' wing. Then we were seated with the coolie-class sweepers at the bottom of the table."

"You must be mistaken! I mean, after all, we're the Terrestrial delegation; surely these Yill must realize our power."

"Precisely, Mr. Magnan. But—"

With a clang of cymbals, the musicians launched a renewed assault. Six tall, helmeted Yill sprang into the center of the floor, paired off in a wild performance, half dance, half combat. Magnan pulled at Retief's sleeve, his mouth moving. Retief shook his head. No one could talk against a Yill orchestra in full cry. Retief sampled a bright red wine and watched the show.

There was a flurry of action, and two of the dancers stumbled and collapsed, their partner-opponents whirling away to pair off again, describe the elaborate pre-combat ritual, and abruptly set to, dulled sabres clashing—and two more Yill were down, stunned. It was a violent dance. Retief watched, the drink forgotten.

The last two Yill approached and retreated, whirled, bobbed, and spun, feinted and postured. And then one was slipping, going down, helmet awry, and the other, a giant, muscular Yill, spun away, whirled in a mad skirl of pipes as coins showered—then froze before a gaudy table, raised the sabre, and slammed it down in a resounding blow across the gay cloth before a lace-and-bow-bedecked Yill. The music stopped with a ringing clash of cymbals.

In utter silence the dancer-fighter stared across the table. With a shout the seated Yill leaped up and raised a

clenched fist. The dancer bowed his head, spread his hands
on his helmet and resumed his dance as the music blared
anew. The beribboned Yill waved a hand negligently, flung
a handful of coins across the floor, and sat down.

Now the dancer stood rigid before the brocaded table—
and the music chopped off short as the sabre slammed
down before a heavy Yill in ornate metallic coils. The
challenged Yill rose, raised a fist, and the other ducked his
head, putting his hands on his helmet. Coins rolled, and
the dancer moved on.

He circled the broad floor, sabre twirling, arms darting
in an intricate symbolism. Then suddenly he was towering before Retief, sabre above his head. The music cut,
and in the startling instantaneous silence, the heavy sabre
whipped over and down with an explosive concussion that
set dishes dancing on the table-top.

The Yill's eyes held on Retief's. In the silence Magnan
tittered drunkenly. Retief pushed back his stool.

"Steady, my boy," Ambassador Spradley called. Retief
stood, the Yill topping his six-foot-three by an inch. In a
motion too quick to follow Retief reached for the sabre,
twitched it from the Yill's grasp, swung it in a whistling arc.
The Yill ducked, sprang back and snatched up a sabre
dropped by another dancer.

"Someone stop the madman!" Spradley howled.

Retief leaped across the table, sending fragile dishes
spinning.

The other danced back, and only then did the orchestra spring to life with a screech and a mad tattoo of high-
pitched drums.

Making no attempt to follow the weaving pattern of the
Yill bolero, Retief pressed the Yill, fending off vicious cuts
with the blunt weapon, chopping back relentlessly. Left
hand on hip, Retief matched blow for blow, driving the
other back.

Abruptly the Yill abandoned the double role. Dancing
forgotten, he settled down in earnest, cutting, thrusting,
parrying. Now the two stood toe to toe, sabres clashing in
a lightning exchange. The Yill gave a step, two, then ral-
lied, drove Retief back, back—

Retief feinted, laid a hearty whack across the grey skull.

The Yill stumbled, his sabre clattered to the floor. Retief stepped aside as the Yill wavered past him and crashed to the floor.

The orchestra fell silent in a descending wail of reeds. Retief drew a deep breath and wiped his forehead.

"Come back here, you young fool!" Spradley called hoarsely.

Retief hefted the sabre, turned, eyed the brocade-draped table. He started across the floor. The Yill sat as if paralyzed.

"Retief, no!" Spradley yelped.

Retief walked directly to the Admirable F'Kau-Kau-Kau, stopped, raised the sabre.

"Not the Chief of State," someone in the Terrestrial Mission groaned.

Retief whipped the sabre down. The dull blade split the heavy brocade and cleaved the hardwood table. There was utter silence.

The Admirable F'Kau-Kau-Kau rose, seven feet of obese grey Yill. His broad face expressionless to the Terran eye, he raised a fist like a jewel-studded ham.

Retief stood rigid for a long moment. Then, gracefully, he inclined his head and placed his finger tips on his temples. Behind him there was a clatter as Ambassador Spradley collapsed. Then the Admirable F'Kau-Kau-Kau cried out, reached across the table to embrace the Terrestrial, and the orchestra went mad. Grey hands helped Retief across the table, stools were pushed aside to make room at F'Kau-Kau-Kau's side. Retief sat, took a tall flagon of coal-black brandy pressed on him by his neighbor, clashed glasses with The Admirable, and drank.

"The feast ends," F'Kau-Kau-Kau said. "Now you and I, Retief, must straddle the Council Stool."

"I'll be honored, Your Admirableness," Retief said. "I must inform my colleagues."

"Colleagues?" F'Kau-Kau-Kau said. "It is for the chiefs to parley. Who shall speak for a king while he yet has tongue for talk?"

"The Yill way is wise," Retief said.

F'Kau-Kau-Kau emptied a squat tumbler of pink beer.

"I'll treat with you, Retief, as viceroy, since as you say your king is old and the space between worlds is far. But there shall be no scheming underlings privy to our dealings." He grinned a Yill grin. "Afterwards we shall carouse, Retief. The Council Stool is hard, and the waiting handmaidens delectable; this makes for quick agreement."

Retief smiled. "The Admirable speaks wisdom."

"Of course, a being prefers wenches of his own kind," F'Kau-Kau-Kau said. He belched. "The Ministry of Culture has imported several Terrestrial joy-girls, said to be top-notch specimens. At least they have very fat watchamacallits."

"Your Admirableness is most considerate," Retief said.

"Let us to it then, Retief. I may hazard a tumble with one of your Terries, myself. I fancy an occasional perversion." F'Kau-Kau-Kau dug an elbow into Retief's side and bellowed with laughter.

As Retief crossed to the door at F'Kau-Kau-Kau's side, Ambassador Spradley glowered from behind the plain tablecloth. "Retief," he called, "kindly excuse yourself. I wish a word with you." His voice was icy. Magnan stood behind him, goggling.

"Forgive my apparent rudeness, Mr. Ambassador," said Retief. "I don't have time to explain now—"

"Rudeness!" Spradley yipped. "Don't have time, eh? Let me tell you—"

"Please lower your voice, Mr. Ambassador," Retief said. "The situation is still delicate."

Spradley quivered, his mouth open. He found his voice, "You—you—"

"Silence!" Retief snapped. Spradley looked up at Retief's face, staring for a moment into Retief's grey eyes. He closed his mouth and swallowed.

"The Yill seem to have gotten the impression I'm in charge," Retief said. "We'll have to maintain the deception."

"But—but—" Spradley stuttered. Then he straightened. "This is the last straw," he whispered hoarsely. "*I* am the Terrestrial Ambassador Extraordinary and Minister Plenipotentiary. Magnan has told me that we've been studiedly and repeatedly insulted, since the moment of our arrival; kept waiting in baggage rooms, transported in refuse lorries, herded about with servants, offered swill at the table. Now I, and my senior staff, are left cooling our heels, without so much as an audience, while this—this multiple Kau person hobnobs with—with—"

Spradley's voice broke. "I may have been a trifle hasty, Retief, in attempting to restrain you. Slighting the native gods and dumping the banquet table are rather extreme measures, but your resentment was perhaps partially justified. I am prepared to be lenient with you." He fixed a choleric eye on Retief.

"I am walking out of this meeting, Mr. Retief. I'll take no more of these personal—"

"That's enough," Retief said sharply. "We're keeping the Admirable waiting."

Spradley's face purpled.

Magnan found his voice. "What are you going to do, Retief?"

"I'm going to handle the negotiation," Retief said. He handed Magnan his empty glass. "Now go sit down and work on the Image."

At his desk in the VIP suite aboard the orbiting Corps vessel, Ambassador Spradley pursed his lips and looked severely at Vice-Consul Retief.

"Further," he said, "you have displayed a complete lack of understanding of Corps discipline, the respect due a senior officer, even the basic courtesies. Your aggravated displays of temper, ill-timed outbursts of violence, and almost incredible arrogance in the assumption of authority make your further retention as an Officer-Agent of the Corps Diplomatique Terrestrienne impossible. It will therefore be my unhappy duty to recommend your immediate—"

There was a muted buzz from the communicator. The Ambassador cleared his throat.

"Well?"

"A signal from Sector HQ, Mr. Ambassador," a voice said.

"Well, read it," Spradley snapped. "Skip the preliminaries . . ."

"Congratulations on the unprecedented success of your

mission. The articles of agreement transmitted by you embody a most favorable resolution of the difficult Sirenian situation, and will form the basis of continued amicable relations between the Terrestrial States and the Yill Empire. To you and your staff, full credit is due for a job well done. Signed, Deputy Assistant Secretary Sternwheeler."

Spradley cut off the voice impatiently. He shuffled papers, then eyed Retief sharply.

"Superficially, of course, an uninitiated observer might leap to the conclusion that the ah . . . results that were produced in spite of these . . . ah . . . irregularities justify the latter." The Ambassador smiled a sad, wise smile. "This is far from the case," he said. "I—"

The communicator burped softly.

"Confound it." Spradley muttered. "Yes?"

"Mr. T'Cai-Cai has arrived," the voice said. "Shall I—"

"Send him in, at once." Spradley glanced at Retief. "Only a two-syllable man, but I shall attempt to correct these false impressions, make some amends . . ."

The two Terrestrials waited silently until the Yill Protocol chief tapped at the door.

"I hope," the Ambassador said, "that you will resist the impulse to take advantage of your unusual position." He looked at the door. "Come in."

T'Cai-Cai stepped into the room, glanced at Spradley, then turned to greet Retief in voluble Yill. He rounded the desk to the Ambassador's chair, motioned him from it, and sat down.

"I have a surprise for you, Retief," he said in Terran. "I myself have made use of the teaching machine you so kindly lent us."

"That's good," Retief said. "I'm sure Mr. Spradley will be interested in hearing what we have to say."

"Never mind," the Yill said. "I am here only socially." He looked around the room.

"So plainly you decorate your chamber; but it has a certain austere charm." He laughed a Yill laugh.

"Oh, you are a strange breed, you Terrestrials. You surprised us all. You know, one hears such outlandish stories. I tell you in confidence, we had expected you to be over-pushes."

"Pushovers," Spradley said tonelessly.

"Such restraint! What pleasure you gave to those of us, like myself of course, who appreciated your grasp of protocol. Such finesse! How subtly you appeared to ignore each overture, while neatly avoiding actual contamination. I can tell you, there were those who thought—poor fools—that you had no grasp of etiquette. How gratified we were, we professionals, who could appreciate your virtuosity—when you placed matters on a comfortable basis by spurning the cats'-meat. It was sheer pleasure then, waiting, to see what form your compliment would take."

The Yill offered orange cigars, then stuffed one in his nostril.

"I confess even I had not hoped that you would honor our Admirable so signally. Oh, it is a pleasure to deal with fellow professionals, who understand the meaning of protocol."

Ambassador Spradley made a choking sound.

"This fellow has caught a chill," T'Cai-Cai said. He eyed Spradley dubiously. "Step back, my man, I am highly susceptible.

"There is one bit of business I shall take pleasure in attending to, my dear Retief," T'Cai-Cai went on. He drew a large paper from his reticule. "His Admirableness is determined that none other than yourself shall be accredited here. I have here my government's exequatur confirming you as Terrestrial Consul-General to Yill. We shall look forward to your prompt return."

Retief looked at Spradley.

"I'm sure the Corps will agree," he said.

"Then I shall be going," T'Cai-Cai said. He stood up. "Hurry back to us, Retief. There is much that I would show you of the great Empire of Yill." He winked a Yill wink.

"Together, Retief, we shall see many high and splendid things."

"Rising above crass materialism, the native piety of Corps diplomats, coupled with a solemn appreciation of universal spiritual values, has enriched Corps annals with no more inspiring example of the reconciliation of alien ideologies than that of Ambassador Straphanger's virtuoso performance among the Hoog. Ever humbly aware of the Great Notebook in the hand of the Big Inspector—whose E.R.'s are written on the parchment of Eternity—Straphanger penetrated the veils of ecclesiastical mystery to base a rapprochement on the firm ground of the realistic doctrine of the Universal Popularity of Sin . . ."

—Vol. II, Reel I, 480 AE (AD 2941)

THE BRASS GOD

The Hoogan chamberlain was tall, black-clad, high-shouldered, with an immense dome-shaped head sloping into massive shoulders, eyes like freshly shelled oysters in a leathery face and over-long, dangling arms. He turned to face the party of Terrestrial diplomats who stood clutching suitcases, dwarfed under the lofty vaulted ceiling of the vast, dark hall. Shafts of eerily colored light filtered through stained-glass loopholes high in the walls to shed a faint glow on the uneven stone floor, the drab-colored murals and hangings depicting the specialties of the seven Hoogan Hells, the mouths of dark corridors radiating from the circular chamber with helmeted and kilted Hoogan pikemen spaced between them, immobile as the gargoyles that peered from high niches.

"His Arrokanze the Bope has kraziously blaced at your disposal these cosy quarters," the chamberlain said in a deep, hollow voice. "You may now zelect rooms on the floors above and array yourselves in the karments provided—"

"Look here, Mr. Oh-Doomy-Gloom," Ambassador Straphanger cut in. "I've been thinking it over, and I've decided that my staff and I will just nip back over to our ship for the night—"

"His Arrokanze will pe eggpecting you at the fête in the Bapal Kardens in one hour's time," the Hoogan bored on. "His Arrokanze tislikes intenzely to be kept waitink."

"Oh, we're all keenly aware of the honor His Arrogance has paid us in offering accommodations here in the Papal Palace, but—"

"One hour," Oh-Doomy-Gloom repeated, his voice echoing across the hall. He turned away, the symbolic chain attached to his neck clanking as he moved. He paused, turned back.

"By the way, you are instrugted to iknore any small ah . . . indrusions. If you zee anything . . . unusual, zummon a guard at once."

"Intrusions?" Straphanger repeated querulously. "What kind of intrusions?"

"The balace," Oh-Doomy-Gloom said, "is haunted."

Four twisting turns of a stone staircase above the reception hall, Second Secretary Magnan tip-toed at Retief's side along an echoing corridor past black, iron-bound doors and mouldy tapestries dimly visible in the light of a flambeau set in a bracket at the far end of the passage.

"Quaint beliefs these bucolics entertain," Magnan said in a tone of forced heartiness. "Haunted indeed! How silly! Ha!"

"Why are you whispering?" Retief inquired.

"Just out of respect for the Pope, of course." Magnan came to an abrupt halt, clutched Retief's sleeve. "Whawhat's that?" he pointed. Along the corridor, something small and dark slipped from the shadow of a pilaster to the shelter of a doorway.

"Probably just our imagination," Retief suggested.

"But it had big red eyes," Magnan protested.

"They're as easy to imagine as any other kind."

"I just remembered: I left my shower cap in my hold baggage. Let's go back."

Retief moved off. "It's just a few doors farther. Six, seven . . . here we are." He inserted the key Oh-Doomy-Gloom's aide had provided; the heavy door swung open with a creak that descended the scale to a low groan. Magnan hurried forward, paused to stare at the nearest wall hanging, showing a group of Hoogans suspended head-down from spikes above leaping flames, while goblins of various shapes prodded them with long barb-tipped spears.

"Curious how similar religious art is from one world to another," he commented. Inside the room, he stared around in dismay at the damp stone walls, the two spartan cots, the carved devils in the corner.

"What perfectly ghastly quarters!" He dropped his suitcase, went over to prod the nearest bunk. "Why, my spine will never endure this mattress! I'll be a physical wreck after the first night! And the draft—I'm sure to catch a chill. And . . . and . . ." He broke off, raised a shaky finger to point at the darkest corner of the narrow chamber, where a tall, bug-eyed demon carved from pale blue stone winked garnet eyes.

"Retief! Something moved over there—it was just like the devils in the pictures! All fuzzy red bristles and eyes that glow in the dark . . . !"

Retief opened his suitcase. "If you see another one, throw a shoe at it. Right now, we'd better be getting into costume; compared with an aroused Ambassador, a few devils are just friendly pets."

Half an hour later, having sponged off at the stone sink, Magnan's eyes were still rolling nervously as he adjusted the folds of his Hoogan ceremonial sarong before the tarnished, rippled mirror.

"I suppose it *is* just nerves," he said. "It's all the fault of that Oh-Doomy-Gloom fellow and his quaint native superstitions! I confess his remarks quite unnerved me for a moment."

Across the room, Third Secretary Retief was loading match-head sized charges into the magazine of an inconspicuous hand-gun.

"Probably just his way of warning us about the mice," he said.

Magnan turned, caught a glimpse of the gun. "Here, Retief! What's that?"

"Just a quaint native cure for spooks—if they get too noisy." He tucked the gun out of sight under the Hoogan sarong. "Just think of it as a sort of good luck charm, Mr. Magnan."

"A knife up the sleeve is an old diplomatic tradition," Magnan said doubtfully. "But a power pistol under the sarong . . ."

"I'll have it along in case something jumps out of the stonework and yells boo!" Retief said reassuringly.

Magnan sniffed, admiring himself in the dark glass.

"I was rather relieved when the Ambassador insisted on native dress for the staff instead of ceremonial nudity for tonight's affair." He turned to study the hang of the uneven hem-line that exposed his bare shins. "One of his finer moments, I fancied. He *does* cut an impressive figure, once his jowls get that purplish tinge. Not even Oh-Doomy-Gloom dared stand up to him. Though I do wish he'd gone just the one step further and demanded the right to wear trousers—" he broke off, his eyes on the black drapes covering the high, narrow window. The heavy cloth twitched.

"Retief!" he gasped. "There it is again!"

"Shhh," Retief watched as the curtain moved again. A tiny red-glowing head appeared at its edge, a foot above the floor; a wire-thin leg emerged, another; a body like a ball of reddish fluff came into view, its red-bead eyes on two inch stalks tilting alertly to scan the chamber. Its gaze fixed on Retief; it moved clear of the curtain, paused, then started toward him on skittery legs—

With a yell, Magnan dived for the door, flung it wide.

"Guards! Help! Goblins! Spooks!" His voice receded along the hall, mingling with the clank of accouterments, the slap of wide Hoogan feet.

The intruder hesitated at the outcry, dithered for a moment, then emitted a cry like a goosed fairy, fumbling with two of its limbs at something attached to its back. Beyond the door, Magnan's voice supplied a shrill counterpoint to the rumble of Hoogan questions.

"Then get someone who speaks Terran!" he yelped. "At this moment my associate is being savaged by the monster!"

Retief crossed quickly to the window, pulled the drapes aside and unlatched a panel, letting in a draft of damp night air.

"This way out, fellow," he said. "You'd better be going before the cops arrive."

The fluff-ball darted across the room, came to a shaky stop before Retief, made quick motions. A folded square of paper fell to the floor at Retief's feet. Then the creature sprang for the opening and was gone as Hoogan feet clumped at the door.

"Where Spism?" a heavy voice demanded in thick Terran. A conical Hoogan head in a flaring helmet swiveled to scan the room. Behind the guard, Magnan craned for a view.

"Where is the beast?" he shrilled. "It was at least four feet high, and its tusks were four inches long at the very least!"

The Hoogan advanced into the room, pointed to the open window with his broad-headed seven-foot pike.

"It was a mouse after all," Retief said. "It got away."

"You let Spism ko?"

"Shouldn't I have?" Retief inquired mildly, pocketing the folded paper.

"Spism pad imp from nether rechions; might bite Terry, get blood boisonink."

"I think you're being impertinent," Magnan said sharply, "biting Terrans is perfectly safe—"

The Hoogan turned to him, pike lowered ominously.

"You will gome with me," it ordered. "The benaldy for consortink with minions of Unterworlt is poilink in oil."

"Here," Magnan said, backing. "Stand back, my man—"

The Hoogan reached for Magnan with a long, snaky hand; Retief stepped up behind him, selected a spot, and struck a sharp blow with bunched fingertips. The guard stumbled, fell past Magnan and hit chin first with a resounding slam. His pike shattered against the wall.

"Retief!" Magnan gobbled. "What are you thinking of? You've laid hands on a member of the Papal Guard!"

"I had the distinct impression this fellow hooked a toe on the rug and fell down. Didn't you notice?"

"Why, you know very well—"

"Just before he reached you, Mr. Magnan."

"Ah . . . why, yes, now that you mention it, he did trip," Magnan's tone was suddenly brisk. "Nasty fall. I rushed up to support him, but alas, too late. Poor fellow. Served him right, the brute. Shall we go through his pockets?"

"Why?"

"You're right; there isn't time. That crash was doubtless heard throughout the palace—"

A second Hoogan appeared at the open door, his helmet bearing the fanged angel indicative of officer rank. He eyed the fallen pikeman.

"You addacked this one?" he demanded.

Magnan glanced at the victim as though noticing him for the first time. "He seems to have fallen down," he observed brightly.

"Against rules to gill Hoogan," the captain said ominously.

"He . . . ah . . . broke his spear," Magnan pointed out helpfully.

"Very bad crime, defile ceremonial spear," the captain said sternly. "Require burification ceremony. Very expensive."

Magnan fumbled in a money pouch at one hip. "I'd love to contribute a little something—"

"Ten Hoogan gredits, forget whole thing. For eggstra five dispose of body—"

The felled Hoogan stirred, mumbled, sat up.

"Ha!" the captain said. "Look like no teal. Put for another eggstra five . . ." He lifted a short, ugly club from his belt. "Finish off unfortunate victim of Terry violence."

"Stop!" Magnan yelled. "Are you out of your mind?"

"Inzult to Overseer caste briest cosd you two more gredits. For you I mage special brice, three for five—"

"Bribery?" Magnan gasped. "Corruption?"

"Three it is," the Hoogan nodded. "How apout you?" he turned to Retief. "You sport like other Terry?"

"Look here, I'm paying you nothing!" Magnan barked.

"Just assist this unfortunate chap out of here, if you please, and we'll get on with our dressing!"

"Small religious contributions fine old Hoogan gustom!" the Overseer protested. "You want to fiolate local tapoos?"

"We Terrans have a few customs of our own," Retief put in smoothly. "We feel that graft should only be paid voluntarily." He offered a note which the officer palmed deftly. The guard was on his feet now, swaying; the captain barked an order; his subordinate gathered up the spear fragments, shot Magnan a poisonous look and departed, followed by the captain.

Retief closed the door behind the departing visitors, fished out the scrap of paper dropped by the fleeing Spism, opened it out:

BY THE OGRE FOUNTAIN AT SECOND
MOONRISE; WEAR A YELLOW DUNGFLOWER

Magnan, busy at the mirror again, heaved a deep sigh.

"Hardly an auspicious beginning," he commented. Then: "Heavens! It's twenty thirty! We're late!" He gave his sarong a final tug, smoothed a thinning lock across his forehead, led the way along the echoing hall and down a spiral stair to an archway debouching onto wide steps above a ragged lawn. Blue lanterns hanging in the branches of skeletal trees shed a wan radiance on the fungus-like ornamental plants, the sculptures representing souls in torment, and the wide tables laden with Terran delicacies hastily unloaded from the Corps transport for the occasion. A dozen grotesquely shaped fountains spread a fine mist and an odor of sulphur across the festive scene. Beyond the high, spike-topped wall, the ominous shape of an immense brass-colored idol reared up half a mile away, its ferocious sculptured grin glowing in the glare of spotlights, its right arm raised in the Hoogan royal salute, elbow straight out, forearm pointing upward with fingers spread, the left hand gripping the right biceps. Magnan shuddered.

"That beastly idol—it's sub-Hoogan," he commented. "Isn't that smoke coming out of its nostrils?"

Retief sniffed. "Something's burning," he agreed.

A dark figure stepped up from dense shadow at Magnan's

elbow. "Only old newsbapers you scent," it rumbled. "Our Hoogan Kods are uzeful; they zerve as gommunity inziner-ators."

"Oh-Doomy-Gloom! You startled me!" Magnan chirped. He slapped at an insect that buzzed his face. "I do hope the evening is a big success. It was so thoughtful of His Arrogance to allow the Corps to act as host tonight; such a gesture of acceptance, sort of."

"Reverze hosbitality is an old Hoogan gustom," Oh-Doomy-Gloom said. "It would be a good idea to know all our old Hoogan gustoms, so as not to end up lige the last Derran Tiplomat."

"Yes, it was unfortunate about Ambassador Straphanger's predecessor getting excommunicated, and all. But really, how was he to know he was supposed to fill the Papal begging bowl with hundred-credit notes?"

"It wasn't zo much not contributink; but pourink the canned beans in spoiled the bill His Arrokanze had planted as a hint."

"A bad scene," Magnan agreed. "But I'm sure this evening will smooth everything over."

The orchestra was tuning up now; lugubrious notes groaned across the lawn. Armed Papal guards were taking up their posts, and sarong-clad diplomats were forming up a receiving line by the stone arch opening on the drive through which the dignitaries would arrive.

"I must hurry alonk now and zee to the kun emplaze-ments," Oh-Doomy-Gloom said. "One lasd suggestion: worldly goods of course mean nothink to His Arrokanze, but the deadliest of the zinz is Stinchiness. His Arrokanze detests a tightwad." He moved off, chains clashing.

"The Ambassador's not out yet," Magnan noted nervously. "Gracious, I hope he puts in an appearance before Pope Ai-Poppy-Googy arrives. I dread the prospect of having to engage His Arrogance in light chitchat."

"According to the Post Report, dealing with the Pope is very simple," Retief said. "Just give him everything in sight, and if that doesn't satisfy him, give him some more."

"I can see that you're getting the hang of diplomacy, Retief," Magnan said approvingly. "Still, I'm worried . . ."

"Since it's your job as Protocol Officer to soften up

difficult guests," Retief said, "why not meet the Pope at the gate and try out a few racy stories on him?"

"I hardly imagine that the Chief of State of a Theocracy would react favorably to biological anecdotes," Magnan said stiffly.

"Oh, biology is a perfectly clean subject here on Hoog; but don't bring up cooking in polite conversation. According to the handbook, there's an unspoken agreement among the cultured element that the stork brings the goodies."

"Really? Heavens, and all the cookies are stamped 'Made in Hong Kong'! I'll have to tell the cook to substitute blintzes. While I'm attending to that, you'd best take your post at the gate. You'll handle the first shift tonight. I'll send Stringwhistle along to relieve you in an hour."

"I could delay the Pope a few minutes for you," Retief offered, as they crossed to the gate. "Suppose I start by demanding to see his invitation—"

"None of your ill-timed japes, Retief! After the last mission's fiasco, establishing a friendly rapport with the Pope tonight could mean promotions all around."

"I think the traditional lawn party is a little too subtle for a fellow like the Pope. We should have used a simpler symbolism—like a few rounds of heavy artillery lobbed into the palace grounds."

"Hardly the diplomatic approach," Magnan sniffed. "For centuries now it's been understood that if enough diplomats go to enough parties, everything will come right in the end."

"I wonder if the Hoogans understand that tradition?"

"Certainly; after all, we're all fellow beings—brothers under the skin, as it were."

"In this case, the skin is an inch thick and tougher than armorplast. I'm not sure we can penetrate to the brotherhood layer in time to save bloodshed."

"Actually, I rather look forward to matching epigrams with His Arrogance tonight," Magnan said loftily, turning to scan the gardens. "As you know, I'm always at my sparkling best with high-ranking guests—and of course, mere size and strength fail utterly to intimidate me—" Magnan turned at a sound behind him, uttered a strangled yelp, and trampled a Hoog waiter's foot as he leaped back from the spectacle of a seven-foot-high, six-foot-wide Hoog wrapped in cloth of gold. The monster's gilded features included one-inch nose holes, huge watery, reddish eyes and a wide mouth set in a formal grimace to display polished gold-capped teeth. Two clusters of ringed fingers gripped the hilt of an immense two-edged sword.

"Somethink smells pat!" the apparition bellowed. He leaned forward, sniffed vigorously at Magnan and snorted.

"Horriple!" he announced, elbowing Magnan aside. "Ko away, vellow! You're invested with an acute P.O.!"

"Why, Your Arrogance—it's just a touch of skin bracer back of my ear—"

"It smelts like pargain night in a choy house. Where's Ambassador Hapstrinker? I drust you have blenty of food reaty. I understant you Terries take a kreat interesd in gooking." The Pope winked a damp pink eye, rammed Magnan under the ribs and guffawed comfortably.

"Oof!" Magnan said. "Why, Your Arrogance!"

The Pope was already striding toward the nearest table, his escort of armed and helmeted guards trailing behind, fingering scimitars and eyeing the diplomats suspiciously.

"I . . . I think I'll just scoot along and see to the refreshments," Magnan bleated. "Retief, you accompany His Arrogance and keep him amused until help arrives—I mean, until the Ambassador puts in an appearance!" He fled.

The Pope dipped a boneless finger into a large crystal container of cheese sauce, studied it at arm's length, sniffed it, then, with a flick of a limber wrist, spattered it across the ruffled shirt-fronts and glassy smiles of the diplomats strung out in the receiving line.

"Who are these loavers?" he demanded loudly. "Bropaply relatives, waitink arount for handouts. I have the same proplem. Or had the same proplem, I should zay. Two weeks ako was Self-Denial Festival. I made the subreme sagrifize ant offered the entire lot to the anzestral spirids."

"Giving up your relatives for Lent is quite an idea," Retief said. "It could catch on."

The Pope picked up a plate of dainty sandwiches, spilled the food off, sniffed the plate, and took a small bite. "I've heard a kreat teal about Terran tishes," he said, chewing noisily. "A bit too crizp, but not bat." He took a second nip from the thin porcelain, offered it to Retief.

"Have a bite," he invited genially.

"No thanks, I filled up on a beer bottle just before Your Arrogance arrived," Retief countered. "Try the dinner plates. They're said to be an epicure's delight."

There was a sudden stir from the vicinity of the wide terrace doors. Ambitious diplomatic underlings sprang to positions of eager anticipation, delighted smiles ready. The squat figure of Career Minister Straphanger, Terrestrial Ambassador Extraordinary and Minister Plenipotentiary to Hoog, waddled into view, stylishly decked out in a short but heavily brocaded Hoogan longhi, a brilliant red sash which all but dragged the ground, and jeweled sandals. At his side puffed a companion of almost identical build and garb, distinguished only by a mop of vivid orange hair. Magnan trailed by two yards.

"Ah, the Ampassador is twints?" the Pope inquired, moving toward the approaching pair.

"No, that's Mrs. Straphanger," Retief said. "If I were Your Arrogance I'd ditch that saucer; she's fierce when aroused."

"Ah, the edernal female, ever conzerned with food gonzervation." The Pope tossed the crust of the plate back of a flowering bush.

"Ah, there, Ampassador Strakhumper!" he bellowed. "And your charming cow! She will be litterink zoon, I trust?"

"Littering? How's that?" Straphanger stared around in confusion.

"I azzume you keep your cows pregnant?" the Pope boomed. "Or possibly thiz one is over-aged. But no matter; doubtless she was a gread broducer in her day."

"Well, I never!" Mrs. Straphanger snapped, bridling.

"By the way," Ai-Poppy-Googy went on, "I hate to disguss finanzes over food, zo I suggesd we deal with the proplem of an abbrobriate kift ad once. I am of gourse quite brebared to vorget the drivial misuntersdandink with the former ampassator ant agcepd any zum in egzess of one million gredits withoud quibblink."

"One million credits?" Straphanger babbled. "Gift?"

"Of gourse, if you wish to avoid aguirink a reputation as a piker, an egstra million would not be taken amiss."

"A million credits of Corps funds? But . . . but whatever for?"

"Ah, ah," the Pope waggled an admonitory tactile member. "No pryink into Hoogan internal matters!"

"Oh, no, indeed, Your Arrogance! I only meant . . . what's the occasion? For the gift, I mean."

"It's Tuesday."

"Oh."

The Pope nodded placidly. "Luggy you didn't throw thiz affaire on Wentsday; thad's douple gifd day." He plucked a glass from a tray offered by a bearer, emptied the contents on the lawn, nipped a chip from the edge with his polished metallic teeth, munched thoughtfully.

"Lackink in flavor," he commented.

"My best crystal," Mrs. Straphanger gasped. "All the way from Brooklyn, yet, and like a goat he's eating it!"

"A koat?" The Pope eyed her suspiciously. "I don't belief I know the term."

"It's a . . . a sort of gourmet," Straphanger improvised. Sweat was glistening on his forehead. "Known for its discriminating tastes."

"Now, about the matter of a bension," the Pope continued. "I zee no neet of oztentation. A mere thousant a day would suvvize as a token of Corps esteem."

"A thousand what a day?" the Ambassador inquired around a frozen diplomatic grin which exposed old-fashioned removable dentures.

"Gredits, of gourse. And then there is the matter of zupzidies to Hoogan industry; zay fifty thousand a month. Don'd give a thoughd to atminisdration; just make the cheggs payable to me perzonally—"

"Hoogan industry? But I was given to understand there are no industries here on Hoog—"

"That's why we reguire a zupzity," the Pope said blandly. Straphanger hitched his smile in place with an effort.

"Your Arrogance, I'm here merely to establish friendly relations, to bring Hoog into the mainstream of Galactic cultural life—"

"What coult be frientlier than money?" the Pope inquired in a loud, final-sounding voice.

"Well," Straphanger conceded, "we might arrange a loan—"

"An oudright krant is zo much zimpler," the Pope pointed out.

"Of course, it would mean extra staff, to handle the administrative load." Straphanger rubbed his hands together, a speculative gleam in his eye. "Say twenty-five for a start—"

The Pope turned as a medium-sized Hoog in tight black-and-silver vestments came up, growled in his ear, waving a rubbery arm toward the house.

"What?" the Pope exploded. He swiveled on Straphanger. "You are harporink tapoo greatures! Givink aid and gomfort to untesirable elements? Sharink your zubstanze with minions of the Opposition?"

"Your Arrogance!" Straphanger's voice quavered against the rising roar of the outraged cleric. "I don't understand! What did that fellow say?"

The Pope bawled commands in Hoogan. His escort scattered, began beating the bushes rimming the garden. The Ambassador trotting at his side, the guest of honor strode to the laden refreshment tables, began stuffing in fragile china, muttering to himself.

"Your Arrogance," Straphanger panted. "If I could just have some explanation! I'm sure it's all just a ghastly mistake! What are these men searching for? I assure you—"

"Out of the gootnezz of my heard, I welgomed you to Hoog!" the Pope roared. "As a great gompliment to you, I abzorbed your language! I was even ready to agzept cash, the zubreme chesture! And now I find that you openly gonzort with the enemies of the Kods!"

Standing on the sidelines of the verbal fray, Retief glanced around the garden, spotted a fountain in the shape of a two-headed Hoogan dwarf with oversized teeth and belly. He moved over to it, turned and surveyed the gesticulating group at the table. There was a tug at his sandal-lace. He looked down. Two bright eyes at the ends of wire-like stalks stared up appealingly from a clump of grass. He glanced around; all eyes were on the Pope.

"Are you looking for me?" Retief asked softly.

"Right!" a squeaky voice piped. "You're a hard man to have a quiet chat with, Mr. Ahh."

"Retief."

"How do, Retief. My name's Jackspurt. The boys appointed me spokesmen to tell you Terries about what's going on. After all, I guess us Spisms got a few rights, too."

"If you can explain what's going on in this filbert factory, I'll be forever in your debt, Jackspurt. Speak your piece."

"It's the Hoogans; they don't give us a minute's peace. Talk about persecution! Do you know those psalm-singing hippos are blaming us for everything from sour milk to loss of potency? It's getting where it's not safe to take a stroll after sundown—"

"Hold on, Jackspurt. Maybe you'd better fill me in one some background. Who are you? Why are the Hoogans after you? And where did you learn to speak Terran with that flawless enunciation of consonants?"

"I used to be a mascot on a Terry trader; I stowed away when she landed here for emergency repairs. It was a good life; but after a while I got homesick for good old Hoog— you know how it is—"

"You're a native of this charming world?"

"Sure—us Spisms have been around longer than the Hoogs. And we got along for thousands of years with no trouble: the Hoogs took the surface, and we settled in nice and comfy underground. Then they got religion and it's been Hell ever since . . ."

"Hold on, Jackspurt: I always heard that religion exercised a beneficent influence on those fortunate enough to possess it."

"That depends on which side you're on."

"That's a point."

"But I haven't given you the big picture yet. These Hoogan priests launched a full-scale propaganda campaign: painted up a lot of religious art with pictures of Spisms poking pitchforks at Hoogs, and pretty soon it got so even the average Hoog in the street started jumping and making X's in the air and mumbling spells everytime one of us came up for a breath of fresh air. The next thing we knew, it was full-scale war! I'm telling you, Retief, us Spisms are in bad shape—and it's gonna get worse!"

A guard was working his way toward the ogre fountain.

"Jiggers, the gendarmes," Retief said. "You'd better get out of sight, Jackspurt. They're beating the bushes for you. Why don't we continue this later—"

The Spism whisked back under cover. "But this is important, Retief!" Jackspurt's voice emanated from the brush. "The boys are counting on me—"

"Shhh! Watch me and take your cue . . ." Magnan had turned and was eyeing Retief suspiciously. He stepped to his junior's side.

"Retief, if you're mixed up in this mix-up . . ."

"Me, Mr. Magnan? Why, I just arrived this afternoon the same time you did—"

"Magnan!" Straphanger's voice cut through the hubbub. "The Pope informs me that some sort of demonic creature was seen here on the Embassy grounds this evening! Of course we know nothing about it, but His Arrogance has drawn the unfortunate implication that we're consorting with denizens of the netherworld!" He lowered his voice as Magnan drew close. "Superstitious poppycock, but we've got to play along; you and the others spread out and go through a show of looking for this mythical imp. I'll pacify His Arrogance."

"Certainly, Mr. Ambassador. But . . . ah . . . what if we find it?"

"Then you're an even greater idiot than I suspect!" Straphanger twisted his working smile into position and turned back to the Pope.

"Retief, you start along there," Magnan indicated the front of the house. "I'll go poke about in the bushes. And whatever you do, don't turn up anything—like that ghastly creature we encountered upstairs—" A startled look spread across his face. "Good lord, Retief! Do you suppose—?"

"Not a chance. I picture something more like a medium-sized dragon."

"Still . . . perhaps I'd better mention it to the Ambassador . . ."

"And confirm the Pope's opinion? Very courageous of you. Mind if I stick around and watch?"

"On the other hand, he's a busy man," Magnan said hurriedly. "After all, why bother him with trivia?" He hurried off to take up a position near the Pope and make a show of stooping and peering among the conifer-like hedges. Retief sauntered back to the table, deserted now except for a lone Hoogan bearer at the far end gathering empties onto a wide tray and tossing damp paper napkins into a capacious waste paper receptacle. Retief picked up an empty sandwich plate said hsst!; the Hoogan looked up as Retief tossed the plate. The Hoogan dropped the big paper bag and caught the tossed crockery.

"Here's some more," Retief offered helpfully. He gathered up and handed over a pair of saucers, three empty glasses and a couple of cheese sandwiches each minus one bite. "You'd better hump along now and police up behind His Arrogance," he suggested. "He's leaving a trail of saucer rims behind him; doesn't seem to like the floral design."

"You dry dell me my chop?" the Hoogan demanded truculently as Retief fumbled a spoon, let it drop to the grass just under the edge of the hanging table cloth.

"Certainly not, old boy," Retief reassured the glowering local. He stooped for the spoon, caught a glimpse of an eye peering from the shadows.

"Get in the bag," he hissed from the corner of his mouth.

"Who you talg to?" the servant ducked and stared under the table. Behind him, the paper trash container rustled softly as the Spism whisked into it.

"Just addressing a few words to the spoon god," Retief said blandly. "Bad luck to drop a spoon, you know."

"Yez?" the Hoogan said. He leaned against the table, got out a much-used toothpick and began plying it on his unpolished teeth. "You voreigners kot grazy iteas. Efrypoty know kood lug trop sboon, bat lug trob forg."

"Back home, falling from a ten-story building is considered an inauspicious omen," Retief rambled on, watching the armed Papal Guard as they worked closer. One came over to the table, gave Retief a sharp look, thrust his head under the table, then reached to check the trash container. "How about a little refreshment?" Retief picked up a cup, dipped it full from a bowl of thick purple punch, took a step toward the warrior and seemed to trip; the sticky fluid struck the Hoogan just below the clasp holding the rainbow-hued cape, spread out in an interesting pattern across his polished breastplate. The bearer grabbed up his tray and bag and backed off hurriedly as the spluttering guard slapped limber fingers at the mess.

"Itiot! Clumpsy oaf!" he choked—

"What, boozink on duty?" a vast voice boomed. The Pope bellied past Retief, planted himself before the confused Hoogan. "The benalty is boilink in oil!" he roared. "Take him away!"

Other guardsmen closed in, grabbed their unfortunate fellow.

"That was my fault, Your Arrogance," Retief started. "I offered him—"

"You would inderfere with the Babal administration of justize?" the Pontiff bellowed, turning on Retief. "You have the demerity to sugchest that the Babal judgment is fallible?"

"Not exactly; you're just wrong," Retief said. "I spilled the punch on him."

The Pope's face purpled; his mouth worked. He swallowed.

"It's ben zo long zinze anyone contradicted me," he said mildly, "that I've vorkotten the bunishment." He waved two fingers in blessing. "You are apzolved, my zon," he said airily. "In vact, I apzolv you for the whole weekent. Have fun; it's on the house."

"Why, isn't that gracious of His Arrogance?" Magnan chirped, popping up beside the Pope. "What a pity we didn't find the demon; but I—"

"That reminds me," the Pope said ominously. He fixed an eye on Ambassador Straphanger as the senior diplomat came up. "I'm still waitink for results!"

"Look here, Your Arrogance! How can we find a demon if there's no demon here?"

"That's *your* broblem!"

There was a yell from the gate. Two guards were manhandling the bearer with the waste-paper bag, who jerked away, making indignant noises. The bag fell, split open, spilling garbage from the midst of which the fugitive Spism burst, sending scraps flying in every direction. With a bound, it was past the astonished guards, heading for the rear gate. More guards appeared in its path, jerking long-barreled guns from tooled holsters. A shot seared a long gouge in the deep grass, narrowly missed other Papal retainers dashing up to get a crack at the action. The Pope yelled, waving his boneless arms.

Cut off, the Spism veered, dashed for the house, was met by a squad charging out from inside. A near-miss smashed dishes on the table beside Magnan, who yelped and hit the dirt.

The Spism skittered, took evasive action, headed for the flower-decked gate letting onto the drive. The guards were all behind it now, the way clear. With a tremendous yell, Pope Ai-Poppy-Googy whipped his giant sword out and leaped to intercept the fleeing creature. As he bounded past Retief, the latter pivoted, thrust out a foot, hooked the papal leg just above a flare-topped bejeweled pink leather shoe. His Arrogance dived forward, struck medals-first, and skidded on his face under the table.

"Why, hi there," Magnan's voice piped from under the muffling canopy of the drooping table cloth. "Just a minute, and I'll scroonch over—"

The Pope roared and rose up, the table lifting with him; dishes, glasses, and food cascaded off on Magnan, crouching on the ground. With a surge, the Pontiff hurled the board aside, roared again, whirling to confront the dancing figure of Ambassador Straphanger, who flapped a napkin at the mud on the ornate canonicals of the guest of honor.

"Treason!" Ai-Poppy-Googy bellowed. "Azzazints! Murderers! Achents of the Unterworlt! Obstructors of chustist! Heretics!"

"Now, now, Your Arrogance! Don't get upset—"

"Upzet! This iz maybe a choke?" The Pope dashed the muddied cloth from Straphanger's hand, bent and snatched up his sword, waved it overhead. The Papal Guard was closing in quickly now.

"I hereby eggsgommunigate the lot of you!" he Pope yelled. "No food, no water, no bolice brotection! Alzo, you will be puplicly eggsecuted! Boys, round them up!"

Guns were suddenly leveled at the huddle of diplomats

surrounding the Ambassador. Magnan yelped. Straphanger's wattles quivered.

"Ton't miss this one!" Ai-Poppy-Googy indicated Retief. "It was his foot I fell over!" A guard poked a gun into Retief's side.

"Ah, I think Your Arrogance is forgetting that Mr. Retief has a Papal dispensation," Straphanger said brightly. "Retief, if you'll just run along to my office and send out a code two-oh-three—or is it three-oh-two—or . . . anyway, a call for aitch ee ell pee—"

"He'll ko along with the rest of you scoundrels!" the Pope yelled. Half a dozen armed Hoogans were herding the remainder of the staff up to join the group now.

"Any more insite?"

"No, Your Arrokants," the captain of the guard reported. "Only a few zervants."

"Poil them in oil for azzociatink with azzazints! As for the rest of you—"

"Your Arrogance," Straphanger spoke up. "Naturally, I don't mind dying, if it's Your Arrogance's pleasure, but then we won't be able to give you the gifts and things, will we...?"

"Tamn!" Ai-Poppy-Googy threw his sword down, narrowly missing Magnan's foot. "I forgot about the gidtz!" He looked thoughtful. "Look, zuppose I make arranchmends for you to write a few chegs in your zell pefore the eggzecution?"

"Oh, I'm afraid that wouldn't do at all, Your Arrogance. I need the Embassy seal, and the check verifying machine, and the code books and—"

"Well . . . bossibly I might make an egzeption; I'll defer punishment until the cash arrives—"

"Sorry, Your Arrogance, but I wouldn't ask you to deviate from tradition just to accommodate me. No, we're all excommunicated, so I suppose we may just as well get comfortable and start starving—"

"Holt it! Don't rush me! Who's doing the eggsgommunigatink, you or me?"

"Oh, you are—"

"Brecizely! And I zay you're not eggsgommunigated!" The Pope stared around truculently. "Now about the gifd!

You can deliver the two million immediately; I juzt happened to pring an armored gar alonk—"

"TWO million? But you said one million!"

"This is touple gift day."

"But you said Wednesday was double-gift day. This is only Tuesday."

"It's now Wentsday, by Babal decree."

"But you can't—I mean, how can you . . . ?"

"Calendar Reform," Ai-Poppy-Googy said. "Lonk overdue."

"Well, I suppose it could be arranged . . ."

"Kood! I herepy grant you a Babal rebrieve. Put that toesn't inglude the resd of these untesiraples!" the Pope waved a hand. "Dake them away, poys!"

"Ah . . . I'm grateful for the pardon, I'm sure," Straphanger said, gaining confidence rapidly; "but of course I won't be able to process the paper work properly without my staff . . ."

Ai-Poppy-Googy glared with large, damp, red eyes. "All righd! Keeb them! They're all rebrieved egzebd thad one!" he aimed a finger at Retief like a gun. "I have sbezial blans for him!" The guards shifted their attention to Retief, ringing him in with aimed guns.

"Maybe His Arrogance would be just a teeny bit lenient this time," Magnan suggested, dabbing at a smear of liver paste along his bare arm, "if Mr. Retief apologized and promised never to do it again."

"Do whad akain?" the Pope demanded.

"Trip you," Magnan said. "You know, like he did just now."

"He dribbed me?" Ai-Poppy-Googy choked. "On burpose?"

"Why, ah, it must have been a mistake—" Straphanger started.

"Your Arrogance has such a keen sense of humor, I'm sure you'll see the comic aspect of it, if you just think about it," Magnan offered.

"Retief! Did you—I mean, surely you didn't—" Straphanger choked.

"Well!" Magnan said indignantly. "I was lying right there—"

"Zearch him!" the Pope bellowed. Guards jumped forward; busy hands grabbed at Retief's kilt-pockets, almost at once came upon the folded paper the Spism had dropped as it fled his room.

"Ah-hah!" the Pope pounced, opened the paper, read the message.

"A gonsbirazy!" he yelled. "Unter my fery nose! But the ironts on him!"

"I must protest!" Straphanger spoke up. "You can't go about chaining up diplomats every time a little indiscretion is committed! Leave the matter to me, Your Arrogance; I'll see that a sharp entry goes in his record—"

"The Kods will nod pe denied their tue!" Ai-Poppy-Googy roared. "Domorrow is the Krant Vestifal of Wentstay—"

"Tomorrow's Thursday," Magnan interjected.

"Domorrow is Wentstay! Totay is Wentstay! I herepy teclare a whole weeg of Wentstays, plast it! Now, as I was sayink—this Derran will bartizibade in the vestifal! Zuch is the Babal will! No more arkuments!"

"Oh, he'll be taking part in a ceremony!" Straphanger said in a relieved tone. "Well, goodness, I suppose we can spare him long enough for that." He offered a small diplomatic chuckle. "The Corps is always ready to promote worship in whatever form, of course—"

"The only dru Kots are the Hookan Kots, py the Kots!" the Pope boomed. "Any more of your Derran heresy, and I'll referse my tisbenzation! Now dake thiz one to the demple and brebare him vor the rides of Wentstay! The resd of you will remain unter arresd, undil the will of the Kots is known!"

"Mr. Ambassador," Magnan quavered, tugging at Straphanger's arm. "Do you think we should allow them—"

"Merely letting His Arrogance save face," Straphanger said in a confidential tone. He winked at Retief. "Don't worry, my boy; good experience for you. You'll get an inside view of the Hoogan religious concept at work."

"But—but, what if they . . . I mean, boiling in oil is so *permanent* . . ." Magnan persisted.

"Quiet, Magnan! I'll have no whiners in my organization!"

"Thanks for thinking of me, Mr. Magnan," Retief said. "I still have my good luck charm."

"Charm?" Magnan looked blank.

"Witchgraft?" the Pope boomed. "I zuzbegted as much!" He turned a large red eye on Straphanger.

"I'll pe zeeing you at the zeremony! Ton't pe lade!" He eyed Retief. "Are you goming beazevully?"

"In view of the number of guns aimed at me," Retief said, "I sincerely hope so."

The cell was narrow, dark, damp, and unfurnished except for a plain table with a bottle of bitter-smelling wine and a narrow bench on which Retief sat, his wrists chained together, listening to a muffled tapping which sounded faintly from beyond the walls. It had been going on now for twelve hours, he estimated—long enough for the Hoogans to have completed their preparations for the religious ceremonies in which he was to play a part.

The tapping abruptly changed tone, sounding louder, nearer. There was a light clatter, as of pebbles tossed on the floor. A moment later, there was a soft scraping sound, a rasping like fingernails on a blackboard; then silence.

"Retief, are you there?" a thin voice chirped through the pitch darkness.

"Sure, Jackspurt! Come on in and join the party. I'm glad to see you eluded the gendarmes."

"Those slobs! Hah! But listen, Retief, I've got bad news . . ."

"Press on, Jackspurt; I'm listening."

"This is Festival Day—and old Googy's scheduled the big all-out push for today, to tie in with the mumbo-jumbo. The Hoogs have been building this king-size fumigator for months—stacking it full of rubbish, old rags, worn-out tires, and what not. At the height of the big ceremony, they set the stuff on fire, and start the smoke-pumps going. They got a system of pipes laid out leading into the burrows, see? There won't be a safe spot for Spisms for miles around. Our boys will come stampeding out of their hideaways, some of which have been in the family for generations, and zowie! the Pope's troops lower the boom! It'll be the finish of Spisms!"

"That's a heart-rending story, Jackspurt—or it would be, if I weren't in such a heart-rending position myself at the moment—"

"Yeah, the Wednesday Rites. You scheduled for the matinee or the big evening spectacular?" Jackspurt broke off as clanking sounded from beyond the door.

"Holy Moses, Retief! Time's up! They're here! Listen, I was supposed to brief you in, like, but it took longer'n I figured tunneling through that wall, and then I got to yakking—"

A key scraped in the keyhole.

"Listen! Did you drink any of what's in the bottle?"

"No."

"Good! It's doped! When I leave, dump it! You'll have to pretend you can't talk or the jig's up! Put on a kind of zombie routine, see? Whatever they tell you—do it! If they get the idea you're putting something over, it's zkkk! for every Terry on Hoog! And remember! Keep your head down and your arms and legs tucked in—"

The lock turned with a rasp of rusty tumblers.

"Got to go! Good luck!" Jackspurt scrambled and was gone. Retief took a step, grabbed up the bottle, poured it down the three-inch hole through which his visitor had fled.

Light blazed as the heavy door swung inward. Three hooded Hoogan pikemen came into the cell, followed by a black-robed priest. Retief stood holding the empty bottle, his body concealing Jackspurt's escape route.

"How to you veel, Derry?" the priest inquired, looking Retief over. He stepped in, thumbed Retief's eyelid up, grunted, took the empty bottle from his hand.

"Goked to the eyeprows," he stated.

"Are you zure?" a pikeman challenged. "I ton'd drust these voreigners."

"Nadurally I'm zure; the hypervasgulations of the subraoccibital whatchamagallids is dypical; a glassic gase. Dake him alonk."

Hemmed in by pikes, Retief followed along a torch-lit passage, up winding stone stairs, to emerge abruptly into blinding light and the susurrus of a multitude of voices, above which one rose like the boom of surf:

" . . . azzure you, my tear Ambassador Hipstinker, our brinzibal teity, Uk-Ruppa-Tooty, is nod only a hantzome degoration and a gonstand reminter to the bobulaze that the nexd tithe is tue—he also brotuzes oragular stadements rekularly efery Wentstay at one B.M. Of gourse, it is nod always kiven to us to undersdant whad he's dalkink apout, bud the evvegd on the beasandry is most zaludory . . ."

Squinting against the sudden sunlight, Retief made out the resplendently-robed figure of the Pope, seated under a vast parasol on a massive throne of dark wood carved with designs of intertwined serpents, flanked on the left by the Terran Ambassador and on the right by a huddle of lesser diplomats, the group ringed in by stony-faced Hoogan guards with bared scimitars.

The priest who had accompanied Retief bowed unctuously before the Papal throne. "Your Arrokanze, the Zoon-to-pe-Elefated One is here," he indicated Retief with a wave of the hand.

"Is he . . . ah . . . ?" Ai-Poppy-Googy looked inquiringly at the escort.

"A glassig gase of hypervasgulations of the thinkamapops," a pikeman spoke up.

"Poil thad one in oil," the Pope said, frowning. "He dalgs doo mudge."

"You appear a bit peaked, Retief," Straphanger commented. "I trust you slept well last night? Comfortable quarters and all that?"

Retief stared absently past the Ambassador's left ear.

"Retief, the Ambassador's addressing you," Magnan said sharply.

"Brobably he's losd in metitations," Ai-Poppy-Googy said hastily. "On with the zeremony—"

"Perhaps he's sick," Magnan said. "Here, you'd better sit down—"

"Ah-ah," Ai-Poppy-Googy held up a limber hand. "The mosd imbortand bortion of the zeremony yed remaints to pe zeleprated."

"Ah, yes, of course," Straphanger sat back. "I'd quite forgotten, Your Arrogance." He glanced around. "We'll have a magnificent view of the proceedings from here . . ."

At a prod from a Papal Guard, Retief turned—and found himself staring directly into the vast brass smile of the Hoogan idol.

❖   ❖   ❖

From Retief's elevated viewpoint atop the two-hundred foot high ziggurat, the head of the god reared up another fifty feet, an immense stylized Hoogan face of polished yellow metal, the vast hand upraised beside it. The eyes were deep hollows at the back of which a sullen red glow gave an impression of malignant intelligence. The nose-holes, a yard each in diameter, drooled a thin trickle of smoke which coiled up past soot-streaked cheeks to dissipate in the clear air. The mouth which split the massive head gaped in a crocodile smile set with spade-shaped teeth with spaces between them, beyond which was visible a curve of polished esophagus agleam with leaping reflections from inner fires below.

Two lesser priests stepped forward to hang assorted ornaments on Retief's shoulders and neck. Another took up a position before him, began intoning a repetitious chant. Somewhere, drums commenced a slow tattoo. A murmur passed over the crowd packing the slopes of the ziggurat and the plaza below. Standing at ease, apparently ignoring his surroundings, Retief noted a two-foot-wide trough cut in the stone platform at his feet, deepening and slanting down as it ran to the abrupt drop-off ten yards distant. An acolyte was busy pouring oil into the hollow and spreading it with swipes of his hands.

"Just what does this phase of the ceremonial involve?" Straphanger inquired in a tone of synthetic diplomatic interest.

"Waid and zee," Ai-Poppy-Googy said shortly.

"Mr. Ambassador," Magnan whispered hoarsely. "His hands are chained!"

"Part of the ceremony, no doubt."

"And that groove," Magnan went on. "It runs from Retief right over to the edge . . . just above that horrible ig-bay outh-may . . ."

"Yes, yes, you needn't play the part of a tourist guide, Magnan. By the way," Straphanger lowered his voice, "you didn't happen to bring along a hip flask, I suppose?"

"Why, no, Mr. Ambassador. I have a nice anti-viral nasal spray, if that would help. But about that chute—"

"Warm, isn't it, Your Arrogance?" Straphanger turned to the Pope. "A bit dry, too . . ."

"You ton't lige our Hoogan weather?" the Pope asked in an ominous tone.

"No, no, it's fine. I love it when it's nice and hot and dry."

"Ah, Your Arrogance," Magnan spoke up. "Just what is it you have in mind doing with Retief?"

"Is kreat honor," the Pope said shortly.

"I'm sure we're all delighted at this opportunity for one of our group to get an inside view of the Hoogan religious philosophy," Straphanger said sharply. "Now kindly sit down and stop that infernal chattering," he added behind his hand.

The Pope was speaking quickly in Hoogan; the attendant priests urged Retief forward a step, grasped his arms and deftly placed him face-down in the oiled channel. The rattle of the drums rose to a crescendo. Flabby Hoogan hands shoved Retief forward down the steepening slope.

"Mr. Ambassador!" Magnan's voice rose to a shrill bleat. "I do believe they're feeding him to that monster!"

"Nonsense, Magnan!" Straphanger's suety voice countered. "It's all symbolic, I'm sure. And I might point out that you're hardly conducting yourself like a seasoned diplomat—"

"Stop!" Retief, sliding rapidly toward the edge, heard Magnan's yelp, the scuffle of rapid footsteps—

There was a wet splat! and bony elbows slammed against him. He twisted, caught a glimpse of Magnan's white face, open mouth and clutching hands as together they shot over the edge and out in a graceful arc toward the waiting jaws of Uk-Ruppa-Tooty.

Keep your arms and legs tucked in, Jackspurt had said; Retief had time to grit his teeth—then he was hurtling past the tombstone sized fangs, Magnan's hands still clutching his legs, dropping down into a blast of searing heat and light, then suddenly, stunningly, slamming against and through a yielding, shredding network of filaments as fine as spiderwebs. He came to a stop, rebounded, caught at a heavier cable that brushed his hand, and was clinging to a coarse rope ladder, Magnan's weight dangling from his heels.

"Bull's-eye!" a tiny voice screeched almost in his ear. "Now let's get out of here fast, before they dope out what happened!"

Retief found a foothold in the snarl of rope, reached down and hauled the rag-limp Second Secretary to his side. The heat from below was scorching, even here in the shelter of a bulge in the god's throat.

"Wha-what-bu-bu—" Magnan babbled, groping for a handhold.

"Hurry up, Retief!" Jackspurt urged. "Up here by the tonsils! It's a secret passage!"

Retief assisted Magnan in scrambling up, boosted him into the narrow, circular burrow that ran back through the solid metal. The Spism in the lead, they moved hurriedly away from the sound of priestly voices raised in puzzled inquiry, reached a set of cramped steps leading down.

"We're OK now," Jackspurt said. "Take a breather, and then we'll go down and meet the boys."

They were in a cavern, floored with rough masonry, lit by a burning wick afloat in a shallow bowl of aromatic oil. All around, twitching Spism eye-stalks stared at the intruders; the close-packed red goblin-forms of Jackspurt and his clan moved restlessly like giant fiddler crabs on some subterranean beach; behind them, tall, pale blue cousins poised on yard-long legs watched from shadowy corners; in niches and crannies in the walls, tiny green Spisms and sluggish orange forms with white spots clung, gazing. Dark purple Spisms, dangling from the ceiling like tumerous stalactites, waved their free legs hypnotically, studying the scene.

Magnan's fingers dug into Retief's arm. "G-great heavens, Retief!" he gasped out. "You—you don't suppose we've died and that my Aunt Minerva was right all along . . . ?"

"Mr. Retief, meet the boys," Jackspurt clambered up to perch on a ledge overlooking the gathering. "A lot of them are pretty shy, but they're a good-natured bunch, always a thousand laughs. When they heard you was in trouble, they all joined in to help out."

"Tell them Mr. Magnan and I said thanks," Retief said. "It was an experience we wouldn't have missed. Right, Mr. Magnan?"

"I'd certainly never miss it," Magnan swallowed audibly. "H-how is it you can talk to these hobgoblins, Retief?" he hissed. "You haven't . . . ah . . . made some sort of pact with the powers of darkness, I trust?"

"Hey, Retief," Jackspurt said. "Your friend got some kind of race prejudice or something?"

"Heavens, no," Magnan said in a strangled voice. "Some of my best friends are fiends—I mean, in our profession, one meets—"

"Mr. Magnan is just a little confused," Retief put in. "He didn't expect to be playing such an active role in today's events."

"Speaking of active, we better get you gents back to the surface fast," Jackspurt said. "The pumps will be starting up any minute now."

"Where are you going when the fumigation begins?"

"We got an escape route mapped out through the sewers that ought to bring us out in the clear a couple miles from town. We're just hoping the Hoog don't have the outfall staked out."

"Where are these smoke pumps located?" Retief asked.

"Up above—in Uk-Ruppa-Tooty's belly."

"Who's manning them?"

"A couple of priests. Why?"

"How do we get there from here?"

"Well, there's a couple passages—but we better not waste any time sight-seeing—"

"Retief, are you out of your mind?" Magnan blurted. "If the priests see us, our goose will be cooked, along with the rest of our anatomies!"

"We'll try to make it a point to see them first. Jackspurt, can you get a couple of dozen volunteers?"

"You mean to climb up in that brass god? I don't know, Retief. The fellas are pretty superstitious . . ."

"We need them to make a diversion while Mr. Magnan and I carry out the negotiation—"

"Who, me?" Magnan squeaked.

"Negotiation?" Jackspurt protested. "Jumping Jehosaphat, how can you negotiate with a Hoog?"

"Ahem," Magnan cleared his throat. "That, Mr. Jackspurt, is after all one's function as a diplomat."

"Well . . ." Jackspurt buzzed briefly to his fellows, then hopped down from his perch as a dozen Spisms of assorted sizes and colors came forward.

"We're game, Mr. Retief. Let's go!"

The dull gleam of the metal walls of the vast chamber that was the interior of the god Uk-Ruppa-Tooty loomed out of dense shadow where Retief and Magnan crouched with their hob-goblin crew. At the center of the gloomy chamber, low-caste Hoogans labored before the open door of a giant, red-glowing furnace, tossing in armloads of rubbish, old shoes, bundled magazines, and broken plastic crockery. A layer of harsh, eye-watering smoke hung in the air. Jackspurt snorted.

"Boy, when they start pumping that stuff into the burrows . . ."

"Where are the priests?" Retief inquired in a whisper.

Jackspurt pointed to a small cubicle at the top of a flight of steps. "Up there, in the control room."

Retief studied the layout. "Jackspurt, you and your men spread out around the room. Give me five minutes. Then take turns jumping out and making faces."

Jackspurt gave instructions to his crew; they faded away into the darkness.

"Maybe you'd better wait here," Retief suggested to Magnan.

"Where are you going?"

"I think I'd better have a chat with the ecclesiastics up in the prompting box."

"And leave me here alone, surrounded by these ghoulish Spisms?"

"All right, but keep it quiet or the smoke of burning diplomats will be added to the other fumes."

Fifty feet above the floor, Retief gripped narrow handholds, working his way around to the rear of the control box, through the dusty windows of which a blue-robed Hoogan priest lounged in a bored attitude, studying a scroll, while a second Hoogan, in the familiar black, stood nervously by. Suddenly the silence below was broken by a mournful wail.

"What's that!" Magnan jumped, slipped, grabbed for a secure grip on a projecting angle-iron supporting a narrow catwalk.

"Our co-workers going into action," Retief said softly. Beside the furnace door, the Hoogan workers were staring round nervously. There was another doleful moan. One of the Hoogans dropped his shovel and muttered. Retief ducked back as the blue-robed priest came to the window, peered down below, then motioned to the other, who went to the door of the tiny chamber, opened it, stepped out on the catwalk, shouted down to the workers. One answered in defiant tones. Two of the workers started toward a door dimly visible at the far side of the furnace room. The priest shouted after them; as his bellow faded and echoed, the thin hoot of a Spism sounded, like the last wail of dying hope. The priest jumped, whirled to dart back inside the control room, slipped, fell from the catwalk, grabbed frantically, caught it and held on by one hand, found himself staring directly into Magnan's startled face. He opened his mouth to roar—

Magnan whipped off his mauve cummerbund and thrust it into the gaping mouth. With a muffled grunt, the Hoogan lost his grip, fell, slammed into the heaped rubbish with a tremendous slam. The stokers fled, shouting. The lone priest flattened his face against the window, peering down into the gloom. With a quick movement, Retief gained the catwalk, stepped through the door. The priest whirled, gaped, leaped for a microphone-like device on the corner table. Retief eased the power pistol from his sarong, aimed it negligently at the priest.

"I wouldn't make any announcements just yet," he said. "The results aren't all in."

"Who are you?" The Hoogan sidled toward a corner cabinet.

"If that's where you keep your prayer books, better let them lie for a while yet."

"Loog here, berhabs you are unaware that I am His Voracity the Arjpishob Um-Moomy-Hooby, and I have gonnegtions—"

"Doubtless. And don't try for the door; I have a confederate out there who's noted for his ferocity."

Magnan came through the door, panting. Um-Moomy-Hooby backed away.

"Whad—whad to you wand?"

"I understand the god is about to utter oracular statements, as the high point of the Wednesday services," Retief said.

"Yez—I was jusd going over my sgribt. Now if you'll eggsguze me—"

"It just happens that it's the script we want to talk about. There are a couple of special announcements I'd like to see inserted—"

"Whad? Damper with holy sgribture?"

"Nothing like that; just a good word for a group of associates of ours and possibly a short commercial for the CDT—"

"Plasphemy! Herezy! Refishionism! Nefer will I pe a barty to zuch zagrileche!"

Retief clicked off the pistol's safety catch.

"—Put, on the other hant, bossiply somethink gould pe arranched," the Archbishop said hastily. "How much did you have in mind offering?"

"I wouldn't think of attempting to bribe a man of the cloth," Retief said smoothly. "You're going to do this for the common welfare."

"Jusd whad is it you hafe in mind?"

"The first item is the campaign you've been waging against the Spisms—"

"Ah, yez! And a wontervul jop our lats hafe peen toing, doo. Uk-Ruppa-Tooty willink, zoon we will zee them stambed oud endirely, and virtue driumvant!"

"The CDT takes a dim view of genocide, I'm afraid. Now, my thought was that we could agree on a reasonable division of spheres of influence—"

"A teal with the Bowers of Tarknezz? Are you oud of your mind?"

"Now, now," Magnan put in, "a more co-operative attitude would do Your Voracity greater credit—"

"You zugchesd that the jurch should gombromize with zin?"

"Not exactly compromise," Magnan said placatingly. "Just work out a sort of peaceful coexistence plan."

"Nefer will I, as arjpishob, gome oud in vafor of doge-therness with Zatan's Imps!"

"There, there, Your Voracity; if you'd just sit down across the table from them, you'd find these imps weren't bad fellows at all . . ."

There was a soft sound from the door. Jackspurt, a jaunty, two-foot sphere of red bristles, appeared, waving his eye-stalks exultantly. A looming blue Spism peered over his shoulder.

"Nice going, Retief!" he called. "I see you caught one. Pitch him down after the other one, and let's clear out of here. This little diversion will give us time to get clear before the smoke starts."

"Jackspurt, do you suppose your fellows could do a fast job of shifting a few hoses around? You'll have to block off the sewers and feed the smoke off in some other direction."

"Say, that's an idea!" Jackspurt agreed. "And I think I know just the direction." He gave instructions to the big blue Spism, who hurried away.

The Archbishop had retreated to a corner, eyes goggling, his hands describing mystic passes in the air. More Spisms were crowding into the room now: tall blue ones, tiny darting green ones, sluggish purple varieties—all cocking their eye-stalks at the prelate.

"Help!" he croaked weakly. "The minions of the nether-worlt are ubon me!"

Magnan drew out a chair from the table. "Just have a seat, Your Voracity," he said soothingly. "Let's just see if we can't work out a *modus vivendi* suitable to all parties . . ."

"Gome to terms with the Enemy? Id will mean the ent of the jurch!"

"On the contrary, Your Voracity; if you ever succeeded in eliminating the opposition, you'd be out of a job. The problem is merely to arrange matters in a civilized fash-ion so that everyone's interests are protected."

"You may hafe somethink there," Um-Moomy-Hooby seated himself gingerly. "Put the nevarious agtifities of these goplins musd pe kebt under sdrigd gondrol—Babal gongrol, thad is."

"Look, my boys got to make a living," Jackspurt started.

"Zellink a vew love-botions, zerdainly," the Archbishop said. "And the jurch is willink to zmile at a modest draffic in aphrodisiags, dope, and raze-drack tips. But beddling filthy menus to teen-agers, no! The zame goes vor sdealing withoud a licenze, and the zale of algoholic peferaches, with the eggzebtion of small amounts of broberly aged sduff for medicinal use py the glerchy, of gourse."

"OK, I think we can go along with that," Jackspurt said. "But you priests will have to lay off the propaganda from now on. I want to see Spisms getting better billing in church art."

"Oh, I think you could work out something lovely in little winged Spisms with haloes," Magnan suggested. "I think you owe it to them, Your Voracity, after all this discrimination in the past."

"Tevils with winks?" Um-Moomy-Hooby groaned. "It will blay hop with our zympolisms—put I zubboze it can be tone."

"And you'll have to have guarantees that everything from two feet under the surface on down belongs to us," Jackspurt added. "We'll leave the surface to you, and throw in the atmosphere, just so you dedicate a few easements so we can come up and sight-see now and then."

"Thad zeems egwidaple," the Archbishop agreed. "Supchegd to vinal approfal py His Arrokanze, of gourze."

"By the way," Jackspurt asked casually, "who's next in line for the Pope's job if anything happens to Ai-Poppy-Googy?"

"Az it habbens, I am," Um-Moomy-Hooby said. "Why?"

"Just asking," Jackspurt said.

A loud thumping started up from the wide floor below.

"What's that?" Magnan yelled.

"The pumps," the Archbishop said. "A bity so many Spisms will tie, but it is manivesdly the will of Uk-Ruppa-Tooty . . ."

"I guess old Uk-Ruppa-Tooty had a last-minute change of heart," Jackspurt said callously. "We shifted the pipes around to feed the fumes back up into the city plumbing system. I guess there's black smoke pouring up out of every john in town by now."

"Touble-grozzer!" the Archbishop leaped up, waving his arms. "The teal's off—"

"Ah, ah, you promised, Your Voracity," Magnan chided. "And besides, Mr. Retief still has the gun."

"And now, if you'll just pick up the microphone, Your Voracity," Retief said. "I think we can initiate the era of good feeling without further delay. Just keep our role quiet, and take all the credit for yourself."

"A pity about poor Ai-Poppy-Googy falling off the ziggurat when the smoke came boiling out of Uk-Ruppa-Tooty's mouth," Ambassador Straphanger said, forking another generous helping of Hoogan chow mein onto his plate. "Still, one must confess it was a dramatic end for a churchman of his stature, shooting down the slide and disappearing into the smoke as he did."

"Yez, alrety the canonization papers are peing brepared," His newly-installed Arrogance, Pope Um-Moomy-Hooby, shot a nervous glance at the Spism seated beside him. "He'll pe the batron zaint of rehabilidated tevils, imps, and koplins."

"A pity you missed all the excitement, Magnan," Straphanger said, chewing. "And you, too, Retief. While you absented yourselves, the Hoogan philosophy underwent a veritable renaissance—helped along, I humbly assume, by my modest peace-making efforts."

"Hah!" the Pope muttered under his breath.

"Frankly, what with all the smoke, I hadn't expected the oracle's pronouncement to be quite so lucid," Straphanger went on, "to say nothing of its unprecedented generosity—"

"Chenerosity?" interrupted Um-Moomy-Hooby, his heavy features reflecting rapid mental recapitulation of his concessions.

"Why, yes, ceding all minerals rights to the formerly persecuted race here on Hoog—a charming gesture of conciliation."

"Mineralts right? Whad mineralts?"

Jackspurt, splendid in the newly tailored tunic of Chief Representative for Spismodic Affairs to the Papal court, spoke up from his place along the table set up on the palace terrace.

"Oh, he's just talking about the deposits of gold, silver, platinum, radium, and uranium, plus a few boulders of diamond, emerald, ruby, and so forth that are laying around below ground. The planet's lousy with the stuff. We'll use our easements to ferry it up to the surface where the freighters will pick it up, so we won't put you Hoogs out at all."

The Pope's alligator-hide features purpled. "You—you knew apout these mineralts?" he choked.

"Why, didn't His former Arrogance mention it to you? That was what brought the mission here; the routine minerals survey our technical people ran from space last year showed up the deposits—"

"And we built our Brincible Kod oud of prass—imborted prass at thad," the Pope said numbly.

"Too scared of a few Spisms to dig," Jackspurt said in a stage whisper.

There was a flicker of lightning in the sky to the east. Thunder rolled. A large rain-drop spattered on Straphanger's plate, followed by another.

"Oh-oh, we'd better head for cover," Jackspurt said. "I know these flash squalls; lightning out the kazoo—"

A brilliant flash cast the looming figure of the god Uk-Ruppa-Tooty into vivid silhouette against a blue-black sky. Dishes rattled on the table as sound rumbled across the sky on wooden wheels. The Pope and his guests rose hastily, as a third jagged electrical discharge ripped across the sky—and struck the giant idol full on the shoulder. A shower of sparks flew; the mighty right arm, raised in the Hoogan gesture of salute, pivoted slowly at the elbow. The yards-wide hand, seen-edge-on with the fingers extended, swung slowly in a great arc, came to rest with the extended thumb resting firmly against the snub nose. Sparks flew as the digit was welded firmly in place.

The Pope stared, then tilted his head back and looked up at the sky, long and searchingly.

"Chusd pedween us men of the worlt," he said hoarsely, "do you zubbose thad phenomenon has any sbezial zignivi-ganze?"

"I think if I were you, Your Arrogance, I'd watch my step," Jackspurt said in an awed tone. "And, uh, by the way, on behalf of the Spisms, I'd like to make a contribution to the Papal treasury."

"Hmmm. Have you ever thought aboud tagink inzdruction?" the Pope inquired. "I'm sure it could be arranged, and as for the little contribution you sboge of, dwenty bercend of the take would zuvvice . . ."

They strolled off along the corridor, deep in conversation. Ambassador Straphanger hurried away to prepare his dispatches to Sector HQ, Magnan at his heels. Retief stepped back out onto the terrace, lit up a dope-stick. Far away, Uk-Ruppa-Tooty loomed, solemnly thumbing his nose at the Papal Palace.

Cheerfully, Retief returned the salute.

... In the face of the multitudinous threats to the peace arising naturally from the complex Galactic situation, the polished techniques devised by Corps theoreticians proved their worth in a thousand difficult confrontations. Even anonymous junior officers, armed with briefcases containing detailed instructions, were able to soothe troubled waters with the skill of experienced negotiators. A case in point was Consul Passwyn's incisive handling of the Jaq-Terrestrial contretemps at Adobe ...

—Vol. II, reel 91 480 A. E. (AD 2941)

SEALED ORDERS

"It's true," Consul Passwyn said, "I requested assignment as Principle Officer at a small post. But I had in mind one of those charming resort worlds, with only an occasional visa problem, or perhaps a distressed spaceman or two a year. Instead, I'm zoo-keeper to these confounded settlers, and not for one world, mind you, but eight." He stared glumly at Vice-Consul Retief.

"Still," Retief said, "it gives an opportunity for travel."

"Travel!" the Consul barked. "I hate travel. Here in this backwater system particularly ..." He paused, blinked at Retief, and cleared his throat. "Not that a bit of travel isn't an excellent thing for a junior officer. Marvelous experience."

He turned to the wall-screen and pressed a button. A system triagram appeared: eight luminous green dots arranged around a larger disc representing the primary. Passwyn picked up a pointer, indicating the innermost planet.

"The situation on Adobe is nearing crisis. The confounded settlers—a mere handful of them—have managed, as usual, to stir up trouble with an intelligent indigenous life form, the Jaq. I can't think why they bother, merely for a few oases among the endless deserts. However, I have, at last, received authorization from Sector Headquarters to take certain action."

He swung back to face Retief. "I'm sending you in to handle the situation, Retief—under sealed orders." He picked up a fat, buff envelope. "A pity they didn't see fit to order the Terrestrial settlers out weeks ago, as I suggested. Now it's too late. I'm expected to produce a miracle—a rapprochement between Terrestrial and Jaq and a division of territory. It's idiotic. However, failure would look very bad in my record, so I shall expect results." He passed the buff envelope across to Retief.

"I understood that Adobe was uninhabited," Retief said, "until the Terrestrial settlers arrived."

"Apparently that was an erroneous impression. The Jaq are there." Passwyn fixed Retief with a watery eye. "You'll follow your instructions to the letter. In a delicate situation such as this, there must be no impulsive, impromptu element introduced. This approach has been worked out in detail at Sector; you need merely implement it. Is that entirely clear?"

"Has anyone at Headquarters ever visited Adobe?"

"Of course not. They all hate travel too. If there are no other questions, you'd best be on your way. The mail run departs the dome in less than an hour."

"What's this native life form like?" Retief asked, getting to his feet.

"When you get back," said Passwyn, "you tell me."

The mail pilot, a leathery veteran with quarter-inch whiskers, spat toward a stained corner of the compartment, and leaned close to the screen.

"They's shootin' goin' on down there," he said. "Them white puffs over the edge of the desert."

"I'm supposed to be preventing the war," said Retief. "It looks like I'm a little late."

The pilot's head snapped around. "War?" he yelped.

"Nobody told me they was a war goin' on on 'Dobe. If that's what that is, I'm gettin' out of here."

"Hold on," said Retief. "I've got to get down. They won't shoot at you."

"They shore won't, sonny. I ain't givin' 'em the chance." He reached for the console and started punching keys. Retief reached out, catching his wrist.

"Maybe you didn't hear me. I said I've got to get down."

The pilot plunged against the restraint and swung a punch that Retief blocked casually. "Are you nuts?" the pilot screeched. "They's plenty shootin' goin' on fer me to see it fifty miles out."

"The mails must go through, you know."

"I ain't no consarned postman. If you're so dead set on getting' killed—take the skiff. I'll tell 'em to pick up the remains next trip—if the shootin's over."

"You're a pal. I'll take your offer."

The pilot jumped to the lifeboat hatch and cycled it open. "Get in. We're closin' fast. Them birds might take it into their heads to lob one this way."

Retief crawled into the narrow cockpit of the skiff. The pilot ducked out of sight, came back, and handed Retief a heavy old-fashioned power pistol. "Long as you're goin' in, might as well take this."

"Thanks." Retief shoved the pistol in his belt. "I hope you're wrong."

"I'll see they pick you up when the shootin's over—one way or another."

The hatch clanked shut; a moment later there was a jar as the skiff dropped away, followed by heavy buffeting in the backwash from the departing mail boat. Retief watched the tiny screen, his hands on the manual controls. He was dropping rapidly: forty miles, thirty nine . . .

At five miles, Retief threw the light skiff into maximum deceleration. Crushed back in the padded seat, he watched the screen and corrected the course minutely. The planetary surface was rushing up with frightening speed. Retief shook his head and kicked in the emergency retro-drive. Points of light arced up from the planet face below. If they were ordinary chemical weapons the skiff's meteor screens should handle them. The screen on the instrument panel flashed brilliant white, then went dark. The skiff leaped and flipped on its back; smoke filling the tiny compartment. There was a series of shocks, a final bone-shaking concussion, then stillness, broken by the ping of hot metal contracting.

Coughing, Retief disengaged himself from the shock-webbing, groped underfoot for the hatch, and wrenched it open. A wave of hot jungle air struck him. He lowered himself to a bed of shattered foliage, got to his feet . . . and dropped flat as a bullet whined past his ear.

He lay listening. Stealthy movements were audible from the left. He inched his way forward and made the shelter of a broad-boled dwarf tree. Somewhere a song lizard burbled. Whining insects circled, scented alien life, and buzzed off. There was another rustle of foliage from the underbrush five yards away. A bush quivered, then a low bough dipped. Retief edged back around the trunk and eased down behind a fallen log. A stocky man in a grimy leather shirt and shorts appeared, moving cautiously, a pistol in his hand.

As he passed, Retief rose, leaped the log, and tackled him. They went down together. The man gave one short yell, then struggled in silence. Retief flipped him onto his back, raised a fist—

"Hey!" the settler yelled. "You're as human as I am!"

"Maybe I'll look better after a shave," said Retief. "What's the idea of shooting at me?"

"Lemme up—my name's Potter. Sorry 'bout that. I figured it was a Flap-jack boat; looks just like 'em. I took a shot when I saw something move; didn't know it was a Terrestrial. Who are you? What you doin' here? We're pretty close to the edge of the oasis. That's Flap-jack country over there." He waved a hand toward the north, where the desert lay.

"I'm glad you're a poor shot. Some of those missiles were too close for comfort."

"Missiles, eh? Must be Flap-jack artillery. We got nothin' like that."

"I heard there was a full-fledged war brewing," said Retief. "I didn't expect—"

"Good!" Potter said. "We figured a few of you boys from

Ivory would be joining up when you heard. You from Ivory?"

"Yes. I'm—"

"Hey, you must be Lemuel's cousin. Good night! I pretty near made a bad mistake. Lemuel's a tough man to explain anything to."

"I'm—"

"Keep your head down. These damn Flap-jacks have got some wicked hand weapons. Come on . . ." He began crawling through the brush. Retief followed. They crossed two hundred yards of rough country before Potter got to his feet, took out a soggy bandanna, and mopped his face.

"You move good for a city man. I thought you folks on Ivory just sat under those domes and read dials. But I guess bein' Lemuel's cousin—"

"As a matter of fact—"

"Have to get you some real clothes, though. Those city duds don't stand up on 'Dobe."

Retief looked down at his charred, torn, sweat-soaked powder-blue blazer and slacks, the informal uniform of a Third Secretary and Vice-Consul in the Corps Diplomatique Terrestrienne.

"This outfit seemed pretty rough-and-ready back home," he said. "But I guess leather has its points."

"Let's get back to camp. We'll just about make it by sundown. And look, don't say nothin' to Lemuel about me thinkin' you were a Flap-jack."

"I won't; but—"

Potter was on his way, loping off up a gentle slope. Retief pulled off the sodden blazer, dropped it over a bush, added his string tie, and followed Potter.

"We're damn glad you're here, mister," said a fat man with two revolvers belted across his paunch. "We can use every man. We're in bad shape. We ran into Flap-jacks three months ago and we haven't made a smart move since. First, we thought they were a native form we hadn't run into before. Fact is, one of the boys shot one, thinkin' it was fair game. I guess that was the start of it." He paused to stir the fire.

"And then a bunch of 'em hit Swazey's farm here. Killed two of his cattle, and pulled back," he said.

"We figure they thought the cows were people," said Swazey. "They were out for revenge."

"How could anybody think a cow was folks," another man put in. "They don't look nothin' like—"

"Don't be so dumb, Bert," said Swazey. "They'd never seen Terries before; they know better now."

Bert chuckled. "Sure do. We showed 'em the next time, didn't we, Potter? Got four—"

"They walked right up to my place a couple days after the first time," Swazey said. "We were ready for 'em. Peppered 'em good. They cut and run—"

"Flopped, you mean. Ugliest-lookin' critters you ever saw. Look just like a old piece of dirty blanket humpin' around."

"It's been goin' that way ever since. They raid and then we raid. But lately they've been bringin' some big stuff into it. They've got some kind of pint-sized airships and automatic rifles. We've lost four men now and a dozen more in the freezer, waiting for the med ship. We can't afford it. The colony's got less than three hundred able-bodied men."

"But we're hangin' onto our farms," said Potter. "All these oases are old sea-beds—a mile deep, solid topsoil. And there's a couple of hundred others we haven't touched yet. The Flap-jacks won't get 'em while there's a man alive."

"The whole system needs the food we can raise," Bert said. "These farms we're tryin' to start won't be enough but they'll help."

"We been yellin' for help to the CDT, over on Ivory," said Potter. "But you know these Embassy stooges."

"We heard they were sendin' some kind of bureaucrat in here to tell us to get out and give the oasis to the Flap-jacks," said Swazey. "We're waitin' for him . . ."

"Meanwhile we got reinforcements comin' up. We put out the word back home; we all got relatives on Ivory and Verde—"

"Shut up, you damn fool!" a deep voice grated.

"Lemuel!" Potter said. "Nobody else could sneak up on us like that—"

"If I'd a been a Flap-jack, I'd of et you alive," the

newcomer said, moving into the ring of the fire. He was a tall, broad-faced man in grimy leather. He eyed Retief.

"Who's that?"

"What do ya mean?" Potter spoke in the silence. "He's your cousin."

"He ain't no cousin of mine," Lemuel said. He stepped to Retief.

"Who you spyin' for, stranger?" he rasped.

Retief got to his feet. "I think I should explain—"

A short-nosed automatic appeared in Lemuel's hand, a clashing note against his fringed buckskins.

"Skip the talk. I know a fink when I see one."

"Just for a change, I'd like to finish a sentence," Retief said. "And I suggest you put your courage back in your pocket before it bites you."

"You talk too damned fancy to suit me."

"You're wrong. I talk to suit me. Now, for the last time: put it away."

Lemuel stared at Retief. "You givin' me orders . . . ?"

Retief's left fist shot out and smacked Lemuel's face dead center. The raw-boned settler stumbled back, blood starting from his nose. The pistol fired into the dirt as he dropped it. He caught himself, jumped for Retief . . . and met a straight right that snapped him onto his back—out cold.

"Wow!" said Potter. "The stranger took Lem . . . in two punches . . ."

"One," said Swazey. "That first one was just a love tap."

Bert froze. "Quiet, boys," he whispered. In the sudden silence a night lizard called. Retief strained, heard nothing. He narrowed his eyes, peering past the fire.

With a swift lunge he seized up the bucket of drinking water, dashed it over the fire, and threw himself flat. He heard the others hit the dirt a split second after him.

"You move fast for a city man," breathed Swazey beside him. "You see pretty good too. We'll split and take 'em from two sides. You and Bert from the left, me and Potter from the right."

"No," said Retief. "You wait here. I'm going out alone."

"What's the idea . . . ?"

"Later. Sit tight and keep your eyes open." Retief took a bearing on a treetop faintly visible against the sky and started forward.

Five minutes' cautious progress brought Retief to a slight rise of ground. With infinite caution he raised himself and risked a glance over an outcropping of rock. The stunted trees ended just ahead. Beyond, he could make out the dim contour of rolling desert: Flap-jack country. He got to his feet, clambered over the stone, still hot after a day of tropical heat, and moved forward twenty yards. Around him he saw nothing but drifted sand, palely visible in the star-light, and the occasional shadow of jutting shale slabs. Behind him the jungle was still. He sat down on the ground to wait.

It was ten minutes before a movement caught his eye; something had separated itself from a dark mass of stone, and glided across a few yards of open ground to another shelter. Retief watched. Minutes passed. The shape moved again, slipped into a shadow ten feet distant. Retief felt the butt of the power pistol with his elbow. His guess had better be right . . .

There was a sudden rasp, like leather against concrete, and a flurry of sand as the Flap-jack charged. Retief rolled aside, then lunged, throwing his weight on the flopping Flap-jack—a yard square, three inches thick at the center, and all muscle. The ray-like creature heaved up, curled backward, its edge rippling, to stand on the flat-tened rim of its encircling sphincter. It scrabbled with its prehensile fringe-tentacles for a grip on Retief's shoulders. Retief wrapped his arms around the creature and struggled to his feet. The thing was heavy, a hundred pounds at least; fighting as it was, it seemed more like five hundred.

The Flap-jack reversed its tactics, becoming limp. Retief grabbed and felt a thumb slip into an orifice.

The creature went wild. Retief hung on, dug the thumb in deeper.

"Sorry, fellow," he muttered between his clenched teeth. "Eye-gouging isn't gentlemanly, but it's effective . . ."

The Flap-jack fell still; only its fringes rippling slowly. Retief relaxed the pressure of his thumb. The creature gave a tentative jerk; the thumb dug in. The Flap-jack went limp again, waiting.

"Now that we understand each other," said Retief, "lead me to your headquarters."

Twenty minutes' walk into the desert brought Retief to a low rampart of thorn branches: the Flap-jacks' outer defensive line against Terry forays. It would be as good a place as any to wait for the next move by the Flap-jacks. He sat down, eased the weight of his captive off his back, keeping a firm thumb in place. If his analysis of the situation was correct, a Flap-jack picket should be along before too long . . .

A penetrating beam of red light struck Retief in the face, then blinked off. He got to his feet. The captive Flap-jack rippled its fringe in an agitated way. Retief tensed his thumb.

"Sit tight," he said. "Don't try to do anything hasty . . ." His remarks were falling on deaf ears—or no ears at all— but the thumb spoke as loudly as words.

There was a slither of sand, then another. Retief became aware of a ring of presences drawing closer.

Retief tightened his grip on the creature. He could see a dark shape now, looming up almost to his own six-three. It appeared that the Flap-jacks came in all sizes.

A low rumble sounded, like a deep-throated growl. It strummed on, then faded out. Retief cocked his head, frowning.

"Try it two octaves higher," he said.

"Awwrrp! Sorry. Is that better?" a clear voice came from the darkness.

"That's fine," Retief said. "I'm here to arrange an exchange of prisoners."

"Prisoners? But we have no prisoners."

"Sure you have. Me. Is it a deal?"

"Ah, yes, of course. Quite equitable. What guarantees do you require?"

"The word of a gentleman is sufficient." Retief released his captive. It flopped once and disappeared into the darkness.

"If you'd care to accompany me to our headquarters,"

the voice said, "we can discuss our mutual concerns in comfort."

"Delighted."

Red lights blinked briefly. Retief, glimpsing a gap in the thorny barrier, stepped through it. He followed dim shapes across warm sand to a low cave-like entry, faintly lit with a reddish glow.

"I must apologize for the awkward design of our comfort-dome," said the voice. "Had we known we would be honored by a visit."

"Think nothing of it," Retief said. "We diplomats are trained to crawl."

Inside, with knees bent and head ducked under the five-foot ceiling, Retief looked around at the walls of pink-toned nacre, a floor like burgundy-colored glass spread with silken rugs, and a low table of polished red granite set out with silver dishes and rose-crystal drinking tubes.

"Let me congratulate you," the voice said. Retief turned. An immense Flap-jack, hung with crimson trappings, rippled at his side. The voice issued from a disk strapped to its back. "Your skirmish-forms fight well. I think we will find in each other worthy adversaries."

"Thanks. I'm sure the test would be interesting, but I'm hoping we can avoid it."

"Avoid it?" Retief heard a low humming coming from the speaker in the silence. "Well, let us dine," the mighty Flap-jack said at last, "we can resolve these matters later. I am called Hoshick of the Mosaic of the Two Dawns."

"I'm Retief." Hoshick waited expectantly. " . . . of the Mountain of Red Tape," Retief added.

"Take your place, Retief," said Hoshick. "I hope you won't find our rude couches uncomfortable." Two other large Flap-jacks came into the room and communed silently with Hoshick. "Pray forgive our lack of translating devices," he said to Retief. "Permit me to introduce my colleagues."

A small Flap-jack rippled into the chamber bearing on its back a silver tray, laden with aromatic food. The waiter served the diners and filled the drinking tubes with yellow wine.

"I trust you'll find these dishes palatable," Hoshick said.

"Our metabolisms are much alike, I believe." Retief tried the food; it had a delicious nut-like flavor. The wine was indistinguishable from Chateau d'Yquem.

"It was an unexpected pleasure to encounter your party here," Hoshick said. "I confess at first we took you for an indigenous earth-grubbing form, but we were soon disabused of that notion." He raised a tube, manipulating it deftly with his fringe tentacles. Retief returned the salute and drank.

"Of course," Hoshick continued, "as soon as we realized that you were sportsmen like ourselves, we attempted to make amends by providing a bit of activity for you. We've ordered out our heavier equipment and a few trained skirmishers and soon we'll be able to give you an adequate show, or so I hope."

"Additional skirmishers?" said Retief. "How many, if you don't mind my asking?"

"For the moment, perhaps only a few hundred. Thereafter . . . well, I'm sure we can arrange that between us. Personally I would prefer a contest of limited scope—no nuclear or radiation-effect weapons. Such a bore, screening the spawn for deviations. Though I confess we've come upon some remarkably useful sports: the ranger-form such as you made captive, for example. Simple-minded, of course, but a fantastically keen tracker."

"Oh, by all means," said Retief. "No atomics. As you pointed out, spawn-sorting is a nuisance, and then too, it's wasteful of troops."

"Ah, well, they are after all expendable. But we agree, no atomics. Have you tried the ground-gwack eggs? Rather a speciality of my Mosaic . . ."

"Delicious," said Retief. "I wonder if you've considered eliminating weapons altogether?"

A scratchy sound issued from the disk. "Pardon my laughter," Hoshick said, "but surely you jest?"

"As a matter of fact," said Retief, "we ourselves try to avoid the use of weapons."

"I seem to recall that our first contact of skirmish-forms involved the use of a weapon by one of your units."

"My apologies," said Retief. "The—ah—skirmish-form failed to recognize that he was dealing with a sportsman."

"Still, now that we have commenced so merrily with weapons . . ." Hoshick signaled and the servant refilled the drinking tubes.

"There is an aspect I haven't yet mentioned," Retief went on. "I hope you won't take this personally, but the fact is, our skirmish-forms think of weapons as something one employs only in dealing with certain specific life-forms."

"Oh? Curious. What forms are those?"

"Vermin. Deadly antagonists, but lacking in caste. I don't want our skirmish-forms thinking of such worthy adversaries as yourself as vermin."

"Dear me! I hadn't realized, of course. Most considerate of you to point it out." Hoshick clucked in dismay. "I see that skirmish-forms are much the same among you as with us: lacking in perception." He laughed scratchily.

"Which brings us to the crux of the matter," Retief said. "You see, we're up against a serious problem with regard to skirmish-forms: a low birth rate. Therefore we've reluctantly taken to substitutes for the mass actions so dear to the heart of the sportsman. We've attempted to put an end to these contests altogether . . ."

Hoshick coughed explosively, sending a spray of wine into the air. "What are you saying?" he gasped. "Are you proposing that Hoshick of the Mosaic of the Two Dawns abandon honor?"

"Sir!" said Retief sternly. "You forget yourself. I, Retief of the Red Tape, merely make an alternate proposal more in keeping with the newest sporting principles."

"New?" cried Hoshick. "My dear Retief, what a pleasant surprise! I'm enthralled with novel modes. One gets so out of touch. Do elaborate."

"It's quite simple, really. Each side selects a representative and the two individuals settle the issue between them."

"I . . . um . . . I'm afraid I don't understand. What possible significance could one attach to the activities of a couple of random skirmish-forms?"

"I haven't made myself clear," Retief said. He took a sip of wine. "We don't involve the skirmish-forms at all; that's quite passé."

"You don't mean . . . ?"

"That's right. You and me."

Outside the starlit sand Retief tossed aside the power pistol and followed it with the leather shirt Swazey had lent him. By the faint light he could just make out the towering figure of the Flap-jack rearing up before him, his trappings gone. A silent rank of Flap-jack retainers were grouped behind him.

"I fear I must lay aside the translator now, Retief," said Hoshick. He sighed and rippled his fringe tentacles. "My spawn-fellows will never credit this. Such a curious turn fashion has taken. How much more pleasant it is to observe the action from a distance."

"I suggest we use Tennessee rules," said Retief. "They're very liberal: biting, gouging, stomping, kneeling, and, of course, choking, as well as the usual punching, shoving, and kicking."

"Hmmm. These gambits seem geared to forms employing rigid endo-skeletons; I fear I shall be at a disadvantage."

"Of course," Retief said, "if you'd prefer a more plebian type of contest . . ."

"By no means. But perhaps we could rule out tentacle-twisting, just to even the balance."

"Very well. Shall we begin?"

With a rush Hoshick threw himself at Retief, who ducked, whirled, and leaped on the Flap-jack's back—and felt himself flipped clear by a mighty ripple of the alien's slab-like body. Retief rolled aside as Hoshick turned on him, jumped to his feet, and threw a punch to Hoshick's mid-section. The alien whipped his left fringe around in an arc that connected with Retief's jaw, spinning onto his back. Hoshick's weight struck Retief like a dumptruck-load of concrete. Retief twisted, trying to roll. The flat body of the creature blanketed him. He worked an arm free and drummed blows on the leathery back. Hoshick nestled closer.

Retief's air was running out. He heaved up against the smothering weight; nothing budged. He was wasting his strength.

He remembered the ranger-form he had captured. The

sensitive orifice had been placed ventrally, in what would be the thoracic area . . .

He groped, feeling tough hide set with horny granules. He would be missing skin tomorrow—if there was a tomorrow. His thumb found the orifice, and he probed.

The Flap-jack recoiled. Retief held fast, probed deeper, groping with the other hand. If the creature were bilaterally symmetrical there would be a set of ready-made hand-holds . . .

There were. Retief dug in and the Flap-jack writhed and pulled away. Retief held on, scrambled to his feet, threw his weight against Hoshick, and fell on top of him, still gouging. Hoshick rippled his fringe wildly, flopped in distress, then went limp. Retief relaxed, released his hold, and got to his feet, breathing hard. Hoshick humped himself over onto his ventral side, lifted, and moved gingerly over to the sidelines. His retainers came forward, assisted him into his trappings, and strapped on the translator. He sighed heavily, adjusting the volume.

"There is much to be said for the old system," he said. "What a burden one's sportsmanship places on one at times."

"Great fun, wasn't it?" said Retief. "Now, I know you'll be eager to continue. If you'll just wait while I run back and fetch some of our gouger-forms—"

"May hide-ticks devour the gouger-forms!" Hoshick bellowed. "You've given me such a sprong-ache as I'll remember each spawning-time for a year."

"Speaking of hide-ticks," said Retief, "we've developed a biter-form—"

"Enough!" Hoshick roared so loudly that the translator bounced on his hide. "Suddenly I yearn for the crowded yellow sands of Jaq. I had hoped . . ." He broke off, drawing a rasping breath. "I had hoped, Retief," he said, speaking sadly now, "to find a new land here where I might plan my own Mosaic, till these alien sands and bring forth such a crop of paradise-lichen as should glut the markets of a hundred worlds. But my spirit is not equal to the prospect of biter-forms and gouger-forms without end. I am shamed before you."

"To tell you the truth, I'm old-fashioned myself,"

said Retief. "I'd rather watch the action from a distance too."

"But surely your spawn-fellows would never condone such an attitude."

"My spawn-fellows aren't here. And besides, didn't I mention it? No one who's really in the know would think of engaging in competition by mere combat if there were any other way. Now, you mentioned tilling the sand, raising lichens—"

"That on which we dined," said Hoshick, "and from which the wine is made."

"The big trend in fashionable diplomacy today is farming competition. Now, if you'd like to take these deserts and raise lichen, we'll promise to stick to the oases and raise vegetables."

Hoshick curled his back in attention. "Retief, you're quite serious? You would leave all the fair sand hills to us?"

"The whole works, Hoshick. I'll take the oases."

Hoshick rippled his fringes ecstatically. "Once again you have outdone me, Retief," he cried, "this time, in generosity."

"We'll talk over the details later. I'm sure we can establish a set of rules that will satisfy all parties. Now I've got to get back. I think some of the gouger-forms are waiting to see me."

It was nearly dawn when Retief gave the whistled signal he had agreed on with Potter, then rose and walked into the camp circle. Swazey stood up.

"There you are," he said. "We been wonderin' whether to go out after you."

Lemuel came forward, one eye black to the cheekbone. He held out a raw-boned hand. "Sorry I jumped you, stranger. Tell you the truth, I thought you was some kind of stool-pigeon from the CDT."

Bert came up behind Lemuel. "How do you know he ain't, Lemuel?" he said. "Maybe he—"

Lemuel floored Bert with a backward sweep of his arm. "Next cotton-picker says some embassy Johnny can cool me gets worse'n that."

"Tell me," said Retief. "How are you boys fixed for wine?"

"Wine? Mister, we been livin' on stump water for a year now. 'Dobe's fatal to the kind of bacteria it takes to ferment liquor."

"Try this." Retief handed over a squat jug. Swazey drew the cork, sniffed, drank, and passed it to Lemuel.

"Mister, where'd you get that?"

"The Flap-jacks make it. Here's another question for you: would you concede a share in this planet to the Flap-jacks in return for a peace guarantee?"

At the end of a half hour of heated debate Lemuel turned to Retief. "We'll make any reasonable deal," he said. "I guess they got as much right here as we have. I think we'd agree to a fifty-fifty split. That'd give about a hundred and fifty oases to each side."

"What would you say to keeping all the oases and giving them the desert?"

Lemuel reached for the wine jug, his eyes on Retief. "Keep talkin', mister," he said. "I think you got yourself a deal."

Consul Passwyn glanced up as Retief entered the office.

"Sit down, Retief," he said absently. "I thought you were over on Pueblo, or Mud-flat, or whatever they call that desert."

"I'm back."

Passwyn eyed him sharply. "Well, well, what is it you need, man? Speak up. Don't expect me to request any military assistance."

Retief passed a bundle of documents across the desk. "Here's the Treaty. And a Mutual Assistance Pact and a Trade Agreement."

"Eh?" Passwyn picked up the papers and riffled through them. He leaned back in his chair, beaming.

"Well, Retief, expeditiously handled." He stopped and blinked at the Vice-Consul. "You seem to have a bruise on your jaw. I hope you've been conducting yourself as befits a member of the Consulate staff."

"I attended a sporting event. One of the players got a little excited."

"Well . . . it's one of the hazards of the profession. One must pretend an interest in such matters." Passwyn rose and extended a hand. "You've done well, my boy. Let this teach you the value of following instructions to the letter."

Outside, by the hall incinerator drop, Retief paused long enough to take from his briefcase a large buff envelope, still sealed, and drop it in the slot.

PART III:
BUT MAGNAN'S STAR RISES

Editor's Note: Magnan appears in almost all of the Retief stories. He provides the ongoing comic relief—the "straight man," as it were, for Retief's wit and sarcasm. In the first three stories, however, Magnan is not *quite* the unmitigated ass he becomes as time goes on. Not that all the raw material isn't there from the very beginning, of course, but early in his career Magnan does show occasional flashes of spirit. An example is the scene in "The Brass God" where Magnan, reacting in a quick and decisive manner which he will soon relinquish, stuffs a cummerbund into the mouth of a Hoogan priest.

Soon enough, however, Magnan adapts completely to the culture of the Corps Diplomatique. From then on, his rise is more or less uninterrupted as Retief's career continues to stagnate due to his awkward habit of ignoring CDT precepts.

Insofar as the Retief stories have an overall architecture, it is provided by two themes: the steady rise of Magnan—who only gets his "just desserts" at the very end of Retief's career, as told in *Diplomat-at-Arms*—and the emergence of the Groaci as Retief's major antagonist (outside, of course, of the ranks of the CDT itself).

In Part III, we examine the first of these.

. . . Ofttimes, the expertise displayed by experienced Terrestrial Chiefs of Mission in the analysis of local political currents enabled these dedicated senior officers to secure acceptance of Corps commercial programs under seemingly insurmountable conditions of adversity. Ambassador Crodfoller's virtuoso performance in the reconciliation of rival elements at Petreac added new lustre to Corps prestige . . .

—Vol VIII, reel 8. 489 A. E. (AD 2950)

PALACE REVOLUTION

Retief paused before a tall mirror to check the overlap of the four sets of lapels that ornamented the vermilion cutaway of a First Secretary and Consul.

"Come along, Retief," Magnan said. "The ambassador has a word to say to the staff before we go in."

"I hope he isn't going to change the spontaneous speech he plans to make when the Potentate impulsively suggests a trade agreement along the lines they've been discussing for the last two months."

"Your derisive attitude is uncalled for, Retief," Magnan said sharply. "I think you realize it's delayed your promotion in the Corps."

Retief took a last glance in the mirror. "I'm not sure I want a promotion. It would mean more lapels."

Ambassador Crodfoller pursed his lips, waiting until Retief and Magnan took places in the ring of Terrestrial diplomats around him.

"A word of caution only, gentlemen. Keep always foremost in your minds the necessity for our identification with the Nenni Caste. Even a hint of familiarity with lower echelons could mean the failure of the mission. Let us remember: the Nenni represent authority here on Petreac; their traditions must be observed, whatever our personal preferences. Let's go along now; the Potentate will be making his entrance any moment."

Magnan came to Retief's side as they moved toward the salon.

"The ambassador's remarks were addressed chiefly to you, Retief," he said. "Your laxness in these matters is notorious. Naturally, I believe firmly in democratic principles myself."

"Have you ever had a feeling, Mr. Magnan, that there's a lot going on here that we don't know about?"

Magnan nodded. "Quite so; Ambassador Crodfoller's point exactly. Matters which are not of concern to the Nenni are of no concern to us."

"Another feeling I get is that the Nenni aren't very bright. Now suppose—"

"I'm not given to suppositions, Retief. We're here to implement the policies of the Chief of Mission. And I should dislike to be in the shoes of a member of the Staff whose conduct jeopardized the agreement that's to be concluded here tonight."

A bearer with a tray of drinks rounded a fluted column, shied as he confronted the diplomats, fumbled the tray, grabbed, and sent a glass crashing to the floor. Magnan leaped back, slapping at the purple cloth of his pants leg. Retief's hand shot out and steadied the tray. The servant rolled his terrified eyes.

"I'll take one of those, now that you're here," Retief said easily, lifting a glass from the tray. "No harm done. Mr. Magnan's just warming up for the big dance."

A Nenni major-domo bustled up, rubbing his hands politely.

"Some trouble here? What happened, Honorables, what, what . . ."

"The blundering idiot," Magnan spluttered. "How dare—"

"You're quite an actor, Mr. Magnan," Retief said. "If I didn't know about your democratic principles, I'd think you were really angry."

The servant ducked his head and scuttled away.

"Has this fellow given dissatisfaction . . . ?" The major-domo eyed the retreating bearer.

"I dropped my glass," Retief said. "Mr. Magnan's upset because he hates to see liquor wasted."

Retief turned and found himself face-to-face with Ambassador Crodfoller.

"I witnessed that," the ambassador hissed. "By the goodness of Providence the Potentate and his retinue haven't appeared yet, but I can assure you the servants saw it. A more un-Nenni-like display I would find it difficult to imagine."

Retief arranged his features into an expression of deep interest. "More un-Nenni-like, sir? I'm not sure I—"

"Bah!" The ambassador glared at Retief. "Your reputation has preceded you, sir. Your name is already associated with a number of bizarre incidents in Corps history. I'm warning you; I'll tolerate nothing." He turned and stalked away.

"Ambassador-baiting is a dangerous sport, Retief," Magnan said.

Retief took a swallow of his drink. "Still, it's better than no sport at all."

"Your time would be better spent observing the Nenni mannerisms; frankly, Retief, you're not fitting into the group at all well."

"I'll be candid with you, Mr. Magnan; the group gives me the willies."

"Oh, the Nenni are a trifle frivolous, I'll concede. But it's with them that we must deal. And you'd be making a contribution to the overall mission if you abandoned that rather arrogant manner of yours." Magnan looked at Retief critically. "You can't help your height, of course, but couldn't you curve your back just a bit—and possibly assume a more placating expression? Just act a little more . . ."

"Girlish?"

"Exactly." Magnan nodded, then looked sharply at Retief.

Retief drained his glass and put it on a passing tray.

"I'm better at acting girlish when I'm well juiced," he said. "But I can't face another sorghum and soda. I suppose it would be un-Nenni-like to slip one of the servants a credit and ask for a Scotch and water."

"Decidedly." Magnan glanced toward a sound across the room.

"Ah, here's the Potentate now . . ." He hurried off.

Retief watched the bearers coming and going, bringing trays laden with drinks, carrying off empties. There was a lull in the drinking now, as the diplomats gathered around the periwigged chief of state and his courtiers. Bearers loitered near the service door, eyeing the notables. Retief strolled over to the service door and pushed through it into a narrow white-tiled hall filled with kitchen odors. Silent servants gaped as he passed and watched him as he moved along to the kitchen door and stepped inside.

A dozen or more low-caste Petreacans, gathered around a long table in the center of the room, looked up, startled. A heap of long-bladed bread knives, carving knives and cleavers lay in the center of the table. Other knives were thrust into belts or held in the hands of the men. A fat man in the yellow sarong of a cook stood frozen in the act of handing a twelve-inch cheese-knife to a tall one-eyed sweeper.

Retief took one glance, then let his eyes wander to a far corner of the room. Humming a careless little tune, he sauntered across to the open liquor shelves, selected a garish green bottle, then turned unhurriedly back toward the door. The group of servants watched him, transfixed.

As Retief reached the door, it swung inward. Magnan stood in the doorway, looking at him.

"I had a premonition," he said.

"I'll bet it was a dandy. You must tell me all about it—in the salon."

"We'll have this out right here," Magnan snapped. I've warned you—" His voice trailed off as he took in the scene around the table.

"After you," Retief said, nudging Magnan toward the door.

"What's going on here?" Magnan barked. He stared at the men and started around Retief. A hand stopped him.

"Let's be going," Retief said, propelling Magnan toward the hall.

"Those knives!" Magnan yelped. "Take your hands off me, Retief! What are you men—"

Retief glanced back. The fat cook gestured suddenly, and the men faded back. The cook stood, arm cocked, a knife across his palm.

"Close the door and make no sound," he said softly.

Magnan pressed back against Retief. "Let's . . . r-run . . ." he faltered.

Retief turned slowly, put his hands up.

"I don't run very well with a knife in my back," he said. "Stand very still, Mr. Magnan, and do just what he tells you."

"Take them out through the back," the cook said.

"What does he mean," Magnan spluttered. "Here, you—"

"Silence," the cook said, almost casually. Magnan gaped at him, then closed his mouth.

Two of the men with knives came to Retief's side, gestured, grinning broadly.

"Let's go, peacocks," said one.

Retief and Magnan silently crossed the kitchen, went out the back door, stopped on command, and stood waiting. The sky was brilliant with stars and a gentle breeze stirred the tree-tops beyond the garden. Behind them the servants talked in low voices.

"You go too, Illy," the cook was saying.

"Do it here," said another.

"And carry them down?"

"Pitch 'em behind the hedge."

"I said the river. Three of you is plenty for a couple of Nenni dandies."

"They're foreigners, not Nenni. We don't know—"

"So they're foreign Nenni. Makes no difference. I've seen them. I need every man here; now get going."

"What about the big guy?"

"Him? He waltzed into the room and didn't notice a thing. But watch the other one."

At a prod from a knife point, Retief moved off down the walk, two of the escort behind him and Magnan, another going ahead to scout the way.

Magnan moved closer to Retief.

"Say," he said in a whisper, "that fellow in the lead— isn't he the one who spilled the drink? The one you took the blame for?"

"That's him, all right. He doesn't seem nervous any more, I notice."

"You saved him from serious punishment," Magnan said. "He'll be grateful; he'll let us go . . ."

"Better check with the fellows with the knives before you act on that."

"Say something to him," Magnan hissed, "remind him."

The lead man fell back in line with Retief and Magnan.

"These two are scared of you," he said, grinning and jerking a thumb toward the knife-handlers. "They haven't worked around the Nenni like me; they don't know you."

"Don't you recognize this gentleman?" Magnan said. "He's—"

"He did me a favor," the man said. "I remember."

"What's it all about?" Retief asked.

"The revolution. We're taking over now."

"Who's 'we'?"

"The People's Anti-Fascist Freedom League."

"What are all the knives for?"

"For the Nenni; and for you foreigners."

"What do you mean?" gasped Magnan.

"We'll slit all the throats at one time; saves a lot of running around."

"When will that be?"

"Just at dawn—and dawn comes early, this time of year. By full daylight the PAFFL will be in charge."

"You'll never succeed," Magnan said. "A few servants with knives; you'll all be caught and executed."

"By who; the Nenni?" The man laughed. "You Nenni are a caution."

"But we're not Nenni—"

"We've watched you; you're the same. You're part of the same blood-sucking class."

"There are better ways," Magnan said. "This killing won't help you. I'll personally see to it that your grievances are heard in the Corps Courts. I can assure you that the plight of the down-trodden workers will be alleviated. Equal rights for all."

"Threats won't help you," the man said. "You don't scare me."

"Threats? I'm promising relief to the exploited classes of Petreac."

"You must be nuts. You trying to upset the system or something?"

"Isn't that the purpose of your revolution?"

"Look, Nenni, we're tired of you Nenni getting all the graft. We want our turn. What good it do us to run Petreac if there's no loot?"

"You mean you intend to oppress the people? But they're your own group."

"Group, schmoop. We're taking all the chances; we're doing the work. We deserve the pay-off. You think we're throwing up good jobs for the fun of it?"

"You're basing a revolt on these cynical premises?"

"Wise up, Nenni; there's never been a revolution for any other reason."

"Who's in charge of this?" Retief said.

"Shoke, the head chef."

"I mean the big boss; who tells Shoke what to do?"

"Oh, that's Zorn. Look out, here's where we start down the slope. It's slippery."

"Look," Magnan said. "You. This—"

"My name's Illy."

"Mr. Illy, this man showed you mercy when he could have had you beaten."

"Keep moving. Yeah, I said I was grateful."

"Yes," Magnan said, swallowing hard. "A noble emotion, gratitude."

"I always try to pay back a good turn," Illy said. "Watch your step now on this sea-wall."

"You'll never regret it."

"This is far enough." Illy motioned to one of the knife men. "Give me your knife, Vug."

The man passed his knife to Illy. There was an odor of sea-mud and kelp. Small waves slapped against the stones of the sea-wall. The wind was stronger here.

"I know a neat stroke," Illy said. "Practically painless. Who's first?"

"What do you mean?" Magnan quavered.

"I said I was grateful; I'll do it myself, give you a nice clean job. You know these amateurs: botch it up and have a guy floppin' around, yellin' and spatterin' everybody up."

"I'm first," Retief said. He pushed past Magnan, stopped suddenly, and drove a straight punch at Illy's mouth.

The long blade flicked harmlessly over Retief's shoulder as Illy fell. Retief took the unarmed servant by the throat and belt, lifted him, and slammed him against the third man. Both screamed as they tumbled from the seawall into the water with a mighty splash. Retief turned back to Illy, pulled off the man's belt, and strapped his hands together.

Magnan found his voice. "You . . . we . . . they . . ."

"I know."

"We've got to get back," Magnan said. "Warn them."

"We'd never get through the rebel cordon around the palace. And if we did, trying to give an alarm would only set the assassinations off early."

"We can't just . . ."

"We've got to go to the source: this fellow Zorn. Get him to call it off."

"We'd be killed. At least we're safe here."

Illy groaned and opened his eyes. He sat up.

"On your feet, Illy," Retief said.

Illy looked around. "I'm sick."

"The damp air is bad for you. Let's be going." Retief pulled the man to his feet. "Where does Zorn stay when he's in town?"

"What happened? Where's Vug and . . ."

"They had an accident. Fell in the pond."

Illy gazed down at the restless black water.

"I guess I had you Nenni figured wrong."

"We Nenni have hidden qualities. Let's get moving before Vug and Slug make it to shore and start it all over again."

"No hurry," Illy said. "They can't swim." He spat into the water. "So long, Vug. So long, Toscin. Take a pull at the Hell Horn for me." He started off along the sea wall toward the sound of the surf.

"You want to see Zorn, I'll take you see Zorn. I can't swim either."

✧   ✧   ✧

"I take it," Retief said, "that the casino is a front for his political activities."

"He makes plenty off it. This PAFFL is a new kick. I never heard about it until maybe a couple months ago."

Retief motioned toward a dark shed with an open door.

"We'll stop here," he said, "long enough to strip the gadgets off these uniforms."

Illy, hands strapped behind his back, stood by and watched as Retief and Magnan removed medals, ribbons, orders, and insignia from the formal diplomatic garments.

"This may help some," Retief said, "if the word is out that two diplomats are loose."

"It's a breeze," Illy said. "We see people in purple and orange tailcoats all the time."

"I hope you're right," Retief said. "But if we're called, you'll be the first to go, Illy."

"You're a funny kind of Nenni," Illy said, eyeing Retief. "Toscin and Vug must be wonderin' what happened to 'em."

"If you think I'm good at drowning people, you ought to see me with a knife. Let's get going."

"It's only a little way now. But you better untie me. Somebody's liable to notice it and start askin' questions and get me killed."

"I'll take the chance. How do we get to the casino?"

"We follow this street. When we get to the Drunkard's Stairs we go up and it's right in front of us. A pink front with a sign like a big luck wheel."

"Give me your belt, Magnan," Retief said.

Magnan handed it over.

"Lie down, Illy."

The servant looked at Retief.

"Vug and Toscin will be glad to see me. But they'll never believe me." He lay down. Retief strapped his feet together and stuffed a handkerchief in his mouth.

"Why are you doing that?" Magnan asked. "We need him."

"We know the way now and we don't need anyone to announce our arrival."

Magnan looked at the man. "Maybe you'd better—ah, cut his throat."

Illy rolled his eyes.

"That's a very un-Nenni-like suggestion, Mr. Magnan," Retief said. "But if we have any trouble finding the casino following his directions, I'll give it serious thought."

There were few people in the narrow street. Shops were shuttered, windows dark.

"Maybe they heard about the coup," Magnan said. "They're lying low."

"More likely they're at the palace checking out knives."

They rounded a corner, stepped over a man curled in the gutter snoring heavily, and found themselves at the foot of a long flight of littered stone steps.

"The Drunkard's Stairs are plainly marked," Magnan sniffed.

"I hear sounds up there . . . sounds of merrymaking."

"Maybe we'd better go back."

"Merrymaking doesn't scare me. Come to think of it, I don't know what the word means." Retief started up, Magnan behind him.

At the top of the long stair a dense throng milled in the alley-like street.

A giant illuminated roulette wheel revolved slowly above them. A loud-speaker blared the chant of the croupiers from the tables inside. Magnan and Retief moved through the crowd toward the wide-open doors.

Magnan plucked at Retief's sleeve. "Are you sure we ought to push right in like this? Maybe we ought to wait a bit, look around."

"When you're where you have no business being," Retief said, "always stride along purposefully. If you loiter, people begin to get curious."

Inside, a mob packed the wide low-ceilinged room and clustered around gambling devices in the form of towers, tables, and basins.

"What do we do now?" Magnan asked.

"We gamble. How much money do you have in your pockets?"

"Why . . . a few credits . . ." Magnan handed the money to Retief. "But what about the man Zorn?"

"A purple cutaway is conspicuous enough, without ignoring the tables. We'll get to Zorn in due course."

"Your pleasure, gents," a bullet-headed man said, eye-ing the colorful evening clothes of the diplomats. "You'll be wantin' to try your luck at the Zoop tower, I'd guess. A game for real sporting gents."

"Why . . . ah . . ." Magnan said.

"What's a Zoop tower?" Retief asked.

"Out-of-towners, hey?" The bullet-headed man shifted his dope-stick to the other corner of his mouth. "Zoop is a great little game. Two teams of players buy into the pot; each player takes a lever; the object is to make the ball drop from the top of the tower into your net. Okay?"

"What's the ante?"

"I got a hundred-credit pot workin' now, gents."

Retief nodded. "We'll try it."

The shill led the way to an eight-foot tower mounted on gimbals. Two perspiring men in trade-class pullovers gripped two of the levers that controlled the tilt of the tower. A white ball lay in a hollow in the thick glass plat-form at the top. From the center an intricate pattern of grooves led out to the edge of the glass. Retief and Magnan took chairs before the two free levers.

"When the light goes on, gents, work the lever to jack the tower. You got three gears; takes a good arm to work top gear. That's this button here. The little knob controls what way you're goin'. May the best team win. I'll take the hundred credits now."

Retief handed over the money. A red light flashed on, and Retief tried the lever. It moved easily, with a ratcheting sound. The tower trembled, slowly tilted toward the two perspiring workmen pumping frantically at their levers. Magnan started slowly, accelerating as he saw the direc-tion the tower was taking.

"Faster, Retief," he said. "They're winning."

"This is against the clock, gents," the bullet-headed man said. "If nobody wins when the light goes off, the house takes all."

"Crank it over to the left," Retief said.

"I'm getting tired."

"Shift to a lower gear."

The tower leaned. The ball stirred and rolled into a concentric channel. Retief shifted to middle gear and worked the lever. The tower, creaking to a stop, started back upright.

"There isn't any lower gear," Magnan gasped. One of the two on the other side of the tower shifted to middle gear; the other followed suit. They worked harder now, heaving against the stiff levers. The tower quivered, then moved slowly toward their side.

"I'm exhausted," Magnan gasped. Dropping the lever, he lolled back in the chair, gulping air. Retief, shifting position, took Magnan's lever with his left hand.

"Shift it to middle gear," he said. Magnan gulped, punched the button and slumped back, panting.

"My arm," he said. "I've injured myself."

The two men in pullovers conferred hurriedly as they cranked their levers; then one punched a button, and the other reached across, using his left arm to help.

"They've shifted to high," Magnan said. "Give up, it's hopeless."

"Shift me to high. Both buttons."

Magnan complied. Retief's shoulders bulged. He brought one lever down, then the other, alternately, slowly at first, then faster. The tower jerked, tilted toward him, farther ... The ball rolled in the channel, found an outlet—

Abruptly, both Retief's levers froze. The tower trembled, wavered, and moved back. Retief heaved. One lever folded at the base, bent down, and snapped off short. Retief braced his feet, gripped the other lever with both hands and pulled. There was a squeal of metal, a loud twang. The lever came free, a length of broken cable flopping into view. The tower fell over as the two on the other side scrambled aside.

"Hey!" the croupier yelled, appearing from the crowd. "You wrecked my equipment!"

Retief got up and faced him

"Does Zorn know you've got your tower rigged for suckers?"

"You tryin' to call me a cheat?"

The crowd had fallen back, ringing the two men. The croupier glanced around. With a lightning motion he pulled out a knife.

"That'll be five hundred credits for the equipment," he said. "Nobody calls Kippy a cheat."

Retief picked up the broken lever.

"Don't make me hit you with this, Kippy."

Kippy looked at the bar.

"Comin' in here," he said indignantly, looking to the crowd for support, "bustin' up my rig, threatenin' me . . ."

"I want a hundred credits," Retief said. "Now."

"Highway robbery!" Kippy yelled.

"Better pay up," somebody said.

"Hit him, mister," another in the crowd yelled.

A broad-shouldered man with greying hair pushed through the crowd and looked around. "You heard him, Kippy. Give."

The shill growled, tucked his knife away, reluctantly peeled a bill from a fat roll and handed it over.

The newcomer looked from Retief to Magnan.

"Pick another game, strangers," he said. "Kippy made a little mistake."

"This is small-time stuff," Retief said. "I'm interested in something big."

The broad-shouldered man lit a perfumed dope-stick, then sniffed at it.

"What would you call big?" he said softly.

"What's the biggest you've got?"

The man narrowed his eyes, smiling. "Maybe you'd like to try Slam."

"Tell me about it."

"Over here." The crowd opened up and made a path. Retief and Magnan followed across the room to a brightly-lit glass-walled box. There was an arm-sized opening at waist height, and inside was a hand grip. A four-foot clear plastic globe a quarter full of chips hung in the center. Apparatus was mounted at the top of the box.

"Slam pays good odds," the man said. "You can go as high as you like. Chips cost you a hundred credits. You start it up by dropping a chip in here." He indicated a slot.

"You take the hand grip. When you squeeze, it unlocks and starts to turn. Takes a pretty good grip to start the globe turning. You can see, it's full of chips. There's a hole at the top. As long as you hold the grip, the bowl turns.

The harder you squeeze, the faster it turns. Eventually it'll turn over to where the hole is down, and chips fall out. If you let up and the bowl stops, you're all through.

"Just to make it interesting, there's contact plates spotted around the bowl; when one of 'em lines up with a live contact, you get a little jolt—guaranteed non-lethal. But if you let go, you lose. All you've got to do is hold on long enough, and you'll get the pay-off."

"How often does this random pattern put the hole down?"

"Anywhere from three minutes to fifteen, with the average grip. Oh, by the way, one more thing. The lead block up there . . ." The man motioned with his head toward a one-foot cube suspended by a thick cable. "It's rigged to drop every now and then: averages five minutes. A warning light flashes first. You can set the clock back on it by dropping another chip—or you can let go the grip. Or you can take a chance; sometimes the light's a bluff."

Retief looked at the massive block of metal.

"That would mess up a man's dealing hand, wouldn't it?"

"The last two jokers who were too cheap to feed the machine had to have 'em off; their arm, I mean. That lead's heavy stuff."

"I don't suppose your machine has a habit of getting stuck, like Kippy's?"

The broad-shouldered man frowned.

"You're a stranger," he said. "You don't know any better."

"It's a fair game, mister," someone called.

"Where do I buy the chips?"

The man smiled. "I'll fix you up. How many?"

"One."

"A big spender, eh?" The man snickered and handed over a large plastic chip.

Retief stepped to the machine and dropped the coin.

"If you want to change your mind," the man said, "you can back out now. All it'll cost you is the chip you dropped."

Retief, reaching through the hole, took the grip. It was leather-padded, hand-filling. He squeezed it. There was a click and bright lights sprang up. The globe began to twirl lazily. The four-inch hole at its top was plainly visible.

"If ever the hole gets in position, it will empty very quickly," Magnan said.

Suddenly, a brilliant white light flooded the glass cage. A sound went up from the spectators.

"Quick, drop a chip," someone yelled.

"You've only got ten seconds . . ."

"Let go!" Magnan pleaded.

Retief sat silent, holding the grip, frowning up at the weight. The globe twirled faster now. Then the bright white light winked off.

"A bluff!" Magnan gasped.

"That's risky, stranger," the grey-templed man said.

The globe was turning rapidly now, oscillating from side to side. The hole seemed to travel in a wavering loop, dipping lower, swinging up high, then down again.

"It has to move to the bottom soon," Magnan said. "Slow it down, so it doesn't shoot past."

"The slower it goes, the longer it takes to get to the bottom," someone said.

There was a crackle, and Retief stiffened. Magnan heard a sharp intake of breath. The globe slowed, and Retief shook his head, blinking.

The broad-shouldered man glanced at a meter.

"You took pretty near a full jolt, that time," he said.

The hole in the globe was tracing an oblique course now, swinging to the center, then below.

"A little longer," Magnan said.

"That's the best speed I ever seen on the Slam ball," someone said. "How much longer can he hold it?"

Magnan looked at Retief's knuckles. They showed white against the grip. The globe tilted farther, swung around, then down; two chips fell out, clattered down a chute and into a box.

"We're ahead," Magnan said. "Let's quit."

Retief shook his head. The globe rotated, dipped again; three chips fell.

"She's ready," someone called.

"It's bound to hit soon," another voice added excitedly. "Come on, mister!"

"Slow down," Magnan said. "So it won't move past too quickly."

"Speed it up, before that lead block gets you," someone called.

The hole swung high, over the top, then down the side. Chips rained out, six, eight . . .

"Next pass," a voice called.

The white warning light flooded the cage. The globe whirled; the hole slid over the top, down, down . . . a chip fell, two more . . .

Retief half rose, clamped his jaw, and crushed the grip. Sparks flew, and the globe slowed, chips spewing. It stopped and swung back. Weighted by the mass of chips at the bottom, it stopped again with the hole centered. Chips cascaded down the chute, filled the box and spilled on the floor. The crowd yelled.

Retief released the grip and withdrew his arm at the same instant that the lead block slammed down.

"Good lord," Magnan said. "I felt that through the floor."

Retief turned to the broad-shouldered man.

"This game's all right for beginners," he said. "But I'd like to talk a really big gamble. Why don't we go to your office, Mr. Zorn?"

"Your proposition interests me," Zorn said, an hour later. "But there's some angles to this I haven't mentioned yet."

"You're a gambler, Zorn, not a suicide," Retief said. "Take what I've offered. Your dream of revolution was fancier, I agree, but it won't work."

"How do I know you birds aren't lying?" Zorn snarled. He stood up and strode up and down the room. "You walk in here and tell me I'll have a squadron of Corps Peace Enforcers on my neck, that the Corps won't recognize my regime. Maybe you're right; but I've got other contacts. They say different." Whirling, he stared at Retief.

"I have pretty good assurance that once I put it over, the Corps will have to recognize me as the legal *de facto* government of Petreac. They won't meddle in internal affairs."

"Nonsense," Magnan spoke up, "the Corps will never deal with a pack of criminals calling themselves—"

"Watch your language, you!" Zorn rasped.

"I'll admit Mr. Magnan's point is a little weak," Retief said.

"But you're overlooking something. You plan to murder a dozen or so officers of the Corps Diplomatique Terrestrienne along with the local wheels. The Corps won't overlook that. It can't."

"Their tough luck they're in the middle," Zorn muttered.

"Our offer is extremely generous, Mr. Zorn," Magnan said. "The post you'll get will pay you very well indeed; as against certain failure of your coup, the choice should be simple."

Zorn eyed Magnan. "I thought you diplomats weren't the type to go around making deals under the table. Offering me a job—it sounds phony as hell."

"It's time you knew," Retief said. "There's no phonier business in the galaxy than diplomacy."

"You'd better take it, Mr. Zorn," Magnan said.

"Don't push me," Zorn said. "You two walk into my headquarters empty-handed and big-mouthed. I don't know what I'm talking to you for. The answer is no. N-i-x, no!"

"Who are you afraid of?" Retief said softly.

Zorn glared at him.

"Where do you get that 'afraid' routine? I'm top man here. What have I got to be afraid of?"

"Don't kid around, Zorn. Somebody's got you under his thumb. I can see you squirming from here."

"What if I let your boys alone?" Zorn said suddenly. "The Corps won't have anything to say then, huh?"

"The Corps has plans for Petreac, Zorn. You aren't part of them. A revolution right now isn't part of them. Having the Potentate and the whole Nenni caste slaughtered isn't part of them. Do I make myself clear?"

"Listen," Zorn said urgently, "I'll tell you guys a few things. You ever heard of a world they call Rotune?"

"Certainly," Magnan said. "It's a near neighbor of yours, another backward—that is, emergent."

"Okay," Zorn said. "You guys think I'm a piker, do you? Well, let me wise you up. The Federal Junta on Rotune is backing my play. I'll be recognized by Rotune, and the Rotune fleet will stand by in case I need any help. I'll present the CDT with what you call a *fait accompli*."

"What does Rotune get out of this? I thought they were your traditional enemies."

"Don't get me wrong. I've got no use for Rotune; but our interests happen to coincide right now."

"Do they?" Retief smiled grimly. "You can spot a sucker as soon as he comes through that door out there—but you go for a deal like this."

"What do you mean?" Zorn looked angrily at Retief. "It's fool-proof."

"After you get in power, you'll be fast friends with Rotune, is that it?"

"Friends, hell. Just give me time to get set, and I'll square a few things with that—"

"Exactly. And what do you suppose they have in mind for you?"

"What are you getting at?"

"Why is Rotune interested in your take-over?"

Zorn studied Retief's face. "I'll tell you why," he said. "It's you birds; you and your trade agreement. You're here to tie Petreac into some kind of trade combine. That cuts Rotune out. They don't like that. And anyway, we're doing all right out here; we don't need any commitments to a lot of fancy-pants on the other side of the galaxy."

"That's what Rotune has sold you, eh?" Retief said, smiling.

"Sold, nothing—" Zorn ground out his dope-stick, then lit another. He snorted angrily.

"Okay—what's your idea?"

"You know what Petreac is getting in the way of imports as a result of the trade agreement?"

"Sure, a lot of junk. Clothes washers, tape projectors, all that kind of stuff."

"To be specific," Retief said, "there'll be 50,000 Tatone B-3 dry washers; 100,000 Glo-float motile lamps; 100,000 Earthworm Minor garden cultivators; 25,000 Veco space heaters; and 75,000 replacement elements for Ford Mono-meg drives."

"Like I said: a lot of junk," Zorn said.

Retief leaned back, looking sardonically at Zorn. "Here's the gimmick, Zorn," he said. "The Corps is getting a little tired of Petreac and Rotune carrying on their two-penny war out here. Your privateers have a nasty habit of picking on innocent bystanders. After studying both sides, the Corps has decided Petreac would be a little easier to do business with; so this trade agreement was worked out. The Corps can't openly sponsor an arms shipment to a belligerent; but personal appliances are another story."

"So what do we do—plow 'em under with back-yard cultivators?" Zorn looked at Retief, puzzled. "What's the point?"

"You take the sealed monitor unit from the washer, the repeller field generator from the lamp, the converter control from the cultivator, et cetera, et cetera. You fit these together according to some very simple instructions; presto! you have one hundred thousand Standard-class Y hand blasters; just the thing to turn the tide in a stalemated war fought with obsolete arms."

"Good lord," Magnan said. "Retief, are you—"

"I have to tell him. He has to know what he's putting his neck into."

"Weapons, hey?" Zorn said. "And Rotune knows about it . . . ?"

"Sure they know about it; it's not too hard to figure out. And there's more. They want the CDT delegation included in the massacre for a reason; it will put Petreac out of the picture; the trade agreement will go to Rotune; and you and your new regime will find yourselves looking down the muzzles of your own blasters."

Zorn threw his dope-stick to the floor with a snarl.

"I should have smelled something when that Rotune agent made his pitch." Zorn looked at the clock on the wall.

"I've got two hundred armed men in the palace. We've got about forty minutes to get over there before the rocket goes up."

In the shadows of the palace terrace, Zorn turned to Retief. "You'd better stay here out of the way until I've spread the word. Just in case."

"Let me caution you against any . . . ah . . . slip-ups, Mr. Zorn," Magnan said. "The Nenni are not to be molested."

Zorn looked at Retief. "Your friend talks too much. I'll keep my end of it; he'd better keep his."

"Nothing's happened yet, you're sure?" Magnan said.

"I'm sure," Zorn said. "Ten minutes to go; plenty of time."

"I'll just step into the salon to assure myself that all is well," Magnan said.

"Suit yourself. Just stay clear of the kitchen, or you'll get your throat cut." Zorn sniffed at his dope-stick. "I sent the word for Shoke," he muttered. "Wonder what's keeping him?"

Magnan stepped to a tall glass door, eased it open, and poked his head through the heavy draperies. As he moved to draw back, a voice was faintly audible. Magnan paused, his head still through the drapes.

"What's going on there?" Zorn rasped. He and Retief stepped up behind Magnan.

". . . breath of air," Magnan was saying.

"Well, come along, Magnan!" Ambassador Crodfoller's voice snapped.

Magnan shifted from one foot to the other, then pushed through the drapes.

"Where've you been, Mr. Magnan?" The ambassador's voice was sharp.

"Oh . . . ah . . . a slight accident, Mr. Ambassador."

"What's happened to your shoes? Where are your insignia and decorations?"

"I—ah—spilled a drink on them. Maybe I'd better nip up to my room and slip into some fresh medals."

The ambassador snorted. "A professional diplomat never shows his liquor, Magnan. It's one of his primary professional skills. I'll speak to you about this later. I had expected your attendance at the signing ceremony, but under the circumstances I'll dispense with that. You'd better depart quietly through the kitchen."

"The kitchen? But it's crowded . . . I mean . . ."

"A little loss of caste won't hurt at this point, Mr. Magnan. Now kindly move along before you attract attention. The agreement isn't signed yet."

"The agreement . . ." Magnan babbled, sparring for time, "very clever, Mr. Ambassador. A very neat solution."

The sound of an orchestra came up suddenly, blaring a fanfare.

Zorn shifted restlessly, his ear against the glass. "What's your friend pulling?" he rasped. "I don't like this."

"Keep cool, Zorn. Mr. Magnan is doing a little emergency salvage on his career."

The music died away with a clatter.

" . . . my God." Ambassador Crodfoller's voice was faint. "Magnan, you'll be knighted for this. Thank God you reached me. Thank God it's not too late. I'll find some excuse. I'll get off a gram at once."

"But you—"

"It's all right, Magnan. You were in time. Another ten minutes and the agreement would have been signed and transmitted. The wheels would have been put in motion. My career would have been ruined . . ."

Retief felt a prod at his back. He turned.

"Double-crossed," Zorn said softly. "So much for the word of a diplomat."

Retief looked at the short-barreled needler in Zorn's hand.

"I see you hedge your bets, Zorn."

"We'll wait here until the excitement's over inside. I wouldn't want to attract any attention right now."

"Your politics are still lousy, Zorn. The picture hasn't changed. Your coup hasn't got a chance."

"Skip it. I'll take up one problem at a time."

"Magnan's mouth has a habit of falling open at the wrong time."

"That's my good luck I heard it. So there'll be no agreement, no guns, no fat job for Tammany Zorn, hey? Well, I can still play it the other way. What have I got to lose?"

With a movement too quick to follow, Retief's hand chopped down across Zorn's wrist. The needler clattered to the ground as Retief's hand clamped on Zorn's arm, whirling him around.

"In answer to your last question," Retief said, "your neck."

"You haven't got a chance, double-crosser," Zorn gasped.

"Shoke will be here in a minute. Tell him it's all off."

"Twist harder, mister. Break it off at the shoulder. I'm telling him nothing."

"The kidding's over, Zorn. Call it off or I'll kill you."

"I believe you. But you won't have long to remember it."

"All the killing will be for nothing. You'll be dead and the Rotunes will step into the power vacuum."

"So what? When I die, the world ends."

"Suppose I make you another offer, Zorn?"

"Why would it be any better than the last one?"

Retief released Zorn's arm, pushed him away, stooped and picked up the needler.

"I could kill you, Zorn; you know that."

"Go ahead."

Retief reversed the needler and held it out.

"I'm a gambler too, Zorn. I'm gambling you'll listen to what I have to say."

Zorn snatched the gun and stepped back. He looked at Retief. "That wasn't the smartest bet you ever made, but go ahead. You've got maybe ten seconds."

"Nobody double-crossed you, Zorn. Magnan put his foot in it; too bad. Is that a reason to kill yourself and a lot of other people who've bet their lives on you?"

"They gambled and lost. Tough."

"Maybe they haven't lost yet—if you don't quit."

"Get to the point."

Retief spoke earnestly for a minute and a half. Zorn stood, gun aimed, listening. Then both men turned as footsteps approached along the terrace. A fat man in a yellow sarong padded up to Zorn.

Zorn tucked the needler in his waistband.

"Hold everything, Shoke," he said. "Tell the boys to put the knives away; spread the word fast; it's all off."

"I want to commend you, Retief," Ambassador Crodfoller said expansively. "You mixed very well at last night's affair; actually, I was hardly aware of your presence."

"I've been studying Mr. Magnan's work," Retief said.

"A good man, Magnan. In a crowd, he's virtually invisible."

"He knows when to disappear, all right."

"This has been in many ways a model operation, Retief." The ambassador patted his paunch contentedly. "By observing local social customs and blending harmoniously with the court, I've succeeded in establishing a fine, friendly, working relationship with the Potentate."

"I understand the agreement has been postponed a few days."

The ambassador chuckled. "The Potentate's a crafty one. Through . . . ah . . . a special study I have been conducting, I learned last night that he had hoped to, shall I say, 'put one over' on the Corps."

"Great Heavens," Retief said.

"Naturally, this placed me in a difficult position. It was my task to quash this gambit, without giving any indication that I was aware of its existence."

"A hairy position indeed."

"Quite casually, I informed the Potentate that certain items which had been included in the terms of the agreement had been deleted and others substituted. I admired him at that moment, Retief. He took it coolly—appearing completely indifferent—perfectly dissembling his very serious disappointment. Of course, he could hardly do otherwise without in effect admitting his plot."

"I noticed him dancing with three girls each wearing a bunch of grapes; he's very agile for a man of his bulk."

"You mustn't discount the Potentate. Remember, beneath that mask of frivolity, he had absorbed a bitter blow."

"He had me fooled," Retief said.

"Don't feel badly; I confess at first I, too, failed to sense his shrewdness." The ambassador nodded and moved off along the corridor.

Retief turned and went into an office. Magnan looked up from his desk.

"Ah, Retief," he said. "I've been meaning to ask you. About the . . . ah . . . blasters; are you—"

Retief leaned on Magnan's desk and looked at him. "I thought that was to be our little secret."

"Well, naturally, I—" Magnan closed his mouth and swallowed. "How is it, Retief," he said sharply, "that you were aware of this blaster business, when the ambassador himself wasn't?"

"Easy," Retief said. "I made it up."

"You what!" Magnan looked wild. "But the agreement— it's been revised. Ambassador Crodfoller has gone on record."

"Too bad. Glad I didn't tell him about it."

Magnan leaned back and closed his eyes.

"It was big of you to take all the . . . blame," Retief

said, "when the ambassador was talking about knighting people."

Magnan opened his eyes. "What about that gambler, Zorn? Won't he be upset when he learns the agreement is off? After all, I . . . that is, we, or you, had more or less promised him—"

"It's all right. I made another arrangement. The business about making blasters out of common components wasn't completely imaginary. You can actually do it, using parts from an old-fashioned disposal unit."

"What good will that do him?" Magnan whispered, looking nervous. "We're not shipping in any old-fashioned disposal units."

"We don't need to. They're already installed in the palace kitchen—and in a few thousand other places, Zorn tells me."

"If this ever leaks . . ." Magnan put a hand to his forehead.

"I have his word on it that the Nenni slaughter is out. This place is ripe for a change; maybe Zorn is what it needs."

"But how can we know?" Magnan said. "How can we be sure?"

"We can't. But it's not up to the Corps to meddle in Petreac's internal affairs." He leaned over, picked up Magnan's desk lighter, and lit a cigar. He blew a cloud of smoke toward the ceiling.

"Right?" he said.

Magnan looked at him and nodded weakly. "Right."

"I'd better be getting along to my desk," Retief said. "Now that the ambassador feels that I'm settling down at last."

"Retief," Magnan said, "tonight, I implore you: stay out of the kitchen—no matter what."

Retief raised his eyebrows.

"I know," Magnan said. "If you hadn't interfered, we'd all have had our throats cut. But at least . . ." He paused. "we'd have died in accordance with regulations."

> ... Highly effective ancillary programs,
> developed early in Corps history, played a vital
> role in promoting harmony among the peace-
> loving people of the Galactic community. The
> notable success of Assistant Attaché (later
> Ambassador) Magnan in the cosmopolitization
> of reactionary elements in the Nicodeman
> Cluster was achieved through the agency of
> these enlightened programs ...
>
> —Vol. III, reel 71 482 A. E. (AD 2943)

CULTURAL EXCHANGE

First Secretary Magnan took his green-lined cape and orange-feathered beret from the clothes tree. "I'm off now, Retief," he said. "I hope you'll manage the administrative routine during my absence without any unfortunate incidents."

"That seems a modest enough hope," said Second Secretary Retief. "I'll try to live up to it."

"I don't appreciate frivolity with reference to this Division," Magnan said testily. "When I first came here, the Manpower Utilization Directorate, Division of Libraries and Education was a shambles. I fancy I've made MUDDLE what it is today. Frankly, I question the wisdom of placing you in charge of such a sensitive desk, even for two weeks; but remember, yours is a purely rubber-stamp function."

"In that case, let's leave it to Miss Furkle, and I'll take a couple of weeks off myself. With her poundage, she could bring plenty of pressure to bear."

"I assume you jest, Retief," Magnan said sadly. "I

should expect even you to appreciate that Bogan participation in the Exchange Program may be the first step toward sublimation of their aggressions into more cultivated channels."

"I see they're sending two thousand students to d'Land," Retief said, glancing at the Memo for Record. "That's a sizable sublimation."

Magnan nodded. "The Bogans have launched no less than four military campaigns in the last two decades. They're known as the Hoodlums of the Nicodeman Cluster. Now, perhaps, we shall see them breaking that precedent and entering into the cultural life of the Galaxy."

"Breaking and entering," Retief said. "You may have something there. But I'm wondering what they'll study on d'Land. That's an industrial world of the poor-but-honest variety."

"Academic details are the affair of the students and their professors," Magnan said. "Our function is merely to bring them together. See that you don't antagonize the Bogan representative. This will be an excellent opportunity for you to practice your diplomatic restraint—not your strong point, I'm sure you'll agree—"

A buzzer sounded. Retief punched a button. "What is it, Miss Furkle?"

"That—bucolic person from Lovenbroy is here again." On the small desk screen, Miss Furkle's meaty features were compressed in disapproval.

"This fellow's a confounded pest; I'll leave him to you, Retief," Magnan said. "Tell him something; get rid of him. And remember: here at Corps HQ, all eyes are upon you."

"If I'd thought of that, I'd have worn my other suit," Retief said.

Magnan snorted and passed from view. Retief punched Miss Furkle's button.

"Send the bucolic person in."

A tall broad man with bronze skin and grey hair, wearing tight trousers of heavy cloth, a loose shirt open at the neck, and a short jacket, stepped into the room, a bundle under his arm. He paused at sight of Retief, looked him over momentarily, then advanced and held out his hand. Retief took it. For a moment the two big men stood, face to face.

The newcomer's jaw muscles knotted. Then he winced. Retief dropped his hand, motioned to a chair.

"That's nice knuckle work, mister," the stranger said, massaging his hand. "First time anybody ever did that to me. My fault, though, I started it, I guess." He grinned and sat down.

"What can I do for you?" the Second Secretary said. "My name's Retief. I'm taking Mr. Magnan's place for a couple of weeks."

"You work for this culture bunch, do you? Funny, I thought they were all ribbon-counter boys. Never mind. I'm Hank Arapoulous. I'm a farmer. What I wanted to see you about was—" He shifted in his chair. "Well, out on Lovenbroy we've got a serious problem. The wine crop is just about ready. We start picking in another two, three months. Now I don't know if you're familiar with the Bacchus vines we grow?"

"No," Retief said. "Have a cigar?" He pushed a box across the desk. Arapoulous took one. "Bacchus vines are an unusual crop," he said, puffing life into the cigar. "Only mature every twelve years. In between, the vines don't need a lot of attention; our time's mostly our own. We like to farm, though. Spend a lot of time developing new forms. Apples the size of a melon—and sweet."

"Sounds very pleasant," Retief said. "Where does the Libraries and Education Division come in?"

Arapoulous leaned forward. "We go in pretty heavy for the arts. Folks can't spend all their time hybridizing plants. We've turned all the land area we've got into parks and farms; course, we left some sizable forest areas for hunting and such. Lovenbroy's a nice place, Mr. Retief."

"It sounds like it, Mr. Arapoulous. Just what—"

"Call me Hank. We've got long seasons back home. Five of 'em. Our year's about eighteen Terry months. Cold as hell in winter—eccentric orbit, you know. Blue-black sky, stars visible all day. We do mostly painting and sculpture in the winter. Then Spring—still plenty cold. Lots of skiing, bobsledding, ice skating—and it's the season for woodworkers. Our furniture—"

"I've seen some of your furniture, I believe," said Retief. "Beautiful work."

Arapoulous nodded. "All local timbers, too. Lots of metals in our soil; those sulphates give the woods some color, I'll tell you. Then comes the Monsoon. Rain—it comes down in sheets—but the sun's gettin' closer; shines all the time. Ever seen it pouring rain in the sunshine? That's the music-writing season. Then summer. Summer's hot. We stay inside in the daytime, and have beach parties all night. Lots of beach on Lovenbroy, we're mostly islands. That's the drama and symphony time. The theatres are set up on the sand, or anchored on barges off-shore. You have the music and the surf and the bonfires and stars—we're close to the center of a globular cluster, you know . . ."

"You say it's time now for the wine crop?"

"That's right. Autumn's our harvest season. Most years we have just the ordinary crops: fruit, grain, that kind of thing. Getting it in doesn't take long. We spend most of the time on architecture, getting new places ready for the winter, or remodeling the older ones. We spend a lot of time in our houses; we like to have them comfortable. But this year's different. This is Wine Year."

Arapoulous puffed on his cigar and looked worriedly at Retief. "Our wine crop is our big money crop," he said. "We make enough to keep us going. But this year . . ."

"The crop isn't panning out?"

"Oh, the crop's fine; one of the best I can remember. Course, I'm only twenty-eight; I can't remember but two other harvests. The problem's not the crop . . ."

"Have you lose your markets? That sounds like a matter for the Commercial—"

"Lost our markets? Mister, nobody that ever tasted our wines ever settled for anything else!"

"It sounds like I've been missing something," said Retief. "I'll have to try them some time."

Arapoulous put his bundle on the desk, pulled off the wrappings. "No time like the present," he said.

Retief looked at the two squat bottles, one green, one amber, both dusty, with faded labels, and blackened corks secured by wire.

"Drinking on duty is frowned on in the Corps, Mr. Arapoulous," he said.

"This isn't drinking, it's just wine." Arapoulous pulled the wire retainer loose and thumbed the cork. It rose slowly, then popped in the air. Arapoulous caught it. Aromatic fumes wafted from the bottle. "Besides, my feelings would be hurt if you didn't join me." He winked.

Retief took two thin-walled glasses from a table beside the desk. "Come to think of it, we also have to be careful about violating quaint native customs." Arapoulous filled the glasses. Retief picked one up, sniffed the deep rust colored fluid, tasted it, then took a healthy swallow. He looked at Arapoulous thoughtfully.

"Hmmm, it tastes like salted pecans, with an undercurrent of crusted port."

"Don't try to describe it, Mr. Retief," Arapoulous said. He took a mouthful of wine, swished it around his teeth, and swallowed. "It's Bacchus wine, that's all." He pushed the second bottle toward Retief. "The custom back home is to alternate red wine and black."

Retief put aside his cigar, pulled the wires loose, nudged the cork, and caught it as it popped up.

"Bad luck if you miss the cork," Arapoulous said, nodding. "You probably never heard about the trouble we had on Lovenbroy a few years back?"

"Can't say that I did, Hank." Retief poured the black wine into the two fresh glasses. "Here's to the harvest."

"We've got plenty of minerals on Lovenbroy," Arapoulous said, swallowing wine. "But we don't plan to wreck the landscape mining 'em. We like to farm. About ten years back some neighbors of ours landed a force. They figured they knew better what to do with our minerals than we did. Wanted to strip-mine, smelt ore. We convinced 'em otherwise. But it took a year, and we lost a lot of men."

"That's too bad," Retief said. "I'd say this one tastes more like roast beef and popcorn over a Riesling base."

"It put us in a bad spot," Arapoulous went on. "We had to borrow money from a world called Croanie, mortgaged our crops; we had to start exporting art work too. Plenty of buyers, but it's not the same when you're doing it for strangers."

"What's the problem?" Retief said, "Croanie about to foreclose?"

"The loan's due. The wine crop would put us in the clear; but we need harvest hands. Picking Bacchus grapes isn't a job you can turn over to machinery—and we wouldn't if we could. Vintage season is the high point of living on Lovenbroy. Everybody joins in. First, there's the picking in the fields. Miles and miles of vineyards covering the mountain sides, crowding the river banks, with gardens here and there. Big vines, eight feet high, loaded with fruit, and deep grass growing between. The wine-carriers keep on the run, bringing wine to the pickers. There's prizes for the biggest day's output, bets on who can fill the most baskets in an hour. The sun's high and bright, and it's just cool enough to give you plenty of energy. Come nightfall the tables are set up in the garden plots, and the feast is laid on: roast turkeys, beef, hams, all kinds of fowl. Big salads and plenty of fruit and fresh-baked breads . . . and wine, plenty of wine. The cooking's done by a different crew each night in each garden, and there's prizes for the best crews.

"Then the wine-making. We still tramp out the vintage. That's mostly for the young folks—but anybody's welcome. That's when things start to get loosened up. Matter of fact, pretty near half our young-uns are born about nine months after a vintage. All bets are off then. It keeps a fellow on his toes though; ever tried to hold onto a gal wearin' nothing but a layer of grape juice?"

"Never did," Retief said. "You say most of the children are born after a vintage. That would make them only twelve years old by the time—"

"Oh, that's Lovenbroy years; they'd be eighteen, Terry reckoning."

"I was thinking you looked a little mature for twenty-eight," Retief said.

"Forty-two, Terry years," Arapoulous said. "But this year—it looks bad. We've got a bumper crop—and we're short-handed. If we don't get a big vintage, Croanie steps in; Lord knows what they'll do to the land.

"What we figured was, maybe you Culture boys could help us out: a loan to see us through the vintage, enough to hire extra hands. Then we'd repay it in sculpture, painting, furniture—"

"Sorry, Hank. All we do here is work out itineraries for

traveling side-shows, that kind of thing. Now if you needed a troop of Groaci nose-flute players—"

"Can they pick grapes?"

"Nope—anyway they can't stand the daylight. Have you talked this over with the Labor office?"

"Sure did. They said they'd fix us up with all the electronics specialists and computer programmers we wanted—but no field hands. Said it was what they classified as menial drudgery; you'd have thought I was trying to buy slaves."

The buzzer sounded. Miss Furkle appeared on the desk screen.

"You're due at the Inter-Group Council in five minutes," she said. "Then afterwards, there are the Bogan students to meet."

"Thanks." Retief finished his glass and stood. "I have to run, Hank," he said. "Let me think this over. Maybe I can come up with something. Check with me day after tomorrow. And you'd better leave the bottles here. Cultural exhibits, you know."

As the council meeting broke up, Retief caught the eye of a colleague across the table.

"Mr. Whaffle, you mentioned a shipment going to a place called Croanie. What are they getting?"

Whaffle blinked. "You're the fellow who's filling in for Magnan, over at MUDDLE," he said. "Properly speaking, equipment grants are the sole concern of the Motorized Equipment Depot, Division of Loans and Exchanges." He pursed his lips. "However, I suppose there's no harm in my telling you. They'll be receiving heavy mining equipment."

"Drill rigs, that sort of thing?"

"Strip mining gear." Whaffle took a slip of paper from a breast pocket and blinked at it. "Bolo Model WV/1 tractors, to be specific. Why MUDDLE's interest in MEDDLE's activities?"

"Forgive my curiosity, Mr. Whaffle. It's just that Croanie cropped up earlier today; seems she holds a mortgage on some vineyards over on—"

"That's not MEDDLE's affair, sir," Whaffle cut in. "I

have sufficient problems as Chief of MEDDLE without probing into MUDDLE's business."

"Speaking of tractors," another man put in, "we over at the Special Committee for Rehabilitation and Overhaul of Underdeveloped Nations' General Economies have been trying for months to get a request for mining equipment for d'Land through MEDDLE—"

"SCROUNGE was late on the scene," Whaffle said. "First come, first served, that's our policy at MEDDLE. Good day, gentlemen." He strode off, a briefcase under his arm.

"That's the trouble with peaceful worlds," the SCROUNGE committeeman said. "Boge is a trouble-maker, so every agency in the Corps is out to pacify her, while my chance to make a record—that is, assist peace-loving d'Land, comes to nought."

"What kind of university do they have on d'Land?" asked Retief. "We're sending them two thousand exchange students. It must be quite an institution—"

"University? D'Land has one under-endowed technical college."

"Will all the exchange students be studying at the Technical College?"

"Two thousand students? Hah! Two hundred students would overtax the facilities of the college!"

"I wonder if the Bogans know that?"

"The Bogans? Why, most of d'Land's difficulties are due to the unwise trade agreement she entered into with Boge. Two thousand students indeed." He snorted and walked away.

Retief stopped by the office to pick up his short violet cape, then rode the elevator to the roof of the 230-storey Corps HQ building and hailed a cab to the port. The Bogan students had arrived early. Retief saw them lined up on the ramp waiting to go through customs. It would be half an hour before they were cleared through. He turned into the bar and ordered a beer. A tall young fellow on the next stool raised his glass.

"Happy days," he said.

"And nights to match."

"You said it." He gulped half his beer. "My name's Karsh.

Mr. Karsh. Yep, Mr. Karsh. Boy, this is a drag, sitting around this place waiting."

"You meeting somebody?"

"Yeah. Bunch of babies. Kids. How they expect— Never mind. Have one on me."

"Thanks. You a scoutmaster?"

"I'll tell you what I am; I'm a cradle-robber. You know," he turned to Retief, "not one of those kids is over eighteen." He hiccuped. "Students, you know. Never saw a student with a beard, did you?"

"Lots of times. You're meeting the students, are you?"

The young fellow blinked at Retief. "Oh, you know about it, huh?"

"I represent MUDDLE."

Karsh finished his beer and ordered another. "I came on ahead: sort of an advance guard for the kids. I trained 'em myself. Treated it like a game, but they can handle a CSU. Don't know how they'll act under pressure. If I had my old platoon—"

He looked at his beer glass, then pushed it back. "Had enough," he said. "So long, friend. Or are you coming along?"

Retief nodded. "Might as well."

At the exit to the Customs enclosure, Retief watched as the first of the Bogan students came through, caught sight of Karsh, and snapped to attention.

"Drop that, mister," Karsh snapped. "Is that any way for a student to act?"

The youth, a round-faced lad with broad shoulders, grinned.

"Guess not," he said. "Say, uh, Mr. Karsh, are we gonna get to go to town. Us fellas were thinkin'—"

"You were, huh? You act like a bunch of school kids— I mean . . . No! Now line up!"

"We have quarters ready for the students," Retief said. "If you'd like to bring them around to the west side, I have a couple of copters laid on."

"Thanks," said Karsh. "They'll stay here until take-off time. Can't have the little darlings wandering around loose. Might get ideas about going over the hill." He hiccuped. "I mean, they might play hookey."

"We've scheduled your re-embarkation for noon tomorrow. That's a long wait. MUDDLE's arranged theatre tickets and a dinner."

"Sorry," Karsh said. "As soon as the baggage gets here, we're off." He hiccuped again. "Can't travel without our baggage, y'know."

"Suit yourself," Retief said. "Where's the baggage now?"

"Coming in aboard a Croanie lighter."

"Maybe you'd like to arrange for a meal for the students here?"

"Sure," Karsh said. "That's a good idea. Why don't you join us?" Karsh winked. "And bring a few beers."

"Not this time," Retief said. He watched the students, still emerging from Customs. "They seem to be all boys," he commented. "No female students?"

"Maybe later," Karsh said, "after we see how the first bunch is received."

Back at the MUDDLE office, Retief buzzed Miss Furkle.

"Do you know the name of the institution these Bogan students are bound for?"

"Why the university at d'Land, of course."

"Would that be the Technical College?"

Miss Furkle's mouth puckered. "I'm sure I've never pried into these details—"

"Where does doing your job stop and prying begin, Miss Furkle?" Retief said. "Personally, I'm curious as to just what it is these students are travelling so far to study—at Corps expense."

"Mr. Magnan never—"

"For the present, Miss Furkle, Mr. Magnan is vacationing. That leaves me with the question of two thousand young male students headed for a world with no classrooms for them . . . a world in need of tractors. But the tractors are on their way to Croanie, a world under obligations to Boge. And Croanie holds a mortgage on the best grape acreage on Lovenbroy."

"Well!" Miss Furkle snapped, her small eyes glaring under unplucked brows. "I hope you're not questioning Mr. Magnan's wisdom!"

"About Mr. Magnan's wisdom there can be no doubts," Retief said. "But never mind. I'd like you to look up an item for me. How many tractors will Croanie be getting under the MEDDLE program?"

"Why, that's entirely MEDDLE business," Miss Furkle said. "Mr. Magnan always—"

"I'm sure he did. Let me know about the tractors as soon as you can."

Miss Furkle sniffed and disappeared from the screen. Retief left the office, descended forty-one stories, and followed a corridor to the Corps Library. In the stacks he thumbed through catalogs and pored over indices.

"Can I help you?" someone chirped. A tiny librarian stood at his elbow.

"Thank you, Ma'am," Retief said. "I'm looking for information on a mining rig: a Bolo model WV tractor."

"You won't find it in the industrial section," the librarian said. "Come along." Retief followed her along the stacks to a well-lit section lettered ARMAMENTS. She took a tape from the shelf, plugged it into the viewer, flipped through, and stopped at a picture of a squat armored vehicle.

"That's the model WV," she said. "It's what is known as a Continental Siege Unit. It carries four men, with a half-megaton/second firepower—"

"There must be an error somewhere," Retief said. "The Bolo model I want is a tractor, model WV M-1—"

"Oh, the modification was the addition of a blade for demolition work. That must be what confused you."

"Probably—among other things. Thank you."

Miss Furkle was waiting at the office. "I have the information you wanted," she said. "I've had it for over ten minutes. I was under the impression you needed it urgently, and I went to great lengths—"

"Sure," Retief said. "Shoot. How many tractors?"

"Five hundred."

"Are you sure?"

Miss Furkle's chins quivered. "Well! If you feel I'm incompetent."

"Just questioning the possibility of a mistake, Miss Furkle. Five hundred tractors is a lot of equipment."

"Was there anything further?" Miss Furkle inquired frigidly.

"I sincerely hope not," Retief said.

Leaning back in Magnan's padded chair with its power swivel and hip-u-matic contour, Retief leafed through a folder labeled "CERP 7-602-Ba; CROANIE (general)." He paused at a page headed INDUSTRY. Still reading, he opened the desk drawer, took out the two bottles of Bacchus wine and two glasses. He poured an inch of wine into each, then sipped the black wine meditatively. It would be a pity, he reflected, if anything should interfere with the production of such vintages . . .

Half an hour later he laid the folder aside, keyed the phone, and put through a call to the Croanie Legation, asking for the Commercial attaché.

"Retief here, Corps HQ," he said airily. "About the MEDDLE shipment, the tractors. I'm wondering if there's been a slip-up. My records show we're shipping five hundred units."

"That's correct. Five hundred."

Retief waited.

"Ah . . . are you there, Mr. Retief?"

"I'm still here. And I'm still wondering about the five hundred tractors."

"It's perfectly in order; I thought it was all settled. Mr. Whaffle—"

"One unit would require a good-sized plant to handle its output," Retief said. "Now Croanie subsists on her fisheries. She has perhaps half-a-dozen pint-sized processing plants. Maybe, in a bind, they could handle the ore ten WV's could scrape up . . . if Croanie had any ore. By the way, isn't a WV a poor choice as a mining outfit? I should think—"

"See here, Retief, why all this interest in a few surplus tractors? And in any event, what business is it of yours how we plan to use the equipment? That's an internal affair of my government. Mr. Whaffle—"

"I'm not Mr. Whaffle. What are you going to do with the other four hundred and ninety tractors?"

"I understood the grant was to be with no strings attached!"

"I know it's bad manners to ask questions. It's an old diplomatic tradition that any time you can get anybody to accept anything as a gift, you've scored points in the game. But if Croanie has some scheme cooking—"

"Nothing like that, Retief! It's a mere business transaction."

"What kind of business do you do with a Bolo WV? With or without a blade attached, it's what's known as a continental siege unit—"

"Great Heavens, Retief! Don't jump to conclusions! Would you have us branded as warmongers? Frankly—is this a closed line?"

"Certainly. You may speak freely."

"The tractors are for trans-shipment. We've gotten ourselves into a difficult situation in our balance of payments. This is an accommodation to a group with which we have strong business ties."

"I understand you hold a mortgage on the best land on Lovenbroy," Retief said. "Any connection?"

"Why ... ah ... no. Of course not."

"Who gets the tractors eventually?"

"Retief, this is unwarranted interference—"

"Who gets them?"

"They happen to be going to Lovenbroy. But I scarcely see—"

"And who's the friend you're helping out with an unauthorized trans-shipment of grant material?"

"Why ... ah ... I've been working with a Mr. Gulver, a Bogan representative."

"And when will they be shipped?"

"Why, they went out a week ago. They'll be halfway there by now. But look here, Retief, this isn't what you're thinking!"

"How do you know what I'm thinking? I don't know myself." Retief rang off and buzzed the secretary.

"Miss Furkle, I'd like to be notified immediately of any new applications that might come in from the Bogan Consulate for placement of students."

"Well, it happens, by coincidence, that I have an application here now. Mr. Gulver of the Consulate brought it in."

"Is Mr. Gulver in the office? I'd like to see him."

"I'll ask him if he has time."

It was half a minute before a thick-necked red-faced man in a tight hat walked in. He wore an old-fashioned suit, a drab shirt, shiny shoes with round toes, and an ill-tempered expression.

"What is it you wish?" he barked. "I understood in my discussions with the other . . . ah . . . civilian there'd be no further need for these irritating conferences."

"I've just learned you're placing more students abroad, Mr. Gulver. How many this time?"

"Three thousand."

"And where will they be going?"

"Croanie—it's all in the application form I've handed in. Your job is to provide transportation."

"Will there be any other students embarking this season?"

"Why . . . perhaps. That's Boge's business." Gulver looked at Retief with pursed lips. "As a matter of fact, we had in mind dispatching another two thousand to Feather-weight."

"Another under-populated world—and in the same cluster, I believe," Retief said. "Your people must be unusually interested in that region of space."

"If that's all you wanted to know, I'll be on my way. I have matters of importance to see to."

After Gulver left Retief called Miss Furkle in. "I'd like to have a break-out of all the student movements that have been planned under the present program," he said. "And see if you can get a summery of what MEDDLE has been shipping lately."

Miss Furkle bridled. "If Mr. Magnan were here, I'm sure he wouldn't dream of interfering in the work of other departments. I . . . overheard your conversation with the gentleman from the Croanie Legation—"

"The lists, Miss Furkle."

"I'm not accustomed," Miss Furkle said, "to intruding in matters outside our interest cluster."

"That's worse than listening in on phone conversations, eh? But never mind. I need the information, Miss Furkle."

"Loyalty to my Chief—"

"Loyalty to your pay-check should send you scuttling for the material I've asked for," Retief said. "I'm taking full responsibility. Now scat."

The buzzer sounded. Retief flipped a key. "MUDDLE, Retief speaking . . ."

Arapoulous' brown face appeared on the desk screen. "How do, Retief. Okay if I come up?"

"Sure, Hank. I want to talk to you."

In the office, Arapoulous took a chair. "Sorry if I'm rushing you, Retief," he said. "But have you got anything for me?"

Retief waved at the wine bottles. "What do you know about Croanie?"

"Croanie? Not much of a place. Mostly ocean. All right if you like fish, I guess. We import some seafood from there. Nice prawns in monsoon time. Over a foot long."

"You on good terms with them?"

"Sure, I guess so. Course, they're pretty thick with Boge."

"So?"

"Didn't I tell you? Boge was the bunch that tried to take us over here a dozen years back. They would have made it, too, if they hadn't had a lot of bad luck. Their armor went in the drink, and without armor they're easy game."

Miss Furkle buzzed. "I have your lists," she said shortly.

"Bring them in, please."

The secretary placed the papers on the desk. Arapoulous caught her eye and grinned. She sniffed and marched from the room.

"What that gal needs is a slippery time in the grape mash," Arapoulous observed. Retief thumbed through the papers, pausing to read from time to time. He finished and looked at Arapoulous.

"How many men do you need for the harvest, Hank?" Retief inquired.

Arapoulous sniffed his wine glass.

"A hundred would help," he said. "A thousand would be better. Cheers."

"What would you say to two thousand?"

"Two thousand? Retief, you're not foolin'?"

"I hope not." He picked up the phone, called the Port Authority, and asked for the dispatch clerk.

"Hello, Jim. Say, I have a favor to ask of you. You know that contingent of Bogan students; they're travelling aboard the two CDT transports. I'm interested in the baggage that goes with the students. Has it arrived yet? Okay, I'll wait . . ."

Jim came back to the phone. "Yeah, Retief, it's here. Just arrived. But there's a funny thing. It's not consigned to d'Land; it's ticketed clear through to Lovenbroy."

"Listen, Jim," Retief said. "I want you to go over to the warehouse and take a look at that baggage for me."

Retief waited while the dispatch clerk carried out the errand. The level in the two bottles had gone down an inch when Jim returned to the phone.

"Hey, I took a look at that baggage, Retief. Something funny going on. Guns. 2nn needlers, Mark XII hand blasters, power pistols—"

"It's okay, Jim. Nothing to worry about. Just a mix-up. Now, Jim, I'm going to ask you to do something more for me. I'm covering for a friend; it seems he slipped up. I wouldn't want word to get out, you understand. I'll send along a written change order in the morning that will cover you officially. Meanwhile, here's what I want you to do . . ."

Retief gave instructions, then rang off and turned to Arapoulous.

"As soon as I get off a couple of TWX's, we'd better get down to the port, Hank. I think I'd like to see the students off personally."

Karsh met Retief as he entered the Departures enclosure at the port.

"What's going on here?" he demanded. "There's some funny business with my baggage consignment; they won't let me see it. I've got a feeling it's not being loaded."

"You'd better hurry, Mr. Karsh," Retief said. "You're scheduled to blast off in less than an hour. Are the students all loaded?"

"Yes, blast you! What about my baggage? Those vessels aren't moving without it!"

"No need to get so upset about a few toothbrushes, is there, Mr. Karsh?" Retief said blandly. "Still, if you're worried—" He turned to Arapoulous.

"Hank, why don't you walk Mr. Karsh over to the warehouse and ... ah ... take care of him?"

"I know just how to handle it," Arapoulous said.

The dispatch clerk came up to Retief. "I caught the tractor shipment," he said. "Funny kind of mistake, but it's okay now. They're being off-loaded at d'Land. I talked to the traffic controller there; he said they weren't looking for any students."

"The labels got switched, Jim. The students go where the baggage was consigned; too bad about the mistake there, but the Armaments Office will have a man along in a little while to dispose of the guns. Keep an eye out for the real luggage; no telling where it's gotten to—"

"Here!" a hoarse voice yelled. Retief turned. A disheveled figure in a tight hat was crossing the enclosure, his arms waving.

"Hi there, Mr. Gulver," Retief called. "How's Boge's business coming along?"

"Piracy!" Gulver blurted as he came up to Retief. "You've got a hand in this, I don't doubt! Where's that Magnan fellow ..."

"What seems to be the problem?" Retief said.

"Hold those transports! I've just been notified that the baggage shipment has been impounded. I'll remind you, that shipment enjoys diplomatic free entry."

"Who told you it was impounded?"

"Never mind! I have my sources!"

Two tall men buttoned into grey tunics came up. "Are you Mr. Retief of CDT?" one said.

"That's right."

"What about my baggage!" Gulver cut in. "And I'm warning you, if those ships lift without—"

"These gentlemen are from the Armaments Control Commission," Retief said. "Would you like to come along and claim your baggage, Mr. Gulver?"

"From what? I ..." Gulver turned two shades redder about the ears. "Armaments ... ?"

"The only shipment I've held up seems to be somebody's arsenal," Retief said. "Now, if you claim this is your baggage ..."

"Why, impossible," Gulver said in a strained voice. "Armaments? Ridiculous. There's been an error."

At the baggage warehouse, Gulver looked glumly at the opened cases of guns. "No, of course not," he said dully. "Not my baggage. Not my baggage at all."

Arapoulous appeared, supporting the stumbling figure of Mr. Karsh.

"What—what's this?" Gulver spluttered. "Karsh? What's happened . . . ?"

"He had a little fall. He'll be okay," Arapoulous said.

"You'd better help him to the ship," Retief said. "It's ready to lift. We wouldn't want him to miss it."

"Leave him to me!" Gulver snapped, his eyes slashing at Karsh. I'll see he's dealt with."

"I couldn't think of it," Retief said. "He's a guest of the Corps, you know. We'll see him safely aboard."

Gulver turned and signaled frantically. Three heavyset men in identical drab suits detached themselves from the wall and crossed to the group.

"Take this man," Gulver snapped, indicating Karsh, who looked at him dazedly.

"We take our hospitality seriously," Retief said. "We'll see him aboard the vessel."

Gulver opened his mouth—

"I know you feel bad about finding guns instead of school books in your luggage," Retief said, looking Gulver in the eye. "You'll be busy straightening out the details of the mix-up. You'll want to avoid further complications."

"Ah . . . yes," Gulver said.

Arapoulous went on to the passenger conveyor, then turned to wave.

"Your man—he's going too?" Gulver blurted.

"He's not our man, properly speaking," Retief said. "He lives on Lovenbroy."

"Lovenbroy?" Gulver choked. "But . . . the . . . I . . ."

"I know you said the students were bound for d'Land," Retief said. "But I guess that was just another aspect of the general confusion. The course plugged into the navigators was to Lovenbroy. You'll be glad to know they're still headed there—even without the baggage."

"Perhaps," Gulver said grimly, "perhaps they'll manage without it."

"By the way," Retief said. "There was another funny mix-up. There were some tractors—for industrial use, you'll recall. I believe you co-operated with Croanie in arranging the grant through MEDDLE. They were erroneously consigned to Lovenbroy, a purely agricultural world. I saved you some embarrassment, I trust, Mr. Gulver, by arranging to have them off-loaded at d'Land."

"D'Land! You've put CSU's in the hands of Boge's bitterest enemies . . . ?"

"But they're only tractors, Mr. Gulver. Peaceful devices. Isn't that correct?"

"That's . . . correct." Gulver sagged. Then he snapped erect. "Hold the ships!" he yelled. "I'm canceling the student exchange."

His voice was drowned out by the rumble as the first of the monster transports rose from the launch pit, followed a moment later by the second. Retief watched them fade out of sight, then turned to Gulver.

"They're off," he said. "Let's hope they get a liberal education."

Retief lay on his back in deep grass by a stream, eating grapes. A tall figure, appearing on the knoll above him, waved.

"Retief!" Hank Arapoulous bounded down the slope. "I heard you were here—and I've got news for you. You won the final day's picking competition. Over two hundred bushels! That's a record! Let's get on over to the garden, shall we? Sounds like the celebration's about to start."

In the flower-crowded park among the stripped vines, Retief and Arapoulous made their way to a laden table under the lanterns. A tall girl dressed in a loose white garment, with long golden hair, came up to Arapoulous.

"Delinda, this is Retief—today's winner. And he's also the fellow that got those workers for us."

Delinda smiled at Retief. "I've heard about you, Mr. Retief. We weren't sure about the boys at first; two thousand Bogans, and all confused about their baggage that went astray. But they seemed to like the picking . . ." She smiled again.

"That's not all; our gals liked the boys," Hank said. "Even Bogans aren't so bad, minus their irons. A lot of 'em will be staying on. But how come you didn't tell me you were coming, Retief? I'd have laid on some kind of big welcome."

"I liked the welcome I got. And I didn't have much notice. Mr. Magnan was a little upset when he got back. It seems I exceeded my authority."

Arapoulous laughed. "I had a feeling you were wheelin' pretty free, Retief. I hope you didn't get into any trouble over it."

"No trouble," Retief said. "A few people were a little unhappy with me. It seems I'm not ready for important assignments at Departmental level. I was shipped off here to the boondocks to get a little more field experience."

"Delinda, look after Retief," said Arapoulous. "I'll see you later. I've got to see to the wine judging." He disappeared in the crowd.

"Congratulations on winning the day," said Delinda. "I noticed you at work. You were wonderful. I'm glad you're going to have the prize."

"Thanks. I noticed you too, flitting around in that white nightie of yours. But why weren't you picking grapes with the rest of us?"

"I had a special assignment."

"Too bad. You should have had a chance at the prize."

Delinda took Retief's hand. "I wouldn't have anyway," she said. "I'm the prize."

"Oft has the Corps, in its steadfast champion-
ing of minority rights, run foul of the massive
influence of entrenched pressure groups. Consul
General (later Secretary) Magnan stirringly
reaffirmed hallowed Corps principles of fair play
in his deft apportionment of minerals properties
in the Belt . . ."

—Vol. III, Reel 21, 481 AE (AD 2942)

SALINE SOLUTION

Consul-General Magnan gingerly fingered a heavily rubber-
banded sheaf of dog-eared documents. "I haven't rushed
into precipitate action on this claim, Retief," he said. "The
consulate has grave responsibilities here in the Belt. One
must weigh all aspects of the situation, consider the rami-
fications; what consequences would arise from a grant of
minerals rights on the planetoid to this claimant?"

"The claim looked all right to me," Retief said. "Sev-
enteen copies with attachments. Why not process it? You've
had it on your desk for a week."

Magnan's eyebrows went up. "You've a personal interest in this claim, Retief?"

"Every day you wait is costing them money; that hulk they
use for an ore-carrier is in a parking orbit piling up demurrage."

"I see you've become emotionally involved in the affairs
of a group of obscure miners; you haven't yet learned the
true diplomat's happy faculty of non-identification with
specifics—or should I say identification with non-specifics?"

"They're not a wealthy outfit, you know. In fact, I
understand this claim is their sole asset—unless you want
to count the ore-carrier."

"The consulate is not concerned with the internal financial problems of the Sam's Last Chance Number Nine Mining Company."

"Careful," Retief said. "You almost identified yourself with a specific that time."

"Hardly, my dear Retief," Magnan said blandly. "The implication is mightier than the affidavit. You should study the records of the giants of Galactic diplomacy: Crodfoller, Wormwell, Spradley, Nitworth, Sternwheeler, Barnshingle; the roll-call of those names rings like the majestic tread of . . . of . . ."

"Dinosaurs?" Retief suggested.

"An apt simile," Magnan nodded. "Those mighty figures, those armored hides—"

"Those tiny brains . . ."

Magnan smiled sadly. "I see you're indulging your penchant for distorted facetiae. Perhaps one day you'll learn the true worth of their contributions."

"I already have my suspicions."

The intercom chimed. Miss Gumble's features appeared on the desk screen.

"Mr. Leatherwell to see you, Mr. Magnan. He has no appointment—"

Magnan's eyebrows went up. "Send Mr. Leatherwell right in." He looked at Retief. "I had no idea Leatherwell was planning a call. I wonder what he's after?" Magnan looked anxious. "He's an important figure in Belt minerals circles. It's important to avoid arousing antagonism, while maintaining non-commitment. You may as well stay. You might pick up some valuable pointers technique-wise."

The door swung wide; Leatherwell strode into the room, his massive paunch buckled into fashionable vests of turquoise velvet and hung with the latest in fluorescent watch charms. He extended a large palm, pumped Magnan's flaccid arm vigorously.

"Ah, there, Mr. Consul-General. Good of you to receive me." He wiped his hand absently on his thigh, eyeing Retief questioningly.

"Mr. Retief, my Vice-Consul and Minerals Officer," Magnan said. "Do take a chair, Mr. Leatherwell. In what capacity can I serve today?"

"I am here, gentlemen," Leatherwell said, putting an immense yellow briefcase on Magnan's desk and settling himself in a power rocker, "on behalf of my company, General Minerals. General Minerals has long been aware, gentlemen, of the austere conditions obtaining here in the Belt, to which public servants like yourselves are subjected." Leatherwell bobbed with the pitch of the rocker, smiling complacently at Magnan. "General Minerals is more than a great industrial combine; it is an organization with a heart." Leatherwell reached for his breast pocket, missed as the chair pitched, tried again.

"How do you turn this damned thing off?" he growled.

Magnan half-rose, peering over Leatherwell's briefcase. "The switch just there—on the arm . . ."

The executive fumbled. There was a click, and the chair subsided with a sigh of compressed air.

"That's better." Leatherwell drew out a long slip of blue paper.

"To alleviate the boredom and brighten the lives of that hardy group of Terrestrials laboring here on Ceres to bring free enterprise to the Belt," he intoned, "General Minerals is presenting to the consulate—on their behalf—one hundred thousand credits for the construction of a Joy Center, to be equipped with the latest and finest in recreational equipment, including a Gourmet Model C banquet synthesizer, a forty-foot sublimation chamber, a five-thousand-tape library—with a number of choice items unobtainable in Boston—a twenty-foot Tri-D tank, and other amenities too numerous to mention." Leatherwell leaned back, beaming expectantly.

"Why, Mr. Leatherwell—we're overwhelmed, of course . . ." Magnan smiled dazedly past the briefcase. "But, I wonder if it's quite proper . . ."

"The gift is to the people, Mr. Consul. You merely accept on their behalf."

"I wonder if General Minerals realizes that the hardy Terrestrials laboring on Ceres are limited to the consular staff?" Retief said. "And the staff consists of Mr. Magnan, Miss Gumble, and myself—"

"Mr. Leatherwell is hardly interested in these details, Retief," Magnan cut in. "A public-spirited offer indeed, sir.

As Terrestrial Consul—and on behalf of all Terrestrials here in the Belt—I accept with a humble awareness of—"

"Now, there was one other little matter," Leatherwell said. He leaned forward to open the briefcase, glancing over Magnan's littered desk-top. He extracted a bundle of papers, dropped them on the desk, then drew out a heavy document, passed it across to Magnan.

"Just a routine claim. I'd like to see it rushed through, as we have in mind some loading operations in the vicinity next week . . ."

"Certainly, Mr. Leatherwell." Magnan glanced at the papers, paused to read. He looked up. "Ah . . ."

"Something the matter, Mr. Consul?" Leatherwell demanded.

"It's just that—ah—I seem to recall—as a matter of fact . . ." Magnan looked at Retief. Retief took the papers, looked over the top sheet.

"95739-A. Sorry, Mr. Leatherwell. General Minerals has been anticipated. We're processing a prior claim—"

"Prior claim?" Leatherwell barked. "You've issued the grant?"

"Oh, no indeed, Mr. Leatherwell," Magnan replied quickly. "The claim hasn't yet been processed—"

"Then there's no difficulty," Leatherwell boomed. He glanced at his finger watch. "If you don't mind, I'll wait and take the grant along with me. I assume it will only take a minute or two to sign it and affix seals and so on?"

"The other claim *was* filed a full week ago—" Magnan started.

"Bah!" Leatherwell waved a hand impatiently. "These details can be arranged." He fixed an eye on Magnan. "I'm sure all of us here understand that it's in the public interest that minerals properties go to responsible firms, with adequate capital for proper development."

"Why, ah," Magnan said.

"The Sam's Last Chance Number Nine Mining Company is a duly chartered firm," Retief said. "Their claim is valid—"

"I know that hole-in-corner concern," Leatherwell snapped. "Mere irresponsible opportunists. General Minerals has spent millions—millions, I say—of the stockholders' funds in minerals explorations. Are they to be balked in realizing a fair return on their investment because these . . . these . . . adventurers have stumbled on a deposit? Not that the property is of any real value, of course," he added. "Quite an ordinary bit of rock. But General Minerals would find it convenient to consolidate its holdings."

"There are plenty of other rocks floating around in the Belt. Why not—"

"One moment, Retief," Magnan cut in. He looked across the desk at his junior with a severe expression. "As Consul-General, I'm quite capable of determining the relative merits of claims. As Mr. Leatherwell has pointed out, it's in the public interest to consider the question in depth—"

Leatherwell cleared his throat, "I might state at this time that General Minerals is prepared to be generous in dealing with these interlopers. I believe we would go so far as to offer them free title to certain GM holdings in exchange for their release of any alleged rights to the property in question—merely to simplify matters, of course."

"That seems more than fair to me," Magnan glowed.

"The Sam's people have a clear priority," Retief said. "I logged the claim in last Friday—"

"They have far from a clear title!" Leatherwell snapped. "And I can assure you GM will contest their claim, if need be, to the Supreme Court!"

"Just what holdings did you have in mind offering them, Mr. Leatherwell?" Magnan asked nervously.

Leatherwell reached into his briefcase, drew out a paper. "2645-P," he read. "A quite massive body; crustal material, I imagine. It should satisfy these squatters' desire to own real estate in the Belt."

"I'll make a note of that," Magnan said, reaching for a pad.

"That's a bona fide offer, Mr. Leatherwell?" Retief asked.

"Certainly!"

"I'll record it as such," Magnan said, scribbling.

"And who knows," Leatherwell said. "It may turn out to contain some surprisingly rich finds . . ."

"And if they won't accept it?" Retief asked.

"Then, I daresay General Minerals will find a remedy in the courts, sir!"

"Oh, I hardly think that will be necessary—" Magnan said.

"Then there's another routine matter," Leatherwell said. He passed a second document across to Magnan. "GM is requesting an injunction to restrain these same parties from aggravated trespass. I'd appreciate it if you'd push it through at once. There's a matter of a load of illegally obtained ore involved, as well."

"Certainly, Mr. Leatherwell. I'll see to it myself—"

"The papers are all drawn up; our legal department will vouch for their correctness. Just sign here . . ." Leatherwell spread out the paper, handed Magnan a pen.

"Wouldn't it be a good idea to read that over first?" Retief said.

Leatherwell frowned impatiently.

"You'll have adequate time to familiarize yourself with the details later, Retief," Magnan snapped, taking the pen. "No need to waste Mr. Leatherwell's valuable time." He scratched a signature on the paper. Leatherwell rose, gathered up his papers from Magnan's desk, dumped them into the briefcase. "Riff-raff, of course. Their kind has no business in the Belt—"

Retief rose, crossed to the desk, and held out a hand. "I believe you gathered in an official document, along with your own, Mr. Leatherwell; by error, of course."

"What's that?" Leatherwell bridled. Retief smiled, waiting. Magnan opened his mouth—

"It was under your papers, Mr. Leatherwell," Retief said. "It's the thick one, with the rubber bands."

Leatherwell dug in his briefcase, produced the document. "Well, fancy finding this here . . ." he growled. He shoved the papers into Retief's hand.

"You're a very observant young fellow." He closed the briefcase with a snap. "I trust you'll have a bright future with the CDT."

"Really, Retief," Magnan said reprovingly. "There was no need to trouble Mr. Leatherwell . . ."

Leatherwell rose, crossed to the door. He paused, directed a sharp look at Retief, turned a bland expression on Magnan. "I trust you'll communicate the proposal to the interested parties. Inasmuch as time is of the essence of the GM position, our offer can only be held open until 0900 Greenwich, tomorrow. I'll call again at that time to finalize matters. I trust there'll be no impediment to a satisfactory settlement at that time. I should dislike to embark on lengthy litigation."

Magnan hurried around his desk to open the door. He turned back to fix Retief with an exasperated frown.

"A crass display of boorishness, Retief," he snapped. "You've embarrassed a most influential member of the business community—and for nothing more than a few miserable forms."

"Those forms represent somebody's stake in what might be a valuable property—"

"They're mere paper until they've been processed!"

"Still—"

"My responsibility is to the Public interest—not to a fly-by-night group of prospectors."

"They found it first."

"Bah! A worthless rock; after Mr. Leatherwell's munificent gesture—"

"Better rush his check through before he thinks it over and changes his mind."

"Good heavens!" Magnan clutched the check, buzzed for Miss Gumble. She swept in, took Magnan's instructions, and left. Retief waited while Magnan glanced over the injunction, then nodded.

"Quite in order. A person called Sam Mancziewicz appears to be the principal. The address given is the Jolly Barge Hotel; that would be that converted derelict ship in orbit 6942, I assume?"

Retief nodded. "That's what they call it."

"As for the ore-carrier, I'd best impound it, pending settlement of the matter." Magnan drew a form from a drawer, filled in blanks, shoved the paper across the desk. He turned and consulted a wall chart. "The hotel is nearby at the moment, as it happens. Take the consulate dinghy. If you get out there right away, you'll catch them before the evening binge has developed fully."

"I take it that's your diplomatic way of telling me that I'm now a process server." Retief took the papers and tucked them into an inside pocket.

"One of the many functions a diplomat is called on to perform in a small consular post. Excellent experience. I needn't warn you to be circumspect. These miners are an unruly lot—especially when receiving bad news."

"Aren't we all?" Retief rose. "I don't suppose there's any prospect of your signing off that claim so that I can take a little good news along, too . . . ?"

"None whatever," Magnan snapped. "They've been made a most generous offer. If that fails to satisfy them, they have recourse through the courts."

"Fighting a suit like that costs money. The Sam's Last Chance Mining Company hasn't got any."

"Need I remind you—"

"I know; that's none of our concern."

"On your way out," Magnan said as Retief turned to the door, "ask Miss Gumble to bring in the Gourmet catalog from the Commercial Library. I want to check on the specifications of the Model C Banquet synthesizer."

An hour later, nine hundred miles from Ceres and fast approaching the Jolly Barge Hotel, Retief keyed the skiff's transmitter.

"CDT 347-89 calling Navy FP-VO-6."

"Navy VO-6 here, CDT," a prompt voice came back. A flickering image appeared on the small screen. "Oh, hi there, Mr. Retief. What brings you out in the cold night air?"

"Hello, Henry. I'm estimating the Jolly Barge in ten minutes. It looks like a busy night ahead. I may be moving around a little. How about keeping an eye on me? I'll be carrying a personnel beacon. Monitor it, and if I switch it into high, come in fast. I can't afford to be held up. I've got a big meeting in the morning."

"Sure thing, Mr. Retief. We'll keep an eye open."

Retief dropped a ten credit note on the bar, accepted a glass and a squat bottle of black Marsberry brandy, and turned to survey the low-ceilinged room, a former hydroponics deck now known as the Jungle Bar. Under the low ceiling, unpruned *Ipomoea batatas* and *Lathyrus odoratus* vines sprawled in a tangle that filtered the light of the S-spectrum glare panels to a muted green. A six-foot trideo screen salvaged from the wreck of a Concordiat transport blared taped music in the style of two centuries past. At the tables heavy-shouldered men, in bright-dyed suit liners played cards, clanked bottles, and carried on shouted conversations.

Carrying the bottle and glass, Retief moved across to an empty chair at one of the tables.

"You gentlemen mind if I join you?"

Five unshaved faces turned to study Retief's six foot three, his closecut black hair, his non-committal grey coverall, the scars on his knuckles. A red-head with a broken nose nodded. "Pull up a chair, stranger."

"You workin' a claim, pardner?"

"Just looking around."

"Try a shot of this rock juice."

"Don't do it, Mister. He makes it himself."

"Best rock juice this side of Luna."

"Say, feller—"

"The name's Retief."

"Retief, you ever play Drift?"

"Can't say that I did."

"Don't gamble with Sam, pardner. He's the local champ."

"How do you play it?"

The black-browed miner who had suggested the game rolled back his sleeve to reveal a sinewy forearm, put his elbow on the table.

"You hook forefingers, and put a glass right up on top. The man that takes a swallow wins. If the drink spills, it's drinks for the house."

"A man don't often win outright," the red-head said cheerfully. "But it makes for plenty of drinkin'."

Retief put his elbow on the table. "I'll give it a try."

The two men hooked forefingers. The red-head poured a tumbler half full of rock juice, placed it atop the two fists. "OK, boys. Go!"

The man named Sam gritted his teeth; his biceps tensed; his knuckles grew white. The glass trembled. Then it moved—toward Retief. Sam hunched his shoulders, straining.

"That's the stuff, Mister!"

"What's the matter, Sam? You tired?"

The glass moved steadily closer to Retief's face.

"A hundred the new man makes it!"

"Watch Sam; any minute now . . ."

The glass slowed, paused. Retief's wrist twitched and the glass crashed to the table top. A shout went up. Sam leaned back with a sigh, massaging his hand.

"That's some arm you got there, Mister," he said. "If you hadn't jumped just then . . ."

"I guess the drinks are on me," Retief said.

Two hours later Retief's Marsberry bottle stood empty on the table beside half a dozen others.

"We were lucky," Sam Mancziewicz was saying. "You figure the original volume of the planet; say 245,000,000,000 cubic miles. The deBerry theory calls for a collapsed-crystal core no more than a mile in diameter. There's your odds."

"And you believe you've found a fragment of this core?"

"Damn right we have. Couple of million tons if it's an ounce—and at three credits a ton delivered at Port Syrtis, we're set for life. About time, too. Twenty years I've been in the Belt. Got two kids I haven't seen for five years. Things are going to be different now."

"Hey, Sam; tone it down. You don't have to broadcast to every claim jumper in the Belt—"

"Our claim's on file at the consulate," Sam said. "As soon as we get the grant—"

"When's that gonna be? We been waitin' a week now."

"I've never seen any collapsed-crystal metal," Retief said. "I'd like to take a look at it."

"Sure; come on, I'll run you over. It's about an hour's run. We'll take our skiff. You want to go along, Willy?"

"I got a bottle to go," Willy said. "See you in the morning."

The two men descended in the lift to the boat bay, suited up, and strapped into the cramped boat. A bored attendant cycled the launch doors, levered the release that propelled the skiff out and clear of the Jolly Barge Hotel. Retief caught a glimpse of a tower of lights spinning majestically against the black of space as the drive hurled the tiny boat away.

Retief's feet sank ankle deep into the powdery surface that glinted like snow in the glare of the distant sun.

"It's funny stuff," Sam's voice sounded in his ear. "Under

a gee of gravity, you'd sink out of sight. The stuff cuts diamond like butter—but temperature changes break it down into a powder. A lot of it's used just like this, as an industrial abrasive. Easy to load, too. Just drop a suction line and start pumping."

"And this whole rock is made of the same material?"

"Sure is. We ran plenty of test bores, and a full schedule of soundings. I've got the reports back aboard *Gertie*—that's our lighter."

"And you've already loaded a cargo here?"

"Yep. We're running out of capital fast. I need to get that cargo to port in a hurry—before the outfit goes into involuntary bankruptcy. With this strike, that'd be a crime. By the time the legal fees were paid off, we'd be broke again."

"What do you know about General Minerals, Sam?"

"You thinking of hiring on with them? Better read the fine print in your contract before you sign. Sneakiest bunch this side of a burglar's convention."

"They own a chunk of rock known as 2645-P. Do you suppose we could find it?"

"Oh, you're buying in, hey? Sure, we can find it. You damn sure want to look it over good if General Minerals is selling."

Back aboard the skiff, Mancziewicz flipped the pages of the chart book, consulted a table. "Yep, she's not too far off. Let's go see what GM's trying to unload . . .

The skiff hovered two miles from the giant boulder known as 2645-P. Retief and Mancziewicz looked it over at high magnification. "It don't look like much, Retief," Sam said. "Let's go down and take a closer look."

The boat dropped rapidly toward the scarred surface of the tiny world, a floating mountain, glaring black and white in the spotlight of the sun. Sam frowned at his instrument panel.

"That's funny; my ion-counter is revving up. Looks like a drive trail, not more than an hour or two old. Somebody's been here . . ."

The boat grounded. Retief and Sam got out. The stony surface was littered with rock fragments varying in size from pebbles to great slabs twenty feet long, tumbled in a loose bed of dust and sand. Retief pushed off gently, drifted up to a vantage point atop an upended wedge of rock. Sam joined him.

"This is all igneous stuff," he said. "Not likely we'll find much here that would pay the freight to Syrtis—unless maybe you lucked onto some Bodean artifacts. They bring plenty."

He flipped a binocular in place as he talked, scanned the riven landscape. "Hey!" he said. "Over there . . ."

Retief followed Sam's pointing glove. He studied the dark patch against a smooth expanse of eroded rock.

"A friend of mine came across a chunk of the old planetary surface two years ago," Sam said thoughtfully. "Had a tunnel in it that'd been used as a storage depot by the Bodeans. Took out over two ton of hardware. Course, nobody's discovered how the stuff works yet, but it brings top prices . . ."

"Looks like water erosion," Retief said.

"Yep. This could be another piece of surface, all right. Could be a cave over there. The Bodeans liked caves, too. Must have been some war—but then, if it hadn't been, they wouldn't have tucked so much stuff away underground where it could weather the planetary break-up."

They descended, crossed the jumbled rocks with light, thirty-foot leaps.

"It's a cave, all right," Sam said, stooping to peer into the five-foot bore. Retief followed him inside.

"Let's get some light in here." Mancziewicz flipped on a beam. It glinted back from dull polished surfaces of Bodean synthetic. Sam's low whistle sounded in Retief's headset.

"That's funny," Retief said.

"Funny, Hell! It's hilarious. General Minerals trying to sell off a worthless rock to a tenderfoot—and it's loaded with Bodean hardware. No telling how much is here; the tunnel seems to go quite a ways back. And there may be more caves around here—"

"That's not what I mean. Do you notice your suit warming up?"

"Huh? Yeah, now that you mention it . . ."

Retief rapped with a gauntleted hand on the satiny black curve of the nearest Bodean artifact. It clunked dully through the suit. "That's not metal," he said. "It's plastic."

"There's something fishy here," Sam said. "This erosion; it looks more like a heat beam . . ."

"Sam," Retief said, turning; "it appears to me somebody has gone to a great deal of trouble to give a false impression here—"

Sam snorted. "I told you they were a crafty bunch." He started out of the cave, then paused, went to one knee to study the floor. "But maybe they outsmarted themselves," he said, his voice tense with excitement. "Look here!"

Retief looked. Sam's beam reflected from a fused surface of milky white, shot through with dirty yellow. He snapped a pointed instrument in place on his gauntlet, dug at one of the yellow streaks. It furrowed under the gouge, a particle adhering to the instrument. With his left hand, Mancziewicz opened a pouch clipped to his belt, carefully deposited the sample in a small orifice on the device in the pouch. He flipped a key, squinted at a dial.

"Atomic weight 197.2," he said. Retief turned down the audio volume on his headset as Sam's laughter rang in his helmet.

"Those clowns were out to stick you, Retief," he gasped, still chuckling. "They salted the rock with a cave full of Bodean artifacts—"

"Fake Bodean artifacts," Retief put in.

"They planed off the rock so it would look like an old beach, and then cut this cave with beamers. And they were boring through practically solid gold!"

"As good as that?"

Mancziewicz flashed the light around. "This stuff will assay out at a thousand credits a ton, easy. If the vein doesn't run to five thousand tons, the beers are on me." He snapped off the light. "Let's get moving, Retief. You want to sew this deal up before they get around to taking another look at it."

Back in the boat, Retief and Mancziewicz opened their helmets. "This calls for a drink," Sam said, extracting a pressure flask from the map case. "This rock's worth as much as mine, maybe more. You hit it lucky, Retief. Congratulations." He thrust out a hand.

"I'm afraid you've jumped to a couple of conclusions, Sam," Retief said. "I'm not out here to buy mining properties."

"You're not—then why—but man! Even if you didn't figure on buying . . ." He trailed off as Retief shook his head, unzipped his suit to reach to an inside pocket, take out a packet of folded papers.

"In my capacity as Terrestrial Vice-Consul, I'm serving you with an injunction restraining you from further exploitation of the body known as 95739-A." He handed a paper across to Sam. "I also have here an Order impounding the vessel *Gravel Gertie II*."

Sam took the papers silently, sat looking at them. He looked up at Retief. "Funny; when you beat me at Drift and then threw the game so you wouldn't show me up in front of the boys, I figured you for a right guy. I've been spilling my heart out to you like you were my old grandma—an old-timer in the game like me." He dropped a hand, brought it up with a Browning 2mm pointed at Retief's chest.

"I could shoot you and dump you here with a slab over you, toss these papers in the john, and high-tail it with the load . . ."

"That wouldn't do you much good in the long run, Sam. Besides which you're not a criminal or an idiot."

Sam chewed his lip. "My claim is on file in the consulate, legal and proper. Maybe by now the grant's gone through and I've got clear title—"

"Other people have their eye on your rock, Sam. Ever meet a fellow called Leatherwell?"

"General Minerals, huh? They haven't got a leg to stand on."

"The last time I saw your claim, it was still lying in the pending file—just a bundle of paper until it's validated by the Consul. If Leatherwell contests it . . . well, his lawyers are on annual retainer. How long could you keep the suit going, Sam?"

Mancziewicz closed his helmet with a decisive snap, motioned to Retief to do the same. He opened the hatch, sat with the gun on Retief.

"Get out, paper-pusher," his voice sounded thin in the headphones. "You'll get lonesome maybe, but your suit will keep you alive a few days. I'll tip somebody off before you lose too much weight. I'm going back and see if I can't stir up a little action at the consulate."

Retief climbed out, walked off fifty yards. He watched as the skiff kicked off in a quickly-dispersed cloud of dust, dwindled rapidly away to a bright speck that was lost against the stars. Then he extracted the locator beacon from the pocket of his suit and thumbed the control.

Twenty minutes later, aboard Navy FP-VO-6, Retief pulled off his helmet. "Fast work, Henry. I've got a couple of calls to make. Put me through to your HQ, will you? I want a word with Commander Hayle."

The young Naval officer raised the HQ, handed the mike to Retief.

"Vice-Consul Retief here, commander. I'd like you to intercept a skiff, bound from my present position toward Ceres. There's a Mr. Mancziewicz aboard. He's armed, but not dangerous. Collect him and see that he's delivered to the consulate at 0900 Greenwich tomorrow.

"Next item: The consulate has impounded an ore-carrier, *Gravel Gertie II*. It's in a parking orbit ten miles off Ceres. I want it taken in tow . . ." Retief gave detailed instruction. Then he asked for a connection through the Navy switchboard to the consulate. Magnan's voice answered.

"Retief speaking, Mr. Consul; I have some news that I think will interest you—"

"Where are you, Retief? What's wrong with the screen? Have you served the injunction?"

"I'm aboard the Navy patrol vessel. I've been looking over the situation, and I've made a surprising discovery. I don't think we're going to have any trouble with the Sam's people; they've looked over the body—2645-P—and it seems General Minerals has slipped up. There appears to be a highly valuable deposit there."

"Oh? What sort of deposit?"

"Mr. Mancziewicz mentioned collapsed-crystal metal," Retief said.

"Well, most interesting." Magnan's voice sounded thoughtful.

"Just thought you'd like to know. This should simplify the meeting in the morning."

"Yes," Magnan said. "Yes, indeed. I think this makes everything very simple . . ."

At 0845 Greenwich, Retief stepped into the outer office of the consular suite.

" . . . fantastic configuration," Leatherwell's bass voice rumbled, "covering literally acres. My xeno-geologists are somewhat confused by the formations. They had only a few hours to examine the site; but it's clear from the extent of the surface indications that we have a very rich find here; very rich, indeed. Beside it, 95739-A dwindles into significance. Very fast thinking on your part, Mr. Consul, to bring the matter to my attention."

"Not at all, Mr. Leatherwell. After all—"

"Our tentative theory is that the basic crystal fragment encountered the core material at some time, and gathered it in. Since we had been working on—that is, had landed to take samples on the other side of the body, this anomalous deposit escaped our attention completely—"

Retief stepped into the room.

"Good morning, gentlemen. Has Mr. Mancziewicz arrived?"

"Mr. Mancziewicz is under restraint by the Navy. I've had a call to the effect that he'd be escorted here."

"Arrested, eh?" Leatherwell nodded. "I told you these people were an irresponsible group. In a way it seems a pity to waste a piece of property like 95739-A on them . . ."

"I understood General Minerals was claiming that rock," Retief said, looking surprised.

Leatherwell and Magnan exchanged glances. "Ah, GM has decided to drop all claim to the body," Leatherwell said. "As always, we wish to encourage enterprise on the part of the small operators. Let them keep the property. After all, GM has other deposits well worth exploiting." He smiled complacently.

"What about 2645-P? You've offered it to the Sam's group—"

"That offer is naturally withdrawn!" Leatherwell snapped.

"I don't see how you can withdraw the offer," Retief said. "It's been officially recorded; it's a bona fide contract, binding on General Minerals, subject to—"

"Out of the goodness of our corporate heart," Leatherwell

roared, "we've offered to relinquish our claim—our legitimate, rightful claim—to asteroid 2645-P; and you have the infernal gall to spout legal technicalities! I have half a mind to withdraw my offer to withdraw!"

"Actually," Magnan put in, eyeing a corner of the room, "I'm not at all sure I could turn up the record of the offer of 2645-P. I noted it down on a bit of scratch paper—"

"That's all right," Retief said, "I had my pocket recorder going. I sealed the record and deposited it in the consular archives."

There was a clatter of feet outside. Miss Gumble's face appeared on the desk screen. "There are a number of persons here—" she began.

The door banged open. Sam Mancziewicz stepped into the room, a sailor tugging at each arm. He shook them loose, stared around the room. His eyes lighted on Retief. "How did you get here . . . ?"

"Look here, Monkeywits or whatever your name is," Leatherwell began, popping out of his chair—

Mancziewicz whirled, seized the stout executive by the shirt front, and lifted him into his tiptoes. "You double-barreled copper-bottomed oak-lined son-of-a—"

"Don't spoil him, Sam," Retief said casually. "He's here to sign off all rights—if any—to 95739-A. It's all yours—if you want it."

Sam glared into Leatherwell's eyes. "That right?" he grated. Leatherwell bobbed his head, his chins compressed into bulging folds.

"However," Retief went on, "I wasn't at all sure you'd still be agreeable, since he's made your company a binding offer of 2645-P in return for clear title to 95739-A."

Mancziewicz looked across at Retief with narrowed eyes. He released Leatherwell, who slumped into his chair. Magnan darted around his desk to minister to the magnate. Behind them Retief closed one eye in a broad wink at Mancziewicz.

" . . . still, if Mr. Leatherwell will agree, in addition to guaranteeing your title to 95739-A, to purchase your output at four credits a ton, FOB his collection station—"

Mancziewicz looked at Leatherwell. Leatherwell hesitated, then nodded. "Agreed," he croaked.

" . . . and to open his commissary and postal facilities to all prospectors operating in the Belt . . ."

Leatherwell swallowed, eyes bulging, glanced at Mancziewicz's face . . . He nodded. "Agreed."

" . . . then I think I'd sign an agreement releasing him from his offer."

Mancziewicz looked at Magnan.

"You're the Terrestrial Consul-General," he said. "Is that the straight goods?"

Magnan nodded. "If Mr. Leatherwell agrees—"

"He's already agreed," Retief said. "My pocket recorder, you know."

"Put it in writing," Mancziewicz said.

Magnan called in Miss Gumble. The others waited silently while Magnan dictated. He signed the paper with a flourish, passed it across to Mancziewicz. He read it, re-read it, then picked up the pen and signed. Magnan impressed the consular seal on the paper.

"Now the grant," Retief said. Magnan signed the paper, added a seal. Mancziewicz tucked the papers away in an inner pocket. He rose.

"Well, gents, I guess maybe I had you figured wrong," he said. He looked at Retief. "Uh . . . got time for a drink?"

"I shouldn't drink on duty," Retief said. He rose. "So I'll take the rest of the day off."

"I don't get it," Sam said, signaling for refills. "What was the routine with the injunction—and impounding *Gertie*? You could have got hurt."

"I don't think so," Retief said. "If you'd meant business with that Browning, you'd have flipped the safety off. As for the injunction—orders are orders."

"I've been thinking," Sam said. "That gold deposit; it was a plant, too, wasn't it?"

"I'm just a bureaucrat, Sam. What would I know about gold?"

"A double-salting job," Sam said. "I was supposed to spot the phoney hardware—and then fall for the gold plant. When Leatherwell put his proposition to me, I'd grab it. The gold was worth plenty, I'd figure, and I couldn't afford a legal tangle with General Minerals. The lousy skunk. And you must have spotted it and put it up to him—"

The bartender leaned across to Retief. "Wanted on the phone."

In the booth, Magnan's agitated face stared at Retief.

"Retief, Mr. Leatherwell's in a towering rage! The deposit on 2645-P; it was merely a surface film, barely a few inches thick! The entire deposit wouldn't fill an ore-boat . . ." A horrified expression dawned on Magnan's face. "Retief," he gasped, "what did you do with the impounded ore-carrier?"

"Well, let me see . . ." Retief said. "According to the Space Navigation Code, a body in orbit within twenty miles of any inhabited airless body constitutes a navigational hazard. Accordingly, I had it towed away."

"And the cargo?"

"Well, accelerating all that mass was an expensive business, so to save the tax-payer's credits, I had it dumped."

"Where?" Magnan croaked.

"On some unimportant asteroid—as specified by Regulations." He smiled blandly at Magnan. Magnan looked back numbly.

"But you said—"

"All I said was that there was what looked like a valuable deposit on 2645-P. It turned out to be a bogus gold mine that somebody had rigged up in a hurry. Curious, eh?"

"But you told me—"

"And you told Mr. Leatherwell. Indiscreet of you, Mr. Consul. That was a privileged communication; classified information, official use only."

"You led me to believe there was collapsed-crystal—"

"I said Sam had mentioned it. He told me his asteroid was made of the stuff."

Magnan swallowed hard, twice. "By the way," he said dully. "You were right about the check. Half an hour ago Mr. Leatherwell tried to stop payment. He was too late . . ."

"All in all, it's been a big day for Leatherwell," Retief said. "Anything else?"

"I hope not," Magnan said. "I sincerely hope not . . ." He leaned close to the screen. "You'll consider the entire affair as . . . confidential? There's no point in unduly complicating relationships—"

"Have no fear, Mr. Consul," Retief said cheerfully. "You won't find me identifying with anything as specific as triple-salting an asteroid."

Back at the table, Sam called for another bottle of rock juice.

"That Drift's a pretty good game," Retief said. "But let me show you one I learned out on Yill . . ."

"For all their professional detachment from emotional involvement in petty local issues, tough-minded CDT envoys have ever opened their hearts to long-suffering peoples striving to cast off the yoke of economic oppression. At Glave, Ambassador Sternwheeler's dedicated group selflessly offered their services, assisting the newly unshackled populace in savoring the first fruits of freedom . . ."

—Vol. IV, Reel 71, 492 AE (AD 2953)

NATIVE INTELLIGENCE

Retief turned back the gold-encrusted scarlet cuff of the mess jacket of a First Secretary and Consul, gathered in the three eight-sided black dice, shook them by his right ear, and sent them rattling across the floor to rebound from the bulkhead.

"Thirteen's the point," the Power Section Chief called. "Ten he makes it!"

"Oh . . . Mr. Retief." A tall thin youth in the black-trimmed grey of a Third Secretary flapped a sheet of paper from the edge of the circle surrounding the game. "The Ambassador's compliments, sir, and will you join him and the staff in the conference room at once . . ."

Retief rose and dusted his knees. "That's all for now, boys," he said. "I'll take the rest of your money later." He followed the junior diplomat from the ward room, along the bare corridors of the crew level, past the glare panel reading NOTICE—FIRST CLASS ONLY BEYOND THIS POINT, through the chandeliered and draped ballroom and along a stretch of soundless carpet

195

to a heavy door bearing a placard with the legend CONFERENCE IN SESSION.

"Ambassador Sternwheeler seemed quite upset, Mr. Retief," the messenger said.

"He usually is, Pete," Retief took a cigar from his breast pocket. "Got a light?"

The Third Secretary produced a permatch. "I don't know why you smoke those things instead of dope-sticks, Mr. Retief," he said. "The Ambassador hates the smell."

Retief nodded. "I only smoke this kind at conferences; it makes for shorter sessions." He stepped into the room. Ambassador Sternwheeler eyed him down the length of the conference table.

"Ah, Mr. Retief honors us with his presence. Do be seated, Retief." He fingered a yellow Departmental dispatch. Retief took a chair, puffed out a dense cloud of smoke.

"As I have been explaining to the remainder of my staff for the past quarter hour," Sternwheeler rumbled, "I've been the recipient of important intelligence." He blinked at Retief expectantly. Retief raised his eyebrows in polite inquiry.

"It seems," Sternwheeler went on, "that there has been a change in regime on Glave. A week ago, the government which invited the dispatch of this mission—and to which we're accredited—was overthrown. The former ruling class has fled into exile, and a popular workers' and peasants' junta has taken over."

"Mr. Ambassador," Counselor Magnan broke in, rising; "I'd like to be the first—" he glanced around the table— "or one of the first, anyway—to welcome the new government of Glave into the family of planetary ruling bodies—"

"Sit down, Magnan!" Sternwheeler snapped. "Of course the Corps always recognizes *de facto* sovereignty. The problem is merely one of acquainting ourselves with the policies of this new group—a sort of blue-collar coalition, it seems. In what position that leaves this Embassy I don't yet know."

"I suppose this means we'll spend the next month in a parking orbit," Counselor Magnan sighed.

"Unfortunately," Sternwheeler went on, "the entire affair

has apparently been carried off without recourse to violence, leaving the Corps no excuse to step in—that is, it appears our assistance in restoring order will not be required."

"Glave was one of the old Contract Worlds," Retief said. "What's become of the Planetary Manager General and the technical staff?—And how do the peasants and workers plan to operate the atmospheric purification system, and weather control station, and the tide-regulation complexes?"

"I'm more concerned at present with the status of the Mission. Will we be welcomed by these peasants and workers, or peppered with buckshot?"

"You say that this is a popular junta, and that the former leaders have fled into exile," someone said. "May I ask the source of this information, Mr. Ambassador?"

"The dispatch cites a 'reliable Glavian source.'"

"That's officialese for something cribbed from a broadcast news tape," Retief commented. "Presumably the Glavian news services are in the hands of the revolution. In that case—"

"Yes, yes, there is the possibility that the issue is yet in doubt; of course, we'll have to exercise caution in making our approach; it wouldn't do to make overtures to the wrong side."

"Oh, I think we need have no fear on that score," the Chief of the Political Section spoke up. "I know these entrenched cliques; once challenged by an aroused populace, they scuttle for safety—with large balances safely tucked away in neutral banks."

"I'd like to go on record," Magnan piped, "as registering my deep gratification at this fulfillment of popular aspirations—"

"The most popular aspiration I know of is to live high off someone else's effort," Retief said. "I don't know of anyone outside the Corps who's managed it."

"I'd like to propose that immediate arrangements be made for a technical mission," Magnan said. "It's my experience that one of the most pressing needs of newly established democracies is—"

"Is someone to tell them how to run what they've stolen after they've kicked out the legitimate owners," Retief suggested.

The Political Officer blinked at Retief. "Are you implying approval of technocratic totalitarianism?"

"I won't know," Retief said, "until I look that up in a dictionary."

"Gentlemen!" Sternwheeler bellowed. "I'm awaiting your constructive suggestions—not an exchange of political views. We'll arrive off Glave in less than six hours. I should like before that time to have developed some notion regarding to whom I shall expect to offer my credentials!"

There was a discreet tap at the door; it opened and the young Third Secretary poked his head in.

"Mr. Ambassador, I have a reply to your message—just received from Glave. It's signed by the Steward of the GFE, and I thought you'd want to see it at once . . ."

"Yes, of course; let me have it."

"What's the GFE?" someone asked.

"It's the revolutionary group," the messenger said, passing the message over.

"GFE? GFE? What do the letters signify?"

"Glorious Fun Eternally," Retief suggested. "Or possibly Goodies For Everybody."

"I believe that's 'Glavian Free Electorate'," the Third Secretary said.

Sternwheeler stared at the paper, lips pursed. His face grew pink. He slammed the paper on the table.

"Well, gentlemen! It appears our worst fears have been realized! This is nothing less than a warning! A threat! We're advised to divert course and by-pass Glave entirely. It seems the GFE wants no interference from meddling foreign exploiters, as they put it!"

Magnan rose. "If you'll excuse me, Mr. Ambassador, I want to get off a message to Sector HQ to hold my old job for me—"

"Sit down, you idiot!" Sternwheeler roared. "If you think I'm consenting to have my career blighted—my first Ambassadorial post whisked out from under me—the Corps made a fool of—"

"I'd like to take a look at that message," Retief said. It was passed along to him. He read it.

"I don't believe this applies to us, Mr. Ambassador."

"What are you talking about? It's addressed to me—by name!"

"It merely states that 'meddling foreign exploiters' are unwelcome. Meddling foreigners we are, but we don't qualify as exploiters unless we show a profit—and this appears to be shaping up as a particularly profitless venture."

"What are you proposing, Mr. Retief?"

"That we proceed to make planetfall as scheduled, greet our welcoming committee with wide diplomatic smiles, hint at largesse in the offing, and settle down to observe the lie of the land."

"Just what I was about to suggest," Magnan said.

"That might be dangerous," Sternwheeler said.

"That's why I didn't suggest it," Magnan said.

"Still it's essential that we learn more of the situation than can be gleaned from official broadcasts," Sternwheeler mused. "Now, while I can't justify risking the entire Mission, it might be advisable to dispatch a delegation to sound out the new regime—"

"I'd like to volunteer," Magnan said, rising.

"Of course, the delegates may be murdered—"

"—but unfortunately, I'm under treatment at the moment." Magnan sat down.

"—which will place us in an excellent position, propaganda-wise."

"What a pity I can't go," the Military Attaché said. "But my place is with my troops."

"The only troops you've got are the Assistant Attaché and your secretary," Magnan pointed out.

"Say, I'd like to be down there in the thick of things," the Political Officer said. He assumed a grave expression. "But, of course, I'll be needed here, to interpret results."

"I appreciate your attitude, gentlemen," Sternwheeler said, studying the ceiling. "But I'm afraid I must limit the privilege of volunteering for this hazardous duty to those officers of more robust physique, under forty years of age—"

"Tsk. I'm forty-one," Magnan said.

"—and with a reputation for adaptability." His glance moved along the table.

"Do you mind if I run along now, Mr. Ambassador?" Retief said. "It's time for my insulin shot."

Sternwheeler's mouth dropped open.

"Just kidding," Retief said. "I'll go. But I have one request, Mr. Ambassador: no further communication with the ground until I give the all-clear."

Retief grounded the lighter in the center of Glave spaceport, cycled the lock, and stepped out. The hot yellow Glavian sun beat down on a broad expanse of concrete, an abandoned service cart, and a row of tall ships casting black shadows toward the silent control tower. A wisp of smoke curled up from the shed area at the rim of the field. There was no other sign of life.

Retief walked over to the cart, tossed his valise aboard, climbed into the driver's seat, and headed for the operations building. Beyond the port, hills rose, white buildings gleaming against the deep green slopes. Near the ridge, a vehicle moved ant-like along a winding road, a dust trail rising behind it. Faintly, the tiny rap! of a distant shot sounded.

Papers littered the ground before the Operations Building. Retief pushed open the tall glass door, stood listening. Slanting sunlight reflected from a wide, polished floor, at the far side of which illuminated lettering over empty counters read IMMIGRATION, HEALTH, and CUSTOMS. He crossed to the desk, put the valise down, then leaned across the counter. A worried face under an over-sized white cap looked up at him.

"You can come out now," Retief said. "They've gone."

The man rose, dusting himself off. He looked over Retief's shoulder. "Who's gone?"

"Whoever it was that scared you."

"Whatta ya mean? I was looking for my pencil."

"Here it is." Retief plucked a worn stub from the pocket of the soiled shirt sagging under the weight of braided shoulder-boards. "You can sign me in as a Diplomatic Representative; a break for you—no formalities necessary. Where can I catch a cab for the city?"

The man eyed Retief's bag. "What's in that?"

"Personal belongings under duty-free entry."

"Guns?"

"No, thanks, just a cab, if you don't mind."

"You got no gun?" the man raised his voice.

"That's right, fellows," Retief called out. "No gun; no knife, not even a small fission bomb; just a few pairs of socks and some reading matter."

A brown-uniformed man rose from behind the Customs counter, holding a long-barreled blast-rifle centered on the Corps insignia stitched to the pocket of Retief's powder-blue blazer.

"Don't try nothing," he said. "You're under arrest—"

"It can't be overtime parking; I've only been here five minutes."

"Hah!" the gun-handler moved out from the counter, came up to Retief. "Empty out your pockets!" he barked. "Hands over head!"

"I'm just a diplomat, not a contortionist," Retief said, not moving. "Do you mind pointing that thing in some other direction?"

"Looky here, Mister, I'll give the orders. We don't need anybody telling us how to run our business—"

"I'm telling you to shift that blaster before I take it away from you and wrap it around your neck," Retief said conversationally. The cop stepped back uncertainly, lowering the gun.

"Jake! Horny! Pud! Come on out!"

Three more brown uniforms emerged from concealment.

"Who are you fellows hiding from? The top sergeant?" Retief glanced over the ill-fitting uniforms, the unshaved faces, the scuffed boots. "Tell you what—when he shows up, I'll engage him in conversation, and you beat it back to the barracks and grab a quick bath—"

"That's enough smart talk." The biggest of the three newcomers moved up to Retief. "You stuck your nose in at the wrong time. We just had a change of management around here."

"I heard about it," Retief said. "Who do I complain to?"

"Complain? What about?"

"The port's a mess," Retief barked. "Nobody on duty to receive official visitors! No passenger service facilities! Why, do you know I had to carry my own bag—"

"All right, all right, that's outside my department. You better see the boss."

"The boss? I thought you got rid of the bosses."

"We did, but now we got new ones."

"They any better than the old ones?"

"This guy asks too many questions," the man with the gun said. "Let's let Sozier answer 'em."

"Who's he?"

"He's the Military Governor of the City."

"Now we're getting somewhere," Retief said. "Lead the way, Jake—and don't forget my bag."

Sozier was a small man with thin hair oiled across a shiny scalp, prominent ears, and eyes like coal chips set in rolls of fat. He glowered at Retief from behind a polished desk occupying the center of a spacious office.

"I warned you off," he snapped. "You came anyway." He leaned forward and slammed a fist down on the desk. "You're used to throwing your weight around, but you won't throw it around here! There'll be no spies pussy-footing around Glave!"

"Looking for what, Mr. Sozier?"

"Call me General!"

"Mind if I sit down?" Retief pulled out a chair, seated himself, and took out a cigar. "Curiously enough," he said, lighting up, "the Corps has no intention of making any embarrassing investigations. We deal with the existing government, no questions asked—" His eyes held the other's. "Unless, of course, there are evidences of atrocities or other illegal measures."

The coal-chip eyes narrowed. "I don't have to make explanations to you or anybody else—"

"Except, presumably, the Glavian Free Electorate," Retief said blandly. "But tell me, General—who's actually running the show?"

A speaker on the desk buzzed. "Hey, Corporal Sozier! Wes's got them two hellions cornered. They're holed up in the Birthday Cake—"

"*General* Sozier, damn you! And plaster your big mouth shut!" He gestured to one of the uniformed men standing by.

"You! Get Trundy and Little Moe up here—pronto!" He swiveled back to Retief. "You're in luck; I'm too busy right now to bother with you. You get back over to the port and leave the same way you came—and tell your blood-sucking friends the easy pickings are over as far as Glave's concerned. You won't lounge around here living high and throwing big parties and cooking up deals to get fat on the expense of the working man."

Retief dribbled ash on Sozier's desk and glanced at the green uniform front bulging between silver buttons.

"Who paid for *your* pot-belly, Sozier?" he inquired carelessly.

Sozier's eyes narrowed to slits. "I could have you shot—"

"Stop playing games with me, Sozier," Retief rapped. "There's a squadron of Peace Enforcers standing by just in case any apprentice statesmen forget the niceties of diplomatic usage. I suggest you start showing a little intelligence about now, or even Horny and Pud are likely to notice."

Sozier's fingers squeaked on the arms of his chair. He swallowed.

"You might start by assigning me an escort for a conducted tour of the capital," Retief went on. "I want to be in a position to confirm that order has been re-established, and that normal services have been restored—otherwise, it may be necessary to send in a Monitor Unit to straighten things out."

"You can't meddle with the internal affairs of a sovereign world—"

Retief sighed. "The trouble with taking over your boss's job is discovering its drawbacks. It's disillusioning, I know, Sozier—but—"

"All right! Take your tour! You'll find everything running as smooth as silk! Utilities, police, transport, environmental control—"

"What about Space Control? Glave Tower seems to be off the air."

"I shut it down. We don't need anything from outside."

"Where's the new Premier keeping himself? Does he share your passion for privacy?"

The general got to his feet. "I'm letting you take your look, Mr. Big Nose. I'm giving you four hours. Then out! And the next meddling bureaucrat that tries to cut atmosphere on Glave without a clearance gets burned!"

"I'll need a car."

"Jake! You stick to this bird. Take him to the main power plant, the water works, and the dispatch center, ride him around town and show him we're doing OK without a bunch of leeches bossing us; then dump him at the port—and see that he leaves."

"I'll plan my own itinerary, thanks. I can't promise I'll be finished in four hours—but I'll keep you advised."

"I warned you—"

"I heard you. Five times. And I only warned you once. You're getting ahead of me," Retief rose, motioned to the hulking guard. "Come on, Jake; we've got a lot of ground to cover before dinner."

At the curb, Retief held out his hand. "Give me the power cylinder out of your rifle, Jake."

"Huh?"

"Come on, Jake. You've got a nervous habit of playing with the firing stud. We don't want any accidents."

"How do you get it out? They only give me this thing yesterday."

Retief pocketed the cylinder. "You sit in back. I'll drive." He wheeled the car off along a broad avenue crowded with vehicles and lined with flowering palms behind which stately white buildings reared up into the pale sky.

"Nice looking city, Jake," Retief said conversationally. "What's the population?"

"I dunno. I only been here a year."

"What about Horny and Pud? Are they natives?"

"Whatta ya mean, natives? They're just as civilized as me."

"My boner, Jake. Known Sozier long?"

"Sure; he useta come around to the club."

"I take it he was in the army under the old regime?"

"Yeah—but he didn't like the way they run it. Nothing but band playing and fancy marching. There wasn't nobody to fight."

"Just between us, Jake—where did the former Planetary

Manager General go?" Retief watched Jake's heavy face in the mirror. Jake jumped, clamped his mouth shut.

"I don't know nothing."

Half an hour later, after a tour of the commercial center, Retief headed toward the city's outskirts. The avenue curved, leading up along the flank of a low hill.

"I must admit I'm surprised, Jake," Retief said. "Everything seems orderly; no signs of riots or panic. Power, water, communications normal—just as the general said. Remarkable, isn't it, considering that the entire managerial class has packed up and left . . ."

"You wanta see the Power Plant?" Retief could see perspiration beaded on the man's forehead under the uniform cap.

"Sure. Which way?" With Jake directing, Retief ascended to the ridge top, cruised past the blank white façade of the station.

"Quiet, isn't it?" Retief pulled the car in to the curb. "Let's go inside."

"Huh? Corporal Sozier didn't say nothing—"

"You're right, Jake. That leaves it to our discretion."

"He won't like it."

"The corporal's a busy man, Jake. We won't worry him by telling him about it."

Jake followed Retief up the walk. The broad double doors were locked.

"Let's try the back."

The narrow door set in the high blank wall opened as Retief approached. A gun barrel poked out, followed by a small man with bushy red hair. He looked Retief over.

"Who's this party, Jake?" he barked.

"Sozier said show him the plant," Jake said.

"What we need is more guys to pull duty, not tourists. Anyway, I'm Chief Engineer here. Nobody comes in here 'less I like their looks."

Retief moved forward, stood looking down at the redhead. The little man hesitated, then waved him past. "Lucky for you, I like your looks."

Inside, Retief surveyed the long room, the giant converter units, the massive bussbars. Armed men—some in uniform, some in work clothes, others in loud sport shirts—

stood here and there. Other men read meters, adjusted controls, or inspected dials.

"You've got more guards than workers," Retief said. "Expecting trouble?"

The red-head bit the corner from a plug of spearmint. He glanced around the plant. "Things is quiet now; but you never know . . ."

"Rather old-fashioned equipment, isn't it? When was it installed?"

"Huh? I dunno. What's wrong with it?"

"What's your basic power source, a core sink? Lithospheric friction? Sub-crustal hydraulics?"

"Beats me, Mister. I'm the boss here, not a dern mechanic."

A grey-haired man carrying a clip-board walked past, studied a panel, made notes, glanced up to catch Retief's eye, moved on.

"Everything seems to be running normally," Retief remarked.

"Sure; why not?"

"Records being kept up properly?"

"Sure; some of these guys, all they do is walk around looking at dials and writing stuff on paper. If it was me, I'd put 'em to work."

Retief strolled over to the grey-haired man, now scribbling before a bank of meters. He glanced at the clip board. *Power off at sunset. Tell Corasol* was scrawled in block letters across the record sheet. Retief nodded, rejoined his guard.

"All right, Jake. Let's have a look at the communications center."

Back in the car, headed west, Retief studied the blank windows of office buildings, the milling throngs in beer bars, shooting galleries, tattoo parlors, billiards halls, pinball arcades, bordellos, and half-credit casinos.

"Everybody seems to be having fun," he remarked.

Jake stared out the window. "Yeah."

"Too bad you're on duty, Jake. You could be out there joining in."

"Soon as the corporal gets things organized, I'm opening me up a place to show dirty tri-di's. I'll get my share."

"Meanwhile, let the rest of 'em have their fun, eh, Jake?"

"Look, Mister, I been thinking: Maybe you better gimme back that kick-stick you taken outa my gun . . ."

"Sorry, Jake; no can do. Tell me, what was the real cause of the revolution? Not enough to eat? Too much regimentation?"

"Naw, we always got plenty to eat. There wasn't none of that regimentation—up till I joined up in the corporal's army."

"Rigid class structure, maybe? Educational discrimination?"

Jake nodded. "Yeah, it was them schools done it. All the time trying to make a feller go to some kind of class. Big shots. Know it all. Gonna make us sit around and view tapes. Figgered they are better than us."

"And Sozier's idea was you'd take over, and you wouldn't have to be bothered."

"Aw, it wasn't Sozier's idea. He ain't the big leader."

"Where does the big leader keep himself?"

"I dunno. I guess he's pretty busy right now." Jake snickered. "Some of them guys call themselves colonels turned out not to know nothing about how to shoot off the guns."

"Shooting, eh? I thought it was a sort of peaceful revolution; the managerial class were booted out, and that was that."

"I don't know nothing," Jake snapped. "How come you keep trying to get me to say stuff I ain't supposed to talk about? You want to get me in trouble?"

"Oh, you're already in trouble, Jake. But if you stick with me, I'll try to get you out of it. Where exactly did the refugees head for? How did they leave? Must have been a lot of them; I'd say in a city of this size they'd run into the thousands."

"I don't know."

"Of course, it depends on your definition of a big shot. Who's included in that category, Jake?"

"You know, the slick-talking ones; the fancy dressers; the guys that walk around and tell other guys what to do. We do all the work and they get all the big pay."

"I suppose that would cover scientists, professional men,

executives, technicians of all sorts, engineers, teachers—all that crowd of no-goods."

"Yeah, them are the ones."

"And once you got them out of the way, the regular fellows would have a chance; chaps that don't spend all their time taking baths and reading books and using big words; good Joes that don't mind picking their noses in public."

"We got as much right as anybody—"

"Jake, who's Corasol?"

"He's—I don't know."

"I thought I overheard his name somewhere."

"Uh, here's the communication center," Jake cut in.

Retief swung into a parking lot under a high blank façade. He set the brake and stepped out.

"Lead the way, Jake."

"Look, Mister, the corporal only wanted me to show you the outside—"

"Anything to hide, Jake?"

Jake shook his head angrily and stamped past Retief. "When I joined up with Sozier, I didn't figger I'd be getting in this kind of mess . . ."

"I know, Jake; it's tough. Sometimes it seems like a fellow works harder after he's thrown out the parasites than he did before."

A cautious guard let Retief and Jake inside, followed them along bright lit aisles among consoles, cables, batteries of instruments. Armed men in careless uniforms lounged, watching. Here and there a silent technician worked quietly.

Retief paused by one, an elderly man in a neat white coverall, with a purple spot under one eye.

"Quite a bruise you've got there," Retief commented heartily. "Power failure at sunset," he added softly. The technician hesitated, nodded, and moved on.

Back in the car, Retief gave Jake directions. At the end of three hours, he had seen twelve smooth-running, heavily guarded installations.

"So far, so good, Jake," he said. "Next stop, sub-station Number Nine." In the mirror, Jake's face stiffened. "Hey, you can't go down there—"

"Something going on there, Jake?"

"That's where—I mean, no; I don't know."

"I don't want to miss anything, Jake. Which way?"

"I ain't going down there," Jake said sullenly.

Retief braked. "In that case, I'm afraid our association is at an end, Jake."

"You mean . . . you're getting out here?"

"No, you are."

"Huh? Now wait a minute, Mister; the corporal said I was to stay with you."

Retief accelerated. "That's settled, then. Which way?"

Retief pulled the car to a halt two hundred yards from the periphery of a loose crowd of brown-uniformed men who stood in groups scattered across a broad plaza, overflowing into a stretch of manicured lawn before the bare, functional facade of Sub-station Number Nine. In the midst of the besieging mob, Sozier's red face and bald head bobbed as he harangued a cluster of green-uniformed men from his place in the rear of a long open car.

"What's it all about, Jake?" Retief inquired. "Since the parasites have all left peacefully, I'm having a hard time figuring out who'd be holed up in the pumping station—and why. Maybe they haven't gotten the word that it's all going to be fun and games from now on."

"If the corporal sees you over here—"

"Ah, the good corporal. Glad you mentioned him, Jake. He's the man to see." Retief stepped out of the car and started through the crowd. A heavy lorry loaded with an immense tank with the letter H blazoned on its side trundled into the square from a side street, moved up to a position before the building. A smaller car pulled alongside Sozier's limousine. The driver stepped down, handed something to Sozier. A moment later, Sozier's amplified voice boomed across the crowd.

"You in there, Corasol. This is General Sozier, and I'm warning you to come out now or you and your smart friends are in for a big surprise. You think I won't blast you out because I don't want to wreck the plant. You see the tank aboard the lorry that just pulled up? It's full of gas—and I got plenty of hoses out here to pump it inside with. I'll put men on the roof and squirt it in the ventilators . . ."

Sozier's voice echoed and died. The militiamen eyed the station. Nothing happened.

"I know you can hear me, damn you!" Sozier squalled. "You'd better get the doors open and get out here fast—"

Retief stepped to Sozier's side. "Say, Corporal, I didn't know you went in for practical jokes—"

Sozier jerked around to gape at Retief.

"What are you doing here!" he burst out. "I told Jake—where is that—"

"Jake didn't like the questions I was asking," Retief said, "so he marched me up here to report to you."

"Jake, you damn fool!" Sozier roared. I gotta good mind—"

"I disagree, Sozier," Retief cut in. "I think you're a complete imbecile. Sitting out here in the open yelling at the top of your lungs. For example: Corasol and his party might get annoyed and spray that fancy car you've swiped with something a lot more painful than words."

"Eh?" Sozier's head whipped around to stare at the building.

"Isn't that a gun I see sticking out?"

Sozier dropped. "Where?"

"My mistake; just a foreign particle on my contact lenses." Retief leaned on the car. "On the other hand, Sozier, most murderers are sneaky about it; I think making a public announcement is a nice gesture on your part. The Monitors won't have any trouble deciding who to hang when they come in to straighten out this mess."

Sozier scrambled back onto his seat. "Monitors?" he snarled. "I don't think so. I don't think you'll be around to do any blabbering to anybody." He raised his voice. "Jake! March this spy over to the sidelines. If he tries anything, shoot him!" He gave Retief a baleful grin. "I'll lay the body out nice and ship it back to your cronies. Accidents will happen, you know. It'll be a week or two before they get around to following up—and by then I'll have this little problem under control."

Jake looked at Retief uncertainly, fingering his empty rifle.

Retief put his hands up. "I guess you got me, Jake," he said. "Careful of that gun, now."

Jake glanced at Sozier, gulped, aimed the rifle at Retief, and nodded toward the car. As Retief moved off, a murmur swept across the crowd. Retief glanced back; a turret on the station roof was rotating slowly. A shout rose; men surged away from the building, scuffling for way; Sozier yelled. His car started up, moved forward, horns blaring. As Retief watched, a white stream arced up from the turret, catching the sun as it spanned the lawn, down to strike the massed men in a splatter of spray. It searched across the mob, came to rest on Sozier's car. Uniformed men scrambled for safety as the terrified driver gunned the heavy vehicle. The hose followed the car, dropping a solid stream of water on Sozier, kicking and flailing in the back seat. As the car passed from view down a side street, water was overflowing the sides.

"The corporal will feel all the better for an invigorating swim in his mobile pool," Retief commented. "By the way, Jake, I have to be going now. It wouldn't be fair to send you back to your boss without something to back up your story that you were outnumbered, so—"

Retief's left fist shot out to connect solidly with Jake's jaw. Jake dropped the gun and sat down hard. Retief turned and headed for the pumping station. The hose had shut down now. A few men were standing, eyeing the building anxiously. Others watched his progress across the square. As Retief passed, he caught scattered comments:

"—seen that bird before."

"—where he's headed."

"—feller Sozier was talkin to . . ."

"Hey, you!" Retief was on the grass now. Ahead, the blank wall loomed up. He walked on, briskly.

"Stop that jasper!" a shout rang out. There was a sharp whine and a black spot appeared on the wall ahead. Near it, a small personnel door abruptly swung inward. Retief sprinted, plunged through the opening as a second shot seared the paint on the doorframe. The door clanged behind him. Retief glanced over the half-dozen men confronting him.

"I'm Retief, CDT, Acting Chargé," he said. "Which of you gentlemen is Manager-General Corasol?"

❖　　　❖　　　❖

Corasol was a tall, wide-shouldered man of fifty, with shrewd eyes, a ready smile, capable-looking hands, and an urbane manner. He and Retief sat at a table at one side of the large room, under a maze of piping, tanks and valves, Corasol poured amber fluid into square glass tumblers.

"We spotted you by the blazer," he said. "Baby blue and gold braid stand out in a crowd."

Retief nodded. "The uniform has its uses," he agreed. He tried the drink. "Say, what is this? It's not bad."

"Sugar-weed rum; made from a marine plant. We have plenty of ocean here on Glave; there's only the one continent, you know, and it's useless for agriculture."

"Weather?"

"That's part of it; Glave is moving into what would be a major glaciation if it weren't for a rather elaborate climatic control installation. Then there are the tides; half the continent would be inundated twice a year when our satellite is at aphelion; there's a system of baffles, locks and deep-water pumps that maintain the shore-line more or less constant; we still keep our cities well inland. Then there are the oxygen generators, the atmosphere filtration complex, vermin control, and so on. Glave in its natural state is a rather hostile world."

"I'm surprised that your mines can support it all."

"Oh, they don't." Corasol shook his head. "Two hundred years ago, when the company first opened up Glave, it was economical enough. Quintite was a precious mineral in those days. Synthetics have long since taken over. Even fully automated, the mines barely support the public services and welfare system."

"I seem to recall a reference in the Post Report to the effect that a Company petition to vacate its charter had been denied . . ."

Corasol nodded, smiling wryly. "The CDT seemed to feel that as long as any of the world's residents desired to remain, the Company was constrained to oblige them. The great majority departed long ago, of course—relocated to other operational areas. Only the untrainables, living off welfare funds—and a skeleton staff of single men to operate the technical installations—have stayed on."

"What do you mean—untrainable?"

"There's always a certain percentage of any population with the conviction that society is a conspiracy to deny them their rights. The right to be totally ignorant of any useful knowledge seems to be the basic one. Most societies can carry the burden of these drones—along with the criminal and idiot classes—as mere minority problems. Here on Glave, they've constituted the population—with the planet operated to maintain them. Some of them have opened small businesses—of the kind that require only a native shrewdness and a stomach for the popular tastes. Of course, they still regard any material advantages possessed by the productive as flagrant evidence of discrimination."

"That explains the mechanics of the recent uprising," Retief said.

The bottle clinked against glasses for a second round. "What about the good corporal?" Retief asked. "Assuming he's a strong swimmer, you should be hearing from him soon."

Corasol glanced at his finger watch. "I imagine he'll be launching his gas attack any minute."

"The prospect doesn't seem to bother you."

"Sozier is a clever enough chap in his own way," Corasol said. "But he has a bad habit of leaping to conclusions. He's gotten hold of a tank of what someone has told him is gas— as indeed it is. Hydrogen, for industrial use. It seems the poor fellow is under the impression that anything masquerading as gas will have a lethal effect."

"He may be right—if he pumps it in fast enough."

"Oh, he won't be pumping it—not after approximately five minutes from now."

"Hmmm. I think I'm beginning to see the light. 'Power off at sunset . . .'"

Corasol nodded. "I don't think he realizes somehow that all his vehicles are operating off broadcast power."

"Still, he has a good-sized crowd of hopefuls with him. How do you plan to get through them?"

"We don't; we go under. There's an extensive system of service ways underlying the city; another detail which I believe has escaped the corporal's notice."

"You'll be heading for the port?"

"Yes—eventually. First, we have a few small chores to

see to. Sozier has quite a number of our technical men working at gun point to keep various services going."

Retief nodded. "It won't be easy breaking them out; I made a fast tour of the city this afternoon; locked doors, armed guards—"

"Oh, the locks are power-operated, too. Our fellows will know what to do when the power fails. I think the sudden darkness will eliminate any problem from the guards."

The lights flickered and died. The whine of the turbines was suddenly noticeable, descending. Faint cries sounded from outside.

Corasol switched on a small portable lantern. "All ready, gentlemen?" he called, rising. "Let's move out. We want to complete this operation before dawn."

Four hours later, Retief stood with Corasol in a low-ceilinged tunnel, white-tiled, brilliantly lit by a central glare strip, watching as the last of the column of men released from forced labor in the city's utilities installations filed past. A solidly-built man with pale blond hair came up, breathing hard.

"How did it go, Taine?" Corasol asked.

"They're beginning to catch on, Mr. Corasol. We had a brisk time of it at Station Four. Everybody's clear now. No one killed, but we had a few injuries."

Corasol nodded. "The last few crews in have reported trouble. "Ah—what about—"

Taine shook his head. "Sorry, Sir. No trace. No one's seen them. But they're probably at the port ahead of us, hiding out. They'd know we'd arrive eventually."

"I suppose so. You sent word to them well in advance . . ."

"Suppose I stand by here with a few men; we'll patrol the tunnels in case they show up. We have several hours before daylight."

"Yes. I'll go along and see to the preparations at Exit Ten. We'll make our sortie at oh-five-hundred. If you haven't seen anything of them by then . . ."

"I'm sure they're all right."

"They'd better be," Corasol said grimly. "Let's be off, Retief."

"If it's all the same to you, Mr. Manager-General, I'll stay here with Taine; I'll join you later."

"As you wish. I don't imagine there'll be any trouble—but if there is, having a CDT observer along will lend a certain air to the operation." He smiled, shook Retief's hand and moved off along the tunnel. The echo of feet and voices grew faint, faded to silence. Taine turned to the three men detailed to him, conversed briefly, sent them off along branching corridors. He glanced at Retief.

"Mr. Retief, you're a diplomat. This errand is not a diplomatic one."

"I've been on a few like that, too, Mr. Taine."

Taine studied Retief's face. "I can believe that," he said. "However, I think you'd better rejoin the main party."

"I might be of some use here, if your missing men arrive under fire."

"Missing men?" Taine's mouth twisted in a sour smile. "You fail to grasp the picture, Mr. Retief. There'll be no missing men arriving."

"Oh? I understood you were waiting here to meet them."

"Not men, Mr. Retief. It happens that Corasol has twin daughters, aged nineteen. They haven't been seen since the trouble began."

Half an hour passed. Retief leaned against the tunnel wall, arms folded, smoking a cigar in silence. Taine paced, ten yards up the corridor, ten yards back . . .

"You seem nervous, Mr. Taine," Retief said.

Taine stopped pacing, eyed Retief coldly. "You'd better go along now," he said decisively. "Just follow the main tunnel; it's about a mile—"

"Plenty of time yet, Mr. Taine." Retief smiled and drew on his cigar. "Your three men are still out—"

"They won't be back here; we'll rendezvous at Exit Ten."

"Am I keeping you from something, Taine?"

"I can't be responsible for your safety if you stay here."

"Oh? You think I might fall victim to an accident?"

Taine narrowed his eyes. "It could happen," he said harshly.

"Where were the girls last seen?" Retief asked suddenly.

"How would I know?"

"Weren't you the one who got word to them?"

"Maybe you'd better keep out of this."

"You sent your men off; now you're eager to see me retire to a safe position. Why the desire for solitude, Taine? You wouldn't by any chance have plans . . . ?"

"That's enough," Taine snapped. "On your way. That's an order!"

"There are some aspects of this situation that puzzle me, Mr. Taine. Mr. Corasol has explained to me how he and his Division Chiefs—including you—were surprised in the Executive Suite at Planetary Control, by a crowd of Sozier's bully-boys. They came in past the entire security system without an alarm. Corasol and the others put up a surprisingly good fight and made it to the service elevators—and from there to the Sub-station. There was even time to order an emergency alert to the entire staff—but somehow, they were all caught at their stations and kept on the job at gun point. Now, I should think that you, as Chief of Security as well as Communications, should have some idea as to how all this came about."

"Are you implying—"

"Let me guess, Taine. You have a deal with Sozier. He takes over, ousts the legal owners, and set himself up to live off the fat of the land, with you as his technical chief. Then, I imagine, you'd find it easy enough to dispose of Sozier—and you'd be in charge."

Without warning, Taine put his head down and charged. Retief dropped his cigar, side-stepped, and planted a solid right on Taine's jaw. He staggered, went to his hands and knees.

"I suppose you'd like to get word to Sozier that his work force is arriving at the port at oh-five-hundred," Retief said. "Of course, he'll want to have a good-sized reception committee on hand as they come out—"

Taine plunged to his feet, threw a vicious left that went past Retief's ear, then abruptly dropped, clamped a lock on Retief's leg, twisted—

The two men rolled, came to rest with Taine on top, Retief face-down, his arm bent back and doubled. Taine, red-faced and puffing, grunted as he applied pressure.

"You know a lot about me," he granted, "but you overlooked the fact that I've been Glavian Judo champion for the past nine years."

"You're a clever man, Taine," Retief said between clenched teeth. "Too clever to think it will work."

"It will work. Glave's never had a CDT mission here before; we're too small. Corasol invited your Embassy in because he had an idea there was something in the wind. That forced my hand. I've had to move hastily. But by the time I invite observers in to see for themselves, everything will be running smoothly. I can even afford to let Corasol and the others go—I'll have hostages for his good behavior."

"You've been wanting to boast about it to someone who could appreciate your cleverness, I see. Sozier must be an unappreciative audience."

"Sozier's a filthy pig—but he had his uses."

"What do you plan to do now?"

"I've been wondering that myself—but I think the best solution is simply break your arm for now. You should be easy to control then. It's quite simple; I merely apply pressure, thus . . ."

"Judo is a very useful technique," Retief said. "But in order to make it work, you have to be a pretty good man . . ." He moved suddenly, shifting his position. Taine grabbed, holding Retief's arm by the wrist and elbow, his own arm levering Retief's back, back . . . Retief twisted onto his side, then his back. Taine grunted, following the movement, straining. Slowly, Retief sat up against Taine's weight. Then, with a surge, he straightened his arm. Taine's grip broke. Retief came to his feet. Taine scrambled up in time to meet a clean uppercut.

"Ah, there you are," Retief said as Taine's eyes fluttered and opened. "You've had a nice nap—almost fifteen minutes. Feeling better?"

Taine snarled, straining against the bonds on his wrists.

"Gold braid has its uses," Retief commented. "Now that you're back, perhaps you can answer a question for me. What's the Birthday Cake?"

Taine spat. Retief went to stand over him.

"Time is growing short, Mr. Taine. It will be dawn in another two hours. I can't afford the luxury of coaxing you. You'd better answer my question."

"You won't get away with this."

Retief looked at the glowing end of his cigar. "This won't be subtle, I agree—but it will work . . ."

"You're bluffing."

Retief leaned closer. "In my place—would you hesitate?" he asked softly.

Taine cursed, struggled to break free, eyes on the cigar. "What kind of diplomat are you?" he snarled.

"The modern variety; throat-cutting, thumb-screws, poison and stiletto work were popular in Machiavelli's time; nowadays we go in more for the administrative approach—but the cigar-end still has its role."

"Look—we can come to an agreement—"

"What's the Birthday Cake?" Retief snapped.

"I'm in a position to do a lot for you—"

"Last chance—"

"It's the official Residence of the Manager-General!" Taine screeched, writhing away from the cigar.

"Where is it? Talk fast!"

"You'll never get close! There's a seven-foot wall and by this time the grounds are swarming with Sozier's men—"

"Nevertheless, I want to know where it is—and the information had better be good. If I don't come back, you'll have a long wait."

Taine groaned. "All right. Put that damned cigar away. I'll tell you what I can . . ."

Retief stood in the shadow of a vine-grown wall, watching the five-man guard detail at the main gate to the Residence grounds. The bluish light of the Glavian satellite reflected from the rain-pocked street, glinted from the leaves of a massive tree ten yards from the gate. The chill in the air cut through Retief's wet clothes; the men at the gate huddled, hands in pockets, coat collars turned up, backs to the wind—and to Retief. He moved silently forward, caught a low branch of the tree, pulled himself up. The men at the gate exchanged muttered remarks. One lit a cigarette. Retief waited, then moved higher. The guards talked in low voices, edged closer to the shelter of the gate-house. Retief lowered himself onto the wall, dropped down onto the sodden lawn, crouched, waiting. There was no alarm.

Through the trees the dark shape of the house loomed

up, its top story defiantly ablaze with lights. Retief moved off silently, from the shadow of one tree to the next, swinging in an arc that would bring him to the rear of the great round structure. He froze as the heavy footfalls of one of Sozier's pickets slogged past five yards from him, then moved on. The glow of a camp-fire flickered near the front of the house. Retief could make out the shapes of men around it—a dozen or two, at least. Probably as many more warmed themselves at each of the other fires visible on the grounds—and most of the rest had doubtless found dryer shelter in the lee of the house itself.

Retief reached the conservatory at the rear of the house, studied the dark path leading to the broad terrace, picked out the squat shape of the utilities manifold behind a screen of shrubbery. So far, Taine's information had been accurate. The next step was to—

There was a faint sound from high above, followed by a whoosh!— Then, with a sharp crack, a flare appeared overhead, rocking gracefully, floating down gently under a small parachute. Below it, inky shadows rocked in unison. In the raw white light, Retief counted eighteen men clinging to handholds on the side of the house, immobile in the pitiless glare. Above them, a face appeared, then a second, peering over the edge of the fourth-story gallery. Both figures rose, unlimbering four-foot bows, fitting arrows to strings—

Whok! Whok! Two men lost their holds and fell, yelling, to slam into the heavy shrubbery. A second flight of arrows found marks. Retief watched from the shadows as man after man dropped to flounder in the wet foliage. Several jumped before the deadly bows were turned on them. As the flare faded, the last of the men plunged down to crash among their fellows. Retief stepped out, ran swiftly to the manifold, forcing his way among the close-growing screen, scrambled to its top. His hand fell on a spent arrow. He picked it up. It was a stout wooden shaft twenty inches long, terminating in a rubber suction cup. Retief snorted, dropped the arrow and started up.

Twenty feet above ground level, the wide windows of the third floor sun terrace presented a precarious handhold as Retief swung back a foot, kicked in a panel. Inside, he dimly made out the shape of a broad carpeted room, curving out of sight in both directions. There were wide-leafed tropical plants in boxes, groups of padded chairs, low tables with bowls of fruit. Retief made his way past them, found an inner door, went into a dark hall. At the far end, voices exchanged shouted questions. Feet pounded. A flicker of light from a hand lantern splashed across the wall, disappeared. Retief found a stair, went up it noiselessly. According to Taine, the elevator to the top floor apartment should be to the left—

Retief flattened himself to the wall. Footsteps sounded near at hand. He moved quickly to a doorway. There was a murmur of voices, the wavering light of lanterns. A party of uniformed men tiptoed past a cross corridor, struggling under the weight of a massive log, two feet in diameter and twelve feet long.

" . . . on signal, hit it all together. Then . . ." someone was saying.

Retief waited, listening. There was the creak of a door, the fumbling of awkwardly-laden feet on a stair, hoarse breathing, a muffled curse.

" . . . got my fingers, ya slob . . ." a voice snarled.

"Shaddup!" another voice hissed.

There was a long moment of silence, then a muffled command—followed an instant later by a thunderous crash, a shout—cut off abruptly by a ponderous blam! followed instantly by a roar like a burst dam, mingled with yells, thumps, crashes. A foamy wash of water surged along the cross corridor, followed a moment later by a man sliding on his back, then another, two more, the log, fragments of a door, more men.

In the uproar, Retief moved along to the elevator, felt over the control panel, located a small knurled button. He turned it; the panel came away. He fumbled cautiously, found a toggle switch, flipped it. A light sprang up in the car; instantly, Retief flipped the light switch; the glow faded. He waited. No alarm. Men were picking themselves up, shouting.

" . . . them broads dropped a hundred gallon bag of water . . ." someone complained.

" . . . up there fast, men. We got the door OK!"

Feet thumped. Yells sounded.

"No good, Wes! They got a safe or something in the way!"

Retief silently closed the lift door, pressed the button. With a sigh, the car slid upward, came to a gentle stop. He eased the door open, looked out into a dim-lit entrance hall. Footsteps sounded beyond a door. He waited, heard the clack of high heels crossing a floor. Retief stepped out of the car, went to the door, glanced into a spacious lounge with rich furniture, deep rugs, paintings, a sweep of glass, and in an alcove at the far side, a bar. Retief crossed the room, poured a stiff drink into a paper-thin glass, and drained it.

The high-heeled steps were coming back now. A door opened. Two leggy young women in shorts, with red-gold hair bound back by ribbons—one green, one blue—stepped into the room. One held a coil of insulated wire; the other carried a heavy-looking grey-enameled box eight inches on a side.

"Now, see if you can tinker that thing to put out about a thousand amps at two volts, Lyn," the girl with the wire said. "I'll start stringing . . ." her voice died as she caught sight of Retief. He raised his glass. "My compliments, ladies. I see you're keeping yourselves amused."

"Who . . . who are you?" Lyn faltered.

"My name's Retief; your father sent me along to carry your bags. It's lucky I arrived when I did, before any of those defenseless chaps outside were seriously injured."

"You're not . . . one of them?"

"Of course he's not, Lyn," the second girl said. "He's much too good-looking."

"That's good," Lyn said crisply. "I didn't want to have to use this thing." She tossed a bright-plated 2mm needler onto a chair and sat down. "Dad's all right, isn't he?"

"He's fine, and we've got to be going. Tight schedule, you know. And you'd better get some clothes on. It's cold outside."

Lyn nodded. "Environmental Control went off the air six hours ago; you can already feel snow coming."

"Don't you suppose we have time to just rig up one little

old circuit?" the other twin wheedled. "Nothing serious; just enough to tickle."

"We planned to wire all the window frames, the trunk we used to block the stair, the lift shaft—"

"And then we thought we'd try to drop a loop down and pick up the gallery guard rail, and maybe some of that wrought-iron work around the front of the house—"

"Sorry, girls; no time."

Five minutes later, the twins were ready, wrapped in fur robes. Retief had exchanged his soaked blazer for a down-lined weatherproof.

"The lift will take us all the way down, won't it?" he asked.

Lyn nodded. "We can go out through the wine cellar."

Retief picked up the needler and handed it to Lyn. "Hang on to this," he said. "You may need it yet."

A cold wind whipped the ramp as dawn lightened the sky.

"It's hard to believe," Corasol said. "What made him do it?"

"He saw a chance to own it all."

"He can have it." Corasol's communicator beeped. He put it to his ear. "Everything's ship-shape and ready to lift," a tiny voice said.

Corasol turned to Retief. "Let's go aboard—"

"Hold it," Retief said. "There's someone coming . . ."

Corasol spoke into the communicator. "Keep him covered, but don't fire unless he does."

The man slogging across the concrete was short, wrapped in heavy garments. Over his head a white cloth fluttered from a stick.

"From the set of those bat-ears, I'd say it was the good corporal."

"I wonder what he wants."

Sozier stopped twenty feet from Retief and Corasol.

"I want to . . . ah . . . talk to you, Corasol," he said.

"Certainly, General. Go right ahead."

"Look here, Corasol. You can't do this. My men will freeze. We'll starve. I've been thinking it over, and I've decided we can reach an understanding."

Corasol waited.

"I mean, we can get together on this thing. Compromise. Maybe I acted a little hasty." Sozier looked from Corasol to Retief. "You're from the CDT. You tell him. I'll guarantee his people full rights . . ."

Retief puffed at his cigar in silence; Sozier started again.

"Look, I'll give you a full voice in running things. A fifty-fifty split. Whatta you say?"

"I'm afraid the proposal doesn't interest me, General," Corasol said.

"Never mind the General stuff," Sozier said desperately. "Listen, you can run it. Just give me and my boys a little say-so."

"Sorry," Corasol shook his head. "Not interested, General."

"OK, OK! You win! Just come on back and get things straightened out! I got a belly fully of running things!"

"I'm afraid I have other plans, General. For some time I've wanted to transfer operations to a world called Las Palmas on which we hold a charter. It has a naturally delightful climate, and I'm told the fishing is good. I leave Glave to the Free Electorate with my blessing. Goodbye, General." He turned to the ship.

"You got to stay here!" Sozier howled. "We'll complain to the CDT! And don't call me General. I'm a Corporal—"

"You're a General now—whether you like it or not," Corasol said bluntly. He shivered. There was a hint of ice in the air. "If you or any of your men ever decide to go to work, General, I daresay we can train you for employment on Las Palmas. In the meantime—Long Live the Revolution!"

"You can't do this! I'll sue!"

"Calm down, Sozier," Retief said. "Go back to town and see if you can get your radio working. Put in a call for Mr. Magnan aboard the CDT vessel. Tell him your troubles. It will make his day. And a word of advice: Mr. Magnan hates a piker—so ask for plenty."

"My boy, I'm delighted," Ambassador Sternwheeler boomed. "A highly professional piece of work. A stirring testimonial to the value of the skilled negotiator! An inspiration to us all!"

"You're too kind, Mr. Ambassador," Retief said, glancing at his watch.

"And Magnan tells me that not only will the mission be welcomed, and my job secure for another year—that is, I shall have an opportunity to serve—but a technical mission has been requested as well. I shall look forward to meeting General Sozier. He sounds a most reasonable chap."

"Oh, you'll like him, Mr. Ambassador. A true democrat, willing to share all you have."

Counselor of Embassy Magnan tapped and entered the office.

"Forgive the intrusion, Mr. Ambassador," he said breathlessly, "but—"

"Well, what is it man! The deal hasn't gone sour . . . ?"

"Oh, far from it! I've been exploring General Sozier's economic situation with him via scope—and it seems he'll require a loan . . ."

"Yes, yes? How much?"

Magnan inhaled proudly. "Twenty. Million. Credits."

"No!"

"Yes!"

"Magnificent! Good lord, Magnan, you're a genius! This will mean promotions all around. Why, the administrative load alone—"

"I can't wait to make planetfall, Mr. Ambassador. I'm all abubble with plans. I hope they manage to get the docking facilities back in operation soon."

"Help is on the way, my dear Magnan. I'm assured the Environmental Control installations will be coming back in operation again within a month or two."

"My, didn't those ice-caps form quickly—and in the open sea."

"Mere scum-ice. As my Counselor for Technical Affairs, you'll be in charge of the ice-breaking operation once we're settled in. I imagine you'll want to spend considerable time in the field. I'll be expecting a record of how every credit is spent."

"I'm more the executive type," Magnan said. "Possibly Retief—"

A desk speaker hummed. "Mr. Corasol's lighter has arrived to ferry Mr. Retief across to the Company ship . . ."

"Sorry you won't be with us, Retief," Sternwheeler said heartily. He turned to Magnan. "Manager-General Corasol has extended Retief an exequatur as Consul General to Las Palmas."

Retief nodded. "Much as I'd like to be out in that open boat with you, breaking ice, I'm afraid duty calls elsewhere."

"Your own post? I'm not sure he's experienced enough, Mr. Ambassador. Now, I—"

"He was requested by name, Magnan. It seems the Manager-General's children took a fancy to him."

"Eh? How curious. I never thought you were particularly interested in infant care, Retief."

"Perhaps I haven't been, Mr. Magnan." Retief draped his short blue cape over his left arm and turned to the door. "But remember the diplomat's motto: be adaptable . . ."

PART IV:
THE GROACI
APPEAR...

Editor's Note: A multitude of alien species appear in the Retief stories. Some of them, such as the Yill and the Soetti, are referred to on several occasions. As a general rule, however, the aliens whom Retief deals with change from one story to the next. Only the Groaci emerge as the ongoing "great opponent" of the Terran Concordiat, beginning with the story "Policy."

As delightful as the Groaci are, however, the aliens who are my personal favorites are the Quopp. They are featured in Laumer's first Retief novel, *Retief's War*, which is included in this section of the volume.

... No jackstraws to be swayed by superficial appearances, dedicated career field personnel of the Corps unflaggingly administered the enlightened concepts evolved at Corps HQ by high-level deep-think teams toiling unceasingly in underground caverns to weld the spirit of Inter-Being amity. Never has the efficacy of close cultural rapport, coupled with Mission teamwork, been better displayed than in the loyal performance of Administrative Assistant Yolanda Meuhl, Acting Consul at Groac, in maintaining the Corps posture laid down by her predecessor, Consul Whaffle ...

—Vol VII, reel 98. 488 A. E. (AD 2949)

POLICY

"The Consul for the Terrestrial States," Retief said, "presents his compliments, et cetera, to the Ministry of Culture of the Groacian Autonomy, and, with reference to the Ministry's invitation to attend a recital of interpretive grimacing, has the honor to express regret that he will be unable—"

"You can't turn down this invitation," Administrative Assistant Meuhl said flatly. "I'll make that 'accepts with pleasure.'"

Retief exhaled a plume of cigar smoke.

"Miss Meuhl," he said, "in the past couple of weeks I've sat through six light concerts, four attempts at chamber music, and God knows how many assorted folk-art festivals. I've been tied up every off-duty hour since I got here."

"You can't offend the Groaci," Miss Meuhl said sharply. "Consul Whaffle would never have—"

"Whaffle left here three months ago," Retief said, "leaving me in charge."

"Well," Miss Meuhl said, snapping off the dictyper. "I'm sure I don't know what excuse I can give the Minister."

"Never mind the excuses. Just tell him I won't be there." He stood up.

"Are you leaving the office?" Miss Meuhl adjusted her glasses. "I have some important letters here for your signature."

"I don't recall dictating any letters today, Miss Meuhl," Retief said, pulling on a light cape.

"I wrote them for you. They're just as Consul Whaffle would have wanted them."

"Did you write all Whaffle's letters for him, Miss Meuhl?"

"Consul Whaffle was an extremely busy man," Miss Meuhl said stiffly. "He had complete confidence in me."

"Since I'm cutting out the culture from now on, I won't be so busy."

"Well! May I ask where you'll be if something comes up?"

"I'm going over to the Foreign Office Archives."

Miss Meuhl blinked behind thick lenses. "Whatever for?"

Retief looked at her thoughtfully. "You've been here on Groac for four years, Miss Meuhl. What was behind the coup d'etat that put the present government in power?"

"I'm sure I haven't pried into—"

"What about that Terrestrial cruiser, the one that disappeared out this way about ten years back?"

"Mr. Retief, those are just the sort of questions we avoid with the Groaci. I certainly hope you're not thinking of openly intruding—"

"Why?"

"The Groaci are a very sensitive race. They don't welcome outworlders raking up things. They've been gracious enough to let us live down the fact that Terrestrials subjected them to deep humiliation on one occasion."

"You mean when we came looking for the cruiser?"

"I, for one, am ashamed of the high-handed tactics that were employed, grilling these innocent people as though they were criminals. We try never to reopen that wound, Mr. Retief."

"They never found the cruiser, did they?"

"Certainly not on Groac."

Retief nodded. "Thanks, Miss Meuhl," he said. "I'll be back before you close the office." Miss Meuhl's thin face was set in lines of grim disapproval as he closed the door.

Peering through the small grilled window, the pale-featured Groacian vibrated his throat-bladder in a distressed bleat.

"Not to enter the Archives," he said in his faint voice. "The denial of permission. The deep regret of the Archivist."

"The importance of my task here," Retief said, enunciating the glottal language with difficulty. "My interest in local history."

"The impossibility of access to outworlders. To depart quietly."

"The necessity that I enter."

"The specific instructions of the Archivist." The Groacian's voice rose to a whisper. "To insist no longer. To give up this idea!"

"Okay, skinny, I know when I'm licked," Retief said in Terran. "To keep your nose clean."

Outside, Retief stood for a moment looking across at the deeply carved windowless stucco facades lining the street, then started off in the direction of the Terrestrial Consulate General. The few Groacians on the street eyed him furtively, and veered to avoid him as he passed. Flimsy high-wheeled ground cars puffed silently along the resilient pavement. The air was clean and cool. At the office Miss Meuhl would be waiting with another list of complaints. Retief studied the carving over the open doorways along the street. An elaborate one picked out in pinkish paint seemed to indicate the Groacian equivalent of a bar. Retief went in.

A Groacian bartender dispensing clay pots of alcoholic drink from the bar-pit at the center of the room looked at Retief, then froze in mid-motion, a metal tube poised over a waiting pot.

"A cooling drink," Retief said in Groacian, squatting down at the edge of the pit. "To sample a true Groacian beverage."

"Not to enjoy my poor offerings," the Groacian mumbled. "A pain in the digestive sacs. To express regret."

"Not to worry," Retief replied. "To pour it out and let me decide whether I like it."

"To be grappled in by peace-keepers for poisoning of . . . foreigners." The barkeep looked around for support, but found none. The Groaci customers, eyes elsewhere, were drifting out.

"To get the lead out," Retief said, placing a thick gold-piece in the dish provided. "To shake a tentacle."

"To procure a cage," a thin voice called from the side-lines. "To display the freak."

Retief turned. A tall Groacian vibrated his mandibles in a gesture of contempt. From his bluish throat coloration it was apparent the creature was drunk.

"To choke in your upper sac," the bartender hissed, extending his eyes toward the drunk. "To keep silent, lit-termate of drones."

"To swallow your own poison, dispenser of vileness," the drunk whispered. "To find a proper cage for this zoo-piece." He wavered toward Retief. "To show this one in the streets, like all freaks."

"Seen a lot of freaks like me, have you?" Retief asked interestedly.

"To speak intelligibly, malodorous outworlder," the drunk said. The barkeep whispered something and two custom-ers came up to the drunk, took his arms, and helped him to the door.

"To get a cage," the drunk shrilled. "To keep the ani-mals in their place . . ."

"I've changed my mind," Retief said to the bartender. "To be grateful as hell, but to have to hurry off now." He followed the drunk out the door. The other Groaci, releas-ing the heckler, hurried back inside. Retief looked at the weaving creature.

"To begone, freak," the Groacian whispered.

"To be pals," Retief said. "To be kind to dumb ani-mals."

"To have you hauled away to a stockyard, ill-odored foreign livestock."

"Not to be angry, fragrant native," Retief said. "To permit me to chum with you."

"To flee before I take a cane to you!"

"To have a drink together."

"Not to endure such insolence." The Groacian advanced toward Retief. Retief backed away.

"To hold hands," he said. "To be buddies—"

The Groacian reached for him, but missed. A passer-by stepped around him, head down, and scuttled away. Retief, backing into the opening to a narrow cross-way, offered further verbal familiarities to the drunken local, who followed, furious. Retief stepped around him, seized his collar and yanked. The Groacian fell on his back. Retief stood over him. The downed native half rose; Retief put a foot against his chest and pushed.

"Not to be going anywhere for a few minutes," he said. "To stay right here and have a nice long talk."

"There you are!" Miss Meuhl said, eyeing Retief over her lenses. "There are two gentlemen waiting to see you. Groacian gentlemen."

"Government men, I imagine. Word travels fast." Retief pulled off his cape. "This saves me the trouble of paying another call at the Foreign Ministry."

"What have you been doing? They seem very upset, I don't mind telling you."

"I'm sure you don't. Come along—and bring an official recorder."

Two Groaci, wearing heavy eye-shields and elaborate crest ornaments indicative of rank, rose as Retief entered the room. Neither offered a courteous snap of the mandibles, Retief noted; they were mad, all right.

"I am Fith, of the Terrestrial Desk, Ministry of Foreign Affairs," the taller Groacian said, in lisping Terran. "May I present Shluh, of the Internal Police."

"Sit down, gentlemen," Retief said. They resumed their seats. Miss Meuhl hovered nervously, then sat down on the edge of a chair.

"Oh, it's such a pleasure—" she began.

"Never mind that," Retief said. "These gentlemen didn't come here to sip tea today."

"True," Fith rasped. "Frankly, I have had a most disturbing report, Mr. Consul. I shall ask Shluh to recount it." He nodded to the police chief.

"One hour ago," Shluh said, "a Groacian national was brought to hospital suffering from serious contusions. Questioning of this individual revealed that he had been set upon and beaten by a foreigner; a Terrestrial, to be precise. Investigation by my Department indicates that the description of the culprit closely matches that of the Terrestrial Consul . . ."

Miss Meuhl gasped audibly.

"Have you ever heard," Retief said, looking steadily at Fith, "of a Terrestrial cruiser, the *ISV Terrific*, which dropped from sight in this sector nine years ago?"

"Really!" Miss Meuhl exclaimed, rising, "I wash my hands—"

"Just keep that recorder going," Retief snapped.

"I'll not be a party—"

"You'll do as you're told, Miss Meuhl," Retief said quietly. "I'm telling you to make an official sealed record of this conversation."

Miss Meuhl sat down.

Fith puffed out his throat indignantly. "You re-open an old wound, Mr. Consul. It reminds us of certain illegal treatment at Terrestrial hands."

"Hogwash," Retief said. "That tune went over with my predecessors, but it hits a sour note with me."

"All our efforts," Miss Meuhl said, "to live down that terrible episode; and you—"

"Terrible? I understand that a Terrestrial Peace Enforcer stood off Groac and sent a delegation down to ask questions. They got some funny answers and stayed on to dig around a little. After a week, they left. Somewhat annoying to you Groaci, if you were innocent—"

"*If!*" Miss Meuhl burst out.

"If, indeed," Fith said, his weak voice trembling. "I must protest your—"

"Save your protests, Fith. You have some explaining to do, and I don't think your story will be good enough."

"It is for you to explain; this person who was beaten—"

"Not beaten; just rapped a few times to loosen his memory."

"Then you admit—"

"It worked, too. He remembered lots of things, once he put his mind to it."

Fith rose, Shluh followed suit.

"I shall ask for your immediate recall, Mr. Consul. Were it not for your diplomatic immunity, I should—"

"Why did the Government fall, Fith, just after the Task Force paid its visit, and before the arrival of the first Terrestrial diplomatic mission?"

"This is an internal matter," Fith cried, in his faint Groacian voice. "The new regime has shown itself most amiable to you Terrestrials; it has outdone itself—"

"—to keep the Terrestrial Consul and his staff in the dark," Retief said, "and the same goes for the few Terrestrial businessmen you've given visas. This continual round of culture; no social contacts outside the diplomatic circle; no travel permits to visit outlying districts or your satellite—"

"Enough!" Fith's mandibles quivered in distress. "I can talk no more of this matter."

"You'll talk to me, or there'll be a squadron of Peace Enforcers here in five days to do the talking," Retief said.

"You can't—" Miss Meuhl gasped.

Retief turned a steady look on Miss Meuhl. She closed her mouth. The Groaci sat down.

"Answer me this one," Retief said, looking at Shluh. "A few years back—nine, to be exact—there was a little parade held here. Some curious-looking creatures were captured, and after being securely caged, were exhibited to the gentle Groacian public. Hauled through the streets. Very educational, no doubt. A highly cultural show.

"Funny thing about these animals: they wore clothes, seemed to communicate with each other. Altogether a very amusing exhibit.

"Tell me, Shluh, what happened to those six Terrestrials after the parade was over?"

Fith made a choked noise, then spoke rapidly to Shluh in Groacian. Shluh, retracting his eyes, shrank down in his chair. Miss Meuhl opened her mouth, then closed it.

"How did they die?" Retief snapped. "Did you cut their throats, shoot them, bury them alive? What amusing end did you figure out for them? Research, maybe. Cut them open to see what made them yell . . ."

"No," Fith gasped. "I must correct this terrible false impression at once."

"False impression, hell," Retief said. "They were Terrans; a simple narco-interrogation would get that out of any Groacian who saw the parade."

"Yes," Fith said weakly. "It is true, they were Terrestrials. But there was no killing—"

"They're alive?"

"Alas, no. They . . . died."

"I see," Retief said. "They died."

"We tried to keep them alive, of course; but we did not know what foods—"

"Didn't take the trouble to find out."

"They fell ill," Fith said. "One by one . . ."

"We'll deal with that question later," Retief said. "Right now, I want more information. Where did you get them? Where did you hide the ship? What happened to the rest of the crew? Did they 'fall ill' before the big parade?"

"There were no more! Absolutely, I assure you!"

"Killed in the crash landing?"

"No crash landing. The ship descended intact, east of the city. The . . . Terrestrials . . . were unharmed. Naturally, we feared them; they were strange to us. We had never before seen such beings."

"Stepped off the ship with guns blazing, did they?"

"Guns? No, no guns—"

"They raised their hands, didn't they, asked for help? You helped them; helped them to death."

"How could we know?" Fith moaned.

"How could you know a flotilla would show up in a few months looking for them, you mean? That was a shock, wasn't it? I'll bet you had a brisk time of it hiding the ship, and shutting everybody up. A close call, eh?"

"We were afraid," Shluh said. "We are a simple people. We feared the strange creatures from the alien craft. We

did not kill them, but we felt it was as well that they . . . did
not survive. Then, when the warships came, we realized
our error, but we feared to speak. We purged our guilty
leaders, concealed what had happened, and . . . offered our
friendship. We invited the opening of diplomatic relations.
We made a blunder, it is true, a great blunder. But we have
tried to make amends . . ."

"Where is the ship?"

"The ship?"

"What did you do with it? It was too big to just walk
off and forget. Where is it?"

The two Groacians exchanged looks.

"We wish to show our contrition," Fith said. "We will
show you the ship."

"Miss Meuhl," Retief said. "If I don't come back in a
reasonable length of time, transmit that recording to Sector
Headquarters, sealed." He stood and looked at the Groaci.

"Let's go," he said.

Retief stooped under the heavy timbers shoring the entry
to the cavern and peered into the gloom at the curving
flank of the space-burned hull.

"Any lights in here?" he asked.

A Groacian threw a switch and a weak bluish glow
sprang up. Retief walked along the raised wooden catwalk,
studying the ship. Empty emplacements gaped below
lenseless scanner eyes. Littered decking was visible within
the half-open entry port. Near the bow the words *'IVS
Terrific B7 New Terra'* were lettered in bright chrome
duralloy.

"How did you get it in here?" Retief asked.

"It was hauled here from the landing point, some nine
miles distant," Fith said, his voice thinner than ever. "This
is a natural crevasse; the vessel was lowered into it and
roofed over."

"How did you shield it so the detectors didn't pick it
up?"

"All here is high-grade iron-ore," Fith said, waving a
member. "Great veins of almost pure metal."

"Let's go inside."

Shluh came forward with a hand-lamp. The party entered

the ship. Retief clambered up a narrow companionway and glanced around the interior of the control compartment. Dust was thick on the deck, the stanchions where acceleration couches had been mounted, the empty instrument panels, the litter of sheared bolts, and on scraps of wire and paper. A thin frosting of rust dulled the exposed metal where cutting torches had sliced away heavy shielding. There was a faint odor of stale bedding.

"The cargo compartment—" Shluh began.

"I've seen enough," Retief said. Silently, the Groacians led the way back out through the tunnel and into the late afternoon sunshine. As they climbed the slope to the steam car, Fith came to Retief's side.

"Indeed I hope that this will be the end of this unfortunate affair," he said. "Now that all has been fully and honestly shown."

"You can skip all that," Retief said. "You're nine years late. The crew was still alive when the Task Force called, I imagine. You killed them—or let them die—rather than take the chance of admitting what you'd done."

"We were at fault," Fith said abjectly. "Now we wish only friendship."

"The *Terrific* was a heavy cruiser, about twenty thousand tons." Retief looked grimly at the slender Foreign Office official. "Where is she, Fith? I won't settle for a hundred-ton lifeboat."

Fith erected his eye stalks so violently that one eye-shield fell off.

"I know nothing of . . . of . . ." He stopped. His throat vibrated rapidly as he struggled for calm.

"My government can entertain no further accusations, Mr. Consul," he said at last. "I have been completely candid with you, I have overlooked your probing into matters not properly within your sphere of responsibility. My patience is at an end."

"Where is that ship?" Retief rapped out. "You never learn, do you? You're still convinced you can hide the whole thing and forget it. I'm telling you you can't."

"We return to the city now," Fith said. "I can do no more."

"You can and you will, Fith," Retief said. "I intend to get to the truth of this matter."

Fith spoke to Shluh in rapid Groacian. The police chief gestured to his four armed constables. They moved to ring Retief in.

Retief eyed Fith. "Don't try it," he said. "You'll just get yourself in deeper."

Fith clacked his mandibles angrily, his eye stalks canted aggressively toward the Terrestrial.

"Out of deference to your diplomatic status, Terrestrial, I shall ignore your insulting implications," Fith said in his reedy voice. "We will now return to the city."

Retief looked at the four policemen. "Sure," he said. "We'll cover the details later."

Fith followed him into the car and sat rigidly at the far end of the seat.

"I advise you to remain very close to your Consulate," Fith said. "I advise you to dismiss these fancies from your mind, and to enjoy the cultural aspects of life at Groac. Especially, I should not venture out of the city, or appear overly curious about matters of concern only to the Groacian government."

In the front seat, Shluh looked straight ahead. The loosely-sprung vehicle bobbed and swayed along the narrow highway. Retief listened to the rhythmic puffing of the motor and said nothing.

"Miss Meuhl," Retief said, "I want you to listen carefully to what I'm going to tell you. I have to move rapidly now, to catch the Groaci off guard.

"I'm sure I don't know what you're talking about," Miss Meuhl snapped, her eyes sharp behind the heavy lenses.

"If you'll listen, you may find out," Retief said. "I have no time to waste, Miss Meuhl. They won't be expecting an immediate move—I hope—and that may give me the latitude I need."

"You're still determined to make an issue of that incident." Miss Meuhl snorted. "I really can hardly blame the Groaci; they are not a sophisticated race; they had never before met aliens."

"You're ready to forgive a great deal, Miss Meuhl. But it's not what happened nine years ago I'm concerned with. It's what's happening now. I've told you that it was only a lifeboat the Groaci have hidden out. Don't you understand the implication? That vessel couldn't have come far; the cruiser itself must be somewhere nearby. I want to know where."

"The Groaci don't know. They're a very cultured, gentle people. You can do irreparable harm to the Terrestrial image if you insist—"

"We're wasting time," Retief said, as he crossed the room to his desk, opened a drawer, and took out a slim-barreled needler.

"This office is being watched; not very efficiently, if I know the Groaci. I think I can get past them all right."

"Where are you going with . . . that?" Miss Meuhl stared at the needler. "What in the world—"

"The Groaci won't waste any time destroying every piece of paper in their files relating to this affair. I have to get what I need before it's too late. If I wait for an official Enquiry Commission, they'll find nothing but blank smiles."

"You're out of your mind!" Miss Meuhl stood up, quivering with indignation. "You're like a . . . a . . ."

"You and I are in a tight spot, Miss Meuhl. The logical next move for the Groaci is to dispose of both of us. We're the only ones who know what happened. Fith almost did the job this afternoon, but I bluffed him out—for the moment."

Miss Meuhl emitted a shrill laugh. "Your fantasies are getting the better of you," she gasped. "In danger, indeed! Disposing of me! I've never heard anything so ridiculous."

"Stay in this office. Close and safe-lock the door. You've got food and water in the dispenser. I suggest you stock up, before they shut the supply down. Don't let anyone in, on any pretext whatever. I'll keep in touch with you via handphone."

"What are you planning to do?"

"If I don't make it back here, transmit the sealed record of this afternoon's conversation, along with the information I've given you. Beam it through on a Mayday priority. Then tell the Groaci what you've done and sit tight. I think you'll be all right. It won't be easy to blast in here and anyway, they won't make things worse by killing you in an obvious way. A Force can be here in a week."

"I'll do nothing of the sort! The Groaci are very fond

of me! You . . . Johnny-come-lately! Roughneck! Setting out to destroy—"

"Blame it on me if it will make you feel any better," Retief said, "but don't be fool enough to trust them." He pulled on a cape, and opened the door.

"I'll be back in a couple of hours," he said. Miss Meuhl stared after him silently as he closed the door.

It was an hour before dawn when Retief keyed the combination to the safe-lock and stepped into the darkened Consular office. Miss Meuhl, dozing in a chair, awoke with a start. She looked at Retief, rose, snapped on a light, and turned to stare.

"What in the world— Where have you been? What's happened to your clothing?"

"I got a little dirty—don't worry about it." Retief went to his desk, opened a drawer, and replaced the needler.

"Where have you been?" Miss Meuhl demanded. "I stayed here."

"I'm glad you did," Retief said. "I hope you piled up a supply of food and water from the dispenser, too. We'll be holed up here for a week, at least." He jotted figures on a pad. "Warm up the official sender. I have a long transmission for Sector Headquarters."

"Are you going to tell me where you've been?"

"I have a message to get off first, Miss Meuhl," Retief said sharply. "I've been to the Foreign Ministry," he added. "I'll tell you all about it later."

"At this hour? There's no one there."

"Exactly."

Miss Meuhl gasped. "You mean you broke in? You burgled the Foreign Office?"

"That's right," Retief said calmly. "Now—"

"This is absolutely the end," Miss Meuhl said. "Thank heaven I've already—"

"Get that sender going, woman! This is important."

"I've already done so, Mr. Retief!" Miss Meuhl said harshly. "I've been waiting for you to come back here." She turned to the communicator and flipped levers. The screen snapped aglow, and a wavering long-distance image appeared.

"He's here now," Miss Meuhl said to the screen. She looked at Retief triumphantly.

"That's good," said Retief. "I don't think the Groaci can knock us off the air, but—"

"I have done my duty, Mr. Retief; I made a full report of your activities to Sector Headquarters last night, as soon as you left this office. Any doubts I may have had as to the rightness of my decision have been completely dispelled by what you've just told me."

Retief looked at her levelly. "You've been a busy girl, Miss Meuhl. Did you mention the six Terrestrials who were killed here?"

"That had no bearing on the matter of your wild behavior. I must say, in all my years in the Corps, I've never encountered a personality less suited to diplomatic work."

The screen crackled, the ten-second transmission lag having elapsed. "Mr. Retief," the face on the screen said sternly, "I am Counselor Nitworth, DSO-1, Deputy Under-Secretary for the Sector. I have received a report on your conduct which makes it mandatory for me to relieve you administratively. Pending the findings of a Board of Inquiry, you will—"

Retief reached out and snapped off the communicator. The triumphant look faded from Miss Meuhl's face.

"Why, what is the meaning—"

"If I'd listened any longer, I might have heard something I couldn't ignore. I can't afford that, at this moment. Listen, Miss Meuhl," Retief went on earnestly, "I've found the missing cruiser. It's—"

"You heard him relieve you!"

"I heard him say he was going to, Miss Meuhl. But until I've heard and acknowledged a verbal order, it has no force. If I'm wrong, he'll get my resignation. If I'm right, that suspension would be embarrassing all around."

"You're defying lawful authority. I'm in charge here now." Miss Meuhl stepped to the local communicator.

"I'm going to report this terrible thing to the Groaci at once, and offer my profound—"

"Don't touch that screen," Retief said. "You go sit in that corner where I can keep an eye on you. I'm going to make a sealed tape for transmission to Headquarters, along with a call for an armed Task Force. Then we'll settle down to wait."

Retief, ignoring Miss Meuhl's fury, spoke into the recorder.

The local communicator chimed. Miss Meuhl jumped up and stared at it.

"Go ahead," Retief said. "Answer it."

A Groacian official appeared on the screen.

"Yolanda Meuhl," he said without preamble, "for the Foreign Minister of the Groacian Autonomy, I herewith accredit you as Terrestrial Consul to Groac, in accordance with the advice transmitted to my Government direct from the Terrestrial Headquarters. As Consul, you are requested to make available for questioning Mr. J. Retief, former Consul, in connection with the assault on two Peace Keepers, and illegal entry into the offices of the Ministry of Foreign Affairs."

"Why . . . why," Miss Meuhl stammered. "Yes, of course, and I do want to express my deepest regrets—"

Retief rose, went to the communicator, and assisted Miss Meuhl aside.

"Listen carefully, Fith," he said. "Your bluff has been called. You don't come in and we don't come out. Your camouflage worked for nine years, but it's all over now. I suggest you keep your heads and resist the temptation to make matters worse."

"Miss Meuhl," Fith replied, "a Peace Squad waits outside your Consulate. It is clear you are in the hands of a dangerous lunatic. As always, the Groaci wish only friendship with the Terrestrials, but—"

"Don't bother," Retief cut in. "You know what was in those files I looked over this morning."

Retief turned at a sound behind him. Miss Meuhl was at the door reaching for the safe-lock release.

"Don't!" Retief jumped . . . too late. The door burst inward, a crowd of crested Groaci pressed into the room, pushed Miss Meuhl back, and aimed scatter guns at Retief. Police Chief Shluh pushed forward.

"Attempt no violence, Terrestrial," he said. "I cannot promise to restrain my men."

"You're violating Terrestrial territory, Shluh," Retief said steadily. "I suggest you move back out the same way you came in."

"I invited them here," Miss Meuhl spoke up. "They are here at my express wish."

"Are they? Are you sure you meant to go this far, Miss Meuhl? A squad of armed Groaci in the Consulate?"

"You are the Consul, Miss Yolanda Meuhl," Shluh said. "Would it not be best if we removed this deranged person to a place of safety?"

"Yes," Miss Meuhl said. "You're quite right, Mr. Shluh. Please escort Mr. Retief to his quarters in this building."

"I don't advise you to violate my diplomatic immunity, Fith," Retief said.

"As Chief of Mission," Miss Meuhl said quickly, "I hereby waive immunity in the case of Mr. Retief."

Shluh produced a hand recorder. "Kindly repeat your statement, madam, officially," he said. "I wish no question—"

"Don't be a fool, woman," Retief said. "Don't you see what you're letting yourself in for? This would be a hell of a good time for you to figure out whose side you're on."

"I'm on the side of common decency!"

"You've been taken in. These people are concealing—"

"You think all women are fools, don't you, Mr. Retief?" She turned to the police chief and spoke into the microphone he held up.

"That's an illegal waiver," Retief said. "I'm Consul here, whatever rumors you've heard. This thing's coming out into the open, in spite of anything you can do; don't add violation of the Consulate to the list of Groacian atrocities."

"Take the man," Shluh said. Two tall Groaci came to Retief's side, guns aimed at his chest.

"Determined to hang yourselves, aren't you?" Retief said. "I hope you have sense enough not to lay a hand on this poor fool here." He jerked a thumb at Miss Meuhl. "She doesn't know anything. I hadn't had time to tell her yet. She thinks you're a band of angels."

The cop at Retief's side swung the butt of his scatter gun and connected solidly with Retief's jaw. Retief staggered against a Groacian, was caught and thrust upright, blood running down onto his shirt. Miss Meuhl yelped. Shluh barked at the guard in shrill Groacian, then turned to stare at Miss Meuhl.

"What has this man told you?"

"I—nothing. I refused to listen to his ravings."

"He said nothing to you of . . . some alleged . . . involvement."

"I've told you," Miss Meuhl said sharply. She looked at the expressionless Groaci, then back at the blood on Retief's shirt.

"He told me nothing," she whispered. "I swear it."

"Let it lie, boys," Retief said, "before you spoil that good impression."

Shluh looked at Miss Meuhl for a long moment. Then he turned.

"Let us go," he said. He turned back to Miss Meuhl. "Do not leave this building until further advice."

"But . . . I am the Terrestrial Consul."

"For your safety, madam. The people are aroused at the beating of Groacian nationals by an . . . alien."

"So long, Meuhlsie," Retief said. "You played it real foxy."

"You'll . . . lock him in his quarters?" Miss Meuhl said.

"What is done with him is now a Groacian affair, Miss Meuhl. You yourself have withdrawn the protection of your government."

"I didn't mean—"

"Don't start having second thoughts," Retief said. "They can make you miserable."

"I had no choice. I had to consider the best interest of the Service."

"My mistake, I guess. I was thinking of the best interests of a Terrestrial cruiser with three hundred men aboard."

"Enough," Shluh said. "Remove this criminal." He gestured to the Peace Keepers.

"Move along," he said to Retief. He turned to Miss Meuhl.

"A pleasure to deal with you, Madam."

The police car started up and pulled away. The Peace Keeper in the front seat turned to look at Retief.

"To have some sport with it, and then to kill it," he said.

"To have a fair trial first," Shluh said. The car rocked

and jounced, rounded a corner, and puffed along between ornamented pastel facades.

"To have a trial and then to have a bit of sport," the Peace Keeper said.

"To suck the eggs in your own hill," Retief said. "To make another stupid mistake."

Shluh raised his short ceremonial club and cracked Retief across the head. Retief shook his head, tensed—

The Peace Keeper in the front seat beside the driver turned and rammed the barrel of his scatter gun against Retief's ribs.

"To make no move, outworlder," he said. Shluh raised his club and carefully struck Retief again. He slumped.

The car, swaying, rounded another corner. Retief slid over against the police chief.

"To fend this animal—" Shluh began. His weak voice was cut off short as Retief's hand shot out, took him by the throat, and snapped him down onto the floor. As the guard on Retief's left lunged, Retief uppercut him, slamming his head against the door post. Retief grabbed the guard's scatter gun as it fell, and pushed it into the mandibles of the Groacian in the front seat.

"To put your pop-gun over the seat—carefully—and drop it," he said.

The driver slammed on his brakes, then whirled to raise his gun. Retief cracked a gun barrel against the head of the Groacian.

"To keep your eye-stalks on the road," he said. The driver grabbed at the tiller and shrank against the window, watching Retief with one eye, driving with another.

"To gun this thing," Retief said. "To keep moving."

Shluh stirred on the floor. Retief put a foot on him, pressing him back. The Peace Keeper beside Retief moved. Retief pushed him off the seat onto the floor. He held the scatter gun with one hand and mopped at the blood on his face with the other. The car bounded over the irregular surface of the road, puffing furiously.

"Your death will not be an easy one, Terrestrial," Shluh said in Terran.

"No easier than I can help," Retief said. "Shut up for now, I want to think."

The car, passing the last of the relief-encrusted mounds, sped along between tilled fields.

"Slow down," Retief said. The driver obeyed.

"Turn down this side road."

The car bumped off onto an unpaved surface, then threaded its way back among tall stalks.

"Stop here." The car stopped, blew off steam, and sat trembling as the hot engine idled.

Retief opened the door, taking his foot off Shluh.

"Sit up," he ordered. "You two in front listen carefully." Shluh sat up, rubbing his throat.

"Three of you are getting out here. Good old Shluh is going to stick around to drive for me. If I get that nervous feeling that you're after me, I'll toss him out. That will be pretty messy, at high speed. Shluh, tell them to sit tight until dark and forget about sounding any alarms. I'd hate to see you split open and spill all over the pavement."

"To burst your throat sac, evil-smelling beast!" Shluh hissed in Groacian.

"Sorry, I haven't got one." Retief put the gun under Shluh's ear. "Tell them, Shluh; I can drive myself, in a pinch."

"To do as the foreign one says; to stay hidden until dark," Shluh said.

"Everybody out," Retief said. "And take this with you." He nudged the unconscious Groacian. "Shluh, you get in the driver's seat. You others stay where I can see you."

Retief watched as the Groaci silently followed instructions.

"All right, Shluh," Retief said softly. "Let's go. Take me to Groac Spaceport by the shortest route that doesn't go through the city, and be very careful about making any sudden movements."

Forty minutes later Shluh steered the car up to the sentry-guarded gate in the security fence surrounding the military enclosure at Groac Spaceport.

"Don't yield to any rash impulses," Retief whispered as a crested Groacian soldier came up. Shluh grated his mandibles in helpless fury.

"Drone-master Shluh, Internal Security," he croaked. The guard tilted his eyes toward Retief.

"The guest of the Autonomy," Shluh added. "To let me pass or to rot in this spot, fool?"

"To pass, Drone-master," the sentry mumbled. He was still staring at Retief as the car moved jerkily away.

"You are as good as pegged-out on the hill in the pleasure pits now, Terrestrial," Shluh said in Terran. "Why do you venture here?"

"Pull over there in the shadow of the tower and stop," Retief said.

Shluh complied. Retief studied a row of four slender ships silhouetted against the early dawn colors of the sky.

"Which of those boats are ready to lift?" Retief demanded.

Shluh swiveled a choleric eye.

"All of them are shuttles; they have no range. They will not help you."

"To answer the question, Shluh, or to get another crack on the head."

"You are not like other Terrestrials, you are a mad dog."

"We'll rough out a character sketch of me later. Are they fueled up? You know the procedures here. Did those shuttles just get in, or is that the ready line?"

"Yes. All are fueled and ready for take-off."

"I hope you're right, Shluh. You and I are going to drive over and get in one; if it doesn't lift, I'll kill you and try the next one. Let's go."

"You are mad. I have told you: these boats have not more than ten thousand ton-seconds capacity; they are useful only for satellite runs."

"Never mind the details. Let's try the first in line."

Shluh let in the clutch and the steam car clanked and heaved, rolling off toward the line of boats.

"Not the first in line," Shluh said suddenly. "The last is the most likely to be fueled. But—"

"Smart grasshopper," Retief said. "Pull up to the entry port, hop out, and go right up. I'll be right behind you."

"The gangway guard. The challenging of—"

"More details. Just give him a dirty look and say what's necessary. You know the technique."

The car passed under the stern of the first boat, then the second. There was no alarm. It rounded the third and shuddered to a stop by the open port of the last vessel.

"Out," Retief said. "To make it snappy."

Shluh stepped from the car, hesitated as the guard came to attention, then hissed at him and mounted the steps. The guard looked wonderingly at Retief, mandibles slack.

"An outworlder!" he said. He unlimbered his scatter gun. "To stop here, meat-faced one."

Up ahead, Shluh turned.

"To snap to attention, litter-mate of drones," Retief rasped in Groacian. The guard jumped, waved his eye stalks, and came to attention.

"About face!" Retief hissed. "To hell out of here—march!"

The guard tramped off across the ramp. Retief took the steps two at a time, slammed the port shut behind himself.

"I'm glad your boys have a little discipline, Shluh," Retief said. "What did you say to him?"

"I but—"

"Never mind. We're in. Get up to the control compartment."

"What do you know of Groacian Naval vessels?"

"Plenty. This is a straight copy from the life boat you lads hijacked. I can run it. Get going."

Retief followed Shluh up the companionway into the cramped control room.

"Tie in, Shluh," Retief ordered.

"This is insane. We have only fuel enough for a one-way transit to the satellite; we cannot enter orbit, nor can we land again! To lift this boat is death. Release me. I promise you immunity."

"If I have to tie you in myself, I might bend your head in the process."

Shluh crawled onto the couch, and strapped in.

"Give it up," he said. "I will see that you are re-instated—with honor. I will guarantee a safe-conduct—"

"Count-down," Retief said. He threw in the autopilot.

"It is death!" Shluh screeched.

The gyros hummed, timers ticked, relays closed. Retief lay relaxed on the acceleration pad. Shluh breathed noisily, his mandibles clicking rapidly.

"That I had fled in time," he said in a hoarse whisper.
"This is not a good death."

"No death is a good death," Retief said, "not for a while
yet." The red light flashed on in the center of the panel,
and sound roared out into the breaking day. The ship
trembled, then lifted. Retief could hear Shluh's whimper-
ing even through the roar of the drive.

"Perihelion," Shluh said dully. "To begin now the long
fall back."

"Not quite," Retief said. "I figure eighty-five seconds
to go." He scanned the instruments, frowning.

"We will not reach the surface, of course," Shluh said.
"The pips on the screen are missiles. We have a rendezvous
in space, Retief. In your madness, may you be content."

"They're fifteen minutes behind us, Shluh. Your defenses
are sluggish."

"Nevermore to burrow in the grey sands of Groac,"
Shluh mourned.

Retief's eyes were fixed on a dial face.

"Any time now," he said softly. Shluh canted his eye
stalks.

"What do you seek?"

Retief stiffened. "Look at the screen," he said. Shluh
looked. A glowing point, off-center, moving rapidly across
the grid . . .

"What—?"

"Later—"

Shluh watched as Retief's eyes darted from one needle
to another.

"How . . ."

"For your own neck's sake, Shluh, you'd better hope this
works." He flipped the sending key.

"2396 TR-42 G, this is the Terrestrial Consul at Groac,
aboard Groac 902, vectoring on you at an MP fix of 91/
54/942. Can you read me? Over."

"What forlorn gesture is this?" Shluh whispered. "You
cry in the night to emptiness."

"Button your mandibles," Retief snapped, listening.
There was a faint hum of stellar background noise. Retief
repeated his call.

"Maybe they hear but can't answer," he muttered. He flipped the key.

"2396, you've got forty seconds to lock a tractor beam on me, before I shoot past you."

"To call into the void," said Shluh. "To—"

"Look at the DV screen."

Shluh twisted his head and looked. Against the background mist of stars, a shape loomed, dark and inert.

"It is . . . a ship," he said, "a monster ship . . ."

"That's her," Retief said. "Nine years and a few months out of New Terra on a routine mapping mission; the missing cruiser, *IVS Terrific.*"

"Impossible," Shluh hissed. "The hulk swings in a deep cometary orbit."

"Right, and now it's making its close swing past Groac."

"You think to match orbits with the derelict? Without power? Our meeting will be a violent one, if that is your intent."

"We won't hit; we'll make our pass at about five thousand yards."

"To what end, Terrestrial? You have found your lost ship; what then? Is this glimpse worth the death we die?"

"Maybe they're not dead," Retief said.

"Not dead?" Shluh lapsed into Groacian. "To have died in the burrow of one's youth. To have burst my throat sac before I embarked with a mad alien to call up the dead."

"2396, make it snappy," Retief called. The speaker crackled heedlessly. The dark image on the screen drifted past, dwindling now.

"Nine years, and the mad one is speaking as to friends," Shluh raved. "Nine years dead, and still to seek them."

"Another ten seconds," Retief said softly, "and we're out of range. Look alive, boys."

"Was this your plan, Retief?" Shluh reverted to Terran. "Did you flee Groac and risk all on this slender thread?"

"How long would I have lasted in a Groaci prison?"

"Long and long, my Retief," Shluh hissed, "under the blade of an artist."

Abruptly the ship trembled, seemed to drag, rolling the two passengers in their couches. Shluh hissed as the restraining harness cut into him. The shuttle boat was pivoting heavily, up-ending. Crushing acceleration forces built. Shluh gasped, crying out shrilly.

"What . . . is . . . it . . . ?"

"It looks," said Retief, "like we've had a little bit of luck."

"On our second pass," the gaunt-faced officer said, "they let fly with something. I don't know how it got past our screens. It socked home in the stern and put the main pipe off the air. I threw full power to the emergency shields, and broadcast our identification on a scatter that should have hit every receiver within a parsec; nothing. Then the transmitter blew. I was a fool to send the boat down, but I couldn't believe, somehow . . ."

"In a way it's lucky you did, Captain. That was my only lead."

"They tried to finish us after that. But, with full power to the screens, nothing they had could get through. Then they called on us to surrender."

Retief nodded. "I take it you weren't tempted?"

"More than you know. It was a long swing out on our first circuit. Then coming back in, we figured we'd hit. As a last resort I would have pulled back power from the screens and tried to adjust the orbit with the steering jets, but the bombardment was pretty heavy. I don't think we'd have made it. Then we swung past and headed out again. We've got a three-year period. Don't think I didn't consider throwing in the towel."

"Why didn't you?"

"The information we have is important. We've got plenty of stores aboard, enough for another ten years, if necessary. Sooner or later I knew a Corps search vessel would find us."

Retief cleared his throat. "I'm glad you stuck with it, Captain. Even a backwater world like Groac can kill a lot of people when it runs amok."

"What I didn't know," the captain went on, "was that we're not in a stable orbit. We're going to graze atmosphere pretty deeply this pass, and in another sixty days we'd be back to stay. I guess the Groaci would be ready for us."

"No wonder they were sitting on this so tight. They were almost in the clear."

"And you're here now," the captain said. "Nine years, and we weren't forgotten. I knew we could count on—"

"It's over now, Captain. That's what counts."

"Home . . . After nine years . . ."

"I'd like to take a look at the films you mentioned," Retief said. "The ones showing the installations on the satellite."

The captain complied. Retief watched as the scene unrolled, showing the bleak surface of the tiny moon as the *Terrific* had seen it, nine years before. In harsh black and white, row on row of identical hulls cast long shadows across the pitted metallic surface of the satellite.

"They had quite a little surprise planned; your visit must have panicked them," Retief said.

"They should be about ready to go, by now. Nine years . . ."

"Hold that picture," Retief said suddenly. "What's that ragged black line across the plain there?"

"I think it's a fissure. The crystalline structure—"

"I've got what may be an idea," Retief said. "I had a look at some classified files last night, at the Foreign Office. One was a progress report on a fissionable stock-pile. It didn't make much sense at the time. Now I get the picture. Which is the north end of that crevasse?"

"At the top of the picture."

"Unless I'm badly mistaken, that's the bomb dump. The Groaci like to tuck things underground. I wonder what a direct hit with a 50 megaton missile would do to it?"

"If that's an ordnance storage dump," the captain said, "it's an experiment I'd like to try."

"Can you hit it?"

"I've got fifty heavy missiles aboard. If I fire them in direct sequence, it should saturate the defenses. Yes, I can hit it."

"The range isn't too great?"

"These are the deluxe models." The captain smiled balefully. "Video guidance. We could steer them into a bar and park 'em on a stool."

"What do you say we try it?"

"I've been wanting a solid target for a long time," the captain said.

✧   ✧   ✧

Half an hour later, Retief propelled Shluh into a seat before the screen.

"That expanding dust cloud used to be the satellite of Groac, Shluh," he said. "Looks like something happened to it."

The police chief stared at the picture.

"Too bad," Retief said. "But then it wasn't of any importance, was it, Shluh?"

Shluh muttered incomprehensibly.

"Just a bare hunk of iron, Shluh, as the Foreign Office assured me when I asked for information."

"I wish you'd keep your prisoner out of sight," the captain said. "I have a hard time keeping my hands off him."

"Shluh wants to help, Captain. He's been a bad boy and I have a feeling he'd like to co-operate with us now, especially in view of the eminent arrival of a Terrestrial ship, and the dust cloud out there," Retief said.

"What do you mean?"

"Captain, you can ride it out for another week, contact the ship when it arrives, get a tow in, and your troubles are over. When your films are shown in the proper quarter, a Peace Force will come out here and reduce Groac to a sub-technical cultural level and set up a monitor system to insure she doesn't get any more expansionist ideas—not that she can do much now, with her handy iron mine in the sky gone."

"That's right, and—"

"On the other hand, there's what I might call the diplomatic approach . . ."

He explained at length. The captain looked at him thoughtfully.

"I'll go along," he said. "What about this fellow?"

Retief turned to Shluh. The Groacian shuddered, retracting his eye stalks.

"I will do it," he said faintly.

"Right," Retief said. "Captain, if you'll have your men bring in the transmitter from the shuttle, I'll place a call to a fellow named Fith at the Foreign Office." He turned to Shluh. "And when I get him, Shluh, you'll do everything exactly as I've told you—or have Terrestrial monitors dictating in Groac City."

"Quite candidly, Retief," Counselor Nitworth said, "I'm rather nonplussed. Mr. Fith of the Foreign Office seemed almost painfully lavish in your praise. He seems most eager to please you. In the light of some of the evidence I've turned up of highly irregular behavior on your part, it's difficult to understand."

"Fith and I have been through a lot together," Retief said. "We understand each other."

"You have no cause for complacency, Retief," Nitworth said. "Miss Meuhl was quite justified in reporting your case. Of course, had she known that you were assisting Mr. Fith in his marvelous work, she would have modified her report somewhat, no doubt. You should have confided in her."

"Fith wanted to keep it secret, in case it didn't work out. You know how it is."

"Of course. And as soon as Miss Meuhl recovers from her nervous breakdown, there'll be a nice promotion awaiting her. The girl more than deserves it for her years of unswerving devotion to Corps policy."

"Unswerving," Retief said. "I'll go along with that."

"As well you may, Retief. You've not acquitted yourself well in this assignment. I'm arranging for a transfer; you've alienated too many of the local people."

"But as you said, Fith speaks highly of me . . ."

"True. It's the cultural intelligentsia I'm referring to. Miss Meuhl's records show that you deliberately affronted a number of influential groups by boycotting—"

"Tone deaf," Retief said. "To me a Groacian blowing a nose-whistle sounds like a Groacian blowing a nose-whistle."

"You have to come to terms with local aesthetic values. Learn to know the people as they really are. It's apparent from some of the remarks Miss Meuhl quoted in her report that you held the Groaci in rather low esteem. But how wrong you were. All the while they were working unceasingly to rescue those brave lads marooned aboard our cruiser. They pressed on, even after we ourselves had abandoned the search. And when they discovered that it had been a collision with their satellite which disabled the craft, they made that magnificent gesture—unprecedented. One hundred thousand credits in gold to each crew member, as a token of Groacian sympathy."

"A handsome gesture," Retief murmured.

"I hope, Retief, that you've learned from this incident. In view of the helpful part you played in advising Mr. Fith in matters of procedure to assist in his search, I'm not recommending a reduction in grade. We'll overlook the affair, give you a clean slate. But in the future, I'll be watching you closely."

"You can't win 'em all," Retief said.

"You'd better pack up; you'll be coming along with us in the morning." Nitworth shuffled his papers together. "I'm sorry that I can't file a more flattering report on you. I would have liked to recommend your promotion, along with Miss Meuhl's."

"That's okay," Retief said. "I have my memories."

---

1) Cf. The original colorful language: "maintenance of a state of tension short of actual conflict." See CDT File 178/b/491, col. VII, spool 12: 745mm (code 2g)

" . . . into the chaotic Galactic political scene of the post-Concordiat era, the CDT emerged to carry forward the ancient diplomatic tradition as a great supranational organization dedicated to the contravention of war.[1] As mediators of disputes among Terrestrial-settled worlds and advocates of Terrestrial interests in contacts with alien cultures, Corps diplomats, trained in the chanceries of innumerable defunct bureaucracies, displayed an encyclopedic grasp of the nuances of Estra-Terrestrial mores as set against the labyrinthine socio-politico-economic Galactic context. Ever-zealous in its enforcement of peace, the Corps traditionally has functioned at its most scintillating level under the threat of imminent annihilation. Facing overwhelming forces at Roolit I, steely-eyed Ambassador Nitworth met the challenge unflinchingly, coolly planning his *coup* . . ."

—extract from the *Official History of the Corps Diplomatique*, Vol I, Reel 2. Solarian Press, New York, 479 A. E. (AD 2940)

ULTIMATUM

Ambassador Nitworth glowered across his mirror-polished, nine-foot platinum desk at his assembled staff.

"Gentlemen, are any of your familiar with a race known as the Qornt?"

There was a moment of profound silence. Nitworth nodded portentously.

"They were a warlike race, known in this sector back

in Corcordiat times—perhaps two hundred years ago. They vanished as suddenly as they had appeared. There was no record of where they went." He paused for effect.

"They have now reappeared—occupying the inner planet of this system!"

"But, sir," Second Secretary Magnan offered. "That's uninhabited Terrestrial territory . . ."

"Indeed, Mr. Magnan . . ." Nitworth smiled icily. "It appears the Qornt do not share that opinion." He plucked a heavy parchment from a folder before him, harrumphed and read aloud:

> HIS SUPREME EXCELLENCY THE QORNT, REGENT OF QORNT, OVERLORD OF THE GALACTIC DESTINY, GREETS THE TERRES-TRIALS AND WITH REFERENCE TO THE PRESENCE IN QORNT MANDATED TERRI-TORY OF TERRESTRIAL SQUATTERS, HAS THE HONOR TO ADVISE THAT HE WILL REQUIRE THE USE OF HIS OUTER WORLD ON THE THIRTIETH DAY: THEN WILL THE QUORT COME WITH STEEL AND FIRE, RECEIVE, TERRESTRIALS, RENEWED ASSURANCES OF MY AWARENESS OF YOUR EXISTENCE, AND LET THOSE WHO DARE GIRD FOR THE CON-TEST.

"Frankly, I wouldn't call it conciliatory," Magnan said. Nitworth tapped the paper with a finger.

"We have been served, gentlemen, with nothing less than an ultimatum!"

"Well, we'll soon straighten these fellows out—" the Military Attaché began.

"There happens to be more to this piece of truculence than appears on the surface," the Ambassador cut in. He paused, waiting for interested frowns to settle into place.

"Note, gentlemen, that these invaders have appeared in force on Terrestrial-controlled soil—and without so much as a flicker from the instruments of the Navigational Monitor Service!"

The Military Attaché blinked. "That's absurd," he said flatly. Nitworth slapped the table.

"We're up against something new, gentlemen! I've considered every hypothesis from cloaks of invisibility to time travel! The fact is—the Qornt fleets are indetectible!"

The Military Attaché pulled at his lower lip. "In that case, we can't try conclusions with these fellows until we have an indetectible drive of our own. I recommend a crash project; in the meantime—"

"I'll have my boys start in to crack this thing," Chief of the Confidential Terrestrial Source Section spoke up. "I'll fit out a couple of volunteers with plastic beaks—"

"No cloak and dagger work, gentlemen! Long range policy will be worked out by Deep-Think teams back at the Department. Our role will be a holding action. Now, I want suggestions for a comprehensive, well-rounded, and decisive course for meeting this threat. Any recommendations?"

The Political Officer placed his fingertips together. "What about a stiff Note demanding an extra week's time?"

"No! No begging," the Economic Officer objected. "I'd say a calm, dignified, aggressive withdrawal—as soon as possible."

"We don't want to give them the idea we spook easily," the Military Attaché said. "Let's delay the withdrawal—say, until tomorrow."

"Early tomorrow," Magnan said. "Or maybe later today."

"Well, I see you're of a mind with me," Nitworth commented, nodding. "Our plan of action is clear, but it remains to be implemented. We have a population of over fifteen million individuals to relocate." He eyed the Political Officer. "I want five proposals for resettlement on my desk by oh-eight-hundred hours tomorrow . . ." Nitworth rapped out instructions; harried-looking staff members arose and hurried from the room. Magnan eased toward the door.

"Where are you going, Magnan?" Nitworth snapped.

"Since you're so busy, I thought I'd just slip back down to Com Inq. It was a most interesting orientation lecture, Mr. Secretary. Be sure to let us know how it works out—"

"Kindly return to your chair," Nitworth said coldly. "A number of chores remain to be assigned. I think you need a little field experience. I want you to get over to Roolit I and take a look at these Qornt personally."

Magnan's mouth opened and closed soundlessly.

"Not afraid of a few Qornt, are you, Magnan?"

"Afraid? Good lord, no, ha ha. It's just that I'm afraid I may lose my head and do something rash."

"Nonsense! A diplomat is immune to heroic impulses. Take Retief along. No dawdling now! I want you on the way in two hours. Notify the transport pool at once."

Magnan nodded unhappily and went out into the hall.

"Oh, Retief," Nitworth said. Retief turned.

"Try to restrain Mr. Magnan from any impulsive moves—in any direction."

Retief and Magnan topped a ridge and looked down across a slope of towering tree-shrubs and glossy violet-stemmed palms set among flamboyant blossoms of yellow and red, reaching down to a strip of white beach with the blue sea beyond.

"A delightful vista," Magnan said, mopping at his face. "A pity we couldn't locate the Qornt. We'll go back now and report—"

"I'm pretty sure the settlement is off to the right," Retief said. "Why don't you head back for the boat, while I ease over and see what I can observe."

"Retief, we're engaged in a serious mission. This is not a time to think of sight-seeing."

"I'd like to take a good look at what we're giving away."

"See here, Retief! One might almost receive the impression that you're questioning Corps policy."

"One might, at that. The Qornt have made their play—but I think it might be valuable to take a look at their cards before we fold. If I'm not back at the boat in an hour, lift without me."

"You expect me to make my way back alone?"

"It's directly down-slope—" Retief broke off, listening. Magnan clutched at his arm. There was a sound of crackling foliage. Twenty feet ahead, a leafy branch swung aside. An eight-foot biped stepped into view; long, thin green-clad legs and back-bending knees moved in quick, bird-like steps. A pair of immense black-lensed goggles covered staring eyes set among bushy green hair above a great bone-white beak. The crest bobbed as the creature cocked its head, listening.

Magnan gulped audibly. The Qornt froze, head tilted, beak aimed directly at the spot where the Terrestrials stood in the deep shade of a giant trunk.

"I'll go for help," Magnan squeaked. He whirled and took three leaps into the brush; a second great green-clad figure rose up to block his way. He spun, darted to the left. The first Qornt pounced, grappled Magnan to its narrow chest. Magnan yelled, threshing and kicking, broke free, turned—and collided with the nine-foot alien, coming in fast from the right. All three went down in a tangle of limbs.

Retief jumped forward, hauled Magnan free, thrust him aside, and stopped, right fist cocked. The two Qornt lay groaning, moving feebly.

"Nice piece of work, Mr. Magnan," Retief said. "You nailed both of them."

"Those, undoubtedly, are the most blood-thirsty, aggressive, merciless countenances it has ever been my misfortune to encounter," Magnan said. "It hardly seems fair; eight feet tall AND faces like that . . ."

The smaller of the two captive Qornt ran long, slender fingers over a bony shin from which he had turned back the tight-fitting green trousers.

"It's not broken," he whistled nasally in passable Terrestrial, eyeing Magnan through the heavy goggles, now badly cracked. "Small thanks to you."

Magnan smiled loftily. "I daresay you'll think twice before interfering with peaceable diplomats in future."

"Diplomats? Surely you jest."

"Never mind us," Retief said. "It's you fellows we'd like to talk about. How many of you are there?"

"Only Zubb and myself—"

"I mean altogether. How many Qornt?"

The alien whistled shrilly.

"Here, no signaling!" Magnan snapped, looking around.

"That was merely an expression of amusement—"

"You find the situation amusing? I assure you, sir, you are in perilous straits at the moment. I MAY fly into another rage, you know."

"Please, restrain yourself. I was merely somewhat astonished—" a small whistle escaped—"at being taken for a Qornt."

"Aren't you a Qornt?"

"I? Great snail trails, no!" More stifled whistles of amusement escaped the beaked face. "Both Zubb and I are Verpp. Naturalists, as it happens."

"You certainly LOOK like Qornt."

"Oh, not at all—except perhaps to a Terrestrial. The Qornt are sturdily-built rascals, all over ten feet in height. And, of course, they do nothing but quarrel. A drone caste, actually."

"A caste? You mean they're biologically the same as you—"

"Not at all! A Verpp wouldn't think of fertilizing a Qornt."

"I mean to say, you're of the same basic stock—descended from a common ancestor, perhaps."

"We are all Pud's creatures."

"What are the differences between you and them?"

"Why, the Qornt are argumentative, boastful, lacking in appreciation for the finer things of life. One dreads to contemplate descending to their level."

"Do you know anything about a Note passed to the Terrestrial Ambassador at Smørbrød?"

The beak twitched. "Smørbrød? I know of no place called Smørbrød."

"The outer planet of this system."

"Oh, yes; we call it Guzzum. I had heard that some sort of creatures had established a settlement there, but I confess I pay little note to such matters."

"We're wasting time, Retief," Magnan said. "We must truss these chaps up, hurry back to the boat, and make our escape. You heard what they said—"

"Are there any Qornt down there at the harbor, where the boats are?" Retief asked.

"At Tarroon, you mean? Oh, yes. A large number; the Qornt are making ready for one of their adventures."

"That would be the invasion of Smørbrød," Magnan said. "And unless we hurry, Retief, we're likely to be caught there with the last of the evacuees—"

"How many Qornt would you say there are at Tarroon?"

"Oh, a very large number. Perhaps fifteen or twenty."

"Fifteen or twenty what?" Magnan looked perplexed.

"Fifteen or twenty Qornt."

"You mean that there are only fifteen or twenty individual Qornt in all?"

Another whistle. "Not at all. I was referring to the local Qornt only. There are more at the other Centers, of course."

"And the Qornt are responsible for the Ultimatum—unilaterally?"

"I suppose so; it sounds like them. A truculent group, you know. And interplanetary relations are rather a hobby of theirs."

Zubb moaned and stirred. He sat up slowly, rubbing his head. He spoke to his companion in a shrill alien clatter of consonants.

"What did he say?"

"Poor Zubb. He blames me for his bruises, since it was my idea to gather you as specimens."

"You should have known better than to tackle that fierce-looking creature," Zubb said, pointing his beak at Magnan.

"How does it happen that you speak Terrestrial?" Retief asked.

"Oh, one picks up all sorts of dialects."

"It's quite charming, really," Magnan said. "Such a quaint, archaic accent."

"Suppose we went down to Tarroon," Retief asked. "What kind of reception would we get?"

"That depends. I wouldn't recommend interfering with the Gwil or the Rheuk; it's their nest-mending time, you know. The Boog will be busy mating—such a tedious business—and of course the Qornt are tied up with their ceremonial feasting. I'm afraid no one will take any notice of you."

"Do you mean to say," Magnan demanded, "that these ferocious Qornt, who have issued an ultimatum to the Corps Diplomatique Terrestrienne—who openly avow their intention to invade a Terrestrial-occupied world—would ignore Terrestrials in their midst?"

"If at all possible."

Retief got to his feet.

"I think our course is clear, Mr. Magnan. It's up to us to go down and attract a little attention."

"I'm not at all sure we're going about this in the right way," Magnan puffed, trotting at Retief's side. "These fellows Zubb and Slun—oh, they seem affable enough—but how can we be sure we're not being led into a trap?"

"We can't."

Magnan stopped short. "Let's go back."

"All right," Retief said. "Of course, there may be an ambush—"

Magnan moved off. "Let's keep going."

The party emerged from the undergrowth at the edge of a great brush-grown mound. Slun took the lead, rounded the flank of the mound, halted at a rectangular opening cut into the slope.

"You can find your way easily enough from here," he said. "You'll excuse us, I hope—"

"Nonsense, Slun!" Zubb pushed forward. "I'll escort our guests to Qornt Hall." He twittered briefly to his fellow Verpp. Slun twittered back.

"I don't like it, Retief," Magnan whispered. "Those fellows are plotting mischief."

"Threaten them with violence, Mr. Magnan. They're scared of you."

"That's true—but the drubbing they received was well-deserved. I'm a patient man, but there are occasions—"

"Come along, please," Zubb called. "Another ten minutes' walk—"

"See here, we have no interest in investigating this barrow," Magnan announced. "We wish you to take us direct to Tarroon to interview your military leaders regarding the Ultimatum!"

"Yes, yes, of course. Qornt Hall lies here inside the village."

"This is Tarroon?"

"A modest civic center, sir, but there are those who love it."

"No wonder we didn't observe their works from the air,"

Magnan muttered. "Camouflaged." He moved hesitantly through the opening.

The party moved along a wide, deserted tunnel which sloped down steeply, then leveled off and branched. Zubb took the center branch, ducking slightly under the nine-foot ceiling lit at intervals with what appeared to be primitive incandescent panels.

"Few signs of an advanced technology here," Magnan whispered. "These creatures must devote all their talents to war-like enterprise."

Ahead, Zubb slowed. A distant susurration was audible, a sustained high-pitched screeching. "Softly, now. We approach Qornt Hall. They can be an irascible lot when disturbed at their feasting."

"When will the feast be over?" Magnan called hoarsely.

"In another few weeks, I should imagine, if, as you say, they've scheduled an invasion for next month."

"Look here, Zubb." Magnan shook a finger at the tall alien. "How is it that these Qornt are allowed to embark on piratical ventures of this sort without reference to the wishes of the majority—"

"Oh, the majority of the Qornt favor the move, I imagine."

"A handful of hotheads are permitted to embroil the planet in war?"

"Oh, they don't embroil the planet in war. It's merely a Qornt enterprise. We Verpp ignore such goings-on."

"Retief, this is fantastic! I've heard of iron-fisted military cliques before, but this is madness!"

"Come softly, now . . ." Zubb beckoned, moving toward a bend in the yellow-lit corridor. Retief and Magnan moved forward. The corridor debouched through a high double door into a vast oval chamber, high-domed, gloomy, paneled in dark wood and hung with tattered banners, scarred halberds, pikes, rusted longswords, crossed spears, patinaed hauberks, pitted radiation armor, corroded power rifles, the immense mummified heads of horned and fanged animals. Great guttering torches in wall brackets and in stands along the length of the long table shed a smoky light that reflected from the mirror polish of the red granite floor, gleamed on polished silver bowls and paper-thin glass, shone jewel-red and gold through dark bottles—and cast long flickering shadows behind the fifteen trolls who loomed in their places at the board. Lesser trolls—beaked, bush-haired, great-eyed—trotted briskly, bird-kneed, bearing steaming platters, stood in groups of three strumming slender bottle-shaped lutes, or pranced in intricately-patterned dance, unnoticed in the shrill uproar as each of the magnificently draped, belted, feathered, and bejeweled Qornt carried on a shouted conversation with an equally noisy fellow.

"A most interesting display of barbaric splendor," Magnan breathed. "Now we'd better be getting back—"

"Ah, a moment," Zubb said. "Observe the Qorn—the tallest of the feasters—he with the headdress of crimson, purple, silver and pink—"

"Twelve feet if he's an inch," Magnan estimated. "And now we really must hurry along—"

"That one is chief among these rowdies. I'm sure you'll want a word with him. He controls not only the Tarroonian vessels but those from the other Centers as well."

"What kind of vessels? Warships?"

"Certainly. What other kind would the Qornt bother with?"

"I don't suppose," Magnan said casually, "that you'd know the type, tonnage, armament, and manning of these vessels? And how many units comprise the fleet? And where they're based at present?"

"They're fully automated twenty-thousand ton all-purpose dreadnoughts. They mount a variety of weapons—the Qornt are fond of that sort of thing—and each of the Qornt has his own, of course. They're virtually identical, except for the personal touches each individual has given his ship."

"Great Heavens, Retief!" Magnan exclaimed in a whisper. "It sounds as though these brutes employ a battle armada as simpler souls might a set of toy sailboats!"

Retief stepped past Magnan and Zubb to study the feasting hall. "I can see that their votes would carry all the necessary weight."

"And, now, an interview with the Qorn himself," Zubb shrilled. "If you'll kindly step along, gentlemen . . ."

"That won't be necessary," Magnan said hastily. "I've decided to refer the entire matter to a committee—"

"After having come so far," Zubb said, "it would be a pity to miss having a cozy chat . . ."

There was a pause.

"Ah . . . Retief," Magnan said. "Zubb has just presented a most compelling argument . . ."

Retief turned. Zubb stood, gripping an ornately decorated power pistol in one bony hand, a slim needler in the other. Both were pointed at Magnan's chest.

"I suspected you had hidden qualities, Zubb," Retief commented.

"See here, Zubb; we're diplomats—" Magnan started.

"Careful, Mr. Magnan; you may goad him to a frenzy."

"By no means," Zubb whistled. "I much prefer to observe the frenzy of the Qornt when presented with the news that two peaceful Verpp have been assaulted and kidnapped by bullying interlopers. If there's anything that annoys the Qornt, it's Qornt-like behavior in others. Now, step along, please."

"Rest assured, this will be reported—"

"I doubt it."

"You'll face the wrath of Enlightened Galactic Opinion—"

"Oh? How big a navy does Enlightened Galactic Opinion have?"

"Stop scaring him, Mr. Magnan. He may get nervous and shoot." Retief stepped into the banquet hall, headed for the resplendent figure at the head of the table. A trio of flute-players broke off in mid-bleat, staring. An inverted pyramid of tumblers blinked as Retief swung past, followed by Magnan and the tall Verpp. The shrill chatter at the table faded.

Qorn turned as Retief came up, blinking three-inch eyes. Zubb stepped forward, gibbered, waving his arms excitedly. Qorn pushed back his chair—a low, heavily padded stool—and stared unwinking at Retief, moving his head to bring first one great round eye, then the other, to bear. There were small blue veins in the immense fleshy beak. The bushy hair, springing out in a giant halo around the grey-ish, porous-skinned face, was wiry, stiff, moss-green, with tufts of chartreuse fuzz surrounding what appeared to be tympanic membranes. The tall headdress of scarlet silk and purple feathers was slightly askew, and a loop of pink pearls had slipped down above one eye.

Zubb finished his speech, fell silent, breathing hard.

Qorn looked Retief over in silence, then belched.

"Not bad," Retief said admiringly. "Maybe we could get up a match between you and Ambassador Sternwheeler. You've got the volume on him, but he could spot you points on timber."

"So," Qorn hooted in a resonant tenor. "You come from Guzzum, eh? Or Smørbrød, as I think you call it. What is it you're after? More time? A compromise? Negotiations? Peace?" He slammed a bony hand against the table. "The answer is NO!"

Zubb twittered. Qorn cocked an eye, motioned to a servant. "Chain him, then . . ." he indicated Magnan. His eyes went to Retief. "This one's bigger; you'd best chain him, too."

"Why, your Excellency—" Magnan started, stepping forward.

"Stay back!" Qorn hooted. "Stand over there where I can keep an eye on you."

"Your Excellency, I'm empowered—"

"Not here, you're not!" Qorn trumpeted. "Want peace, do you? Well, I don't want peace! I've had a surfeit of peace these last two centuries! I want action! Loot! Adventure! Glory!" He turned to look down the table. "How about it fellows? It's war to the knife, eh?"

There was a momentary silence.

"I guess so," grunted a giant Qornt in iridescent blue with flame-colored plumes.

Qorn's eyes bulged. He half rose. "We've been all over this!" he bassooned. He clamped bony fingers on the hilt of a light rapier. "I thought I'd made my point . . ."

"Oh, sure, Qorn."

"You bet."

"I'm convinced."

Qorn rumbled and resumed his seat. "All for one and one for all, that's us."

"And you're the one, eh Qorn?" Retief commented.

Magnan cleared his throat. "I sense that some of you gentlemen are not convinced of the wisdom of this move," he piped, looking along the table at the silks, jewels, beaks, feather-decked crests, and staring eyes.

"Silence!" Qorn hooted. "No use your talking to my loyal lieutenants anyway," he added. "They do whatever I convince them they ought to do."

"But I'm sure that on more mature consideration—"

"I can lick any Qornt in the house," Qorn said. "That's why I'm Qorn." He belched again.

A servant came up staggering under a weight of chain, dropped it with a crash at Magnan's feet. Zubb aimed the guns while the servant wrapped three loops around Magnan's wrists, snapped a lock in place.

"You, next!" The guns pointed at Retief's chest. He held out his arms. Four loops of silvery-grey chain in half-inch links dropped around them. The servant cinched them up tight, squeezed a lock through the ends and closed it.

"Now," Qorn said, lolling back in his chair, glass in hand. "There's a bit of sport to be had here, lads. What shall we do with them?"

"Let them go," the blue and flame Qornt said glumly.

"You can do better than that," Qorn hooted. "Now, here's a suggestion: we carve them up a little—lop off the external labiae and pinnae, say—and ship them back—"

"Good lord! Retief, he's talking about cutting off our ears and sending us home mutilated! What a barbaric proposal!"

"It wouldn't be the first time a Terrestrial diplomat got a trimming," Retief commented.

"It should have the effect of stimulating the Terries to put up a reasonable scrap," Qorn said judiciously. "I have a feeling that they're thinking of giving up without a struggle."

"Oh, I doubt that," the blue-and-flame Qornt said. "Why should they?"

Qorn rolled an eye at Retief and another at Magnan. "Take these two," he hooted. "I'll wager they came here to negotiate a surrender!"

"Well," Magnan started.

"Hold it, Mr. Magnan," Retief said, "I'll tell him."

"What's your proposal?" Qorn whistled, taking a gulp

from his goblet. "A fifty-fifty split? Monetary reparations? Alternate territory? I can assure you, it's useless. We Qornt LIKE to fight—"

"I'm afraid you've gotten the wrong impression, Your Excellency," Retief said blandly. "We didn't come to negotiate. We came to deliver an ultimatum . . ."

"What?" Qorn trumpeted. Behind Retief, Magnan spluttered.

"We plan to use this planet for target practice," Retief said. "A new type hell bomb we've worked out. Have all your people off of it in seventy-two hours, or suffer the consequences."

"You have the gall," Qorn stormed, "to stand here in the center of Qornt Hall—uninvited, at that—and in chains—"

"Oh, these," Retief said. He tensed his arms; the soft aluminum links stretched, broke. He shook the light metal free. "We diplomats like to go along with colorful local customs, but I wouldn't want to mislead you. Now, as to the evacuation of Roolit I—"

Zubb screeched, waved the guns. The Qornt at the table craned, jabbering.

"I told you they were brutes," Zubb shrilled.

Qorn slammed his fist down on the table. "I don't care what they are!" he honked. "Evacuate, hell! I can field eighty-five combat-ready ships—"

"And we can englobe every one of them with a thousand Peace Enforcers, with a hundred megatons/second firepower each."

"Retief—" Magnan tugged at his sleeve. "Don't forget their superdrive—"

"That's all right; they don't have one."

"But—"

"We'll take you on!" Qorn French-horned. "We're the Qorn! We glory in battle! We live in fame or go down in—"

"Hogwash," the flame-and-blue Qornt cut in. "If it wasn't for you, Qorn, we could sit around and feast and brag and enjoy life without having to prove anything."

"Qorn, you seem to be the firebrand here," Retief

said. "I think the rest of the boys would listen to reason—"

"Over my dead body!"

"My idea exactly," Retief said. "You claim you can lick any man in the house. Unwind yourself from your ribbons and step out here on the floor, and we'll see how good you are at backing up your conversation."

Magnan hovered at Retief's side. "Twelve feet tall," he moaned. "And did you notice the size of those hands?"

Retief watched as Qorn's aides helped him out of his formal trappings. "I wouldn't worry too much, Mr. Magnan. This is a light-Gee world. I doubt if old Qorn would weigh up at more than two-fifty standard pounds here."

"But that phenomenal reach—"

"I'll peck away at him at knee level; when he bends over to swat me, I'll get a crack at him."

Across the cleared floor, Qorn shook off his helpers with a snort.

"Enough! Let me at the upstart!"

Retief moved out to meet him, watching the upraised backward-jointed arms. Qorn stalked forward, long lean legs bent, long horny feet clacking against the polished floor. The other aliens—both servitors and bejeweled Qornt— formed a wide circle, all eyes unwaveringly on the combatants.

Qorn struck suddenly, a long arm flashing down in a vicious cut at Retief, who leaned aside, caught a lean shank below the knee. Qorn bent to haul Retief from his leg—and staggered back as a haymaker took him just below the beak. A screech went up from the crowd as Retief leaped clear.

Qorn hissed and charged. Retief whirled aside, then struck the alien's off-leg in a flying tackle. Qorn leaned, arms windmilling, crashed to the floor. Retief whirled, dived for the left arm, whipped it behind the narrow back, seized Qorn's neck in a stranglehold, and threw his weight backward. Qorn fell on his back, his legs squatted out at an awkward angle. He squawked, beat his free arm on the floor, reaching in vain for Retief.

Zubb stepped forward, pistols ready. Magnan stepped before him.

"Need I remind you, sir," he said icily, "that this is an official diplomatic function? I can brook no interference from disinterested parties."

Zubb hesitated. Magnan held out a hand. "I must ask you to hand me your weapons, Zubb."

"Look here," Zubb began.

"I MAY lose my temper," Magnan hinted. Zubb lowered the guns, passed them to Magnan. He thrust them into his belt with a sour smile, turned back to watch the encounter.

Retief had thrown a turn of violet silk around Qorn's left wrist, bound it to the alien's neck. Another wisp of stuff floated from Qorn's shoulder. Retief, still holding Qorn in an awkward sprawl, wrapped it around one outflung leg, trussed ankle and thigh together. Qorn flopped, hooting. At each movement, the constricting loop around his neck jerked his head back, the green crest tossing wildly.

"If I were you, I'd relax," Retief said, rising and releasing his grip. Qorn got a leg under him. Retief kicked it. Qorn's chin hit the floor with a hollow clack. He wilted, an ungainly tangle of over-long limbs and gay silks.

Retief turned to the watching crowd. "Next?" he called.

The blue and flame Qornt stepped forward. "Maybe this would be a good time to elect a new leader," he said. "Now, my qualifications—"

"Sit down," Retief said loudly. He stepped to the head of the table, seated himself in Qorn's vacated chair. "A couple of you finish trussing Qorn up; then stack him in the corner—"

"But we must select a leader!"

"That won't be necessary, boys. I'm your new leader."

"As I see it," Retief said, dribbling cigar ashes into an empty wine glass, "you Qornt like to be warriors, but you don't particularly like to fight."

"We don't mind a little fighting—within reason. And, of course, as Qornt, we're expected to die in battle. But what I say is—why rush things?"

"I have a suggestion," Magnan said. "Why not turn the reins of government over to the Verpp? They seem a level-headed group—"

"What good would that do? Qornt are Qornt; and it seems

there's always one among us who's a slave to instinct—and, naturally, we have to follow him."

"Why?"

"Because that's the way it's done."

"Why not do it another way?" Magnan offered. "Now, I'd like to suggest Community singing—"

"If we gave up fighting, we might live too long; then what would happen?"

"Live too long . . ." Magnan looked puzzled.

"When estivating time comes, there'd be no burrows for us; and anyway, with the new Qornt stepping in next Awakening—"

"I've lost the thread," Magnan said. "Who are the new Qornt?"

"After estivating, the Verpp moult, and then they're Qornt, of course. The Gwil become Boog, the Boog become Rheuk, the Rheuk metamorphosize into Verpp—"

"You mean Slun and Zubb—the mild-mannered naturalists—will become warmongers like Qorn?"

"Very likely; 'the milder the Verpp, the wilder the Qornt,' as the old saying goes."

"What do Qornt turn into?" Retief asked.

"Hmmmm. That's a good question. So far, none have survived Qornthood."

"Have you thought of forsaking your warlike ways?" Magnan asked. "What about taking up sheepherding and regular church attendance—"

"Don't mistake me. We Qornt like a military life. It's great sport to sit around roaring fires and drink and tell lies and then go dashing off to enjoy a brisk affray and some leisurely looting afterward. But we prefer a nice numerical advantage. Now, this business of tackling you Terrestrials over on Guzzum—that was a mad notion. We had no idea what your strength was—"

"But now that's all off, of course," Magnan chirped. "Now that we've had diplomatic relations and all—"

"Oh, by no means. The fleet lifts in thirty days; after all, we're Qornt; we have to satisfy our drive to action."

"But Mr. Retief is your leader, now. He won't let you . . ."

"Only a dead Qornt stays home when Attack Day comes.

And even if he orders us all to cut our own throats, there are still the other Centers—all with their own leaders. No, gentlemen, the invasion is definitely on."

"Why don't you go invade somebody else?" Magnan suggested. "Now, I could name some very attractive prospects—outside my sector, of course."

"Hold everything," Retief said. "I think we've got the basis of a deal here . . ."

At the head of a double column of gaudily caparisoned Qornt, Retief and Magnan strolled across the ramp toward the bright tower of the CDT Sector HQ. Ahead, gates opened, and a black Corps limousine emerged, flying an Ambassadorial flag below a plain white banner.

"Curious," Magnan commented. "I wonder what the significance of the white ensign might be?"

Retief raised a hand. The column halted with a clash of accoutrements, a rasp of Qornt boots. Retief looked back along the line. The high white sun flashed on bright silks, polished buckles, deep-dyed plumes, ceremonial swords, the polished butts of pistols, the soft gleam of leather.

"A brave show indeed," Magnan commented approvingly. "I confess the idea has merit—"

The limousine pulled up with a squeal of brakes, stood on two fat-tired wheels, tyros humming softly. The hatch popped up. A portly diplomat stepped out.

"Why, Ambassador Nitworth," Magnan glowed. "This is very kind of you—"

"Keep cool, Magnan," Nitworth said in a strained voice. "We'll attempt to get you out of this . . ." He stepped past Magnan's outstretched hand and looked hesitantly at the ramrod-straight line of Qornt, eighty-five strong—and beyond at the eighty-five tall Qornt dreadnoughts.

"Good afternoon, sir . . . ah, Your Excellency," Nitworth said, blinking up at the leading Qornt. "You are Commander of the Strike Force, I assume?"

"Nope," the Qornt said shortly.

"I . . . ah . . . wish to request seventy-two hours in which to evacuate the Headquarters," Nitworth plowed on.

"Mr. Ambassador," Retief said. "This—"

"Don't panic, Retief. I'll attempt to secure your release," Nitworth hissed over his shoulder. "Now—"

"You will address our leader with more respect!" the tall Qornt hooted, eyeing Nitworth ominously from eleven feet up.

"Oh, yes indeed, sir . . . Your Excellency . . . Commander. Now, about the invasion—"

"Mr. Secretary," Magnan tugged at Nitworth's sleeve.

"In heaven's name, permit me to negotiate in peace!" Nitworth snapped. He rearranged his features. "Now, Your Excellency, we've arranged to evacuate Smørbrød, of course, just as you requested—"

"Requested?" the Qornt honked.

"Ah . . . demanded, that is. Quite rightly of course. Ordered. Instructed. And, of course, we'll be only too pleased to follow any other instructions you might have—"

"You don't quite get the big picture, Mr. Secretary," Retief said. "This isn't—"

"Silence, confound you!" Nitworth barked. The leading Qornt looked at Retief. He nodded. Two bony hands shot out, seized Nitworth, and stuffed a length of bright pink silk into his mouth, then spun him around and held him facing Retief.

"If you don't mind my taking this opportunity to brief you, Mr. Ambassador," Retief said blandly, "I think I should mention that this isn't an invasion fleet. These are the new recruits for the Peace Enforcement Corps."

Magnan stepped forward, glanced at the gag in Ambassador Nitworth's mouth, hesitated, then cleared his throat. "We felt," he said, "that the establishment of a Foreign Brigade with the P E Corps structure would provide the element of novelty the Department has requested in our recruiting, and at the same time would remove the stigma of Terrestrial chauvinism from future punitive operations."

Nitworth stared, eyes bulging. He grunted, reaching for the gag, caught the Qornt's eye on him, dropped his hands to his sides.

"I suggest we get the troops in out of the hot sun," Retief said. Magnan edged closer. "What about the gag?" he whispered.

"Let's leave it where it is for a while," Retief murmured. "It may save us a few concessions."

An hour later, Nitworth, breathing freely again, glowered across his desk at Retief and Magnan.

"This entire affair," he rumbled, "has made me appear to be a fool!"

"But we who are privileged to serve on your staff already know just how clever you are," Magnan burbled.

Nitworth purpled. "You're skirting insolence, Magnan," he roared. "Why was I not informed of the arrangements? What was I to assume at the sight of eighty-five war vessels over my headquarters, unannounced?"

"We tried to get through, but our wave-lengths—"

"Bah! Sterner souls than I would have quailed at the spectacle of those armed horrors advancing."

"Oh, you were perfectly justified in panicking—"

"I did NOT panic!" Nitworth bellowed. "I merely adjusted to the apparent circumstances. Now, I'm of two minds as to the advisability of this foreign legion idea of yours. Still, it may have merit. I believe the wisest course would be to dispatch them on a long training cruise in an uninhabited sector of space—"

The office windows rattled. "What the devil—!" Nitworth turned, stared out at the ramp where a Qornt ship rose slowly on a column of pale blue light. The vibration increased as a second ship lifted, then a third—

Nitworth whirled on Magnan. "What's this! Who ordered these recruits to embark without my permission?"

"I took the liberty of giving them an errand to run, Mr. Secretary," Retief said. "There was that little matter of the Groaci infiltrating the Sirenian System. I sent the boys off to handle it."

"Call them back! Call them back at once!"

"I'm afraid that won't be possible. They're under orders to maintain total communications silence until completion of the mission."

Nitworth drummed his fingers on the desk top. Slowly, a thoughtful expression dawned. He nodded. "This may work out," he said. "I should call them back, but since the fleet is out of contact, I'm unable to do so, correct? Thus,

I can hardly be held responsible for any over-enthusiasm in chastising the Groaci." He closed one eye in a broad wink at Magnan.

"Very well, gentlemen, I'll overlook the irregularity this time. Magnan, see to it the Smørbrødian public are notified they can remain where they are. And by the way, did you by any chance discover the technique of the indetectible drive the Qornt use?"

"No, sir. That is, yes, sir."

"Well? Well?"

"There isn't any. The Qornt were there all the while. Underground."

"Underground? Doing what?"

"Hibernating—for two hundred years at a stretch."

Outside in the corridor, Magnan came up to Retief, who stood talking to a tall man in a pilot's coverall.

"I'll be tied up, sending through full details on my—our—your recruiting scheme, Retief," Magnan said. "Suppose you run into the city to assist the new Verpp Consul in settling in."

"I'll do that, Mr. Magnan. Anything else?"

Magnan raised his eyebrows. "You're remarkably compliant today, Retief. I'll arrange transportation—"

"Don't bother, Mr. Magnan. Cy here will run me over. He was the pilot who ferried us over to Roolit I, you recall."

Magnan nodded curtly.

"I'll be with you as soon as I pack a few phone numbers, Retief," the pilot said. He moved off. Magnan followed him with a disapproving eye. "An uncouth sort, I fancied. I trust you're not consorting with his kind socially . . ."

"I wouldn't say that, exactly," Retief said. "We just want to go over a few figures together."

"The ancient defender of the principle of self-determination of peoples threw the elite of its diplomatic shock troops into the fight when local tradition was threatened at Elora. Holding himself aloof from internal bickering, Ambassador Hidebinder dealt shrewdly with diverse elements of the power picture, to forge a bright new page in Corps history . . ."

—Vol. VIII, Reel 7, 450 AE (AD 2951)

THE PRINCE AND THE PIRATE

Retief reined in the tall-shouldered urze-beast with a jangle of the hunting-bells attached to the long-legged mount's harness. The trail of the dirosaur led straight ahead, into a dense thicket of iron-rod trees fifty feet distant, now bent and twisted by the passing of the wounded monster. Far away, the hunting horns of the main party sounded; Retief smiled. Prince Tavilan would employ a choice selection of royal oaths when he learned that a mere diplomat had beaten him to the quarry's turn-at-bay . . .

A windy screech sounded from the depths of the thicket; Retief raised his saddle-horn, blew an answering blast. There was a clanging of branches, a scraping of armored hide on metallic bark. Retief dropped the horn to swing at the pommel; with a pull of a lever, he cocked his cross-bow, sat his mount, waiting. A tiny head, mostly jaws, armed with a foot-long spike below the mouth, snaked out from the grove, hissing a ferocious warning. Retief's urze-beast stirred, tossed its head at the scent of the dirosaur. Trees shuddered aside as the great carnivore forced its bulk between them, its golden-yellow eyes fixed on the man. A clawed foreleg as big as a man's body set with rusty scales raked the ground, dragging the predator's multi-ton bulk into the clear. With a final clangorous flick of its log-like tail, the dirosaur broke free, reared its head into striking position, and charged. Retief raised the cross-bow, took aim—

The cross-bow bucked; Retief spurred aside; he had a momentary glimpse of a two-foot shaft of polished steel protruding from the eye socket of the monster as it blundered past, the long neck falling, to collapse in a cloud of dust, lie twitching, then still.

It was five minutes before the hunt galloped into view, Prince Tavilan's black crested urze-beast in the lead. He slowed to a canter, rode up beside the fallen dirosaur, sat looking down at the open-jawed head, the yellow eyes, glazing in death.

"That's another barrel of royal vintage I owe you, Retief," he said. "If I ever see the palace cellars again." He was a tall, wide, sandy-haired man with a turned-up sunburned-nose. His leather forest garb was well worn; there were cockleburrs in the snow-tiger facings of his royal Eloran blue cape. The cross-bow slung across his back was his only weapon.

"We're wasting time hunting game," a rider at the prince's side said. "There's a plentiful supply of cross-bow bolts at the lodge; I propose we ride down to Elora City and distribute them among the good Prime Minister's Greenbacks—point first."

"The King still has hopes the CDT will revise its policy," Tavilan glanced at Retief. "If the triple-damned embargo were lifted, Minister Prouch and his talk of a regency would evaporate faster than the royal treasury has under his control."

"Oh, it's not an Embargo, Your Highness," Retief said. "I believe Ambassador Hidebinder refers to it as a unilateral shift in emphasis balance-of-trade-wise to a more group-oriented—"

"What it adds up to is the Royal Eloran Navy grounded, while traitors plot in the palace and Dangredi's pirates raid shipping at the edge of Eloran atmosphere!" Tavilan smacked a fist into his palm. "I've got the finest corps of naval-combat commanders in the Eastern Arm, forty-five battle-ready ships of the line—and, thanks to CDT policy, no fuel! So much for my co-operation with your Ambassador, Retief!"

"Didn't he explain that, Your Highness? If you had the Big Picture, it would all make sense. Of course, I'm a Small Picture man myself, so I'm afraid I can't be of much help."

"It's not your doing, Retief. But ten million Elorans are about to have a dictatorship clamped on them because I lack a few megaton/seconds of firepower . . ."

"Your great-grandfather's mistake was in being a romantic. If he'd named his planet Drab Conformity, set up a committee of bureaucrats to run it and used the forest to supply paper mills instead of hunting in them, you'd be the apple of the collective CDT eye today."

"The old man led a hard life; when he found Elora it was a wilderness. He made his fortune—and then arranged matters here to suit himself—and we Elorans still like parties!"

Retief glanced at the sun. "Speaking of which, I'd better be starting back; the Grande Balle d'Elore is tonight and Mr. Magnan will be upset if I'm not there to help him hover nervously for at least an hour before the Ambassador comes down."

"Retief, you're not riding back to the city . . . ?" Count Arrol looked up from cutting out the dirosaur's chin-horn. He stood. "I told you what my man reported. Your sympathies are too well-known to suit Prouch. Tonight, at the ball—"

"I don't think the worthy Prime Minister will go that far. He's dependent on the good will of the CDT—and diplomat-killing is bad publicity."

"The Palace Guard is still loyal," Tavilan said. "And remember the lad, Aric; you can trust him with any mission within his strength. He's working in the palace as a mess-servant." He laughed bitterly. "Think of us as you dance with the fair ladies of the court, Retief. If you see my father, tell him that my Invincibles and I will continue to skulk here in the Deep Forest as he commands—but we long for action."

"I'll get word to you, Tavilan," Retief said. "My

conspiratorial instinct tells me that there'll be action enough for everybody before sunrise tomorrow."

In the Grand Ballroom at the Palace of Elora, Retief cast an eye over the chattering elite of the court, the gorgeously gowned and uniformed couples, the glum representatives of the People's Party, the gaudily uniformed diplomats from Yill, Fust, Flamme, and half a hundred other worlds. A cluster of spider-lean Groaci whispered together near a potted man-eating plant, one leaf of which quivered tentatively, seemed to sniff the aliens, withdrew hastily. Retief plucked a glass from a wide silver tray offered by a bright-eyed mess-boy in a brocaded bolero jacket and a cloth-of-gold turban, who glanced quickly around the crowded ballroom, then stepped close to whisper:

"Mr. Retief—the rascals are forcing the lock on your room!"

Retief passed the glass under his nose, sipped.

"Exactly which rascals do you mean, Aric?" he murmured. "We've got about four sets to choose from."

Aric grinned. "A couple of the Groaci Ambassador's boys," he whispered. "The ones he usually uses for high-class back-alley work."

Retief nodded. "That would be Yilith and Sith, formerly of the Groaci Secret Police. Things must be coming to a head. It's not like old Lhiss to take such direct action." He finished the drink in his hand, put the empty glass on a black marble table.

"Come on, Aric. Ditch that tray and let's take a walk."

In the broad mirror-hung corridor, Retief turned to the right.

"But, Mr. Retief," Aric said. "Your apartment's in the other direction . . ."

"They won't find anything there, Aric—and it would be embarrassing for all concerned if I caught them red-handed. So while they're occupied, I'll just take this opportunity to search their rooms."

At the top of the wide spiral staircase that led from the public areas of the palace to the living quarters assigned to foreign diplomatic missions, Retief paused.

"You wait here, Aric." He went along the corridor to the third door, a simple white-painted panel edged with a tiny carved floral design. He tried the large gold door-knob, then took a slender instrument from an inner pocket of his silver-epauletted tangerine mess jacket and delicately probed the lock. The bolt snicked back. He eased the door open, glanced around, then stepped back out and beckoned Aric to him.

"How'd you get it open, Mr. Retief?"

"Locks are a hobby of mine. Patrol the corridor, and if you see anybody, cough. If it's one of my Groaci colleagues, have a regular paroxysm. I won't be long."

Inside the room, Retief made a fast check of the desk, the dresser drawers, the undersides of furniture. He slapped sofa cushions, prodded mattresses for telltale cracklings, then opened the closet door. Through the wall, faint voices were audible, scratchy with the quality of narrow-range amplification. He stooped, plucked a tiny earphone from a miniature wall bracket. Ambassador Lhiss, it appeared, was not immune from eavesdropping by his own staff.

Retief put the 'phone to his ear.

" . . . agreed, then," Ambassador Hidebinder's voice was saying. "Seventy-two hours from now, and not a moment before."

"Just see that you keep your end of the bargain," a thin Groaci voice lisped. "This would be a poor time for treachery . . ."

"I want it clearly understood that our man will be treated in a reasonably civilized fashion, and quietly released to us when the affair is completed."

"I suggest you avoid over-complicating the arrangements with last minute conditions," the Groaci voice said.

"You've done very well in this affair," Hidebinder came back. "Your profits on the armaments alone—"

"As I recall, it was you who proposed the scheme; it is you who wish to place homeless Soetti rabble on Elora, not we . . ."

Retief listened for another five minutes before he snapped the phone back in its bracket, stepped quickly to the door; in the hall, Aric came to meet him.

"Find anything, Mr. Retief?"

"Too much . . ." Retief took a pen from his pocket, jotted a note.

"See that this gets to Prince Tavilan at the lodge; tell him to get the Invincibles ready, but to do nothing until I get word to him—no matter what."

"Sure, Mr. Retief, but—"

"Let's go, Aric. And remember: you're more help to me outside than inside . . ."

"I don't follow you, Mr. Retief . . ." Aric trotted at his side. "Outside what . . . ?"

"We'll know in a few minutes; but wherever I wind up, watch for a signal . . ."

From the head of the Grand Staircase, Retief saw the glint of light on steel. Two men in the dull black and green of the People's Volunteers stood in the corridor.

"Hey, Mr. Retief," Aric whispered. "What are Greenbacks doing in the palace . . . ?"

"Simple, Aric. They're standing guard over my door."

"Maybe somebody caught those Groaci trying to break in . . ."

"Drop back behind me, Aric—and remember what I said . . ."

Retief walked up to his door, took out an old-fashioned mechanical key, inserted it in the lock. One of the two armed soldiers stepped up, made a threatening motion with his rifle butt.

"Nobody goes in there, you," he growled. He was a broad-faced blonde, a descendant of the transported felons who had served as contract labor on Elora a century earlier.

Retief turned casually, moved to one side far enough that the man before him was between him and his companion, then moved suddenly, caught the stock of the rifle in his left hand and with his right yanked the barrel forward; the butt described a short arc, smashed against the soldier's chin. He gave a choked yell, stumbled back. Retief jerked the door open, slipped inside, slammed it behind him. He shot the bolt, then started a fast check of his room. The door rattled; heavy poundings sounded. Retief pulled open the desk; a loose heap of unfamiliar papers lay there. A glance at one showed the letterhead of the Office of the Commercial Attaché, Terrestrial Embassy. It appeared to be a delivery order for one hundred thousand rounds of fractional-ton ammunition made out to a Bogan armaments exporter. Another was an unsigned letter referring to drop-points and large sums of money. A heavy parchment caught Retief's eye. It was stamped in red: UTTER TOP SECRET. Below the seal of the Eloran Imperial Department of War was a detailed break-out of the disposition of units of the Imperial Fleet and the Volunteer Reserve.

The telephone buzzed. Retief picked it up. There was a sound of breathing at the other end.

"Yilith . . . ?" a faint voice inquired.

"No, you damned fool!" Retief snapped. "They finished up ten minutes ago. When do the Greenbacks arrive?"

"Why, they should be there now. The pigeon has left the ballroom—" There was a pause. "Who is this?"

Retief slammed down the phone, whirled to the wide fireplace, flipped the switch that started a cheery blaze licking over the pseudo-logs. He grabbed up a handful of papers from the desk, tossed them into the fire, started back for another—

With a rending of tough plastic panels, the door bulged, then slammed open. Half a dozen Greenbacks charged into the room, short bayonets fixed and leveled. Retief's hand went behind him, felt over the small table at his back, plucked open the drawer, fished out a tiny slug gun, dropped it into a back pocket.

A tall man with a small head, a body like a bag of water, and tiny feet bellied his way through the armed men. He wore a drab cutaway of greyish-green adorned with the star of the Order of Farm Production. Behind him, the small, spindle-armed figure of the Groaci Military Attaché was visible, decked out in formal jewel-studded eyeshields and a pink and green hip-cloak.

"Don't touch anything!" the water-bag man called in a high, excited voice. "I want everything undisturbed!"

"What about the fire, Mr. Minister?" the Groaci lisped. "The miscreant seems to have been burning something . . ."

"Yes, yes. Rake those papers out of there!" The large man wobbled his chin agitatedly. He fixed Retief with eyes like peeled eggs. "I'm warning you, don't make any violent moves—"

"Let me have a crack at him," a Greenback said. "He fixed Horney so he won't be able to eat nothing but mush for six months—"

"None of that!" the big-bellied man folded his arms. A striped vest bulged under his voluminous frock coat like a feather mattress. "We'll just hold him for the criminal authorities."

"Any particular reason why you and your friends came to play in my room?" Retief inquired mildly. "Or were you under the impression it was my birthday?"

"Look here," a man called from across the room. "Under the mattress . . ." He held up a paper. "A letter from the pirate, Dangredi, addressed to Retief, thanking him for the latest consignment of arms and supplies!"

"If you'll wait just a minute," Retief said, "I'll get my scrapbook; it's full of all kinds of incriminating evidence I've been saving for just this occasion."

"Ah, then you confess! Where is it?" the Groaci whispered hoarsely, pushing to the fore.

"Oh, I forgot; when I heard you coming, I ate it."

There was a stir at the rear of the group. The ranks parted and a short, round Terrestrial with a stiff white moustache and a mouth like a change-purse pushed through. He yanked at the overlapping lapels of a grape-juice colored mess-jacket caked with decorations.

"Here, what's this, Mr. Retief! Contraband? Pilfered documents? Evidence of traffic with piratical elements?"

"No, Mr. Ambassador," Retief said, "I'm only charging them with breaking and entering, assault with a deadly weapon, abuse of diplomatic privilege, and loitering. If you'll—"

"Here, don't let him confuse the issue, Ambassador Hidebinder!" The egg-like eyes rolled toward the stout diplomat. "He stands self-convicted—"

"Don't say too much, Mr. Minister," Retief cut in. "After all, you haven't had time yet to read those scraps the boys are fishing out of the fire, so it wouldn't do for you to know what they are."

"Enough of this pointless chatter!" Prime Minister

Prouch piped. "Obviously, there's treason afoot here!" He jabbed a finger at the Terrestrial Ambassador. "In view of the seriousness of the offense—in a time of grave crisis in inter-world affairs—I demand that you suspend this criminal's diplomatic immunity!"

The Groaci spoke up: "As a neutral party, I propose that he be turned over to my mission for restraint until the time of trial."

"Well . . ." Ambassador Hidebinder blinked. "I'm not at all sure . . ."

"We'll tolerate no stalling tactics!" the Minister squeaked. "The security of Elora is at stake!" He motioned. The troops closed in around Retief.

"I propose to take this man into custody at once," he bulged his eyes at Hidebinder. "I trust there will be no protest . . . !"

Hidebinder looked around at the room, the scattered papers, the smoldering fire, then past Retief's ear.

"Your penchant for mischief is well-known, Mr. Retief," he said solemnly. "I'm sure this fits the pattern nicely."

"Not as nicely as you seem to imagine," Retief said. "Maybe you'd better think it over—without any help from Ambassador Lhiss."

Hidebinder purpled; he sputtered. "The man's insane! You have my permission to place him under protective restraint!" He stamped from the room.

General Hish stepped forward. "Soldiers, you heard the order of the Minister," he hissed. "Take the criminal away . . ."

The cell was ten feet square, with a twelve by eighteen inch opening just under the ten-foot high ceiling. The furnishings included a plastic cot with one blanket, the minimum in plumbing facilities, one small, unshielded neon lamp, numerous large roaches, and a bristly rat over a foot long, which sat by the open floor drain from which it had emerged, regarding Retief with beady eyes.

Retief's hand went slowly to the small, hard pillow on the cot beside him. He picked it up, pegged it suddenly; with a squeal of rage, the rat dove for cover, scrabbled for a moment in a frantic attempt to squirm past the cushion, now wedged in the drain; then it darted for the darkest corner of the cell.

Retief picked up the blanket and a length of yarn worked from it earlier, moved toward the rat. It crouched, making a sound like a rusty-bed-spring. Suddenly it leaped—straight at Retief's face—and met the enveloping blanket in mid-air. Cautiously, Retief folded back the blanket to expose the chinless, snouted face, armed with back-slanting yellow fangs half an inch long. He looped the string over the vicious head, drew it snug, and knotted it.

He went to the drain, kicked the obstruction from it, then released the tethered rat. It dived down the dark opening and was gone. The carefully coiled string paid out rapidly, loop after loop. It slowed, then fed down the drain more slowly as the rat traveled through the piping. The guard's footsteps approached, Retief jumped for the cot; he was stretched out at ease when the sentry looked in. When he had passed, Retief looped the end of the string over his finger, pulled in the slack. In the gloomy light of the neon lamp, the thread was invisible against the dark floor. He sat on the bunk and waited.

An hour passed. The barred rectangle of moonlight slanting through the window crept across the floor. Regularly, at nine minute intervals, feet sounded in the passage outside the metal slab door. Suddenly the string in Retief's hand twitched, once, twice, three times. He gave three answering tugs. For a moment there was no response; then there was a single firm tug. Aric was on the job . . .

Retief pulled at the string; it dragged heavily. He hauled it in slowly, hand over hand. Twice it caught on some obstruction far away in the drain line; he tugged gently until it came free. He thrust the accumulating pile of thread under the mattress. Each time the guard looked in, he was sitting quietly, staring at the wall. Suddenly, the end of a half-inch rope appeared, securely tied to the end of the string. Retief let it slip back a few inches, waited until the sentry passed, then quickly began hauling in the rope.

Five minutes later, a hundred feet of polyon cable was tucked out of sight under the mattress. Retief slipped the bundle of hacksaw blades which had been tied to the end

of the rope into the pocket of the gold-braided white
trousers which he had been allowed to retain along with
his short boots. He stood under the window, gauged the
distance, then jumped; he pulled himself up, got a firm
grip on the bars, then took out a saw and started in.

An hour later, both bars were cut through, ready to be
removed by a single firm twist. Retief waited for the guard
to pass, then dropped the blades down the drain, looped
the cable over his shoulder and leaped up to the window
again. Far below, he could see the moonlight sparkling on
a fountain in the palace garden; the shadows of trees and
hedges were dark against the grass. On the graveled walks,
armed sentries passed.

Retief wrenched the bars free, tied the rope to one,
tossed the coil of rope through the window, then pulled
himself up, and carefully fitted the short bar across the
corner of the window opening on the inside. Keeping
pressure on the rope, he eased out, then slid quickly
down.

Twenty feet below, Retief dropped onto a narrow balcony before a rank of darkened glass doors. With a flick,
he freed the upper end of the rope; the bar clattered
against the stone wall as it fell; he pulled the rope in,
dropped it in a heap, then tried door handles, found one
that turned. He stepped in through heavy drapes, felt his
way across to a door, opened it and looked out into a wide
corridor. At the far end, two ornately uniformed guards
stood stiffly at attention. There was no one else in sight.
Retief slipped the slug gun into the palm of his hand,
stepped out, walked boldly toward the guards. They stood
unmoving. As he passed, one spoke quietly from the corner of his mouth:

"Greenback patrolling one flight up . . ."

"They're on the look-out for any suspicious activity," the
other sentry added.

"If you see any, let us know," the first said.

"I'll do that," Retief said softly. "If you hear any loud
noises, pay no attention. General Hish will be entertaining
a guest . . ."

Retief followed the corridor, took a turn to the left, then

a right, found the passage housing the Groaci Embassy, now brightly lit. The apartment of the Military Attaché was on the left, four doors along . . .

A black-booted Greenback officer stepped into view from the far end of the passage, paused at sight of Retief striding unconcernedly toward him. The Greenback narrowed his eyes uncertainly, started along the corridor toward Retief. At fifteen feet, sure now of the identity of the intruder, he snapped back the flap covering his sidearm, tugged at the heavy power pistol. Retief brought the slug gun up, fired at point-blank range. At the muffled whoomp! the officer slammed back, hit the floor and lay sprawled; his gun bounced against the wall. Retief scooped it up, turned to the door of the Groaci General's quarters, needle-beamed the lock at low power. The hardware dissolved in a wash of blue flame, an acrid stink of burned plastic and metal. He kicked the door wide, caught the fallen Greenback by the ankles, dragged him inside. A swift examination of the room revealed that it was deserted. He picked up the phone, dialed.

"Post number twenty-nine," a crisp voice answered promptly.

"This is the General's guest," Retief said. "The light in the hall might hurt the General's eyes; corridor 9-C. Think you could douse it?"

"We've had some trouble with fuses in that wing lately; I've got a feeling one might go out any minute now—and it will take maybe an hour to fix." The phone clicked off.

Retief flipped off the lights in the room, went into the small, lavishly equipped kitchen, rummaged through the supplies of Groaci delicacies, found a one-pound jar of caviar and a package of grain wafers. He ate hurriedly, keeping an eye on the door, drank a small bottle of Green Yill wine, then returned to the living room. He stripped the Greenback, donned the drab uniform.

The phone buzzed. Retief went to it, lifted the receiver.

"Two minute alert," a low voice said. "He's alone . . ."

Retief went to the door, opened it half an inch, stood in the shadows beside it. He heard the soft approach of mincing Groaci footsteps, then a soft exclamation—

He swung the door open, reached out, caught the Groaci

by the throat and dragged him inside. He grunted as a booted foot caught him in the ribs; then he jammed the pistol hard against the Groaci's horny thorax.

"No loud noises, please, General; it's my hour for meditation . . ."

Retief pushed the door shut with a foot, leaned against the light button; a soft glow sprang up. Retief released the Groaci, holding the gun aimed at a three-inch broad *Grand Cordon* of the Legion d'Cosme crossing the bulging abdomen.

"I'm going out; you're coming with me. Better hope we make it."

He holstered the pistol, showed the small, smooth-stone-shaped slug gun. "This will be a foot from your back, so be a good little soldier and give all the right answers."

The Groaci's throat sacs dilated, vibrating. He cast a sidelong glance at the stripped body of the Greenback.

"The swift inevitability of your death," he hissed in Groaci. "To anticipate with joy your end in frightful torment . . ."

"To button your mandible and march," Retief interrupted. He pulled the door open. "After you, General . . ."

The blaze of stars scattered from horizon to horizon above the palace roof gleamed on the polished fittings of a low-slung heli parked on the royal pad. As Retief and his prisoner emerged from the service stair into the cold night air, there was a crunch of boots on gravel, the snick! of a power gun's action. A dark shadow moved before Retief. Abruptly a searchlight's beam glared in his eyes.

"Stand aside, idiot!" the Groaci hissed. The light flashed across to him; five beady, stemmed eyes glinted angrily at the guard.

"General Hish, sir . . ." The guard snapped off the light, presented arms hurriedly. Other boots sounded, coming across the rooftop helipad.

"What's going on here? Tell these—" the voice broke off. In the gloom, barely relieved by starlight, Retief saw the newcomer start, then put a hand to his pistol butt.

"We require the use of the royal gig," Hish whispered. "Stand aside!"

"But the orders—" the first guard started.

"General, drop!" the second bawled, hauling his gun out. Retief shot him, took a short step and drove a hard punch to the jaw of the first Greenback, then caught the Groaci's arm, jumped for the heli. Yells sounded across the roof. A yard-wide light-cannon, gymbal-mounted atop the guard shack, winked on, throwing a grey-blue tunnel of light into the sky; it pivoted, depressed, swept a burning disc across to Retief—

He drew the power pistol, thumbed it to narrow beam, blasted the light; it exploded in a shower of tinkling glass, a billow of orange smoke that faded, winked out.

Retief shoved the slender Groaci ahead of him, yanked wide the heli's entry hatch, tumbled his prisoner in, jumped after him. He flipped switches, rammed the control lever to EMERGENCY FULL CLIMB. With a whine of power, the finely-engineered craft leaped from the roof, surged upward in a buffet of suddenly stirred air. From below, the blue and yellow flashes of blasters winked briefly against the discs of the screaming rotors; then they dwindled away and were gone.

Half an hour later, Retief dropped the heli in low over the black tree-tops of the Deep Forest. A gleam of light reflected across rippling water. He edged the machine forward, swung out over the lake; below, the water churned in the down-draft from the rotors as the heli settled gently into two feet of water. Retief cut the engine and popped the hatch. Cold mountain air swirled in; somewhere, water lizards shrilled.

"What place of infamy is this?" the captive general hissed. He stared out into the darkness. "Do you bring me here to slay me unseen, vile disrespecter of diplomatic privilege?"

"The idea has merit," Retief said, "but I have other plans for you, General." He climbed down, motioned the Groaci out. Hish grumbled, scrambling down into the icy water of the lake, slogging to shore. From the darkness, a night-fowl called. Retief whistled a reply. There was the sound of a footstep in the brush, the click! of a cross-bow's cocking mechanism.

"It's Retief," he called. "I have a guest: General Hish, of the Groaci Embassy."

"Ah, welcome, Retief," a soft voice drawled. "We're honored, General. Good of you to call. His Highness was hoping you'd be along soon . . ."

Inside the high-beamed lodge, Prince Tavilan came across the room; behind him, Aric grinned.

"I caught the rat all right, Mr. Retief—"

"Retief!" Tavilan clapped him on the shoulder. "Aric reached me with your message an hour ago. I heard the news of your arrest on Tri-D; they broke into a concert to announce that a plot involving the CDT and reactionary Royalist elements had been uncovered."

"Hidebinder will be very unhappy with that version of events," Retief said. "The agreement was that it was all to be blamed on a rotten apple in the Corps barrel, namely me—"

"We were saddling up to storm the palace and free you, when your message reached me—"

"How many reliable men do you have available on short notice, Your Highness?" Retief cut in.

"I have thirty-eight of the Invincibles with me here; at least three others are under arrest on various pretexts. Four more managed to report in that they're pinned down by 'protective escorts' but we can still strike—"

Retief shook his head. "That was the idea of arresting me, Your Highness—as a personal challenge to you, since my sympathies are well-known. Prouch wanted to bring you out into the open. An armed attack was just what he needed—and he was ready for you. He has at least two hundred Greenbacks in the palace—armed to the nines. Your raid would have been the signal for his take-over—to preserve the domestic tranquility, of course—and your death in the fighting would have left him a clear field."

"What about the Palace Guard? They haven't gone over . . . ?"

"Of course not . . ." Retief accepted a cigar, took a seat by the fire. "They're standing fast, playing it by ear. The Grand Ball tonight gave them an excuse for full dress, including weapons, of course. The Greenbacks aren't quite ready to start anything with them—yet."

Tavilan stamped across the fire-beast-hide rug. "Blast it, Retief, we can't sit here and watch Prouch and his mob move in unopposed! If we hit them now—before they've had time to consolidate—"

"—you'll get every Royalist supporter in Elora City killed," Retief finished for him. "Now, let's consider the situation. Item: the Royal Fleet is grounded, courtesy of CDT policy. Item two: Prouch's People's Volunteer Naval Reserve Detachment of late-model Bogan destroyers is sitting in its launch-cradles at Grey Valley, fifteen miles from here—"

"They're no threat to us; they can't operate without fuel either."

"They won't have to," Retief said, pulling out smoke. "Corps policy is nothing if not elastic. It seems that the Big Picture called for the supplying of the Volunteer Reserve with full magazines—"

"What!"

"—and the topping off of all tanks."

Tavilan's face was pale. "I see," he said quietly, nodding. "The CDT talked disarmament to me while it was arming Prouch's revolutionaries. It never intended to see the monarchy survive."

"Well, Your Highness, the CDT is a very clean-minded organization, and it heard somewhere that 'monarchy' was a dirty word—"

"All right!" Prince Tavilan turned to Count Arrol. "We have mounts for every man—and plenty of cross-bow bolts. There'll be Greenback blood on the palace floors before the night is out—"

"If I might make a suggestion . . . ?"

"You're not involved in this, Retief. Take the copter and get clear—"

"Clear to where? I've been disowned by my colleagues and slapped in jail by the Prime Minister. To get back to the Little Picture: I see no point in our riding into Elora City and being shot down at long range by Greenbacks—"

"We'll ride in at the Marivale Gate, move up through the fire-lanes—"

"If you'll pardon my saying so," Retief said, "I've got a better idea. It's only fifteen miles to the Grey Valley . . ."

"So?"

"So I suggest we take a ride over and look at the Volunteer Navy."

"You just told me Prouch's renegades are armed to the teeth . . ."

Retief nodded. "Since we need guns, Your Highness, I can't think of a closer place to get 'em . . ."

At the head of the troop of thirty-eight riders, including General Hish, lashed to a mount, Retief and Tavilan reined in at the crest of the slope that faced the barracks of the Peoples' Volunteer Naval Reserve, a blaze of light all across the narrow valley. On the ramp a quarter of a mile beyond the administrative and shop areas, fifty slim destroyers loomed, bathed in the glare of polyarcs. Prince Tavilan whistled.

"Prouch and the CDT seem to have struck it off even better than I thought. That's all brand-new equipment."

"Just defensive, of course," Retief said. "I believe Minister Prouch has given assurances that the elimination of Dangredi's free-booters will be carried out with dispatch—just as soon as the CDT recognizes his regime."

Tavilan laughed shortly. "I could have swept Dangredi off the space lanes six months ago—if the CDT hadn't blockaded me."

"Such are the vagaries of Galactic policy—"

"I know: the Big Picture again." Tavilan turned to Arrol. "We'll split into two parties, work around both ends of the valley, and pick our targets at close range. Retief, you ride with me. Let's move out."

It was a forty-minute ride along the forested slopes walling the valley to the rendezvous point Prince Tavilan had designated, a sheltered ravine less than a hundred yards from the nearest of the parked war vessels. The access ladder was down, and light spilled from the open entry port. A Reservist in baggy grey and green lounged in the opening. Two more stood below, power rifles slung across their backs.

"You could pick those three off from here," Retief
remarked. "Cross-bows are a nice quiet weapon—"

Tavilan shook his head. "We'll ride down in formal battle-
order. No war's been declared. They won't fire on the
Prince Royal."

"There may be forty more inside—to say nothing of the
crews of the next ships in line, sentries, stand-by riot
squads, and those two pill-boxes commanding the ends of
the valley."

"Still—I must give those men their chance to declare
themselves."

"As the Prince wishes—but I'll keep my blaster loose
in its holster—just in case . . ."

The Prince rode in the lead with his guidon at his left,
followed by thirty-five men, formed up in a precise triangle
of seven ranks, with two honor guards out on the flanks. The
rear guard followed, holding the reins of the mount to which
General Hish, still hissing bitter complaints, was lashed.

The Invincibles moved down the slope and out onto the
broad tarmac, hooves clattering against the paved surface.
The two men on the ramp turned, stoop gaping. The one
above at the ship's entry port whirled, disappeared inside.

The troop rode on; they were halfway to the ship now.
One of the waiting Greenbacks unlimbered his power gun,
cranked the action, the other followed suit. Both stepped
forward half a dozen paces, brought their weapons up
uncertainly.

"Halt! Who the Hell's there!" one bawled.

Tavilan flipped the corner of his hunting cape forward
over his shoulder to show the royal Eloran device, came
on in silence.

The taller of the two Greenbacks raised his rifle, hesitated, half-lowered it. Riding half a pace behind Tavilan,
Retief eased his pistol from its holster, watching the doorway above. On his right, Count Arrol held his crossbow
across his knee, a bolt cocked in the carriage, his finger
on the trigger.

Ten feet from the two Greenback sentries, Prince Tavilan
reined in.

"Aren't you men accustomed to render a proper salute

when your Commander makes a surprise inspection?" he said calmly.

The Greenbacks looked at each other, fingering their guns.

"It looks as though the word had gone out," Arrol whispered to Retief.

"You cover the Prince; I'll handle the entry port," Retief murmured.

At that moment a figure eased into view at the port; light glinted from the front sight of a power gun as it came up, steadied—

Retief sighted, fired; in the instantaneous blue glare, the man at the port whirled and fell outward. The Greenback nearest Tavilan made a sudden move to swing his gun on the Prince—then stumbled back, a steel quarrel from Arrol's cross-bow standing in his chest. The second Greenback dropped his weapon, stood with raised hands, his mouth open and eyes wide, then turned and ran.

Tavilan leaped down from his steed, dashed for the access ladder, his cross-bow ready. As though on command, four men followed him, while others scattered to form a rough semi-circle at the base of the ladder. Sheltered behind a generator unit, Retief and Arrol covered the port. Tavilan disappeared inside, the men at his heels. There was a long half-minute of dead silence. Then a shout sounded from the next vessel in line, a hundred yards distant. Tavilan reappeared, gestured.

"Everybody in," Arrol called. The men went for the ladder, sprang up in good order; those waiting on the ramp faced outward, covering all points.

A light flashed briefly from the adjacent vessel; a sharp report echoed. A man fell from the ladder; others caught him, lifted him up. Far away, a harsh voice bellowed orders.

"They aren't using any heavy stuff," Arrol said. "They wouldn't want to nick the paint on their new battle wagon . . ."

A squad of men appeared, running from the shadows at the base of the ship from which the firing had come. Most of the troop were up the ladder now; two men hustled the struggling Groaci up. Beside Retief, Arrol launched three bolts in rapid-fire order. Two of the oncoming men fell. The blue flashes of power guns winked; here and there, the surface of the tarmac boiled as wild shots struck.

"Come on . . ." The two men ran for the ladder; Arrol sprang for it, swarmed up. Retief followed; molten metal spattered as a power-gun bolt vaporized the handrail. Then hands were hauling him inside.

"Hit the deck," Arrol yelled. "We're lifting . . . ?"

"We took one burst from an infinite repeater," an officer reported, "but no serious damage was done. They held their fire just a little too long."

"We were lucky," Prince Tavilan said. "One man killed, one wounded. It's fortunate we didn't select the next ship in line; we'd have had a hornet's nest on our hands."

"Too bad we broke up the battalion crap game," Retief commented. "But by now they'll be lifting off after us— a few of them, anyway."

"All right—we'll give them a warm welcome before they nail us—"

"If I may venture to suggest—"

Tavilan waved a hand, grinning. "Every time you get too damned polite, you've got some diabolical scheme up your sleeve. What is it this time, Retief?"

"We won't wait around to be nailed. We'll drive for Deep Space at flank speed—"

"And run into Dangredi's blockage? I'd rather use my firepower on Prouch's scavengers."

"That's where our friend the General comes in." Retief nodded toward the trussed Groaci. "He and Dangredi are old business associates. We'll put him on the screen and see if he can't negotiate a brief truce. With the approval of Your Highness, I think we can make an offer that will interest him . . ."

The flagship of the pirate fleet was a four-hundred-year-old, five-hundred-thousand-ton dreadnought, a relic of pre-Concordiat times. In the red-lit gloom of its cavernous Command Control deck, Retief and Prince Tavilan relaxed in deep couches designed for the massive frames of the Hondu corsairs. Opposite them, Dangredi, the Hondu chieftain, lounged at ease, his shaggy, leather-strapped, jewel-spangled 350-pound bulk almost overflowing his throne-like chair. At Retief's side, General Hish perched nervously. Half a dozen of Tavilan's Invincibles stood around the room, chatting with an equal number of Dangredi's hulking officers, whose greenish fur looked black in the light from the crimson lamps.

"What I failing to grasp," Dangredi rumbled, "is reason for why suddenly now changing of plan previously okayed."

"I hardly think that matters," Tavilan said smoothly. "I've offered to add one hundred thousand Galactic Credits to the sum already agreed on."

"But the whole idea was compensate me, Grand Hereditary War Chief of Hondu people, for not fight; now is offering more pay for stand and give battle . . ."

"I thought you Hondu loved war," an Eloran officer said.

Dangredi nodded his heavy green-furred head, featureless but for two wide green-pupiled eyes. "Crazy mad for warring, and also plenty fond of cash. But is smelling rodent somewhere in woodpile . . ."

"It's very simple, Commodore," Retief said. "General Hish here had arranged with you to flee when the People's Volunteer forces attacked; now changing conditions on Elora make it necessary that you fight—and in place of the loot you would otherwise so rightly expect, you'll collect a handsome honorarium—"

Suddenly the Groaci leaped to his feet, pointed at Retief. "Commodore Dangredi," he hissed. "This renegade diplomat beside me holds a gun pointed at my vitals; only thus did he coerce me to request this parley. Had I guessed his intention, I would have dared him to do his worst. Seize the traitor, Excellency!"

Dangredi stared at the Groaci.

"He—and these strutting popinjays—plot against the security of the People's State of Elora!" Hish whispered urgently. "The plan remains unchanged! You are to flee engagement with the forces of Minister Prouch!"

The great green head bobbed suddenly; hooting laughter sounded. A vast hand slapped a thigh like a shaggy beer keg.

"Aha! At last is getting grasp of situation," Dangredi

bellowed. "Now is little honest treachery, kind of dealing Hondu understanding!" He waved a hand at a servitor standing by. "Bringing wassail bowl, plenty meat!" He brought his hands together with a dull boom, rubbed them briskly. "Double-cross, plenty fighting, more gold at end of trail! Is kind of operation I, Dangredi, Hereditary War chief, dreaming of in long nights of tooth-shedding time!"

"But these—these criminal kidnappers have no authority to deal—"

"Groaci-napping is harmless pastime—like stealing wine-melons when cub. Unless, maybe . . ." he cocked a large emerald eye at Hish " . . . you maybe raising ante?"

"I . . . I will match the offer of the saboteurs of inter-planetary amity! One hundred thousand in Groaci gold!"

Dangredi considered briefly. "No good. What about fighting? You give Hondu gunners targets in sights? Or maybe chance for rough-and-tumble, hand-to-hand, cold steel against enemy blades?"

General Hish shuddered. "In the name of civilization, I appeal—"

"Shove civilization in ventral orifice! Hondu taking good, crooked, blood-thirsty barbarians every time. Now disappearing quietly, Groaci, while I and new buddies planning strategy. Maybe later I sending for you and bending arms and legs until you tell all about enemy battle plan . . ."

"The Groaci is our hostage," Tavilan said as the general was led away. "He's not to be bent without my prior approval."

"Sure; just having little joke." Dangredi leaned back, accepted a vast drumstick and a tank of wine, waited while his guests accepted proffered delicacies.

"Now, Retief, you say attack coming when . . . ?"

"I must confess," Counselor Magnan said, "I don't quite understand how it happened that after trouncing the Eloran Volunteers, the pirate Dangredi voluntarily gave himself up and offered the services of his entire fleet as a reserve force to replace the very units he destroyed."

"Never mind that, Magnan," Ambassador Hidebinder said. "As seasoned campaigners must, we shall accept the *fait accompli*. Our resettlement plans are set back a year, at least. It's doubly unfortunate that Prime Minister Prouch suffered a fall just at this time. Magnan, you'll attend the funeral."

"With pleasure, Mr. Ambassador," Magnan said. "That is, I'll be honored—"

"Retief . . ." Hidebinder glared across the table. "I'm not going to press civil charges, since the Eloran government, at the behest of Prince Tavilan, has dropped the case. However, I may as well tell you at once—your future with the Corps is non-existent. A trifling embezzlement of official funds, I could wink at. Embellished reports, slack performance of duty, cowardice in the face of the enemy—these I could shrug off as youthful peccadilloes. But foot-dragging in the carrying out of Corps policy—" his fist thumped the desk. "Intolerable!"

A messenger entered the conference room, handed a note to Magnan, who passed it to Hidebinder; he opened it impatiently, glanced at it. His jaw dropped. He read it through again. His mouth closed; his jowls paled, quivering.

"Mr. Ambassador—what is it?" Magnan gasped.

Hidebinder rose and tottered from the room. Magnan snatched up the paper, read it through, then stared at Retief.

"He's been—declared *persona non grata*—The Imperial government gives him twelve hours to leave Elora . . . !"

Retief glanced at the wall clock. "If he hurries, he can catch the mail boat."

"And you, Retief . . . !"

Retief raised his eyebrows. Magnan glanced around the table. "If you gentlemen will excuse us for a few moments . . . ?" Half a dozen frowning diplomats filed from the room. Magnan cleared his throat. "This is *most* irregular, Retief! The imperial government requests that you present credentials as Minister Plenipotentiary and Ambassador Extraordinary at once . . . they will accept no other appointee . . ."

Retief tsked. "I told Prince Tavilan I wouldn't have time for a ceremonial job. I have a suggestion, Mr. Magnan: suppose I nominate you for the post?"

"Over the heads of a hundred senior officers?" Magnan gasped. "Retief, dear boy . . ."

"That is, if your distaste for monarchies isn't overwhelming . . . ?"

"Eh? Oh, well, as to that," Magnan sat erect, tugged his lapels into place. "I've always had a sneaking admiration for absolute royalty."

"Fine. Dangredi will be along in a few minutes to arrange for supplies; it seems there are a few shiploads of CDT-sponsored undesirables already landing on the northern continent who'll have to be warned off. It's probably just a slip. I'm sure our former Ambassador wouldn't have jumped the gun in violation of solemn treaties."

"Ah," Magnan said.

"And, of course, the Royal Navy will require provisioning—just to be sure the new Reservists don't get any large ideas . . ."

"Uh . . ."

"And, of course, a new treaty plainly guaranteeing the territorial integrity of Elora will have to be worked up at once . . ."

"Oh . . ."

Retief rose. "All of which I'm sure you'll handle brilliantly, Mr. Ambassador. And by the way—I think I could best serve the mission in some other capacity than as Admin Officer . . ."

Magnan pulled at his collar, waiting . . .

"I think I'd better work closely with Prince Tavilan, the heir apparent," Retief said blandly. "He does a lot of hunting, so perhaps you'd better designate me as Field and Stream Attaché . . ." He picked up his cross-bow from the corner.

"I leave the details to you, Mr. Ambassador. I'm going hunting."

"The interposition of the stern Corps presence, unflinching champion of underdogs, has
more than once frustrated the colonial-
imperialist urges of expansion-minded states.
At Yalc, Minister Barnshingle, braving every
peril in single-handed confrontation with the
forces of tyranny, gallantly reaffirmed the
hallowed principle of fair play for all."

—Vol. II, reel 161, 481 AE (AD 2942)

THE CASTLE OF LIGHT

Retief scaled his pale burgundy afternoon informal beret
across the office, narrowly missing the clothes tree, and
dumped the heavy carton he was carrying on his desk. A
shapely brunette with a turned-up nose appeared at the
connecting door to the next office.

"Miss Braswell," he said before she could speak. "I have
here two handsome half-liter wine glasses which I'm about
to field-test. Will you join me?"

She made a shushing motion, rolling her eyes toward
the inner office. A narrow, agitated face appeared over her
shoulder.

"Retief!" Consul-General Magnan burst out. "I've been
at wit's end! How does it happen that every time catas-
trophe strikes you're out of the office?"

"It's merely a matter of timing," Retief said soothingly, stripping paper from the package. He pulled out a
tulip-shaped goblet which seemed to be made of coils of

jewel-colored glass welded together in an intricate pattern, held it up to the light.

"Pretty, eh? And barely cool from the glass-blower—"

"While you idled about the bazaar," Magnan snapped, his face an angry pink above a wide, stiff collar of yellow plastiweave, "I've been coping single-handedly with disaster! I suggest you put aside your baubles; I'm calling a formal Emergency Staff Meeting in two minutes!"

"That means you, me and Miss Braswell, I take it, since the rest of the staff is off crater-viewing—"

"Just you and I." Magnan mopped at his face with a vast floral-patterned tissue. "This is a highly classified emergency."

"Oh, goody, I'll take the rest of the afternoon off and watch the festivities." Miss Braswell winked at Retief, extended the tip of her tongue in salute to the Consul-General's back, and was gone.

Retief plucked a bottle from his desk drawer and followed Magnan into the inner office. The senior officer yanked at his stiff collar, now wilting with perspiration.

"Why this couldn't have waited until Minister Barnshingle's return, I don't know," he said. "He's already a day overdue. I've tried to contact him, to no avail; this primitive line-of-sight local telescreen system—" he broke off. "Retief, kindly defer your tippling until after the crisis!"

"Oh, this isn't tippling, Mr. Magnan. I'm doing a commodity analysis for my next report. You fobbed the detail of Commercial Attaché on me, if you recall—"

"As Chargé d'affaires in the absence of the Minister, I forbid drinking on duty!" Magnan roared.

"Surely you jest, Mr. Magnan; it would mean the end of diplomacy as we know it—"

"Well, not until after lunch, at least. And I hereby authorize you to postpone market research until further notice; we're facing a possible holocaust in a matter of hours!"

"What's it all about?"

Magnan plucked a sheet of yellow paper from his desk and handed it across to Retief. "This came in over the auto-typer forty minutes ago."

❖ ❖ ❖

UNIDENTIFIED CONVOY COMPRISING FIFTY
UHLAN CLASS VESSELS SIGHTED ON COURSE
FOR YALC III ETA 1500 GST 33 OCT GSC.
SIGNED POMFROY, ENSIGN PATROL NAVY
786-G.

"Uhlans," Retief said. "Those are thousand-man transports. And oh-nine-hundred on the thirty-third is just about
two hours from now."

"This could be an invasion, Retief! A major breach of
the peace! Can you imagine how it would look in my record
if the planet were invaded under my very nose!"

"Tough on the natives, too," Retief commented. "What
action have you taken so far?"

"Action? Why, I've canceled this afternoon's social
engagements, checked out-going passenger schedules, and
sharpened a number of pencils."

"Have you tried contacting this Ensign Pomfroy for a
little more detail?"

"There's no one on duty in the Message Center but a
local Code Clerk; he's trying to raise him now." Magnan
depressed a button on his desk. "Oo-Gilitit, have you met
with any success?"

"Pomfroy-Tic all same have organ cluster up ventral
orifice—"

"Gilitit, I've warned you to watch your language!"
Magnan roared. "It's no habit for a communications man
to get into!" He clicked off. "Confounded locals! It's hopeless, of course; our equipment was never designed for pin-
pointing moving patrol boats at four A-U's."

"How do the Yalcans feel about the situation?"

Magnan blinked. "Why, as to that, I, ah . . . was just going
to call Oo-Rilikuk." Magnan punched keys, tuned in a bland
yellow and blue face with eyes like gold pinheads and
vertically-hinged jaws busy with an oily drumstick.

"Ah, there, Magnan," a voice like an unoiled wheel said.
"Just finishing up my lunch. Roast haunch of giant locust.
Delicious." A tongue like a length of green silken rope
flicked a tidbit from a corner of the lipless mouth.

"Oo-Rilikuk, do you know anything of a large convoy
due here today?"

Rilikuk dabbed at his chin with a gossamer napkin. "I seem to recall issuing a number of visas to Groaci nationals in recent weeks."

"Groaci? Fifty shiploads of them?"

"Something like that," the Yalcan said carelessly. "By the way, if you haven't already made arrangements, perhaps you'd care to join my Bachelor's Group for the upcoming festivities—"

"You're not concerned? Perhaps you're not aware of the insidious reputation the Groaci enjoy—"

"I don't mind saying I've exercised a trifle of influence to procure a choice mud pocket; the rich, oleaginous kind, you know. And there'll be no shortage of nubile females along—though you're not organized to appreciate the latter, it's true—"

"May I ask the state of the planetary defenses, Rilikuk? I'm warning you, these Groaci are not to be trusted—"

"Planetary defenses?" Rilikuk issued a chirp of amusement. "As confirmed pacifists, we've never felt the need for such an extravagance. Now, I'll be leaving the office in a few minutes; suppose I drop by for you—we'll go on to my place for dinner, then off to the bog—"

"You're leaving the Foreign Office at a moment like this?" Magnan yelped. "They'll be landing in a matter of minutes!"

"I fear I'll have no time to devote to tourism this week, Magnan," Rilikuk said. "They'll just have to manage alone. After all, Voom Festival time comes but once in ninety-four standard years—"

Magnan rang off with a snort. "We'll receive scant help from that quarter." He swiveled to gaze out the unglazed window across the gay tiles of the plaza, lined with squat, one-story shops of embossed and colored ceramic brick to the glittering minarets of the mile-distant temple complex.

"If these idlers invested less energy in shard-sorting and more in foreign affairs, I wouldn't be faced with this contretemps," he grumbled.

"If the CDT would talk Groac into selling them a few thousand tons of sand, they wouldn't have to sort shards."

"There are better uses for CDT bottoms than hauling sand, Retief, though I notice the local scrap pile is about depleted. Possibly now they'll turn to more profitable pursuits than lavishing the artistry of generations on tenantless shrines." He indicated the cluster of glass towers sparkling in the sun. "They might even consent to export a reasonable volume of glassware in place of the present token amounts."

"Rarity keeps the price up; and they say they can't afford to let much glass off-world. It all goes back in the scrap piles when it's broken, for reuse."

Magnan stared across the plain, where the white plumes of small geysers puffed into brief life, while the pale smoke rising from the fumaroles rose straight up in the still air. Far above, a point of blue light twinkled.

"Odd," Magnan said, frowning. "I've never seen one of the moons in broad daylight before . . ."

Retief came to the window.

"You still haven't. Apparently our Groaci friends are ahead of schedule. That's an ion drive, and it's not over twenty miles out."

Magnan bounded to his feet. "Get your hat, Retief! We'll confront these interlopers the moment they set foot on Yalcan soil! The Corps isn't letting this sort of thing pass without comment!"

"The Corps is always a fast group with a comment," Retief said. "I'll give it that."

Outside, the plaza was a-bustle with shopkeepers glittering in holiday glass jewelry, busily closing up their stalls, erecting intricate decorations like inverted chandeliers before their shuttered shops, and exchanging shouted greetings. A long-bodied pink-and-red-faced Yalcan in a white apron leaning in the open door of a shop waved a jointed forearm.

"Retief-Tic! Do me honor of to drop in for last Voom cup before I lock up. Your friend, too!"

"Sorry, Oo-Plif; duty calls."

"I see you've established your usual contacts among the undesirable element," Magnan muttered, signaling a boat-shaped taxi edging through the press on fat pneumatic wheels. "Look at these lackwits! Completely engrossed in their frivolity, while disaster descends scarcely a mile away."

Retief eyed the descending ship as it settled in beyond the glittering glass spires of the temple-city.

"I wonder why they're landing there instead of at the port."

"They've probably mistaken the shrine for the town," Magnan snapped. "One must admit that it makes a far more impressive display than this collection of mud huts!"

"Not the Groaci; they do their homework carefully before they start anything."

The cab pulled up and Magnan barked directions at the driver, who waved his forearms in the Yalcan equivalent of a shrug.

"Speak to this fellow, Retief!" Magnan snapped. "Obscure dialects are a hobby of yours, I believe."

Retief gave the driver instructions in the local patois and leaned back against the floppy cushions. Magnan perched on the edge of the seat and nipped at a hangnail. The car cleared the square, racketed down a side street streaming with locals headed for the bog, gunned out across the hard-baked mud-flat, swerving violently around the bubbling devil's cauldrons of hot mud that dotted the way. A small geyser erupted with a whoosh!, spattering the open vehicle with hot droplets. A whiff of rotten-egg smoke blew past. Off to the left, the sunlight glinted from the wide surface of the swamp, thickly scattered with exotic lily-like flowers. Here and there, tree-ferns grew in graceful clumps from the shallow water. Along the shore, bright-colored tents had been erected, and local celebrants clustered in groups among them, weaving to and fro and waving their multiple arms.

"It's disgraceful," Magnan sniffed. "They're already staggering and their infernal festival's hardly begun!"

"It's a native dance," Retief said. "Very cultural."

"What's the occasion for this idiotic celebration? It seems to have completely paralyzed whatever elementary sense of responsibility these flibbertigibbets possess."

"It's related in some way to the conjunction of the four moons," Retief said. "But there's more to it than that. It seems to have an important religious significance; the dances are symbolic of death and rebirth, or something of the sort."

"Hmmph! I see the dancers are now falling flat on their faces! Religious ecstasy, no doubt!"

As they swept past the reeling locals, the driver made cabalistic signs in the air, grabbed the steering bar just in time to swerve past a steam-jet that snorted from a cleft boulder. Ahead, a cloud of dust was rolling out from the landing spot where the Groaci ship had settled in, a scant hundred yards from an outlying shrine, a sparkling fifty-foot tower of red, yellow, and green glass.

"They're coming perilously close to violating the native holy place," Magnan observed as the taxi pulled up beside the ship. "There may be mob violence at any moment."

A pair of locals, emerging from one of the many fanciful glass arches adorning the entrances to the shrine complex, cast no more than a casual glance at the vessel as a port opened in its side and a spindle-legged Groaci in golfing knickers and loud socks appeared.

Magnan climbed hurriedly from the cab. "I want you to note my handling of this, Retief," he said behind his hand, "a firm word now may avert an incident."

"I'd better say a firm word to the driver, or we'll be walking back."

"Look, Mac-Tic, I got a reserved slot in a hot pocket of mud waiting for me," the driver called as he wheeled the car around. "Five minutes, OK?"

Retief handed the cabbie a ten credit token and followed Magnan across the scorched ground to the landing ladder. The Groaci descended, all five eye-stalks canted in different directions. One fixed on Magnan.

"Minister Barnshingle," he said in his faint Groaci voice before Magnan could speak. "I am Fiss, Tour Director for Groac Planetary Tours, Incorporated. I assume you've come to assist in clearing my little flock through the Customs and Immigration formalities. Now—"

"Tour Director, did you say, Mr. Fiss?" Magnan cut in. "Fifty shiploads of tourists?"

"Quite correct. I can assure you that passports and visas are all in order, and immunization records are up-to-date. Since we Groaci have no diplomatic mission to Yalc, it is most kind of the CDT to extend its good offices—"

"Just a minute, Mr. Fiss. How long are your tourists

planning to stay on Yalc? Just during Voom Festival, I assume?"

"I believe our visas read . . . ah . . . indefinite, Mr. Minister . . ."

"I'm Magnan, Chargé in the absence of the Minister," Magnan said.

Fiss waved his eyes. "The Minister is not here?"

"No, he's off mountain climbing. Very keen on sports. Now, ah, may I ask where your other forty-nine vessels might be?"

"Just where is the Minister to be found?" Fiss inquired.

"I really can't say," Magnan sniffed. "We've had no word for two days. Now, about your other ships—"

"There are, I believe, forty-nine cities here on this charming little world," Fiss said smoothly. "One transport is calling at each."

"Curious way to conduct a tour—" Magnan broke off as a cargo port rumbled open and a heavy six-wheeled vehicle churned out. Rows of multi-eyed Groaci heads peered over open sides, on which the words GROAC PLANETARY TOURS, INC. had been hastily lettered. A second vehicle followed the first, and then a third and fourth. Magnan gaped as the emerging carriers took up positions in an orderly double file.

"Here, what's this, Fiss?" he blurted. "These are tourists?"

"Of course? What else? Please note the presence of the ladies and also a number of lovable Groaci grubs. Yes, innocent, fun-loving tourists all."

"Why are they in armored cars?" Magnan watched as the vehicles moved off in the direction of the towering glass temples. "Here, where are they going?"

"Since the entire local populace is fully occupied with Voom Festival activities," Fiss hissed blandly, "Groac Tours has thoughtfully arranged to occupy available unused housing . . ."

"Why, that's the local Holy of Holies," Magnan expostulated. "You can't go in there . . . !"

"The structures are not in use," Fiss whispered. "And I see no objection on the part of the aborigines." He indicated the cab driver who was watching indifferently as the first tractor moved under a graceful crystalline arch into the sparkling glass-bricked avenue.

"Hey, Mac-Tic," the driver called to Retief in Yalc. "Time's up. I wanna get there before the mud cools . . ."

"Are you out of your mind, Mr. Fiss?" Magnan demanded. "You're deliberately precipitating an incident! I'm warning you, I'll refer this to Sector HQ and call for a squadron of Peace Enforcers—"

"What need for Peace Enforcers, my dear fellow?" Fiss murmured. "Peace reigns! We are unarmed; no act of violence is contemplated."

"We'll see about this!" Magnan fumed. He turned and stamped toward the waiting taxi.

"So thoughtful of you to welcome us," Fiss's faint voice followed him. "I shall be calling at the Legation later to arrange a number of formalities—all quite legal, I assure you."

"It's worse than I thought," Magnan groaned to Retief as he climbed into the cab. "When a Groaci starts citing statutes, you can be sure there's mischief afoot."

"This is incredible!" Magnan barked at the screen where Oo-Rilikuk's multi-colored visage nodded blandly against a background of sinuously moving Yalcan dancing-wenches. "You calmly admit that these foreigners are occupying every pagoda on the planet, strewing dope-stick butts and algae-bar wrappers—"

"This is Voom season, Mr. Magnan," Rilikuk said reasonably. "What could be more fitting?"

"Your concept of propriety confounds me. There are fifty thousand of these fellows—and I have the distinct impression they're planning an extended stay!"

"Very likely," Rilikuk agreed, twitching in time to the music in the background. "And now, if you'll excuse me . . ." The screen blanked.

Magnan threw up his hands. "I don't like it, Retief; there's an aspect of this we're missing—"

A chime sounded; the door opened and the Groaci Fiss bustled in, breathing noisily under the weight of a heavy briefcase.

"Ah, Mr. Magnan! So good of you to await me. I have

the papers here . . ." He hoisted the case onto the desk and undid stout straps. "I'm sure you'll find all in order: Territorial claims, governmental charter, application for League membership—"

"What's this?" Magnan scanned the heavy documents. "What are you saying, sir? That Yalc—that the Groaci— that you—"

"Quite right," Fiss nodded. "This world is now Groaci property."

There was a loud crash from the direction of the now deserted street. Magnan swiveled, stared out at a band of business-like Groaci, hard at work on a shuttered shop with pry-bars.

"What are they doing?" he yelped. "Mr. Fiss, order those vandals away at once! The situation is getting out of hand!"

"Not at all; those chaps are merely following my instructions. And now if you have any belongings you wish to take along, please feel free—"

"Eh? Belongings? I'm not going anywhere!"

"Permit me to contradict you," Fiss hissed softly, prodding a paper with a damp-looking finger. "This is the eviction order. I find that this humble structure will adequately fulfill my requirement for a field-office here in the village."

"F-field office?"

"I expect we shall be busy here for a few days," Fiss said. "Transferring useful items to our quarters." He waved airily toward the sparkling towers beyond the swamp.

"You're violating the Legation?" Magnan's eyes bulged.

"There has been a change of status quo since my arrival," Fiss pointed out. "No formal relations exist between my government and the CDT; therefore, this is merely an office, and you are unregistered aliens—"

"This is an outrage!" Magnan sputtered. "I'm not leaving!"

"So?" Fiss murmured. He stepped to the door, opened it, waved in a quartet of bigger-than-average Groaci.

"To intimidate the soft ones," he hissed in Groaci. "To make threatening gestures."

Two of the newcomers stepped to Retief. He took them casually by their thin necks, escorted them to the window, and tumbled them out. The second pair jumped at him in time to meet a stiff-arm which slammed both of them onto their backs. Fiss emitted a weak but impassioned bleat.

"Unhand them, brute! These are lawfully appointed bailiffs—"

Retief tossed the stunned Groaci after their fellows and took a step toward Fiss. The Tour Director squeaked and darted through the door.

"Retief!" Magnan yelped. "Stop! After all, these papers—"

Retief gathered in the parchments, tossed them after the intruders. The outraged face of Tour Director Fiss appeared at the opening.

"Ruffians! Bandits! Our legal and just claim—"

"—isn't worth the plastic it's printed on," Retief stated. "And if any more tourists wander into the Legation I won't be so polite with them."

Fiss turned and made frantic gestures to the foraging crew. "To enter and evict the madmen!" he hissed. "To cast them forth bodily!"

The several dozen Groaci who had gathered moved in a body toward the Legation door.

"I'm disappointed in you, Fiss," Retief said, shaking his head sadly. "I thought you were going to pretend that this was all perfectly legal, and here you are about to violate a diplomatic mission in broad daylight."

Fiss hesitated, then hissed an order to his men. They halted.

"Very well, Soft One," he whispered. "What need of force? Unlike the higher races, you require water at frequent intervals, I believe. Since, alas, I cannot authorize further deliveries through the village mains, you will soon emerge to seek it. We will be waiting."

Magnan tottered to Retief's side. "Mr. Fiss," he croaked. "This is madness! You can't possibly hope to justify this outrageous seizure—"

"On the contrary, Mr. Magnan," Fiss waved a fistful of paper. "If you will re-read your Colonial Code, Title Three, Section XXI, paragraph 9b, you will find that, and I quote, 'any planetary body lacking an indigenous culture may be considered as available for homesteading by any Power covenant to these articles—'"

"Surely, Fiss, you don't imply that Yalc is uninhabited! Great Heavens, the world is known throughout the Sector for the beauty of its glass and ceramics work—"

"I refer further to paragraph 12d, *ibidem*," Fiss bored on, "which provides the following criteria for determination of cultural level within the meaning of the Code: (a) an active, organized government competent to represent native interests; (b) a degree of social organization characterized by cities of at least one thousand inhabitants; and (c) individual or group IQ (as applicable), averaging .8 (standard) as evidenced by GST Test scores—"

"Have you lost your wits?" Magnan cut in. "You're standing in the midst of a Yalcan City! I deal daily with representatives of the Yalcan government! And as for intelligence—"

"*Inhabited* city, Mr. Magnan, permit me to remind you minimum population, one thousand individuals." Fiss waved a hand at the empty street. "I see no individuals here."

"But they're all away participating in a festival—"

"As for government," Fiss continued blandly, "I have been totally unsuccessful in discovering any *active* organization. I confess I have been unable to secure a specimen of the local fauna for IQ Testing, but I feel sure any such effort would be unrewarded."

"You deliberately timed this coup to take advantage of local customs!" Magnan said in shocked tone. "The Code will be amended, Fiss—!"

The Groaci vibrated his throat sac, a contemptuous gesture. "Ex post facto legal manipulations can hardly be expected to affect the present situation retroactively, my dear Magnan."

Magnan clutched the edge of the window. "Retief," he gasped weakly. "This is insane, but I have a sudden, awful conviction that he's legally on firm ground."

"Of course," Fiss went on, "article 68 of the Code expressly prohibits occupation by force of any world, cultured or otherwise. However, since our arrival was carried out in complete tranquility, this is hardly germane—"

"The festival will be over tomorrow," Magnan burst out. "What then?"

"Now that we have established legal possession of this planet," Fiss whispered, "it will, of course, be necessary to enforce the just laws which are even now being enacted. To this end, certain arms are of course necessary." He spat rapid Groacian at a trio of newcomers in black hip-cloaks, who silently produced heavy particle-guns from sequined holsters strapped to their thighs.

"You aren't planning—violence?" Magnan gasped. "Not against *us!*"

"As to that," Fiss whispered, "I was about to point out that naturally, a formal request for diplomatic status addressed to the present regime would, of course, receive consideration."

"Tour Director Fiss—" Magnan gulped.

"Planetary Coordinator *Pro Tem* Fiss, if you please," the Groaci hissed. "A pity the large Soft One acted in such haste, but I am prepared to overlook the incident."

"Why, ah, very good of you, I'm sure, Pla—"

"You're out of luck, Fiss," Retief cut in. "You'll have to conduct your piracy without CDT sanction."

Magnan tugged at Retief's sleeve. "Here, Retief, this is hardly a time for truculence—"

"It's as good a time as any, Mr. Magnan. And Minister Barnshingle might be irritated if he came back and discovered that these squatters had been recognized as a legal government."

Magnan groaned. "I . . . I suppose you're right."

"So? But, no matter, Soft One," Fiss whispered. "Why treat with underlings, eh? My scouts report a party of Terrestrials in difficulty on an awkward slope some leagues from here. Doubtless the person Barnshingle of whom you speak will be grateful for relief. A timely rescue by self-less Groaci homesteaders will establish a correct mood for initiation of formal relations."

"The Minister's in trouble?" Magnan squeaked.

"He is at present dangling over a crevasse of awesome depth by a single strand of rope. Diplomat muscles appear unequal to the task of drawing him up—"

There was a rending crash from a shop across the plaza as a barred door collapsed under the impact of a power ram. Swarms of Groaci were systematically looting the stalls already opened, loading foodstuffs, glassware, and other merchandise into wheeled vehicles.

"This is wholesale hijackery!" Magnan yelped. "Open pillage! Highway robbery!" You can't do this without a license!"

"Curb your tongue, sir!" Fiss hissed. "I shall for a while indulge your arrogant preemption of Groaci property out of sentimental respect for the niceties of diplomatic usage, but I shall tolerate no insult!"

"Threats, Mr. Fiss?" Magnan choked.

"Call it what you will, Soft One," Fiss said. "When you are ready to indicate your acquiescence, send word to me. Meantime, leave this building at your peril!"

Dusk had fallen. The sounds of shattering locks and maneuvering vehicles continued in the streets outside. Beyond the window, booted Groaci Peace-keepers paced monotonously, heavy blast guns at the ready. Now and then, in a momentary lull, the sound of Yalcan voices raised in song could be heard emanating from the bog, where torches flared, reflecting from the mirror-dark waters. The two lesser moons were high in the sky in their slow orbits; the third had risen above the horizon and cast purple shadows across the floor of the silent Legation office.

"It's nearly dark," Magnan muttered. "Retief, perhaps I'd better accompany you. Fiss may change his mind and batter the door down—"

"He could come in through the window anytime he decided to," Retief said. "He's nicely bluffed for the present, Mr. Magnan, and someone has to stay here to maintain occupancy of the Legation—"

"On second thought, I'm changing my instructions," Magnan said decisively. "You'd better not go. After all, if Minister Barnshingle wishes to recognize the coup, I see no reason—"

"I don't think the Minister will be reasoning at his most lucid level while dangling over a precipice. And there's also Miss Braswell to consider. She's out there somewhere."

"Retief, you can't hope to find her without being apprehended! The city is swarming with armed Groaci!"

"I think I know the back streets better than they do;

I'll stay out of sight. If I can reach Barnshingle before he signs anything, it may save a lot of embarrassment all around."

"Retief, as Chargé—"

"Don't give me any instructions I can't follow, Mr. Magnan," Retief took a hand-light from a desk drawer, clipped it to his belt. "Just lie low and ignore whatever Fiss says to you. I'll be back in a few hours."

Retief stepped from a doorless opening into the shadows of a narrow alley running behind the Legation. He waited until a knob-kneed Groaci in an elaborate helmet had strolled past the lighted intersection fifty feet distant, then jumped, pulled himself up onto the low, tiled roof of the adjacent building. In the light of the rising fourth moon, he moved quietly to the far side, lay flat looking down on a side street littered with items discarded by the looters. One or two windows showed lights. A single armed Groaci stood under a corner street-lamp. Silently Retief worked his way along the roofs, jumping gaps between buildings, until he reached a narrow space leading back into darkness a few yards from the corner. He groped, found a chip of broken tile, tossed it down into the alley. The Groaci cocked his eyes alertly, swung his gun around and came over to investigate. Retief tossed down another pebble; as the sentry entered the dark way, Retief dropped behind him, yanked him backward off his feet, and caught the falling gun. He put the muzzle against the Groaci's pulsating throat sac.

"Tell me where the Terry female is being held," he growled, "and maybe I won't tie knots in your eye-stalks."

"Iiiikkk!" the Groaci said. "To unhand me, demonic one!"

"Of course, you may not know," Retief said. "In that case I'd have to regretfully kill you and strike up a new acquaintance, which would be a nuisance for both of us."

"The impropriety of assaulting an innocent tourist! To lodge a complaint with the Travelers Aid Society!"

"No, that was this morning," Retief corrected his prisoner. "This afternoon you're a peaceful homesteader. You can think of me as an unpacified aborigine, if it will help any." He jabbed with the gun. "Make up your mind. I'm on a tight schedule."

"The ghastliness of your fate," the Groaci hissed.

"Well, I have to hurry along," Retief said. "Pardon my thumbs; shooting is such a messy business, and noisy, too."

"To restrain yourself, prowler in the night! To show you the way to the Soft She—and to savor the moment when you writhe on the hooks!"

"That's right," Retief said agreeably. "Think about something cheerful." He prodded the captive guard to his feet. "In the meantime—" he switched to Groaci—"To play your cards right and maybe to live to see the dawn."

In a shadowy arcade running beside a rare two-story structure, Retief studied the dark windows in the wall opposite. Faint light gleamed behind two of the glassless openings.

"I'll have to leave you here, I'm afraid, Tish," Retief said softly. "I'll just pop you into one of these convenient garbage storage units; they have nicely-fitted air tight doors, but you'll be all right for an hour or so. If your information is accurate, with luck I'll be back in plenty of time to let you out before you suffocate. Of course, if anything happens to delay me—well, that's just the little risk we have to run, eh?"

"To . . . to try the rear window first," Tish whispered.

"Whatever you say," Retief opened the door to the refuse bin and urged the Groaci inside. The alien clinched his olfactory sphincters tight and perched disconsolately on a heap of fruit rinds, locust carapaces, and pottery shards, his head ducked under the low ceiling.

"To remember this trusting one," he said shakily. "To carefully avoid being killed before returning to release me."

"With a motivation like that, I'm sure to survive." Retief clamped the door shut, looked both ways, and darted across the street. The wall tiles were deeply incised with decorative floral motifs; he found finger and toeholds, climbed quickly to the level of the windows, eased through one into a dark room. He paused to listen; there were faint Groaci voices somewhere. In the dim-lit hall, they were more distinct. He moved silently along to the nearmost room. The door opened at a touch.

Miss Braswell jumped up from a long, low Yalcan couch,

her mouth open for a scream, cut off as she recognized Retief in the gloom.

"Why—Mr. Retief—"

"Shhh." He crossed to her. A length of rope was tied firmly to her ankle and looped around a massive clay sculpture. She was barefooted, and her brown hair was in a state of mild disarray; there was a streak of dirt along one cheek.

"What in the world is it all about?" she whispered. "I was just about to buy the darlingest hand-decorated chamber pot, when all of a sudden a whole bunch of these nasty little creatures popped out of nowhere waving their eyes at me—"

"How many are in the building now?" Retief attacked the heavy knots in the rope.

"Heavens, I have no idea. It's been pretty quiet for the last hour." She giggled. "That tickles. I tried to untie it, but I only broke a fingernail."

The knot yielded and Retief tossed the rope aside.

"Do you feel equal to a short climb?"

Miss Braswell came close to Retief. "Whatever you say, Mr. Retief," she murmured.

"Where are your shoes?"

"I kept kicking them when they were tying me up, so they took them. Ugh! Those creepy, damp hands!"

"If we should get separated, head for the Legation. Mr. Magnan is holding the fort."

"You mean—these awful little Groaci are there, too?"

"Haven't you heard? They're colonizing the place."

"Why, the nerve!"

There was a sudden hiss of nearby voices. Retief flattened himself against the wall just inside the door. Miss Braswell whirled and sat on the chaise lounge. There was the soft clap of Groaci feet. A small figure stepped into the room.

"Ah, young woman," a soft Groaci voice hissed. "Time to be going along."

"Where?" the girl demanded loudly.

"To more comfortable quarters in more attractive surroundings—"

"If it wasn't so ridiculous, I'd think you were on the make, you sticky little monster. Keep away from me!"

"You mammals are all alike," the Groaci whispered. "But it's pointless to flaunt those ugly udders at me, my girl..." Two more Groaci had followed the first, who signaled. "To make fast its arms," he snapped. "Mind its talons—"

Miss Braswell jumped up and swung an open-handed slap that sent the flimsy alien reeling back; Retief stepped quickly behind the other two, cracked their heads together sharply, thrust them aside and chopped a hand across the leader's neck.

"Time to go," he breathed. At the window, he glanced out, then swung a leg over the sill. "It's easy; just hang on with your toes."

Miss Braswell giggled again. "It's so sort of sexy, being barefooted, isn't it?"

"That depends on what's attached to the feet," Retief said. "Hurry up, now. We're in enemy territory."

"Mr. Retief," she said from above, "do you think I flaunt my ah..."

"Certainly not, Miss Braswell. They flaunt themselves."

There was a sudden drumming from the shadows of the arcade across the way.

"It just occurred to my friend Tish to use a little initiative," Retief called softly. He dropped to the street a few feet below. "Jump—I'll catch you."

The thumping continued. Miss Braswell squealed and let go, slammed against Retief's chest. He set her on her feet. "The Groaci have good ears. Come on—" They dashed for the nearest dark alley as a squad of armed Groaci Peace-keepers rounded a corner. There was a weak shout, a clatter of accouterments as the four aliens broke into a run. Gripping Miss Braswell's hand, Retief dashed along the narrow way. Ahead, a wall loomed, blocking the passage. They skidded to a halt, turned to face the oncoming pursuers.

"Get to the roof," Retief snapped. "I'll slow them down—!"

Between Retief and the Groaci, a six-foot-long grating set in the pavement suddenly dropped open with a clank of metal. The leading Groaci, coming on at a smart clip, plunged over the edge, followed an instant later by the second. Retief brought his light up, shone it in the eyes of the other two as the third Groaci reached the pitfall, dropped from sight. As the last of the four faltered, sensing something amiss, the long, sinuous form of a Yalcan native glided from a door set in the wall, gave the Groaci a hearty push, dusted both sets of hands, and inclined its head in a gracious nod.

"Ah, Retief-Tic—and Braswell Ticcim! What jolly surprise! Please do honor to enter humble abode for refreshing snort before continuing!"

"Nice timing, Oo-Plif," Retief said. "I thought you'd be off to the festival by now."

The Yalcan reached inside the door, fumbled. The grating swung back in place. "I was busy with brisk trade when Five-eyes arrive," he explained. "Decide stick around keep eye on store. Plenty time make scene at bog yet."

Miss Braswell shuddered as she crossed the grate. "What's down there?"

"Only good honest sewage, nice change for Five-eyes. After brisk swim, fetch up in bog, join in merry-making."

"I thought you Yalcans were pacifists," Retief commented, stepping inside a roughly-finished passage running parallel with the outer wall of the building.

"All Yalcan love peace. More peaceful now noisy Five-eyes enjoying swim. Besides, only open drain cover; visitors dive in of own free will."

"I had the impression you helped that last fellow along."

"Always try to be helpful when possible. Now for snort."

They followed Oo-Plif along interior passages to emerge behind the bar of the darkened dram-shop, took seats at a low bench and accepted elaborate glasses of aromatic liquor.

"Oo-Plif, I'd appreciate it if you'd see Miss Braswell back to the Legation," Retief said. "I have to leave town on an urgent errand."

"Better stay close, Retief-Tic, come along to bog in time for high point of Voom Festival; only couple hours now."

"I have an errand to run first, Oo-Plif; I've been delegated to find Minister Barnshingle and notify him that the Legation's under siege and that he shouldn't sign anything without reading the fine print."

"Barnshingle Tic-Tic? Skinny Terran with receding lower mandible and abdomen like queen ripe with eggs?"

"Graphically put, Oo-Plif. He's supposed to be hanging around a mountain somewhere, if the Groaci haven't yet swooped down to the rescue."

Oo-Plif was wobbling his head, now enameled in orange and green holiday colors, in the Yalcan gesture of affirmation.

"Barnshingle Tic-Tic here in city at present moment; arrive half-hour ago amid heavy escort of Five-eyes."

"Hmmm. That simplifies matters, perhaps. I was expecting to have to steal a Groaci heli and hunt him down in the wilds. Did he seem to be a prisoner, Oo-Plif?"

"Hard to say, not get too good look. Busy helping Five-eyes find way to bog."

"Via the sewer, I take it?"

"Sure; plenty gratings round town. Must be fifty Five-eyes in swim now; plenty company."

"Are you sure they can swim?"

"Details, details," Oo-Plif said soothingly. "You want go now, pay visit to Barnshingle Tic-Tic?"

"As soon as Miss Braswell's taken care of."

"I'm going with you," the girl said quickly. "I wouldn't dream of missing the excitement."

"This system of hidden passages is certainly handy," Retief said. "How much farther?"

"Close now. Not really hidden passages; just space in double walls. Yalcan like build plenty strong."

They emerged into another of the innumerable alleys that characterized the town, crossed it, entered another door. Oo-Plif cautioned silence. "Place swarm with Five-eyes. We sneak up and get lie of land, find way of rescue Barnshingle Tic-Tic from rescuers."

Five minutes later, crowded into a narrow, dusty passage in the heart of the sprawling building, Retief heard the booming tones of Barnshingle's voice nearby, and the breathy reply of a Groaci.

"Opening in back of closet just ahead," Oo-Plif whispered. "Get earful of proceedings there."

Retief edged forward. Through the half-open closet door he caught a glimpse of Minister Barnshingle seated awkwardly in a low Yalcan easy chair, dressed in dusty hiking clothes. Half a dozen Groaci in vari-colored mufti surrounded him.

"—an exceedingly hairy experience, to be sure," Barnshingle was saying. "Most gratifying to see your heli appear, Drone-master Fiss. But I don't quite grasp the import of the present situation. Not that I'm suggesting that I'm being held against my will, you understand, but I really must hurry back to my office—"

"No need for haste, Mr. Minister," Fiss reassured him. "Everything has been conducted with scrupulous regard for legality, I assure you."

"But there seemed to be hundreds of your . . . ah . . . esteemed compatriots about in the streets," Barnshingle pressed on. "And I had the distinct impression that there were a number of highly irregular activities in progress—"

"You refer perhaps to the efforts of some of our people to remove certain obstacles—"

"Breaking down doors, to be precise," Barnshingle said a trifle snappishly. "As well as hauling away wagon-loads of merchandise from shops, the owners of which appeared to be absent."

"Ah, yes, impulse buying; hardly consonant with domestic thrift. But enough of this delightful gossip, Mr. Minister. The matter I wished to discuss with you . . ." Fiss gave the Minister a glowing account of his peaceful take-over, citing chapter and verse each time the astounded diplomat attempted to rumble a protest.

"And, of course," he finished, "I wished to acquaint your Excellency with the facts before permitting you to be subjected to ill-advised counsel by hot-heads."

"B-but, Great heavens, Drone-master—"

"Planetary Coordinator *Pro Tem*," Fiss interjected smoothly. "Now, I shall, of course, be happy to inspect your credentials at once in order to regularize relations between the Corps and my government."

"My credentials? But I've presented my credentials to Mr. Rilikuk of the Foreign Office—"

"This is hardly the time to reminisce over vanished regimes, Mr. Minister. Now . . ." Fiss leaned forward confidentially. "You and I are, if I may employ the term, men of the world. Not for us the fruitless expense of emotional energy over the *fait accompli*, eh? As for myself, I am most eager to show you around my offices in the finest of the towers of my capitol—"

"Towers? Capitol?"

"The attractive edifices just beyond the swampy area where the local wild-life are now disporting themselves," Fiss explained. "I have assigned—"

"You've violated the native Sanctum Sanctorum?" Barnshingle gasped.

"An unfortunate choice of words," Fiss hissed. "Would you have me establish my ministries here in this warren of one-story clay huts?"

"The Yalcans—" Barnshingle said weakly.

"The name of the planet is now Grudlu," Fiss stated. "In honor of Grud, the patron Muse of practicality."

"Look here, Fiss! Are you asking me to turn my back on the Yalcans and recognize you as the *de jure* government here? Simply on the basis of this absurd legalistic rationalization of yours?"

"With the exception of a number of slanted adjectives, very succinctly put," Fiss whispered.

"Why in the world would I do a dastardly thing like that?" Barnshingle demanded.

"Why, good for him," Miss Braswell breathed behind Retief.

"Ah, yes, terms," Fiss said comfortably. "First, your Mission would, of course, be raised at once to Embassy level, at Grudlun insistence, with yourself requested by name as Ambassador, naturally. Secondly, I have in mind certain local commercial properties which might make a valuable addition to your portfolio; I can let you in at investor's prices—the entire transaction to be conducted with the utmost discretion, of course, so as not to arouse comment among the coarse-minded. Then, of course, you'll wish to select a handsome penthouse for yourself in one of my more exclusive towers . . ."

"Penthouse? Ambassador? Portfolio?" Barnshingle babbled.

"I marvel at the patience Your Excellency has displayed in tolerating the thinly-veiled insult implied in your assignment to grubby quarters in this kennel," Fiss commented. "Why, a person could disappear in this maze of old crockery and never be heard from again . . ."

"Disappear?" Barnshingle croaked. "And wha-what if I refuse . . . ?"

"Refuse? Please, Mr. Minister—or more properly, Mr. Ambassador—why release the fowl of fancy to flutter among such morbid trees of speculation?"

"What about my staff? Will they . . . ah . . . ?"

"Suitable bribes will be offered," Fiss whispered crisply. "Pray don't give it another thought. All surviving members of the Mission will present a united front—with the exception of the two criminals now skulking in the former Legation, of course," he added.

"Magnan? Why, he's one of my most reliable men . . ."

"Perhaps something could be managed in the case of Mr. Magnan, since you express an interest. As for the other—he will return to Groac to stand trial for assorted crimes against the peace and dignity of the Groacian state."

"I really must protest . . ." Barnshingle said weakly.

"Your Excellency's loyalty is most touching. And now, if you'd just care to sign here . . ." An underling handed Fiss a document which he passed to Barnshingle.

"Why, the old phoney!" Miss Braswell gasped. "He's going to do it!"

"It's time to break this up," Retief whispered to Oo-Plif. "I'll take care of Fiss; you hit the others—"

"On contrary, Retief-Tic," the Yalcan replied. "Most improper to interfere with natural course of events."

"Maybe you don't understand; Barnshingle's about to sign away your rights to Yalc. By the time you drag it though the courts and recover, you may all be dead. The Groaci are zealous in the field of wildlife control—"

"No matter; we Yalcans pacifistic folk; not like butt in."

"In that case, I'll have to do it alone. You'll take care of Miss Braswell—"

"No, not even alone, dear Retief-Tic. Not in spirit of Yalcan Pacifism." Something hard prodded Retief's chest; he looked down at the power gun in Oo-Plif's lower right hand.

"Why, you old stinker," Miss Braswell said. "And I thought you were sweet!"

"Hope soon to recoup good opinion, Braswell Ticcim," Oo-Plif said. "Now silence, please."

In the room, Barnshingle and Fiss were making congratulatory noises at each other.

"Matter of fact," Barnshingle said, "I never felt these Yalcans were ready for self-government. I'm sure your wardship will be just what they need."

"Please—no meddling in internal affairs," Fiss said. "And, now, let us away to more appropriate surroundings. Just wait until you see the view from your new suite, Mr. Ambassador . . ." They departed, chattering.

"Well, you've had your way, Oo-Plif," Retief said. "Your pacifism has a curiously spotty quality. Just why do you object to preventing our unfortunate Minister from making an idiot of himself?"

"Forgive use of weapon, Retief-Tic. Foolishness of Barnshingle Tic-Tic-Tic not important—"

"He's a three-tic man now?"

"Promotion just received at hands of Five-eyes. Now away to bog, all buddies together, eh?"

"Where's the rest of Barnshingle's staff? They were together on the crater-viewing expedition."

"All tucked away in house few alleys from here. Better get wiggle on now; climax of festival arrive soon."

"Good night, does your silly old carnival mean more to you than your own planet?" Miss Braswell demanded.

"Voom Festival of great national importance," Oo-Plif stated, opening and closing his bony mandibles like the two halves of a clam—a mannerism indicating polite amusement.

Following the Yalcan's instructions, Retief squeezed through narrow passages, found his way out into the inevitable dark alley, Miss Braswell's hand holding tightly to his. The sounds of looters and their vehicles had diminished to near-silence now. A turbine growled along a nearby street, going away. They came out into a side street, surveyed the deserted pavement, the scattered discards of the Groaci homesteaders. Above the low roof-lines, the mile-distant towers of the shrine were a blaze of gorgeous light.

"It looks so pretty, all lit up," Miss Braswell said. "I'm just amazed that you'd let those nasty little Groaci walk in and take it all away from you."

Oo-Plif laughed, a sound like sand in a bearing. "Towers tributes to deities. Fate of towers in deities' hands now."

"Hmmmph. They could have used a little help from you," Miss Braswell sniffed.

"Looks like the new owners have cleared out for now," Retief said. "All over at the towers, throwing a party in honor of Independence Day."

"Time go to dandy hot bog," Oo-Plif said. "Big event soon now."

Moving briskly along the empty street under the light of the fourth moon, now high in the sky, they reached the corner. Down the wide cross-avenue, the flaring torches of the revelers at the bog sparkled cheerfully. The faint sound of Yalcan voices raised in song were audible now in the stillness.

"Just what is this big event we're hurrying to make?" Retief inquired.

Oo-Plif indicated the large satellite overhead. "When number four moon reach position ten degrees west of zenith—Voom!"

"Oh, astrological symbolism."

"Not know big word—but only one time every ninety-four years standard all four moon line up. When this happen—Voom time here!"

"Voom," Retief said. "Just what does the word signify?"

"Fine old Yalcan word," Oo-Plif said. "Terry equivalent . . . ummm . . ."

"Probably untranslatable."

Oo-Plif snapped the fingers of his upper left hand.

"I remember," he said. "Mean 'earthquake'!"

Retief stopped dead.

"You did say—'earthquake'?"

"Correct Retief-Tic—"

Retief's left fist slammed out in a jack-hammer punch to the Yalcan's midriff plates. The tall creature oofed, coiled into a ball, all four legs scrabbling, the four arms groping wildly.

"Sorry, pal," Retief muttered, catching up the power gun. "No time to argue." He grabbed Miss Braswell's hand and started off at a dead run down the deserted avenue toward the towering castle of light.

They skidded to a halt at a gleam from an opening door ahead. A pipe-stem-legged Groaci hurried from a building, a bulging sack over one knobby shoulder. A second helmeted looter trotted behind, lugging a handsome ten gallon spittoon.

"They've got a heli," Retief said softly. "We need it. Wait here."

Miss Braswell clutched his hand even tighter. "I'm scared!"

The two scavengers were clambering into their dark machine now. Running lights sprang into diamond brilliance. The turbos whirred. Retief disengaged his hand, ran across the thirty feet of open pavement and jumped, just as the heli lifted. There were faint, confused cries from the startled Groaci; one fumbled out a power rifle in time for Retief to jerk it from his grasp, toss it over the side. The heli canted wildly, narrowly missing a decorated cornice. Retief got a grip on a bony neck, propelled the owner over the side, heard a faint yelp as he hit. An instant later, the second followed. Retief caught the controls, brought the heli around in a tight turn, dropped it in beside Miss Braswell.

"Oh! I was afraid it was you that fell overboard, Mr. Retief!" She scrambled up beside him, lent a hand to tumble the gaboon out to smash thunderously on the tiles. On a nearby roof, the two dispossessed Groaci keened softly, like lost kittens. The heli jumped off, lifted swiftly and headed for the glass towers.

The city of glass spread over forty acres, a crystalline fantasy of towers, minarets, fragile balconies suspended over space, diaphanous fretwork, airy walkways spun like spiderwebs between slim spires ablaze with jewel-colored light. Retief brought the heli in high, settled in a stomach-lifting swoop toward the tallest of the towers.

"Miss Braswell, you can operate this thing, can't you?"

"Sure, I'm a good driver, but—"

Retief threw the drive into auto-hover three feet above a tiny terrace clinging to the spire. "Wait here; I'll be back as soon as I can. If anybody else shows up, get out of here fast and head for the bog!"

"The . . . the bog?"

"It'll be the safest place around when the quake hits . . . !" He was over the side, across the five-foot wide shelf of water-clear glass, and through an opening arched with intertwined glass vines hung with sparkling scarlet and purple berries. A narrow stair wound down, debouching into a round chamber walled with transparent murals depicting gardens in the sun. Through the glass, lighted windows in the next tower were visible, and beyond, the silhouettes of half a dozen Groaci and a tall, paunchy Terrestrial.

Retief found more stairs, leaped down them, whirled through an archway of trellised glass flowers. A narrow crystal ribbon arched across the void to the lighted entry opposite. He pulled off his shoes, crossed the bridge in five quick steps.

Voices were audible above, and dark shadows moved to the pebble-glass ceiling. Retief went up, caught a brief glimpse of five richly-draped Groaci under an ornate chandelier, fingering elaborate Yalcan wine glasses and clustering about the stooping, chinless figure of Minister Barnshingle.

"—pleasure to deal with realists like yourselves," the diplomat was saying. "Pity about the natives, of course, but as you pointed out, a little discipline—"

Retief knocked two Groaci spinning, caught Barnshingle by the arm, slopping his drink over the crimson cuff of his mess jacket.

"We've got to go—fast, Mr. Minister! Explanations later!"

Fiss hissed orders; two Groaci darted away and another rushed in to be stiff-armed. Barnshingle choked, spluttered, jerked free. His face had turned an unflattering shade of purple.

"What's the meaning of this outburst—"

"Sorry, Mr. Minister . . ." Retief slammed a clean right cross to the side of Barnshingle's jaw, caught the diplomat as he folded, stooped to hoist the weight to his shoulders, and ran for the door.

Suddenly, Groaci were everywhere. Two bounced aside from Retief's rush; another ducked, swung a power gun up, fired just as Fiss leaped in and knocked his hand aside.

"To endanger the bloated one," he hissed—and went over backward as Retief slammed him aside. A helmeted Groaci Peace-keeper tackled Retief from behind; he paused to kick him across the room, bowling over others. A blaster bolt bubbled glass above his head. The air hissed with weak Groaci shouts as Retief plunged down stairs. Behind him, there was a terrific crash; over his shoulder he caught a glimpse of glass chips showering from the fallen chandelier. He was at the bridge now. Barnshingle groaned and flapped his arms feebly. Retief stepped onto the narrow span, felt it sway under his weight. He took two steps, put a foot over the edge, teetered—

There was a crystalline tinkle, and a ten-foot spear of canary-yellow glass fell past him. He caught his balance, took another step, wobbled as the bridge quivered, leaped clear as the glass shattered into ten thousand glittering shards that sparkled as they fell.

He went up stairs three at a time. A sudden lurch threw him against the wall, where mosaiced glass figures depicted glass blowers at work. A huge chunk of the scene fell backward, letting in a gust of cool night air. Retief scrambled for footing, went up, felt a glass slab drop from underfoot as he gained the terrace. Wind beat down from the heli, hovering a few yards distant. The sparkling tower that had loomed nearby was gone. A sustained crashing, as of nearby surf, drowned the whine of the heli's turbos as it darted in close.

Retief lowered Barnshingle, now pawing weakly and blinking vague eyes, half lifted, half shoved him into the rear seat.

"Hurry, Mr. Retief! It's going . . . !" The noise was deafening now. Retief grasped a strut to pull himself up, and suddenly he was hanging by one hand, his feet treading air. The heli surged, lifting. He looked down. The tower was dropping away below, a cloud of vari-colored glass splinters puffing out as the upper stories thundered down into the depths. A slender sapphire spire, thrusting up almost alone now, rippled like a dancer, then broke into three major fragments, dropped gracefully from view. Retief hauled himself up, got a foot inside the heli, pulled himself into the seat.

"Mr. Retief, you're bleeding!" He put a hand up, felt slickness across his cheek.

"A lot of splinters flying around. It was a little too close—"

"Mr. Retief . . . !" Miss Braswell worked frantically at the controls. "We're losing altitude!"

There was a harsh droning noise. Retief looked back. A heavy armored heli with Groaci markings was dropping toward them.

"Make for the bog!" Retief called over the racket.

There was a buzz, and garish light glared across the struts above Retief's head, bubbling paint.

"Hang on!" Miss Braswell shouted. "Evasive action!" The heli tilted. Barnshingle yelled. The heli whipped up in the opposite direction, spun, dropped like a stone, darted ahead. The futile buzzing of the Groaci's blaster rattled around the faltering vehicle.

"Can't do much more of that," Miss Braswell gasped. "Losing altitude too fast—"

A vast, dark shadow flitted overhead.

"We're sunk," Miss Braswell squeaked. "Another one—"

There was a flare of actinic blue from above and behind, followed by a muffled clatter. Retief caught a glimpse of the Groaci heli, its rotors vibrating wildly falling away behind them. Something huge and shadowy swept toward them from the rear in a rising whistle of air.

"Get set," Retief called. He brought up the blaster he had taken from Oo-Plif, steadied his hand against the heli—

The shadow dropped close; the running lights of the heli gleamed on thirty-foot canopies of translucent tracery spread wide above a seven-foot body. Oo-Plif's gaily painted face beamed down at them. He floated on spread wings, arms and legs folded close.

"Ah, Retief-Tic! Punch in thorax hasten metamorphosis. Got clear of chrysalis just in time!"

"Oo-Plif!" Retief yelled. "What are you doing here?"

"Follow to warn you, dear buddy! Not want you meet gods with crowd of Five-eyes! Now on to bog for festivities!"

Below, the torch-lit surface of the swamp rushed up. Miss Braswell braked, threw herself into Retief's arms as the battered heli struck with a massive splatter at the edge of the mud. Painted Yalcan faces bobbed all around.

"Welcome, strangers!" voices called. "Just in time for fun!"

❖   ❖   ❖

Barnshingle was groaning, holding his head.

"What am I doing here, hip-deep in mud?" he demanded. "Where's Magnan? What happened to that fellow Fiss?"

"Mr. Magnan is coming now," Miss Braswell said. "You bumped your head."

"Bumped my head? I seem to recall . . ."

Someone floundered up, gasping and waving skinny, mud-caked arms.

"Mr. Minister! These primitives dragged me bodily from the street—"

"I thought you were going to stay inside the Legation," Retief said.

"I was merely conducting a negotiation," Magnan huffed. "What are you doing here, Retief—and Miss Braswell!"

"What were you negotiating for, a private apartment just below the Ambassadorial penthouse?" she snapped.

"Miss Braswell! Kindly bend your knees! You're exposing yourself!"

"I've got a quarter-inch layer of black mud on; that's more than I wear to the office!"

"Here, what's this?" Barnshingle exclaimed. "What's happened to my clothes? I'm stark naked!"

"Why, it's a sort of symbolic shedding of the chrysalis, as I understand it, sir," Magnan babbled. "One must go along with native religious observances, of course—"

"Gee, Mr. Retief," Miss Braswell murmured. "It's sort of sexy at that, isn't it?"

"Wha-whatever's happened?" Barnshingle burst out. "Where's the city gone?" He stared across at the glowing heap that marked the site of the fallen towers.

"It seems to have—ah—been offered to the local deities," Magnan said. "It seems to be the custom."

"And all those nasty little bug-eyes with it," Miss Braswell put in.

"Really, Miss Braswell! I must ask you to avoid the use of racial epithets!"

"It's really too bad about the towers; they were awfully pretty."

Oo-Plif, perched like a vast moth on a nearby tree-fern,

spoke up. "Is OK; re-use glass; make plenty bowl and pot from fragments."

"But, what about all those Groaci mixed in with the pieces?"

"Impurities make dandy colors," Oo-Plif assured her.

"My jaw," Barnshingle grated. "How did I fall and hit my jaw?"

"Retief-Tic arrive in nick of time to snatch you from sacrificial pile. Probably bump chin in process."

"What in the world were you doing there, Mr. Minister?" Magnan gasped. "You might have been killed."

"Why, ah, I was trepanned there by the Groaci—quite against my will, of course. They . . . ah . . . had some fantastic proposal to make. I was just on the point of daring them to do their worst, when you appeared, Retief. After that, my recollection grows a bit hazy."

"These head-blows often have retroactive effects," Retief said. "I'll wager you don't recall a thing that was said from the time they picked you off the mountain.

"It's even possible that Oo-Plif has forgotten some of the things he overheard—about penthouses and gilt edge stocks," Retief went on. "Maybe it was the excitement generated by your announcement that Yalc will be getting some large shipments of fine grey silica sand from Groac suitable for glass-making, courtesy of the CDT."

"Announcement?" Barnshingle gulped.

"The one you're going to make tomorrow," Retief suggested gently.

"Oh . . . that one," the Minister said weakly.

"Time to go along now to next phase of celebration," Oo-Plif called from his perch.

"How jolly," Magnan said. "Come along, Mr. Minister—"

"Not you, Magnan-Tic, and Barnshingle Tic-Tic," Oo-Plif said. "Mating rite no place for elderly drones. You scheduled for cozy roost in thorn-tree as ceremonial penitence for follies of youth."

"What about us?" Miss Braswell asked breathlessly.

"Oh, time for you to get in on youthful follies, so have something to repent later!"

"You said . . . mating rite. Does that mean . . . ?"

"Voom Festival merely provide time, place, and member of opposite gender," Oo-Plif said. "Rest up to you . . ."

RETIEF'S WAR

One

Jame Retief, Second Secretary and Consul of the Terrestrial Embassy to Quopp, paused in his stroll along the Twisting Path of Sublime Release to admire the blaze of early morning sunlight on the stained glass window of a modest grog shop wedged between a stall with a sign in jittery native script announcing Bargain Prices in Cuticula Inlays, and the cheery facade of the Idle Hour Comfort Station, One Hundred Stalls, No Waiting. He took out a long cigar of the old-fashioned type still hand-rolled on Jorgensen's Worlds, glanced back along the steep, narrow street. Among the crowd of brilliantly colored Quoppina—members of a hundred related native species mingling freely here in the Great Market of Ixix—the four Terrans who had been trailing him for the past half hour stood out drably.

Retief drew on the cigar, savoring the aroma, turned and stepped through the low arch into the tavern. From a high stool within the raised ring-bar at the center of the gaily lit chamber, the barkeeper—a medium-sized, short-abdomened individual of the Herpp tribe, with chipped wing cases of faded baby blue and four dexterous arms of bristly wine-red on one of which a Terran wristwatch was strapped—manipulated the controls of the dispenser console, exchanged banter with the customers, made change, and kept a pair of eyes on the free lunch simultaneously. He saw Retief, tilted his anterior antennae in friendly greeting.

"I am Gom-Goo, and I dance the Dance of Welcome," he susurrated in Quopp trade dialect, his voice reminiscent of fingernails on a blackboard. "What'll it be, Retief?"

"I'm Retief, and I dance the Dance of Glad Arrival," the diplomat replied in the same tongue. "How about a shot of Bacchus brandy?"

"Red or black?"

"Black." The other customers made room as Retief moved up, unclipped a carefully charred wooden bowl from the serving panel, got it under the proper bright-plated nozzle just in time to catch the tar-colored syrup as it jetted forth.

"That's pretty good stuff," Gom-Goo said; he lowered his voice. "But for a real kick, you ought to try a shot of Hellrose—cut ten to one, of course. That'll put a charge on your plates."

"I tried it once. Too sweet for a Terry. We like our sugar fermented."

"Sourballs?" The Herpp indicated an assortment of pea-sized lumps of yellow, white, purple, and green.

Retief shook his head. "I prefer salt peanuts to salt-peter," he confided.

"Well, every tribe to its own poison."

"Here's oil in your crankcase," Retief toasted formally, nibbling the brandy.

"Oil," Gom-Goo responded. "You haven't been in lately, Retief. Been dormant?"

"No more so than usual, Gom-Goo. Ambassador Longspoon's been imposing non-union hours on the staff, I'm afraid. Wouldn't do to let the Groaci steal a march on us and get a Bolshoi-type ballet theater built before we can get a Yankee-stadium type sports arena off the drawing board."

Gom-Goo worked his dorsal mandibles in the gesture that expressed courteous skepticism. "Frankly, Retief, we

Quoppina aren't much interested in watching Terries hobble around. After all, only two legs and no wings . . ."

"I know; but it's traditional in these diplomatic competitions to build something conspicuously inappropriate."

Gom-Goo tilted his oculars toward the door, where a pair of Quoppina with highly polished black carapaces were rolling past, twirling nightsticks.

"Speaking of Terry programs, Retief, just between you and me, what's behind this business of buffing up these Voion ne'er-do-wells and setting them to cruising the streets waving clubs at the rest of us?"

"Well, Gom-Goo, it appears that in some quarters the view is held that you Quoppina are a little too fond of brawling, anarchy, and dueling in the streets to qualify as natural democrats. Ergo, a native police force."

"Uh-huh—but why pick the Voion for the job? Their tribe's made its living by waylaying honest Quoppina in back alleys ever since the Great Egg first hatched—"

A heavy foot clumped behind Retief. He turned to find the four Terrans ringing him in, ominous expressions on their weathered features.

"We're just in from the Trading Post at Rum Jungle," the lean, scar-faced member of the quartet said flatly. "We want to have a little talk with you, Mister." He put his left fist carefully against the palm of his right hand and twisted it, looking around nervously.

Retief nodded. "Go ahead," he said pleasantly. A large man with thick, protuberant ears and thin sandy hair eased the scarred man aside.

"Not in this dump," he said in a voice like a cannon-ball rolling downstairs. "Outside."

"If it's a private matter, maybe you'd better drop by my office—"

"We already been to the Embassy; talked to some bird named Magnan," the big man said. "He acted like his lace drawers was itching him; no joy there."

"Don't argue with this chump, Big Leon," a squatty fellow with a bluish chin and a steel front tooth advised. "Bring him along."

The bartender leaned over and buzzed sharply. "My name is Gom-Goo," he started. "I—"

"Better get your wiring checked, low-pockets," Scar-face cut him off. "Sounds like you got a short in your talk box." He jerked his head at Retief. "Let's walk, Mister."

"I haven't quite finished my drink," Retief said mildly. "Why don't you go stand outside; I'll be along presently."

The fourth man, yet to be heard from, edged close. "Ah, sir, we have a problem," he began. "We—"

"Skip it, Jerry," Scar-face snapped. He hooked a thumb over his shoulder, glowered at Retief. "Outside, you, like Big Leon said."

"Sorry," Retief said. "Some other time, maybe."

Scar-face narrowed his eyes, reached a large-knuckled hand for Retief's collar; Retief leaned aside, caught the hand, and flipped it over, his fingers against the palm, his thumb against the scarred knuckles, doubled it back over the wrist. Scar-face went to his knees with a yowl. Retief tsked.

"A very poor lead, Lefty," he said reproachfully. "It's a good thing I wasn't an enemy of yours."

"Hey," the big man said, stepping in. "Let him up."

Retief looked at the wide face that topped his own six-three by an inch. "Why do they call you Big Leon?"

Big Leon set himself. "Put Seymour down and I'll show you," he grated.

Retief shifted his grip, lifted the scarred man clear of the floor, hoisted him chest-high. "Here, you have him," he offered, and tossed him at the big man. Leon staggered back, *oof*ed, thrust Seymour aside, frowned, doubled a large fist, and moved in—

There was a shrill rasp of sound. A thick, five-foot Quoppina with a glistening black carapace decked out in elaborate silver ornaments rolled between Retief and Big Leon.

"Outside, foreign grubs!" the intruder keened. He waved a long billy club of black wood, jabbed it at the scar-faced man, who had stumbled to his feet. There were other club-wielders behind the first—two, three, half a dozen or more, all wearing the new black and silver trappings of the CDT-sponsored Federal Police. The Voion captain waved his palps, giving Retief a glimpse down a yellow-green throat set with silvery needles.

"All of you are under arrest," he rasped. "Place your manipulative members above your sense-organ clusters and proceed hence!"

"What's the charge?" Retief asked in the Voion dialect.

"Trespassing in forbidden territory, alien, not that it matters! The example may remind your fellows to remain in the ghetto graciously assigned to them by the indulgence of the Planetary Government!"

"Just a minute," the barkeeper interrupted from his perch above. "I am Gom-Goo and—"

"Silence, panderer to alien perversions," the Voion snapped. "Or I'll find dungeon space for you, too!"

The other Voion were unlimbering clubs now. Over their heads, Retief caught Big Leon's eye, jerked his head minutely to the right; the big man narrowed his eyes, nodded quickly. As the Voion before Retief brought his club back for a jab to the sternum, Leon reached, caught the alien by the upper pair of arms, lifted him clear of the floor, whirled him, and slammed him at his fellows. Two of them went over with a crash. Retief spun, intercepted an eager junior closing in from the left, caught him by his vestigial wing cases, sent him reeling back to collide with his partner as Scar-face feinted, twisted the club from the two-pronged grip of the nearest cop, ducked, and jammed it through the spokes of the alien's yard-high main wheels. The victim stopped with a screech and a twanging of broken spokes. Big Leon met a second charging Voion with a roundhouse swipe, yelled as his fist glanced off the armored and thorned thorax, then landed a blow that spun the creature aside. Retief, ready, spiked its main wheels with the club he had wrenched from his last victim, just as the sole undamaged Voion struck Big Leon a vicious blow behind the ear. Leon turned with a roar, picked up the cop bodily, and slammed him against the barkeeper's podium.

"Here!" the barkeeper shrilled. "I am Gom-Goo and I dance the Dance of Distress—"

"Let's get out of here!" Scar-face ducked aside as a Voion's club whistled, charged for the door. Quoppina of all sizes and colors scattered before him. Leon aimed a blow at a cop renewing the attack; Jerry took the arm of the fourth Terran, staggering from a bloody cut across the scalp, plunged through the crowd. Retief, backed against the podium by the last two Voion still in action, keeping their distance and swinging their clubs in whistling arcs, plucked a tall bottle from a display, got in a hearty crack across the head of one as Gom-Goo leaned down and laid the other out with a bung starter.

"Retief!" The Herpp called above the chatter of the clientele who had been enjoying the free show. "I am Gom-Goo and I dance the Dance of Apology—"

"This dance is on me," Retief panted. "I think I'd better be off now, Gom-Goo; sorry about the damage—"

"It was entirely the fault of these jacks-in-office," the bartender clashed his wing cases in agitation. "Interfering in a friendly dispute among cash customers! Tum-Tuk . . ." He signaled to his two table waiters. "Haul these Voion troublemakers out into the alley, to survive or not, just as they please." He leaned over to eye the one Big Leon had thrown against the podium. "As for this fellow, stuff him in the incinerator. He's shouldered his last free citizen off the parking-ledge."

"We'd better dust, Mister," Leon said. "That Bug was a cop and he's got plenty of pals . . ."

There was a distant clanging of gongs.

"You'd best transfer the scene of your diversions elsewhere for the nonce, Retief," Gom-Goo called. "One of these spoil-sports has summoned his fellow black-guards . . ."

"We were just leaving; and thanks for tapping that last fellow; he was getting too close for comfort."

"My pleasure, Retief. The rascals have been getting pushier by the day. They're up to something, mark my words! And remember: After the wheels, the juncture between the parietal plates is the best spot to go for on a Voion."

"I'll remember that. Ta ta."

In a quieter grog shop half a mile from the scene of the action, Retief and four Terrans found a table at the back of the room from which they could keep an eye on the street. Through the wide, doorless arch, Voion cops could be seen hurrying past, grim and businesslike in their black and silver trappings. Big Leon blew on his skinned fist, looked at Retief almost shyly.

"Sorry about the rough stuff, uh, Mister, uh . . ."

"Retief. No apology needed. I see now why they call you Big Leon."

Leon nodded. "You looked pretty good in there yourself, Mister. Maybe those Bugs'll think about it before they tackle a bunch of Terries again."

"What's got into them Bugs?" the scarred man demanded. "They been giving us a hard time out in the field, but I figured they'd be minding their manners here in town."

"That's what we came here to talk about," Big Leon said, "Something's stirring the Voion tribe up. I thought it was just us planters and traders they were out to get, but they've got the whole town sewed up like a dead sailor."

"We pretty near didn't get into the city," the steel-toothed man said. "There's a patrol around the port; a man could get the idea he wasn't welcome."

"The new police force was designed to bring law and order to Quopp," Retief said. "According to the official T.O. there are supposed to be no more than a hundred of them assigned to the city, with smaller detachments at the major trading towns."

"A hundred my uncle Edgar," Leon growled. "The whole town's swarming with 'em—and there must be another ten thousand between here and Rum Jungle."

"Yes, I'd say our friends the Voion have answered the call to civic duty in surprising numbers," Retief said.

"They say Longspoon's the one behind it," Scar-face said. "Sometimes I wonder whose side you CDT boys are on."

"The motivation of the diplomat is an enigma that even his best friend, if he had one, would be hard put to define," Retief confided. "Technically, the Corps Diplomatique Terrestrienne is dedicated to the protection of Terran interests, Galaxy-wide. Of course, figuring out what those interests really are can get a little complicated."

"Like equipping local cops with clubs to pound Terry heads, using fees squeezed out of Terry businessmen," Seymour growled.

"What does the Corps want here, anyway?" Leon demanded. "Quopp was doing all right—with a little help from Terry free enterprises; then along comes a bunch of CDT Johnnies getting everything organized, and all of a sudden us Terries are undesirable aliens."

Retief refilled glasses. "Admittedly, some of the measures selected by our Chief of Mission may seem paradoxical at first glance. But that's just because you haven't entered into the spirit of the game. All of the measures Ambassador Longspoon has taken—restrictions on private enterprise by Terrans, establishment of the Planetary Police, free goods for the indigent, subsidies for Voion commercial enterprise, and the rest—are designed to bring peace and plenty to the downtrodden locals whom you fellows have been exploiting."

"What do you mean, exploiting?" Big Leon's fist hit the table. "Why, a hundred years ago, when the first Terries hit Quopp, there was nothing here but wild Bugs living in grass huts and eating each other. We laid out the towns, built trails, started 'em in on a little cottage industry and intertribal trade. We brought in electronics men to be country G.P.'s, developed new lines of merchandise to make life more beautiful for the Quopp in the street, and taught 'em the idea of civilization. Sure, we made a good profit—but they've got their money's worth every step of the way!"

"Still, Leon, now that you've put Quopp on the star maps, competition has set in. Our friends the Groaci aren't going to let this world drift into the Terry camp without a struggle. They've set up a string of trading posts along the other coast of Continent One, and they're doing a brisk trade in miniature Tri-D's, artificial limbs and wheels, and electronic Mah-Jongg sets—"

"Direct competition with us!" Jerry burst out. "The copycats!"

"Of course," Retief went on, "no self-respecting diplomat could let the challenge pass without making an effort to out-enlighten the opposition. Whatever the Groaci do, we have to do bigger—"

"Why?" Seymour grunted.

"Why does a golfer have to hit the golf ball?" Retief riposted. "Such is the challenge of diplomacy."

"But why this sudden compulsion to unite the planet

under a single government—and with the Voion in charge, of all people!" Jerry looked indignant.

"You know we can't even travel inland to look over the markets?" Big Leon said.

"You know why? The Voion! They're all over like a land-lubber's lunch—waving clubs and telling *us* where we can and can't go!"

"Longspoon's made a mistake, backing the Voion," Big Leon said. "There's not a Bug on the planet doesn't hate their main windings. Slavers and dope-runners, con artists, highway robbers, and second-story men—that's what they were—until this idea of reforming 'em and putting badges on 'em came along."

"His Excellency envisions the day when a trained cadre of reformed Voion will lead the newly enlightened masses to a new era of planetary unity," Retief explained. "Or so he frequently says."

"Retief, how long you been here on Quopp?" Leon inquired.

"Only a few weeks, I'm afraid."

"You talk the dialects pretty good."

"I've spent a few hours on the encephalotapes."

"Uh-huh," Leon nodded. "Well, I was born here, Retief. Hell, I haven't been off the planet half a dozen times in my life. And I can tell you—these devils have got something up their sleeve!"

"I'm inclined to agree their police badges seem to have gone to their heads—"

"It ain't just that," Seymour said. "There's something in the wind! We saw it, out in the jungle—and now here in town! It's getting ready to pop! Pushing Terries around—that's bad medicine, Mister!"

"And I'll tell you something else," the steel-toothed man said. "Those Bugs are tapping CDT shipments at the port—in broad daylight!"

Retief frowned. "You're sure of that?"

"Been down to the port lately?" Big Leon inquired.

"Not in the past month."

"Come on," Leon rose. "Let's go take a look-see. There's a CDT shipment on the pad right now big enough to put half the Terries on Quopp out of business." As he stood, a buzzing three-inch yellow-green flyer sailed by, settled to a puddle of spilled liquor on the floor. Big Leon raised a size thirteen shoe—

"Don't do it," Retief said. "He probably needs a drink as bad as we did."

"That's just a Phip," Seymour said. "You talk like they was human."

"You never can tell," Retief said, skirting the small creature. "He just might be somebody's cousin George."

Outside, the five Terrans hailed two massive peach-colored Wumblums, mounted to the creaking velvet-lined seats strapped to the heavy creatures' backs, relaxed as their mounts trundled off on broad leather-shod wheels toward the space port, groaning up the steep slopes, puffing down the declines, shouting for way among the thronging Quoppina packing the route. Clear of the main shopping streets, the Wumblums made better time, wheeling along briskly under the crisp morning sky. Overhead, the glaring crescent of Joop, Quopp's sister world, swung toward its twice-daily eclipse of the distant sun, a blinding point of white light casting short midmorning shadows across the intricately surfaced buildings that thrust up everywhere like giant, lumpy loaves of pastel-toned bread.

"You gents coming back?" Retief's mount inquired in a voice like the E-string on a bass cello. It tilted an auditory receptor to pick up the reply over the noise of wheels of pavement. "Ten percent off for a round trip."

"Not right away," Retief said. "Better not wait for us."

"I'll stick around anyway; Voom-Voom's the name. Ask for me when you're ready to go. Not much action this morning. All these Zilk and Jackoo in town from the villages, they'd wear out their wheels rubbernecking before they'd hail a ride—and these Voion cops all over the place—they're not helping business any."

The Wumblum behind Retief's swung out, came alongside. "Looks like we got company," Big Leon called, pointing over his shoulder with a large, blunt thumb. Retief glanced back; a pair of Voion were trailing fifty yards behind, black shells glistening, light winking from their recently applied police insignia.

"There are two more flanking us on the right," Retief

said. "I'd guess we're covered on the left, too. They don't want us to be lonely."

"Maybe you'd better cut out of here," Leon suggested. "I guess they're still mad. Me and the boys'll handle this."

"It's a nice day for a drive," Retief said. "I wouldn't think of missing it."

The Wumblum took a quick look back at Retief. "Some of those Voion giving you gents trouble?"

"They're trying, I'll concede, Voom-Voom."

"Don't worry about a thing, boss. I'll say a word to my sidekick Rhum-Rhum, and we'll lead those grub-eaters down a couple of side streets to a cul-de-sac I know and work 'em over for you."

"That's friendly of you, old-timer, but we don't have time for any more horseplay today."

"All part of the service," Voom-Voom said.

The port came into view as the party emerged from the twisting avenue; a hundred acre expanse of hilly ground ringed by a sagging wire fence, paved and scabbed over with a maze of flimsy temporary structures, some now nearly a century old, among which the tall shapes of scattered vessels thrust up, festooned with service cables and personnel rigging. As Retief watched, a vast black shadow swept down the hillside beyond the ships, rushed across the port blanking out the gleam of sun on chromalloy and concrete and corrugated aluminum, then enveloped them, plunging the street into abrupt, total darkness. Retief looked up; the great fire-edged disk of Joop loomed black against the midnight blue sky. Voom-Voom lowered his head, and the beam of dusty light from his luminescent organ cut a path through the gloom ahead.

"You know, you Terries have done us Quoppina a lot of good," he said, slowing now to pick his way with more care. "Like the focusing lenses for us Wumblums' head-lights; a real boon. And the rubber wheel-shoes like some of the fellows wear; a useful item. And the synthetic lubricants— and the surgical spares—you've kept a lot of fellows on the street earning a living at the time o' life when our dads would have been laid up for good. But these Voion cops, and this one-world, one-government idea: It's a mistake. It's always been every tribe for itself, and a good system, too—"

"Watch out, Retief," Big Leon called quietly. There was a soft swish of tires on clay pavement, the abrupt stab of yellowish light beams as fast-moving forms closed in on both sides.

"Halt!" a Voion accent came from the darkness. "Pull up here, you Wumblums, in the name of the law!"

"You small-time chiselers have got the gall to pull that routine on me?" Voom-Voom trumpeted, accelerating. "Stay out of my way, or I'll leave my tread-marks down your backs!"

"That's an order, you great bumbling lout!" One of the Voion, apparently carried away by his own recently acquired rank, swung too close; Voom-Voom shot out an arm like a ship-grapple, gathered the luckless creature in, tossed him aside to slam the pavement with a clang of metallo-organic body plates. A second Voion, veering aside, gave a shriek, disappeared under the massive wheels of Rhum-Rhum. The others sheered off, fell back, as the Wumblums sped off toward the lights now gleaming all across the port. Retief held on to the worn leather hand-straps as the solid wheels hammered over the potholed road.

"A good thing the CDT hasn't gone as far as handing out power guns to those Jaspers," Seymour shouted as Rhum-Rhum came up on the starboard beam.

"Look there—" Jerry leaned forward beside Retief. "There are Voion swarming all over the port!"

"Don't worry, gents," Voom-Voom hooted. "Rhum-Rhum and me will stand by. That was the first time I've had my wheels on a Voion since the last time I caught one prying the lid off my fare-box. It felt good."

There was a flood-lit gate ahead, flanked by a pair of Voion who rolled forward officiously—and darted back as Voom-Voom barreled past them, slammed through the fence, hurtled on without slowing. They were in among the tall ships now, threading their way among stacked packing cases, dangling cargo nets, hurrying stevedores, and Vorch cargo-carriers, the latter squat Quoppina with three thick functional wheels and broad, labor-scarred carapaces. Ahead Retief saw the familiar CDT code stenciled on the sides of stacked cases being unloaded by Voion stevedores from the hold of a battered tramp trader under a battery of polyarcs.

"You notice they're not shipping the stuff in Corps vessels," Big Leon pointed out as their mounts pulled up at a signal from Retief. "It's all handled pretty cagey; looks like there's angles to this that Longspoon doesn't want publicity on. It just happens I know that cargo-mark."

A pair of bustling Voion were at work on the cargo net, overseeing the placement of the crates. Others stood about, as though on guard—humbler specimens than the elite police, Retief noted; their dull black wing cases lacked the high polish and brightwork of their favored tribesmates. One, wearing the armband of a Ramp Master, wheeled across to confront the visitors. He was an oldster, beginning to silver around the edges, his thickened wing cases showing the marks of repeated paring.

"What d'ye seek here, sirs?" he chirped in tribal Voion, in what was meant to be an authoritative tone, meanwhile working his anterior antennae in frantic Voion thieves' code.

"Shift . . . cases . . . conceal . . . special . . . consignment . . ." Retief deciphered. He noted a sudden stir of activity among the Voion at the net. A pair of the patrolling stick-wielders rolled in to help. The center of attention appeared to be a stack of cases conspicuously tagged with large red cards reading "For the Terran Ambassador."

"We takee look-see," Seymour was saying in trade pidgin. "We lookee gift-gift Terry friend-friend send."

"Very good," the oldster shifted to the same tongue. "Looky see, plenty ski pants, snowshoe, smoked oyster, bagels, tennis racquet, paint-by-number kit; all stuff keep tiny Quoppina tot alive all winter."

"You hear that, Retief?" Big Leon growled. "Some of my hottest trade items, those are. You'd think Longspoon was deliberately trying to put us traders out of business." He pointed suddenly. "Hey, look there!" A Voion in tribal dress, with the feathery antennae of a Flying Jarwheel strapped to his head, was maneuvering a pink Timblum— a smaller cousin of the mighty Wumblum—into position. There was a squat cart hitched behind the mount.

"That's Smuk; he's a retired slaver; used to be one of my best customers. Now look at him, freeloading! No wonder I don't see him around the warehouse sales anymore!"

Retief climbed down from his seat, strolled across to study the stacked crates. The Ramp Master trailed him, his wheels squeaking on the dry bearings of old age. Behind the façade of hurriedly places boxes, Retief counted at least half a dozen of the red-marked cases, identical with the others except for the prominent diplomatic address. The Voion twittered nervously at his heels.

"Nice Terry gentleman take look-see next side, see plenty nice box, you bet," he creaked.

"What's in those, Ramp Master?" Retief asked in tribal Voion, indicating the half-concealed boxes.

"Eee, the sir speaks good Tribal," the old Voion clacked his palps in a gesture indicating Respectful Congratulation. "Why, as to those cases there, they contain educational material, yes, sir, that's what they contain. Now, over here . . ."

Big Leon had come up beside Retief. "Feel like sticking your nose into trouble?" Retief asked softly.

Leon nodded. "Sure, why not?"

"Why don't you go stir up a little activity over there, on the far side of the landing jack—say in about ten minutes?"

"Huh? Oh, I gotcha." Leon gave Retief a quizzical look, went over and spoke to Seymour. Beside Retief, the old Voion signaled with his antennae. A pair of cargo-handlers wheeled casually over to hover near the Terrans, trailing as they sauntered off, looking over the scene of bustling activity.

Retief moved on along the deep-shadowed lane between stacked cargo, paused before a heap of crates, pointed to the manila envelopes stapled to their sides.

"Mind if I look?" he inquired.

"As the sir desires," the oldster said quickly. Retief pulled a folded copy of a bill of lading from the pocket, opened it out. It indicated that the crate contained bound volumes of the *Pest Control Journal*, consigned to the Information Service Library in the care of the Terran Consulate at Groon—a small city a hundred miles upriver in Deep Jungle. He went on, casually checking packing lists, rounded the end of the line of stacked crates, came up the back side. Directly behind the red-tagged cases, he found a pile of boxes, containing blank forms destined for the Terran Chancery. At that moment, an outcry came from beyond the looming bulk of the ship. Retief turned to his guide, who was now jittering nervously and looking in the direction from which the disturbance emanated.

"By the way, I forgot to mention it, but one of my companions—the large one—is something of a practical joker. He may have taken it into his head to start a fire or plant a couple of small choke-bombs. Maybe you'd better wheel over and check on him."

"The sir jests . . . ?" The Ramp Master looked around for a courier, saw the last of his crew curving sharply out of sight on one wheel, headed for the scene of the growing uproar. "If the sir will excuse . . ." he shot off at surprising speed.

At once, Retief turned to the nearest red-tagged crates, used a handy pry-bar to lever a slot free. A layer of oil-impregnated plastic barred his view of the contents of the box. He took out a compact pocket knife, snapped the blade out, slit the liner, reached in, felt a lump coolness of a plastic coated object. He managed a two-fingered grip, drew it out. It was a bulky, heavy package, roughly triangular, larger than Retief's hand, its outlines obscured by the protective cocoon. He slit it, peeled it back; the polished butt of a Mark XXX power gun nestled in his hand.

Retief glanced around; none of the port personnel were in view. He stripped away the oily covering from the gun, dropped the weapon in his pocket, then tucked the empty plastic back inside, folded the liner over it, pressed the slat back in position.

The noises from Big Leon's direction were gaining in timbre and volume, accompanied by splintering sounds. Voom-Voom glanced at Retief. "Say, boss, that racket—"

"Just boyish high spirits; it won't last much longer," Retief said. "Meanwhile, see that nobody disturbs me for the next five minutes." Voom-Voom waved one arm, clicked his luminescent organ on, and rolled forward to cover the approach. Retief set to work moving the barricade of boxes aside and removing red tags from the special consignment. The riot continued, still growing in volume. With the red tags free, Retief moved back to the crates marked for Groon, quickly removed the tags, used the butt of his pocket knife to hammer labels removed from the consignment of forms in place in their stead, then hurried on to the crated forms, placed the red tags on the boxes.

"Better hurry it up, boss," Voom-Voom hooted softly. "I think the excitement's dying down over there—" He broke off to rumble suddenly into action. Retief heard the shrill of Voion voices. He glanced up at the black disk of Joop; a glowing bulge was showing at one edge now; the eclipse would be over in another half-minute. He hurried back to the special consignment, attached the cards from the library shipment intended for Groon. Behind him, voices shrilled; Voom-Voom was still blocking the lane, loudly demanding why he should move merely to let a pack of Voion riffraff through. Retief stepped quickly to Rhum-Rhum.

"If you backed up carelessly, you might just ram that pile of boxes," he said. "They *might* get all mixed up together . . ."

"They might, at that," the Wumblum agreed. "Take those scalpers half their siesta hour to unscramble 'em." He straightened his wheels, glanced back, and moved suddenly, slammed into the neatly stacked crates. They skidded, toppled with a crash. Voom-Voom, watching the byplay with one pair of eyes, whirled about in mock alarm, dumped another row. Excited Voion shot past him, shrilling, just as the glare of returned sunlight sprang across the hills, scythed down the slope and on across the crowded tarmac to bathe the scene of chaos in brilliant day.

Big Leon appeared, looming over the scurrying cargo-tenders. He looked around, frowning.

"What the Sam Hill happened here?" he demanded loudly.

"Big brute of a dumb Wumblum makee big mess-mess," the old Voion cargo master shrieked. "Great clumsy louts gotee no damn pidgin here!"

"Don't spin your wheels, grandpa," Voom-Voom rumbled carelessly. He leaned over to put his armored cranium near Retief's. "How'd I do, chief?"

"Very effective," Retief said approvingly. He walked over to the sidelines where a dull-eyed Vorch cargo-carrier was squatting, watching the activity.

"There are half a dozen crates marked for the Terry Library at Groon," he said in trade dialect to the heavyweight. "I wonder if you know of an unused shed nearby where they might accidentally be tucked away out of sight for a few days." He dropped a strip of embossed plastic trade wampum in the Vorch's nearest hand, which immediately twitched it out of sight.

"What's this—a bribe?" the carrier swiveled his wide head to bring his silicon-lensed rear eyes to bear.

"Just a gratuity for services rendered," Retief reassured him.

"That's OK then; just so you don't offer me no graft." The Vorch pointed with a short, thick arm. "The little bonded warehouse over there—the one with the red carving on the front. I'll stack the stuff in there."

Retief nodded and rejoined the party.

"Hey, what gives, Mr. Retief?" Seymour demanded. "Leon says—"

"Maybe you better not ask too many questions," the big man put in. "I think we made our point. Let's settle for that and head back for Rum Jungle. Something's ready to pop, and I want to be minding the store when it happens."

"Maybe you better come with us, Retief," Steel-tooth said. "The post is a pretty fair fort if push comes to shove."

"Don't talk foolish, Lester," Leon said. "Retief's got a job to do here."

"Yeah," Steel-tooth said, "but when the job blows up in your face, remember Rum Jungle. We'll need every man— and then it won't be enough."

Two

At the Terran Chancery in the Path of Many Sporting Agents, Retief stepped down from his perch and handed a strip of credit to his mount.

"Call on me any time, boss," the Wumblum said. "I kind of like your style." He nodded toward the irregularly surfaced Embassy complex, a cluster of standard Quopp-style buildings perched on the uneven ground, painted ocher,

Indian red, and dusty aquamarine, perforated by irregularly shaped windows at random intervals. "First time I ever hauled a Terry," the Wumblum went on in a confidential tone. "Between you and me, I heard you folks were a tight crowd with a credit and not much in the sporting line, if you know what I mean."

"A base canard, Voom-Voom. A diplomat considers a day wasted if he isn't playing at least three games at once."

As Retief stepped through the main entry, incongruously aluminum-framed and glass-doored, First Secretary Magnan hurried up, a thin, harassed figure in the limp yellow seersucker shorts and dickey of subtropical undress kit.

"Retief," he called. "Wherever have you been? The ambassador is furious! And Colonel Underknuckle's been calling for you for an hour! I've been frantic!"

"Why? Can't they be furious without me?"

"The sight of you seems to stimulate the condition, that I grant," Magnan said witheringly. "Come along now. I've told the colonel you were probably out gathering material for the quarterly Sewage Report. I trust you'll say nothing to dispel that impression."

"I've been cementing relations with the Terran business community," Retief explained as he accompanied the senior diplomat along the wide, tiled, office-lined corridor which had been installed to replace the warren of tiny, twisting passages and cubicles originally filling the interior of the structure.

"Hmmm. I'm not sure that was wise, in view of the present down-playing of Terran private enterprise here on Quopp. You know how Prime Minister Ikk frowns on that sort of thing."

"Oh, prime minister, eh? Who gave him that title?"

"Why, he advised the ambassador that it was conferred early this morning by unanimous vote of the Council of Drones." Retief followed Magnan into the lift; the doors closed with a soft *whoosh!* of compressed air. The car lurched, started heavily upward.

"Let's see," Retief mused. "That's the dummy legislature he set up to satisfy the ambassador's passion for democracy, isn't it? It was fortunate he had seventy-three senile uncles handy to appoint; saved the bother of breaking in strangers."

"Yours is a distorted view of the evolution of representational government here on Quopp," Magnan said reprovingly. "Closer attention to your *Daily Bulletin from the Bird's Nest* would go far toward homogenizing your thinking on the subject."

"I thought that was something they did to milk."

"The term refers to voluntary alignment of viewpoint toward a group-oriented polarity; a sort of linkage of moral horsepower for maximal thrust toward the objective."

"I'm not sure that pasteurized thinking is rich enough in intellectual vitamins to satisfy my growing curiosity about just what Ikk is up to."

"It should be apparent even to you, Retief," Magnan said sharply, "that the Corps can hardly accredit a full Mission to a nonexistent planetary government. Ergo, such a ruling body must be formed—and who better qualified than the Voion to undertake the task?"

"You might have something there; their past history has given them a firm grounding in the basics of politics; but with the other tribes outnumbering them a hundred to one, it's a little hard to see how they're planning to impose planet-wide enlightenment on a race that's as fond of anarchy as the Quoppina."

"That, my dear Retief, is Ambassador Longspoon's problem, not ours. It was his idea to groom the Voion for leadership; our task is merely to implement his policies."

"And if in the process we saddle the other ninety-nine percent of the population with a dictatorship, that's a mere detail."

"Ah, I can see you're beginning to get the picture. Now . . ." The elevator halted and Magnan led the way out, paused at the heavy door barring the public from the Chancery wing. "I hope you'll restrain your unfortunate tendency to essay japes at the expense of decorum, Retief. Colonel Underknuckle is in no mood for facetiae." He pushed through, nodded mechanically at the small, gray Voion female buffing her chelae at a small desk of polished blue wood at one side of the red-carpeted corridor. She clacked her palps indifferently, blew a large bubble of green spearmint, and popped it with lively report.

"Impertinence!" Magnan sniffed under his breath. "A few months ago the baggage was an apprentice slop-drudge in a local inn of most unsavory repute; now, after we've trained her and given her that expensive set of chrome inlays, a derisive pop of the gum is considered adequate greeting for her benefactors."

"That's the trouble with uplifting the masses; they get to believing it themselves."

Magnan stopped at an austere slab door marked MILITARY ATTACHE, fitted an expression on his narrow features appropriate for greeting a Grade Seven employee, pushed through into deep-carpeted silence.

"Ah, there, Hernia, I believe Colonel Underknuckle wished to see Mr. Retief . . ."

The fat woman behind the desk patted a coil of mummified hair with a hand like a glove full of lard, showed Magnan a simper suitable for a first secretary, thumbed a button on a console before her. A chime sounded beyond the half-open door.

"Yes, confound it, what is it this time!" a voice like splitting canvas snarled from the desk speaker. "What in the name of perdition's become of Magnan? If he's not here in five minutes, send along that memo to the ambassador I keep handy—"

"It is I," Magnan said stiffly. "And—"

"Don't use grammar on me, Magnan!" the attaché shouted. "Come in here at once! There's been another communication from that benighted vessel! The saucy minx at the controls insists she's bringing her in, clearance or no clearance. And where the devil's that fellow, Retief?"

"I have him right here, Colonel . . ." As his callers entered the room, Underknuckle, a lean, high-shouldered man with bushy white hair, hollow, purplish cheeks, and a lumpy, clay-colored nose, his immaculately tailored midafternoon semiformal uniform awry, spun in his hip-u-matic contour chair, causing the power-swivel mechanism to whine in protest. He glared at Retief.

"So there you are at last! What's the meaning of this,

sir? Is it possible that you're unaware of the new restrictions on tourism here on Quopp?" The colonel lowered his voice. "Schemes are all about us, gentlemen. We'll have to look sharp to our fences to keep our powder dry!"

"But just one little shipload of ladies—and in difficulty at that—" Magnan began.

"Orders are orders!" Underknuckle hit the desk with his fist, winced, slung his fingers as though drying them.

"Let me assure you, when Ambassador Longspoon imposed entry quotas on sightseers, there was an excellent reason for it!" He barked through a grimace of pain.

"Gracious, yes, Colonel," Magnan chirped. "We all know Prime Minister Ikk doesn't like Terries."

"Ikk's likes and dislikes have nothing to do with it! It was the ambassador's decision!"

"Of course, Colonel. What I meant was, *you* don't like Terries—"

"Don't like Terrans? Why, I'm a Terran myself, you idiot!"

"I didn't mean to give the wrong impression, I'm sure, Fred," Magnan said breathlessly. "Personally, I *love* Terries—"

"Not *these* Terries!" Underknuckle snatched up a paper and waved it. "A boatload of females! Giddy, irresponsible, women! Idlers—or worse! Parasites! And no visas, mind you! And the ringleader, Mr. Retief"—the colonel thrust a mobile lower lip at him—"is demanding to speak to *you*, sir! By name!"

"Retief!" Magnan turned on him. "What can you be thinking of, importing luxury goods—"

"It's clear enough what he's thinking of," Underknuckle snapped. "And I needn't point out that such thoughts are hardly in consonance with tight military security!"

Magnan assumed a troubled-but-determined expression. "Did the young lady give a name?"

"Harrumph! Indeed she did. 'Tell him it's Fifi,' she said—as though the military attaché were a common messenger boy!"

"Heavens—such cheek!" Magnan sniffed.

"The name itself conjures up images of rhinestone-clad doxies," Underknuckle snorted. "I confess it's difficult to understand how a diplomat has occasion to make the acquaintance of persons of such stripe!"

"Oh, I'm sure Mr. Retief can fix you up, Fred," Magnan volunteered. "He seems to have a knack—"

"I do not wish to be fixed up!" Underknuckle roared. "I wish to make it clear to these junketing trollops that they will not be permitted to make planetfall here! Now, if you, Mr. Retief, will be so kind as to report to the Message Center and so inform your, ah, *petite amie*—"

"I don't have an *amie* at the moment, Colonel, *petite* or otherwise," Retief said. "And, as it happens, I don't know any young ladies named Fifi. Still, it's never too late to rectify the omission. I'll be happy to talk to her."

"I'm gratified to hear that," Underknuckle said coldly. "And if that vessel lands on this planet, young man, I'll hold you solely responsible!"

Back in the corridor, Magnan trotted at Retief's side, offering advice. "Now, just tell this young person, kindly but firmly, that your time is fully occupied by your duties and that if she'll just flit along to Adobe, say—there's a fascinating museum there with a lovely display of mummified giant spiders—"

"I won't presume to plan any itineraries," Retief interrupted gently. "I think it might be better to find out what the girls are up to, first."

"Yes, it does seem odd they'd plan a vacation on Quopp; after all, there's nothing here but jungle, with a few thousand tribal villages and three or four dozen market towns."

They turned in at the Message Center, showed badges; electro-locks clicked and the inner door slid back, revealing a bright-lit room crammed with lock-files and coding machines.

"Oh boy, am I glad to see you, Mr. Retief," a freckled youth with thick contact lenses and a struggling mustache blurted, coming forward. "That babe aboard the yacht's a dish, all right, but she's got a way of flashing her eyes at a fellow when she doesn't get her way—"

"If you don't mind, Willis, Mr. Retief and I are in

something of a hurry," Magnan cut him off. "Which screen are they on?"

"The yacht's over the horizon at the moment," the boy said. "She'll make reentry on the next pass; a couple more minutes, I guess."

"What's a yacht doing out here, Willy?" Retief asked. "Quopp's a long way off the regular tourist runs."

"Beats me, Mr. Retief. She's a nice job—ten thousand tons, loaded with all the latest comm gear. Too bad all we have is this obsolete line-of-sight stuff." He gestured at the banked equipment panels. "Tough about those girls losing their celestial tracking circuit, too. Even if they could get in here, they'd be stuck for months waiting for a replacement. That Mark XXXIV stuff is hard to come by."

"Emergency letdown, eh? What kind of help are we giving them?"

The youth shrugged. "None—Longspoon's orders. Says they've got no business coming in on Quopp."

"Did you tell him about the tracker?"

"He said they could go on to the next system on manual tracking—"

"Two months of staring into a tracker scope could get tiring," Retief said. "And a good chance of fatigue error and no planet-fall at the end of it. Let's get 'em down."

"Yeah, but the ambassador's orders—"

"I'll take the responsibility of countermanding them. Get the yacht on the SDR and start feeding her data as soon as she makes contact again."

"Look here, Retief," Magnan held up an admonitory hand. "I can't stand idly by while you exceed your authority! I confess it seems a trifle surprising the ambassador hasn't authorized aid to a distressed Terran vessel, but—"

"We don't need authorization in a Deep Space emergency. Check Title Nine, Article Twelve, Section three-B of the Uniform Code."

"Hey, that's right," Willis blinked. "The code overrides any planetary authority, it says so right in—"

"See here, Retief," Magnan moved to Retief's side, speaking low. "Quoting technicalities is all very well, but afterward one still has the problem of an overridden ambassador to deal with. Hardly a shrewd move, career-wise . . ."

"We'll get the ladies down first, and carry out career salvage afterward," Retief said soothingly. "Maybe it would be better if you went down to spot-check the commissary while I attend to this."

Magnan frowned, settled his dickey in place. "Never mind," he said shortly. "I'll stand by."

A blare of static burst from the center screen on the console across the room, followed by rapidly flickering bars of light; then the image steadied into focus. A girl's face appeared, framed in red-blond hair, a headset clamped in place. Other feminine faces were visible behind her, all young, all worried.

"Hello, Quopp Control," she said calmly. "It looks as though the rock that hulled us did more than take out the tracker. I have no horizontal gyros, and damned little control in my left corrector banks. I'm going to have to do this by the seat-of-the-pants method. I'd appreciate it if you'd loosen up and feed me some trajectory data."

Retief flipped the SEND key.

"Quopp Control here, young lady. Listen closely; there won't be time for a repeat. You have two choices on impact areas; one is the commercial port here at Ixix. If you've got a fix on me, you know the general location. I'm throwing the R and D fixer beam on the line now; lock into it if you can—"

The girl frowned. "Sorry, Quopp Control. No response from my R and D. I have a fix on your transmission, though, and—"

"Your other possibility is an unimproved patch of rocky desert about fifty miles north-north-west. Try to align on my signal here; if you miss, you'll have the other as a backup."

"Roger, Quopp Tower. I've got some speed to kill if I want to make you on this pass—"

"This pass is it," Retief rapped out. "I'm clocking you on a descending spiral with an intersect this orbit. Damp that velocity fast!"

The image on the screen jittered and jumped; Retief waited while the girl worked the controls, watching the glowing red blip moving rapidly across the R and D screen, dropping steadily closer to the line representing the horizon.

"More grief," the girl said briskly. "I've got about half power on the forward main tubes. I'm afraid I'm going to have to give your beacon a miss and try for the desert."

"Throw everything you've got to your retros, let 'em blast and keep blasting! You're going to overshoot by a hundred miles on your present course, and there's nothing out there but nineteen thousand miles of unexplored jungle!"

There was a long moment of tense silence as the girl's hands moved out of sight. Then she shook her head, gave a quick, flashing smile. "That's it, Quopp Control. A fizzle. Did you say nineteen thousand miles?"

"As the Phip flies. How many are there aboard?"

"Ten of us."

"I've got a tracker on you; try to nurse her in as easy as you can. Got any flares aboard?"

"If not, there are a few cases of hundred and sixty proof Imperial Lily gin; I'm sure the intended recipient won't mind if I light them off." Already, her voice was growing fuzzy as the hurtling ship neared the horizon.

"Hold her steady on your present course. Looks like you'll intersect ground zero about eighty miles out."

"I'm not reading you, Quopp. I hope you get here before all the gin's—" Her voice broke off. Then it came again, faint and far away: "Quopp . . . er, a . . . ing in . . . make it . . ." The voice was gone in a rising hiss of random noise.

"Good Lord, I hope the poor girls land safely," Magnan gasped; he dabbed at his forehead with a large floral-patterned tissue. "Imagine being down in that horrible wilderness, swarming with unpacified Quoppina—"

"I'll get an Embassy heli on the way to make the pickup," Retief said; he glanced at the wall clock. "No time to waste if we're going to collect them by dark."

"Retief—are you *sure* you don't know this Fifi person?" Magnan queried as they turned to the door.

"Regrettably, no. But I hope to correct the omission soon—"

The interoffice communicator screen burped; an angular female face with stiff-looking hair and a porridgy complexion blinked into focus.

"There you are," she snapped at Retief. "The ambassador wants to see you in his office—right away!"

"Tsk," Magnan said. "I warned you about stretching those coffee breaks . . ."

"Hi, Fester," Retief greeted the woman. "Is it business, or should I bring my tennis racket?"

"You can save the wisecracks," she sniffed. "There are two Planetary Police officers with him."

"Goodness, I'd be glad to give His Excellency a character reference," Magnan burbled. "What did they catch—that is, what's the charge?"

"It's not Ambassador Longspoon who's in trouble," Fester said coldly. "It's Mr. Retief they want to see."

Ambassador Longspoon was a small man with bright, close-set eyes in a parchment-yellow face, a mouth which would have been inconspicuous on a carp, and a shiny skull over which a few strands of damp-looking hair were combed for maximum coverage. He sat behind a nine-foot ambassadorial desk of polished platinum, flanked by two Voion, one ornately crested and jeweled, whose oculars followed Retief unwaveringly as he entered the room.

"Commissioner Ziz, Mr. Retief," Longspoon said in a voice like a dry bearing. There was silence as he looked expectantly from one of the Voion to the other.

"Well, how about it, Xif," the commissioner buzzed in harsh tribal Voion to his companion. "Is this the one?"

"That's him, chief," the other cop confirmed. "He was the ringleader."

"Here, Commissioner, I must ask you to speak Terran!" Longspoon rasped.

"Just advising my associate that he mustn't harbor grudges for the brutal treatment he received," Ziz said smoothly. "I assured him Your Excellency will make full amends."

"Amends. Yes." Longspoon favored Retief with a look like a jab from an old maid's umbrella. "It appears there's been some sort of free-for-all in an unsavory local drinking spot." He put bony fingers on the desk top and pinched them together. "I trust you have some explanation?"

"Explanation of what, Mr. Ambassador?" Retief inquired pleasantly.

"Of just what would possess an Embassy Officer to attack

members of the Planetary Police in the performance of
their duties!" Purplish color was creeping up from under
Longspoon's stiff midmorning informal collar.

Retief shook his head sympathetically. "No, I certainly
couldn't explain a thing like that."

Longspoon's lower jaw dropped. "Surely you have *some*,
ah, justification to offer?" He shot a quick side glance at
the Voion.

"It would be pretty hard to justify attacking a policeman," Retief offered. "In the performance of his duties at
that."

"Look here . . . !" Longspoon leaned toward Retief.
"You're supposed to be a diplomat!" he hissed from the
corner of his mouth. "You might at least try lying a little!"

Retief nodded agreeably. "What about?"

"Confound it, sir!" Longspoon waved a hand. "When a
police commissioner rolls into my office and charges one
of my staff with aggravated breach of the peace, you can
hardly expect me to simply ignore the situation!"

"Certainly not," Retief said firmly. "Still I think if you
explain to him that invading the Terrestrial Embassy to
make unsupported charges is impolite, and warn him never
to try it again, it won't be necessary to demand his resignation—"

"His resignation!" Longspoon's mouth was open again.
"Hmmm . . ." He swiveled to face the commissioner. "Per-
haps I should point out that invading the Terrestrial
Embassy to make unsup—"

"One moment!" Ziz cut in harshly. "The question here
is one of appropriate punishment to lawless foreigners who
engage in the murder of harmless, grub-loving Voion! I
demand that the culprit be turned over to me for a fair
Trial by Internal Omens!"

"As I recall, the method requires a surgical operation
to study the evidence," Longspoon mused. "What happens
if the victim, er, I mean patient, is innocent?"

"Then we weld him back up and give him a touching
funeral ceremony."

"No, Ziz," Longspoon wagged a finger playfully. "If we
simply turned our diplomats over to anyone who wanted
them, we'd be stripped of personnel in no time."

"Just the one," Ziz suggested delicately.

"I'd like to oblige, my dear Commissioner, but the precedent would be most unfortunate."

The desk screen chimed apologetically.

"Yes, Fester?" Longspoon eyed it impatiently. "I told you I wasn't to be disturbed—"

"It's His Omnivoracity," Fester squeaked excitedly. "He presents his second best compliments and insists on speaking to you at once, Mr. Ambassador!"

Longspoon twitched a bleak smile at the police commissioner. "Well, my good friend Ikk seems to be a bit outside himself today. Just tell him I'll ring him up later, Fester—"

"He says it's about an educational shipment," the female cut in. "Heavens, what language!"

"Ah, yes, educational material," Longspoon said. "Well, I'm always most concerned about educational affairs; perhaps I'd best just see what he has in mind . . ." He turned the volume down low, listened as a tiny voice chirped angrily.

"Are you sure?" he muttered. "Six cases?"

There was more shrill talk from the communicator.

"Nonsense!" Longspoon snapped. "What possible motive—"

Ikk buzzed again. Longspoon glanced at Retief with a startled expression. "No," he said. "Quite out of the question. See here, I'll call you back. I have, er, callers at the moment." He rang off. The police commissioner relaxed the auditory members which had been straining forward during the exchange.

"You still refuse to remand this one to my custody?" He pointed at Retief.

"Have you all gone mad?" Longspoon barked. "I'll deal with Mr. Retief in my own way—"

"In that case . . ." Ziz turned to his retainer. "Put phase two into operation," he snapped in Tribal. "Just sending the lad along to water the jelly flowers down at headquarters," he added soothingly as Longspoon drew breath to protest. Xif wheeled across to the door, left silently. Ziz rolled to the lopsidedly hexagonal window, glanced out into the street.

"A pity Your Excellency didn't see fit to assist the police in the maintenance of law and order," he said, turning to Longspoon. "However, I shall take the disappointment philosophically . . ." He broke off, waving both posterior antennae. "Hark!" he said. "Do I scent a suspicious odor?"

Longspoon cleared his throat hurriedly. "My throat balm," he said. "My physician insists . . ." He sniffed again. "Smoke!" He jumped to his feet. At that moment, a shrill bell jangled into strident life somewhere beyond the door.

"Flee for your lives!" Ziz keened. He shot to the door, flung it wide. A billow of black smoke bulged into the room. Longspoon dithered for a moment, then grabbed up a code book and the Classified Dispatch reel, tossed them into his desk-side safe, slammed it shut just as a pair of Voion charged into the room, hauling a heavy fire hose with a massive brass nozzle from which a weak stream of muddy water dribbled into the deep-pile carpeting. Ziz barked a command and pointed at Retief; the firemen dropped the hose—and were bowled aside as Ambassador Longspoon hurtled between them, his basketball-sized paunch jouncing under overlapping vests. Ziz spun, reached for Retief with a pair of horny grasping members; the Terran leaned aside, caught one of the Voion's arms and jerked; Ziz went over with a crash.

Retief whirled to the window from which the commissioner had glanced a moment before, saw a crowd of crested and ornamented Voion police pressing toward the Embassy doors.

"Fast action," he murmured. He stepped past the overturned firemen into the corridor; wide-eyed staff members were appearing from doors, batting at smoke clouds. Shouts and squeals sounded. Retief pushed through toward an open door from which dense yellowish clouds were pouring, layering out at chest height. He reached the far wall of the room, groped for and found an overturned typist's chair, slammed it at the dim glow of a small triangular window. The colored glass fell outward with a musical tinkle. At once, the smoke—boiling from an overturned wastebasket, Retief saw—was swept toward the opening by a strong draft. He picked up the smoking wastebasket and contents, stepped into the lavatory and doused it with water; it died with a prolonged hiss. Retief lifted a small, soot-blackened plastic canister from the basket; a small wisp of smoke was still coiling from it; incised on its base were what appeared to be Groaci hieroglyphs.

Back in the hall, First Secretary Magnan appeared from a smoke cloud, coughing, eyes blurred.

"Retief! The service door's jammed with people! We're trapped!"

"Let's try another route." Retief started toward the front of the building, Magnan trailing.

"But—what about the others!"

"I predict the fire scare will give them excellent appetites for dinner."

"Scare?"

"It seems to be just smoke bombs."

"You mean—Retief! You didn't—"

"No, but somebody did." They reached the wide hall before the main Embassy entrance door, packed now with excited diplomats and semihysterical stenographers milling in the smoke, and swarms of Voion firemen, wheeling authoritatively through the press, shrilling the alarm. More Voion were struggling in the door to breast the tide of escape-bent Terrans.

"All personnel must evacuate the premises at once," a cop with a bright red inlay across his ventral plates keened. "Collapse is imminent! The danger is frightful! Remember, you are all highly combustible . . . !"

"I don't know what the game is, but we'd better have a fast look around." Retief headed for a side corridor. A stout diplomat with four boneless chins flapped a hand at him.

"I say, young man, all these locals invading the Terrestrial Embassy—it's irregular! Now, I want you to speak to Chief Sskt, and point out—"

"Sorry, Counselor Eggwalk; rush job." Retief pushed past, forced his way through a shouting knot of entangled police and Terrans, rounded a curve in the corridor. A small door marked MAINTENANCE PERSONNEL ONLY caught his eye. It stood ajar; the lock, Retief noted, was broken.

"Mr. Magnan, if you see any volunteer firemen headed this way, give me a fast yell."

"Retief! What are you—"

Magnan's voice cut off as Retief slid through the door, went down a narrow ramp into the cool of a low-ceilinged cellar. There was a scurry of sound ahead; he ducked under insulated air ducts, saw a flicker of motion down a shadowy passage, heard the scrape of wheels scuffling on uneven pavement.

"Come on out," he called. "Nothing back there but a couple of sump pumps and some bilge water."

The sounds had ceased now. Retief took a step—and a three-foot yellow-green Quoppina of the Dink tribe shot out of the darkness, ducked under his arm, veered around the looming bulk of the furnace, disappeared into the dark mouth of a narrow crawlway. Retief paused, listening. There was a soft buzzing from far back in the recess where the Dink had hidden. He ducked his head, moved toward the source of the sound. Above, the thudding of feet and the shouts of Terran and Voion voices were faint, remote. Somewhere, water dripped.

Retief followed the sound, traced it to a dark crevice behind the metal-clad housing of an air-processing unit. He reached in, brought out a foot-long ovoid, plastic-surfaced. It hummed busily; he could feel the tiny vibration against his hands. He spun, headed for the ramp.

Back in the hall, Magnan was nowhere in sight. Ten feet away, a Voion cop stood on relaxed, outward-slanting wheels, talking into a small field microphone. He broke off when he saw Retief, jerked two arms in a commanding gesture.

"Out! Fire has reached boilers!" he rasped in badly accented trade dialect.

Retief balanced the humming object on one outstretched hand. "You know what this is?" he inquired casually.

"No time for ball games," the Voion shrilled. "Fool Terry—" He stopped, snapped his anterior eyes forward, made a whistling noise between his palps, then spun, dug off with a squeak of new Terry-issue neoprene. Retief turned toward a side exit. Two Voion appeared ahead, skidded to a halt at sight of him.

"That's him!" one shrilled. "Get him, boys!" More Voion shot into view, closing in. "Don't move, stilter!" the cop commanded. "What's that you're holding?"

"This?" Retief juggled the ovoid. "Oh, this is just an old Plooch egg. I was just cleaning out my collection, and—"

"You lie, unwheeled crippling!" The cops crowded in reaching. "I'll wager a liter of Hellrose it's part of the loot!" one keened. "It'll mean promotions all around when we bring *this* in!"

"Give me that, you!" eager Voion manipulative members grabbed for the buzzing object. "We'll take it out the back way!"

"Sure, you have it, fellows," Retief offered genially. "Just hurry back to your boss with it—"

"Bribes will do you no good, Terran," a cop shrilled as the find was passed from one gleeful fireman to another. "His Omnivoracity wants to see you—in person." He jabbed with his club at Retief, who caught the heavy weapon, jerked it from its owner's grip, slammed it across his wrist with a metallic clang. More clubs flashed; Retief fended off blows, then charged, slamming Voion in all directions. A club whistled past his ear; a harsh voice shrilled, "Stop him!" Ahead, a dim blue light glowed over a side door. Retief skidded to a halt, tried it: locked. He stepped back, kicked at the lock; the door burst wide. Retief plunged through into a narrow street—and stopped dead facing a solid rank of Voion who ringed him in with leveled spears featuring prominently barbed heads.

"Welcome to our midst," a police lieutenant with an enameled badge hissed. "You will now accompany us without resistance, or you will die, unseen by your fellows."

"Ah-ah," Retief chided. "Ikk will be annoyed if you do anything rash."

"An excellent point," the cop agreed. "I suppose after all we shall have to satisfy ourselves with merely poking holes in you here and there. The effect will be the same."

"Your logic is inescapable," Retief conceded. "I'll be delighted to call on His Omnivoracity."

There was a sharp tremor underfoot, followed instantly by a dull Boom! and a shower of plaster dust from the nearby windows. Shrill Voion sounds broke out, questioning. Retief turned, surveyed the wall of the Embassy tower. A large crack had appeared some yards to the right of the door.

"I guess it wasn't a Plooch egg after all," he said judiciously.

The spearheads had jumped a foot closer at the explosion. "Watch him!" the lieutenant barked.

"Steady, boys," Retief cautioned. "Don't louse up an important pinch with any hasty moves."

"Button your mandibles," the cop rasped. "You'll have your chance to work them soon enough!" He motioned and an avenue opened through the warriors. Retief moved off, spear-points at his back.

Three

Prime Minister Ikk was a larger than average Voion with a sixteen-coat lacquer job, jeweled palps, and an elaborately crested headpiece featuring metallic turquoise curlicues and white Rhoon plumes. He lounged at ease in his office, a wide, garishly decorated room the floor of which, Retief noted, was scattered with blank CDT forms. The Voion's main wheels were braced in padded, satin-lined frames; a peculiarly vile-smelling dope-stick of Groaci manufacture was clamped in one manipulative member. He waved the latter at the guards standing by, dribbling ashes carelessly on the rug.

"Leave us," he snapped in Tribal. "And no spying, either!" The cops filed out silently. Ikk waited until the door closed, then swiveled to stare at Retief.

"So, you are the person." He canted both sets of antennae forward alertly. "It seems we had a busy morning, eh?" His voice had an edge like torn metal.

"Rather dull, actually," Retief said easily. "Sight-seeing, you know."

"And what sort of sights did you see . . . ?"

"Some rather interesting samples of Navajo beadwork and a nice display of hand-painted Groaci back-scratchers. Then there was—"

"Save your flippancy, Terran!" Ikk snapped. "Your activities are known! It remains merely to fill in certain, ah, details!"

"Perhaps you'd care to be a little more specific," Retief suggested. "After all, nobody's listening."

"You were seen at the port," Ikk grated. "You created a disturbance, after which certain items were found to be missing."

"Oh? What items?"

"Six large cases, newly arrived aboard a chartered freight vessel," Ikk snapped. "They contained educational material destined to play an important role in my program for the uplift of the downtrodden Quoppina masses."

"I see; and you think I may have picked them up and strolled off without noticing."

"An end to your insolence," Ikk snarled. "What have you done with the purloined consignment?"

Retief shook his head. "I haven't seen your school books, Mr. Prime Minister."

"Bah; enough of this verbal pussyfooting! You know what the cases contain as well as I—"

"I believe you mentioned educational material—"

"What could be more educational than guns?" Ikk screeched. "The truth, now!"

"The truth is, you're making a blunder, Ikk. Your fellow Quoppina aren't as ready for compulsory education as you seem to imagine."

"If they've grown wise at my expense—through *your* meddling," Ikk cut in, "I promise you an enlightening experience under the implements of a staff of experienced speech tutors!"

"I'm sure your training aids are tucked safely away out of circulation," Retief said soothingly. "That being the case, I suggest you reappraise the whole indoctrination program and try a less ambitious approach."

"Ah, I see it now!" Ikk shrilled. "Longspoon thinks to unseat me, replace me with some compliant puppet—a Herpp, perhaps, or one of those wishy-washy Yerkle! Well, it won't work!" He lowered his voice suddenly. "See here, my good fellow, I'm sure we could work out something. Just tell me where you've hidden the guns and I'll see to it you're appropriately rewarded after the enlightenment."

"That's a fascinating proposal, Mr. Prime Minister. But I'm afraid I'd lie awake nights wondering what you considered appropriate. No, on the whole I think I'd prefer to take my chances on my own."

"An opportunity you are hardly likely to enjoy," Ikk grated, "considering the fact that I have fifty thousand crack troops in the city at this moment, all of them between you and your friends."

"Fifty thousand, you say," Retief countered. "That's not a big enough army for a first class victory parade, to say nothing of taking over a planet with a population of five billion argumentative Quoppina."

"The fifty thousand I mentioned are merely my household detachment," Ikk purred. "Every Voion on Quopp answers to me—two million of them! They've been training for a year at secret camps in the Deep Jungle. They are now ready!"

"Except for the guns," Retief said. "Still, there were only a few hundred of them; they wouldn't have helped you much—"

"Today's shipment was but the first of many! But enough of this gossip! For the last time: Give up your secret and enjoy my lasting favor!"

"You mean if I tell you, you'll give me an escort back to the Embassy, no hard feelings?"

"Certainly, my dear chap! I'll even concoct a stirring tale of your abduction by unscrupulous elements from whom I effected your rescue, not neglecting to mention your own brisk resistance to their wiles."

"Brisker than you anticipated, perhaps," Retief said. "I think I've learned enough to satisfy my curiosity, so—if you'll just move away from that desk and back up against the wall . . ."

Ikk erected his oculars violently. "Eh—" He broke off, looking at the gleaming new power gun in Retief's hand.

"What's this?" he squeaked. "I've offered you safe conduct . . . !"

"Now, Ikk, you don't really think I'd expect a campaigner of your experience to let me off scot-free, do you?"

"Well, my fellows might have to employ just a few little measures on you to be sure you weren't holding anything back—but then I'll have them patch you up nicely afterward."

"Sorry—but I have a strong intuitive feeling that your

Torture Department may not realize just how fragile human hide is."

"I shall know in a moment." The prime minister started toward Retief—six feet of armored hostility, four arms like sheet-metal clubs tipped with bolt cutters cocked for action.

"I can see that Your Omnivoracity hasn't yet sampled Terran educational methods personally," Retief commented. "Another foot and I'll give you your first lesson."

Ikk halted. "Would you dare?" he keened.

"Sure. Why not? Now, don't make any sudden moves. I'm going to tie you up. Then I'm leaving."

Ikk hissed but submitted as Retief plucked the ministerial flag from its place, thrust the staff through his spokes and bound it in place, then tied all four arms firmly.

"There, now, you'll be all right until the sweepers arrive along about dinner time."

"You're a fool!" Ikk shrilled. "You'll never get clear of the building!"

"Perhaps not," Retief said. "In that case, education may never come to Quopp." He went to the intercom. "When I flip the key, tell them I'm coming out," he said. "Tell them to trail me at a respectful distance, because I'm suspicious. Also, you're not to be disturbed until further notice. Sound like you mean it."

Ikk clacked his palps.

"And," Retief added in fluent Voion thieves' dialect, "don't make any mistakes." He pressed the key.

"What is it this time?" a sharp Voion voice came back. Retief held the gun aimed at Ikk's center ventral plate while the prime minister delivered the message.

"Well done, Ikk." Retief flipped off the switch, bent it out of line to render it inoperative. "You may yell all you like now; I have great confidence in ministerial soundproofing."

"Listen to me, Terry!" Ikk keened. "Give up this madness! My troops will hunt you down without mercy! And what can you hope to accomplish alone?"

"Ah, that's the question, isn't it, Ikk?" Retief went to the door. "And on that note I'll leave you . . ."

In the outer office the bodyguards standing by swiveled their oculars nervously at Retief.

"Ikk's tied up for the rest of the afternoon," he said breezily. "He's busy pondering some surprising new developments." He stepped into the corridor, made his way along narrow, strange-smelling passages, winding, dipping, curiously angled, lit by chemical lamps and lined with cubicles from which bright Voion eyes glinted. He emerged in a cramped courtyard surrounded by high, curving, decoration-crusted walls of faded Burgundy and Prussian blue, gleaming in the eerie light of Second Eclipse. There were, if anything, more police gathered now than an hour before. A ripple seemed to pass across the crowd as Retief appeared—twitching antennae semaphoring a message. At once, a path opened through the press.

In the open street the mob was scarcely less dense. Voion—both polished police and dull-finished tribesmen—stood in rows, packed the parking ledges, jostled for wheel-space in the narrow thoroughfare. Here and there a tall bottle-green Yerkle or blue-and-white Clute hurried, a furtive touch of color against the sea of restless black. Through lighted shop windows, Quoppina of other tribes were visible, gathered in tight groups, watching the street. Except for a steady, subdued buzzing in the Voion dialects, the city was ominously silent.

Retief strode along briskly, the Voion continuing to unobtrusively edge from his path. On a street corner he paused, glanced back. A pair of crested Special Police were shouldering through, keeping a fifty-foot interval between themselves and the object of the prime minister's instructions. A third Voion came up behind them, shrilled a command. The two came on at a quick roll. Retief pushed on across the street, turned down a narrow sideway. Ahead, there was a stir. More of the tall Special Police appeared, keening orders to those about them. A message rippled across the crowd. To the right, three more cops had come into view, pushing through toward him, clubs prominently displayed.

"Maybe you'd better step in to avoid the crowd, Terry," a thin voice said at Retief's back. He turned. A small, purplish, lightly built Quopp of the Flink tribe stood in the doorway of a tiny shop. He stepped back; Retief followed, glanced around at shelves loaded with trinkets; Yalcan glasswork, Jaq beaten copper-ware, wooden objects from far-off Lovenbroy, a dim-lit display of Hoogan religious mosaics featuring the Twelve Ritual Dismemberments.

"That one caught your eye, didn't it?" the Flink said. "That's always been a snappy seller with you Terries."

"It's a winner," Retief agreed. "There wouldn't be a back way out of here, I suppose?"

The Flink was staring out at the street. "Ikk's up to something big this time; such a force he never had in town before. Half his tribe he's got in the streets, just standing around like it was a signal they was waiting for." He turned to look at Retief. "Yep, there's a back way—but you won't get far; not if Ikk's bully boys are looking for you. Right now, you must be the only Terry in Ixix still running around loose."

"That's a distinction I'd like to retain," Retief pointed out.

"Terry, I'd like to help you out," the Flink waggled his head. "But you're as easy to spot as an off-color grub at a hatching ceremony—" He broke off, twitched vestigial wing cases, producing a sharp pop. "Unless . . ." he said. "Terry, are you game to try something risky?"

"It couldn't be any riskier than standing here," Retief said. "The cops are closing in from all four directions."

"Come on." The Flink flipped aside a hanging, waved Retief through into an even tinier chamber behind the shop, from which a number of dark tunnel-mouths opened—mere holes, two feet in diameter.

"You'll have to crawl, I'm afraid," he said.

"One of the basic diplomatic skills," Retief said. "Lead on."

It was a five-minute trip through the cramped passage, which twisted and writhed, doubled back, rose suddenly, then dropped, did a sharp jag to the left, and opened into a leather-and-wax smelling chamber, lit by a sour-yellow chemical lamp inside a glass bowl. The room was stacked with curiously shaped objects of all sizes and colors. Retief snapped a finger against the nearest—a large, shield-shaped panel of a shimmering pearly pink. It gave off a metallic bong.

"These look like fragments of native anatomy," he said.

"Right. This is the back room of Sopp's Surgical Spares; Sopp has the best stock in the district. Come on."

Hobbling on small wheels better adapted to trolley service than ground-running, the Flink led the way past heaped carapace segments of glossy chocolate brown, screaming orange, butter-yellow, chartreuse, magenta, coppery red. Some of the metallo-chitinous plates bore ribs, bosses, knobs, spikes; some were varicolored, with polka dots and ribbons of contrasting color, or elaborate silver-edged rosettes. A few bore feathers, scales or bristles. At one side were ranged bins filled with gears, bearings, shafts, electronic components.

"Yep, for anything in the used parts line, old Sopp's the Quopp to see," the Flink said. "He can pull this off if anybody can. Wait here a minute." He stepped through an arched opening into the display room beyond.

"Hey, Sopp, close the blinds," Retief heard him say. "I've got a friend with me that doesn't want to attract any attention . . ." There was an answering twitter, a clatter of wooden shutters, followed by more low-voiced conversation punctuated with exclamations from the unseen proprietor. Then the Flink called. Retief came through into a neat showroom with cases filled with bright-colored objects of obscure function, presided over by a frail-looking Yerkle with a deep green carapace half-concealed under a silken paisley-patterned shawl. He stared at Retief, looking him over like a prospective purchaser.

"Well, what about it, Sopp?" the Flink demanded. "You're the best in the business. You think you can do it?"

"Well . . . I can give it a try."

"Great!" the Flink chirped. "If this works, it'll be the slickest caper pulled in this town since you rigged Geeper out as a Blint and he fertilized half the rolling stock in the Municipal Car-Barns!"

"Well," the Yerkle said two hours later. "It's not perfect, but in a bad light you may pass."

"Sopp, it's your masterpiece." The Flink, whose name was Ibbl, rolled in a circle around Retief. "If I didn't know different, I'd swear he was some kind of a cross-breed Jorp in town for the bright lights! That set of trimmed down Twilch rotors is perfect!"

"Just so you don't try to fly," Sopp said to Retief. "It's a wonder to me how some of these life-forms get around, with nothing but chemical energy to draw on. I've tucked a few Terry food bars in the hip pouch to help keep you running."

Creaking slightly, Retief stepped to the nearest window, a roughly hexagonal panel of rippled amber glass, backed by a closed shutter of dark wood. His reflection, distorted by the uneven surface, was startling: curving plates of deep maroon metallo-chitin had been snipped, warped, then neatly welded to form a suit of smoothly articulated armor which covered him from neck to toe. Over his hands, Sopp had fitted a pair of massive red snipping claws salvaged from a Grunk, operable from within by a system of conveniently arranged levers, while a dummy abdominal section from a defunct Clute, sprayed to match the over-all color scheme, disguised the short Terran torso. A handsome set of vestigial pink wing cases edged in a contrasting shade of purplish black lent a pleasant accent to the shoulder region that went far to camouflage their width. The headpiece, taken from a prime specimen of the Voion tribe, sprayed a metallic red-orange and fitted with a crest of pink-dyed Jarweel plumes, fitted lightly over Retief's face, a hinged section closing down to clamp in place behind.

"Of course, those big, long, thick legs are a bit odd," Sopp said. "But with the rotating members adapted for rotor use, naturally the anterior arms have to fill in as landing gear. There's a few tribes that have gone in for stilting around, and developed them into something quite useful."

"Sure," Ibbl agreed. "Look at the Terries: no wheels, but they manage OK. I tell you, he looks like a natural! Outside of a few unreconstructed Voion trying to flog him a set of gold inlays or some snappy photos of the tribal ovumracks, nobody'll give him a second look."

"Gentlemen," Retief said, "you've produced a miracle. It's even comfortable. All it needs now is a service test."

"Where will you go? Ikk's got the whole town sewed up tight as a carapace in molting season."

"I'll head for the Terry Embassy. It's not far."

Sopp looked doubtful. "Farther than you think, maybe."
He turned to a wall display, selected a two-foot broadsword
fashioned from the iridescent wing case of a Blang. "Better take this. It may come in handy to, shall we say, cut
your way through the undergrowth."

The long twilight of Quopp was staining the sky in vivid
colors now; through a chink in the shutter, Retief saw lights
glowing against the shadows blanketing the hushed street
where the Voion waited, silent. Up high, the carved facades
still caught the light, gleaming in soft pastels against the
neon-bright sky.

"I think it's time to go," he said. "While I still have light
enough to see where I'm going."

"You want to be careful, Terry." Ibbl was scanning the
street from the other window. "Those Voion are in a nasty
mood. They're waiting for something. You can feel it in
the air."

"I'm subject to moods myself," Retief said. "At the
moment I think I could spot them high, low, and jack and
still win it in a walkaway." He took a final turn up and down
the room, testing the action of the suit's joints; he checked
the location of the power pistol with his elbow; it was
tucked inconspicuously behind the flare of a lateral hip
flange, accessible for a fast draw.

"Thanks again, fellows. If our side wins, the brandies
are on me."

"Good luck, Terry. If your side wins, remember me when
it's time to let the contract to junk out the police force."

"You'll be first on the list." Retief worked the lever that
clacked his anterior mandibles in the gesture of Reluctant
Departure on Press of Urgent Business and stepped out
into the street.

It was a brisk fifteen minutes walk to the Path of Many
Sporting Agents, every yard of the way impeded by Voion
who stared, gave ground reluctantly. Retief came in sight
of the Embassy complex, saw Voion clustered before the
main doors in a solid mass. He forced his way closer,
eliciting complaints from jostled sightseers. Behind the wide
glass panels, the darting shapes of Dinks were working

busily; a steady stream of Voion were coming and going, with much shrilling of commands and waggling of signals. There were no Terrans in evidence.

Retief pushed into a narrow shop entry across the street from the scene of the activity, scanned the upper Embassy windows. There were lights on there, and once or twice a shape moved behind the colored glass panes.

There was a distant, thudding clatter. Retief looked up, saw the vast shape of an immense flying Rhoon soar on its wide rotors across the strip of sky between buildings, followed a moment later by a second. Then a tiny heli appeared, bilious yellow-green in color, flitting low above the Chancery Tower. As Retief watched, a head appeared over the cockpit rim—the merest glimpse of stalked eyes, a pale throat bladder—

"That one's no Voion, nor no Terry, either," a reedy voice said at Retief's elbow. He looked around to see an aged Kloob, distinguished by a metallic vermilion abdomen and small, almost atrophied wheels.

"Whoever he was, he seems to be on good terms with the Rhoon," Retief said.

"Never saw that before," the Kloob said. "There's unnatural things going on in the world these days: Rhoon flying over town. Like they was patrolling, like."

"I don't see any of the Terry diplomats around," Retief said. "What's been going on here?"

"Ha! What hasn't been going on? First the smoke and the big bang; then the Voion cops swarming all over . . ." The Kloob clacked his ventral plates with a rippling noise indicating total lack of approval. "Things are coming to a pretty pass when a bunch of Voion trash can take over the Terry Embassy and make it stick."

"So it's like that, eh?" Retief said. "What happened to the Terries?"

"Dunno. I'm taking a short siesta and I wake up and all I can see is cops. Too bad, too. The Terries were good customers. I hate to see 'em go."

"Maybe they'll be back," Retief said. "They've still got a few tricks left."

"Maybe—but I doubt it," the Kloob said glumly. "Ikk's

got 'em buffaloed. The rest of us Quoppina better head for the tall grass."

"Not a bad idea. I wonder where I could pick up a map."

"You mean one of those diagrams showing where places are? I've heard of 'em—but I could never quite figure out what they were for. I mean, after all, a fellow knows where he is, right? And he knows where he wants to go . . ."

"That's one of the areas in which we Stilters are a little backward," Retief said. "We seldom know where we are, to say nothing of where we're going. The place I'm looking for is somewhere to the northeast—that way." He pointed.

"More that way." The Kloob indicated a direction three degrees to the right of Retief's approximation. "Straight ahead. You can't miss it. That where your tribe hangs out? Never saw one like you before."

"There's a group of my tribesfellows in trouble out there," Retief said. "About eighty miles from here."

"Hm. That's a good four days on a fast Blint if the trails are in shape."

"How does the port look?"

"Guards on every gate. The Voion don't want any of us traveling, looks like."

"I'm afraid I'll have to argue that point with them."

The Kloob looked dubiously at Retief. "Well, I can guess who'll win the argument—but good luck to you anyway, Stilter."

Retief pushed through the loosely milling crowd for half a block before one of the stick-twirling Planetary Police thrust out an arm to halt him.

"You, there! Where are you going?" He hummed in Voion tribal.

"Back where a fellow can dip a drinking organ in a short Hellrose and nibble a couple of sourballs without some flat-wheel flapping a mandible at him," Retief replied shortly. "One side, you, before I pry that badge off your chest to give to the grubs for a play-pretty."

The Voion retreated. "Tell the other hicks to stay clear of the city," he rasped. "Now get rolling before I run you in."

Retief thrust past him with a contemptuous snap of his

left chela. The sun was almost down now, and few lamps
had gone on in the shops to light the way. There were no
other Quoppina in sight, only the sullen black of the Voion,
many of them with the crude shell inlays and filed fangs
of tribesmen. The port, Retief estimated, would be off to
the right, where the last purplish gleam of sunset still
showed above the building tops. He headed that way, one
elbow touching the butt of the power gun.

Clustered polyarcs gleamed down from tall poles to
reflect on the space-scarred hulls of half a dozen trade
vessels as Retief came up to the sagging wire fence surrounding the port. More lights gleamed by the gate where
four Voion were posted, twirling clubs.

"Which one of you blackwheels do I bribe to get in?"
Retief called out in Tribal.

All four Voion spoke at once; then one waved an arm
for silence. "I'm corporal of the guard here, rube," he
buzzed. "What have you got in mind?"

"Well, now, what's the going price?" Retief sauntered
casually to a position two yards from the open gate.

"You talking Village, or Terry credit?"

"Do I look like I'm hauling thirty or forty pounds of
Rock around with me?" Retief inquired. "I just peddled
a cargo of country booze down at the barracks. I've got
enough Terry credit to hang the four of you with."

"Have you, now?" The quartet shifted positions to
encircle Retief, a move which placed two of them farther
from the gate than himself.

"You bet." He reached into the pouch slung at his hip,
pulled out a tangle of plastic, gained another step toward
the corporal, who canted his oculars at the cash.

"Here, catch." Retief tossed the credit. As the NCO
reached to snare it, the other three Voion said "hey!" and
converged on him. Retief stepped through the gate,
slammed it, clicked the hanging padlock shut, leaving the
four guards outside.

"Hold on there, you!" the corporal keened. "You can't
go in there!"

"I figured you sharpies would hold out on me," Retief
said. "Well, I'm in now. You can yell for the sergeant and

turn the bundle over to him, or you can forget you saw me and work out a fair split. So long."

"Hey," one of the Voion said. "Look at the way that Stilter walks! Like a Terry, kind of . . ."

"Are you kidding?" the corporal inquired.

"Look, fellows, the way I see it, what's it to us if this yokel wants to sight-see . . . ?"

Retief moved off as the foursome settled down to quarreling over the loot, headed for the nearest of the five ships in sight, a battered thousand tonner with the purple and yellow comet insignia of the Four Planet Line. The few lounging locals in sight ignored him as he went to the rear access ladder, swung up and stepped inside. A startled Voion looked up from a litter of papers and clothes spilled from a locker, the door of which had been pried from its hinges. As the looter reached for a club lying on a table, Retief caught his outstretched arm, spun him around, planted a foot against his back, and launched him toward the open entry. The Voion emitted a thin screech as he shot through, yelped as he hit the pavement below with a splintering crash.

Retief swarmed up the ladder to the cargo deck, rode the one-man lift to the control compartment, cycled the other lock shut, then quickly checked gauges.

"Swell," he said softly. "Just enough fuel to stage a blazing reentry." He whirled to the lifeboat bay, cycled the hatch. Two tiny one-man shells rested in their slings. Retief wiped dust from the external inspection panel of the nearest, saw the dull red glow of panic lights indicating low accumulator charge, a leaky atmosphere seal, and over-aged fuel. He checked the second boat; its accumulators read full charge, though it, too, was leaking air and indicating a decayed fuel supply. Retief went back to the panel, flipped a key, glanced at the ground-view screens. Voion were closing in on the vessel from three sides; he recognized the evicted impulse shopper in the van, limping on an out-of-round wheel.

He went back to the Number Two lifeboat, popped the canopy, climbed inside, fitting himself into the cramped seat, taking care to settle his rotors and wing cases comfortably, then closed the hatch. He activated the warm-up

switch; panel lights blinked on. The boat was flyable—
maybe. Retief kicked in the eject lever and slammed back
in the padded seat as the rocket blast hurled the tiny boat
skyward.

Level at five thousand feet, Retief set a northeast course.
As he looked back at the pattern of city lights below, a
brilliant red light glowed, climbed upward from a point near
the center of the town, burst in a shower of whirling pin-
wheels of green, yellow, magenta. A second rocket went
up, then three together, more, shedding a carnival glow over
the clustered towers of the city. Retief punched a button
on the tiny panel, twirled a dial.

" . . . laration of the establishment of a new era of
Quopp-wide peace and plenty," a voice boomed from the
radio, "under the benign and selfless leadership of His
Omnivoracity, our glorious leader, Prime Minister Ikk! All
loyal Quoppina are instructed to remain in their village or
other place of residence until tax assessors, draft board
officials, and members of the emergency requisition team
have completed initial surveys. All citizens will be required
to purchase a copy of *New Laws and Punishments*, for sale
at all newsstands for a low, low nine ninety-eight, plus tax.
Failure to possess a copy will be punishable by Salvage.
And now, a word from our effulgent chief, the great lib-
erator of Quopp, Prime Minister Ikk!"

There was a prolonged burst of shrill prerecorded applause
that made Retief's eardrums itch, then the familiar tones of
the Voion leader:

"Fellow Voion, and you other, shall I say, honorary
Voion," he started. "Now that the planet is free, certain
changes will be made; no longer will the unenlightened
struggle on, following erroneous tribal customs! We Voion
have figured out all the answers, and—"

Retief flicked off the radio, settled down for the eighty
mile run ahead.

The lifeboat rocked abruptly, as though it had glanced
off a giant, spongy pillow. Retief banked to the right,
scanned the sky above. A wide, dark shape swooped quickly
past; there was a sudden buffeting as the small craft pitched

in the backwash of the thirty-foot rotors of a giant Rhoon. It swung in a wide circle, climbing, then pivoted sharply, stooped again, hurtling straight at him like a vast pouncing eagle. Retief slammed the controls full over, felt the lifeboat flip on its back, drop like a stone toward the jungle below. He rolled out, shot away at full thrust, at right angles to his previous course. Off to the right the Rhoon tilted up in a sharp turn, faint starlight gleaming from its spinning rotors, swelling enormously as it closed. Again Retief dove under it, pulled out to find it close on his port side, angling in across his bows. He gave the boat full throttle, shot under the Rhoon's yellow-green head, then pulled the nose up, climbing . . .

The skiff was sluggish under him, staggering; he reduced the angle of climb, saw the Rhoon dropping in from his port quarter. Again he dived, leveled out this time a scant thousand feet above the dark jungle below. A glance to the right showed the Rhoon banking in for another pass; its mighty rotors drove it effortlessly at twice the speed the skiff could manage on its outdated fuel. Retief saw its four ten-foot-long armored fighting members, its gaping jaws armed with saw-edged fangs that could devour any lesser Quoppina in two snaps. At the last moment, he rolled to the right, went over on his back, snapped out of the maneuver to whip off to the left, coming around sharply on the Rhoon's flank. With a jerk at the release handle, he jettisoned the canopy; it leaped clear with a dull boom, and a tornado of air whipped at Retief's face. He jerked the power gun clear of its holster, took aim, and as the Rhoon banked belatedly to the right, fired for the left rotor. Yellow light glared from the whipping blades as Retief held the beam full on the spinning hub; a spot glowed a dull red; then a puff of vapor whiffed up—and suddenly the air was filled with whining fragments, whistling past Retief's exposed head and ricocheting off the skiff's hull. Retief held the beam on target another five seconds, saw the Rhoon tilt almost vertically, vibrating wildly as the damaged rotor shook itself to pieces; something small and dark seemed to break from the Rhoon then, clung for a moment, dropped free. Then the great predator was on its back, a glimpse of gray belly plates and folded legs, then gone as the boat shot past. At that moment, a violent shock slammed Retief hard against the restraining harness. He grabbed the controls, fought to pull the boat up. A flat expanse of black wilderness swung up past the nose, rolled leisurely over the top, then slid down the left side . . .

The controls bit into the air then; fighting vertigo, Retief hauled the boat out of the spin. The motor barked once, twice, snarled unevenly for a moment, then died. The ship bucked, wanting to fall off on its port stub-wing. A glance showed torn metal, a dark stain of leaking coolant. The skiff was no more than a hundred feet above tree level now; ahead a tall spike-palm loomed. Retief banked to the right, felt the boat drop under him. He caught a momentary glimpse of the immense wreckage of the Rhoon strewn across half an acre of bushy treetops; then he was crashing through yielding foliage, the boat slamming left, then right, then upended, tumbling, dropping to a final splintering crash of metalwood, a terrific impact that filled the tiny cockpit with whirling fireworks even brighter than the ones over the city, before they faded into a darkness filled with distant gongs . . .

Four

Something sharp poked Retief in the side, a vigorous jab that bruised even through the leather strip that joined the dorsal and ventral plates of his costume. He made an effort, sat up, reached to investigate the extent of the skull fracture, felt the metallic clang as his claw touched the painted Voion headpiece. The tough armor, it seemed, had its uses. He pushed the helmet into alignment, looked around at a torch-lit clearing among the boles of great trees, and a ring of three-foot blue-green Quoppina, members, he saw, of the Ween tribe, all eyeing him with faintly luminous oculars, their saber-like fighting claws ready, their scarlet biting apparatus cleared for action.

"Hoo. Meat-fall-from-sky moving around," a tiny, penetrating voice keened in heavily accented Tribal. "Us better slice it up quick, before it get clean away."

Retief got to his feet, felt for the gun with his elbow. It was gone—lost in the crash. One midget meat-eater, bolder than the rest, edged closer, gave a tentative snap of his immense white-edge claw. Retief worked levers, clacked back at him.

"Stand back, little fellow," he said. "Don't you recognize a supernatural apparition when you see one?" He moved to put his back to a tree.

"What you mean, big boy?" one of the natives demanded. "What that big word mean?"

"It means it's bad medicine to cook a stranger," Retief translated.

"Hmm, that mean we is got to eat you raw. How is you, tough?"

Retief drew the short sword. "Tough enough to give you a bellyache, I'd estimate."

"Hey, what kind of Quopp is you, anyway?" someone inquired. "I ain't never see one like you before."

"I'm a diplomat," Retief explained. "We mostly lie up during the day and come out at night to drink."

"A Dipple-mac. Hmmm. Ain't never heard of that tribe before, is you, Jik-jik?"

"Can't say as I is. Must come from over the mountain."

"How you get here, Meat-from-sky?" somebody called. "You ain't got the wingspan for no flying."

"In that." Retief nodded toward the smashed shell of the skiff.

"What that?" one native inquired. Another prodded the machine with a small wheel, adapted for rough jungle trails. "Whatever it is, it dead." He looked at Retief. "You friend no help to you now, big boy. You is all alone."

"You a long way out of your territory, Stilter," another said. "Ain't never see one like you before. What you doing here in Ween country?"

"I'm just passing through," Retief said. "I'm looking for a party of Terrans that wandered off-course. I don't suppose you've seen them?"

"I heard of them whatchacallums—Terrans. They twelve

feet high and made out of jelly, I hears; and they takes their wheels off at night and leaves 'em outside."

"That's the group. Any sign of them in these parts?"

"Nope," the Ween crossed their rear oculars, indicating negation.

"In that case, if you'll stand aside, I'll breeze on my way and let you get back to whatever you were doing when I dropped in."

"What we was doing, we was starving, Meat-from-sky. Your timing good."

"Jik-jik, you all the time talking to something to eat," someone said from the ranks. "What you all say to a nice barbecue sauce on this meal, with greens on the side?"

There was a sudden flurry of sound from the near distance, punctuated by shrill cries.

"Get your feather-picking members off me, you ignorant clodhoppers!" a thin Voion voice screeched. "I'm a member of the Planetary Armed Forces! There's a big reward—" the speech cut off in mid-sentence; threshing sounds followed. Moments later, three Ween pushed into the clearing, hauling the limp figure of a bright-polished member of the Planetary Police. He groaned as they dropped him; one of his wheels, badly warped, whirled lopsidedly.

"Hoo, this evening shaping up," someone said. The Voion was lying on his back, waving all four arms feebly.

"You can't do this to me," the captive tweeted. "In the name of the Wo—" The Ween standing closest to the fallen policeman brought his immense claw around and with a sound like a pistol shot nipped off the newcomer's head with a single snap.

"Well, that the first of them big noises I see trimmed up like he ought to be," Jik-jik said. "You got him just in time, Fut-fut, before he call on the Name of the Worm—" He broke off, looked at Retief.

"In the Name of the Worm," Retief said, "what about a little hospitality?"

"You and your big vocalizing apparatus," someone said disgustedly. "Well, back to camp. At least us can fry up some policeman to tide us over." A quartet of Ween lifted the limp body; someone picked up the head.

"Lucky for you you call on the Name of the Worm," Jik-jik said conversationally. "Old Hub-hub ready to dine right now, what I mean."

"Mentioning the Worm takes me off the menu, eh?"

"Well, it give you time to get you thoughts in order, anyway."

"I have a feeling that remark is pregnant with meanings, none of them pleasant."

"Hoo, it simple enough, big boy. It mean us keep you pen up for five days, and then skin you out for a old-fashioned tribal blowout."

An aggressive-looking Ween pushed forward. "How about if us trim off a few edges now—just to sample the flavor?"

"Get back there, Hub-hub," Jik-jik admonished. "No snacking between meals."

"Come on, Meat-from-sky," the aggressive pygmy called. "Get you wheels in gear." He reached out with his claw to prod Retief—and jumped back with a screech as the heavy sword whipped down, lopped off an inch of the member's pointed tip.

"Look what he do to my chopper!" he shrilled.

"You ask for it, Hub-hub," Fut-fut said.

"I like a lot of space around me," Retief said, swinging the sword loosely in his hand. "Don't crowd me."

The Ween edged back, fifty or more small, dark-glittering creatures like oversized army ants in a wide ring around Retief, his armor a splash of vivid color in the gloom. Hub-hub jittered, holding his damaged claw high, torchlight glinting on his metallic sides. "I is hereby taking this piece of meat off the chow list!" he screeched. "I is promoting him to the status of folks!"

"Hey, Hub-hub, is you gone out of you head? What the idea of doing a trick like that . . . ?" A chorus of protest broke out.

Jik-jik confronted the outraged tribesman.

"He chop off a piece of you, and now you chumming up to him. What the idea?"

"The idea is now I ain't got to wait no five days to get a piece back!" Hub-hub keened. "Get back, all of you . . ." He waved the two-foot long, steel-trap claw in a commanding gesture. "I is now going to snip this Stilter down to size!"

The Ween drew back, disappointed but obedient to tribal custom. Hub-hub danced before Retief, who waited, his back to the tree, the sword held before him, torchlight glinting along its steel-hard razor-sharp edge. Hub-hub darted in, legs twinkling, snick-snacked a double feint high and low with the big fighting arm, lashed out viciously with a pair of small pinchers, then struck with the big claw, eliciting a loud clang! from Retief's chest armor—and staggered as the flat of Retief's blade knocked him spinning.

"Hoo!" Jik-jik shrilled. "Old Hub-hub chew off more than he can bite this time!"

"Let's call this off, Shorty," Retief suggested. "I'd hate to have to skewer you before we've really gotten acquainted—"

The Ween danced in, pivoting on spider legs, feinted, struck with his fighting claw—

Retief's sword flashed in a lightning arc, sang as it bit through steel-hard metallo-chitin. The oversized claw dropped to the ground.

"He . . . he done chop off my chopper . . . !" Hub-hub said faintly. "Now he going to stick me for sure . . ." He crouched, waiting, a drop of syrupy dark fluid forming on the stump.

"Serve you right, Hub-hub," someone called.

"Suppose I let you go?" Retief stepped forward and prodded the Ween's slender neck with the sword point. "Promise to be good and speak only when spoken to?"

"Way I feels now, I done talking for good," Hub-hub declared.

"Very well." Retief lowered the blade. "Go with my blessing."

"Well, that a neat trick, big boy," Jik-jik commented. "Take him six months to grow a new arm, and meantime he learn to keep his mandibles buttoned."

Retief looked around. "Anybody else?" he inquired. There were no takers.

"In that case, I'll be on my way. You're sure you haven't noticed a ship crashing in the vicinity in the past few hours?"

"Well, now, that different," Jik-jik stated. "They was a big smash over yonder way a while back. We was looking for it when we found you, Stilter."

"The name's Retief. Now that we're all friends and tribesfellows, how about a few of you showing me the spot where it came down?"

"Sure, Tief-tief. It not far from where you was."

Retief walked over to examine the body of the decapitated Voion. He had obviously been a member of Ikk's police—or army—complete with brand-new chromalloy inlays and an enameled cranium insignia with a stylized picture of what looked like a dragonfly.

"I wonder what this fellow was doing out here, so far from town," Retief said.

"I don't know," Jik-jik said; "but I got a feeling when us finds out us ain't going like it."

The bright disk of Joop was high above the treetops, shedding a cold white light on the village street. Retief followed as Jik-jik and two other tribesmen led the way along a trail worn smooth by the wheels of generations of forest dwellers. It was a fifteen minute trek to the spot where Pin-pin halted and waved an arm. "Yonder's where I found that policeman," he said. "Back in the brush. I heard him cussing up a cyclone back there."

Retief pushed through, came to a spot where fallen limbs and scattered leaves marked the position of the injured Voion. Above, the silvery ends of broken branches marked a trajectory through the treetops.

"What I wondering, how he get up there?" Pin-pin inquired. "Funny stuff going on around here. Us heard the big crash—that why us out here—"

"The big crash—which way was that?" Retief asked.

"Yonder," Pin-pin pointed. Again he led the way, guided by the unerring Quoppina instinct for direction. Fifty feet along the trail, Retief stooped, picked up a twisted fragment of heavy, iron-gray metallo-chitin, one edge melted and charred. He went on, seeing more bits and pieces—a bright-edge shred here, swinging from a bush, a card-table-sized plate there, wedged high in a tree. Then suddenly the dull-gleaming mass of a major fragment of the wrecked Rhoon loomed through the underbrush, piled against the ribbed base of a forest giant.

"Hoo, that big fellow hit hard, Tief-tief," Pin-pin said. "Wonder what bring him down?"

"Something he tried to eat disagreed with him." Retief made his way around the giant corpse, noting the blaster burns on the stripped hub of the rotors, the tangle of internal organic wiring exposed by the force of the crash, the twisted and shattered landing members. The rear half of the body was missing, torn away in the passage through the trees.

"Wonder what a Rhoon meet big enough to down him?" Pin-pin wondered. "He the toughest critter in this jungle; everybody spin gravel when a Rhoon flit overhead." The Ween dipped a finger in a smear of spilled lubricant, waved it near an olfactory organ.

"Fool!" he snorted. "That gone plumb rancid already! I guess we don't make no meal off this fellow!"

Retief clambered up the side of the downed behemoth, looked down into an open cavity gouged in the upper side of the thorax, just anterior to the massive supporting structures for the rotating members. Wires were visible; not the irregular-diametered organic conduits of the Quoppina internal organization, but bright-colored cables bearing lettering . . .

"Hey, Tief-tief!" Pin-pin called suddenly. "Us better get scarce! This boy's relations is out looking for him!"

Retief looked up; a great dark shape was visible, hovering a few hundred feet above treetop level. By the bright light of Joop, a second and a third Rhoon appeared, cruising slowly back and forth over the position of their fallen comrade.

"They going to spot him any minute now," Pin-pin said. "I say let's get!"

"They can't land here," Retief said. "They've already spotted him; they're patrolling the location . . ." He looked around, listening. There was the whine of the breeze among metallic leaves, the high throb of idling Rhoon rotors, a distant rustle of underbrush . . .

"Somebody's coming," Retief said. "Let's fade back and watch."

"Look, Tief-tief, I just remembered, I got a roof needs patching—"

"We'll lie low and pull back if it's more than we can handle, Pin-pin. I don't want to miss anything."

"Well . . ." The three Ween went into a hurried consultation, then clacked palps in reluctant agreement. "OK—but if it's a bunch of them no-good Voion coming to see what can they steal, us leaving," Pin-pin announced. "They getting too quick with them clubs lately."

It was five minutes before the first of the approaching group came into view among the great scarlet- and purple-boled trees, laden with full field packs and spare tires.

"What I tell you?" Pin-pin whispered shrilly. "More of them policemen! They all over the place!"

Retief and the Ween watched as more and more Voion came up, crowding into the clearing leveled by the passage of the Rhoon, all chattering in a subdued buzz, fingering their blackwood clubs and staring about them into the forest.

"Plenty of them," a Ween hissed. "Must is six sixes of sixes if they's a one . . ."

"More than that. Look at 'em come!"

An imposing-looking Voion with a jewel in his left palp appeared; the others fell back, let him through. He rolled up beside the dead Rhoon, looked it over.

"Any sign of Lieutenant Xit?" he demanded in trade dialect.

"What he say?" Pin-pin whispered.

"He's looking for the one you fellows found," Retief translated.

"Oh-oh; they ain't gonna to like it if they finds him."

The conversation among the Voion continued:

" . . . trace of him, Colonel. But there a native village not far away; maybe they can help us."

The colonel clacked his palps. "They'll help us," he grated. "Which way?"

The Voion pointed. "Half a mile—there."

"All right, let's march." The column formed up, started off in a new direction.

"For a minute I figure they mean Weensville," Pin-pin said. "But they headed for the Zilk town."

"Can we skirt them and get there first?" Retief asked.

"I reckon—but I ain't hungry just now—and besides, with them policemens on the way—"

"I'm not talking about grocery shopping," Retief said. "Those Voion are in a mean mood. I want to warn the villagers."

"But they's Zilk. What we care what happen to them babies?"

"The Terries I'm looking for might be there; I'd prefer to reach them before the Voion do. Beside which, you villagers should stick together."

"Tief-tief, you is got funny ideas, but if that's what you wants . . ."

Retief and his guides pushed through a final screen of underbrush, emerged at the edge of a cleared and planted field where the broad yellow leaves of a ripening crop of alloy plants caught the Jooplight.

"Them Zilk a funny bunch," Pin-pin said. "Eats nothing but greens. Spends all they time grubbing in the ground."

"In that case, I don't suppose they have to wait until a policeman drops in to plan a meal," Retief pointed out. He started across the open field.

"Hoo, Tief-tief!" Pin-pin hurried after him. "When I say they don't eat folks, that don't mean they don't snap a mean chopper! Us is tangled with them before, plenty of times! You can't just wheel in on 'em!"

"Sorry, Pin-pin. No time for formalities now. Those cops aren't far behind us."

A tall, lean Quoppina appeared at the far side of the field—a bright yellow-orange specimen with long upper arms tipped with specialized earth-working members, shorter, blade-bearing limbs below.

"Oh-oh; they sees us. Too late to change our minds now." Jik-jik held his fighting claw straight up in a gesture indicating peaceful intentions.

"What d'ye want here, ye murderous devils?" a high, mellow voice called.

"I'm looking for a party of Terrans whose boat crash-landed near here a few hours back," Retief called. "Have you seen them?"

"Terrans, is it?" the Zilk hooted. "I've not seen 'em—
and if I had, I'd not be likely to turn 'em over to the likes
o' you."

Other Zilk were popping from the low, domed huts now,
fanning out, moving forward on both flanks in an encircling pincer movement. At close range, Retief could see
the businesslike foot-long scythes tipping the lower arms.

"Listen here, you Zilk," Jik-jik called in a voice which
may have quavered a trifle. "In the Name of the Worm—
us ain't just here to ask foolish questions; us is got news
for you folks."

"And we've got news for you—not that ye'll ever have
the chance to spread it about—"

"Us come to tip you folks off," the Ween persisted.
"They a mob of mean-looking Voion on the way! Less you
wants to tangle with 'em, you better head for the brush!"

"Don't try to put us off with wild tales, Ween!"

"It's the truth, if I ever told it."

"Why would ye tell us—if t'were true?"

"It beat me; it were Tief-tief here had the idea."

"What kind o' Quoppina is he?" the Zilk called. "I've
seen no Stilter wi' half the length o' member that one
shows."

"He a out-of-town boy; just passing through."

"T'is a trick, Wikker," a Zilk beside the spokesman
hooted. "I'd not trust the little butchers as far as I could
kick 'em—nor the big Stilter, neither."

"The Voion are looking for a friend of theirs," Retief
said. "They have an idea you'll help them look."

"We'll help 'em off our land," a Zilk stated. "I seen a
mort o' the scoundrels about the acreage lately, running
in packs and trampling the crops—"

"They're armed and they mean business," Retief said.
"Better get ready."

The Zilk were closing in now; the three Ween crowded
up against Retief, their fighting claws clicking like casta-
nets. Retief drew his sword.

"You're making a mistake," he told the advancing Zilk
leader. "They'll be here any minute."

"A sly trick, ye heathens—but we Zilk are too shrewd
for ye—"

"Hey!" A Zilk called. The others turned. The lead elements of the Voion column were just emerging from the forest. At once, the Zilk formation broke, fell back in confusion toward the town.

"Get the females and grubs clear," the Zilk chief honked, and dashed away with the rest. The Voion colonel, seeing the tribesmen in confusion, barked an order; his troops rolled forward through the fields, clubs ready.

"Let them have the town." Retief seized the arm of the chief as he shot by. "Disperse in the jungle and you can reform for a counterattack!"

The Zilk jerked free. "Well—maybe. Who'd ha' thought a crowd of Ween were telling the truth?" He rushed away.

The Voion were well into the village now; startled Zilk, caught short, dashed from the huts and wheeled for cover burdened with hastily salvaged possessions, only to drop them and veer off, with hoots of alarm, as fast-wheeling Voion intercepted them.

"Us better back off," Jik-jik proposed from the shelter of a hut on the sidelines.

"Scout around and try to round up the survivors," Retief said. "Pin-pin, you make it back to Weensville and bring up reinforcements. The Voion need a little lesson in inter-tribal cooperation before their success goes to their heads."

Half an hour later, from a screen of narrow pink leaves that tinkled in the light breeze, Retief, several dozen Zilk, and seventy-odd Ween watched by the waning light of the fast-sinking Joop as a swarm Retief estimated at three hundred Voion, a few showing signs of a brisk engagement, prodded their captives into a ragged lineup.

"I don't know what's got into them babies," Jik-jik said. "Used to be they garbage-pickers, slipping around after Second Joop, looking for what they could pick up; now here they is, all shined up and acting like they rule the roost."

"They've gotten a disease called ambition," Retief said. "The form they have causes a severe itch in the acquisitive instinct."

"Not much meat on a Zilk," someone mused. "What you reckon they want over here? Can't be they just looking for they boy; them Voion never frets over no trifles like that."

"Hoo!" Fut-fut said, coming to Retief's side. "Look what they up to now!"

The Voion, having arranged the captive Zilk in two columns of a dozen or so individuals of both sexes, were busy with strips of flexible metallo-plastic, welding shackles to the arms of the first in line, while others of their number poised with raised clubs to punish any resistance. The lead Zilk, seeing the chain about to be linked to him, lashed out suddenly with his scythe, severing a Voion arm at the first joint, then plunged through the circle around him, dashed for the jungle. A Voion wheeled into his path, brought his club around in a whistling arc—and bounced aside as the Zilk snapped out an overlong digging arm, just as two more Voion closed from the off side, brought their clubs down in unison. The Zilk skidded aside, arms whirling, crashed in a heap and lay still.

"Nice try, Wikker," the Zilk chief muttered. "Don't reckon I'd endure chains on me, either."

"That's what happens when you play it their way," Retief said. "I suggest we work out some new rules. We'll decoy them into the jungle, break up their formation, and take them one at a time."

"What you mean, Tief-tief? Us going to tackle them ugly babies?"

"Sure, why not?"

"Well, I guess you is right. Us ain't got nothing else scheduled for the evening."

"Good," Retief said. "Now, here's what I've got in mind . . ."

Three Voion working busily to pry the lid from the Zilk town grain bin paused in their labors. Again the thin cry sounded from the forest near at hand.

"Sounds like a lost grub," one said. "A little tender roast meat wouldn't go bad now; pounding in the skullplates of farmers is hard work."

"Let's take a look. The colonel's busy overseeing the looting; he won't notice us."

"Let's go." The three dropped their pry-bars, wheeled briskly across to the deep shadow of the thicket whence the sound emanated. The first in line thrust branches aside, rolled slowly forward, peering through the shadows. There was a dull *snack!* and he seemed to duck down suddenly. The Voion behind him hurried forward. "Find it?" he inquired, then skidded to a halt. "Juz!" he whistled. "Where's your head . . . ?" Something small and blue-green sprang up before him, a huge claw opening—

At the sound—a sharp *whock!*—the third Voion halted. "Huj?" he called. "Juz? What's go—" A scythe swung in a whistling arc, and his head bounced off to join those of his comrades. Jik-jik and Tupper, the Zilk leader, emerged from the brush.

"Work like a charm," the Ween said. "Let's do it again."

Behind him, Retief turned from surveying the work in progress in the town.

"I think the colonel's beginning to suspect something; he's falling his men in for a roll call. How many have we given haircuts to so far?"

"Half a six of sixes, maybe."

"We'll have to stage a diversion before he figures out what's going on. Tell Fut-fut and his group to wait five minutes, then kick up a disturbance on the far side of the trail we came in on."

Jik-jik keened orders to a half-grown Ween who darted away to spread the word.

"Now we'll string out along the trail. They'll probably come out in single file. Keep out of sight until their lead unit's well past our last man; at my signal, we'll hit them all together and pull back fast."

"It sounds slick. Let's roll."

Three minutes later, as a Voion sergeant continued to bark out names, the small messenger darted up to the position where Retief and Jik-jik waited beside the trail. "Old Fut-fut, he ready, he say," the lad chirped breathlessly. "Hey, Jik-jik, can I get me one?"

"You ain't got the chopper for it, Ip-ip; but you can scout around the other side of the town, and soon as you hear them policemen's heads popping, you set up a ruckus. That'll keep 'em guessing—them that still has guessing equipment. Now scat; it's time for the fun to begin."

A shrill yell sounded from Fut-fut's position, then an angry yammer of Ween voices, accompanied by sounds of scuffling. From his concealment behind a yard-wide tree with a trunk like pale blue glass, Retief saw a stirring in the Voion ranks as they looked toward the outcry. The colonel barked an order. A squad of Voion fell out, rolled quickly to the trail mouth. There was a moment of confusion as the troops milled, not liking the looks of the dark tunnel; then, at a shrill command from a sergeant, they formed a single file and started in. The first rolled past Retief's position, his club swinging loosely in his hand; he was followed closely by another, and another. Retief counted twenty before they stopped coming. He stepped from behind the tree, glanced toward the village; the roll call went on. He drew his sword, put two fingers in his mouth, and gave a shrill blast. At once, there was a crash of underbrush, a staccato volley of snicks and snaps, followed in an instant by a lone Voion yell, quickly cut off. The last Voion in the column, ducking back from the attacking Ween, spun, found himself confronting Retief. He brought his club up, gave a shrill yelp as Retief, with a roundhouse stroke, cut through the weapon near the grip.

"Go back and tell the colonel he has two hours to get to town," Retief said. "Any Voion found loose in the jungle after that will be roasted over a slow fire." He implemented the command with a blow of the flat of the blade that sent the Voion wobbling villageward; then he whirled and plunged into the dense growth, made for a vantage point overlooking the village.

There was a high-pitched cry from the far side of the town—Ip-ip at work. The Voion were milling now, unsettled by the sudden noises. The one whose club Retief had clipped off charged into the midst of the platoon, shrilling and waving the stump of the weapon.

"... forest demon," he was yelling. "Nine feet high, with wheels like a juggernaut, and a head like a Voion, except it was red! Hundreds of them! I'm the only one got away ...!"

Branches rustled and clanked as Jik-jik came up. "Hoo, Tief-tief, you quite a strategist. Got a passel of the trash that time! What's next?"

The colonel was shrilling orders now, the roll call abandoned; Voion scurried to and fro in confusion.

"Let them go. I see they're not bothering with their prisoners."

The Voion were streaming away down the wide trail in considerable disorder, flinging loot aside as they went. In two minutes the village was deserted, with the exception of the ranks of chained Zilk, staring fearfully about, and the crumpled bodies of their relatives.

"We'll go in quietly so as not to scare them to death," Retief said. "And remember, the idea is to make allies of them; not hors d'oeuvres."

Fifty-one Zilk, three of them badly dented, had survived the attack. Now they sat in a circle among their rescuers, shaking their heads mournfully, still not quite at ease in the presence of seventy fighting Ween.

"Ye warned us, I'll gi' ye that," one said ruefully. "Never thought I'd see the day a bunch of Voion'd jump us Zilk, face to face—even if they did have us six to one."

"The Voion have a new mission in life," Retief said. "Their days of petty larceny are over. Now they're after a whole planet."

"Well, I guess we fix them, hey Tief-tief?" Jik-jik chuckled. "The way them babies run, they going to need retreads before they gets to town."

"That was just a minor scuffle," Retief said. "They're shaken up at the moment, but they'll be back."

"You sure enough reckon?" Fut-fut executed a twitch of the palps indicating sudden alarm.

"For a Stilter what just hit town at First Joop, you sure is take in a lot of ground in a hurry," Jik-jik said plaintively. "If you knowed them rascals coming back, how come you tell us to mix it in the first place?"

"I thought it would save a lot of talk all around if you Ween saw a demonstration of Voion tactics first hand. Then, too, it seemed worthwhile to help out the Zilk."

"We lost good old Lop-lop," Jik-jik pointed out. "His head plumb bashed in. He was a good eater."

"They lost thirty-five club swingers," Retief said. "We've gained fifty-one new recruits."

"What that?" Jik-jik clacked his secondary claws with a

br-r-rapp! "You ain't talking about these here greens-eaters . . . ?"

"Why, ye murdering spawn o' the mud devil, d'ye think we Zilk'd have any part of ye'r heathen ways?" one of the rescuees hooted, waving his scythe. "Ye can all—"

"Hold it, fellow," Retief said. "If it comes to a fight with the city boys, you tribes will stick together or lose. Which will it be?"

"Where you get a idea like that, Tief-tief? They always been a few Voion sneaking around, getting they antennae in—"

"Just before I arrived here, Ikk declared himself proprietor of the planet; if the rest of you are good, he promises to make you honorary Voion."

There was a chorus of indignant buzzes and hoots from Ween and Zilk alike.

"Well, I'm glad to see an area of agreement at last," Retief said. "Now, if you Zilk are recovered, we'd better be pulling out—"

"What about our crop?" Tupper protested. "It's all ready to harvest—"

"This here grass?" Jik-jik contemptuously plucked a wide golden leaf from the row beside him, waved it under his olfactory organ. "Never could figure out what a Quoppina thinking of, all the time nibbling leaves . . ." He paused, sniffed at the leaf again. Then he bit off a piece with a sound like a sardine can being torn in two, chewed thoughtfully.

"Hey," he said. "Maybe us been missing something. This plumb good!"

Fut-fut snorted his amusement, plucked a leaf and sniffed it, then bit.

"Hoo!" he announced. "Taste like prime Flink, dog if it don't!"

In a moment, every Ween in sight was busily sampling the Zilk greens.

"Don't s'pose it matters," a Zilk grumbled. "We'll never get the crop in anyway, wi' these Voion robbers on the loose."

"Don't worry about that," a Ween called. "Us'll have these here greens in in ten minutes flat!"

Jik-jik nodded, still masticating. "Maybe us Ween and

you Zilk could work together after all," he said. "Us'll do the fighting and you fellows grow the greens."

Retief, Jik-jik and Tupper watched by the trail as the last of the grubs were carted away by nervous mothers to shelter in the deep jungle along with the village pots and pans, and the newly acquired store of alloy plants. Suddenly Topper pointed.

"Look up there," he boomed. "A flight of Rhoon—big ones! Coming this way!"

"Scatter!" Retief called. "Into the woods and regroup on the trail to the north!"

Ween and Zilk darted off in every direction. Retief waited until the lead Rhoon had dropped to almost treetop level, heading for a landing in the village clearing; then he faded back into the shadows of the jungle. One by one ten great Rhoon settled in, their rotors flicking back glints of Jooplight as they whirled to a stop. In the gloom, dark figures moved: Voion, filing out from between the parked leviathans, forming up a loose ring among the deserted huts, fanning outward, clubs ready.

"Come on, Tief-tief," Jik-jik said softly. "If them Rhoon wants the place I says let 'em have it—" He broke off. "Look there!" he hissed. "Voion—swarms of 'em—wheeling right under them big babies' snappers!"

"They got here a little sooner than I expected," Retief said softly. "They must have already set up a field HQ nearby."

"Tief-tief, you know what I'm thinking? I'm thinking them Voion and them Rhoon is working together! But they can't! Ain't no tribe never worked with no other tribe, not since the Worm's first Wiggle!"

"The Ween and the Zilk got together," Retief pointed out. "Why not the Voion and the Rhoon?"

"But that ain't fair, Tief-tief! Ain't nobody can fight a Rhoon! And they always been such peaceable babies. Just set on their mountaintops and leave the flatland to us."

"It seems they've changed their ways. We'll have to fall back. Spread the word to the troops to move off—and keep it quiet."

"Sure is getting dark fast," Jik-jik commented nervously. "Us Ween figure it bad luck to move around in the dark of Joop."

"It'll be worse luck if we stay here. They're forming up to sweep this stretch of jungle clear."

"Well—if you says so, Tief-tief," Jik-jik conceded. "I'll spread the word."

Half an hour later, the party paused on the trail, in total darkness now.

Tupper was peering through the blackness. "I'd give a pretty to know where we are," he said. "Stumping along a trail in the dark—'tis no fit occupation for a sane Quopp."

"We'll have to call a halt until Second Jooprise," Retief said. "We can't see where we're going, but neither can the Voion. They're not using torches either."

"But I can hear 'em; they're not far behind us—the night-crawling heathen!"

"It'll be Second Jooprise in another half hour, maybe," Jik-jik said. "I hopes them Voion is as smart as we is and set still for a while instead of cooking up surprises."

"I don't like it," Tupper stated. "There's something about this spot—I got a feeling hostile eyes are on me!"

"They'll be hostile clubs on you, if you keeps talking so loud," Jik-jik said. "Hush up now and let's all set and rest whiles we can."

Tupper was moving carefully about in the darkness. "Oh-oh," he said softly.

"What that?" Jik-jik demanded.

"It feels like . . ."

"What it feel like?" Jik-jik asked breathlessly.

"Tief—better give us a light," Tupper said tensely.

Retief stepped to his side, took out a lighter, fired a torch supplied by a Ween. The oily brand flared up, cast dancing light on a purplish-gray mound blocking the path.

"Was there something?" a deep voice boomed out.

"Now we is done it," Jik-jik choked out. "Us is right smack dab in the middle of Jackooburg!"

Five

At once, a dozen torches flared ahead; Retief looked around at a sprawling collection of wide mud and leaf sheds spotted at random under the shelter of a grove of vast green-barked nicklewood trees. There was a wide yard, beaten to concrete smoothness by heavy wheels; about it were parked a dozen massive, low-slung creatures, five feet at the shoulder and ten feet long, with dusty magenta back plates, foot-thick rear wheels a yard in diameter, and a pair of smaller wheels forward, evolved from the lower pair of arms. The upper arms, flexible and spade-tipped, were coiled under the wide, flat duckbilled heads.

"Well?" the same voice, like heavy syrup, insisted. "I hope you have *some* excuse for bursting in on our nightly contemplation hour!"

"Just leaving, big boy," Jik-jik spun his wheels backward, raising dust that roiled in the torchlight. With a low rumble, a pair of Jackoo wheeled to cut off retreat. Another pair gave low, rumbling honks, took up positions flanking the intruders on the left. More Jackoo appeared from the darkness and still more emerged from shelter among the trees ringing the yard.

"Not in such a darned hurry, skinny-wheels," the Jackoo purred. "Before I roll you out into a pretty orange rug, I'd like to know what you thought you could snitch here."

"I'm looking for a missing party of Terrans," Retief said. "Have you seen them?"

"Terrans? What on Quopp are those?"

"A type of Stilter; they look a little like me, actually, except that they have tender skins."

"Hmm. Sounds tasty. Tell you what; whoever catches them first divvies up with the others, all right?"

"They're not to be eaten," Retief corrected. "I want them whole."

"Oh, greedy, eh?" More Jackoo rolled to complete the encirclement.

"Oh-oh," Jik-jik twittered. "Us surrounded."

"That's fine," Retief said. "Now we won't have any Voion sneaking up on us."

❖   ❖   ❖

"Tief-tief, us don't want to tangle with those boys," Jik-jik hissed. "They is tough customers. They ain't fast on they wheels, but when they starts, it take a mountain to stop 'em. They flatten whatever they meets!"

"Good. They'll make excellent heavy armor."

"Tief-tief, you is got strange ideas. These Jackoo ain't got a friend in the jungle. They grubbers, and they don't care what kind they gets—Ween, Zilk, Flink—"

"Maybe we can offer them a change of diet."

"If you have any last words, better get them said." The Jackoo were closing in, ponderous as Bolo combat units.

"You boys is got wrong ideas," Jik-jik crowded against Retief. "Us just dropped in to say howdy. I mean, us figured—I mean Tief-tief figured—"

"What he means is," Tupper amplified hastily, "the club-swinging rogues ha' carried out a dastardly attack on Zilk Town, and—"

"And you boys is next," Jik-jik added. "So—"

"Heavens, one at a time!" the Jackoo bellowed. "Gracious, a person can't even hear himself think! Now, let me get this straight: Just which of you is offering what others for sale?"

"The cute one with the long stilts," a Jackoo suggested from the background. "He's the owner, and these other two—"

"Nonsense, Fufu; the sour-looking one owns the squatty one, and the Stilter is some kind of a flack—"

"You're both wrong," a third hollow voice chimed in. "The little jumpy one with the big bitey thing obviously—"

"Gentlemen . . ." Retief held up both gauntleted hands. "I wonder if you've noticed a small conflagration in the near distance?"

"Gracious, yes," the Jackoo named Fufu said. "I thought it was morning and woke up hour early."

"A large party of Voion calling themselves Planetary Police have raided Zilk Town. They'll be here next."

"Well, dandy! Maybe they'll have some succulent grubs for sale. Last time—"

"This isn't like last time," Retief said. "They're not small-time free-lance bushrangers anymore; they've incorporated as a government and gone into the wholesale end. They've started off by levying a modest hundred percent property tax; after collecting that, they draft the survivors into government service, in what capacity we haven't yet determined."

"Ummm, no," the nearest Jackoo thumped heavy palps together in the gesture of Invitation Declined. "We're content as we are, living our peaceful, contemplative lives, bothering no one—"

"What about all them grubs you steals?" Jik-jik put in.

"Well, if you're going to be *picky* . . ."

"What Fufu means is that we don't want to sign up for the program," a Jackoo explained. "Naturally, we think enterprise is ducky, but—"

"It's not exactly an invitation," Retief said. "More of an ultimatum. Your village is on their route of march. They should be here by First Jooprise."

"Well, they'll just have their trouble for nothing," Fufu snorted. "Having one salesman call is one thing, but whole squads of them is simply out of the question!"

"Sure is glad us settle this thing when us did," Pin-pin said heartily. "Now us better disappear in a hurry. Them Voion done snuck up on us; they about six deep all the way around the town."

"I just remembered," Jik-jik said. "I got cousins on the far side of the valley. I believes I'll just go pay them Ween a call—"

"Hey, that a good idea, Jik-jik," a nearby Ween chimed in. "Ain't seen old Grandpa since I a nipper. I believes I'll just go along . . ."

"It a shame the way us been neglecting our kin . . ." another offered.

"I has a yen to travel myself . . ." a third realized aloud.

"Hold on," Retief called as a general surge toward the surrounding foliage gathered force. "Running away won't help. The Voion will catch you, whichever way you go."

"It was satisfying, getting the hook into a few o' the murdering no-goods," Tupper keened. "But there's too many o' 'em; our only chance is to slip off, quiet-like . . ."

"Why, you bunch of spoilsports!" Fufu honked. "Do you

mean you're going to run away just because a few worthless lightweights might be decapitated?"

"Us worthless lightweights wheeling out of here while the wheeling good," Fut-fut declared. "Rest of you can do what you likes; it a free country!"

"That's right, Tief-tief," Jik-jik sighed. "You Dipple-macs is good fighters, but us knows when us licked."

"Just listen to them chatter," Fufu grunted. "A shameful display of arrant cowardice. Luckily, we Jackoo are simply too brave for words. Unfortunately, we can't see in the dark, so we'll have to bow out of night operations. In fact, I think it might be a good idea to slip quietly away to quieter territory now and recharge our plates. It *has* been rather an unsettling evening—"

"Gentlemen," Retief called, "you're all talking like idiots. They have us hemmed in on all sides. There's only one way to get out of this trap—and that's fight our way out."

"How in the world did we get mixed up in this, Fufu?" a Jackoo boomed. "Why don't we just mash these noisy creatures and get back to sleep?"

"Listen at them," Jik-jik said. "They ready to quit. Only us Ween doing any fighting talk. Too bad we is got to sneak off with the rest of them—"

"Ween, ha!" Tupper shrilled. "Tief-tief's no Ween."

"He a honorary Ween," Jik-jik said sullenly.

"We're wasting time arguing," Retief said. "If we hit them hard, we can punch our way through. They won't be expecting attack."

"I've got an idea," Fufu said. "Since Tief-tief is the one who wants to start trouble, why doesn't he go do it—alone? Then in the confusion, the rest of us can just steal away . . ."

"Hey, that not a bad idea," Jik-jik nodded judiciously. He eased over beside Retief.

"This you big chance to impress me," he whistled. "Not only will you hog all the glory, but if you get annihilated, nobody miss you. What you say?"

"Very well," Retief said. "I'll lead the attack—if you'll permit me to sit on your back, Fufu—and if the rest of you will follow my lead."

"Well . . . us Ween is fighting sons of guns," Jik-jik said. "But seeing as them Zilk done pooped the party . . ."

"It was you Ween started this talk o' desertion," Tupper honked. "We Zilk will stick as long as any o' ye—if you go first, Tief."

"That's settled, then," Retief said. "Sharpen up your cutting edges, everybody, and we'll see what we can do."

"One thing about being a Stilter," Jik-jik said almost enviously, eyeing Retief, sitting astride Fufu. "You sticks up there like you was welded on. Can't no fellow with wheels manage that trick."

"Get ready," Retief called. Brush was stirring across the yard. A big, tall Voion rolled into view, a jewel glinting in one palp. He crossed his upper arms, propped the lower ones on what would have been hips in a vertebrate.

"You, there!" he shrilled in tribal dialect. "This village is under arrest! Now, all of you Jackoo lie down and roll over on your backs, and if you happen to catch those out-of-town agitators under you, so much the better!"

Fufu's oculars, plus both pairs of antennae, snapped erect.

"*What* did he say?"

"He wants you to lie down and play dead," Retief explained.

"A Jackoo lie down? He *must* be having us on," the great creature honked. "Once a Jackoo is off his wheels, he's— well, I shouldn't noise this about, but since we're allies now—"

"I know; he can't get up again."

"Well?" the Voion colonel shrilled. "You have exactly one minute to do as you're told, or my troops will fire the underbrush and burn you and your village into slag!"

"These huts of yours; they burn pretty well, don't they, Fufu?" Retief inquired.

"Well, we *do* use magnesium-bearing leaves for our roofs; they're light and easy to manage."

"What we going do now, Tief-tief?" Jik-jik demanded. "Them salesmen means business."

"They've formed up a nice envelopment all the way around our position," Retief said. "And they have all the strategic advantages. That leaves it up to us to score a tactical victory."

"What them words mean?" a Ween demanded.

"They mean the Voion have us outnumbered, outgunned, and outflanked; so we'll have to beat the wheels off them in a fashion they're not expecting."

"How we going do that?"

"Just follow my lead."

"I'm waiting!" the Voion screeched.

"Just be patient another ten seconds," Retief said soothingly.

The glow of approaching Jooprise was bright in the east; abruptly the fast-moving body leaped into view, a vivid edge of greenish light that swelled into a white glare as the great disk swept upward.

Retief drew his sword, pointed it at the Voion.

"Let's go, Fufu," he said. The Jackoo leader gave a mighty honk, and with a surge of power lunged into motion—his tribesmen at his back.

Retief could see leaves tremble on the trees ahead as the ground shook to the charge of the forty multiton Quoppina. For a startled moment, the colonel stood his ground. Then he backed, spun, shot into the underbrush a scant ten yards ahead of Fufu. Retief ducked as his mighty mount thundered in among the trees; leafy branches whipped aside with a screech and clatter of twisted metallo-wood. A polished Voion flashed into sight, gunned aside barely in time, whirled to thrust a bright lance head at Retief, who struck it aside, heard a screech cut off abruptly as the next Jackoo in line pounded across the spot where the invader had stood. More Voion were in sight ahead now, scattering before the avalanche of Jackoo. There was a loud *twang!* and a heavy arrow glanced off Retief's chest armor, whined away over his shoulder. Fufu slammed full tilt into a six-inch tree, bounced it aside as though it were a bundle of straw, veered slightly to miss a two-foot trunk, flushed a Voion who darted ahead, tripped, disappeared under Fufu's blind charge. Two Voion popped up at once, leveling lances, Retief crouched low, struck one spear aside with his sword point, saw Fufu's grubber knock the other flying.

Behind and on both sides a heavy crashing of underbrush attested to the presence of other units of Federation heavy armor charging in line abreast. Above, leaves tinkled and clanged to the passage of moving bodies.

Reflected Joop-light winked from the accoutrements of half-concealed Voion soldiery.

"Wheee!" Fufu hooted. "This is perfectly thrilling! I never thought I'd be charging into battle with a generalissimo sitting on me."

"Just be sure I'm still in place when you charge out again," Retief instructed.

A portable searchlight winked on ahead, silhouetting scurrying Voion against a bluish haze as they rushed to form up a defensive line against the thunder of approaching attackers.

"Oh, that's lovely," Fufu panted. "I can see them ever so much better now!"

The Voion ahead were dashing hither and thither, each seemingly reluctant to hog the glory of placing himself in the path of the oncoming enemy.

"Swing to the left now," Retief called. A Voion shot across the path ahead, whirled, brought a handgun up as Fufu veered to slam the gunner under his wheels. Two more Voion popped up, leaped aside, gave despairing yelps as Fufu's flankers steamrollered them. Fufu was running parallel to the Voion front now, fifty feet inside the besieging line, half a dozen yards behind a tribesfellow. Voion were racing alongside the turf-pounding line now, loosing off arrows which clacked harmlessly off Jackoo armor. One shot in close, fired at Retief, who ducked, thrust with the sword, saw the Voion wobble wildly, go over, bounce high, and slam into a tree.

The crashing of metallo-chitin under horny wheels was like the thundering of a heavy surf, punctuated by belated screeches of alarm as the Voion rear ranks caught glimpses of the doom rushing down at them. Spears arced up, falling as often among the Voion as among the rebellious tribesmen; blasters fired wildly, and here and there a club swung in a vain blow at a racing Quoppina. Then suddenly Fufu was through the main body, slamming past astonished rearguardsmen who gaped, dithered, fired too late.

"Swing left!" Retief called. "Maybe we can isolate this bunch!"

Now the Jackoo raced parallel to the outer fringes of a sizable detachment of the foe, cut off from the main body.

Behind them, the Ween and Zilk who had made their dash trailing close along the lanes opened up by the heavyweights charged on, disappeared into the surrounding forest in hot pursuit of the demoralized main body. Locked in a solid mass of entangled wheels, the entrapped herd cut off by the rebels battled hopelessly to retreat. Those who eluded the freight-train column and fled to the shelter of the woods seemed to disappear abruptly as soon as they reached cover.

The Voion captives were now compressed to the consistency of a single interlocked traffic jam, screeching mournfully and huddling back from the patrolling heavyweights.

"Hold it up, Fufu," Retief called. The Jackoo puffed to a halt, wheezing heavily. His tribesmates, following his lead, closed ranks, buzzing and humming, radiating heat like big purple boilers. The ensnarled Voion squalled, drew ever closer together as the mighty creatures stared at them, their sides heaving from the run. The few Planetary Police still mobile darted to and fro, then threw down their weapons and huddled against their embattled fellows. Behind Retief, the concealed combat teams emerged from the brush, snappers snapping, scythes waving.

"Fall out for a ten-minute break, gentlemen," Retief addressed his fighters. "They'll be back in a few minutes; but with about three hundred cops in our custody, we may find the opposition in a mood to talk terms."

"Tief-tief, I is got to hand it to you," Jik-jik stated. "Our plan work out pretty good! Us leave a trail of wide, skinny policemens all the way back to where Jackooburg use to be!"

"Used to be?" Jackoo heads turned.

"Sure; what you think that smoke is?"

"Why—they wouldn't dare . . . !"

"Never mind," Jik-jik said. "It wasn't much of a place anyhow. But Tief-tief—like I says, you is a credit to honorary Weenhood; only thing I don't see is, how come you won't let us get on with breaking them Voion down into bite-size? Way they jumbled up, it take 'em six months to figure out whose wheels belongs to which!"

"This bunch we've rounded up is just a small part of the Voion army," Retief pointed out. "We'll get the maximum use from them as negotiating material—but not if they're disassembled."

"Hey, Tief-tief . . . !" A Ween who had been posted as lookout hurried up, pointing skyward. "Some kind of flying wagon coming."

Retief and the others watched as a foreign-made heli settled in nearby. A small, undernourished-looking Voion with an oversized head lowered himself from the cockpit, unfurled a white flag, and approached, moving unsteadily on wheels several spokes of which were flapping loose.

"All right, let him come—and try to remember not to remove his head before he gets here," Retief cautioned.

"You are Tief-tief, the rebel commander?" the newcomer called in a curiously weak voice.

Retief looked the envoy over carefully, nodded.

"We, ah, admire your spirit," the Voion went on. "For that reason we are considering offering you a general amnesty . . ."

Retief waited.

"If, er, we could discuss the details in private . . . ?" the emissary proposed in a hoarse whisper.

Retief nodded to Jik-jik and Tupper. "Would you fellows mind stepping aside for a minute or two?"

"Ok, Tief-tief—but keep both oculars on that customer; he look to me like a slick one." They moved off a few yards.

"Go ahead," Retief said. "What's your proposition?"

The Voion was staring at him; he made a dry rasping sound. "Forgive my mirth," he hissed. "I confess I came here to salvage what I could from a debacle—but that voice—those legs . . ." The Voion's tone changed to a confident rasp: "I have just revised my terms. You will relinquish command of this rabble at once and accompany me as a prisoner to Planetary Field HQ!"

"Why," Retief inquired interestedly, "would I do that?"

"For an excellent reason. In fact, for ten excellent reasons, my dear Retief!" The Voion reached to its head, fumbled—then lifted off a hollow headpiece to reveal a pale gray face and five inquisitive eye stalks.

"Well, General Hish of the Groaci Legation," Retief said. "You're out of your territory."

Hish fixed two pairs of eyes on Retief. "We have in our custody the person of ten Terry females, removed from a disabled vessel illegally on Voion soil," he said coldly. "They are scheduled to be shot at dawn. I offer you their lives in return for the surrender of yourself!"

Six

"When you coming back, Tief-tief?" Jik-jik inquired worriedly. "How come you going off with this here policeman in this here apparatus?"

"I'll be back as soon as I can," Retief said. "Keep up the hit and run tactics—and recruit every tribe you meet."

"To get aboard," the disguised alien said in Groaci. "To make haste to arrive before the executions."

Retief stepped into the two-man heli in which the emissary had arrived. The latter strapped in, started up, lifted from the wheel-scarred field, then turned in the seat and cocked three unoccupied eyes at Retief. "I congratulate you on your wisdom in coming along quietly," he whispered in excellent Terran. "I of course disapprove of bloodshed, but without the compelling argument which your presence at Planetary HQ will present, I fear my protests would never have availed to preserve intact the prisoners."

"You still haven't told me what a Groaci military man is doing out here in the brush, General—"

"Please—address me merely as Hish. My Voion associates know me only as a helpful adviser. If my voice is to be effective in securing clemency for the captives, no complicating new elements must be introduced into the present rather fragile equation."

"For a group enjoying the services of a high-powered military adviser," Retief said, "the Planetary Army shows a surprising ignorance of the elements of warfare."

"I've only just arrived in the field today," Hish said. "As for these native levies—hopeless. But no matter. In the absence of your restraining presence your irregulars will doubtless devise a suitable disposition for them. The survivors, if any, will perhaps have learned a lesson or two from the experience which will stand them in good stead during coming campaigns under my tutelage."

There was a heavy satchel on the floor by Retief's feet, its top gaping open. "I see you're taking a practical view of matters," Retief commented. He studied a dull-glinting shape inside the bag. "I confess I'm curious as to just what it is you Groaci expect to net from the operation." As he spoke, he reached casually, lifted out the inert form of a two-inch Quoppina, a harsh yellow in color, remarkably heavy. Beneath it, he saw another, similar trophy, this one a soft silvery color. He replaced the dead specimens.

"Shall we say—new customers . . . ?" Hish whispered, staring ahead at the jungle below.

"The prospect of opening up a new market for your usual line of hardware isn't sufficient inducement to launch a hardheaded group like yourselves on a risky adventure under the collective CDT nose."

"Ah, but perhaps the new Planetary Government, sensible of the close ties binding them to the Groaci state, will spurn continued intervention in internal affairs by reactionary Terran influences . . ."

"Booting the Terries is part of the deal, eh? There's still something you're not being perfectly candid about, Hish. What's in it for the Groaci?"

"One must keep a few little secrets," Hish chided. "And now I must give my attention to landing; such an awkward business, laboring under the weight of this bulky disguise. Still, it's necessary; the rank and file of my associates seem to suffer from the sort of anti-foreign animus so typical of bucolics."

There were lights below, the dark rectangle of tents, the raw scars of hastily scraped camp streets, packed with the hurrying ant-shapes of Voion. To one side of the field headquarters, Retief saw a rank of parked Rhoon, unnaturally still as technicians crawled over them under the glare of portable polyarcs. The heli dropped in to a bumpy landing, was at once surrounded by Voion, nervously fingering weapons. Hish replaced his headpiece, opened the hatch and scrambled out. An officious-looking Voion staff officer bustled up, gave Retief a hostile look.

"Who's this, Hish-hish?" he demanded. "Their truce representative, I suppose?"

"By no means, Xic," Hish whispered in his weak Groaci voice. "Instruct your chaps to keep a sharp eye on this fellow; he's my prisoner."

"What do we want with more prisoners—and a Stilter at that? I've already suffered a number of nasty dents from the legs of those Terry cows you insisted we bring in—"

"Enough, Xic; I've had a trying evening—"

"What did you manage in the way of truce terms? I suppose they're demanding outrageous reparations for those few trivial villages that accidentally caught on fire—"

"On the contrary, they demand nothing. I left them to their own devices. Now—"

"What about our troops? Those rabble are holding an entire brigade of highly polished soldiers immobilized out there! Why, the cost of inlays alone—"

"The fortunes of war, my dear Major. Now, if you please, I have important matters to discuss—"

"What's more important than salvaging my brigade?" the outraged officer shrilled. "How can I be adjutant of an organization that's been scrapped by the enemy?"

"A neat problem in administration, sir. Possibly if you carry them on your morning report as 'Missing in action' . . ."

"Hmmm. That might work—at least until next payday. Meanwhile, why not disassemble this Stilter and get on with planning our next victory?"

"This Stilter will play an important part in that happy event, Xic. He happens to be the rebel commander."

"Him?" Xic canted his oculars alertly at Retief. "How in Quopp did you manage to capture him?"

"I have a certain skill in these matters. Bring him along now to my tent—"

"Not until the prisoners are released," Retief said. "I want to see them put aboard a couple of helis and on their way."

"What's this? A prisoner dictating terms?" Xic keened.

"No matter; the wenches have served their purpose. I had in mind ransoming them off for concessions from the Terry ambassador, but the present arrangement has a certain euphony. Go along to the stockade and see that they're released at once."

"I'll go with you," Retief said.

"You'll do as you're ordered!" Major Xic snapped. "Or I'll shorten those stilts of yours by a joint to bring you down to a more manageable size!"

"No, you won't. You'll carefully keep me intact and reasonably well pleased with things. Hish-hish would like it that way."

"We'll indulge his fancy for the moment, Major," the Groaci hissed. "Kindly lead the way."

The Voion clacked his palps angrily and rolled off toward a stoutly palisaded enclosure looming above the lines of low tents along the company streets. At a heavy gate made of stout logs welded together, a guard produced a foot-long key, opened a huge padlock, hauled the portal wide, then shouted to a compatriot above. Lights sprang on at the corner towers. Xic motioned a squad of Voion through, then followed, Hish close on his heels, Retief and an additional squad behind him.

There was an outcry ahead. Four Voion shrilled simultaneously, an effect not unlike the vocalizations of mating cats, though magnified. The Voion around Retief jerked up their clubs. Hish darted ahead. Retief pushed after him, came up beside the Voion officer who was waving all four arms and swiveling his oculars excitedly while the soldiers peered about the thirty-yard square enclosure, all explaining at once.

"Where are the Terrans?" Hish whispered. "What have you done with my prisoners?"

"Quiet!" the major shrieked. He turned to Hish, assuming a nonchalant angle of the antennae.

"Too bad, Hish-hish," he said airily. "It appears they've excavated a tunnel and departed."

"It was the one with the copper-colored cranial filaments!" a guard explained. "It demanded digging tools so that it and its fellows could eplivate the ratesifrans . . ."

"What's that?" Hish demanded.

"I don't know!" the major yelled. "Something to do with a tribal taboo; and if you think my boys are going to call down the wrath of the Worm—"

"Beware . . . lest you call down a more immediate ill temper," Hish snarled. He calmed himself with a visible effort, turned on Retief. "An unexpected development—but the females appear to be free, just as you desired—"

"Not exactly," Retief cut him off. "I desired to see them turned loose with a fighting chance of getting across a hundred miles of jungle and back to Ixix."

"Ah, well, life is filled with these trifling disappointments, my dear Retief. Suppose we go along to my tent now and proceed with business . . ."

"Thanks, but I won't be able to make it," Retief said affably. "I have to be getting back to the wars."

"Be realistic, Retief," Hish urged. "My end of the bargain was fulfilled in a rather informal manner, true, but surely you are not so naïve as to imagine that detail nullifies the spirit of our agreement . . . ?"

Retief glanced at the looming stockade walls, the Voion ringing him in. "What spirit would that be?"

"One of cooperation," Hish purred. "I suggest we move along from these depressing surroundings now and conduct our little chat in more comfortable circumstances—"

"I'm afraid you've gotten a couple of false impressions along the line somewhere," Retief said. "I just agreed to come with you; I didn't promise to do your homework for you."

"Surely the supplying of certain information was implicit in your surrender!"

"Why natter with the scoundrel?" the Voion major put in. "I have specialists on my staff who'll put him into a talking mood!"

"Don't be tiresome, Retief," Hish whispered. "I can squeeze the truth out of you; but why force me to these uncouth tactics?"

"Oh, maybe I have an idea you don't know just where I stand, and that you're a little reluctant to damage CDT property—"

"What's he talking about?" the Voion demanded. "What has this to do with interloping Terries?"

"Silence!" Hish snapped. "Go busy yourself with executing the slackers responsible for the escape, or some other routine task—"

"Who do you think you're talking to?" the major keened. "Some headquarters goldbrick sent you out here to poke around and count paper clips, but if you think you can talk that way to me and get away with it—"

"Calm yourself, Major! I should dislike to employ my influence with Prime Minister Ikk to have you transferred to duty on—certain other fronts . . ." Hish turned back to Retief. "You will now give me full particulars on rebel troop concentrations, or suffer the consequences!"

"Suppose we just jump directly along to the consequences," Retief proposed. "It will save time all around."

"As you will, then." Hish turned back to Xic. "Since your stockade has proven inadequate to requirements, what other facilities can you offer for the restraint of the prisoner?"

"Well—there's a nice little room behind post headquarters, specially built to house the officers' stimulant supply—if we ever get any. If it's good enough to keep my kleptomaniacs out of the Hellrose, it ought to keep this Stilter in."

"Very well," Hish snapped. "Take him there and chain him to the wall."

The cell was a cramped, low-ceilinged chamber with damp mud walls retained by log pilings only the upper foot of which were above ground level; through the narrow openings between uprights, Retief could see the muddy polyarc-lit acres of the camp stretching a hundred yards to the nearest jungle perimeter. The crowd of Voion who had escorted him there crowded in, watching as the head jailer shook out a length of tough chain, welded one end to a projecting stub on an ironwood corner post, then approached Retief.

"Just sit quiet now, Stilter," he ordered, "while I throw a loop around your neck—and no backchat, or I'll weld your mandibles shut."

"How about putting it on my left stilt instead," Retief proposed. "That way it won't interfere with my thinking nice thoughts about you, just in case my side wins."

"Confidentially," the welder said in a low voice. "Just how strong *are* you boys?"

"Well, let's see," Retief considered. "There are five billion

Quoppina on Quopp; subtract two million Voion, and that leaves—"

"Wow!" a gaping guard said. "That's better'n two to one, pretty near—"

"Shut up, Vop!" the warder buzzed. "Stick out that stilt, Stilter!" Retief complied, watched as the Voion threw two loops of stout chain around his ankle, welded the links together.

"That ought to hold you until Hish-hish gets through arguing with the major and comes down to work you over." The Voion snapped off his portable welder. "If you need anything, just yell. The exercise'll do you good."

"What time is breakfast served?" Retief inquired.

"Oh, I'll throw a couple slabs of over-aged Dink in to you after a while—if I think of it." The guards filed from the cell, taking their torches with them, the warder bringing up the rear. He looked back from the door.

"That bad?" he queried. "Five billion of youse?"

"Worse," Retief agreed solemnly. "Some of us vote twice."

There was silence after the door clanked shut. Along the narrow gap between the top of the excavation and the sagging log ceiling half a dozen inquisitive Voion faces were ducked down, staring in at the dark pit; they saw nothing, tired of the sport, rolled off to other pastimes. Retief picked a relatively dry spot, sat down, quickly unsnapped the leather soled foot-covering from his chained leg, pulled off the shoe, then unbuckled the greavelike shin armor, worked it out from under the loops. A moment later his leg was free. He resumed the leg- and foot-pieces, shook out the chain and arranged a slip noose for use in the event of sudden callers, then scouted the small room. The metallo-wood posts were deep-set, six inches apart. He chipped at one with the clawed gauntlet on his right hand; it was like scratching at a fireplug. The air space above the wall was hardly more promising; the clearance under the ceiling was no more than eight inches, and the gap between verticals hardly a foot . . .

A movement beyond the barrier caught Retief's eye; a pattern of glowing, greenish dots danced in the air a few yards distant, bobbed, came closer.

"Tief-tief!" a tiny voice peeped. "Tief-tief caught-caught!"

"Well—you know my name." Something small and bright green buzzed through the opening, hovering on three-inch rotors.

"Save-save George-George," the tiny flyer said. "Tief-tief pal-pal!"

Retief held out his hand. The six-inch Quoppina—a Phip—settled on it, perched like a jeweled ornament, its head a deep green, its short body a brilliant chartreuse with forest green stripes, its four straw-thin legs a bright sunshine yellow.

"Phip-phip help-help," it stated in its tiny voice.

"That's a very friendly offer," Retief said. "There might be something you could do, at that. How about rounding up a couple of your friends and see if you can find a few things for me . . ."

Retief studied the six-foot-long, two-foot-deep trench he had scooped in the stiff clay of the cell floor, rimmed on one side by a low parapet heaped up from the excavated material.

"That will have to do," he said to the half dozen Phips who perched along the sill, watching the proceedings. "Old Hish will be hotfooting it down here any time now to see if durance vile has softened me up."

A last flight of Phips buzzed in through the wall opening, deposited their bean-sized contributions in the small heaps laid out on a mat of leaves flown in for the purpose.

"All-all," one hummed. "Gone-gone."

"That's all right," Retief assured the small creature. "I've got enough now." He lifted a wide leaf heaped with shredded bark selected by the Phips for its high cellulose content, placed it atop the heaped-earth revetment beside the foxhole. "Somebody give me a light," he called. A Phip settled in, struck its rear legs together with a sound like a file on glass. At the third try a spark jumped. Retief blew gently on it, watched as the fuel glowed, burst into a bright green flame. He covered the small blaze with another broad leaf; yellowish smoke boiled out. He held the damper in place until the low-oxygen combustion was complete, then lifted it to reveal a double handful of black residue.

"That ought to do the job; now let's prepare the rest of the ingredients."

He picked up a rough-surfaced slab of ironwood previously split off a post, began grating sourballs into a fine powder.

Half an hour later, Retief packed the last pinch of the finely divided mixture into the container he had improvised from nicklewood leaves, carefully wrapped with lengths of tough wire-vine. He crimped down the top, inserted a fuse made from a strip of shirt-sleeve impregnated with the home-made gunpowder.

"Now, when I give the word, light it off," he instructed the hovering Phips. "Just one of you; the rest will have to stand back at a good distance. And as soon as it's lit—head for the tall timber, fast! Don't wait around to see what happens."

"Kay-kay, Tief-tief," a Phip chirped. "Now-now?"

"In just a minute . . ." He hefted the bomb. "A good point and a half; that ought to have a salutary effect." He placed the rude package on the ledge against an upright, pressed it firmly in position, then packed clay around it, leaving the fuse clear.

"That's it," he said. He stepped into the trench, settled himself face-down.

"Light it off, fellows—and don't forget to hightail it . . ."

There was the busy humming of small rotors, then a harsh rasping as the selected Phip struck a spark. A brief sputtering followed, accompanied by the hasty whine of the departing Phil, then silence. Retief waited. He sniffed. Was there a faint odor of burning rag . . . ?

The *boom!* lifted Retief bodily, slammed him back against the floor of his retreat under an avalanche of mud and screaming wood fragments. He thrust himself clear, spat dirt, his head ringing like a giant gong. There was a harsh stink of chemicals, a taste in his mouth like charred sneakers. Cool air blew from a gaping cavern where the wall had been. A timber sagged from above; beyond it he could see smoke swirling in a room littered with shattered lumber.

A Phip buzzed close. "Fun-fun," it shrilled. "Gain-gain!"

"Some other time," Retief said blurrily. "And remind me to use smaller amounts . . ." He ducked under the fallen ceiling beams, went up the blast-gouged slope, emerged into the open. Voion shot past him, inaudible in the shrill ringing in Retief's ears. Out of the smoke haze, the slight figure of General Hish appeared, arms waving. Retief straight-armed the Groaci, saw him go end over end, one artificial wheel bouncing free to go rolling off into the brush. He sprinted, dodged a pair of Voion who belatedly skittered into his path, plunged into the dark wall of the jungle.

Seven

The trail left by the fleeing prisoners was not difficult to follow; bits of lacy cloth, dropped hankies, candy wrappers, and the deep prints of spike heels served to indicate their direction of flight as plainly as a set of hand-painted signposts. The girls had pushed through dense thickets for a hundred yards, then encountered a well-defined trail leading in an approximately westward direction. It was now after Second Jooprise, and Retief moved along in multi-colored gloom beneath towering trees of a thousand varieties, each bearing metal-bright leaves in gay tones, which rustled and tinkled, clashing with soft musical notes as the arching branches stirred to the wind.

Half an hour's walk brought him to a stream of clear water bubbling over a shallow, sandy bottom bright with vivid-colored pebbles. Small aquatic Quoppina the size of Phips darted to and fro in the sun-dappled water, propelled by rotating members modified by evolutionary processes into twin screws astern.

The water looked tempting. Retief hung his sword on a convenient branch, lifted off the helmet he had been wearing for the past eighteen hours, unstrapped the leather side-buckles and shed the chest and back armor, then splashed into the stream and dashed cold water over his face and arms. Back on shore, he settled himself under a mauve-barked tree, took out one of the concentrated food bars Ibbl had provided.

From above, a plaintive keening sounded. Retief looked up into the tree, saw something move in the Jooplight, striking down through branches and glittering dark foliage— a flash of vivid purple among the blackish-red leaves. There was a second movement, lower down. Retief made out the almost invisible form of a wiry, slender Quoppina, gorgeous violet where the light struck him, decorated with white-edged purple rosettes, a perfect camouflage in the light-mottled foliage. The creature hung motionless, wailing softly.

Retief jumped, caught a branch, pulled himself up, then climbed higher, avoiding the knife-edged leaves. From a position astride a stout limb twenty feet up, he could make out the cleverly concealed lines of a narrow-mesh net in which the captive—a Flink, Retief saw—hung, a tangle of purple limbs, twisted ropes, and anxiously canted oculars.

"What happened, fellow? Pull the wrong string and catch yourself?"

"I'm laughing," the Flink said glumly, in a high, thin voice.

"So go ahead, gloat," a second Flink voice called from above. "Rub it in."

"Just a minute and I'll cut you down," Retief offered.

"Hey, me first," the upper Flink called. "It was him started the trouble, remember? Me, I'm a peaceful Flink, bothering nobody—"

"It's a different Stilter, you lowlife," the nearer Flink called hastily. "This ain't the one from before."

"Oh, you've seen other Stilters around?" Retief inquired interestedly.

"Maybe; you know how it is. You meet all kinds of people."

"You're not being completely candid, I'm afraid. Come on—give."

"Look," the Flink said. "Such a crick I've got: How about cutting me down first and we'll chat after?"

"*He's* got a crick," the other Flink shrilled hoarsely. "Ha! In *his* lousy net I'm hanging! Six cricks I've got, all worse than his!"

"You think this noose is maybe comfortable?" the first came back hotly. "Rope burns I'm getting—"

"Let's compare notes later," Retief interrupted. "Which way did the Stilters go?"

"You look like a nice, kind sort of Stilter," the nearest Flink said, holding his oculars on Retief as he swung in a gentle arc past him. "Let me down and I'll try to help you out with your problem. I mean, in such a position, who could talk?"

"Cut him down, and he's gone like a flash," the other called. "Now, I happen to like your looks, so I'll tell you what I'll do—"

"Don't listen," the roped Flink said in a confidential tone. "Look at him—and he claims to be number one tribal woodsman, yet. Some woodsman!"

"A woodsman like you I shouldn't be, even without you was hanging in my noose," the other countered. "Take it from me, Stilter, Ozzl's the biggest liar in the tribe, and believe me, competition he's got!"

"Fellows, I'm afraid I can't stay for a conference after all," Retief cut in. "Sorry to leave you hanging around in bad company, but—"

"Hold it!" the Flink called Ozzl screeched. "I've thought it over and I've decided: A nice fellow like you I want my family to meet—"

"Don't trust him! I'll tell you what: Get me out of this lousy rope, and I'm your Flink—"

"You expect this Stilter—such a fine-looking Quopp— he should believe that? As soon as I'm loose, everything I own is his!"

"So what'll he do with a pile of empties? My deal is better, believe me, Mister; you and me, such a talk we'll have, you wouldn't believe—"

"You're right; he wouldn't. Him and me, together a long chat we'll have—"

There was a flash of green, a sharp humming; the Phip was back, hovering before Retief's face.

"Tief-tief, flip-flip," it churped. "Flip-flip Flink-flink!"

"Don't listen!" Ozzl screeched. "What does this midget know?"

"Flip-flip Flink-flink!" the Phip repeated.

"Hmmm. I seem to remember hearing somewhere that a Flink's word is good as long as he's standing on his head," Retief mused. "Thanks, partner." He gripped Ozzl's lower arms—in his species specialized as landing gear—and inverted the captive tree-dweller.

"If I cut you down, will you tell me where the Stilters are?"

"OK, OK, you got me," the Flink chirped glumly. "Cut me down and the whole miserable story I'll give you."

Retief extracted a similar promise from the second Flink.

"Look out, now," the latter cautioned. "All around is nets."

Retief made out the cleverly concealed lines of other nets and nooses, some small, some large enough to gather in a fair-sized Quoppina.

"Thanks for the warning," Retief said. "I might have walked right in to one of those."

Five minutes later both captives had been lowered to the ground and cut free. They sprawled, groaning, working their arms and experimentally revving up their rotation members: small pulleylike wheels which they customarily hooked over vines or branches for fast travel.

"Well," Ozzl sighed. "Me and Nopl, first class trappers we're supposed to be. Such a picture, the two of us in our own ropes hung up!"

"Nothing's busted," Nopl said. "Boy, such a experience!"

"Don't stall, gentlemen," Retief said. "The time has come to tell all: Where did you see the Stilters, how long ago, and which way did they go when they left?"

"A promise is a promise—but listen—you won't tell, OK?"

"I won't tell."

Ozzl sighed. "All right. It was this way . . ."

" . . . so I turned around, and zzzskttt! The Stilter with the copper-colored head filaments—the one the others called Fi-fi—pulls the trip wire—such a dummy I was to explain it—and there I am, downside up. It was humiliating!"

"Under the circumstances, a little humility seems appropriate," Retief suggested. "And after the Stilter tricked you into your own net, what then?"

"Then the two-timer cuts down the rest of the Stilters, and off they go—thataway." Ozzl pointed.

"Yeah," the other Flink said aggrievedly. "So there we hung until you come along—and all because we try to be polite and show that Stilter how the nets work, such an interest it was expressing."

Retief nodded sympathetically. "We Stilters are a tricky lot, especially when anybody tries to violate our tribal taboo against being eaten. And on that note I must leave you—"

"What's the rush?" Ozzl demanded. "Stick around awhile; a little philosophy we'll kick around."

"What about a drink, fellows?" Ozzl proposed. He took a hip flask from the flat pouch strapped to his lean flank, quaffed deeply, rose to his full three foot six, flexed his arms. "A new Quopp that'll make out of you," he announced and passed the bottle to Retief. He took a swallow; like all Quoppina liquors, it was thin, delicately flavored, resembling dilute honey. He passed the flask to Nopl, who drank, offered sulphurous sourballs which Retief declined.

"They're a good two hours ahead of me," he said. "I have to make up some time—"

The Phip was back, buzzing around Retief's head.

"Tief-tief," the Phip hummed. "Nip-nip!"

"Sure, give the little stool pigeon a shot," Nopl offered. "Whoopee! Life is just a bowl of snik-berries!"

"My pal, Tief-tief!" Ozzl slung one long, pulley-wheeled member across the lower portion of Retief's back in comradely fashion. "You're a shrewd dealer for a . . . a . . . whatever kind of Quoppina you are!"

Nopl took another pull at the flask. "Tief-tief, you should meet the crowd," he shrilled cheerfully. "A swell bunch, am I right, Ozzl?"

"Such a swell bunch, I'm crying," the Flink replied. "When I think what a swell bunch they are I wonder, what did I do to deserve it?"

"They're a lousy crowd teetotaling small-timers, but so what?" Nopl caroled. "Tief-tief they should meet."

"Sorry," Retief said. "Some other time."

Ozzl made a noise like a broken connecting rod, the Flink expression of suppressed merriment. "Guess again,

Tief-tief," he caroled, and waved a wheeled member in an all-encompassing gesture. "Meet the boys!"

Retief glanced upward. From behind every leafy branch and vine-shrouded shrub, a purple Quoppina materialized, a rope or net in hand, a few nocking arrows to small bows, one or two armed with long, flexible tridents.

"About time," Nopl said and hiccuped. "I thought you boys would never show."

Retief stood in the center of the patch of open, Jooplit sward beneath the big tree from which a hundred silent Flink hung like grotesque fruits. An overweight Flink with the wine-purple carapace of mature age tilted myopic oculars at him. "These two loafers I send out, they should check the traps and with a drinking buddy they come reeling back," he commented bitterly.

"Who's reeling? Am I reeling? Look at me," Ozzl invited.

"What about the Stilter?" someone called. "He looks like prime stock—with a cheese sauce, maybe he should be served—"

"My pal, Tief-tief, nobody cuts up! First I'll drop dead!"

"This I could arrange," the oldster cut him off. "Now, if we slice up this Stilter, a snack for everybody he'll make—"

"Stop right there," Nopl shrilled. "A businessman like Tief-tief we couldn't eat! Cannibalism, yet, it would be! Instead, we'll truss him up and sell him—or maybe disassemble him for spares . . ."

Cries rang back and forth as the Flink discussed the various proposals.

"Such a head I've got," Nopl groaned during a momentary lull. "I think I need another little snort."

"That booze of yours works fast," Retief commented. "You got through the buzz and into the hangover stage in record time."

"Hung over or no, Ozzl and me will stick by you, Tief-tief. If they vote to sell you, I'll put in a good word we should hold out for top price."

"Marked down you'll not be while I'm around," Ozzl agreed.

The elderly Flink emitted a shrill cry for silence. "The

pros and cons we've discussed," they announced. "It looks like the cons have it." A rustle ran through the Flink ranks. The encircling tribesmen moved in closer, shaking out nets and ropes as they maneuvered for favorable positions, Retief drew his sword, stepped back against the nearest tree trunk.

"Hey," the oldster called. "What's that sharp thing? It looks dangerous! Put it away like a nice piece of merchandise before somebody gets hurt."

"It's an old tribal custom among us Stilters that we make owning us as expensive as possible," Retief explained. "Who's going to be first to open an account?"

"It figures," the elder said judiciously. "Price supports, yet."

"Still, we try to be reasonable," Retief amplified. "I doubt if I'll disassemble more than a dozen Flink before you get a rope on me."

"Six," the Flink said flatly. "That's my top offer."

"I'm afraid we're not going to be able to get together," Retief said. "Maybe we'd better call off the whole deal."

"He's right," someone stated. "Worth twelve Flink, including maybe me, he's not."

Retief started forward, swinging the sword loosely. "Just step back, gentlemen," he suggested. "I have important business to transact, and no time to continue this delightful discussion—"

A noose whirled at him; he spun, slashed; the severed line dropped to the ground.

"Hey! That's expensive rope you're cutting," someone protested, hauling in the damaged lariat.

"Let him go," another suggested. "My rope I ain't risking."

"What's that?" the elder shrilled. "You want I should let valuable merchandise go stilting right out of sight?"

"Listen, Tief-tief," Ozzl called. "There's only the one trail, and it leads straight to the rock spire. Now, with us, you get sold for parts, so OK, there you are. But you climb up there and a Rhoon picks you up and flies off—I'm asking: Where are you?"

"Did you say Rhoon?" Retief inquired.

"On top of the rock spire they're thick like Phips on a jelly flower. A chance you haven't got!"

"Still, I think I'll risk it," Retief said. He moved toward the trail and two Flink rushed in, nets ready; he knocked them spinning, dodged two nets and a lasso, leaped for the dark tunnel of the trail and ran for it with a horde of Flink baying in hot pursuit.

Later, on a rocky slope a hundred yards above the tops of the thick jungle growth below, Retief pulled himself up onto a flat boulder, turned and looked down at the Flink tribe clustered below, staring up and shaking fists.

"Dirty pool, Tief-tief," Ozzl yelled. "This kind terrain, our wheels ain't meant for."

"Thanks for escorting me this far," Retief called. "I'll find my way from here."

"Sure." The Flink waved a member at the steep escarpments rising above. "Just keep climbing. The Rhoon roost is only about a mile—straight up. If you don't fall off and get killed, the Rhoon you'll find after a while—or they'll find you." He clicked his antennae in the Gesture of Sentimental Farewell. "You were a good drinking buddy, Tief-tief. Hang loose."

Retief scanned the slope above; he had a stiff climb ahead. He lifted off his helmet, pulled off the gauntlets, slung them by a thong to his belt. He shook his canteen; nearly empty. He took a last look at the valley and started up the almost vertical slope.

It was an hour after dawn when Retief reached a narrow ledge a thousand feet above the jungle valley below. The wind whistled here, unimpeded by Quoppian flora; in the distance, a pair of white flyers of medium size wheeled and dipped under the ominous sky of approaching First Eclipse, where the fire-edged disk of Joop rushed to its rendezvous with the glaring Quopp sun. Far above, a mere spec in the dark blue sky, a lone Rhoon circled the towering peak where the giant flyers nested.

Retief studied the rock face above; it was a smooth expanse of black slatelike stone rising sheer from the ledge. The route upward, it appeared, ended here.

One of the white aerialists was dropping lower, coming in to look over the intruder. Retief donned his headpiece, shifted his sword hilt to a convenient angle, waited for the visitor. He could hear the beat of its rotors now, see the pale coral markings along the underside of the body, the black legs folded against the chest region, the inquisitive oculars canted to look him over.

"What seek you here upon the wind slopes, groundling?" a thin voice called down to him, tattered by the gusty breeze. "There's naught for your kind here but unforgiving rock spires and the deep, cold air."

"They say the Rhoon have their nests up there," Retief called.

"That do they—up a-high, where low clouds scrape their bellies and death blooms grow amid the moss as black as night." The flying creature dropped closer; the slipstream from its ten-foot rotors battered at Retief, whirling dust into his face. He gripped the rock, braced his feet apart.

"Aiiii!" the flyer called. "If a zephyr from my passing can come nigh to spill you from your perch, how will you fare when some great lordling of the Rhoon comes like a cyclone to attend you here?"

"I'll work on that one when I get to it," Retief shouted over the tumult.

"If you've come to steal my eggs, you've picked a lonely death."

"Is there any other kind?"

The flyer settled lower, reached out and gripped a buttress of rock with black talons; its rotors whined to a stop.

"Perhaps you've tired of life, chained to the world, and you've come here to launch yourself into one glorious taste of flight," it hazarded.

"Just paying a social call," Retief assured the creature. "But I seem to have run out of highway. You wouldn't happen to know an easier route up?"

"A social call? I see you wish a braver death than a mere tumble to the rocks."

"I'd like to sample the view from the top; I hear it's very impressive."

"The view of raging Rhoonhood stooping to defend a nest is said to be the fearsomest on Quopp," the flyer agreed. "However, few eyewitness tales of the experience are told."

Retief studied the creature's rotors, spinning slowly as the wind sighed over the thin, curved blades.

"How much weight can you lift?" he inquired.

"I once plucked up a full-grown Flink and dropped him in the river, yonder," the flyer motioned with one limber arm. "I doubt if he'll come thieving 'round my nest again."

"I weigh more than a Flink," Retief pointed out.

"No matter that: You'd fall as fast as any Flink, and make a better splash."

"I'll bet you can't lift me," Retief challenged. The flyer revved its rotors, shifting its grip on its perch.

"Most groundlings plead for life when once I catch them on the rock spires. Now you invite my wrath."

"Oh no, I'm just talking about flying me up there." Retief pointed to the peaks towering above.

"Fly you . . . ?"

"Sure. I can't walk up a vertical wall, and it wouldn't be convenient to go down and look for another route."

"Can you be serious, poor earthbound grub? Would you indeed trust life and limb to me?"

"Most Quoppina will keep their word to a harmless stranger. Why should you be any different?"

"A curious rationale," the flyer said, "and yet, withal, a most refreshing one. I'd come to think of crawlers all as timid things, who cling and whimper out their fear when I come on them here among the lonely peaks. And now here's one who speaks as boldly as a flyer born!"

"Just put me down anywhere in climbing range of Rhoon country," Retief suggested.

"A strange anomaly is this: A wingless one who dares to come among the masters of the sky!" The flyer whirled its rotors, lifted, drifted, hovering, toward Retief. "I'll put you to the test then, groundling! Perhaps you'll weight me down, and then together we'll go tumbling toward our death below. But if my rotors hold, I'll bear you up, my life upon it!"

"Fair enough." Retief sheathed his sword, squinting against the down-blast of air. He reached for the steel-hard grapples of the flyer, gripped, held on. Air screamed as the whirling blades raced, biting for purchase; then he was lifting, floating up, wind screaming past his face, the mountainside dwindling away below.

❖   ❖   ❖

The flying creature rose swiftly for a hundred feet; then it slowed, gained another fifty feet, inched upward, its rotors laboring now. A gust of wind tilted it, and it dropped, then righted itself, struggled upward again, paralleling the smooth face of rock at a distance of thirty feet, Retief estimated. A small white flower growing from a crevice caught his eye; slowly it dropped below him as the flyer gained altitude foot by foot. Above, Retief could see a tiny ledge where the vertical face ended, and above it a long sweep, only slightly less steep, to a lone spire thrusting up another five hundred feet against the darkening sky.

"How say you, groundling?" the laboring flyer's voice rang out, "will you trust me to press on, or shall I give it up and place you safe below?"

"Just a little way now," Retief called. "You can do it, old timer."

"I like the groundling's spirit, wings or no!" the Quoppina shouted into the wind. "We'll hazard all . . . and win or die . . . and none can say we quailed before the test!"

"You'd better save your wind for flying," Retief called. "We'll stage a self-congratulation session after we get there."

The wind whipped, buffeting. The cliff face moved past with agonizing sloth. Retief's hands were numb from the strain; the ledge was still twenty feet above, inching closer. The Quoppina's breathing was loud, wheezing; the sound of the rotors had changed timbre. They seemed to flutter now, as though the blades were loose. Then another sound was audible—a sharp whirring, coming closer . . .

Retief twisted his head. A second flying Quoppina had come up from the port beam; it hovered, studying the situation with alert oculars.

"That one's too big to eat, Gulinda!" it called. "I'll wager he's as tough as Wumblum wheel rim!"

"I'll place him . . . safe above . . . or die . . ." Retief's flyer got out.

"Ah—then it's a wager! Well, I suggest you waste no time. A Rhoon has seen you now, and half a minute hence he'll be here."

Retief's flyer grunted a reply, settled down to steady pulling. Ten feet more, five, three . . .

There was a deep thrumming, a beat of wind that
bounced the flyer closer to the cliff face. Retief craned,
saw the huge-bodied shape of a fast-descending Rhoon
silhouetted against the vast, glittering disks of its spinning rotors. With a final, gear-screeching effort, the
smaller flyer surged upward the final yard, banked toward
the ledge. "Farewell!" it screamed. Retief dropped,
slammed stony ground, fetched up against the rising wall
above as the Rhoon pounced, hissing, its fanged eating
jaws wide. Retief rolled away as the Rhoon struck out
with a barbed hind leg, missed and struck again, sent
stone chips flying. A narrow crevice split the rock a yard
distant; Retief dived for it, wedged himself in just as the
disk of Joop cut off the blackish sunlight like a snapped
switch. Long Rhoon talons raked against the rock, sending a shower of bright sparks glimmering against the sudden dark. Then, with a hoarse scream, the Rhoon lifted
away; the beat of its rotors faded. Retief leaned back
in his cramped refuge, let out his breath with a long
sigh, alone now with the stars that twinkled in the false
night of the eclipse and the moaning wind that searched
among the rock crannies.

Retief rested while Joop edged across the bright corona
of the distant sun; the glowing halo bulged, then burst into
full light as the transit was completed. He scanned the sky;
a pair of Rhoon circled far above, light flicking from their
rotors. He squeezed out of his hideaway, looked over the
edge of the two-foot shelf on which he stood. Far below,
the ledge from which he had hitched the ride to his present
position showed as a thin line against vertical rock—and
far below that, the jungle stretched like a varicolored carpet
across low hills to distant haze.

He looked up; striated rock loomed, topped by a rock
spire that thrust up like a knife blade a final hundred feet.
Retief turned back to the cranny in which he had hidden.
It narrowed sharply into darkness—but a steady flow of cold
air funneled from it. He went to hands and knees, pushed
through the first narrowing, found that the passage widened slightly. Above, the sky was a bright blue line between
the rising walls of rock. He rose, crunching brittle debris

underfoot, braced his back against one face of the chimney, started upward.

Halfway up, Retief found an outthrust shoulder of rock on which to rest. He ate half a food bar, took a swallow of water—the last in his canteen. Then he went on.

Once the cleft narrowed, then widened out into a near-cave, from which a cloud of tiny gray-black Quoppina no bigger than hummingbirds swarmed in alarm, battering at his face, uttering supersonic cries. Again, the black shadow of a Rhoon swept across the strip of sky above, momentarily blacking out the meager light. The armor chafed, cutting into his back; his hands were cut in a dozen places from the sharp-edged rock.

The crevasse widened again ten feet from the top. Retief made the last few yards in a scramble up a deeply scored slope half-choked with weathered and faded fragments of Quoppina exoskeleton and sun-bleached organic gears looped by tangles of corroded internal wiring. The Rhoon, it appeared, were messy eaters.

Keeping in black shadow, Retief studied the open sky; a thousand feet above, two Rhoon wheeled lazily, unaware of the intruder in their domain. He stood, dusted himself off, looked around at an oval platform fifteen by twenty feet, backed at one side by a spear of rock that rose ten feet to a needle point, edged on the remainder of its periphery by a void that yawned across to a stupendous view of high, lonely peaks, only a few of which topped his present vantage point. Closer at hand, a heap of round boulders caught his eye: Butter-yellow spheres eighteen inches in diameter. He went to them, tapped the smooth surface of one; it gave off a hollow, metallic bong. There were six of them—Rhoon eggs, piled here to hatch in the sun.

Retief glanced toward the monster parents circling above, still apparently serenely ignorant of his presence.

The big eggs were heavy, unwieldy in their lopsidedness. He lifted down the topmost spheroid, rolled it across to the cliff's edge, propped it, delicately poised, just above the brink. The next two eggs he ranged beside the first. Two more eggs formed a short second rank, with the final orb positioned atop the others. Retief dusted his hands, resumed the helmet and gauntlets he had laid aside earlier, then posted himself squarely before the gargantuan Easter display and settled down to wait.

Eight

A cold wind whipped down from the deep blue sky. Retief watched the mighty Rhoon elders wheeling in the distance, tireless as the wind—a description which, he reflected, did not apply equally to himself.

Half an hour passed. Retief watched the high white clouds that marched past like gunboats hurrying to distant battles. He shifted to a more comfortable position leaning against a convenient boulder, closed his eyes against the brightness of the sky . . .

A rhythmic, thudding whistle brought him suddenly wide awake. A hundred feet above, an immense Rhoon swelled visibly as it dropped to the attack, its giant rotors hammering a tornado of air down at him, swirling up dust in a choking cloud. The Rhoon's four legs were extended, the three-foot-long slashing talons glinting like blue steel in the sunlight, the open biting jaws looking wide enough to swallow an ambassador at one gulp.

Retief braced himself, both hands on the topmost of the pyramid of eggs as the flying behemoth darkened the sun—

At the last possible instant the Rhoon veered off, shot past the peak like a runaway airliner, leaving a thin shriek trailing in the air behind it. Retief turned, saw it mount up into view again, its thirty-foot propellers flexing under the massive acceleration pressures. It swung in to hover scant yards away.

"Who comes to steal Gerthudion's eggs?" the great creature screamed.

"I want a word with you," Retief called. "The egg arrangement is just a conversation piece."

"High have you crept to reach my nest, and slow was your progress," the Rhoon steam-whistled. "I promise you a quicker return passage!" It edged closer, rocking in the gusty wind.

"Careful with that draft," Retief cautioned. "I feel a sneeze coming on; I'd hate to accidentally nudge your future family over the edge."

"Stand back, egg-napper! If even one of my darlings falls, I'll impale you on a rock spike to dry in the sun!"

"I propose a truce; you restrain your violent impulses and I'll see to it no accidents happen to your eggs."

"You threaten me, impudent mite? You'd bribe me with my own precious Rhoonlets?"

"I sincerely hope so. If you'll just perch somewhere, I'll tell you what it's all about."

"Some reason must there be for such madness under the morning sun! To hear the why of it, I confess I'm curious!" The Rhoon mother swung across the platform, settled in at the far edge in a flurry of dust, clinging to the rock with four jointed legs like lengths of polished gray pipe. Her yard-long head reared up a full fifteen feet to stare down at Retief, the shadows of her rotors flicking across her horny features as the blades slowed to a leisurely wind-driven twirl.

"Mind you don't twitch, now, and send what remains of your short future tumbling down into the abyss," the huge flyer admonished in a voice that boomed like a pipe organ. "Now, tell me: Why chose you this peculiar means of dying?"

"Dying isn't exactly what I had in mind," Retief corrected. "I'm looking for a party of Terrans—Stilters, somewhat like me, you know—and—"

"And you think to find them here?"

"Not exactly; but I have an idea you can help me find them."

"I, Gerthudion, lend aid to the trivial enterprises of a planet-bound mite? The thin air of the steps has addled your wits!"

"Still, I predict you'll take an interest before long."

The Rhoon edged closer, stretching its neck. "Your time grows short, daft groundling," she rumbled. "Now tell me what prompts you to dare such insolence!"

"I don't suppose you've been following recent political developments down below?" Retief hazarded.

"What cares Gerthudion for such?" the Rhoon boomed. "Wide are the skies and long the thoughts of the Rhoon-folk—"

"Uh-huh. I'm a long-thought fan myself," Retief put in. "However, a brand of mite called the Voion have been cutting a lot of people's thinking short lately—"

"How could any petty dirt-creeper cut short the thoughts of a free-born Rhoon?"

"I'll get to that in a minute," Retief promised. "Is it true that you Rhoon have keen eyesight . . . ?"

"Keen is our vision, and long our gaze—"

"And your wind's not bad, either. Too bad you're too big for a career in diplomacy; you could keep a round of peace talks going for a record run. Now, tell me, Gertie, have you noticed the smoke columns rising from the forest over there to the north?"

"That I have," the Rhoon snapped. "And lucky for you my eggs you're embracing, else I'd tumble you over the edge for your impertinence!"

"Those are tribal villages burning. The Voion are setting out to take over the planet. They have very specific ideas of what constitutes a desirable citizen: no Quoppina who isn't a Voion seems to qualify—"

"Get to the point!"

"You Rhoon, not being Voion, are going to have to join the fight—"

"A curious fancy, that!" the Rhoon bassooned. "As though the lofty Rhoon-folk would stoop to such petty enterprise!"

"I wonder if that keen vision of yours has detected the presence of a number of Rhoon cruising around at tree-top level over the jungle in the last few days?"

"Those did I note, and wondered at it," the Rhoon conceded. "But a Rhoon flies where he will—"

"Does he?" Retief countered. "Those particular Rhoon are flying where the Voion will."

"Nonsense! A Rhoon, servant to a creeping mite who'd not a goodly swallow make?"

"They have at least two squadrons of Rhoon in service now, and unless someone changes their plans for them, there'll be more recruits in the very near future. You, for example—"

"Gerthudion, slave to a verminous crawler on the floor of the world?" The Rhoon spun its wide rotors with an ominous buzzing sound. "Not while I live!"

"Exactly," Retief agreed.

"What mean you?" the Rhoon croaked. "What mad talk is this . . . ?"

"Those Rhoon the Voion are using are all dead," Retief said flatly. "The Voion killed them and they're riding around on their corpses."

Gerthudion sat squatted on folded legs, her stilled rotors canted at non-aeronautical angles.

"This talk, it makes no sense," she tubaed. "Dead Rhoon, their innards to replace with wires imported from a factory on another world? Power cells instead of stomachs? Usurping Voion strapped into saddles in place of honest Rhoonish brains?"

"That's about it. You Quoppina all have organo-electronic interiors, and there's enough metal in your makeup to simplify spot welding the necessary replacement components in position. A nuclear pack the size of a fat man's lunch will supply enough power to run even those king-sized rotors of yours for a year. I didn't have time to examine the dead Rhoon I saw in detail, but I'd guess they've even rigged the oculars to a cockpit display screen to take advantage of your natural vision. Riding their zombies, the Voion can probably fly higher and faster than you can—"

"They'd dare?" the Rhoon burst out, vibrating her posterior antennae in the universal Gesture of Propriety Outraged. "Our airy realm to usurp—our very members to employ? Aunt Vulugulei—for a week her dainty tonnage I've not seen; could it be . . . ?"

"Quite possibly she's been fitted out with a windshield and rudder pedals," Retief nodded. "And some shined-up Voion's probably sitting where her main reactor used to be, carving his initials on her side and revving her rotors—"

"Enough! No more!" The Rhoon waggled her oculars in a dizzying pattern. She rose, creaking, on legs quivering with emotion, started her rotors up. "I'm off, my fellow Rhoon to consult," she called over the rising tumult of air. "If what you say is true—and I've a horrid feeling it is—we'll join in, these ghouls to destroy!"

"I had an idea you'd see it that way, Gertie. And don't forget to ask if any of them have seen a party of Stilters in the jungle."

"Inquire I will; meanwhile, my eggs from that precarious edge withdraw. If one should slip, your ragtag horde will lack a leader!" In a hailstorm of blown pebbles, the Rhoon leaped off, beating her way eastward toward a cluster of tall peaks.

Retief turned at a sound—a loud *scrongg!* like a sheet-metal roof being lifted off a shed by a high wind. The heap of eggs which he had stacked safely back where he had found them quivered. The ripping noise came again; a gleaming spike poked out through the polished curve of the center spheroid in the bottom row, ripped a foot-long tear. An ungainly shape thrust through the opening—a head like a chromalloy pickax equipped with a pair of alert eyes which fixed on Retief. The beak opened.

"Quopp!" the fledgling Rhoon squalled. "Quopppp!" It struggled frantically, snapping the impressive jaws, lined, Retief noted, with a row of triangular razors. A clawed leg appeared, gained the newcomer another six inches of freedom. As the broached egg rocked, those above trembled, then toppled with a crash like spilled milk cans. One, badly dented, bounced to a stop at Retief's feet. A six-inch split opened to reveal a second baby face, complete with meat shredders. The first Rhoonlet gave a final kick, sprawled free of the shell, which skidded across the platform, driven by the wind, disappeared over the side. A third egg gave a jump; a bright needle point punctured its side.

The first of the newborn Rhoon was unsteadily on its feet now, trying out six short, unspecialized limbs, claw-tipped, the rear pair showing only knobby buds where later the rotating members would develop—a form not unlike the ten-million-year remote ancestor of all the Quopp tribes. The hatchling wobbled, steadied, then charged, jaws gaping. Retief sidestepped, noting that infant number two was now half clear of his prison, while number three was surveying the scene with interested eyes. Dull clunks and clangs attested to activity within the other three eggs.

The eldest infant managed to halt its rush just short of the cliff edge, teetered for a moment staring down into the awesome depths over which it would soar later in life, backed away, hissing, then remembered lunch and rushed Retief again in time to collide with younger brother, freshly on the scene. While the two tangled, squalling, Retief hastily maneuvered half a dozen scattered rocks in place to form a rude barricade, stationed himself behind it. The argument ended as a third young appetite shot past the combatants, zeroing in on the free lunch. The trio hit the barrier with a metallic crash, rebounded, came on again—and now there were four.

The beat of heavy rotors sounded above. Gerthudion, flanked by two immense males distinguished by gold and red cranial plumes, dropped in with a tornado of air that sent her young slithering and squawking across the rocky platform—and over the edge.

"Hey!" Retief called. "Your kids . . ."

The Rhoon settled in. "That's all right; obnoxious creatures, those. It's only the eggs I'm concerned about, their hatching to ensure. Anyway, they'll be all right. It's good experience. As for the call to war, we're with you—"

A small head appeared over the edge; scrabbling claws pulled a hungry Rhoonlet up, the others close behind. Retief stepped to the giant parent, scaled the massive side and straddled the back just behind the head. "Let's get moving," he called over the pound of idling rotors. "I'm beginning to share your view of the younger generation."

"As for your Terries," Gerthudion honked, "Lundelia reports he's seen such a group as you described near the village of the Herpp, a few miles west."

"Then just drop me off there, if you don't mind."

The Rhoon leaped into the air, the backwash from her pounding rotors a howling typhoon.

"I'll take you there," she boomed over the uproar. "Then thereafter you'll guide me to these ghoulish Voion, my vengeance to wreak."

It was a swift flight from the chill altitudes of the rock spires down across rolling jungle to the bend of the river where the pinkish copperwood huts of the Herpp nestled in the shelter of the trees. Gerthudion settled in to a bouncy landing on a sand spit where there was clearance for her rotors, and Retief slid down, settled his sword belt into position for a quick draw, scanning the silent village with its neat wheelways, orderly flower beds, and colorful awnings.

"Nobody in sight, Gertie; I think the inhabitants beat a hasty retreat when they saw you coming."

"Or mayhap they crouch behind their doorposts with drawn bows," the flyer suggested.

"Yeah—mayhap. I guess there's just one way to find out." He walked across the sand, climbed a grassy bank, stood at the end of the village street beside a long table heaped with bright-colored fruits and fragments of husk—a task apparently hastily abandoned.

"I am Tief-tief," he called. "And I dance the Dance of Friendly Intentions."

There was a flicker of motion at a window. The polished tip of an arrow poked into view, followed by a pale blue head.

"I am Nop-Nee, and I dance the Dance of Fair Warning," a squeaky-chalk voice piped.

"I'm looking for some friends of mine," Retief called. "Don't let Gerthudion bother you. She's tame—"

The Rhoon snorted loudly behind Retief.

" . . . and she won't eliminate your village unless you carelessly initiate hostilities by letting fly with that arrow."

The aimed weapon disappeared. The Herpp rose, emerged cautiously from the door, the arrow still nocked but aimed off-side now.

"What makes you think your friends are here?" he chirped.

"Oh, word gets around. There are ten of them—Stilters, you know. Where are they?"

"Never saw them," the Herpp snapped. "Now you better get back on that monster of yours and dust back off where you came from, before we clobber the both of you."

"Don't do anything hasty, Nop-Nee," Retief cautioned. "Gerthudion is a patient Rhoon, but you *might* annoy her with that kind of talk—"

"Bah, we've seen enough Rhoon in the last twelve

hours to last us," the Herpp snapped. "A round dozen of the devils flew over and dropped stones on us last night; told us to surrender, before they set the whole place on fire!"

"That's unfortunate," Retief agreed. "But those were outlaw Rhoon. Gerthudion's on her way to hunt them down right now—"

"Then she'd better get started. We've got catapults and ballistae rigged, and by now they're zeroed in and ready to fire. So . . ." he raised the bow. "Scat!"

"I admire your spirit," Retief said. "But first I want the ten Terrans."

Nop-Nee drew the bowstring farther back. "Not on your life! I'm not turning harmless foreigners over to the likes of you and your oversized cronies! They're guests of Quopp, and they'll receive hospitable treatment. I am Nop-Nee and I dance the Dance of Ferocious Defiance!"

"And I'm Retief and I dance the Dance of Mounting Impatience—"

"You can dance the Dance of Apoplexy for all I care," Nop-Nee yelped. "Git!"

Retief cupped a hand beside his mouth.

"Girls, if you're in there, come on out!" He called in Terran. "I'm here on behalf of the Terry Embassy at Ixix . . ."

The Herpp jumped back in alarm. "Here, I'm Nop-Nee and I dance the Dance of Confusion! That sounded like Terry talk . . ."

A door banged wide on the third hut in line, and a slim brunette Terry female in torn flying togs appeared. She shaded her eyes at Retief, while other girls crowded out behind her. Retief executed a sweeping bow.

"Ladies, I'm enchanted to find you," he said. "I hope none of you were hurt in the crash."

"Who are you?" the brunette asked. She had a snub nose and blue eyes and was not over nineteen. "I thought I heard a Terran voice . . ."

"That was me, I'm afraid. I'm known as Tief-tief. I'm here to help you."

Nop-Nee was jittering restlessly, keeping the drawn bow aimed at Retief's chest.

"You're not from that nasty little Voion who locked us up in a corral?" the girl asked.

"By no means. He and I are confirmed antagonists, ever since I blew up his liquor vault."

The girls were in a huddle now, whispering together. A small blonde with green eyes spoke urgently, with emphatic gestures.

"Well," the brunette said. "I guess we may as well take a chance; Aphrodisia likes your voice." She smiled and came forward. "I'm Rene. It's very nice of you to trouble about us, Mr. Tief-tief."

Nop-Nee lowered his bow. "I dance the Dance of Utter Bafflement," he complained. "What's going on?"

"Girls, now that I've located you, I can make arrangements to fly you out. I'm afraid Ixix isn't a healthy place for Terries right now, but there's a trading post at Rum Jungle where you'll be reasonably safe for the present." Retief looked over the little group, all young, all pretty, all showing signs of a difficult day and night in the jungle.

"Which one of you is Fifi?" he inquired.

The girls looked at each other. Rene bit her lip. "She's not here, I'm afraid. We heard that a rebel army was organizing to fight the Voion, and she started out early this morning alone to try to reach them."

"You ladies just sit tight until you hear from me," Retief called down from his perch on Gerthudion's back. "I'll round up a few Rhoon and be back for you as soon as I can."

"I am Nop-Nee and I dance the Dance of Apology," the Herpp keened. "Who would have thought that a Stilter on Rhoonback would mean anything but trouble?"

"You did just the right thing, Nop-Nee," Retief assured the agitated Herpp. "Take good care of the girls until I get back, and we'll all dance the Dance of Mutual Congratulation."

"She wouldn't *let* any of us go with her," Aphrodisia wailed. "She said we'd slow her down . . ."

"Don't worry. We should be able to spot her from the air." Retief waved; Gerthudion lifted off with a great battering of air, climbed to three hundred feet, headed south. It was high noon now; the sun glared down from a cloudless pale sky. Retief watched the trail below, saw a scurry of small Quoppina fleeing the shadow of the giant flyer passing overhead—but no sign of the missing girl.

It was a twenty-minute flight to the spot where the victorious troops of the Federated Tribes had been encamped eight hours earlier. Gerthudion settled in to a landing on the wheel-trampled ground, deserted now and littered with the debris of battle—and of hasty evacuation.

"Looks like our prisoners sneaked off when nobody was looking," Retief observed. He studied the maze of trails leading off in all directions. "Which way did our lads go?" he inquired of a pair of Phips, hovering nearby.

"Here-here, there-there," the nearest cheeped. "Run-run, quick-quick!"

"Don't tell me," Retief said. "Some of our more impulsive members started in on the chore of sawing the Voion up into convenient lengths, thereby panicking them into breaking out of the jam."

"Check-check!" a Phip agreed. "All-all scat-scat!"

"And by now they're scattered over a hundred square miles of jungle, with several thousand highly irritated Voion in pursuit. So much for the grass-roots movement—"

"Tief-tief!" a Phip buzzed in excitedly from a reconnoiter of the nearby cover. "Thing-thing, there-there!"

Retief drew his sword. "What kind of thing, small stuff? A Voion left over from the party?"

"Big-big, long-long, stilt-stilt!"

"A Stilter? Like me? Gertie, wait here!" Retief followed the Phip for a hundred yards, then paused, listening.

There was a crackling in the underbrush. A heavy-shouldered biped stalked into view—an unshaven Terran in a tattered coverall and scuffed boots, holding a heavy old-style power pistol gripped in one immense fist.

"Hold it right there, Bug," Big Leon growled in tribal dialect. "I got a couple bones to pick with you."

Retief smiled behind the mask, put a hand up to lift the disguising headpiece—

"Keep the flippers out from the sides," Leon growled

in dialect. "And drop the sticker. Maybe you never saw one of these before—" he gestured with the gun "—but it'll blow a hole through you, tree and all."

Retief tossed the sword aside. Leon nodded. "Smart Bug. Now, there's just one thing I want out of you, wiggly-eyes: I hear there's a native leader that's popped up out here in the brush, organizing the yokels." He motioned at the spare-parts littered ground. "It looks like there was a little action here, not too many hours back. I don't know which side you were on, and I don't care—just tell me where to find that Bug leader—fast."

"Why?" Retief demanded.

Leon frowned at him. "For a Bug, you've got kind of a funny voice—but to hell with it. I want to ask him for help."

"What kind of help?"

Leon drew a finger across his forehead like a wind-shield wiper, slung sweat from it. "Help in staying alive," he said. "There's forty-six of us Terries over at Rum Jungle. Ikk's got us surrounded with about half a million troops and he swears he's going to eat us for breakfast."

"I see," Retief nodded. "And you'd ask a Bug for help?"

"We'll take any help we can get," Leon stated flatly.

"What makes you think you can get it?"

Leon grunted. "You got a point there—but let's can the chatter. Where'll I find this Tief-tief character?"

Retief folded his arms. "That's what they call me," he said.

"Huh?" Leon's mouth closed slowly. "Uh-huh," he nodded. "It figures. The only Quopp on the planet I want to make pals with, and I stick a gun in his chest-plates." He holstered the weapon. "Well, how about it?"

"I'd like to help you—" Retief said.

"Great. That's settled, then. Call your army out of the bushes and let's get rolling. Something tells me the Voion will hit us at dawn—"

"As I was saying," Retief interrupted, "I'd like to help you Terries, but unfortunately I seem to have misplaced my army."

Leon's hand went to his gun. "What kind of a stall is this?" he grated.

"My hundred seasoned veterans wandered off while I wasn't looking," Retief explained.

"A hundred!" the big Terran burst out. "I heard you had half the Bugs on Quopp with you! I heard you were cutting Ikk's troops into Christmas tree ornaments! I heard—"

"You heard wrong. The Federated Tribes were a spark glimmering in the night. Now they're not even that."

Big Leon let out a long breath. "So I had a little walk for nothing. OK. I should have known better. Now all I've got to do is get back through the Voion lines so I can help the boys pick off as many of those Jaspers as we can before they ride over us." He half turned away, then faced Retief again. "A hundred against an army, huh? Maybe you Bugs are all right—some of you." He turned and was gone.

Retief motioned a hovering Phip over.

"No sign of any other Stilters in the neighborhood?"

"Not-not," the Phip stated.

"How each one of you fellows knows what all the other ones know beats me," Retief said. "But that's a mystery I'll have to investigate later. Keep looking for her; she can't have gotten far through this growth in the dark with a Voion behind every third clump of brush."

"Sure-sure, Tief-tief! Look-look!" the Phip squeaked and darted off. Retief pulled off his helmet, unbuckled the chest and back armor, laid it aside with a sigh of relief. He removed the leg coverings gingerly; there was a nasty blister above the ankle where the Voion jailer had plied his torch carelessly. Clad in the narrow-cut trousers and shirt he had retained when donning his disguise in Sopp's shop, he stacked the armor together, tied it with a loop of wire vine, concealed it behind a bush, then made his way back to the place where he had left Gerthudion.

"All right, let's go, Gertie," he called, coming up her port quarter. The Rhoon started nervously, tilted a foot-long ocular over her dorsal plates, then gave a rumbling growl.

"It's all right," Retief soothed. "I'm wearing a disguise."

"You look like a Terry," Gerthudion accused.

"That's right; it's all part of an elaborate scheme I'm rapidly getting wrapped up in like King Tut."

"Kink Tut? Who's he? Sounds like a Voion. Now royal they'll declare themselves—"

"Steady, girl. Just a literary allusion."

"But now, Tief-tief, what of dear Aunt Vulugulei, I long to seek her out, or her destroyers to rend!"

"I'm afraid you Rhoon are on your own, Gertie. Those fighting tribes I told you about won't be available to carry out their end of the war after all."

"No matter; even now the tribal host circles far to the west in a wide sweep, our enemies to spy. Then retribution will me take in full measure—allies or no."

"How long would it take them to get here?"

"Many hours, Tief-tief—if their search they'd abandon to heed a call."

"Do you know where Rum Jungle is?"

"Certainly—if by that you mean that clustering of huts yonder to the south, whence emanate curious odors of alien cookery with a disfavorable wind—"

"That's the place. I need a lift in there. And there's another Stilter up ahead; he's wearing the same kind of disguise I am. We can gather him in on the way."

"As you wish, Tief-tief."

"Gertie, now that the Federated Tribes are dispersed, I can't hold you to our agreement. This is a dangerous trip I'm asking you to make. You might run into the whole Voion Air Force."

"Why then, I'll know where to find the ghouls!" Gerthudion honked. "Mount up, Retief! Fly where I will, that will I—and let the villains beware!"

"That's the way to talk, Gertie."

Retief climbed into position on the Rhoon's back. "Now let's go see if things at Rum Jungle are as bad as reported— or worse."

Nine

"I don't get it," Big Leon said between clenched teeth from his position just behind Retief atop Gerthudion's ribbed shoulder-plates. "How'd you get out here in the woods? How'd you spot me? And how in the name of the Big Worm did you tame this man-eater? In forty years in the jungle I never—"

"You never tried," Retief finished for him.

"I guess I didn't," Leon sounded surprised. "Why would I?"

"We're sitting on one reason. I'll go into the other answers later, when things quiet down."

Gerthudion's rotors thumped rhythmically; wind whistled past Retief's head. A thousand feet below, the jungle was a gray-green blanket, touched with yellow light here and there where the afternoon sun reached a tall treetop.

"Hey, Retief!" Leon called above the whine of the slipstream. "Has your friend here got a friend?"

Retief looked back, following Big Leon's pointing arm. Half a mile behind, a Rhoon was rapidly overhauling the laden Gerthudion.

"Goblin at seven o'clock," Retief called to her. "Anyone you know, Gertie?"

The Rhoon lifted her massive head, then swung her body sideways—a trick she performed with only a slight lagging of forward motion.

"That's—but it couldn't be! Not Aunt Vulugulei!" the great creature honked. At once, she banked, swept in a tight curve back toward the trailing Rhoon, now closing fast.

"Aunt Vulgy!" she trumpeted. "Where in Quopp have you been? I've been worrying myself into a premature molt—"

The other Rhoon, a scant five hundred yards distant now, banked up suddenly, shot away, rising fast, its rotors whick-whicking loudly. Gerthudion swerved, causing her riders to grab for better holds, gave chase.

"Auntie! It's me, Gerthudion! Wait . . . !" The agitated flyer was beating her rotors frantically as she fell behind the unladen Rhoon, a quarter of a mile ahead now and two hundred feet higher. Sunlight glinted on spinning rotors as the strange Rhoon tilted, swung in a tight curve, swept down at top speed on its pursuer.

"Duck!" Retief called. "It's a zombie!"

Yellow light winked from a point behind the pouncing

Rhoon's head. The buzz of a power gun cut through the tumult of rushing air. There was a harsh rattle of sound from behind Retief; blue light glared and danced at close hand as a pencil-thin beam lanced out, picked out the attacking Rhoon's left rotor, held on it as Gerthudion wheeled to the left, dropped like a stone, rocking violently in the air blast as the enemy flyer shot past.

"I nicked him," Leon growled. "The range is too long for a handgun to do much damage."

"He's got the same problem." Retief leaned forward. "Gertie, I'm sorry about Aunt Vulugulei, but you see how it is. Try to get above him; he can't fire through his rotors."

"I'll try, Tief-tief," Gerthudion wailed. "To think that my own auntie—"

"It's not your aunt anymore, Gertie; just a sneaky little Voion getting a free ride."

Gerthudion's rotors labored. "I can't gain on her—or it," she bawled. "Not with this burden . . ."

"Tell her not to try dumping us off," Leon barked. "My gun is the only thing that'll nail that Jasper! Just get me in position!"

The Voion-controlled Rhoon cadaver was far above now, still climbing. Gerthudion, her rotors thumping hard, was losing ground.

"He'll drop on us again in a minute," Retief said. "Gertie, as he gets within range, you're going to have to go into a vertical bank to give Leon a clear shot . . ."

"Vertical? I'll fall like a stone from a frost-shattered peak!"

"That's the way it's got to be, I'm afraid. Lead him down—and don't flare out until we're at treetop level. If we give him time to think, it will dawn on him all he has to do is stay right over us and pour in the fire!"

"I'll try . . ." The Rhoon was in position now, above and slightly off-side to the right. It stooped then, moving in for an easy kill. Gerthudion held her course; abruptly the enemy gun fired, a wide-angle beam at extreme range that flicked across Retief's exposed face like a breath from a blast furnace.

"Now," Retief called. Instantly, Gerthudion whipped up on her left side, her rotors screaming in the sudden release of load, and in the same moment Leon, his left arm clamped around Retief, lanced out with his narrow-beam weapon. A spot of actinic light darted across the gray belly-plates of the zombie, then found and held steady on the left rotor.

The fire from above was back on target now, playing over Gerthudion's exposed side-plates with an odor like hot iron.

"Stay with that wide beam another ten seconds, and you're a gone Bug," Leon grated out. The Rhoon above dipped to one side now, feeling the sting of the blaster, but Leon followed, held the rotor in the beam while air shrieked up past him like a tornado.

"Right myself now I must, or perish!" Gerthudion honked. "Which is it to be, Tief-tief?"

"Pull out!" Retief grabbed for handholds as the great body shifted under him, surging upward with a crushing pressure. The whirling vanes bit into air, hammering; Leon broke off his fire—

"Hey, look!" The attacking Rhoon had veered off at the last possible instant, gun still firing; now lazily it rolled over, went into a violent tumble. Pieces flew; then the zombie was gone against the darkness below.

"I think you burned through his wiring," Retief called. "Gertie, stay low now; it's only another couple of miles."

"Low shall I stay, like it or no," the Rhoon called. "I thought my main armature, its windings I would melt!"

Retief felt the heat of the overworked body scorching his legs. "If we meet another one in the air we've had it."

"If far it is, we're lost," she wheezed. "I'm all but spent . . ."

"There it is!" Leon pointed to a tiny cluster of buildings against the sweep of jungle ahead, ringed by tilled fields.

Gerthudion flew on, dropping even lower, until she labored just above the high crowns of trees whose leaves glittered in her backwash like rippling water. The forest ended abruptly, and she was swooping across the fields that surrounded the trading town, packed solid now with Voion soldiery.

"Look at 'em," Leon called. "Jammed in so tight they

can't even maneuver! If those Bugs knew anything about siege tactics, they'd have wiped us out the first night!"

"Better try some evasive action," Retief called. "They may have some big stuff down there."

Gerthudion groaned, complied sluggishly.

"If they have, they're holding it back," Leon yelled behind him. "All they hit us with so far is a lot of talk, plenty of rocks and arrows, and a few handguns."

Blasters winked below now, searching after the Rhoon as she threw her massive weight from one side to another, flying a twisting course toward the squatty palisade ahead and the cluster of low buildings behind it. Leon took careful aim, poured a long burst from his power gun into a Voion gun crew. There was a flicker, then a violent burst of pale yellow light that puffed outward in a dingy smoke cloud, faded quickly as fragments whistled past Gerthudion's head and clattered against her rotors. Then the giant flyer staggered over the wall in a billow of dust, slammed the ground at the center of the wide central plaza of the town. Men appeared, running toward the Rhoon.

"Hold your fire!" Big Leon bellowed. "It's me—and Retief! This Rhoon's a tame one! The first bushwhacker lays a hand on her's got me to answer to!"

The embattled Terrans were all around now, gaping as Retief and Leon slid down from their places.

"Jumping jinkberries, Leon—how'd you catch that critter?"

"You sure it don't bite?"

" . . . thought you was one of them that been buzzing us all day—"

"Quiet, the lot of you!" Leon held up his hands. "The bug rebels are out of the picture. We're on our own." He motioned to Retief. "I picked up a recruit, name's Retief."

"Well, you're just in time for the massacre, Mister," someone greeted.

"Hey, Leon—what about this Rhoon of yours? Maybe it could airlift us out of here—"

"I'll carry no burden . . . this day," the Rhoon gasped out. Her rotors sagged as she squatted, her massive keel against the ground. "Grave damage . . . to my windings . . . I fear

I've done . . . such burdens to bear up . . . the while I gamboled like a Phip . . ."

"You did OK, Gertie," Leon said. "Just take it easy, girl." He faced the crowd of some forty unshaven, unwashed frontiersmen. "What's been going on while I was gone?"

"They hit us again just after First Eclipse," a wide, swarthy man with a low-slung pistol belt said. "Same old business: Come at us in a straight frontal assault, whopping it up and shooting arrows; a couple Rhoon making passes, dropping leaflets and stones; our guns—we still got three working—kept 'em at a safe altitude. We kept our heads down and peppered 'em and they pulled back before they hit the stockade. They been quiet since noon—but they're up to something. Been working since before dawn on something."

Leon grunted. "After a while those Bugs are going to figure out all they have to do is hit us from four sides at once, get a couple magnesium fires going against the walls, and we've had it."

"Their tactics are likely to improve suddenly," Retief said. "There's a Groaci military adviser in the area. I imagine he'll take the troops in hand before many hours pass. In the meantime, we'd better start making some plans—"

"Some wills, you mean," someone corrected. "They'll flatten us like a tidal wave once they get rolling."

"Still, we don't want to make it too easy for them. Leon, what have you got in the way of armaments, other than those three guns I heard mentioned?"

"My iron makes four; it's got about half a charge left. There's a couple dozen heavy-duty hunting bows; some of the boys are pretty good with 'em—and I had Jerry trying to tinker up a rig to drop a few thousand volts to the perimeter wall—"

"I have it going, Leon," Jerry called. "Don't know how long it will last if they throw a big load on the line."

"We finished up the ditching while you was gone, Leon," a man called. "If they get past the stockade, they'll hit a six-foot trench; that ought to slow 'em down some."

"This is all just peanuts," Leon said. "Sure, we'll take a few hundred with us—but that won't stop us from going."

"It will be dusk in another few hours," Retief said. "I

think we can count on a go-for-broke attack before then, with General Hish calling the plays. Let's see if we can't arrange a suitable reception."

From a top-floor room in a tower that formed one corner of the compound at Rum Jungle Retief studied the ranks of the Voion that moved restlessly all across the half-mile of cleared ground surrounding the fortress.

"Uh-huh, our Groaci military expert is on the scene," he said. "That formation's not exactly a parade-ground effect, but it's a long way from the mob we flew over on the way in."

"It's not that that gives me the willies," a thick-set man with a short blond beard said. "It's them damned Rhoon circling up there." He motioned toward floating dots far overhead that indicated the presence of a pair of the huge flyers.

"If they knew Gertie's crowd were out looking for them, they'd be a little less carefree up there," Retief commented. "But I'm afraid our aerial allies are combing the wrong stretch of sky."

A man hurried in, breathing hard. "OK, Big Leon," he said. "I guess that does it: We rigged the ropes and the tank-traps, and all the boys are posted up as high as they could get. Les's got a good head o' steam up on both boilers, and—"

"All right, Shorty," Leon said. "Just tell everybody to look sharp and don't make a move before the signal goes up."

"Get ready," Retief said. "I think something's starting down there now."

Barely visible in the dim light, the Voion were crowding back, opening narrow lanes through their ranks; bulky shapes were trundling forward along the paths thus formed.

"Oh-oh, looks like they got some kind of heavy equipment," Shorty said.

"Nope—not equipment; friends," Leon stated. "Those are Jackoo. I guess that cuts it. Those boys can steamroller right through the walls."

"Correction," Retief said. "Six, two, and even those are zombies—like the Rhoon."

"What do you mean?" Leon and the other stared at

Retief. He gave them a brief explanation of the Voion technique of installing an energy cell and a pilot in a dead Quoppina.

"The drive mechanism and circuitry are all there," he concluded. "All they have to do is supply the power and the guidance."

"That's far from simple," Jerry said. "Ye gods, the technical knowledge that implies . . . ! Maybe we've been underestimating these Voion!"

"I think the Groaci have a digit in the pie," Retief said.

"Groaci, huh," Jerry nodded, looking worried. "It fits; they're skillful surgeons as well as exporters of sophisticated electronic and mechanical devices—"

"How can they butt in here?" Shorty demanded. "I thought that kind of stuff was frowned on by the CDT."

"You have to get within frowning range first," Retief pointed out. "They've done a good job of keeping under cover."

"Looks like they're getting set to hit the wall, all right," Leon said. "I count eight of 'em. The game'll be over quicker'n I figured."

Retief studied the maneuvers below, dim in the pre-dawn light. "Maybe not," he said. "See if you can get me seven volunteers, and we'll try to stretch it into extra innings."

Retief waited, flattened against the wall of a one-story structure the back of which was no more than ten feet from the timber wall surrounding the compound.

"Get ready," Shorty called from the roof above. "They're rolling now; boy, look at 'em come! Brace yourself—he's gonna hit right—"

There was a thunderous smash; a section of wall six feet wide bowed, burst inward; amid a hail of splinters, the dull magenta form of a two-ton Jackoo appeared, wobbling from the terrific force of the impact, but still coming on, veering past the corner of the structure half in its path, gathering speed again now as it plunged past Retief at a distance of six feet—

He swung out behind the bulky shape, took three running steps, jumped, pulled himself up on the wide back— even broader than Fufu's ponderous dimensions, he noted in passing. Directly before him, in a hollow chopped out behind the massive skull—the brain location in all Quoppina species—the narrow back of a Voion crouched, a heavy helmet of gray armor plate protecting the head. Retief braced himself, reached forward, hauled the driver bodily from his cockpit, propelled him over the prow; there was a heavy ker-blump! as the broad wheels slammed over the unfortunate Quoppina. Clinging to the now unguided zombie, Retief reached into the cockpit, flipped up a large lever dabbed with luminescent orange paint. The groan of the drive ceased instantly; the juggernaut slowed, rolled to a stop a foot from the six-foot moat dug by the defenders.

There was a confused shrilling behind; Retief turned, saw the leaders of a column of Voion pressing through the broached wall.

"Now!" someone shouted from a rooftop. At once, a brilliant cascade of electric blue sparks leaped across the packed mass of invaders struggling on high wheels across the shattered timbers; the two foremost members squalled, shot forward; those behind also squalled, but impeded by the uneven ground and the efforts of their fellows, failed to dart clear. The high voltage continued to flow—here leaping a gap to the accompaniment of miniature lightnings, there bringing adjacent patches of Voion to red heat before welding them together. More Voion, coming up fast from the rear, joined the press, found themselves instantly joined in the wild dance of arcing current and randomly stimulated nerves and gear trains.

Retief returned to the task at hand, flipped the "back" switch, hastily maneuvered the captured ram to face in the direction from which it had come. The two Voion who had leaped clear of the confusion dashed toward him, seeking refuge. Retief grabbed up the issue club dropped by the former operator in his hasty exit in time to slam the gun from the grip of one of them, knock the other spinning with a backhanded swipe to the head. Then he pushed the "go" lever into the forward position, threw the speed control full over, and vaulted over the side.

"Cut the power," Shorty yelled from above. At once, the showering sparks from the electrified attack column died, leaving only the dull red glow of hot spots; then the riderless zombie was into the welded mess, slamming through the obstruction to disappear into the mob beyond.

"Get them cables back in place!" a voice yelled. Men darted out, hauled at the one-inch steel lines, stretching them across the gap three feet from ground level. Retief looked around. Across the compound, other dark gaps showed in the wall. Here and there lay the slumped form of a Voion, and one Jackoo bulked, immobile.

"Six of 'em busted through," Big Leon's voice said, coming up beside Retief, breathing hard. "One got stuck in his own hole; another one was damaged—couldn't get him going again. The boys sent the others back to spread joy according to plan."

"Any casualties?"

"Les got a busted arm; he was kind of slow knocking over a Bug that got through. Your scheme worked out neat, Retief."

"It slowed them a little. Let's see how Gertie's doing."

They walked across to where the big flyer still rested, her four legs sprawled, her eyes dull.

"Gertie, they'll make it through on the next try," Retief said. "How are you feeling?"

"Bad," the Rhoon groaned. "My circuitry I've overloaded. A month's nest-rest I'll require to be myself again."

"You're going to have to lift off in a few minutes or you'll wind up being somebody else," Big Leon said. "Think you can do it?"

Gerthudion lifted an eye, gazed distastefully across at the signs of the recent fray. "If I must, I must. But I'll wait until the last, my powers to recover."

"Gertie, I have an important mission for you," Retief said.

He outlined the plan while Gerthudion breathed sonorously, like a pipe organ being tuned.

" . . . that's about it," he concluded. "Can you do it?"

" 'Tis no mean errand you dispatch me on, Retief; still, I'll aloft, these dastards to forestall. Then I'll return, your further needs to serve."

"Thanks, Gertie. I'm sorry I got you into this."

"I came willingly," she honked with a show of spirit. "Sorry am I my fellow Rhoon so far afield have flown, else a goodly number of the rascals we'd have disassembled for you." She started her rotors with a groan, lifted off, a vast dark shadow flitting upward in the gloom, tilting away toward the dark wall of the jungle.

Ten

"Hey," Shorty shouted from his rooftop. "There's a bunch shaping up to hit the gap over here—and looks like the same down the line at Jerry's spot . . ."

Other calls rang out from the spotters posted on the roofs.

"Trying to catch us off-balance," Big Leon said. "OK," he yelled up to Shorty. "You know the plan; don't let yourselves get cut off!" He turned to Retief as they started for the buildings at a run. "That Groaci general's spending Bugs like half-credit chips in an all-night Zoop Palace."

"He's getting them free," Retief said. "So far they haven't bought him much."

"Here they come . . ." Shorty's voice was drowned in a shrill battle cry as the lead elements of the new wave of Voion shot through the breaks in the stockade, coming fast along the paths trodden out by the Jackoo. The first in line—a big fellow with gaudy tribal inlays—saw Retief and Leon, veered toward them raising a barb-headed spear, struck the stretched cable and slammed to a stop, bent almost double—and was instantly engulfed by others charging in to collide from behind with a sound like empty garbage cans falling off a truck.

"Sock it to 'em!" Les yelled from his vantage point in the corner tower. Again a display of fireworks sprang up as ten thousand volts surged through the strung cable.

"The generators can't take that load for long," Big Leon yelled above the uproar of crackling current, screeching Voion, and enthusiastic human yells.

There was a brief tremor underfoot, a vivid glare from the direction of the power plant. Retief and Leon threw themselves flat as a dull boom rumbled across the

compound accented by the whine of shrapnel passing overhead. The glow at the fence line died.

"Shorty!" Leon called.

"He's down," a voice rang from the next post in line.

Leon swore, jumped to his feet. "Fall back on the post
office," he yelled. "Pass the word!" He turned, ran for the
building where Shorty had been posted. The Voion crowded
in the gap in the wall were shrilling, fighting to free
themselves—those who had survived the overload. A large
specimen broke free, shot forward to cut Leon off. Retief
reached him in time to lay a solid blow across the side of
his head, then spiked his wheels with his own club. Ahead,
Leon jumped, caught the eaves, pulled himself up. A second
Voion disentangled himself, came thumping forward on a
warped wheel, gun in hand—

There was the crackle of a power gun from the upper
window of the adjacent corner tower. The Voion's head
disappeared in a spatter of vaporized metallo-chitin as the
dead chassis slammed on to crash against the wall. Leon
reappeared, lowering the inert form of Shorty. Retief caught
the wounded man, draped him over a shoulder as Leon
dropped down beside him.

"Let's spring," the big man said. "They'll cut us off . . . !"

Half a dozen Voion wheeled around the corner of the
next structure in line, charged the two Terrans. Retief
pivoted aside from a blaster shot, clubbed the next Voion
in line as shots burped from the tower. At his side, Leon
ducked under a swinging club, caught a Voion by the wheel,
flipped him. Then they were through, sprinting for the
plank laid across the six foot ditch. Leon spun, flipped the
board into the trench. Shots scored the doorframe as they
dived through it.

"Close," Leon panted. "How's Shorty?"

"Breathing." Retief took the stairs three at a time,
whirled into the room previously selected as a last-ditch
stronghold, lowered the small man to the floor, then jumped
to the window. Below, Voion were pouring into the
compound—and stopping short at the moat barring their
path, in which some dozens of their more impetuous comrades were already trapped, floundering on broken wheels
and waving frantic arms. More Voion pressed from behind,

crowding those in front. The rank lining the ditch was fighting now to pull back from the brink of disaster but as Retief watched, one, then three more, then half a dozen together went over, dropped with a smash as those behind pressed forward to share in the loot.

"That's one way to bridge it," a man said beside Retief. More men were coming into the room behind him. Across the compound, Retief saw two men drop from a roof, start across, change course as Voion blaster shots crackled near them. A power gun buzzed beside Retief, laying down a covering fire.

"Everybody's here but Sam and Square-deal Mac," somebody yelled.

"They're OK—so far," the man beside Retief called. He fired again, nailed a Voion who had struggled across the Voion-filled moat. One of the two men stumbled, spun, fell on his back. The other bent, slung him over his shoulders in a fireman's carry, came on, disappeared into the door below.

"All in," somebody called. "Button her up!"

There was a sound of heavy timbers falling as a previously prepared barricade dropped into position blocking the door below.

"Henry's had it," somebody said. "Steel splinter in the skull . . ."

"How many we lose?" Leon demanded.

"Henry's dead. Shorty don't look good. Three more with medium bad blaster burns and a couple bruised up."

"Pretty good," somebody called. "We must of put a couple hundred of them devils out of commission just on that last go-round!"

"Their turn comes next," Les said from the window. "They're across the ditch now . . ."

The compound was rapidly filling with Voion, pouring through the shattered wall and across the choked ditch. The late afternoon light was failing rapidly now.

"They'll fire the building next," Retief said. "Leon, let's get the best shooters at the windows and try to discourage them from getting in close."

Leon snapped orders. Men moved to firing positions, readying bows and power guns.

"We're down to three guns," Leon said, "and not enough arrows to make a fellow start any long books."

"We'll make 'em count," someone said. A bowstring twanged, then another. A blaster buzzed. Below, a group of Voion who had reached the embattled post office withdrew hastily, leaving three former comrades lying on their sides, wheels spinning lazily. The enemy horde filled the compound now, formed up in a dense-packed ring around the Terran-occupied tower.

"The boys in the front rank are a little reluctant to grab the glory," Retief commented.

"But the boys behind won't let 'em stop," Big Leon growled. "It's like fighting high tide."

The circle closed; arrows sped, slammed through armor with solid *clunks!* or glanced off a helmet or shoulder-plate to fly high in the air.

"Save the guns for the ones out front," Leon called. "Watch for fire-makers."

Beside Retief, a man made a choked sound, fell backward, an arrow quivering high in his chest. Retief caught up his bow, nocked a bolt, took aim, picked off a Voion wheeling in fast firing a blaster. The gunner veered, crashed over on his side.

"This is fun," somebody called. "But it won't buy us much. Look at them babies come!"

"Hey, they shot some kind of fire-arrow over here," a man yelled from across the wide room. "It's stuck in the wall, burning like a fused tube-lining!"

There were bright flares among the Voion ranks now, then streaks that arced up across the glowing sky, trailing white-hot embers. Most fell short, one or two among the front ranks of the attackers, but there were two solid thuds against the roof overhead. Acrid, chemical-smelling smoke was coiling in the windows from the first hit.

"How about it, men: Do we stay in here and roast, or go out and take a few of 'em with us?" Leon called.

"Let's go get those Jaspers," someone called. There was a shout of agreement. Men were coughing now; there were more thumps against walls and roof. A flaming arrow shot through a glassless window, elicited yells as it slammed the wall opposite, scattering burning globlets of magnesium.

A man plucked it out, set it against his bowstring, let fly; there were yells as it sank home against the chest of a big Voion almost directly below. Someone had the door open now; smoke and sparks billowed in. Big Leon cupped his hands to his mouth to shout above the roar of fire and battle:

"You boys at the windows stick till the rest of us are out; keep pouring it to 'em!" He turned, plunged out through smoke.

Retief waited with his bow drawn, the feathers just under his chin. Big Leon appeared below, behind the tumbled logs of the barricade; a Voion charged to meet him, intercepted Retief's arrow instead. Below Retief's window the Voion were pressing close again, driven by the inexorable pressure of those behind. There were three fires burning briskly along Retief's side of the wall now. He loosed an arrow, saw more Voion crowd in; one, hustled by his fellows, fought helplessly, fell into a flame-spouting puddle of melted wood, flared up in a bright green glaze, only to be smothered by others crushing in against him. From behind the barricade, Leon and the other Terrans fired steadily, building up a heap of casualties. Leon vaulted the barrier, climbed up on the stacked Voion, firing down into the press. Retief picked off a Voion with a gun, set another arrow, loosed it, another . . .

"That's it," a man called. "Out of ammo; I'm going down and see if I can't get me a couple barehanded." He disappeared into the smoke, coughing.

At the barricade, Leon was still firing, an arrow entangled in the sleeve of his leather jacket. Retief saw him throw the gun aside, jump down into the small clear space before the tangle of downed Voion, laying about him with a Voion club.

"I guess it's all over," the last of Retief's fellow archers declared. "No more arrows. Reckon I'll go down and meet 'em in the open. Don't much like the idea of frying up here—"

"Hold it," Retief said. "Look there . . ."

Beyond the palisade, a disturbance had broken out on the Voion left flank. A horde of varicolored Quoppina had appeared from the jungle on that quarter, and were rapidly cutting their way through toward the palisade, led by a wedge of Jackoo, one of which, larger than its fellows, a varicolored Quoppina bestrode. Close behind, a fast-moving column of blue-green fighters followed, their fighting claws snapping left and right; behind them, a detachment of yellow-orange warriors swinging bright-edged scythes mowed a path through the Voion ranks. Small purple shadows appeared among the trees, casting ropes which plucked targets from the fleeing Voion rabble to dangle, arms windmilling, above their fellows.

"Hey! That must be that rebel army," the bowman yelled. "Look at 'em come!"

Down below, the clear space before Big Leon was wider now; all across the compound breaks in the Voion ranks were opening. At the walls, Voion backs were visible as the confused attackers crowded out through the ragged gaps broached by the Jackoo zombies to confront the new threat, before which their fellows were streaming away in disorder.

The Jackoo vanguard dozed onward, cutting a swathe toward the embattled stockade; the varicolored Quoppina rider whirled a flashing blade above a bright red Voion-like head. A small organized group of Voion barred their path, led by a small officer with wobbly wheels; they stood their ground for half a minute, then broke and fled. Below, Leon's men were across the barricade now, firing at retreating backs, jumping huddled dead and wounded to get clear shots at the confused enemy.

"It's a blooming miracle!" a man shouted.

"That must be them guerilla fighters we heard about!" someone called. "Yippee!"

Retief left the window, went down through the churning smoke, emerged in the front entry hall where two Terrans lay on their backs behind the barricade of logs. He climbed the latter, clambered across fallen Voion, jumped down to stand beside Leon, bleeding from a cut across the cheek.

"I guess that Bug leader just didn't like my looks," the big man said. "Look yonder . . ."

The bright-colored Quoppina who had led the charge jumped down from the Jackoo, stepped through the nearest gap in the wall—a tall creature with posterior arms well developed for walking, shorter upper members, rudimentary rotors above each shoulder, a bright red-orange face resembling a Voion with the exception of color.

"Yep," Leon said. "That's Tief-tief, all right. Come on; I guess we owe that Bug some thanks . . ."

Retief studied the varicolored Stilter as it strode across the battle-littered ground, sword in hand, casually skirting the smoking bodies of electrocuted Voion, detouring around victims shot, incinerated, or crushed in the disorderly scene just concluded.

"That was good timing," Big Leon called in the Voion tribal dialect. "Glad you changed your mind."

The Stilter came up, halted facing Retief and Leon, sheathed the sword. "My grasp of the Voion tongue is rather limited," the Quoppina said in clear, accentless Terran, looking around at the shambles. "It seems you gentlemen have been busy."

Leon grunted. "We'll be busy again if those Bugs decide to turn around and come back. How many troops you say you've got?"

"I haven't counted lately," the Stilter said coolly. "However, they're rallying to the colors in satisfying numbers." One armored manipulative member waved. "Are you in command of this deathtrap?"

Leon frowned. "Me and Retief been making most of the decisions," he said flatly. "I'm no general, if that's what you mean."

"Retief?" the Stilter's oculars swiveled. "Which one is he?"

Leon jerked a thumb at him. "You called this place a deathtrap," he started. "What—"

"Later," the biped said quickly, looking at Retief. "I thought—I understood he was a diplomat . . ."

"There are times when the wiliest diplomacy seems inadequate," Retief said. "This appeared to be one of them."

"I'd like to speak to you—in private," the Stilter said, sounding breathless.

"Hey, Retief, better watch this character—"

"It's all right, Leon," Retief said. He indicated an uncrowded spot a few feet distant. The Stilter stepped to it, then went on, paused inside the doorway to a building the roof of which was burning briskly, turned and faced Retief. The two upper arms went to the scarlet head, rumbled for a moment—

The mask lifted off, to reveal an oval face with wide blue eyes, a cascade of strawberry blond hair, a brilliant smile.

"Don't . . . don't you know me?" the girl almost wailed as Retief studied her approvingly. "I'm Fifi!"

Retief shook his head slowly. "Sorry—and I do mean sorry—"

"It's been quite a few years," the girl said appealingly, "but I thought . . ."

"You couldn't be over twenty-one," Retief said. "It would take more than twenty-one years to forget that face."

The girl tossed her head, her eyes sparkling. "Perhaps you'll recall the name Fianna Glorian . . . ?"

Retief's eyes widened. "You mean *little* Fifi . . . ?"

The girl clapped her gauntleted hands together, eliciting a loud clang. "Cousin Jame—I thought I'd *never* find you . . . !"

Eleven

"I don't get it," Big Leon declared. "I turn my back for five minutes to see how the wounded are making out, and this Tief-tief character disappears back into the brush—and this little lady pops out of no place!"

"Not exactly no place, Mr. Caracki," Fifi corrected gently. "I was with the army."

"Yeah—and how you got there beats me; I've lived out here forty years and it's the first time—"

"I told you about the yacht crashing—"

"Sure—and then you bust out of a Voion jail and a couple Phips take you in hand—"

"The little green ones? They're cute!" Fifi said. "They led us to the Herpp village and told us about the rebel army—"

"Hey, Leon," a bearded Terran came up, gave Fifi an

admiring look. "Looks like they're getting set for one more push before full dark—and this time they'll make it."

Leon growled. "The reinforcements are nice," he said. "But not enough. Them Bugs will be all over us like army ants in a few minutes. Sorry you had to get into this, young lady. I wish there was some way to smuggle you out of here—"

"Don't fret, Mr. Carnacki," Fifi said coolly. "I have a weapon." She held up an efficient-looking short-sword. "I wouldn't dream of missing the action."

"Hmmm . . . That looks like the one that Bug Tief-tief was carrying . . ."

"He gave it to me."

Leon grunted, turned away to bark an order. Retief leaned close to Fifi.

"You still haven't told me how you managed to take over my army."

"After I got the other girls settled in the native village, the little Phip led me to your scare-suit," Fifi whispered. "Of course, I didn't know whose it was, but I thought it would be a good disguise. As soon as I got it on, the Phips flew off buzzing like mad. The next thing I knew, there were Quoppina arriving from every direction. They seemed to accept me as their general, and I just went along . . ."

"You seemed to be playing the role to the hilt when I first caught sight of you, Fifi."

"I've listened to enough war stories to know a little tactics—which is more than can be said for the Voion."

A sharp hubbub broke out nearby; Retief stepped out to see Jik-jik, Tupper, several other Zilk and Ween, a pair of heavy Jackoo, half a dozen Herpp and a cluster of blue and white Clute and high-wheeled Blang, striking in lemon accented with orange polka dots.

"Where our war chief?" Jik-jik shrilled. "I wants to see Tief-tief, and I means now!"

"Steady, troops," Retief soothed. "Here I am."

"What you mean, here I is?" Jik-jik yelped. "I looking for a fighting Quopp name of Tief-tief, not some foreign-type Terry!"

"Shhh. I'm in disguise. Don't give me away."

"Oh." Jik-jik looked Retief over carefully. "Pretty good," he said in a conspiratorial tone. "Almost fooled me."

"Is it you, Tief?" Tupper hooted. "I feared ye were dead, the way ye dropped out of sight."

"Just a tricky bit of undercover work," Retief assured the group.

"Things is got worse since we seen you last," Jik-jik said. "Voion using new stuff on us!"

"Them Voion throwing thunderbolts now, for sure!" a Ween said. "Come nigh to melting my tail wheel down!" He displayed the two-inch coaster depending from the tip of his anterior segment.

"Hoo! It melted half away!" Jik-jik looked at Retief. "What this mean, War Chief?"

"It means the Federated Tribes are in trouble," he said. "The Voion are using guns."

"Where'd they get those whatchacallums, guns?" a Clute inquired. "I ain't never hear of nothing like that before. Melt a fellow down before he gets in harpoon range."

"I'm afraid there's been some meddling in Quopp's internal affairs," Retief said. "After we've cured the Voion of their interest in governing the planet, we'll have to reverse that trend." He looked over the delegation. "I see you've picked up a few recruits. How did you manage it?"

"Well, Tief-tief," Jik-jik announced. "I got to thinking about my uncle Lub-lub and some of them other Ween in the next village, so I bribed a Phip to scatter over there and invite 'em to join the party. Seem like word got around, because volunteers done been coming in all day. Them Voion sure is got a heap of folks riled at 'em."

"Nice work, Jik-jik—you, too, Tupper."

"What about me?" Fufu demanded. "While I was out on patrol, I caught a nosy Voion creeping up on us and flattened him single-wheeled!"

"Way I heard it, you was sneaking off the back way and run into the whole Voion army," Fut-fut commented. "It scare you so bad you come rolling back fast!"

"The idea! I'd just slipped away for a little solitary contemplation—"

"We'll compose a suitable military history of the

operation later," Retief interposed. "We'll put in all the things we wish we'd done, and leave out the embarrassing mistakes. For now, we'll stick to practical politics."

"Ain't nothing practical about the fix us in," Jik-jik stated. "Us done cut our way right into a trap. They is got us outnumbered a six of sixes to one or I is a Voob's nephew."

"I resent that, you!" a small red-orange Quoppina said cockily, snapping a couple of medium-sized claws at the Ween. "We Voob—"

"Even you Voob can see they packed together out there like grubs in a brood-rack—"

"Watch y'r language, ye Wormless cannibal—" a Zilk grated.

"No bickering," Retief broke in. "Tonight we're all Quoppina together, or tomorrow we'll be spare parts!"

It was full dark now. A pale glow in the south announced the imminent appearance of Joop. A Phip, its tiny pale green running lights glowing, dropped in, rotors whining, to settle on Retief's outstretched arm.

"Ween-ween set-set," it reported in a penny-whistle chirp. "Zilk-zilk chop-chop, Flink-flink swing-swing!"

"All right, we're as ready as we'll ever be," Retief said softly to Jik-jik, standing by with the other members of the general staff, one from each of the tribes now represented in the Federation, plus Leon, Fifi, and Seymour.

Retief swung up onto Fufu's back. "Leon, wait until our diversion has penetrated as far as the edge of the jungle; then hit them with all the firepower we've got. With a little luck, they might panic and pull out."

"And if a Dink had rotors, he wouldn't spin his wheels so much," a Blang muttered.

"All right, you Quoppina in the commando party; don't do anything brave and don't get captured," Retief directed. "Just stick to the plan and try to cause as much confusion as possible."

"Let's go," a Flink mounted astride a Jackoo whined. "Already nervous prostitution I got."

"All right—roll out!" Fufu huffed and started forward, rolling over a mat of flattened Voion, bursting out through the broached fence, sending Voion flying. Ahead, the suddenly aroused enemy were closing in, clubs waving and here and there the wink of a power gun, firing with wild inaccuracy.

Retief crouched over Fufu's neck, his sword held extended low on the right side. A Voion darted into his path, raised a gun—and slammed back as the point took him under the chest-plates. Another leveled a spear, jumped aside in the nick of time as Fufu thundered past, the others of the assault column close behind.

"Those city wheels," Fufu snorted. "No good at all for this sort of thing!" A Voion dashing to firing position among the trees ahead threw up his arms, arced gracefully into the air, paused, started a return swing, suspended by the neck from a length of purple rope. Another veered suddenly as a filmy net dropped to engulf him, went head over wheels in a cloud of dead leaves, tripping a pair of comrades.

"Those Flink are a caution," Fufu panted. "Shall I head back out now?"

"Affirmative—and look out for that big fellow with the harpoon—"

Fufu honked, swerved as a long barb-headed spear shot past his head, clattered off his side.

"Tief-tief, are you all right?" he shouted.

"Sure; nice dodging!" The Jackoo curving back now, racing through the trees for the shelter of the stockade. Behind him, Voion non-coms shrilled commands; a steady fire slashed after the retreating heavyweights. Fufu shied as a beam flicked across his flank, shifted into high gear.

"Yiiiii!" he bucked wildly. "That *stings!*"

Retief looked back; a pack of Voion were in close pursuit; light winked as they fired at the run, keeping to the six foot trail flattened by Fufu's hasty passage. More Voion packed the way ahead. Fufu plowed into the press, dozing the hapless Planetary forces aside like Indian clubs— but more popped up to fill their places.

"I'm getting . . . winded," the heavy mount called back over his shoulder. "There are so many of them . . ."

"Break it off, Fufu," Retief came back. "Looks like we can't make the stockade; we'll take to the woods and harass their flanks . . ."

"I'll try—but . . . I'm almost . . . pooped . . ."

"As soon as you hit the edge of the jungle, we'll form up a defensive ring," Retief called. He countered a swinging club in the grip of a Voion, ducked under a spear thrust, leaned aside from the flare of a power gun. Behind him, the other Jackoo of the detachment were in similar straits, hemmed in from all sides by a crushing press of Voion, those behind forcing the front rank unwillingly under the flattening treads of the heavy creatures.

"We'll form a circle," he shouted back to them. "Close spacing, and heads facing out; you Flink dismount and beat them off as long as you can!"

At the edge of the jungle now, Fufu wheezed to a halt; Bubu came alongside, wheeled to face the forward-surging enemy; the others quickly took up positions to complete the ring. The oncoming Voion met wild swings from the embattled Jackoo's digging members, supported by vigorous resistance from Flink-wielded clubs and spears, captured from the Voion. Retief wrenched a power gun from the grip of a Voion who had managed to evade Fufu's shovel-tipped arms, blasted him with it, then downed another. A heap of damaged Voion grew around the tiny fortress; now the Voion attackers were forced to scale a mound of casualties to fire down into the enclosure.

Beside Retief, one Flink after another yelled, toppled backward, smoking from a hit. The few remaining rebels had all captured guns now; they fired steadily, but nearly as inaccurately as the Voion. Retief picked off one attacker after another, while the weapon grew hot in his hand. Then it buzzed dolefully and died. A Voion above him took aim, and Retief threw the gun, saw it clang off the Voion's armored head, knocking him backward—

There was a sudden change in the quality of the sounds of conflict: a high, thin shriek cut through the squalling of the Voion and the crackle of gunfire and fiercely burning metallo-wood. Dust rose in a swirl; a miniature tornado seemed to press at the crowded Voion, then hurl them backward.

Into the cleared patch thus created, something vast and dark slammed down with a ground-shaking impact, a boom! like a falling cliff. In the stunned silence that followed, pieces rattled down all around as shrill Voion cries rang out. Dust rolled away to show the pulverized remains of a Rhoon scattered across the field among windrows of felled Voion. A second huge dark shape appeared, beating across the scene of battle at low level, rotors hammering. The bright flash of a power gun winked above its lights.

"That does it, Tief-tief," Ozzl gasped. "Who could fight lightning from the sky?"

Something dropped from the Rhoon's underside, slammed down among the Voion, bounced high, hit again, cutting a swathe through ranks still stunned by the crash of the first of the giant creatures.

"Tief-tief!" a vast voice boomed, floating across the sky as the Rhoon lifted. "Tief-tief . . ."

"Listen!" Ozzl choked. "He's—he's calling you? What could it mean?"

Retief jumped up on Fufu's broad back. All around, the Voion were breaking and fleeing now, while the steady crackle and *bzzapp!* of power guns sounded from the vast dark shadows hanging above on hammering rotors.

"It means the fight's over!" Retief shouted above the hurricane. "It's Gertie and her friends with reinforcements from the city—and two hundred smuggled power pistols!"

An hour later, in an unburned room of the battered post office, Retief and his victorious allies sat around a wide table, sampling Terran trade rum, Bacchus brandy, and Quoppina Hellrose, cut three to one to stretch.

"Those blasters turned the trick, all right, Retief," Leon said. "What sleeve did you have them up?"

"Oh, they were stored conveniently in the customs shed. I hoped we wouldn't have to use them, but once the Voion started it, there wasn't much choice."

"You're a funny kind of diplomat, if you don't mind my mentioning it," Seymour commented. "I mean, sending Gertie to collect contraband guns so you could blast the government army—it was a neat move, don't get me wrong—but what'll Longspoon say?"

"Actually, Seymour, I hadn't intended to tell him."

"I hope all of you gentlemen will display the most

complete discretion," Fifi said sweetly. "Otherwise, I'll come gunning for you personally."

"Retief did what he had to do," Leon growled. "What good's a dead diplomat?"

"That's a question we'd better not examine too closely," Retief said. "And since we're now in position to present the authorities with a *fait accompli*, I don't think anyone will pursue it to its logical conclusion."

"You is got my guarantee," Jik-jik announced. "The new Federated Tribes ain't going ask no embarrassing questions."

A Terran planter thrust his head into the room. "The Bugs—*our* Bugs, I mean—just brought in the Voion general. Ugly-looking little devil. What do you think we ought to do with him?"

"Retief, you want to talk to this Jasper?" Leon demanded. "Or should I just throw him back?"

"Maybe I'd better have a word with him." Retief and Fifi followed Leon along to the room where the captive Voion huddled on splayed wheels, his drooping antennae expressive of profound dejection. One ocular twitched as he saw Retief.

"Let me talk to him—alone," he squeaked in a weak voice. Retief nodded. Leon frowned at him.

"Every time somebody gets you off to the side, funny things start happening, Retief; I've got an idea you're not telling all you know."

"Just my diplomatic reflex, Leon. I'll be with you in five minutes."

"Watch that bird; he may have a spare sticker under his inlay."

As soon as the two Terrans had left, the Voion lifted off his headpiece to reveal the pale gray visage of General Hish.

"To give you credit, Terry," he hissed in Groaci. "To have sucked me in neatly with the pretense of disorganization."

"Don't feel too badly, General; if you only knew how I labored over the timing—"

"To not forget the miserable quality of the troops under my command," Hish added anxiously. "To wish the lot of them disassembled and exported—" He broke off. "But I tire you with these recriminations," he went on smoothly in

Voion. "Now, as a fellow member of a foreign mission, I assume you'll accord me the usual courtesies . . ."

Retief looked thoughtful. "Let me see; as far as I can recall, the courtesies I received the last time I was a guest of the Groaci—"

"Now, now, my dear Retief, we mustn't hold grudges, eh? Just give me an escort to my heli and we'll let bygones be bygones—"

"There are a few little points I'd like for you to clear up for me first," Retief said. "You can start by telling me what the Groaci Foreign Office had in mind when it started arming the Voion."

Hish made a clicking noise indicating surprise. "But my dear chap—I thought it was common knowledge that it was your own Ambassador Longspoon who conceived the notion of supplying, ah, educational material . . . ?"

"Terry power guns make a blue flash, Hish," Retief said patiently. "Those of Groaci manufacture make yellow ones—even when they're tricked out with plastic covers to look like Terry guns. It was one of your flimsier deceptions—"

"Speaking of deceptions," Hish mused, "I feel sure your own clever impersonation will cause quite a stir among your troops, once it's known—to say nothing of the reaction among your colleagues when they discover you've been leading an armed insurrection—and against your own CDT-supported faction at that."

"It might—if there were anyone alive who knew about it—and felt gabby," Retief agreed.

"I'm alive," Hish pointed out. "And while 'gabby' is not perhaps the word I would have employed—"

"There's not much I can do about your gabbiness," Retief cut in. "But as for your being alive—"

"Retief! You wouldn't? Not a fellow alien! A fellow diplomat! A fellow illegal operator!"

"Oh, I might," Retief said. "Now, suppose you demonstrate that gabbiness you were boasting about a few seconds ago . . ."

" . . . in the strictest confidence," Hish croaked, mopping at his throat sac with a large green hanky. "If Ambassador

Schluh ever suspected—that is, if he knew of my professional confidences—"

There was a scrape of feet outside the door. Hish hastily donned his head as the yellow-bearded Terran came into the room. "Hey, Mr. Retief," he said. "There's a fellow out here just made a sloppy landing in a heli. Says he's from the Terry Embassy at Ixix. Leon says you better talk to him."

"Certainly," Retief got to his feet. "Where is he?"

"Right here . . ." the blond man motioned. A second figure appeared in the door—muddy, tattered, his clothing awry, his cheeks unshaved; Leon, Fifi, Seymour, and a crowd of others were behind him.

"Retief!" Magnan gasped. "Then you—how—I thought—but never mind. They let me go—that is, they sent me—Ikk sent me—"

"Maybe you'd better sit down and collect yourself, Mr. Magnan," Retief put a hand under the First Secretary's elbow, guided him to a chair. Magnan sank down.

"He has them—all of us—the entire staff," he choked. "From Ambassador Longspoon—locked up in his own Chancery, mind you—down to the merest code clerk! And unless the Federated Tribes instantly lay down their arms, disband their army, and release all prisoners, he's going to hang them right after breakfast tomorrow!"

"All I got to say is," Seymour announced, hitching up his pants, "we ain't about to give up what we won just to save a bunch of CDT slickers from a necktie party. Serves 'em right for chumming up to them Voion in the first place."

"Retief didn't ask you to," Big Leon snapped. "Shut up, Seymour. Anyway, we didn't win the fight—the Bugs did."

"But the sixty-one prisoners," Magnan protested breathlessly. "Twenty women—"

"Longspoon ought to appreciate being strung up by his pals," a man put in. "Those Quopp tribesmen will sure do the job if the Voion don't."

"It's a tough deal," Leon cut in. "But even if we went along, we got no guarantee Ikk wouldn't hang 'em anyway—and us alongside of 'em."

"I'm afraid doing business with Ikk is out of the

question," Retief agreed. "The former prime minister is one of those realistic souls who never let a matter of principle stand in the way of practical matters. Still, I think hanging the whole staff is a bit severe."

"He must be out of his mind," someone said. "He'll have a couple squadrons of CDT Peace Enforcers in here before you can say Jack Dools—"

"Ikk is an end-of-the-world type," Retief said. "He's not concerned about consequences—not until they jump out and grab him by the back of the neck."

"I say let's get the Bug army together—"

"The Federated Tribes," Retief corrected gently.

"Yeah—OK, the Federated Tribes. We march 'em straight through to Ixix, with plenty of Rhoon cover, take over the town, kick out the Voion garrison, tell old Ikk to hang up his toolbox, and put in a call for CDT Monitors—"

"CDT Monitors, hell," Seymour growled. "What did the CDT ever do for Quopp except give the Voion big ideas?"

"Gentlemen, it's apparent that the next target for the Federation is the capital," Retief said. "I want you to wait one day before starting, however."

"Hell, let's hit 'em now, before they get a chance to pull themselves together—"

"That ain't likely—not with their general cooling his wheels here." Seymour nodded toward Hish, sitting silently in a corner.

"What do you want us to wait for, Retief?" Les demanded.

"Don't sound any dumber'n you got to," Big Leon growled. "He needs a few hours to try to spring the ambassador and his rappies before Ikk strings 'em up." He looked at Retief. "Seymour and me'll go with you."

"Three Terries would be just a trifle too conspicuous in Ixix tonight," Retief said. "But I think I'll take our friend the general along for company."

Hish jumped as though stung by a zinger. "Why me?" he whispered.

"You'll be my guide," Retief said blandly.

"How do you figure to make your play?" Leon asked.

"There are a few supplies I'll need. Then I'll have to go over to the Federation camp and talk to the local headmen," Retief said. "We'll work out something."

Leon looked at him with narrowed eyes. "There's angles to this I'm not getting," he said. "But that's OK. I guess you know what you're doing."

Fifi put a hand on his arm. "Jame—have you really got to . . . ? But that's a stupid question, isn't it?" She managed a smile. Retief put a finger under her chin.

"Better send out some Jackoo and an escort and get the girls in here to camp and ready to march. Tomorrow night you'll all be celebrating with a big party aboard a Corps Transport."

"But we c-came to see *you* . . . !"

"You will," Retief said. "I claim the first dance."

"Yeah," Shorty said under his breath. "Let's hope he's got both feet on the floor when he gets it."

Twelve

With his Quoppina armor in an inconspicuous bundle under one arm and Hish, still in Voion trappings, trailing dismally, Retief followed a guiding Phip to the Ween encampment a mile from Rum Jungle. Startled veterans of the morning's action jumped up, fighting claws ready, as he walked into the clearing around their main campfire, the Groaci close on his heels. Jik-jik came forward.

"Well, you must be one of them Terries us saved the bacon for," he shrilled, coming up close. "Hmmm; you looks tender and juicy . . ."

"We've already been through this routine, Jik-jik," Retief said in a low voice. "Don't you know me?"

"Oh, uh, yeah," Jik-jik made a fast recovery. "Well, Terry, just step on in and sit down. Just be a little bit careful one of the boys don't get kind of curious and nip off a small bite."

"I'm poison," Retief said loudly. "You get terrible belly cramps if you eat a Terry, and afterward your cuticula falls off in big patches." He took a seat on a fallen log; Hish hovered close, looking nervously at the Ween fighting claws gleaming all around. "I have to get into town, Jik-jik," Retief said. "I'm going to need some help from the tribes with what I have in mind . . ."

Retief, once again clad in his bright-colored armor, scanned the ground below as the immense male Rhoon on which he rode beat its way southward in company with a dozen picked companions. To the left flew the steed of General Hish, a mount specially equipped with a dummy cockpit astride which the terrified Groaci sat, a gay red scarf fluttering from his neck. "It looks as though the ground troops have rounded up most of the refugees from last night's fiasco," Retief called to his Rhoon. "I see a few small parties huddled together here and there, but no concentrations."

"Except the fifty thousand of the rascals who still behind the city's towers hide," the deep voice boomed. "My hope it is they'll venture up, their stolen Rhoonish corpses to employ against us."

"I doubt if you'll get your wish," Retief said. "Gerthudion and her friends have pretty well cleared the skies, I think."

With the Rhoon carrying Hish a hundred yards in advance, Retief's flyer descended steadily, passed over the port at five hundred feet, aiming for the rooftop heli pad that crowned the Terran Chancery Tower.

"That gun crew down there is tracking us," Retief said. "But they're not quite sure enough to shoot."

"That's but a trivial hazard, Tief-tief, compared with challenging the Blackwheel's stronghold."

"Let's hope Hish remembers his lines."

"The prospect of Lundelia's rending claws will him inspire to a flawless performance," the Rhoon croaked. Ahead, the lead Rhoon settled in to the pad, Hish clinging to his saddle, his jaunty scarf fluttering downward now in the air blast from Lundelia's rotors. Two Voion posted on the roof rolled to meet him, guns in hand. Hish lowered himself awkwardly, cast a nervous glance at the looming head of his mount; his arms waved as he spoke to the police. He pointed to Retief's Rhoon, now dropping in to light beside Lundelia. The big flyer braked his rotors to a stop with a final whop-whop-woooppp of displaced air.

" . . . prisoner," Hish was whispering. "Just stand aside, fellow, and I'll take him along to His Omnivoracity."

As Retief jumped down, Hish waved the power gun from which the energy cell had been removed. "I'm sure the prime minister will be interested in meeting the rebel chieftain, Tief-tief," he amplified.

"So that's the bandit, eh?" One of the Voion rolled over, peering through the failing light of the sun, now a baleful spotlight behind flat purple clouds on the horizon. "He's a queer-looking Quopp; how'd you snare him?"

"I snatched him single-handed from under the noses of his compatriots, killing dozens and injuring hundreds more," Hish snapped in his breathy Groaci voice. "Now clear my path before I lose my temper and add you to the list of casualties."

"OK, OK, don't get huffy," the guard said sullenly. He waved the pair toward the door. "For your sake I hope that's the genuine article you've got there," he muttered as Hish rolled awkwardly by on his prosthetic wheels.

"Oh, I'm genuine," Retief said. "You don't think he'd lie to you?"

Inside, Retief went ahead of Hish, glanced along the short hall, turned to Hish.

"You're doing fine, General. Now don't get excited and blow this next scene; it's the climax of the morning's entertainment." He took the gun, fitted the kick-stick back in the butt, slipped it into his concealed hip holster, then adjusted his face mask.

"How do I look?"

"Like an insomniac's nightmare," Hish whispered. "Let me go now, Retief! When you're shot down for the idiot you are, it would be a pity if I were caught in the overkill."

"I'll see that your passing won't be accidental," Retief reassured the Groaci. He checked to see that the bulky pouch slung over his left hip was in place; its contents shifted with a dull clank of glass.

"All right, Hish," he said. "Let's go down."

"How can I negotiate these stairs, wheeled as I am?" the Groaci demanded.

"No stalling, General; just bump down the way the Voion do, not forgetting to use the handrails."

Hish complied, grumbling. In the wide corridor one flight down, Voion sentries posted at intervals turned cold oculars on the pair.

"Sing pretty," Retief said softly.

"You there," Hish keened at the nearest Voion. "Which are the chambers of His Omnivoracity?"

"Who wants to know, wobbly-wheels?" the cop came back. "What's this you've got in tow? A Terry-Quopp half-breed?" He made the scratchy sound that indicated Appreciation of One's Own Wit.

"What wandering cretin fertilized your tribal ovum racks just prior to your hatching?" Hish inquired pointedly. "But I waste time with these pleasantries. Show me the way to the prime minister or I'll see to it your component parts are added to the bench stock in a front line reppo deppo."

"You will, eh? Who the Worm you think you are—"

Hish tapped his narrow, Voion-armored thorax with a horny pseudoclaw, eliciting a hollow clunk. "Is it possible you don't know the insignia of a general officer?" he hissed.

"Uh—is that what you are?" the fellow hesitated. "I never saw one—"

"That omission has now been rectified," Hish announced. "Quickly now! This prisoner is the insurgent commander-in-chief!"

"Yeah?" The guard rolled closer. Others in hearing pricked up their auditory antennae, moving in to follow the conversation.

"To watch your step," Retief said quietly in Groaci. "To remember that if I have to shoot, you'll be in my line of fire . . ."

"Stop!" Hish snapped hoarsely, waving back the curious Voion. "Resume your posts at once! Clear the way—"

"Let's have a look at this Stilter," a Voion shrilled.

"Yeah, I'd like to get a piece of the Quopp that blew the wheels off a couple of former associates of mine!"

"Let's work him over!"

Hish crowded back against Retief. "One step closer, and you die!" he choked. "I can assure you a gun is aimed at your vitals at this instant—"

"I don't see any guns—"

"Let's see if this Stilter's arms bend—"

There was the crash of a door slamming wide, an ear-splitting screech of Voion rage; the sentries whirled to see the oversized figure of Prime Minister Ikk, Jarweel feathers atremble with rage, confronting them, flanked by armed guards.

"You pond scum have the unmitigated insolence to conduct a free-for-all at my very door?" he shrilled. "I'll have the organ-clusters off the lot of you! Niv! Kuz! Shoot them down where they stand!"

"Ah . . . if I might interject a word, Your Omnivoracity . . . ?" Hish raised a hand. "I hope you remember me—General Hish? I just happened along with my prisoner—"

"Hish? Prisoner? What—" The irate leader clacked his jeweled palps with a sound like a popped paper bag, staring at the disguised Groaci. "You mentioned the name of, ah, General Hish . . ."

"Ah—there was the matter of a suitable, er, cover identity . . . ?"

"Cover . . ." Ikk rolled up, waving the chastened sentries aside. He stared closely at Hish. "Hmmm. Yes," he muttered. "I see the joints now; nice job. You look like a tribal reject with axle rickets and shorted windings, but I'd never have guessed . . ." He looked at Retief. "And this is a prisoner, you say, Hish?"

"This, my dear Ikk, is the leader of the rabble forces."

"What—are you sure?" Ikk rolled quickly back, looking Retief up and down. "I heard he was a Stilter . . . maroon cuticula . . . rudimentary rotors . . . by the Worm, it fits! How did you manage—but never mind! Bring him along!" He whirled; his eye fell on the sentries huddled in a clump under the watchful oculars of the bodyguards.

"Send these good fellows along," he shrilled merrily. "See that they all get promotions. Nothing like a show of spirit, I always say. Shows morale's up." Buzzing a merry tune, the Voion leader led the way through the wide door into the ambassadorial office, took up his pose under the large portrait of himself hanging where the Corps Ensign had been on Retief's last visit.

"Now," he rubbed his grasping members together, eliciting a sound effect reminiscent of a hacksaw cutting an oil drum. "Let's have a look at the dacoit who had the effrontery to imagine he could interfere with my plans!"

"Ah, Ikk," Hish made a fluttery gesture. "There are aspects to the present situation I haven't yet mentioned . . ."

"Well?" Ikk canted his oculars at the Groaci. "Mention them at once! Not that they can be of any importance, with this fellow in my hands. A capital piece of work, Hish! For this, I may allow you to . . . But we'll go into that later."

"It's rather private," Hish whispered urgently. "If you wouldn't mind sending these fellows along . . . ?"

"Umph." Ikk waved an arm at his bodyguards. "Get out, you two. And while you're at it, tell Sergeant Uzz and his carpenters to hurry up with the ten-Terry gibbet. No need to wait until morning now."

The two Voion rolled silently to the door, closed it gently behind them. Ikk turned to Retief, making a clattering sound with his zygomatic plates indicative of Pleasure Anticipated.

"Now, criminal," he purred. "What have you to say for yourself?"

Retief lifted the holster flap, snapped out the power gun and leveled it at Ikk's head. "I'll let this open the conversation," he said genially.

Ikk crouched, slumped down over his outward-slanting wheels, his lower arms slack, his upper pair picking nervously at his chest inlays.

"You!" he addressed Hish. "A traitor! I trusted you! I gave you full powers, listened to your counsels, turned over my army to you! And now this!"

"Surprising how these matters sometimes turn out," Hish agreed in his whispery voice. He had his headpiece off now and was smoking one of Ikk's imported dope-sticks. "Of course, there was the little matter of the assassins assigned to eliminate me from the picture as soon as you had achieved your modest goal, but of course that was to be expected."

Ikk's oculars twitched. "Who, me?" he said dazedly. "Why . . ."

"Naturally, I eliminated them the first day; a small needle fired into their main armatures did the trick neatly—"

There was a small sound at the door; it snapped wide and Ikk's two bodyguards rolled quickly through, guns at the ready, flipped the door shut behind them. Ikk came to life then, dropped behind the platinum ambassadorial desk as the two swiveled to face Hish. Behind the Groaci, Retief held the gun steady against his hostage's back-plates.

"Shoot them down, Kuz!" Ikk shrilled. "Blast them into atoms! Burn them where they stand; never mind about the rug . . ." His voice faded off. He extended an ocular above tabletop level, saw the two Voion standing, guns at their sides.

"What's this?" he shrilled. "I order you to shoot them at once!"

"Please, my dear Ikk!" Hish objected. "Those supersonic harmonics are giving me a splitting headache!"

Ikk rose up, his palps working spasmodically. "But—but I summoned them! I pushed my secret button right here under my green and pink inlay . . ."

"Of course. But naturally, your bodyguards are on my payroll. But don't feel badly; after all, my budget—"

"But—" Ikk waved his arms at the Voion. "You can't mean it, fellows! Traitors to your own kind?"

"They're a couple of chaps you ordered disassembled for forgetting to light your dope-stick," Hish said. "I countermanded the order and planted them on you. Now—"

"Then—at least let them shoot the Stilter!" Ikk proposed. "Surely you and I can settle our little differences—"

"The Stilter has the drop on me, I'm afraid, Ikk. No, these two good lads will have to be locked in the W.C. Attend to it, will you, there's a good fellow."

"You handled that properly, Hish," Retief commended as Ikk rolled dejectedly back after snapping the lock behind his former adherents. "Now, Ikk, I think we'd better summon Ambassador Longspoon here to make the party complete."

Ikk grumbled, pressed a button on the silver mounted call box, snapped an order. Five minutes dragged past. There was a tap at the door.

"You'll know just how to handle this," Retief suggested gently to the prime minister.

Ikk twitched his oculars. "Send the Terry in!" he snapped. "Alone!"

The door opened cautiously; a sharp nose appeared past its edge, then an unshaved, receding chin, followed by the rest of the Terran ambassador. He ducked his head at Ikk, shot a glance at Retief and Hish, whose face was again concealed behind the Voion mask. He let the door click behind him, tugged at the upper set of chrome-plated lapels of his mauve after-midnight extra-formal cutaway, incongruous in the early evening light that gleamed through the hexagonal window behind Ikk.

"Ahh . . . there you are, Mr. Prime Minister," he said. "Er, ah . . ."

"Hish, tell him not to get in my line of fire," Retief said in Tribal. Longspoon's eyes settled on Retief, still fully armored, jumped to the disguised Groaci, then back to the prime minister. "I'm not sure I understand . . ."

"The person behind me is armed, my dear Archie," Hish said. "I fear he, not our respected colleague, the prime minister, controls the situation."

Longspoon stared blankly at Retief, his close-set eyes taking in the maroon chest-plates, the scarlet-dyed head, the pink rotors.

"Who—who is he?" he managed.

"He's the Worm-doomed troublemaker who's had the effrontery to defeat my army," Ikk snapped. "So much for visions of a Quopp united in Voionhood."

"And," Hish put in quickly, "you'll be astonished to learn that his name is . . ." He paused as though remembering something.

"Why, I know the bandit's name," Longspoon's mouth clamped in an indignant expression. "As a diplomat, it's my business to keep in touch with these folk movements. It's, ah, Tough-tough or Toof-toof or something of the sort."

"How clever of Your Excellency," Hish murmured.

"Now that the introductions are out of the way," Retief said in Tribal, "we'd better be getting on with the night's work. Ikk, I want the entire Embassy staff taken to the port and loaded aboard these foreign freighters you've impounded and permitted to lift. Meanwhile, we'll use the hot line to Sector HQ to get a squadron of CDT Peace Enforcers headed out this way. I hope they arrive in time to salvage a few undamaged Voion for use as museum specimens."

"What's he saying?" Longspoon pulled at his stiff ver-milion collar, his mouth opening and closing as though he were pumping air over gills.

"He demands that you and your staff leave Quopp at once," Ikk said quickly.

"What's that? Leave Quopp? Abandon my post? Why, why, this is outrageous! I'm a fully accredited Terran emissary of Galactic Good Will! How could I ever explain to the under-secretary—"

"Tell him you departed under duress," Ikk suggested. "Driven out by lawless criminals wielding illegal firearms."

"Firearms? Here on Quopp? But that's . . . that's—"

"A flagrant violation of Interplanetary Law," Hish whis-pered piously. "Shocking . . ."

"Give the orders, Ikk," Retief said. "I want the opera-tion concluded before Second Jooprise. If I have to sit here any longer with my finger on the firing stud it may begin to twitch involuntarily."

"What? What?" Longspoon waited for a translation.

"He threatens to kill me unless I do as he commands," Ikk said. "Much as I regret seeing you depart under such, ah, humiliating circumstances, Archie, I fear I've no choice. Still, after your dismissal from the Corps for gross derelic-tion of duty in permitting shipments of Terry-manufactured arms to the rebels—"

"I? Nonsense! There are no Terran weapons on Quopp—"

"Look at the gun even now being aimed at my Grand Cross of the Legion d'Cosme," Ikk snapped. "I assume you know a Terran power pistol when it's pointed between your eyes!"

Longspoon's face sagged. "A Browning Mark XXX," he gasped.

Hish canted an eye to look at Retief. Retief said nothing.

"Still," Ikk went on, "you can always write your memoirs— under a pseudonym of course, the name Longspoon having by then acquired a Galaxy-wide taint—"

"I'll not go!" Longspoon's Adam's apple quivered with indignation. "I'll stay here until this is covered up—or, rather, until I'm able to clarify the situation!"

"Kindly advise the ambassador this his good friend Ikk intends to hang him," Retief instructed Hish.

"Lies!" Ikk screeched in Terran. "All lies! Archie and I have sucked the Sourball of Eternal Chumship!"

"I'll not stir an inch!" Longspoon quavered. "My mind is made up!"

"Let's have a little action, Ikk," Retief ordered. "I can feel the first twitch coming on."

"You wouldn't dare," Ikk keened faintly. "My loyal troops would tear you wheel from wheel . . ."

"But you won't be here to see it." Prodding Hish ahead of him, Retief went up to the desk, leaned on it, put the gun to Ikk's central inlay. "Now," he said.

Behind him there was a rustle, a wheeze of effort—

He stepped back, whirled in time to see a chair wielded by the ambassador an instant before it crashed down across his head.

"Ah," Ikk purred, like a knife sawing through corn husks. "Our rabble-rouser is now in position to see matters in a new light . . ." He made rattling noises in tribute to the jest. Retief, strapped into the same chair with which Longspoon had crowned him, many loops of stout cord restraining his arms, held his headpiece half turned away from the lamp which had been placed to glare into his oculars. A pair of heavy-armed Voion interrogation specialists stood by, implements ready. Hish was parked in a corner, striving to appear inconspicuous. Longspoon, lapels awry, hooked a finger under the rope knotted about his neck.

"I . . . I don't understand, Your Omnivoracity," he quavered. "What's the nature of the ceremony I'm to take part in?"

"I promised you'd be elevated to a high post," Ikk snapped. "Silence, or we'll settle for a small informal ritual right here in your office." He rolled over to confront Retief. "Who supplied the nuclear weapons with which you slaughtered my innocent, fun-loving, primitively armed freedom fighters? The Terrans, no doubt? A classic double cross."

"The Terrans supplied nothing but big ideas," Retief confided, "and you Voion got all those."

"A claw-snap for their ideas." Ikk clicked his claws in discharge of the obligation. "You imagine I intended to conduct the planet's business with a cold Terran nose in all my dealings, carping at every trifling slum-clearance project that happened to involve the disassembly of a few thousand Sub-Voion villagers? Hah! Longspoon very generously supplied sufficient equipment to enable me to launch the Liberation; his usefulness ended the day the black banner of United Voionhood went up over Ixix!" He turned back to Retief. "Now, you will at once supply full information on rebel troop dispositions, armaments, unit designations—"

"Why ask him about troop dispositions, Ikk?" one of the interrogators asked. "Every Quopp on the planet's headed this way; we won't have any trouble finding them—"

"It's traditional," Ikk snapped. "Now shut up and let me get on with this!"

"I thought we were the interrogators," the other Voion said sullenly. "You stick to your prime-ministering and let Union Labor do their job—"

"Hmmmph. I hope the Union will enter no objection if my good friend Hish assists with the chore in the capacity of technical adviser?" He canted an ocular at the disguised Groaci. "What techniques would you recommend as being the most fun as well as most effective?"

"Whom, I?" Hish stalled. "Why, wherever did you get an idea like that . . . ?"

"To keep them occupied," Retief said quickly in Groaci. "To remember which side of the bread substitute has the ikky-wax on it."

"What's that?" Ikk waggled his antennae alertly at Retief. "What did you say?"

"Just invoking the Worm in her own language," Retief clarified.

"What language is that?"

"Worman, of course."

"Oh yes. Well, don't do it any more—"

"Ikk!" Hish exclaimed. "A most disturbing thought has just come to me . . ."

"Well, out with it." Ikk tilted his eyes toward the Groaci.

"Ah—er . . I hardly know how to phrase it . . ."

Ikk rolled toward him. "I've yet to decide just how to deal with you, Hish; I suggest you endear yourself to me immediately by explaining what these hems and haws signify!"

"I was thinking . . . that is, I hadn't thought . . . I mean, have you happened to think . . ."

Ikk motioned his torturers over. "I warn you, Hish—you'll tell me what this is all about at once, or I'll give my Union men a crack at some overtime!"

As Hish engaged the Voion in conversation, Retief twisted his arm inside the fitted armor sheath, slipped his hand free of the gauntlet; the confining rope fell away. He reached to the pouch still slung at his side, lifted the flap, took out a small jar of thick amber fluid.

"Awwwwkk!" Ambassador Longspoon pointed at him, eyes goggling. "Help! It's liquid smashite! He'll blow us all to atoms—"

Ikk and his troops spun on their wheels; one Voion scrabbled at a holster, brought up a gun as the jar arched through the air, smashed at his feet; a golden puddle spread across the rug in an aroma of pure Terran clover honey. There was a moment's stunned silence.

"Sh—shoot him!" Ikk managed. The Voion with the gun dropped the weapon, dived for the fragrant syrup; an instant later, both interrogators were jackknifed over the honey, quivering in ecstasy, their drinking organs buried in nectar a thousand times stronger than the most potent Hellrose. Ikk alone still resisted, his antennae vibrating like struck gongs. He groped, brought up a gun, wavered, dithered, then with a thin cry dropped it and dived for the irresistible honey.

Retief shook the ropes from his arms, undid the straps and stood.

"Well done, General," he said. "I think that concludes this unfortunate incident in Quopp history. Now you and I had better have that little private chat you mentioned earlier . . ."

THIRTEEN

It was almost dawn. Ambassador Longspoon, freshly shaved and arrayed in a crisp breakfast hour informal dickey in puce and ocher stripes, stared glumly across the width of his platinum desk at Retief, now back in mufti. Beside him, Colonel Underknuckle rattled a sheet of paper, cleared his throat, beetled his eyebrows.

"The report indicates that after the accused was seen with the bomb—just before being reported absent without leave—a cursory inspection of his quarters revealed, among other curiosities, the following: a dozen pairs of hand-tooled polyon undergarments with the monogram 'L,' absent for some weeks from the wardrobe of Your Excellency; three cases of aged Pepsi from the ambassadorial private stock; a voluminous secret correspondence with unnamed subversive elements; a number of reels of high-denomination credit reported missing from the Budget and Fiscal Office; and a collection of racy photos of unfertilized ova."

"Gracious," Magnan murmured. "Did you find all those things yourself, Fred?"

"Of course not," the military attaché snapped. "The Planetary Police turned them up."

"What's this?" Longspoon frowned. "Considering subsequent events, I hardly think we can enter *their* findings as evidence. Let's confine ourselves to the matter of the bomb, and the irregularities at the port—and of course, the AWOL."

"Hmmmph! Seems a pity to waste perfectly good evidence . . ."

"Mr. Ambassador," Magnan piped. "I'm sure it's all just an unfortunate misunderstanding. Perhaps Retief wasn't at the port at all . . ."

"Well?" Longspoon waited, eyes boring into Retief.

"I was there," Retief said mildly.

"But—but, maybe it wasn't really a bomb he had," Magnan offered.

"It was a bomb, all right," Retief conceded.

"Well, in that case," Longspoon began—

"Ah—gentlemen, if I may put in a word . . . ?" General Hish, minus his Voion trappings and dapper in a dun-colored hip-cloak and jeweled eye-shields, hitched his chair forward. "The bomb . . . ah . . . it was, er, that is to say, I, ah . . ."

"Yes, yes, get on with it, General," Longspoon snapped.

"I've a number of other questions to ask you as soon as this distasteful business is cleared up."

"It was my bomb," Hish whispered.

"*Your* bomb?" Underknuckle and Longspoon said in chorus.

"I, ah, had been led astray by evil companions," Hish said, arranging his mandibles at angles indicative of deprecation. "That is, I had supplied the infernal machine to a group whom I understood intended to employ it to er, ah, carry out patriotic measures directed against reactionary elements. Little did I suspect that it was the Terran Embassy which was thus so ungenerously characterized. At the last moment, learning of the full intent of these insidious schemers, I, um, advised Mr. Retief of its whereabouts—"

"Heavens, nobly done!" Magnan gushed. "Gracious, and I always thought your Groaci had sort of a teentsy little prejudice against us Terrans."

"Ignoring for the moment the matter of Groaci interference in Quopp's internal affairs," Underknuckle barked, "there's still the matter of the stolen publications! What about that, eh? Can't wiggle out of this one, can you, by golly!"

"Oh, I wanted to mention," Magnan said. "Those bound volumes of the *Pest Control Journal*—"

"You didn't say *Pest Control Journal*, did you, Magnan?" Longspoon demanded.

"Yes, indeed I did way *Pest Contr*—"

"What idiot shipped that particular periodical in here?" Longspoon bellowed. "The entire journal's devoted to methods of annihilating arthropods with chitinous exoskeletons and ventral ladder-type nervous systems! If that sort of thing were ever released among the Quoppina—why, we'd be hailed as the greatest murderers since Attila the Hung!"

"Hun," Magnan corrected.

"Well, I trust he was hung eventually! And the same goes for the nincompoop who ordered the PCJ!"

"Gee, Fred." Magnan looked at Underknuckle. "Wasn't it you who—"

"Well, so that's taken care of," Underknuckle said briskly. "That seems to leave nothing outstanding but the unauthorized absence," Longspoon commented. "We can deal with this charge at the local level, I think, Fred."

"Pity, in a way." The attaché blinked at Retief. "I'd intended to ship him out under guard for examination by a Board of Interrogators, after which he'd be stripped of rank in a most colorful ceremony—"

The desk screen buzzed. "The Revolutionary Council is here to see you, Mr. Ambassador," a vinegary voice announced.

"Show them in at once, Fester." Longspoon arranged his features, faced the door expectantly. "I'll just quickly establish my ascendancy over these fellows," he explained. "May as well get matters off on the correct footing . . ."

Magnan leaned toward Retief. "I love watching him work," he murmured. "It only took him an instant to decide on Hearty Congratulation plus Alert Awareness of Irregularities, and just the teeniest bit of Latent Severity, all tied together with a touch of Gracious Condescension."

"A great technician," Retief agreed. "Too bad you can't tell the result from Stunned Incredulity."

"Umm. Still, the Quoppina won't know the difference."

The door opened; Fester appeared, ushering in the newly buffed figure of Jik-jik, his scarlet-cuticula gleaming under multiple coats of wax, a new Jarweel feather bobbing behind his left rear antennae. Behind him was the tall figure of Tupper, similarly glorified; Ozzl followed, with half a dozen other representatives of the victorious Federation.

"Ah, Mr. Tief-tief, I presume?" Longspoon rose, extended a hand. Jik-jik waved it off.

"No thanks, not hungry. Besides, us is got a new rule: Greens for Grubs and Grown-ups. Allies is better than Entrées."

"What's he saying?" Longspoon muttered.

"He's just explaining the Federation's new dietary arrangements," Retief explained.

"A food faddist, eh?" Longspoon nodded wisely.

Jik-jik glanced about the room; his oculars settled on Retief. "Hey," he said. "Ain't you—"

"Still working under cover," Retief said quickly. "Pretend you don't know me."

"Tell Mr. Tief-tief that I'm much disturbed by the recent disorders," Longspoon instructed. "Still, I'll listen to an explanation."

"Did you get the Terry females into the city safely?" Retief asked the Ween.

"Sure did, Tief-tief; they at the port, waiting for that Terry Peace Enforcer coming in this morning."

"What did he say?" Longspoon demanded.

"He'll examine your credentials presently, Mr. Ambassador. Meanwhile, keep your manipulative members out of Quopp's affairs."

"He said *that?*" Longspoon's face darkened.

"I'm giving a free translation," Retief explained. "Meanwhile, what about CDT recognition of the new regime?"

"Recognition? Hmmm. There *was* the matter of a certain understanding with the Voion . . ."

"Shall I remind him of that?"

"By no means! Tell him, ah, that I shall look forward to regularization of relations between our two peoples as soon as one or two points are ironed out. Now, we'll want an understanding on commercial matters; I think a thousand-man Trade Mission would be about right . . ."

"Did you find the remains of the yacht the girls were in?" Retief inquired of Jik-jik.

"Uh-huh. Just like you say, Tief-tief: It blasted by some kind of big fire gun. Big hole busted in the side."

Retief glanced at Hish, who aimed his five eyes at different corners of the room, began humming the opening bars of *You tell Me Your Dream, I'll Tell You Mine.*

"Well?" Longspoon barked.

"He says there's to be no Terry interference in Quopp's tradition of free enterprise," Retief advised the ambassador. "And no more harassment of the traders at Rum Jungle and the other market towns."

"Eh? But what about the land reform program . . . ?"

"There'll be a big party tonight aboard the Terry ship," Retief said to the delegates. "The ambassador hopes you can make it."

"Nothing like a little socializing to take the boys' mind off the fun they missing not getting to loot the town," Jik-jik said. "Us'll be there."

"The Federated Tribes will tolerate no political intervention of any kind," Retief relayed to Longspoon. "They specifically reject anything with the word 'reform' in it."

"Gad! This fellow's a reactionary of the worst stripe! Surely he won't object to my Jungle Slum clearance plan, my Pretties for the Underprivileged Program, and my Spiraling Price Support formula—"

"I hope you followed my advice and disarmed the Voion instead of annihilating them," Retief said to Jik-jik.

"Head-chopping hard work," the Ween agreed. "Us worked out a nice arrangement where one Voion assigned to each village to keep the sanitary drains open. It working out good."

"They like the jungle the way it is," Retief informed Longspoon. "No one gets any privileges unless he can manage them for himself; and prices will be controlled by supply and demand."

"I see I've underrated this fellow," Longspoon muttered to his aides. "He's obviously an exponent of some rather far-out economic theories." He adjusted a smile expressing the unspoken rapport existing between Men of the World. "Tell him that I've been considering the size of the development loan I'll be prepared to recommend, and I've decided that the sum of, ah . . ." He glanced at Magnan. "Ten million . . . ?"

"Twenty," Magnan murmured. "Per year," he added.

"Plus the military aid program," Underknuckle put in. "I'd estimate a hundred-man Advisory Group—"

"Twenty-five million per annum," Longspoon said decisively. "With a cost-of-dying increase built in—plus a sliding scale to compensate for seasonal fluctuations."

"Fluctuations in what?" Magnan asked alertly.

"Anything that fluctuates, dammit!" the ambassador snapped.

Retief nodded solemnly. "Did you collect the guns?" he asked Jik-jik. "All of them?"

Jik-jik wiggled his oculars uncomfortably. "Uh, well, Tief-tief, it like this—"

"Bury 'em, Jik-jik," Retief said sternly. "Along with all the captured guns. We agreed that firearms take all the fun out of fighting."

Jik-jik gave the soft squeal that was the Ween equivalent of a sigh. "OK; I guess you right, Tief-tief. Me and Tupper here already done a little scrapping over what tribe get 'em. I guess I rather bury 'em all than wind up looking down the barrel next time they a little intertribal rumble."

"What does he say?" Longspoon demanded.

"No loan," Retief translated.

"Oh, he's holding out for an outright grant," Longspoon rubbed his hands together. "Well, I think that could be arranged. Naturally, that will call for closer control: Say an additional staff of fifty—"

"No grants, either," Retief interjected.

"See here," Longspoon clamped his mouth. "If the fellow's going to be unreasonable . . ."

"All he wants is a Monitor Service station in a quarter-million mile orbit to ensure that no cargoes move between Groac and Quopp—in either direction."

General Hish made a choking sound. Colonel Underknuckle brightened. "That's reasonable," he stated. "Now let me see; the station would fall under my command, naturally; for a medium-sized unit, say thirty men—"

"There's one other thing," Retief said. "Terran honey will have to be added to Narcotics Control's list of excluded items as far as Quopp is concerned."

"Hmmph." Longspoon eyed Jik-jik sourly. "I must say this chap is a shrewder negotiator than I'd anticipated. I can see we're all going to have to tighten our belts and settle down to a long campaign before we can bring Quopp to readiness for membership in the Free Liaison of Organized Planets."

Magnan sniffed. "From what I've seen of these confounded rebels—that is, the freedom-loving standard-bearers of the aroused populace—they may never be ready for FLOP."

"Nonsense, Magnan; just give us a few more sessions at the conference table; they'll come around. I may even take time to absorb the language—not that I don't already have a good working knowledge of it," he added. "You handled the interpretation fairly well, Retief, but you missed a few of the finer nuances."

"I thought the nuances were the best part," Retief commented.

"Maybe you'd better invite these fellows along to the military ball tonight," Underknuckle announced. "After all, as the rebel leaders, we can consider them as honorary military men, even though they lack formal training."

"By all mean," Longspoon said. "An excellent opportunity to make a few points; or rather, to implement our sincere and heartfelt sense of solidarity with the forces of popular aspiration."

"Oh, well put, Mr. Ambassador," Magnan gasped.

"It will be a gala affair," Underknuckle said. "A fitting conclusion to the excitement of the week, as well as a tribute to General Tief-tief and his gallant warriors of the Federated Tribes." He looked at Retief severely. "Tell 'em that; that'll soften 'em up."

"Remember now," Retief said to the callers. "No fighting at tonight's big social event. Colonel Underknuckle abhors violence."

"OK, Tief-tief," Jik-jik said. "By the way, we is heard they going to be some extra good stuff on board . . ." He worked his oculars in a Quoppian wink. "I hopes that ain't no mere rumor."

"I'll personally spike the punch bowl," Retief assured him. He turned to Underknuckle. "He wants to know if he should wear his medals."

"By all means!" Underknuckle boomed. "Full dress, medals and orders! A real military occasion." He gave Retief a cold eye. "As for yourself, sir—inasmuch as you're under charges for AWOL, I suggest you consider yourself confined to quarters until further notice."

Retief and Jik-jik stood together at the arched entrance to the mirror-floored grand ballroom aboard the CDT Armed Monitor Vessel *Expedient*, watching the brilliantly gowned and uniformed diplomats of a dozen worlds gathered under the chandeliers to celebrate the new independence of Quopp.

"Well, Tief-tief," the Ween said. "Look like all the excitement over for a while. I going to miss it. Cutting greens not near as good exercise as snipping Voion down to size."

He sighed. "Us going to miss you, too, when you goes back to Stiltsville."

"You'll find that fighting in defense of peace will absorb all your spare energy, now that you're civilized," Retief reassured him.

"I is a great believer in peaceful settlements," Jik-jik assured him. "Ain't nobody as peaceful as a dead trouble-maker."

"Just keep it within reason, or you'll have the Terries on your neck. They tend to be spoilsports when it comes to good old-fashioned massacres."

"Sound like a good tip; I'll keep it in mind." Jik-jik leaned close to Retief. "Beat me how that disguise of yours fool these Terries, even right up close. It ain't *that* good."

"Let me know if it starts to slip."

Big Leon appeared, uncomfortable in a brand-new black dress coverall and white tie.

"Looks like old Longspoon learned something while that rope was around his neck," he said. "Seems like maybe us traders are going to get a square deal now."

"Most people are willing to give up their misconceptions," Retief said. "Once they have them tattooed on their hide with a blunt instrument."

"Yeah. Uh . . ." Leon looked at Jik-jik. "I guess I had a bunch of wrong ideas about you boys, too. You looked pretty good charging in out of the jungle yesterday."

"You Terries done heap up a big stack of arguments yourselves. Maybe us ought to work out some kind of mutual insistence agreement."

"Yeah—and while we're at it, why don't you boys come around the store sometime; I go a line of luminous neckties coming in that'll tie knots in your oculars . . ."

General Hish caught Retief's eye; he strolled over to join the small Groaci, now resplendent in formal kit including a gold fringe that dragged the floor and three honorary head-bladders, one with fig-leaf cluster.

"Really, Retief, I think you went a bit far when you banned Groaci shipping from an entire volume of space," Hish whispered. "I fear I shall have to insist on a relaxation of that stricture, as well as certain other concessions in the field of, ah, minerals exploration."

A waiter offered drinks; Hish accepted a clay pot of thick black brandy. Retief lifted a slender-stemmed glass of pale pink liqueur. "Don't confuse your terminology, Hish," Retief said. "I didn't ban your arms-runners and smugglers; it was the wish of Tief-tief, remember?"

"Come, come," Hish hissed. "Out of regard for a colleague, I refrained from advising your ambassador of the rather baroque role you played in the upsetting of his plans—but—"

"Tsk, tsk, Hish. I thought we'd settled this earlier."

"That was before you overplayed your hand in presuming to dictate the terms of the Terran-Quoppina accord," Hish said crisply. "I think now that, all things considered—"

"Ah, but have all things been considered?" Retief sampled his drink, eyed the Groaci.

"Your departure from the role of diplomat to lead the rebel forces was a trifling breech of protocol compared with deluding your chief of Mission in his own sanctum sanctorum," Hish pointed out. "Still, if you arrange matters to permit a few teams of Groaci prospectors to pan a little gravel in the interior, perhaps I'll forget to mention the matter."

"I think you'd better suppress any impulses you may have in the direction of overly candid disclosures," Retief advised. "At least until after the Board of Inquiry into the matter of the downed yacht. The investigation is being pressed rather vigorously by His Imperial Majesty, Ronare the Ninth of Lily; it was his yacht, you know—"

"A great pity—but I fail to see what—"

"It was just luck that the missile that hit the vessel failed to detonate and was found, nearly intact, wedged in among what was left of the stern tubes—"

"Retief! Have you . . . ?"

"The shell is in the hands of the Federated Tribes. They can't read Groaci, so they have no way of knowing who supplied it. Still, now that the evidence has been deposited in a safe place—"

"Blackmail?" Hish whispered urgently. "And after I risked my existence to get you into Ikk's office—"

"The famous Groaci instinct for backing a winner was operating that day," Retief said. "Now, I believe we agreed that nothing was to be gained by mentioning the unfortunate error that caused Groaci guns to be substituted for Terran propaganda—"

"If you expose me, I'll inform the Galaxy of your dastardly role in the affair," the Groaci hissed.

"I confess I might find that personally embarrassing," Retief said. "But my report will place all Groac in a very dim light—"

"Not so loud!" Hish warned, looking around.

" . . . but we still haven't discussed the moral implications of your scheme to import from Quopp large volumes of parts for your justly famed transistorized Tri-D sets, mechanical egg timers, and electronic pleasure-center stimulators—"

"But Quopp manufactures no such components," Hish said weakly.

"Now, we both know better than that, don't we?" Retief reproved gently. "The Voion were to handle the harvesting, disassemble and sort the victims, and deliver them to the port, and you were to pay them off in armaments. What the Voion didn't know was that the entire scheme was merely a cover-up for something else."

"My dear Retief, you've gotten a touch of the sun," Hish whispered. "You're raving . . ."

"Once comfortably established, it would have been a simple matter to dispense with your Voion helpers and proceed to the real business at hand; turning the whole planet into a breeding ground for a number of rather rare species of Quoppina inhabiting the central regions of the Deep Jungle."

"What a perfectly fantastic allegation," Hish said breathlessly. "Why on Quopp would we Groaci go in for breeding aliens?"

"Every creature on the planet—and every plant, for that matter—assimilates metal into its makeup. Most of the varieties in this region use iron, copper, antimony, arsenic, and so on. It just happens that there are a number of little-known tribes inhabiting the Deep Jungle on the other side of the planet who sequester silver, gold, uranium, platinum, and traces of a few other useful materials."

"Really? Why, who would have thought it . . ."

"You might have," Retief said bluntly. "Inasmuch as I discovered specimens in your luggage."

"You searched my luggage?" Hish's jeweled eye-shields almost fell off.

"Certainly; you carelessly left it aboard the heli you used to pay your call at my camp just before I was forced to blow up the Voion officer's field mess."

"I claim diplomatic immunity!" Hish croaked. "I demand the right to consult a lawyer—"

"Don't panic; I haven't confided these matters in any-one yet; I thought you might want an opportunity to smooth things over in a quieter way."

"But, my dear Retief, of course, any little thing I can do—"

"Here," a loud Terran voice said behind Retief. "I thought I confined you to your quarters, sir!" Retief turned. The portly figure of Colonel Underknuckle confronted him, the broad mud-colored lapels of his full-dress uniform sagging over his hollow chest, his shoulder boards droop-ing under the weight of gold braid. "You'll leave this ves-sel at once and . . . and . . ." His jaw sagged back against a cushion of fat, exposing inexpensive GI plates. His eyes goggled at Retief's bronze-black uniform, the dragon ram-pant insignia of a battle commander worked in gold thread on the collar, the short cape of dark velvet, silver-lined, the rows of medals, orders, jeweled starbursts . . .

"Here," he said weakly. "What's this . . . impersonating an officer . . . ?"

"I believe reservists are required to wear appropriate uniforms at a military ball," Retief said.

"A battle commander? A general officer? Impossible! You're a civilian! An imposter! A fake!"

"Oh no, he's quite genuine," a mellow feminine voice said behind the colonel. He spun. A breathtaking girl in a silvery gown and a jeweled coronet smiled at him.

"And—and how would you know?" he blurted.

"Because he hold his commission in the armed forces of my world."

"Your world?" He blinked at her. "Here, aren't you the person who ignored my orders not to land here?"

"My dear Colonel," General Hish interjected, placing a

limp Groaci hand on Underknuckle's arm. "Is it possible you don't know? This young lady is Her Highness Princess Fianna Glorian Deliciosa Hermoine Arianne de Retief et du Lille."

"B—b—but I gave orders—"

"And I countermanded them, Colonel. I knew you'd understand." She smiled radiantly.

"And, now, Colonel, I think you and General Hish would like to have a little chat," Retief put in. "He wants to tell you all about his plans for a Groaci surgical and prosthetics mission to improve the lot of the Quoppina wounded, past and future." He looked at the Groaci. "Right, General?"

"Quite correct, my dear Battle Commander," Hish whispered in a resigned tone. "And the other matters we were discussing . . . ?"

"I've forgotten what they were."

"Ahh . . . to be sure. So have I, now that you mention it." Hish moved off, whispering to Underknuckle. Retief turned to Fifi, inclined his head.

"If I may crave the honor . . . ?"

"You'd better," she said, taking his hand and turning to the dance floor. "After coming all this way just to lead a charge in sheet-metal underwear, I think I deserve a little attention . . ."

"Patiently toiling in humble consulates on many a remote world, Junior Corps officers, ever-mindful of the welfare of emergent non-Terrestrial peoples, labored on in their unending quest to bring the fruits of modern technology to supplement native arts and crafts, enriching their halcyon days with the awareness of the profound effect their efforts might have on entire populations. The examples set by such dedicated public servants as Vice-consuls Pird and Wimperton stand as an inspiration to us all . . ."

—Vol. VII, Reel 21, 487 AE (AD2948)

WICKER WONDERLAND

Consul-General Magnan clutched his baggy chartreuse velvet beret against the blast of air from the rotor of the waiting heli, beckoned Retief closer.

"I'll be candid with you, Retief," he said from the side of his mouth. "I'm not at all happy about leaving you here as deputy chief under a Groaci superior; the combination of unpredictable elements is an open invitation to disaster."

"I've never known disaster to wait for an invitation, where our Groaci colleagues were concerned," Retief commented.

"Naturalizing a Groaci was irregular enough in itself—" Magnan went on. "Tendering him an appointment in the Corps smacks of folly."

"Don't underestimate the boys at headquarters," Retief said cheerfully. "Maybe this is just the first step in a shrewd scheme to take over Groac."

"Nonsense! No one at HQ would want to go on record as favoring such a policy . . ." Magnan looked thoughtful. "Besides, what does Groac have that we need?"

"Their cast-iron gall would be a valuable acquisition— but I'm afraid that's the sort of intangible that will elude the wiliest diplomacy."

Magnan pursed his lips. "Take care, Retief: if anything goes awry, I'll hold you fully responsible." The senior diplomat turned to the other staff members waiting nearby on the tower-top helipad, moved among them shaking hands, then scrambled into the heli; it lifted, beat it way eastward against a backdrop of vermilion-bellied clouds in a sky of luminous violet. Behind Retief, the voice of Vice-Consul Wimperton rose to a shrill bark.

"No want um basket! No need um beads! Want um heavy metal, you blooming idiot!"

Retief turned. A short-legged, long-torsoed local draped in a stiff lime-green garment stood round-shouldered before the Commercial Attaché dwarfed under a load of fancifully woven and beaded baskets.

"No want um?" the Poon inquired in a voice that seemed to thrum in his chest. "Plenty too cheap—"

"No bloody want um! How many times do I have to tell you, you bug-eyed—"

A curtain twitched aside from a narrow doorway; a spindle-legged Groaci in Bermuda shorts, argyle socks and a puce and magenta aloha shirt peered out.

"Mr. Wimperton," he said faintly, "I must request that you refrain from abusing the locals so loudly; I have a splitting headache . . ."

The deck lifted, creaking, sank back gently. The Groaci put a hand against his midriff and clutched the doorframe.

"My, that was a dandy," Wimperton said. "Felt like my stomach came right up and bumped my chin!"

"I'm sure we're all aware of the motion, Mr. Wimperton— all too aware . . ."

"Say, you don't look at all well, Mr. Consul-General," Wimperton said solicitously. "It's this constant rocking, up and down, to and fro; you can never tell which way the tower will lean next—"

"Yes, yes, a penetrating observation, Mr. Wimperton."

The Consul-General tilted two eye-stalks toward Retief. "If you'd step inside a moment, Mr. Retief . . . ?" He held the curtain aside, let it drop behind Retief.

Late sunlight filtering through the open-work walls of the consulate splashed a checkered pattern across colorful rugs of kelp fibre, low couches, desks, and chairs of woven wickerwork. Consul-General Dools looked at Retief nervously.

"Mr. Retief," he said in his faint voice. "Now that our previous chief, Mr. Magnan, has departed, I, of course, find myself in charge . . ." He paused while the floor lifted and sank; his eye-stalks waved sickeningly.

"As a newcomer, perhaps you've noticed . . . ah . . . irregularities in our little organization here . . ." Four of his eyes studied different corners of the room. Retief said nothing.

"I wished merely to caution you: It would be unwise to evince excessive curiosity . . ."

Retief waited. The tower leaned to the steady pressure of the rising gale. The floor slanted. Consul-General Dools clung to a desk, his throat-sacs vibrating.

"There are many ways," he started, "in which accidents could befall one here . . ."

The floor sagged, rose abruptly. Dools gulped, threw Retief a last despairing glance and fled as Wimperton came in, still muttering. He looked after the departing Groaci.

"Consul-General Dools isn't a very good sailor," he commented. "Of course, in the week you've been here, you haven't seen a real blow yet—"

The native peddler poked his round head through the door hanging, padded across the room on large, bare webbed feet, paused before Retief.

"You want um basket?" The round, amber-and-olive patterned face gazed hopefully at him.

"I'll take that one," Retief said in the native language, pointing.

The lipless mouth stretched wide in the local equivalent of a delighted grin.

"A sale! I was beginning to think you High-Pockets— excuse me, sir—you Terries were tighter than weed-ticks in a belly-button." He lowered his wares, extracted the basket.

"You shouldn't encourage him," Wimperton said snappishly. "For months I've been indoctrinating him to bring in some gold nuggets; the land-masses are practically solid with them—but no, they build their town on a raft of seaweed in mid-ocean and weave baskets!"

"They evolved in the weed," Retief said mildly. "And if they lifted the embargo on gold, in six months the planet would be swarming with prospectors, dumping their tailings into the ocean. They like it the way it is."

The Poon caught Retief's eyes, jerked his head toward the doorway, then ducked out through the door hanging.

Retief waited half a minute, then rose lazily, stepped out on the wide observation deck. All around, lesser towers, intricately patterned, rose from the miles-long mat of yellow-green seaweed far below, moving restlessly with the long ocean swells. Sea fowl with weed-colored backs and sky-blue undersides wheeled and screamed. Between the swaying pinnacles, a spider-web complex of catwalks swung in hundred-yard festoons. A continuous creaking of rattan filled the air. Far away, the white-flecked surface of the open sea was visible.

Retief crossed to where the Poon waited by the stairwell entry.

"You seem like a good fellow," the native said as Retief came up. "So I'll give you some free advice." He glanced around at the color-drenched sky. "There'll be a Big Blow tonight. Get down below—don't waste any time." He hitched at his load of baskets, turned to the stairs. "And don't bother to tell those clowns—" he jerked his head toward the consular offices. "They're bad medicine." He bobbed his head and was gone.

Retief threw a sharp glance at the clouds, got out a cigar and lit up, turned from the rail.

A tall, broad-shouldered man in a somber uniform stood by the catwalk mouth. He looked Retief over casually, then came across the close-woven deck, thrust out a large, well-tanned hand.

"My name's Klamper, Planetary Monitor Service. I guess you're the new man."

Retief nodded.

"Let me give you some advice: watch out for the natives.

They're sly, tricky devils . . ." He paused. "You were talking to one just now. Don't let him lure you into going down into the native quarter. Nothing down there but natives and dark holes to fall into. A helluva place for a Terry. Knifings, poisonings—Nothing there worth climbing down thirty flights of wicker steps to look at."

Retief puffed at his dope-stick. The wind swirled the smoke away.

"Sounds interesting," he said. "I'll think it over."

"Plenty to do right up here in the consulate tower," Klamper said. "I guess you've seen the Tri-D tank—a twenty-footer—and the sublimation chamber—and there's a pretty good auto-banquet. And don't overlook the library. They've got a few dandy sense-tapes there; I confiscated them from a Joy-boat in a twelve-mile orbit off Callisto last year." The Constable got out a dope-stick, cocked an eye at Retief.

"What do you think of your Groaci boss, Consul-General Jack Dools?"

"I haven't seen much of him, he's been seasick ever since I got here."

"First time I ever ran into a Groaci in the CDT," Klamper said. "A naturalized Terry, I hear. Well, maybe he hasn't got all five eyes on an angle—but I'd say watch him." Klamper hitched up his gun belt. "Well, I'll be shoving off." He glanced at the stormy sky. "Looks like I've got a busy night ahead tonight . . ."

Retief stepped back into the office. A small, round man with pale hair and eyebrows looked up from the chair by Wimperton's desk.

"Oh," Wimperton blinked at Retief. "I thought you'd gone for the day . . ." He folded a sheaf of papers hurriedly, snapped a rubber band around them, turned and dropped them in the drawer of the filing cabinet. The round man hooked a small, glassy smile in position.

Wimperton rose. "Well, I'll be nipping along to dorm tower, I believe, before the wind gets any worse. This breeze is nothing to what we get sometimes. I'd suggest you take care crossing the catwalk, Mr. Retief. It can be dangerous. In a cross-wind, it sets up a steady ripple . . ." His limber hands demonstrated a steady ripple. "Other times it seems to float up and down." He eyed Retief. "I hope the motion isn't bothering you . . . ?"

"I like it," Retief said. "As a boy, I had a habit of eating candy bars—you know, the sticky kind—while standing on my head on a merry-go-round."

Wimperton's eyes stared fixedly at Retief. A fine sweat popped out on his forehead.

"Feels like it's building up, all right," Retief said genially. "Feel that one?"

A distant, thoughtful look crept over Wimperton's face.

"It's good and hot in here, too," Retief went on. "And there's that slight odor of fish, or octopus, or whatever it is . . ."

"Uh . . . I'd better see to the goldfish," Wimperton gasped. He rushed away.

Retief turned to the round-faced man. "How was your trip, Mr. Pird?"

"Ghastly," Pird piped. His voice sounded like a rubber doll. "I visited continents One and Two. Bare rock. No life higher than insects, but plenty of those. You know, it never rains on Poon. All five continents are deserts, and the heat—"

"I understood the Zoological Investigation and Liaison Council Headquarters had financed a couple of wildlife census stations over there," Retief said.

"To be sure, facilities were provided by ZILCH, but, unhappily, no volunteers have come forward to man them." Pird smiled sourly. "A pity; Consul-General Dools has expressed a passionate interest in wildlife." Pird grabbed at a paperweight as it slid across the desk-top. The walls creaked; wind shrilled, flapping the door hanging. The floor heaved, settled back. Pird swallowed, looking pale.

"I believe I'd best be going." He started toward the door.

"Hold it," Retief called. Pird jerked. His eyes blinked.

"Aren't you going to warn me about anything?"

Pird stared for a moment, then scurried off.

Alone, Retief stood with braced feet in the consular office, gloomy now in the eerie light of the stormy sunset. He crossed to the filing cabinet, took a small instrument from a leather case, went to work on the lock. After five minutes' work, the top drawer popped out half an inch.

Retief pulled it open; it was empty. The second contained a dry sandwich and a small green flask of blended whiskey. In the bottom drawer were four dog-eared copies of *Saucy Stories*, a prospectus in full-dimensional color illustrating Playtime on Paradise, the Planet with a Past, glossy catalogs describing the latest in two-seater sport helis, and a fat document secured by a wide rubber band.

Retief extracted the latter, opened the stiff paper. It was an elaborately worded legal instrument. In the fifth paragraph, he read:

" . . . *whereas such body is otherwise uninhabited, unimproved and subject to no prior claim filed with the proper authorities as specified in paragraph 2A (3) d and;*

Whereas claimant has duly established, by personal occupancy for a period of not less than six Standard Months, or by improvement to a value of . . ."

Retief read on, then removed the elaborately engraved cover sheet of the document, folded the rest and fitted it into an inside pocket. Outside, the wind rose to a howling crescendo; the floor shuddered, the walls tilted precariously. Retief took a magazine from the drawer, fitted the document cover over it, folded it and snapped the red rubber band in place, then replaced it in the drawer and closed it. The lock seated with a snick. He left the consulate and crossed the swaying catwalk to the next tower.

Retief stood in the doorway of his room, smoking a cigar. Pird, just starting down the stairway, clucked. "Better hurry, sir. Everyone else has gone down. The wind is rising very rapidly."

"I'll be along," Retief looked down the empty corridor, undulating in the dim late-evening light, then went along to a curtain-hung doorway, stepped out onto a windswept balcony from which a swaying wicker catwalk launched itself in a dizzy span to the consulate tower, a hundred yards distant. A dim light winked on in the consular offices, moved above slowly. Retief watched for a moment, then turned up the collar of his windbreaker, stepped off into the dark tunnel of the wildly swinging passage. The gale buffeted at it with a ferocity that had increased even in the quarter-hour he had spent in the dorm tower. The sky had darkened to an ominous mauve, streaked with fiery crimson. Below, lights sparkled all across the lower levels.

Abruptly, the catwalk dropped three feet, came to a stop with its floor canted at a sharp angle. Retief steadied himself, then went on, climbing now. Ten feet ahead, the yellow and blue hanging at the end of the passage was visible. It moved. The slight figure of Consul Dools appeared for a moment, wrapped in a dark poncho, then whisked back out of view.

Retief made another two yards against the bucking of the sloping passage. He could hear a rasping now, a harsh sawing sound. A wedge of electric-purple sky appeared through the wicker roof ahead, widened . . .

With an abrupt crackling of breaking fibers, the end of the catwalk broke free and dropped like an express elevator. Retief locked his fingers in the twisted rattan and held on. The face of the tower flashed past; then the end of the catwalk whipped aside; Retief slid two feet, caught himself with his torso half out the open end. Air shrieked past his face. A foot from his eyes, the severed end of the supporting cable whipped in the wind—cut clean.

Retief looked down, saw the massed lights of the native section swooping up to meet him. A wall rushed close; Retief felt the whistle of air as he brushed it; then he was hurtling past low towers with lighted windows behind which alien faces gaped briefly. He swept low over a narrow street ablaze with colored lights, felt a shock as the catwalk brushed a building somewhere above; then the street was falling away below as the free-swinging catwalk cracked-the-whip, soaring upward, slowing now . . .

A wall loomed before him with a narrow balcony before lighted windows. For an instant, it seemed to hang before his face—and Retief lunged, kicked his legs free of the twisted wicker—and caught the heavy rattan guard rail. He hung on, groping with his feet, with the gale tearing at, shrieking in his ears . . .

Hands gripped him, hauling him up. He shook his head to clear it, felt a heavy hanging brush his face. Then he was standing on a yielding floor, blinking in the soft light of a primitive incandescent lamp, feeling the warmth and strange, spicy odor of an alien room.

A five-foot native stood before him, staring up anxiously with large protruding green eyes in a smooth, olive-colored face. A wide, almost human mouth opened, showing a flash of pink interior.

"Are you all right, buddy?" a strangely resonant voice inquired in the bubbly local tongue.

Retief felt of his jaw, moved his shoulders gingerly. "A little dazed by the speed with which the boys work, but otherwise fine," he replied.

"You speak Poon like a native, by Hoop!" the alien said. "Here, sit down. How about a drink of yiquil?" He indicated a low couch heaped with varicolored cushions, turned to a cupboard, wide webbed feet in bright yellow sandals gripping the swaying floor.

"You fell off a catwalk, eh?"

"Something like that," Retief accepted a deep two-handled porcelain jug, delicately shaped. He sniffed the drink, then sipped.

"My name's Url Yum. I'm a netter for Matwide Fooderies."

"I'm Retief. I'm with the Terran Consulate." He glanced around the room. "Handsome apartment you have here."

"Oh, it's all right—" There was a sharp whistle at the door.

"You feel like meeting a bunch of people? I guess they saw you fall, and they'll be crowding in now to take a look at you; we don't often see Terries here in town, you know."

"I'd rather not go on exhibit right now, Yum."

"Sure, I know how you feel. I had to go over to Dryport on business a few months back, and every other do-gooder wanted to have me in for tea and look me over."

The whistle sounded again at the door. Url Yum padded across to the closet, brought out a large satchel, pulled out bright-colored gear of plastic and metal.

"I was just about to go for a swim. Why don't you join me? You don't want to go back up tonight—in this wind. We can go down the back way. How about it?"

"A swim? In this weather?"

"The best time. Hunting's good; the small stuff shelters under the Mat, and the big stuff is in there hunting them— and we hunt the big stuff." He held up a polished spear-head.

"Look, Yum, I'm just a Terry; I can't hold my breath more than a minute or two."

"Neither can I. That's what the gear's for. You burn oxygen, same as we do, don't you?"

The whistle came again, more peremptory now. "Hey, Yum!" a voice called.

Retief finished his drink. "That yiquil's great stuff, Yum; it's already affecting my judgment. Let's go!"

They stood in a narrow way that wound between high walls hung with lights and signboards, studded with balconies from which pennants fluttered, crowded with brilliantly mantled and jeweled Pupoony, filled with the shriek of wind, the chatter of whistled conversation, and over all the polyphonic creaking of the city.

"I've heard of twisting roads," Retief called. "This is the first time I ever saw one that fit the description."

Yum put his mouth close to Retief's ear. "You know the whistle dialect?"

"I can understand it," Retief shouted back. "But I can't whistle it."

Yum motioned, led the way down a side alley to a seashell ornamented hanging, pushed into a low room with couches along one wall, open shelves on another. A portly Poon waddled forward.

"Oi, Yum! Oi, stranger."

"Oi," Yum said. "Gipp, this is Retief. We're going down. Can you fix him up with a spray job?"

"Lucky you came to my place, Yum. I happen to have a compound specially prepared for Terry requirements, a fresh batch, just concocted yesterday."

"Good. Retief, put your stuff over there . . ." Yum opened his satchel, took out equipment, laid it out on a low table. He selected a pair of goggles, handed them to Retief. "These are a little big, but I think they'll seat all right." He handed over a heavy cylinder the size and shape of a beer bottle, added other items.

"OK: propulsion, communication, lights, breathing apparatus, emergency gear. Now, after you strip and get your equipment buckled on, Gipp will fit you with water foils, and spray you in."

Retief donned the gear, watched with interest while the portly proprietor shaped a putty-like material to his feet, forming large fins which stiffened to a rubbery consistency, then brought out a portable apparatus with a tank, compressor, and hose with a wide nozzle.

"Give him a Striding Devil job, Gipp," Yum ordered.

Gipp hesitated, looking at Retief. "I suppose you've had a lot of experience . . . ?"

"He'll be all right," Yum put in. "He catches on fast, and he's got a good arm."

"Whatever you say, Yum—but you ought to warn him that a Death Angel will jump a Strider on sight."

"Sure—that way we don't have to go looking for 'em."

"Well, if you get one, remember I'm paying top sprud for stones."

"You'll get first crack."

Gipp started up the compressor, twiddled knobs, then directed a heavy spray of viscous, greenish fluid on Retief's chest, working it in a pattern that covered him to the knees, then shut down and set about changing hoses.

"What's this stuff for?" Retief inquired, studying the thick, soft layer hardening on his skin.

"Protective covering; it's tough as yuk skin. And it has an osmotic action; passes oxygen in, and CO_2 out. The color disguises you so you don't scare off the game—and the finished job holds all your gear in place. It's a good insulation, too. That water's cold. It strips off easily when you come back in."

Gipp worked for another five minutes. Retief craned his neck to look at himself. His back, he saw, was a dull black, with red and white flecks, separated from the glossy green front by pale grey sides. Broad pink gill-flaps flared from throat to shoulders. The ankles and fin-covered feet were a vivid red-orange.

"He's got the build for it," Gipp said, looking him over. "If I hadn't done the job myself, I'd swear he was a Strider, by Hoop!"

"That's the idea, Gipp. Now just give me a straight Big Mouth outfit." Yum took a flask from a side pocket, offered it to Retief, who took a generous pull, then passed it to Gipp, busy with his apparatus.

"No thanks; I don't need any delusions of grandeur tonight. I hope to do a good volume of business before the storm hits its peak." He worked carefully, covered Yum with a uniform dull grey, added a peaked crest of garish yellow.

"All right, Retief." Yum handed him a light, short-barreled rifle from the muzzle of which a razor-edged spear head protruded. "Let's go down."

Gipp led the way to a back room, opened a wide wicker cover set in the floor. Retief looked down at the sloping surface of a three-foot tube of close-woven strips.

"Follow me," Yum said, and dived, head first, out of sight. Retief gripped his spear-gun, waved Gipp a cheery farewell, and dived after him.

The water was ink-black, alive with darting lights in red and yellow, ponderous-moving patterns of green and blue, and far below, dull gleams of violet. Retief kicked his feet, watched lights scatter before him in a boil of phosphorescence.

A dark shape darted from the gloom, hovered before him; he recognized Yum's yellow crest, waving gently in the moving water.

"Only peaceful place in town, when the wind's working," Yum's voice crackled in Retief's ears. "Let's work our way east to get clear of the activity around here; then we'll see if we can't bait an Angel up."

"How deep are we?"

"The Mat's thirty meters thick here; we're going to work Underside first; if that's no go, we'll move down."

Yum darted off with a flick of webbed feet. Retief followed. Above, the mass of the floating continent of weed was a fairyland tangle of waving fronds, fantastically shaped corals, moving lights.

"Use the knob on your left hip as a jet control," Yum said. "Steer with your feet—and keep your rifle ready. If you see anything that looks like you, let him have it."

Retief tried the knob, felt water churn past his knees; he leaped ahead, driving through the water with a speed that blurred the weedscape above. A slight twist of the ankles sent him angling sharply toward the depths; a minute adjustment brought him back to Yum's side. His eyes adjusted to the darkness, picked out the shapes behind the lights now. Massive, sluggish swimmers cruised, wide jaws open. Slim torpedo shapes darted and wheeled. A nebulous form, glowing with a nacreous pink, rose up, reached out with feathery arms; Yum swerved away, Retief following fifteen feet to one side of his bubble-trail.

After a ten-minute run, Yum slowed, rose until he brushed the tops of the coral trees, then reached up with his feet, planted them in a swirl of smoky mud, and stood, inverted. Retief came alongside, twisted, felt the soft ooze under his feet.

"It's a little confusing at first," Yum's voice came clear in Retief's ears. "But you'll get used to it."

Retief looked around. The undulating surface of the weed mass stretched away into deep gloom, studded with waving fronds, stiff-branched trees of red-violet, orange and chartreuse coral, feathery banks of leafy undergrowth set with multi-colored flowers as big as dinner plates, among which moving lights sparkled and played.

"I'll pace you, off to the left," Yum said. "Move along with big, leaping strides. Anything your size except another Strider will give you a wide berth. If you see one, hit him fast. Aim for the mid-section. Now, if we pick up an Angel, you'll notice the shadow first. Just keep moving; I'll get under him and hit him where it hurts. When he turns, give it to him near the big red spot on his back. Got it?"

"How many rounds in this rifle?"

"Five in the magazine, and a spare magazine on your left shoulder."

"How do we know there aren't other hunters around? I'd hate to spear a friend of yours by mistake."

"You'll get a recognition tone in your phones if anybody gets within fifteen yards—maybe. That's part of the game. I got a nice barb cut out of my left leg last year—some joker wanted a Big Mouth for cut bait." Yum waved and flicked away. Retief picked an open avenue between towering corals and started off. Walking was not too difficult after the first few steps; rather like tramping the dusty surface of an asteroid, he reflected—except that the diving gear was considerably less bulky than a space suit.

There was a movement to Retief's right. A tall biped stalked into view ten yards distant, barely visible in the glow of phosphorescence. Retief halted, brought the gun around. The newcomer moved on in great floating leaps. Retief turned to follow.

"Never mind the Strider," Yum said. "He didn't see you; must have just fed. We'll work off to the right here and let him have this territory."

Retief watched as the biped bounded off into the gloom, then moved on. Ahead, the darkness seemed deeper; a cow-sized creature with warts and glowing rings around wide eyes blundered past, rocking him with a surge of water. Tiny fish flashed past. The gloom deepened.

"Action!" Yum's voice came, tense in the earphones. "Keep going; we've got a big one coming up to take a look . . ."

Retief twisted to look toward the depths, like a black sky in which a dark cloud moved. He went on.

"That's the stuff, act like you don't notice him; otherwise he'll let fly with his musk, and we'll be working in the dark . . ."

The shadow moved, spreading. All around, the scene darkened. A last sluggish sea-creature humped past, raising a trail of mud-fog.

"Hey," Yum's voice came. "He's by-passing us, moving on . . ."

"Maybe he's just not hungry tonight—"

"It's that Strider we saw; he's after him. Let's go!"

Retief turned, saw a swirl of phosphorescence, jetted after it. The surface of the weed sloped, an inverted hill. Retief moved up beside Yum, following the immense shadow that fled across the rolling surface. The Strider came into view, leaping back toward the two hunters.

"Take him!" Yum barked. "I'll get under the big boy . . ." He swirled away. Retief brought the rifle to his shoulder, aimed—

A brilliant light flashed from the Strider's chest. The creature reached, grabbing at its back . . .

"Hold it!" Yum's voice snapped. "That's no Strider . . . !"

The long greenish beam of the searchlight swung, flashing from coral trees, glowing through drifting mud-clouds.

"The damned fool! He'd better douse that light . . . !"

The Death Angel closed, like a hundred-foot blanket of black jelly settling in; the stranger backed, worked frantically to fit a magazine to his rifle, bringing it up—

The Angel struck; for a moment it hugged the surface of the weed, rippling its edges—then it heaved, recoiling violently—

"Good-O!" Yum yelled. "I planted one fair and square! Move in and hit the hot-spot, Retief, and we'll be up half the night counting gold over a bottle of hundred-year yiquil!"

Retief hurled himself forward, kicked clear of the weed-bed, centered his sights on a foot-wide patch of luminous red at the center of the vast writhing shape, and fired, fired again, then went tumbling as the turbulence caught him and bowled him over.

Retief and Yum crouched by the prone body of the Angel's victim.

"He's a Terry, all right, Retief. I wonder what he was doing Underside—alone?"

"Probably a tourist, out to see the sights—though I hadn't heard of any travelers registered with the consulate."

"You may be right. We're not far from the Tap Root; he was headed that way, and he seemed to know where he was going."

Retief checked the man's equipment, noted his pulse and respiration.

"He seems to be all right."

"Sure. He just took a good jolt of current. We didn't give the Big Boy a chance to get his shredding hooks into him."

"We'd better take him up."

"Sure—soon as we stone out our Angel, before the Big Mouths get him. There's a Public Entry Well not far away; probably the one he used. We'll just tow him along with us. He'll be OK."

The vast bulk of the Angel drifted fifty yards from the crowns of the coral trees. They swam to it, shooed off an inquisitive scavenger, moved around to the red spot on the expanse of black hide. A short spear stood, half its length buried dead center in the target. A second spear protruded a foot away.

Yum whistled. "You work close, Retief. Nice shooting." He unclipped a slim-bladed knife, made an incision, plunged an arm into the rubbery body, brought out a lumpy organ the size of a grapefruit. He whistled again.

"This must be the beachmaster of all Angels! Look at the size of that pouch!" He slit the leathery bag carefully, dipped in two fingers and extracted a black sphere as big as a large grape.

"Retief, we make a great team! Look at those stones!"

"What do you use them for?"

"We grind them up and sprinkle them on our food. A great delicacy."

"Yum, what's this Tap Root you mentioned?"

"Eh? Why, its—well, it's the root that supplies the Mat."

"Just one—for all this weed?"

"Sure; it's all one plant—the whole Mat."

"I'd like to take a look at it. I can't picture a Terry swimming around down here at the height of a storm, just to rubberneck—not unless it's a pretty spectacular sight."

"It doesn't look like much; just a big, tough cable, running down into the Big Deep." Yum tucked the pearls into a pouch clipped to his belt and led the way along the sloping weed surface, indicated a dark mass ahead.

"That's it—back in that tangle of rootlets there. The Tap's a hundred feet in diameter and over a mile long. It anchors the Mat, and feeds it, too."

"Let's take a closer look."

Retief moved in among the waving rootlets.

"Say—what's that?" Yum's voice came over the earphones. Ahead, a large dark shape nestled among the entwining roots. Retief swam up alongside.

"It's a scout boat—Terry design . . ." He swam to the entry port, found it locked. "Let's reconnoiter a little, Yum."

The two moved over the waving mass of rootlets, cruising beside the moss-grown, barnacled wall of the immense root. Retief caught a glimpse of a white object, fluttering in the dark water. He headed for it. It was a plastic tag, wired to a spike driven into the husk of the root. Below it hung a small box, metal covered, with an insulated cable projecting from one side.

"What is it? Who'd come here and tamper with the Root?" Yum asked, puzzled.

"It's a detonator," Retief said. "The cable is designed to plug into a packaged explosive charge—"

"Explosive! Here, by the Root?"

"How long would the weed last with the root cut?"

"Last? It wouldn't last a day. You can cut a sprig of the weed, it crumbles in a matter of minutes. Oh, the fruit, leaves, husks, are tough enough—but the main mass would disintegrate like a sugar lump in a mug of hot *roca*."

"Somewhere there's a bomb to go with the detonator, Yum," Retief said. "Probably aboard the boat. Our swimmer was on the way to get it, I'd guess. Let's check him for keys."

Yum fumbled over the limp body. "He's clean, Retief. He must have lost them in the fight."

"All right; let's get him to the surface and see what he has to say . . ."

In the damp-smelling cavern of the Public Entry Well, Retief stood over the unconscious man. Water dripped from him, puddled on the heavy-duty rattan ramp that sloped up from the water. The attendant on duty came forward, clucked at the sight of the inert body.

"He left here, not fifteen minutes ago. Wouldn't accept my offer of a guide. I warned him . . ."

"Where are his clothes?" Retief asked.

"On the shelf—there." The attendant pointed to a coat, trousers, boots, a tangle of heavy leather belts, and am empty holster in a neat pile.

"A cop?" Retief said. He examined the garments. "No identification," he said. "And no keys."

"What happened?" the attendant asked.

"An angel hit him."

"He'll be out for hours, then," the attendant said. "A big angel gives a pretty good shock. Hah! These tourists are all alike."

"Yum, you don't have a police force here—or an army . . . ?"

"No, what would we need with those?"

"Can you get a few friends together—volunteers, to watch the patrol boat?"

"Sure, Retief. All you want."

"Station about a dozen in the underbrush around the boat; tell them to keep out of sight—we don't want to scare anybody off. But be careful—a spear-gun is no match for a Mark IV blaster."

"I'll call the boys." Yum went into the attendant's office, emerged five minutes later.

"All set," he declared. "What about him?" he indicated the sleeping cop.

"Have the fellow on duty watch him until your friends get here—meanwhile, he'd better put him somewhere out of sight."

"What about the bomb?"

"We'll have to try to stampede somebody. Whoever sent our friend here doesn't know he didn't make it."

Retief looked at Yum, frowning in thought. "Yum, peel out of that scare suit and put the uniform on." He began stripping off the Striding Devil disguise. "I'll borrow some local garb."

"You've got an idea?"

"Not much of one. Just a wild hunch."

Yum kicked free of the last of the diving gear, pulled on the shapeless patrol outfit. It hung ludicrously on his squat frame.

"Retief, I wouldn't fool anybody in this . . ."

"That's just the point, Yum. Now let's move . . . !"

Yum stopped before a dark entry, pointed up at a lighted floor above. "This is it," he called over the howling wind. Retief's long violet cloak whipped at his ankles; Yum held onto his Patrolman's cap with one hand.

"All right." Retief leaned close to Yum and shouted. "You wait five minutes, Yum; then just move off down the street. Move as though you were in a hurry. Then you'd better go back and help out the boys. If anybody comes close, let him get the port open; then hit him fast."

"Well—I guess you know what you're doing."

Retief climbed the trembling wicker stairway, gripping the handrail as a violent gust bounced him against the swaying wall. Two flights up he pushed aside a hanging lettered TERRESTRIAL CONSULATE-GENERAL—EMERGENCY QUARTERS.

Wimperton and Pird looked up from a table on which a meal of emergency rations was laid out in the bleak light of a feeble DC lamp. Wimperton's mouth opened wide. Pird scrambled up and stood wiping his fingers on his pink vest.

"Hi, boys," Retief said cheerfully. "Damnedest thing happened to me. You'll never guess."

"Ah . . . you fell out a window?" Wimperton hazarded.

"Close, but no dope-stick; the catwalk broke under me. Quite a ride." He strolled to the window. "Some wind out there. Say . . ."

"Yes, indeed, quite a wind, you're right," Pird piped.

"Look here," Retief said. "Is that a Patrolman? Wonder what he's doing out in the storm!"

Wimperton and Pird jumped to the window, craned. Below, Yum's ungainly figure waddled briskly along the pitching street, turned a corner.

"Hey, that's—" Wimperton started.

"Yes, that's strange, all right," Pird cut in. "Poor weather for a stroll."

"But that wasn't—"

"Wasn't anything for us to worry about, ha ha," Pird babbled. He pretended to yawn. "Well, about time to turn in, eh?" He patted his mouth, watching Retief.

"I'm glad you suggested that," Retief said. "I was afraid you'd want to sit up and talk."

"Just take that first room there," Pird said eagerly. "Lovely room. Just lie right down and drift right off. Wimperton, you show Mr. Retief the room and I'll just . . . ah . . . check a few things."

Retief glanced back from the door, caught a glimpse of Pird darting past the outer hanging. He stepped into the room. There was a tidy bunk, an easy chair, a rug, a tri-D set.

"This is dandy." He patted the bed. "Well, Wimperton, have a pleasant night."

"Yes indeed—you too . . ." Wimperton disappeared. Retief flipped the light off, lay back and waited. A minute passed. The door curtain twitched aside for a moment, dropped back. Lights winked off in the outer room.

Retief rose, glanced out. The shelter was deserted. He crossed to the outer hanging, went down the swaying wicker stairs three at a time, stepped out into the storm-whipped street. Pird and Wimperton, each dragging a suitcase, staggered out of sight around the corner. Retief wrapped the cloak close and followed.

Standing in the shadows by the straining wicker-work wall of a Public Entry Well, Retief watched Wimperton and Pird as they paced the ramp. Pird glanced at a finger watch.

" . . . any time now . . ." the words came faintly through the hammer of the wind and the groaning of wicker. Pird stopped before Wimperton, apparently asking a question.

Wimperton reached inside his coat, brought out a thick packet of papers restrained by a red rubber band, waved them at Pird, put them back. Retief edged closer.

" . . . don't like it either," Wimperton's nasal voice stated. "Either the locals are wise—or they've got a deal with . . ." The wind whirled the words away.

Retief stepped back into the street, saw the pink glow of a public phone fifty yards distant. He fought his way to it through the wind, dialed, asked for Yum.

"No action here yet," the native said. "How did the routine go over?"

"Our pigeons flew the coop, all right. They know they've got troubles, but they're not sure just what kind. They're at a Public Entry near the consulate, waiting for a pick-up."

"They'll have a long wait; their driver's still asleep."

"Yum, I have a feeling the bomb's timed to go off at the peak of the storm. How long will that be?"

"Oh, about two hours, I'd say."

"What will conditions be like at the top of the consulate tower now?"

"Rough. The towers lean to the wind. The ceilings fold right down against the floors in a good blow—and this one's a dandy."

"We're about out of time, Yum—and there are two parties still unaccounted for. I'm afraid I have one more trip in this wind."

"You're coming back here?"

"I'm going up—and I'd better get moving while there's still crawl space in the consulate."

A howling gale struck Retief's head as he hauled himself up from a dark opening onto the thirtieth-floor balcony, looked up the long slant of the tower face. Forty feet above, the guard rail lining the terrace of the consulate penthouse was dimly visible in the murk.

Under Retief, the tower wall trembled and moved like a living thing. He reached for a handhold, started up the thirty-degree slope. Gusts tore at him; he rested, hugging the surface, then went on. Ten minutes later he pulled himself over, lay full length on the steep slope of the tower roof.

The wind was less, here in the shelter of the canted floor. Retief slid down, then jumped, tumbled through the wind-tattered entry hanging, caught himself and blinked through the gloom of the deserted office.

From the far wall, a grunt sounded. Retief made his way across the room, flicked a wall switch. Dim light glowed, showed him the trussed form of Consul-General Jack Dools huddled in the angle of wall and floor. Five bloodshot eye-stalks quivered appealingly at Retief.

He went to a tilted desk, extracted a letter knife from a clip, came back and sawed at the cords binding the Groaci, then pulled the gag free of the mandibles.

"Ah, the shining of the sun on your ancestral egg-hill," Dools gasped in Groaci. "To express heartfelt gratitude; to vow eternal chum-ship . . ."

"Think nothing of it, Mr. Dools. You feel well enough to travel? We'll have to go down the outside; the stairs are collapsed."

"How pleasant to see you alive, dear fellow," Dools went on in Terran. "I feared the miscreants had done their worst. I tried to interfere, but alas—"

"I saw you; at the time, I had the idea you were doing the sawing, but then I got to thinking about the booze and girly-book supply in the filing cabinet. Alcohol would poison you; and as for unadorned mammals—"

"Mr. Retief, take care," Dools hissed. "My hearing is keen; someone comes . . ."

Retief looked toward the doorway, then hastily tucked the cut ends of the rope out of sight under Dools' body. "Play 'em close to your thorax, Mr. Dools," he cautioned.

A tall figure climbed through the flapping door hanging, crouched on the sloping floor, braced by one hand. The other held a power pistol, aimed at Retief.

"Just stay where you are, bright boy," Klamper called over the screech of the wind. "Don't bother untying him. My errand won't take but a minute."

He half-slid, half-crawled to the filing cabinet, keeping both eyes on Retief, fumbled a key from a pocket. He opened the top drawer, then the next, rummaged, tried the last drawer, then turned on Retief, showing even white teeth in an expression that was not a smile.

"I ought to have my head examined. I let those two light-weights sell me a story. What an act; Wimperton gobbled like a turkey when he opened up that phoney cover and got a load of the funnybooks inside. So I let 'em sucker me into a goose-chase—unless you've got it?" He came closer. "Turn out your pockets, hot-shot."

Retief shook his head. "If you're looking for the papers, forget it. I left them in my other suit."

"You loused up six months' work, greenhorn. But I'll be back to fill out some fresh forms. Too bad you won't be here to watch."

He raised the power pistol; behind him, Dools lunged for the Patrolman's ankle. A bolt of blue fire crackled harmlessly past Retief's ear as he leaned aside, chopped at Klamper's gun hand, followed up with a knee to the face. Klamper rolled with the blow, scrambled over a sagging desk, and dived for the doorway. Dools grabbed up the gun, started after him.

"Let him go, Mr. Dools," Retief said. "I think I know where he's headed. Now let's get out of here before we get our clothes pressed with us in 'em."

At the Public Entry Well, Yum and a group of well-muscled locals met Retief.

"Our man was here about ten minutes ago," Yum said blandly. "Big fellow, in a hurry."

"You let him through?"

"That's right."

"Then you warned the boys at the boat to stop him . . . ?"

"Well, no, Retief. I told them to let him go. As you pointed out, he had a blaster . . . He's several hundred miles out by now . . ."

Retief folded his arms. "There's something funny going on here, Yum. What about the bomb? It's probably timed to go off at the height of the storm—say in another ten minutes."

"Oh, that. I found it. It's taken care of."

"Found it where? And how do you take care of a sealed titanite charge . . . ?"

"It was aboard the boat. You were right about that—"

"Come on, Yum. Give!"

"Well, Retief, I was a little curious; you can't blame me, after meeting you under such—unusual circumstances. I took a look through your clothes. I found this . . ." He held up the document Retief had extracted from the consulate files. "A fancy piece of paper laying claim to the whole damned planet of Poon—which it states is uninhabited—which it would have been if the bomb idea had worked out. The Mat would have broken up in the wind, and when the sky cleared, it would look like just another natural disaster. And in a few months, all five continents would be one big gold mine."

"So?"

"So I held out on you. Our slumbering pal had keys, all right. I went back and opened up the boat. There sat the bomb—a nice little ten-kilo charge of titanite, all labeled and ready to go—"

"Except for the detonator; that was wired to the root—"

"Uh-huh. A safety precaution. But I found another one. It wasn't hard to install. I had an idea the owner would be along to see about it before zero hour; but I didn't like the sight of the thing sitting out in the middle of the floor, so I tucked it away."

"Where?"

"In the chart storage bin."

Retief whirled to the discarded Terran uniform, jerked the communicator from the lapel clip, keyed it on the official frequency.

"Klamper, if you can hear me, answer—fast!"

After a moment, Klamper's voice came back, a thin piping in the miniature ear-phone. Yum and Dools leaned close.

"Klamper here. Who're you?"

"This is Retief, Klamper—"

"Oh, yeah, the bright young official. Well, I predict a big change in the near future for you. In about thirty seconds, to be exact."

"Klamper, there's a bomb—"

"Well, well, so you found out about that, too. Sorry I can't help you. So long, su—" The earphones went dead.

"Klamper!"

Yum looked at his watch. "Right on the button," he said.

"At least," Dools said, "he lived long enough to exonerate Mr. Retief . . ."

There was a patter of hurried footsteps. Retief and Yum turned. In the door, Wimperton and Pird stood like ruffled birds, staring.

"I'm afraid you lads missed the boat," Retief called. Yum signaled with his hand. Half a dozen local citizens fanned out to hem in the newcomers.

"Ah, why, Mr. Retief . . . what are you doing out of bed?" Pird squeaked.

"Oh, I just dropped down to offer you boys a crack at a peachy new opportunity in the Achievement Corps. Consul-General Dools here has need of two volunteers to man the new wildlife census stations over on continents One and Two. I'm going to give you first grabs at it. We'll go over to the Shelter and type out your resignations from the CDT, and a couple of five-year enlistment contracts in the A.C.—on a non-compensatory basis, of course."

Wimperton's mouth sagged open.

"And I have a number of micro-tape recordings I'll contribute," Dools said. "They're quite exciting—all about bombs and land claims and gold mines. You can play them over during your leisure time—during sandstorms, perhaps."

"But—Mr. Retief," Pird cried. "We—we've found conditions here somewhat less than congenial . . ."

"What if—if we refuse?" Wimperton gulped.

"In that case, Yum and his associates would like to interview you on the subject of homesteading . . ."

"Your pen or mine?" Pird said hastily.

"I'll ask a couple of the boys to help these two philanthropists over to the consulate," Yum said. "Let the business wait till morning. You and I have a bottle of yiquil to finish, Retief."

"Show Mr. Dools a few of those pearls we netted, Yum."

Yum fished out the stones, handed them to Dools, who canted two pairs of eye-stalks at the lustrous one-inch spheres.

"Gentlemen—this is precisely the product I need to qualify Poon as a Class One commercial world! Can these be supplied in any volume? Say, a dozen a month?"

"I think it could be arranged," Yum said in heavily accented Terran. "Why don't you join Retief and the boys and me in a snort?"

"Well, I really don't think . . ."

"I know a barman who can concoct a suitable booze for any metabolism," Yum urged. "And a hangover cure afterward."

Retief linked arms with the slender Groaci. "Come along, Mr. Consul-General," he said. "We won't take no for an answer."

PART V:
MAGNAN MAKES GOOD!

Editor's Note: All of the stories contained in this volume were written by Laumer in the early '60s. He would continue to write Retief stories for many years thereafter, but even by the end of this first period the true hero of the series has emerged triumphant:

Magnan, of course—who ends this volume having achieved the august status of Ambassador himself.

"Ever mindful of its lofty mission as guardian
of the territorial integrity of Terrestrial-settled
worlds against forays by non-social-minded alien
groups, the Corps, in time of need, dispatched
inobtrusive representatives to threatened areas,
thus dynamically reaffirming hallowed Corps
principles of Terrestrial solidarity. The unflinching support tendered by Deputy Ass't Under-
Secretary Magnan to Jorgensen's Worlds in their
hour of crisis added a proud page to Corps
history . . ."

—Vol. X, Reel 9, 493 AE (AD 2954)

COURIER

"It *is* rather unusual, Retief," Deputy Assistant Under-
Secretary Magnan said, "to assign an officer of your rank
to courier duty; but this is an unusual mission."

Retief drew on his cigar and said nothing. Just before
the silence grew awkward, Magnan went on.

"There are four planets in the group," he said. "Two
double planets, all rather close to an unimportant star listed
as DRI-G 814369. They're called Jorgensen's Worlds, and
in themselves are of no importance whatever. However, they
lie deep in the sector into which the Soetti have been
penetrating.

"Now," Magnan leaned forward and lowered his voice,
"we have learned that the Soetti plan a bold step forward.
They've been quietly occupying non-settled worlds. Since

they've met no opposition so far in their infiltration of Terrestrial space, they intend to seize Jorgensen's Worlds by force."

Magnan leaned back, waiting for Retief's reaction. Retief drew carefully on his cigar and looked at Magnan. Magnan frowned.

"This is open aggression, Retief, in case I haven't made myself clear. Aggression on Terrestrial-occupied territory by an alien species. Obviously, we can't allow it." He drew a large folder from his desk.

"A show of resistance at this point is necessary. Unfortunately, Jorgensen's Worlds are backward, technologically undeveloped areas. They're farmers, traders; their industry is limited to a minor role in their economy—enough to support the merchant fleet, no more. The war potential, by conventional standards, is nil."

Magnan tapped the folder before him.

"I have here," he said solemnly, "information which will change that picture completely." He leaned back, blinked at Retief.

"All right, Mr. Secretary," Retief said. "I'll play along; what's in the folder?"

Magnan spread his fingers, folded one digit down.

"First," he said, "the Soetti War Plan—in detail. We were fortunate enough to make contact with a defector from a party of renegade Terrestrials who've been advising the Soetti." He folded another finger. "Next, a battle plan for the Jorgensen's people, worked out by the Theory Group." He wrestled a third finger down. "Lastly, an Utter Top Secret schematic for conversion of a standard anti-acceleration field into a potent weapon—a development our Systems people have been holding in reserve for just such a situation."

"Is that all? You've still got two fingers sticking up."

Magnan looked at the fingers and put them away. "This is no occasion for flippancy, Retief. In the wrong hands, this information could be catastrophic. You'll memorize it before you leave this building—"

"I'll carry it, sealed," Retief said. "That way nobody can sweat it out of me."

"As you wish. Now, let me caution you against personal emotional involvement here. Overall policy calls for a defense of these backwater worlds; otherwise, the Corps would prefer simply to allow History to follow its natural course, as always."

"When does this attack happen?"

"In less than four weeks."

"That doesn't leave me much time."

"I have your itinerary here. Your accommodations are clear as far as Aldo Cerise. You'll have to rely on your ingenuity to get you the rest of the way."

"And what do I rely on to get me back?"

Magnan looked casually at his fingernails. "Of course you *could* refuse the assignment . . ."

Retief smiled, directed a smoke ring past Magnan's ear. "This antiac conversion; how long does it take?"

"A skilled electronics crew can do the job in a matter of minutes. The Jorgensens can handle it very nicely; every second man is a mechanic of some sort."

Retief opened the envelope Magnan handed him and looked at the tickets inside.

"Less than four hours to departure time," he said. "I'd better not start any long books."

"You'd better waste no time getting over to Indoctrination," Magnan said.

Retief stood up. "If I hurry, maybe I can catch the cartoon."

"The allusion escapes me," Magnan said coldly. "And one last word: the Soetti are patrolling the trade lanes into Jorgensen's Worlds. Don't get yourself interned."

"I'll tell you what," Retief said soberly; "in a pinch, I'll mention your name."

"You'll be traveling with Class X credentials," Magnan snapped. "There must be nothing to connect you with the Corps."

"I'll pose as a gentleman. They'll never guess."

"You'd better be getting started." Magnan shuffled papers.

"You're right. If I work at it, I might manage a snootful by take-off." He went to the door, looked back.

"No objection to my checking out a needler, is there?"

Magnan looked up. "I suppose not. What do you want with it?"

"Just a feeling I've got."

"Please yourself."

"Some day," Retief said, "I may take you up on that."

Retief put down the heavy, travel-battered suitcase and leaned on the counter, studying the schedules chalked on the board under the legend "ALDO CERISE INTERPLANETARY." A thin clerk in a faded sequined blouse and a plastic snakeskin cummerbund groomed his fingernails and watched Retief from the corner of his eye; he nipped off a ragged corner with rabbit-like front teeth, spat it on the floor. "Was there something?" he said.

"Two-twenty-eight, due out today for the Jorgensen group. Is it on schedule?"

The clerk nibbled the inside of his right cheek, eyed Retief.

"Filled up. Try again in a couple of weeks."

"What time does it leave?"

The clerk smiled pityingly. "It's my lunch hour. I'll be open in an hour." He held up a thumb nail, frowned at it.

"If I have to come around this counter," Retief said, "I'll feed that thumb to you the hard way."

The clerk looked up, opened his mouth, caught Retief's eye. He closed his mouth and swallowed.

"Just as it says there," he said, jerking the thumb at the board. "Lifts in an hour. But you won't be on it," he added.

Retief looked at him.

"Some . . . ah . . . VIPs required accommodation," the clerk said. He hooked a finger inside the sequined collar. "All tourist reservations were canceled," he went on. "You'll have to try to get space on the Four-Planet Line ship next—"

"Which gate?" Retief said.

"For . . . ah . . . ?"

"Two-twenty-eight for Jorgensen's Worlds."

"Well," said the clerk. "Gate 19," he added quickly. "But—"

Retief picked up his suitcase and walked away toward the glare sign reading "To gates 16-30."

"Smart-alec," the clerk said behind him.

Retief followed the signs, threaded his way through

crowds, found a covered ramp with the number 228 posted over it. A heavy-shouldered man with a scarred jawline and small eyes, wearing a rumpled grey uniform, put out a hand as Retief started past him.

"Lessee your boarding pass," he growled.

Retief pulled a paper from an inside pocket, handed it over.

The guard blinked at it. "Whassat?"

"A 'gram confirming my space. Your boy on the counter says he's out to lunch."

The guard crumbled the 'gram, dropped it on the floor, lounged back against the handrail.

"On your way, bum," he said.

Retief put his suitcase down carefully, took a step and drove a right into the guard's midriff, stepped aside as the man doubled and went to his knees.

"You were wide open, ugly. I couldn't resist." Retief picked up his bag. "Tell your boss I sneaked past while you were resting your eyes." He stepped over the man and went up the gangway into the ship. A pimply youth in stained white came along the corridor.

"Which way to cabin fifty-seven?" Retief asked.

"Up there." The boy jerked his head, hurried on. Retief made his way along the narrow hall, found signs, followed them to cabin fifty-seven. The door was open. Inside, unfamiliar baggage was piled in the center of the floor. A tall florid man with an expensive coat belted over a massive paunch stood in the open door. He looked at Retief. Retief looked back. The florid man clamped his jaws together, turned to speak over his shoulder.

"Somebody in the cabin. Get 'em out." He rolled a cold eye at Retief, backed out of the room. A short thick-necked man appeared.

"What are you doing in Mr. Tony's room?" he barked. "Never mind; clear out of here, fellow. You're keeping Mr. Tony waiting."

"Too bad," Retief said. "Finders keepers."

"You nuts or something?" The thick-necked man stared at Retief. "I said it's Mr. Tony's room."

"I don't know Mr. Tony. He'll have to bull his way into other quarters."

"We'll see about you, mister." The man turned and went out. Retief sat on the bunk and lit a cigar. There was a sound of voices in the corridor. Two burly baggage-smashers appeared, straining at an oversized trunk. They maneuvered it through the door, lowered it with a crash, glanced at Retief, and went out. The thick-necked man appeared again.

"All right, you; out," he growled. "Or have I got to have you thrown out?"

Retief rose, clamped the cigar between his teeth. He gripped a handle of the brass-bound trunk in each hand, bent his knees and heaved the trunk up to chest level, then raised it overhead. He turned to the door.

"Catch," he said between clenched teeth. The trunk slammed against the far wall of the corridor and burst. Retief turned to the baggage on the floor, tossed it into the hall. The face of the thick-necked man appeared cautiously around the door jamb.

"Mister, you must be—"

"If you'll excuse me," Retief said. "It's time for my nap." He flipped the door shut, pulled off his shoes, and stretched out on the bed.

Five minutes passed before the door rattled and burst open. Retief looked up. A gaunt leathery-skinned man wearing white ducks, a blue turtleneck sweater, and a peaked cap tilted raffishly over one eye stared at Retief.

"Is this the joker?" he grated.

The thick-necked man edged past him, looked at Retief, snorted. "That's him, sure."

"I'm captain of this vessel," the gaunt man said. "You've got two minutes to haul your freight out of here. Get moving, Buster."

"When you can spare the time," Retief said, "take a look at Section Three, Paragraph One, of the Uniform Code. That spells out the law on confirmed space on vessels engaged in interplanetary commerce."

"A space lawyer." The captain turned. "Throw him out, boys," he called.

Two big men edged into the cabin, stood looking at Retief. "Go on, pitch him out," the captain snapped.

Retief put his cigar in an ashtray, swung his feet off the bunk. One of the two wiped his nose on a sleeve, spat on his right palm, and stepped forward, then hesitated.

"Hey," he said. "This the guy tossed the trunk off the wall?"

"That's him," the thick-necked man called. "Spilled Mr. Tony's possessions right on the deck."

"Deal me out," the bouncer said. "He can stay put as long as he wants to. I signed on to move cargo. Let's go, Moe."

"You'd better be getting back to the bridge, Captain," Retief said. "We're due to lift in twenty minutes."

The thick-necked man and the captain both shouted at once. The captain's voice prevailed. "—twenty minutes . . . Uniform Code . . . gonna do?"

"Close the door as you leave," Retief said.

The thick-necked man paused at the door. "We'll see you when you come out."

Four waiters passed Retief's table without stopping. A fifth leaned against the wall nearby, a menu under his arm. At a table across the room, the captain, now wearing a dress uniform and with his thin red hair neatly parted, sat with a table of male passengers. He talked loudly and laughed frequently, casting occasional glances Retief's way.

A panel opened in the wall behind Retief's chair. Bright blue eyes peered out from under a white chef's cap.

"Givin' you the cold shoulder, heh, mister?"

"Looks like it, old timer. Maybe I'd better go join the skipper; his party seems to be having all the fun."

"Fella has to be mighty careless who he eats with to set over there."

"I see your point."

"You set right where you're at, mister. I'll rustle you up a plate."

Five minutes later, Retief cut into a thirty-two-ounce Delmonico nicely garnished with mushrooms and garlic butter.

"I'm Chip," the chef said. "I don't like the cap'n. You can tell him I said so. Don't like his friends, either. Don't like them dern Sweaties; look at a man like he was a worm."

"You know how to fry a steak, Chip," Retief said. He poured red wine into a glass. "Here's to you."

"Dern right," Chip said. "Dunno who ever thought up broiling 'em. I got a Baked Alaska comin up in here for dessert. You like brandy in yer coffee?"

"Chip, you're a genius."

"Like to see a fella eat. I gotta go now; if you need anything, holler."

Retief ate slowly. Time always dragged on shipboard. Four days to Jorgensen's Worlds. Then, if Magnan's information was correct, there would be four days to prepare for the Soetti attack. It was a temptation to scan the tapes built into the handle of his suitcase; it would be good to know what Jorgensen's Worlds would be up against.

Retief finished the steak, and the chef handed out the Baked Alaska and coffee. Most of the other passengers had left the dining room. Mr. Tony and his retainers still sat at the captain's table.

As Retief watched, four men arose from the table, sauntered across the room. The first in line, a stony-faced thug with a broken ear, took a cigar from his mouth as he reached the table, dipped the lighted end in Retief's coffee, looked at it, dropped it on the tablecloth.

The others came up, Mr. Tony trailing.

"You must want to get to Jorgensen's pretty bad," the thug said in a grating voice. "What's your game, hick?"

Retief looked at the coffee up, picked it up.

"I don't think I want my coffee," he said. He looked at the thug. "You drink it."

The thug squinted at Retief. "A wise hick," he began.

With a flick of the wrist, Retief tossed the coffee into the thug's face, then stood and slammed a straight right to the chin. The thug went down.

Retief looked at Mr. Tony, who stood open-mouthed.

"You can take your playmates away now, Tony," he said. "And don't bother to come around yourself. You're not funny enough."

Mr. Tony found his voice. "Take him, Marbles," he growled.

The thick-necked man slipped a hand inside his tunic,

brought out a long-bladed knife. He licked his lips and moved in.

Retief heard the panel open beside him. "Here you go, mister," Chip said. Retief darted a glance; a well-honed French knife lay on the sill.

"Thanks, Chip. I won't need it for these punks."

Thick-neck lunged and Retief hit him square in the face, knocking him under the table. The other man stepped back, fumbled a power pistol from his shoulder holster.

"Aim that at me, and I'll kill you," Retief said.

"Go on, burn him, Hoany!" Mr. Tony shouted. Behind him the captain appeared, white-faced.

"Put that away, you!" he yelled. "What kind of—"

"Shut up," Mr. Tony said. "Put it away, Hoany. We'll fix this bum later."

"Not on this vessel, you won't," the captain said shakily. "I got my charter to—"

"Ram your charter," Hoany said harshly. "You won't be needing it long—"

"Button your floppy mouth, damn you," Mr. Tony snapped. He looked at the two men on the floor. "Get Marbles out of here. I ought to dump the slobs . . ." He turned and walked away. The captain signaled and two waiters came up. Retief watched as they carted the casualties from the dining room.

The panel opened. "I usta be about your size, when I was your age," Chip said. "You handled them pansies right. I wouldn't give 'em the time o' day."

"How about a fresh cup of coffee, Chip?"

"Sure, mister. Anything else?"

"I'll think of something," Retief said. "This is shaping up into one of those long days."

"They don't like me bringing yer meals to you in yer cabin," Chip said. "But the cap'n knows I'm the best cook in the Merchant Service; they won't mess with me."

"What has Mr. Tony got on the captain, Chip?" Retief asked.

"They're in some kind o' crooked business together. You want some more of that smoked turkey?"

"Sure. What have they got against my going to Jorgensen's Worlds?"

"Dunno; hasn't been no tourists got in there fer six or eight months. I sure like a fella that can put it away. I was a big eater when I was yer age."

"I'll bet you can still handle it, old-timer. What are Jorgensen's Worlds like?"

"One of 'em's cold as hell and three of 'em's colder. Most o' the Jorgies live on Svea; that's the least froze up. Man don't enjoy eatin' his own cookin' like he does somebody else's."

"That's where I'm lucky, Chip. What kind of cargo's the captain got aboard for Jorgensen's?"

"Derned if I know. In and out o' there like a grasshopper, ever few weeks. Don't never pick up no cargo. No tourists any more, like I says. Don't know what we even run in there for."

"Where are the passengers we have aboard headed?"

"To Alabaster; that's nine days' run in-sector from Jorgensen's. You ain't got another of them cigars, have you?"

"Have one, Chip. I guess I was lucky to get space on this ship."

"Plenty of space, mister. We got a dozen empty cabins." Chip puffed the cigar alight, then cleared away the dishes, poured out coffee and brandy.

"Them Sweaties is what I don't like," he said.

Retief looked at him questioningly.

"You never seen a Sweaty? Ugly-lookin' devils. Skinny legs, like a lobster; big chest, shaped like the top of a turnip; rubbery-lookin' head; you can see the pulse beatin' when they get riled."

"I've never had the pleasure."

"You'll prob'ly have it perty soon. Them devils board us nigh ever trip out; act like they was the Customs Patrol or somethin'."

There was a distant clang, and a faint tremor ran through the floor.

"I ain't superstitious ner nothin'," said Chip, "but I'll be triple-danged if that ain't them boardin' us now."

Ten minutes passed before bootsteps sounded outside the door, accompanied by a clicking patter. The doorknob rattled, then a heavy knock sounded.

"They got to look you over," Chip whispered. "Nosey damn Sweaties."

"Unlock it, Chip." The chef threw the latch, opened the door.

"Come in, damn you," he said.

A tall and grotesque creature minced into the room, tiny hoof-like feet tapping on the floor. A metal helmet shaded the deep-set compound eyes, and a loose mantle flapped around the knobbed knees. Behind the alien, the captain hovered nervously.

"Yo' papiss," the alien rasped.

"Who's your friend, captain?" Retief said.

"Never mind; just do like he tells you."

"Yo' papiss," the alien said again.

"Okay," Retief said. "I've seen it. You can take it away now."

"Don't horse around," the captain said. "This fellow can get mean."

The alien brought up two tiny arms from the conceal-ment of the mantle, clicked toothed pincers under Retief's nose. "Quick, soft one."

"Captain, tell your friend to keep its distance. It looks brittle, and I'm tempted to test it."

"Don't start anything with Skaw; he can clip through steel with those snappers."

"Last chance," said Retief. Skaw stood poised, open pincers an inch from Retief's eyes.

"Show him your papers, you damned fool," the captain said hoarsely. "I got no control over Skaw."

The alien clicked both pincers with a sharp report, and in the same instant Retief half turned to the left, leaned away from the alien, and drove his right foot against the slender leg above the bulbous knee-joint. Skaw screeched, floundered, greenish fluid spattering from the burst joint.

"I told you he was brittle," Retief said. "Next time you invite pirates aboard, don't bother to call."

"Jesus, what did you do! They'll kill us!" the captain gasped, staring at the figure flopping on the floor.

"Cart poor old Skaw back to his boat," Retief said. "Tell him to pass the word; no more illegal entry and search of Terrestrial vessels in Terrestrial space."

"Hey," Chip said. "He's quit kickin'."

The captain bent over Skaw, gingerly rolled him over. He leaned close, sniffed.

"He's dead." The captain stared at Retief. "We're all dead men. These Soetti got no mercy."

"They won't need it. Tell 'em to sheer off; their fun is over."

"They got no more emotions than a blue crab—"

"You bluff easily, captain. Show a few guns as you hand the body back. We know their secret now."

"What secret? I—"

"Don't be dumber than you gotta, Cap'n," Chip said. "Sweaties dies easy; that's the secret."

"Maybe you got a point," the captain said, looking at Retief. "All they got's a three-man scout. It could work."

He went out, came back with two crewmen. They circled the dead alien, hauled him gingerly into the hall.

"Maybe I can run a bluff on the Soetti," the captain said, looking back from the door. "But I'll be back to see you later."

"You don't scare us, Cap'n," Chip called as the door closed. He grinned at Retief. "Him and Mr. Tony and all his goons. You hit 'em where they live, that time. They're pals o' these Sweaties. Runnin' some kind o' crooked racket."

"You'd better take the captain's advice, Chip. There's no point in your getting involved in my problems."

"They'd of killed you before now, mister, if they had any guts. That's where we got it over these monkeys; they got no guts."

"They act scared, Chip. Scared men are killers."

"They don't scare me none." Chip picked up the tray. "I'll scout around a little and see what's goin' on. If the Sweaties figure to do anything about that Skaw fella they'll have to move fast; they won't try nothin' close to port."

"Don't worry, Chip. I have reason to be pretty sure they won't do anything to attract a lot of attention in this sector just now."

Chip looked at Retief. "You ain't no tourist, mister. I

know that much. You didn't come out here for fun, did you?"

"That," said Retief, "would be a hard one to answer."

Retief awoke at a tap on his door.

"It's me, mister: Chip."

"Come on in."

The chef entered the room, locked the door. "You shoulda had that door locked." He stood by the door, listening, then turned to Retief.

"You want to get to Jorgensen's pretty bad, don't you, mister?"

"That's right, Chip."

"Mr. Tony give the captain a real hard time about old Skaw. The Sweaties didn't say nothin'; didn't even act surprised, just took the remains and pushed off. Mr. Tony and that other crook they call Marbles—they was fit to be tied. Took the cap'n in his cabin and talked loud at him fer half an hour. Then the cap'n come out and give some orders to the mate."

Retief sat up and reached for a cigar.

"Mr. Tony and Skaw were pals, eh?"

"He hated Skaw's guts. But with him it was business. Mister, you got a gun?"

"A 2mm needler. Why?"

"The orders Cap'n give was to change course fer Alabaster; we're by-passin' Jorgensen's Worlds. We'll feel the course change any minute."

Retief lit the cigar, reached under the mattress and took out a short-barreled pistol. He dropped it in his pocket, looked at Chip.

"Maybe it was a good thought, at that. Which way to the captain's cabin?"

"This is it," Chip said softly. "You want me to keep a eye on who comes down the passage?"

Retief nodded, opened the door, and stepped into the cabin. The captain looked up from his desk, then jumped up. "What do you think you're doing, busting in here—"

"I hear you're planning a course change, Captain."

"You've got damn big ears."

"I think we'd better call in at Jorgensen's."

"You do, huh?" The captain sat down. "I'm in command of this vessel. I'm changing course for Alabaster."

"I wouldn't find it convenient to go to Alabaster. So just hold your course for Jorgensen's."

"Not bloody likely." The captain reached for the mike on his desk, pressed the key. "Power Section, this is the captain," he said. Retief reached across the desk, gripped the captain's wrist.

"Tell the mate to hold his present course," he said softly.

"Let go my hand, Buster," the captain snarled. With his eyes on Retief's, he eased a drawer open with his left hand, reached in. Retief kneed the drawer. The captain yelped, dropped the mike.

"You busted my wrist, you—"

"And one to go," Retief said. "Tell him."

"I'm an officer of the Merchant Service—"

"You're a cheapjack who's sold his bridge to a pack of back-alley hoods."

"You can't put it over, hick. The landing—"

"Tell him."

The captain groaned, keyed the mike.

"Captain to Power Section. Hold your present course until you hear from me." He dropped the mike, looked up at Retief. "It's eighteen hours yet before we pick up Jorgensen control; you going to sit here and bend my arm the whole time?"

Retief released the captain's wrist, turned to Chip. "Chip, I'm locking the door. You circulate around, let me know what's going on. Bring me a pot of coffee every so often. I'm sitting up with a sick friend."

"Right, mister. Keep an eye on that jasper; he's slippery."

"What are you going to do?" the captain demanded.

Retief settled himself in a chair.

"Instead of strangling you, as you deserve, I'm going to stay here and help you hold your course for Jorgensen's Worlds."

The captain looked at Retief. He laughed, a short bark. "Then I'll stretch out and have a little nap, farmer. If you feel like dozing off some time during the next eighteen hours, don't mind me."

Retief took out the needler and put it on the desk before him.

"If anything happens that I don't like," he said, "I'll wake you up with this."

"Why don't you let me spell you, mister," Chip said. "Four hours to go yet; you're gonna hafta be on yer toes to handle the landing."

"I'll be all right, Chip. You get some sleep."

"Nope. Many's the time I stood four, five watches runnin', back when I was yer age. I'll make another round."

Retief stood up, stretched his legs, paced the floor, stared at the repeater instruments on the wall. Things had gone quietly so far, but the landing would be another matter. The captain's absence from the bridge during the highly complex maneuvering would be difficult to explain . . .

The desk speaker crackled.

"Captain, Officer of the Watch here. Ain't it about time you was getting up here with the orbit figures?"

Retief nudged the captain. He awoke with a start, sat up. "Whazzat?" He looked wild-eyed at Retief.

"Watch Officer wants orbit figures," Retief said, nodding toward the speaker.

The captain rubbed his eyes, shook his head, picked up the mike. Retief released the safety on the needler with an audible click.

"Watch Officer, I'll . . . ah . . . get some figures for you right away. I'm . . . ah . . . busy right now."

"What the hell you talking about, busy?" the speaker blared. "You ain't got the figures ready, you'll have a hell of a hot time getting 'em up in the next three minutes. You fergot your approach pattern or something?"

"I guess I overlooked it," the captain said, looking sideways at Retief. He smiled crookedly. "I've been busy."

"One for your side," Retief said. He reached for the captain.

"I'll make a deal," the captain squalled. "Your life for—"

Retief took aim, slammed a hard right to the captain's jaw. He slumped to the floor.

Retief glanced around the room, yanked wires loose from

a motile lamp, trussed the man's hands and feet, stuffed his mouth with paper and taped it.

Chip tapped at the door. Retief opened it and the chef stepped inside, looked at the man on the floor.

"The jasper tried somethin', huh? Figured he would. What we goin' to do now?"

"The captain forgot to set up an approach, Chip. He out-foxed me."

"If we overrun our approach patterns," Chip said, "we can't make orbit at Jorgensen's on automatic, and a manual approach—"

"That's out. But there's another possibility."

Chip blinked. "Only one thing you could mean, mister. But cuttin' out in a lifeboat in deep space is no picnic."

"They're on the port side, aft, right?"

Chip nodded. "Hot damn!" he said. "Who's got the 'tater salad?"

"We'd better tuck the skipper away out of sight."

"In the locker."

The two men carried the limp body to a deep storage chest, dumped it in, closed the lid.

"He won't suffercate; lid's a lousy fit."

Retief opened the door, went into the corridor, Chip behind him.

"Shouldn't oughta be nobody around now," the chef said. "Everybody's mannin' approach stations."

At the D deck companionway Retief stopped suddenly. "Listen."

Chip cocked his head. "I don't hear nothin'," he whispered.

"Sounds like a sentry posted on the lifeboat deck," Retief said softly.

"Let's take him, mister."

"I'll go down. Stand by, Chip."

Retief started down the narrow steps, half stair, half ladder. Halfway, he paused to listen. There was a sound of slow footsteps, then silence. Retief palmed the needler, went down the last steps quickly, emerged in the dim light of a low-ceilinged room. The stern of a five-man lifeboat bulked before him.

"Freeze, you!" a cold voice snapped.

Retief dropped, rolled behind the shelter of the lifeboat as the whine of a power pistol echoed off metal walls. A lunge, and he was under the boat, on his feet. He jumped, caught the quick-access handle, hauled it down. The lifeboat's outer port cycled open.

Feet scrambled at the bow of the boat, and Retief whirled, fired. The guard rounded into sight and fell head-long. Above, an alarm bell jangled. Retief stepped on a stanchion, hauled himself into the open port. A yell rang, then the clatter of feet on the stair.

"Don't shoot, mister!" Chip shouted.

"All clear, Chip," Retief called.

"Hang on; I'm comin' with ya!"

Retief reached down, lifted the chef bodily through the port, slammed the lever home. The outer door whooshed, clanged shut.

"Take number two, tie in! I'll blast her off," Chip said. "Been through a hundred 'bandon ship drills . . ."

Retief watched as the chef flipped levers, pressed a fat red button. The deck trembled under the lifeboat.

"Blew the bay doors," Chip said, smiling happily. "That'll cool them jaspers down." He punched a green button.

"Look out, Jorgensen's . . ." With an ear-splitting blast, the stern rockets fired, a sustained agony of pressure . . .

Abruptly, there was silence, weightlessness. Contracting metal pinged loudly. Chip's breathing rasped in the stillness.

"Pulled nine Gs there for ten seconds," he gasped. "I gave her full emergency kick-off."

"Any armament aboard our late host?"

"A pop-gun; time they get their wind, we'll be clear. Now all we got to do is set tight till we pick up a R and D from Svea Tower: maybe four, five hours."

"Chip, you're a wonder," Retief said. "This looks like a good time to catch that nap."

"Me too. Mighty peaceful here, ain't it?"

There was a moment's silence.

"Durn!" Chip said softly.

Retief opened one eye. "Sorry you came, Chip?"

"Left my best carvin' knife jammed up 'tween Marbles' ribs," the chef said. "Comes o' doin' things in a hurry."

✧　　✧　　✧

The blond girl brushed her hair from her eyes and smiled at Retief.

"I'm the only one on duty," she said. "I'm Freya Dahl."

"It's important that I talk to someone in your government, miss," Retief said.

The girl looked at Retief. "The men you want to see are Thor Stahl and Bo Bergman. They will be at the lodge by nightfall."

"Then it looks like we go to the lodge," Retief said. "Lead on, ma'am."

"What about the boat?" Chip asked.

"I'll send someone to see to it tomorrow," the girl said.

"You're some gal," Chip said admiringly. "Dern near six feet, ain't you? And built too, what I mean."

They stepped out of the building into a whipping wind.

"Let's go across to the equipment shed, and get parkas for you," Freya said. "It will be cold on the slopes."

"Yeah," Chip said, shivering. "I've heard you folks don't believe in ridin' ever time you want to go a few miles uphill in a blizzard."

"It will make us hungry," Freya said.

Across the wind-scoured ramp abrupt peaks rose, snow-blanketed. A faint trail led across white slopes, disappeared into low clouds.

"The lodge is above the cloud layer," Freya said. "Up there the sky is always clear."

It was three hours later, and the sun was burning the peaks red, when Freya stopped, pulled off her woolen cap, and waved at the vista below.

"There you see it. Our valley."

"It's a mighty perty sight," Chip gasped. "Anything this tough to get a look at ought to be."

Freya pointed to where gaily painted houses nestled together, a puddle of color in the bowl of the valley. "There," she said. "The little red house by itself; do you see it? It is my father's home-acre."

"I'd appreciate it a dern sight better if my feet were up to that big fire you was talking about, Honey," Chip said.

The climbed on, crossed a shoulder, a slope of broken

rock, reached the final slope. Above, the lodge sprawled, a long low structure of heavy logs, outlined against the deep-blue twilight sky. Smoke billowed from stone chimneys at either end, and yellow light gleamed from the narrow windows, reflected on the snow. Men and women stood in groups of three or four, skis over their shoulders. Their voices and laughter rang in the icy air.

Freya whistled shrilly. Someone waved.

"Come," she said. "Meet all my friends."

A man separated himself from the group, walked down the slope to meet them. Freya introduced the guests.

"Welcome," the man said heartily. "Come inside and be warm."

They crossed the trampled snow to the lodge, pushed through a heavy door into a vast low-beamed hall, crowded with people talking, singing, some sitting at long plank tables, others ringed around an eight-foot fireplace at the far side of the room. Freya led the way to a bench near the fire, made introductions, found a stool to prop Chip's feet on near the blaze. He looked around.

"I never seen so many perty gals before," he said delightedly.

A brunette with blue eyes raked a chestnut from the fire, cracked it, and offered it to Retief. A tall man with arms like oak roots passed heavy beer tankards to the two guests.

"Tell us about the places you've seen," someone called. Chip emerged from a long pull at the mug, heaved a sigh.

"Well," he said. "I tell you I been in some places . . ."

Music started up, ringing above the clamor of talk. Freya rose. "Come," she said to Retief. "Dance with me."

When the music stopped, Retief rejoined Chip, who put down his mug and sighed. "Derned if I ever felt right at home so quick before." He lowered his voice. "They's some kind o' trouble in the air, though. Some o' the remarks they passed sounds like they're lookin' to have some trouble with the Sweaties. Don't seem to worry 'em none, though."

"Chip," Retief said, "how much do these people know about the Soetti?"

"Dunno. We useta touch down here regler, but I always

jist set in my galley and worked on ship models or somethin'. I hear the Sweaties been nosin' around here some,
though."

Two girls came up to Chip. "I gotta go now, mister,"
he said. "These gals got a idea I oughta take a hand in
the kitchen."

"Smart girls," Retief said. He turned as Freya came up.

"Bo Bergman and Thor aren't back yet," she said. "They
stayed to ski after moonrise."

"That moon is something. Almost like daylight."

"They will come soon, now. Shall we go to see the
moonlight on the snow?"

Outside, long black shadows fell like ink in silver. The
top of the cloud layer below glared white under the
immense moon.

"Our sister world, Göta," Freya said. "Nearly as big as
Svea. I would like to visit it someday, although they say
it's all stone and ice."

"Freya," Retief said, "how many people live on Jorgensen's
Worlds?"

"About fifteen million, most of us here on Svea. There
are mining camps and ice-fisheries on Göta. No one lives
on Vasa or Skone, but there are always a few ice-wolf
hunters there."

"Have you ever fought a war?"

Freya turned to look at Retief. "Don't be afraid for us,
Retief. The Soetti will attack our worlds, and we will fight
them. We have fought before. These planets were not
friendly ones . . ."

"I thought the Soetti attack would be a surprise to you,"
Retief said. "Have you made any preparation for it?"

"We have ten thousand merchant ships. When the enemy
comes, we will meet them."

Retief frowned. "Are there any guns on this planet? Any
missiles?"

Freya shook her head. "We have a plan of deployment—"

"Deployment hell! Against a modern assault force you
need modern armament."

"Look!" Freya touched Retief's arm. "They're coming
now."

Two tall grizzled men came up the slope, skis over their

shoulders. Freya went forward to meet them, Retief at her side.

The two came up, embraced the girl, shook hands with Retief.

"He has come to help us," Freya said.

"Welcome to Svea," Thor said. "Let's find a warm corner where we can talk."

Retief shook his head, smiling as a tall girl with coppery hair offered a vast slab of venison. "I've caught up," he said, "for every hungry day I ever lived."

Bo Bergman poured Retief's beer mug full. "Our captains are the best in space," he said. "Our population is concentrated in half a hundred small cities all across the planet. We know where the Soetti must strike us. We will ram their major vessels with unmanned ships; on the ground, we will hunt them down with small-arms."

"An assembly line turning out penetration missiles would have been more to the point."

"Yes," Bo Bergman said. "If we had known sooner."

"We've seen very few of the Soetti," Thor said. "Their ships have landed and taken on stores. They say little to us, but we've felt their contempt. They envy us our worlds. They come from a cold land."

"Freya says you have a plan of defense," Retief said. "A sort of suicide squadron idea, followed by guerilla warfare."

"It's the best we can devise, Retief. If there aren't too many of them, it might work."

Retief shook his head. "It might delay matters—but not much."

"Perhaps; but our remote control equipment is excellent; we have plenty of ships, albeit unarmed. And our people know how to live on the slopes—and how to shoot."

"There are too many of them," Retief said. "They breed like flies and, according to some sources, they mature in a matter of months. They've been feeling their way into the sector for years now; set up outposts on a thousand or so minor planets—cold ones, the kind they like. They want your worlds because they need living space."

"Retief must not be trapped here," said Freya to her

compatriots. "His small boat is useless now; he must have a ship."

"Of course," Thor said. "And—"

"Retief," a voice called. "A message for you; the operator has phoned it up. A 'gram . . ."

Retief took the slip of paper, unfolded it. It was short, in verbal code, and signed by Magnan.

"You are recalled herewith," he read. "Assignment canceled. Agreement concluded with Soetti relinquishing all claims so-called Jorgensen system. Utmost importance that under no repeat no circumstances classified intelligence regarding Soetti be divulged to locals. Advise you depart instanter; Soetti occupation imminent."

Retief looked thoughtfully at the scrap of paper, then crumpled it, dropped it on the floor.

"Any answer?" the messenger asked.

"No," Retief said. "As a matter of fact, I didn't even get the message." He turned to Bo Bergman, took a tiny reel of tape from his pocket.

"This contains information," he said. "The Soetti attack plan, a defensive plan worked out at Corps HQ, and instructions for the conversion of a standard anti-acceleration unit into a potent weapon. If you have a screen handy, we'd better get started; we have about seventy-two hours."

In the Briefing Room at Svea Tower, Thor snapped off the projector.

"Our plan would have been worthless against that," he said. "We assumed they'd make their strike from a standard in-line formation. This scheme of hitting all our settlements simultaneously, in a random order from all points—we'd have been helpless."

"It's perfect for this defensive plan," Bo Bergman said. "Assuming this antiac trick works."

"It works," said Retief. "I hope you've got plenty of heavy power cable available."

"We export copper," Thor said.

"We'll assign about two hundred vessels to each settlement. Linked up, they should throw up quite a field."

"It ought to be effective up to about fifteen miles, I'd estimate," Retief said.

A red light flashed on the communications panel. Thor went to it, flipped a key.

"Tower, Thor here," he said.

"I've got a ship on the scope, Thor," a voice said. "There's nothing scheduled; ACI 228 by-passed at 1600 . . ."

"Just one?"

"A lone ship; coming in on a bearing of 291/456/653; on manual, I'd say."

"How does this track key in with the idea of ACI 228 making a manual correction for a missed automatic approach?" Retief asked.

Thor talked to the tower, got a reply.

"That's it," he said.

"How long before he touches down?"

Thor glanced at a lighted chart. "Perhaps eight minutes."

"Any guns here?"

Thor shook his head.

"If that's old 228, she ain't got but the one 50mm rifle," Chip said. "She cain't figure on jumpin' the whole planet."

"Hard to say what she figures on," Retief said. "Mr. Tony will be in a mood for drastic measures."

"I wonder what kind o' deal the skunk's got with the Sweaties," Chip said. "Prob'ly he gits to scavenge, after the Sweaties kill off the Jorgensens."

"He's upset about our leaving him without saying goodbye. And you left the door hanging open, too."

Chip cackled. "Old Mr. Tony don't look so good to the Sweaties now, hey, mister?"

Retief turned to Bo Bergman. "Chip's right. A Soetti died on the ship, and a tourist got through the cordon. Tony's out to redeem himself."

"He's on final now," the tower operator said. "Still no contact."

"We'll know soon enough what he has in mind," Thor said.

"Let's ta e a look."

Outside, the four men watched the point of fire grow, evolve into a ship ponderously settling to rest. The drive faded and cut; silence fell.

Inside the briefing room, the speaker called out. Bo

Bergman went inside, talked to the tower, motioned the others in. "This is the tower talking to the ship," he said.

"—over to you," the speaker was saying. There was a crackling moment of silence; then another voice:

"—illegal entry. Send the two of them out, I'll see to it they're dealt with."

Thor flipped a key. "Tower, switch me direct to the ship."

"Right."

"You on ACI 228," he said. "Who are you?"

"What's that to you?" the speaker crackled.

"You weren't cleared to berth here. Do you have an emergency aboard?"

"Never mind that, you," the speaker rumbled. "I tracked this bird in; I got the lifeboat on the screen now. They haven't gone far in six hours. Let's have 'em."

"You're wasting your time."

There was a momentary silence.

"You think so, hah?" the speaker blared. "I'll put it to you straight: I see two guys on their way out in one minute, or I open up."

"He's bluffin'," Chip said. "The pop-gun won't bear on us."

"Take a look out the window," said Retief.

In the white glare of the moonlight a loading cover swung open at the stern of the ship, dropped down, formed a sloping ramp. A squat and massive shape appeared in the opening, trundled down onto the snow-swept tarmac.

Chip whistled. "I told you the captain was slippery," he muttered. "Where the devil'd he git that at?"

"What is it?" Thor asked.

"A tank," Retief said. "A museum piece, by the look of it."

"I'll say," Chip said. "That's a Bolo *Resartus*, Model M. Built mebbe two hundred years ago in Concordiat times. Packs a wallop too, I'll tell ye."

The tank wheeled, brought a gun muzzle to bear in the base of the tower.

"Send 'em out," the speaker growled. "Or I blast 'em out."

"One round in here, and I've had a wasted trip," Retief said. "I'd better go out."

"Wait a minute, mister. I got the glimmerins of a idear."

"I'll stall them," Thor said. He keyed the mike. "ACI 228, what's your authority for this demand?"

"I know that machine," Chip said. "My hobby, old-time fightin' machines. Built a model of a *Resartus* once, inch to the foot; a beauty. Now lessee . . ."

The icy wind blew snow crystals stingingly against Retief's face. Chip carried a short length of iron bar thrust into his belt. He looked across at the tank. "Useta think that was a perty thing, that *Resartus*," he said. "Looks mean, now."

"You're getting the target's eye view," Retief said. "Sorry you had to get mixed up in this, old-timer."

"Mixed myself in. Dern good thing too." Chip sighed. "I like these folks. Them boys didn't like lettin' us come out here, but I'll give 'em credit; they seen it had to be this way, and they didn't set to moanin' about it."

"They're tough people, Chip."

"Funny how it sneaks up on you, ain't it, mister? Few minutes ago we was eatin' high on the hog; now we're right close to bein' dead men."

"They want us alive."

"It'll be a hairy deal. But t'hell with it. If it works, it works."

"That's the spirit."

"I hope I got them fields o' fire right—"

"Don't worry; I'll bet a barrel of beer we make it."

"We'll find out in about ten seconds," Chip said. "Here we go . . ."

As they reached the tank the two men broke stride and jumped. Retief leaped for the gun barrel, swung up astride it, ripped off the fur-lined leather cap he wore, and, leaning forward, jammed it into the bore of the cannon. The chef sprang for a perch above the fore scanner antenna. With an angry whuff! anti-personnel charges slammed from apertures low on the sides of the vehicle. Retief swung around, pulled himself up on the hull.

"Okay, mister," Chip called. "I'm goin' under." He slipped down the front of the tank, disappeared between the treads. Retief clambered up, took a position behind the turret, lay flat as it whirled angrily, sonar eyes searching for the tank's tormentors. The vehicle shuddered, backed, stopped, moved forward, pivoted.

Chip reappeared at the front of the tank.

"It's stuck," he called. He stopped to breathe hard, clung as the machine lurched forward, spun to the right, stopped, rocking slightly.

"Take over here," Retief said. He crawled forward, watched as the chef pulled himself up, slipped down past him, feeling for the footholds between the treads. He reached the ground, dropped on his back, hitching himself under the dark belly of the tank. He groped, found the handholds, probed with a foot for the tread-jack lever.

The tank rumbled, backed quickly, turned left and right in a sine curve. Retief clung grimly, inches from the clashing treads. He found the lever, braced his back, pushed. The lever seemed to give minutely. He set himself again, put both feet against the frozen bar, and heaved. With a dry rasp it slid back. Immediately, two rods extended themselves, slid down to grate against the pavement, drove on irresistibly. The left track raced as the weight went off it. Retief grabbed for a hold as the right tread clashed, heaving the fifty-ton machine forward, jacks screeching as they scored the tarmac. The tank pivoted, chips of pavement flying. The jacks lifted the clattering left track clear of the surface and the tank spun like a hamstrung buffalo.

The tank stopped, sat silent, canted now on the extended jacks. Retief emerged from under the machine, jumped, pulled himself above the anti-personnel apertures as another charge rocked the tank. He clambered to the turret, crouched beside Chip. They waited, watching the entry hatch.

Five minutes passed.

"I'll bet old Tony's givin' the chauffeur hell," Chip said.

The hatch moved, cycled open. A head came cautiously into view in time to see the needler in Retief's hand.

"Come on out," Retief said.

The head dropped, and Chip snaked forward, rammed the iron rod under the hatch near the hinge. The hatch began to cycle shut, groaned, stopped. There was a sound of metal failing, and the hatch, popped, stood open. Retief half rose, aimed the needler. The walls of the tank rang as the metal splinters ricocheted inside.

"That's one keg o' beer I owe you, mister," Chip said. "Now let's git outa here before the ship lifts and fries us."

"The biggest problem the Jorgensen's people will have is decontaminating the wreckage," Retief said.

Magnan leaned forward. "Amazing," he said. "They just kept coming, did they? Had they no inter-ship communication?"

"They had their orders. And their attack plan. They followed it."

"What a spectacle! Over a thousand ships, plunging out of control one by one as they entered the stress-field."

"Not much of a spectacle. You couldn't see them; too far away. They all crashed back in the mountains."

"Oh." Magnan's face fell. "But it's as well they did; the bacterial bombs—"

"Too cold for bacteria. They won't spread."

"Nor will the Soetti," Magnan said smugly, "thanks to the promptness with which I acted in dispatching you with the requisite data." He looked narrowly at Retief. "By the way, you're sure no . . . ah . . . message reached you after your arrival?"

"I got something," Retief said, looking Magnan in the eye. "It must have been a garbled transmission. It didn't make sense."

Magnan coughed, shuffled papers. "This information you've reported," he said hurriedly. "This rather fantastic story that the Soetti originated in the Cloud, that they're seeking a foothold in the main galaxy because they've literally eaten themselves out of subsistence; how did you get it? The one of two Soetti we attempted to question . . . ah," Magnan coughed again. "There was an accident," he finished. "We got nothing from them."

"The Jorgensens took a Soetti from a wreck, still alive but unconscious. They managed to get the story from him."

"It's immaterial, actually," Magnan said. "The Soetti violated their treaty with us the day after it was signed. Had no intention of fair play. Far from evacuating the agreed areas, they had actually occupied half a dozen additional minor bodies in the *Whate* system."

Retief clucked sympathetically. "You don't know who to trust, these days," he said. Magnan looked at him coldly.

"Spare me your sarcasm, Retief." He picked up a folder from his desk, opened it. "While you're out that way, I have another little task for you. We haven't had a comprehensive wildlife census report from Brimstone lately—"

"Sorry," Retief said. "I'll be tied up. I'm taking a month off. Maybe more."

"What's that?" Magnan's head came up. "You seem to forget—"

"I'm trying, Mr. Secretary. Goodbye now." Retief reached out and flipped the key. Magnan's face faded from the screen. Retief stood up.

"Chip, we'll crack that keg when I get back." He turned to Freya.

"Freya," he said, "do you think you could teach me to ski by moonlight?"

> "For all its spirit of detachment from petty
> local issues, the Corps was never slow to
> interpose its majestic presence in the path of
> injustice. Under-Secretary Sternwheeler's classic
> approach to the problem of Aga Kagan aggres-
> sion at Flamme testified to the efficacy of tried
> diplomatic procedures backed by the profound
> prestige of the Corps . . ."

> —Vol. XV, Reel 3, 494 AE (AD 2955)

PROTEST NOTE

"I'm not at all sure," Under-Secretary Sternwheeler said,
"that I fully understand the necessity of your absenting
yourself from your post of duty at this time, Mr. Retief.
Surely this matter could have been dealt with in the usual
way—assuming any action is necessary."

"I had a sharp attack of writer's cramp, Mr. Secretary,"
Retief said. "So I thought I'd better come along in person—
just to be sure of making my point."

"I seem to recall seeing a dispatch or two on the subject," Deputy Under-Secretary Magnan put in. "Unfortunately, this being end-of-the-fiscal-year time, we found
ourselves quite inundated with reports. Reports, reports,
reports—"

"Not criticizing the reporting system, are you, Mr.
Magnan?" the Under-Secretary barked.

"Gracious, no. I love reports—"

"It seems nobody's told the Aga Kagans about fiscal
years," Retief said. "They're going right ahead with their
program of land-grabbing on Flamme. So far, I've

persuaded the Boyars that this is a matter for the Corps, and not to take matters into their own hands."

The Under-Secretary nodded. "Quite right. Carry on along the same lines. Now, if there's nothing further—"

"Thank you, Mr. Secretary," Magnan said, rising. "We certainly appreciate your guidance—"

"There is a little something further," said Retief, sitting solidly in his chair. "What's the Corps going to do about the Aga Kagans?"

The Under-Secretary turned a liverish eye on Retief. "As Minister to Flamme, you should know that the function of a diplomatic representative is merely to . . . what shall I say . . . ?"

"String them along?" Magnan suggested.

"An unfortunate choice of phrase," the Under-Secretary said.

"However, it embodies certain realities of Galactic politics. The Corps must concern itself with matters of broad policy—"

"Sixty years ago the Corps was encouraging the Boyars to settle Flamme," Retief said. "They were assured of Corps support."

"I don't believe you'll find that in writing," said the Under-Secretary blandly. "In any event, that was sixty years ago. At that time a foothold against Neo-Concordiatist elements was deemed desirable. Now the situation has changed."

"The Boyars have spent sixty years terraforming Flamme," Retief said. "They're cleared jungle, descummed the seas, irrigated deserts, set out forests. They've just about reached the point where they can begin to enjoy it. The Aga Kagans have picked this as a good time to move in. They've landed thirty detachments of 'fishermen'—complete with armored trawlers mounting 40mm infinite repeaters—and two dozen parties of 'homesteaders'—all male and toting rocket launchers."

"Surely there's land enough on the world to afford space to both groups," the Under-Secretary said. "A spirit of cooperation—"

"The Boyars needed some co-operation sixty years ago. They tried to get the Aga Kagans to join in, help them beat back some of the saurian wildlife that liked to graze on people. The Aga Kagans didn't want to play. The Corps didn't like the idea either; they wanted to see an undisputed anti-Concordiatist enclave. But now that the world is tamed, the squatters are moving in."

"The exigencies of diplomacy require a flexible policy—"

"I want a firm assurance of Corps support to take back to Flamme," Retief said. "The Boyars are a little naïve; they don't understand diplomatic triple-speak. They just want to hold onto the homes they've made out of a wasteland."

"I'm warning you, Retief!" the Under-Secretary snapped, leaning forward, wattles quivering. "Corps policy with regard to Flamme includes no inflammatory actions based on outmoded concepts. The Boyars will have to accommodate themselves to the situation!"

"That's what I'm afraid of," Retief said. "They're not going to sit still and watch it happen. If I don't take back concrete evidence of Corps backing, we're going to have a nice hot little shooting war on our hands."

The Under-Secretary pushed out his lips, drummed his fingers on the desk. "Confounded hot-heads," he muttered. "Very well, Retief. I'll go along to the extent of a Note; but no further."

"A Note? I was thinking of something more like a squadron of Corps Peace Enforcers running through a few routine maneuvers off Flamme—"

"Out of the question. A stiffly worded Protest Note is the best I can do. That's final."

Back in the corridor, Magnan turned to Retief. "When will you learn not to argue with Under-Secretaries? One would think you actively dislike the idea of a promotion. I was astonished at the Under-Secretary's restraint. Frankly, I was stunned when he actually agreed to a Note. I, of course, will have to draft it." Magnan pulled at his lower lip thoughtfully. "Now, I wonder, should I view with deep concern an act of open aggression, or merely point out an apparent violation of technicalities . . ."

"Don't bother," Retief said. "I have a draft all ready to go."

"But how—?"

"I had a feeling I'd get paper instead of action. I thought I'd save a little time all around."

"At times your cynicism borders on impudence."

"At other times it borders on disgust. Now, if you'll run the Note through for signature, I'll try to catch the six o'clock shuttle."

"Leaving so soon? There's an important reception tonight. Some of our biggest names will be there. An excellent opportunity for you to join in the diplomatic give-and-take."

"No, thanks. I want to get back to Flamme and join in something mild, like a dinosaur hunt."

"When you get there, I hope you'll make it clear that this matter is to be settled without violence."

"Don't worry. I'll keep the peace, if I have to start a war to do it."

On the broad veranda at Government House, Retief settled himself comfortably in a lounge chair, accepted a tall glass from a white-jacketed waiter, and regarded the flamboyant Flamme sunset, a gorgeous blaze of vermilion and purple that reflected from a still lake, tinged the broad lawn with color, silhouetted tall poplars among flower beds.

"You've done great things here in sixty years, Georges," said Retief. "Not that natural geological processes couldn't have produced the same results, given a couple of hundred million years."

"Don't belabor the point," the Boyar Chef d'Regime said, "—since we seem to be on the verge of losing it."

"You're forgetting the Note."

"A Note," Georges said, waving his cigar. "What the purple polluted hell is a Note supposed to do? I've got Aga Kagan claim-jumpers camped in the middle of what used to be a fine stand of barley, cooking sheep's brains over dung fires not ten miles from Government House—and up-wind at that."

"Say, if that's the same barley you distill your whiskey from, I'd call that a first-class atrocity."

"Retief, on your say-so, I've kept my boys on a short leash. They've put up with plenty. Last week, while you were away, these barbarians sailed that flotilla of armor-plated junks right through the middle of one of our best oyster breeding beds.

It was all I could do to keep a bunch of our men from going out in private helis and blasting 'em out of the water."

"That wouldn't have been good for the oysters, either."

"That's what I told 'em. I also said you'd be back here in a few days with something from Corps HQ. When I tell 'em all we're got is a piece of paper, that'll be the end. There's a strong vigilante organization here that's been outfitting for the last four weeks. If I hadn't held them back with assurances that the CDT would step in and take care of this invasion, they would have hit them before now."

"That would have been a mistake. The Aga Kagans are tough customers. They're active on half a dozen worlds at the moment. They've been building up for this push for the last five years. A show of resistance by you Boyars without Corps backing would be an invitation to slaughter— with the excuse that you started it."

"So what are we going to do? Sit here and watch these goat-herders take over our farms and fisheries?"

"Those goat-herders aren't all they seem. They've got a first-class modern navy."

"I've seen 'em. They camp in goat-skin tents, gallop around on animal-back, wear dresses down to their ankles—"

"The 'goat-skin' tents are a high-polymer plastic, made in the same factory that turns out those long flowing bullet-proof robes you mention. The animals are just for show; back home they use helis and ground cars of the most modern design."

The Chef d'Regime chewed his cigar.

"Why the masquerade?"

"Something to do with internal policies, I suppose."

"So we sit tight and watch 'em take our world away from us. That's what I get for playing along with you, Retief. We should have clobbered these monkeys as soon as they set foot on our world."

"Slow down, I haven't finished yet. There's still the Note."

"I've got plenty of paper already; rolls and rolls of it."

"Give diplomatic processes a chance," said Retief. "The Note hasn't even been delivered yet. Who knows? We may get surprising results."

"If you expect me to supply a runner for the purpose,

you're out of luck. From what I hear, he's likely to come back with his ears stuffed in his hip pocket."

"I'll deliver the Note personally," Retief said. "I could use a couple of escorts—preferably strong-arm lads."

The Chef d'Regime frowned, blew out a cloud of smoke. "I wasn't kidding about these Aga Kagans," he said. "I hear they have some nasty habits. I don't want to see you operated on with the same knives they use to skin out the goats."

"I'd be against that myself. Still the mail must go through."

"Strong-arm lads, eh? What have you got in mind, Retief?"

"A little muscle in the background is an old diplomatic custom," Retief said.

The Chef d'Regime stubbed out his cigar thoughtfully. "I used to be a pretty fair elbow-wrestler myself," he said. "Suppose I go along . . . ?"

"That," said Retief, "should lend just the right note of solidarity to our little delegation." He hitched his chair closer. "Now, depending on what we run into, here's how we'll play it . . ."

Eight miles into the rolling granite hills west of the capital, a black-painted official air car flying the twin flags of Chief of State and Terrestrial Minister skimmed along a foot above a pot-holed road. Slumped in the padded seat, the Boyar Chef d'Regime waved his cigar glumly at the surrounding hills.

"Fifty years ago this was bare rock," he said. "We've bred special strains of bacteria here to break down the formations into soil, and we followed up with a program of broad-spectrum fertilization. We planned to put the whole area into crops by next year. Now it looks like the goats will get it."

"Will that scrub-land support a crop?" Retief said, eyeing the lichen-covered knolls.

"Sure. We start with legumes, follow up with cereals. Wait until you see this next section. It's an old flood plain, came into production thirty years ago. One of our finest—"

The air car topped a rise and the Chef dropped his cigar,

half rose, with a hoarse yell. A herd of scraggly goats tossed
their heads among a stand of ripe grain. The car pulled
to a stop. Retief held the Boyar's arm.

"Keep calm, Georges," he said. "Remember, we're on
a diplomatic mission. It wouldn't do to come to the conference table smelling of goats."

"Let me at 'em!" Georges roared. "I'll throttle 'em with
my bare hands!"

A bearded goat eyed the Boyar Chef sardonically, jaw
working.

"Look at that long-nosed son of a—!" The goat gave a
derisive bleat and took another mouthful of ripe grain.

"Did you see that?" Georges yelled. "They've trained the
son of a—"

"Chin up, Georges," Retief said. "We'll take up the goat
problem along with the rest."

"I'll murder 'em—!"

"Hold it, Georges. Look over there . . ."

A hundred yards away a trio of brown-cloaked horsemen topped a rise, paused dramatically against the cloudless
pale sky, then galloped down the slope toward the car, rifles
bobbing at their backs, cloaks billowing out behind. Side
by side they rode, through the brown-golden grain, cutting three narrow swaths that ran in a straight sweep from
the ridge to the air car where Retief and the Chef d'Regime
hovered, waiting.

Georges scrambled for the side of the car. "Just wait
till I get my hands on the son of a—"

Retief pulled him back. "Sit tight and look pleased,
Georges. Never give the opposition a hint of your true
feelings. Pretend you're a goat lover—and hand me one
of your cigars."

The three horsemen pulled up in a churn of chaff and
a clatter of pebbles. Georges coughed, batting a hand at
the settling dust. Retief peeled the cigar unhurriedly, sniffed
at it, thumbed it alight. He drew at it, puffed out a cloud
of smoke, and glanced casually at the trio of Aga Kagan
cavaliers.

"Peace be with you," he intoned in accent-free Kagan.
"May your shadows never grow less."

The leader of the three, a hawk-faced man with a

heavy beard, unlimbered his rifle, fingered it, frowning ferociously.

"Have no fear," Retief said, smiling graciously. "He who comes as a guest enjoys perfect safety."

A smooth-faced member of the threesome barked an oath, leveled his rifle at Retief.

"Youth is the steed of folly," Retief said. "Take care that the beardless one does not disgrace his house."

The leader whirled on the youth, snarled an order; he lowered the rifle, muttering. Blackbeard turned back to Retief.

"Begone, interlopers," he said. "You disturb the goats."

"Provision is not taken to the house of the generous," Retief said. "May the creatures dine well ere they move on."

"Hah! The goats of the Aga Kaga graze on the lands of the Aga Kaga." The leader edged his horse close, eyed Retief fiercely. "We welcome no intruders on our lands."

"To praise a man for what he does not possess is to make him appear foolish," Retief said. "These are the lands of the Boyars. But enough of these pleasantries. We seek audience with your ruler."

"You may address me as 'Exalted One,'" the leader said. "Now dismount from that steed of Shaitan—"

"It is written, 'If you need anything from a dog, call him 'sir,' " Retief said. "I must decline to impute canine ancestry to a guest. Now you may conduct me to your headquarters."

"Enough of your insolence—!" The bearded man cocked his rifle. "I could blow your heads off—"

"The hen has feathers, but it does not fly," Retief said. "We have asked for escort. A slave must be beaten with a stick; for a free man, a hint is enough."

"You mock me, pale one. I warn you—"

"Only love makes me weep," Retief said. "I laugh at hatred."

"Get out of the car!"

Retief puffed at his cigar, eyed the Aga Kagan cheerfully. The youth in the rear moved forward, teeth bared.

"Never give in to the fool, lest he say, 'He fears me,'" Retief said.

"I cannot restrain my men in the face of your insults,"

the bearded Aga Kagan roared. "These hens of mine have feathers—and talons as well!"

"When God would destroy an ant, he gives him wings," Retief said. "Distress in misfortune is another misfortune."

The bearded man's face grew purple.

Retief dribbled the ash from his cigar over the side of the car.

"Now, I think we'd better be getting on," he said briskly. "I've enjoyed our chat, but we do have business to attend to."

The bearded leader laughed shortly. "Does the condemned man beg for the axe?" he inquired rhetorically. "You shall be allowed audience with the Aga Kaga, then. Move on—and make no attempt to escape, else my gun will speak you a brief farewell."

The horsemen glowered, then at a word from the leader, took positions around the car. Georges started the vehicle forward, following the leading rider. Retief leaned back and let out a long sigh.

"That was close," he said. "I was about out of proverbs."

"You sound as though you'd brought off a coup," Georges said. "From the expression on the whiskery one's face, we're in for trouble. What was he saying?"

"Just a routine exchange of bluffs," Retief said. "Now when we get there, remember to make your flattery sound like insults and your insults sound like flattery, and you'll be all right."

"These birds are armed—and they don't like strangers," Georges said. "Maybe I should have boned up on their habits before I joined this expedition."

"Just stick to the plan. And remember: a handful of luck is better than a camel-load of learning."

The air car followed the escort down a long slope to a dry river bed, across it, through a barren stretch of shifting sand, to a green oasis, set with canopies.

The armed escort motioned the car to a halt before an immense tent of glistening black, before which armed men lounged under a pennant bearing a lion *couchant* in crimson on a field vert.

"Get out," Blackbeard ordered. The guards eyed the

visitors, drawn sabers catching sunlight. Retief and Georges stepped from the car onto rich rugs spread on the grass, followed the ferocious gesture of the bearded man through the opening into a perfumed interior of luminous shadows. A heavy odor of incense hung in the air, and the strumming of stringed instruments laid a muted pattern of sound behind the decorations of gold and blue, silver and green. At the far end of the room, among a bevy of female slaves, a large and resplendently clad man with blue-black hair and a clean-shaven chin popped a grape into his mouth, wiped his fingers negligently on a wisp of silk offered by a hand-maiden, belched loudly, and looked the callers over.

Blackbeard cleared his throat. "Down on your faces in the presence of the Exalted One, the Aga Kaga, ruler of the East and West—"

"Sorry," Retief said firmly. "My hay-fever, you know."

The reclining giant waved a hand languidly.

"Never mind the formalities," he said. "Approach."

Retief and Georges crossed the thick rugs. A cold draft blew toward them. The reclining man sneezed violently, wiped his nose on another silken scarf, and held up a hand.

"Night and the horses and the desert know me," he said in resonant tones. "Also the sword and the guest and paper and pen—" He paused, wrinkled his nose, and sneezed again.

"Turn off that damned air-conditioner," he snapped. He settled himself, motioned the bearded man to him; the two exchanged muted remarks. Then the bearded man stepped back, ducked his head, and withdrew to the rear.

"Excellency," Retief said, "I have the honor to present M. Georges Duror, Chef d'Regime of the Planetary government—"

"Planetary government?" The Aga Kaga spat grape seeds on the rug. "My men have observed a few squatters along the shore. If they're in distress, I'll see about a distribution of goat-meat."

"It is the punishment of the envious to grieve at another's plenty," Retief said. "No goat-meat will be required."

"Ralph told me you talk like a page out of Mustapha

ben Abdallah Katib Jelebi," the Aga Kaga said. "I know a few old sayings myself. For example, 'A Bedouin is only cheated once.'"

"We have no such intentions, Excellency," Retief said. "Is it not written, 'Have no faith in the Prince whose minister cheats you'?"

"I've had some unhappy experiences with strangers," the Aga Kaga said. "It is written in the sands, 'All strangers are kin.' Still, he who visits rarely is a welcome guest. Be seated."

Hand-maidens brought cushions, giggled, and fled. Retief and Georges settled themselves comfortably. The Aga Kaga eyed them in silence.

"We have come to bear tiding from Corps Diplomatique Terrestrienne," Retief said solemnly. A perfumed slave girl offered grapes.

"Modest ignorance is better than boastful knowledge," the Aga Kaga said. "What brings the CDT into the picture?"

"The essay of the drunkard will be read in the tavern," Retief said. "Whereas the words of kings . . ."

"Very well, I concede the point." The Aga Kaga waved a hand at the serving maids. "Depart, my dears. Attend me later. You too, Ralph. These are mere diplomats: men of words, not deeds."

The bearded man glared and departed. The girls hurried after him.

"Now," the Aga Kaga said. "Let's drop the wisdom of the ages and get down to the issues. Not that I don't admire your repertoire of platitudes. How do you remember them all?"

"Diplomats and other liars require good memories," Retief said. "But, as you point out, small wisdom to small minds. I'm here to effect a settlement of certain differences between yourself and the planetary authorities. I have here a Note, which I'm conveying on behalf of the Sector Under-Secretary. With your permission, I'll read it."

"Go ahead." The Aga Kaga kicked a couple of cushions onto the floor, eased a bottle from under the couch, and reached for glasses.

"The Under-Secretary for Sector Affairs presents his

compliments to his Excellency the Aga Kaga of the Aga Kaga,
Primary Potentate, Hereditary Sheik, Emir of the—"

"Yes, yes; skip the titles."

Retief flipped over two pages.

" . . . and with reference to the recent relocation of
persons under the jurisdiction of his Excellency, has the
honor to point out that the territories now under settlement comprise a portion of that area, designated as Sub-
sector Alpha, which, under terms of the Agreement entered
into by his Excellency's predecessor, and as referenced in
Sector Ministry's Notes numbers G-175846573957-b and
X-7584-736 c-1, with particular pertinence to that body
designated in the Revised Galactic Catalogue, tenth edi-
tion, as amended, Volume Nine, reel 43, as 54 Cygni Alpha,
otherwise referred to hereinafter as Flamme—"

"Come to the point," the Aga Kaga cut in. "You're here
to lodge a complaint that I'm invading territories to which
someone else lays claim, is that it?" He smiled broadly,
offered dope-sticks, and lit one. "Well, I've been expecting a call. After all, it's what you gentlemen are paid for.
Cheers."

"Your Excellency has a lucid way of putting things,"
Retief said.

"Call me Stanley," the Aga Kaga said. "The other routine is just to please some of the old fools—I mean the
more conservative members of my government. They're still
gnawing their beards and kicking themselves because their
ancestors dropped science in favor of alchemy and got
themselves stranded in a cultural dead-end. This charade
is supposed to prove they were right all along. However,
I've no time to waste in neurotic compensations. I have
places to go and deeds to accomplish."

"At first glance," Retief said, "it looks as though the
places are already occupied and the deeds are illegal."

The Aga Kaga guffawed. "For a diplomat, you speak
plainly, Retief. Have another drink." He poured, eyeing
Georges. "What of M. Duror? How does he feel about it?"

Georges took a thoughtful swallow of whiskey. "Not bad,"
he said. "But not quite good enough to cover the odor of
goats."

The Aga Kaga snorted. "I thought the goats were

overdoing it a bit myself," he said. "Still, the greybeards insisted. And I need their support."

"Also," Georges said distinctly, "I think you're soft. You lie around letting women wait on you, while your betters are out doing an honest day's work."

The Aga Kaga looked startled. "Soft? I can tie a knot in an iron bar as thick as your thumb." He popped a grape into his mouth. "As for the rest, your pious views as to the virtues of hard labor are as childish as my advisors' faith in the advantages of primitive plumbing. As for myself, I am a realist. If two monkeys want the same banana, in the end one will have it, and the other will cry morality. The days of my years are numbered, praise be to God. While they last, I hope to eat well, hunt well, fight well, and take my share of pleasure. I leave to others the arid satisfactions of self-denial and other perversions."

"You admit you're here to grab our land then," Georges said. "That's the damndest piece of bare-faced aggression—"

"Ah, ah." The Aga Kaga held up a hand: "watch your vocabulary, my dear sir. I'm sure that 'justifiable yearnings for territorial self-realization' would be more appropriate to the situation. Or possibly 'legitimate aspirations for self-determination of formerly exploited peoples' might fit the case. Aggression is, by definition, an activity carried on only by those who have inherited the mantle of 'Colonial Imperialism.'"

"Imperialism! Why, you Aga Kagans have been the most notorious planet-grabbers in Sector history, you—you—"

"Call me Stanley." The Aga Kaga munched a grape. "I merely face the realities of popular folk lore. Let's be pragmatic; it's a matter of historical association. Some people can grab land and pass it off lightly as a moral duty; others are dubbed imperialist merely for holding onto their own. Unfair, you say. But that's life, my friends. And I shall continue to take every advantage of it."

"We'll fight you!" Georges bellowed. He took another gulp of whiskey and slammed the glass down. "You won't take this world without a struggle—"

"Another?" the Aga Kaga said, offering the bottle. Georges glowered as his glass was filled. The Aga Kaga held the glass up to the light. "Excellent color, don't you agree?" He turned his eyes on Georges.

"It's pointless to resist," he said. "We have you outgunned and outmanned. Your small nation has no chance against us. But we're prepared to be generous. You may continue to occupy such areas as we do not immediately require until such time as you're able to make other arrangements."

"And by the time we've got a crop growing out of what was bare rock, you'll be ready to move in," the Boyar Chef d'Regime snapped. "But you'll find we aren't alone!"

"Quite alone," the Aga Kaga said. He nodded sagely. "Yes, one need but read the lesson of history. The Corps Diplomatique Terrestrienne will make expostulatory noises, but it will accept the *fait accompli*. You, my dear sir, are but a very small nibble. We won't make the mistake of excessive greed; we shall inch our way to empire—and those who stand in our way shall be dubbed warmongers."

"I see you're quite a student of history, Stanley," Retief said. "I wonder if you recall the eventual fate of most of the world-be empire nibblers of the past?"

"Ah, but they grew incautious; they went too far, too fast."

"The confounded impudence," Georges rasped. "Tells us to our face what he has in mind . . ."

"An ancient and honorable custom, from the time of *Mein Kampf* and the *Communist Manifesto* through the *Porcelain Wall* of Leung. Such declarations have a legendary quality; it's traditional that they're never taken at face value."

"But always," Retief said, "there was a critical point at which the man on horseback could have been pulled from the saddle—"

"COULD have been," the Aga Kaga chuckled. He finished the grapes and began peeling an orange. "But they never were. Hitler could have been stopped by the Czech Air Force in 1938; Stalin was at the mercy of the primitive atomics of the West in 1946; Leung was grossly overextended at Rangoon. But the onus of that historic role could not be overcome. It has been the fate of your spiritual forebears to carve civilizations from the wilderness, and then, amid tearing of garments and the heaping of ashes of self-accusation on your own confused heads, to withdraw, leaving the spoils for local political opportunists and mob leaders, clothed in the mystical virtue of native birth. Have a banana."

"You're stretching the analogy a little too far," Retief said. "You're banking on the inaction of the Corps. You could be wrong."

"I shall know when to stop," the Aga Kaga said.

"Tell me, Stanley," Retief said, rising. "Are we quite private here?"

"Yes, perfectly so. None would dare to intrude in my council." He cocked an eyebrow at Retief. "You have a proposal to make in confidence? But what of our dear friend Georges? One would not like to see him disillusioned . . ."

"Don't worry about Georges. He's a realist, like you. He's prepared to deal in facts. Hard facts, in this case."

The Aga Kaga nodded thoughtfully. "What are you getting at?"

"You're basing your plan of action on the certainty that the Corps will sit by, wringing its hands, while you embark on a career of interplanetary piracy—"

"Isn't it the custom?" the Aga Kaga smiled complacently.

"I have news for you, Stanley. In this instance, neck-wringing seems more in order than hand-wringing . . ."

The Aga Kaga frowned. "Your manner—"

"Never mind our manners!" Georges blurted, standing. "We don't need any lessons from goat-herding land-thieves!"

The Aga Kaga's face darkened. "You dare to speak thus to me, pig of a muck-grubber—"

With a muffled curse Georges launched himself at the potentate. The giant rolled aside, grunted as the Boyar's fist thumped in his short ribs, then chopped down on Georges' neck. The Chef d'Regime slid off onto the floor as the Aga Kaga bounded to his feet, sending fruit and silken cushions flying.

"I see it now!" he hissed. "An assassination attempt!" He stretched his arms, thick as tree-roots—a grizzly in satin robes. "Your heads will ring together like gongs before I have done with you . . . !" He lunged for Retief. Retief came to his feet, feinted with his left, and planted a short right against the Aga Kaga's jaw with a solid smack. The potentate stumbled, grabbed; Retief slipped aside. The Aga Kaga whirled to face Retief.

"A slippery diplomat, by all the houris in Paradise!" he grated, breathing hard. "But a fool. True to your medieval code of chivalry, you attacked singly, a blunder I would never have made. And you shall die for your idiocy!" He opened his mouth to bellow—

"You sure look foolish, with your fancy hair-do down in your eyes," Retief said. "The servants will get a big laugh out of that—"

With a choked yell, the Aga Kaga dived for Retief, missed as he leaped aside. The two went to the mat together, rolled, sending a stool skittering. Grunts and curses were heard as the two big men strained, muscles popping. Retief groped for a scissors hold; the Aga Kaga seized his foot, bit hard. Retief bent nearly double, braced himself, and slammed the potentate against the rug. Dust flew. Then the two were on their feet, circling.

"Many times have I longed to broil a diplomat over a slow fire," the Aga Kaga snarled. "Tonight will see it come to pass . . ."

"I've seen it done often at staff meetings," said Retief. "It seems to have no permanent effect—"

The Aga Kaga reached for Retief, who feinted left, hammered a right to the chin. The Aga Kaga tottered. Retief measured him, brought up a haymaker. The potentate slammed to the rug—out cold.

Georges rolled over, sat up. "Let me at the son of a—" he muttered.

"Take over, Georges," Retief said, panting. "Since he's in a mood to negotiate now, we may as well get something accomplished."

Georges eyed the fallen ruler, who stirred, groaned lugubriously. "I hope you know what you're doing. But I'm with you in any case." Georges straddled the prone body, plucked a curved knife from the low table, prodded the Aga Kaga's Adam's apple. He groaned again and opened his eyes.

"Make one little peep and your wind-bag will spring a leak," Georges said. "Very few historical figures have accomplished anything important after their throats were cut."

"Stanley won't yell," Retief said. "We're not the only ones who're guilty of cultural idiocy. He'd lose face something awful if he let his followers see him like this." Retief settled himself on a tufted ottoman. "Right, Stanley?"

The Aga Kaga snarled.

Retief selected a grape, ate it thoughtfully. "These aren't bad, Georges. You might consider taking on a few Aga Kagan vine-growers—purely on a yearly contract basis, of course."

The Aga Kaga groaned, rolling his eyes.

"Well, I believe we're ready to get down to diplomatic proceedings now," Retief said. "Nothing like dealing in an atmosphere of realistic good-fellowship. First, of course, there's the matter of the presence of aliens lacking visas." He opened his briefcase, withdrew a heavy sheet of parchment. "I have the document here, drawn up and ready for signature. It provides for the prompt deportation of such persons, by Corps Transport, all expenses to be borne by the Aga Kagan government. That's agreeable, I think?" Retief looked expectantly at the purple face of the prone potentate. The Aga Kaga grunted a strangled grunt.

"Speak up, Stanley," Retief said. "Give him plenty of air, Georges."

"Shall I let some in through the side?"

"Not yet. I'm sure Stanley wants to be agreeable."

The Aga Kaga snarled.

"Maybe just a little then, Georges," Retief said judiciously. Georges jabbed the knife in far enough to draw a bead of blood. The Aga Kaga grunted.

"Agreed!" he snorted. "By the beard of the Prophet, when I get my hands on you . . ."

"Second item: certain fields, fishing grounds, et cetera, have suffered damage due to the presence of the aforementioned illegal immigrants. Full compensation will be made by the Aga Kagan government. Agreed?"

The Aga Kaga drew a breath, tensed himself; Georges jabbed with the knife point. His prisoner relaxed with a groan. "Agreed!" he grated. "A vile tactic! You enter my tent under the guise of guests, protected by diplomatic immunity—"

"I had the impression we were herded in here at sword point," said Retief. "Shall we go on? Now, there's the little matter of restitution for violation of sovereignty, reparations for mental anguish, payment for damaged fences, roads, drainage canals, communications, et cetera, et cetera. Shall I read them all?"

"Wait until the news of this outrage is spread abroad—"

"They'd never believe it. History would prove it impossible. And on mature consideration, I'm sure you won't want it noised about that you entertained visiting dignitaries flat on your back."

"What about the pollution of the atmosphere by goats?" Georges put in. "And don't overlook the muddying of streams, the destruction of valuable timber for camp fires, and—"

"I've covered all that sort of thing under a miscellaneous heading," Retief said. "We can fill it in at leisure when we get back."

"Bandits!" the Aga Kaga hissed. "Thieves! Dogs of unreliable imperialists!"

"It's disillusioning, I know," Retief said. "Still, of such little surprises is history made. Sign here." He held the parchment out and offered a pen. "A nice clear signature, please. We wouldn't want any quibbling about the legality of the treaty, after conducting the negotiation with such scrupulous regard for the niceties."

"Niceties! Never in history has such an abomination been perpetrated!"

"Oh, treaties are always worked out this way, when it comes right down to it. We've just accelerated the process a little. Now, if you'll just sign like a good fellow, we'll be on our way. Georges will have his work cut out for him, planning how to use all this reparations money."

The Aga Kaga gnashed his teeth; Georges prodded. The Aga Kaga seized the pen and scrawled his name. Retief signed with a flourish. He tucked the treaty away in his briefcase, took out another paper.

"This is just a safe-conduct, to get us out of the door and into the car," he said. "Probably unnecessary, but it won't hurt to have it, in case you figure out some way to avoid your obligations as a host."

The Aga Kaga signed the document after another prod from Georges.

"One more paper, and I'll be into the jugular," he said.

"We're all through now," said Retief. "Stanley, we're going to have to run now. I'm going to strap up your hands and feet a trifle; it shouldn't take you more than ten minutes or so to get loose, stick a band-aid over that place on your neck, and get back in your grape-eating pose."

"My men will cut you down for the rascals you are!"

"—By that time, we'll be over the hill," Retief continued. "At full throttle, we'll be at Government House in an hour, and of course I won't waste any time transmitting the treaty to Sector HQ. And the same concern for face that keeps you from yelling for help will ensure that the details of the negotiation remain our secret."

"Treaty! That scrap of paper—"

"I confess the Corps is a little sluggish about taking action at times," Retief said, whipping a turn of silken cord around the Aga Kaga's ankles. "But once it's got signatures on a legal treaty, it's extremely stubborn about all parties' adhering to the letter. It can't afford to be otherwise, as I'm sure you'll understand." He cinched up the cord, went to work on the hands. The Aga Kaga glared at him balefully.

"To the Pit with the Corps! The ferocity of my revenge—"

"Don't talk nonsense, Stanley. There are several squadrons of Peace Enforcers cruising in the Sector just now. I'm sure you're not ready to make any historical errors by taking them on." Retief finished and stood up.

"Georges, just stuff a scarf in Stanley's mouth. I think he'd prefer to work quietly until he recovers his dignity." Retief buckled his briefcase, selected a large grape, and looked down at the Aga Kaga.

"Actually, you'll be glad you saw things our way, Stanley," he said. "You'll get all the credit for the generous settlement. Of course, it will be a striking precedent for any other negotiations that may become necessary if you get grabby on other worlds in this region. And if your advisors want to know why the sudden change of heart, just tell them you've decided to start from scratch on an unoccupied world. Mention the virtues of thrift and hard work. I'm confident you can find plenty of historical examples to support you."

"Thanks for the drink," said Georges. "Drop in on me at Government House some time and we'll crack another bottle."

"And don't feel bad about your project's going awry," said Retief. "In the words of the Prophet, 'Stolen goods are never sold at a loss.'"

"A remarkable about-face, Retief," Magnan said. "Let this be a lesson to you. A stern Note of Protest can work wonders."

"A lot depends on the method of delivery," Retief said.

"Nonsense. I knew all along the Aga Kagans were a reasonable, peace-loving people. One of the advantages of senior rank, of course, is the opportunity to see the big picture. Why, I was saying only this morning—"

The desk screen broke into life. The mottled jowls of Under-Secretary Sternwheeler appeared.

"Magnan! I've just learned of the Flamme affair. Who's responsible?"

"Why, ah . . . I suppose that I might be said—"

"This is your work, is it?"

"Well . . . Mr. Retief did play the role of messenger—"

"Don't pass the buck, Magnan!" the Under-Secretary barked. "What the devil went on out there?"

"Why, just a routine Protest Note. Everything is quite in order—"

"Bah! Your over-zealousness has cost me dear. I was feeding Flamme to the Aga Kaga to consolidate our position of moral superiority for use as a lever in a number of important negotiations. Now they've backed out. The Aga Kaga emerges from the affair wreathed in virtue. You've destroyed a very pretty finesse in power politics, Mr. Magnan! A year's work down the drain!"

"But I thought—"

"I doubt that, Mr. Magnan. I doubt that very much!" The Under-Secretary rang off.

"This is a fine turn of events," Magnan groaned. "Retief, you know very well Protest Notes are merely intended for the historical record; no one ever takes them seriously."

"You and the Aga Kaga ought to get together," said Retief. "He's a great one for citing historical parallels. He's not a bad fellow, as a matter of fact. I have an invitation from him to visit Kaga and go mud-pig hunting. He was so impressed by Corps methods that he wants to be sure we're on his side next time. Why don't you come along?"

"Mmmm. Perhaps I should cultivate him. A few high-level contacts never do any harm. On the other hand, I understand he lives in a very loose way, feasting and merry-making. Frivolous in the extreme. No wife, I understand, but hordes of light-clad women about. And in that connection, the Aga Kagans have some very curious notions as to what constitutes proper hospitality to guests."

Retief rose, pulled on the powder blue cloak and black velvet gauntlets of a Career Minister.

"Don't let it worry you," he said. "You'll have a great time. And as the Aga Kaga would say, 'Ugliness is the best safeguard of virginity.'"

> . . . Supplementing broad knowledge of
> affairs with such shrewd gambits as identifica-
> tion with significant local groups, and the
> consequent deft manipulating of inter-group
> rivalries, Corps officials on the scene played
> decisive roles in the preservation of domestic
> tranquility on many a far-flung world. At Fust,
> Ambassador Magnan forged to the van in the
> exercise of the technique . . .
>
> —Vol. VII, reel 43. 487 A. E. (AD 2948)

AIDE MEMOIRE

Across the table from Retief, Ambassador Magnan, rustling
a stiff sheet of parchment, looked grave.

"This aide memoire," he said, "was just handed to me
by the Cultural Attaché. It's the third on the subject this
week. It refers to the matter of sponsorship of Youth
groups."

"Some youths," Retief said. "Average age: seventy-five."

"The Fustians are a long-lived people," Magnan snapped.
"These matters are relative. At seventy-five, a male Fustian is at a trying age."

"That's right; he'll try anything in the hope it will maim
somebody."

"Precisely the problem," Magnan replied. "But the Youth
Movement is the important news in today's political situation here on Fust, and sponsorship of Youth groups is a
shrewd stroke on the part of the Terrestrial Embassy. At
my suggestion, well nigh every member of the mission has
leaped at the opportunity to score a few p— that is, to
cement relations with this emergent power group: the

leaders of the future. You, Retief, as Counselor, are the outstanding exception."

"I'm not convinced these hoodlums need my help in organizing their rumbles," Retief said. "Now, if you have a proposal for a pest control group—"

"To the Fustians, this is no jesting matter," Magnan cut in. "This group," he glanced at the paper, "known as the Sexual, Cultural and Athletic Recreational Society, or SCARS, for short, has been awaiting sponsorship for a matter of weeks now."

"Meaning they want someone to buy them a clubhouse, uniforms, equipment, and anything else they need to plot against the peace in style," Retief said.

"If we don't act promptly, the Groaci embassy may well anticipate us. They're very active here."

"That's an idea," said Retief, "let 'em. After a while they'll be broke—instead of us."

"Nonsense. The group requires a sponsor. I can't actually order you to step forward. However . . ." Magnan let the sentence hang in the air. Retief raised one eyebrow.

"For a minute there," he said, "I thought you were going to make a positive statement."

Magnan leaned back, lacing his fingers over his stomach. "I don't think you'll find a diplomat of my experience doing anything so naïve," he said.

"I like the adult Fustians," said Retief. "Too bad they have to lug half a ton of horn around on their backs. I wonder if surgery—"

"Great heavens, Retief," Magnan spluttered. "I'm amazed that even you would bring up a matter of such delicacy. A race's unfortunate physical characteristics are hardly a fit matter for Terrestrial curiosity."

"Well, I've only been here a month. But it's been my experience, Mr. Ambassador, that few people are above improving on nature; otherwise you, for example, would be tripping over your beard."

Magnan shuddered. "Please—never mention the idea to a Fustian."

Retief stood. "My own program for the day includes going over to the dockyards. There are some features of this new passenger liner the Fustians are putting together that I want to look into. With your permission, Mr. Ambassador . . . ?"

Magnan snorted. "Your preoccupation with the trivial disturbs me, Retief. More interest in substantive matters—such as working with youth groups—would create a far better impression."

"Before getting too involved with these groups, it might be a good idea to find out a little more about them," Retief said. "Who organizes them? There are three strong political parties here on Fust; what's the alignment of this SCARS organization?"

"You forget, these are merely teen-agers, so to speak," Magnan said. "Politics mean nothing to them . . . yet."

"Then there are the Groaci. Why their passionate interest in a two-horse world like Fust? Normally they're concerned with nothing but business; and what has Fust got that they could use?

"You may rule out the commercial aspect in this instance," said Magnan. "Fust possesses a vigorous steel-age manufacturing economy. The Groaci are barely ahead of them."

"Barely," said Retief. "Just over the line into crude atomics . . . like fission bombs."

Magnan, shaking his head, turned back to his papers. "What market exists for such devices on a world at peace?" he said. "I suggest you address your attention to the less spectacular but more rewarding work of insinuating yourself into the social patterns of the local youth."

"I've considered the matter," Retief said, "and before I meet any of the local youth socially I want to get myself a good blackjack."

Retief left the sprawling bungalow-type building that housed the chancery of the Terrestrial Embassy, hailed one of the ponderous slow-moving Fustian flat-cars, and leaned back against the wooden guard rail as the heavy vehicle trundled through the city toward the looming gantries of the shipyards. It was a cool morning with a light breeze carrying the fish odor of Fustian dwellings across the broad cobbled avenue. A few mature Fustians lumbered heavily along in the shade of the low buildings, audibly wheezing under the burden of their immense carapaces. Among them, shell-less youths trotted briskly on scaly stub legs. The driver of the flat-car, a labor-caste Fustian with his guild colors emblazoned on his back, heaved at the tiller, swung the unwieldy conveyance through the shipyard gates, and creaked to a halt.

"Thus I come to the shipyard with frightful speed," he said in Fustian. "Well I know the way of the naked-backs, who move always in haste."

Retief, climbing down, handed him a coin. "You should take up professional racing," he said. "Dare-devil."

Retief crossed the littered yard and tapped at the door of a rambling shed. Boards creaked inside, then the door swung back. A gnarled ancient with tarnished facial scales and a weathered carapace peered out at Retief.

"Long may you sleep," Retief said. "I'd like to take a look around, if you don't mind. I understand you're laying the bed-plate for your new liner today."

"May you dream of the deeps," the old fellow mumbled. He waved a stumpy arm toward a group of shell-less Fustians standing by a massive hoist. "The youths know more of bed-plates than do I, who but tend the place of papers."

"I know how you feel, old-timer," Retief said. "That sounds like the story of my life. Among your papers do you have a set of plans for the vessel? I understand it's to be a passenger liner."

The oldster nodded. He shuffled in a drawing file, rummaged, pulled out a sheaf of curled prints, and spread them on the table. Retief stood silently, running a finger over the uppermost drawing, tracing lines . . .

"What does the naked-back here?" a deep voice barked behind Retief. He turned. A heavy-faced Fustian youth, wrapped in a mantle, stood at the open door. Beady yellow eyes set among fine scales bored into Retief.

"I came to take a look at your new liner," said Retief.

"We need no prying foreigners here," the youth snapped. His eye fell on the drawing; he hissed in anger.

"Doddering hulk!" he snapped at the ancient, moving toward them. "May you toss in nightmares! Put aside the plans!"

"My mistake," Retief said. "I didn't know this was a secret project."

The youth hesitated. "It is not a secret," he muttered. "Why should it be a secret?"

"You tell me."

The youth worked his jaws and rocked his head from side to side in the Fustian gesture of uncertainty. "There is nothing to conceal," he said. "We merely construct a passenger liner."

"Then you don't mind if I look over the drawings," Retief said. "Who knows, maybe some day I'll want to reserve a suite for the trip out."

The youth turned and disappeared. Retief grinned at the oldster. "Went for his big brother, I guess," he said. "I have a feeling I won't get to study these in peace here. Mind if I copy them?"

"Willingly, light-footed one," said the old Fustian. "And mine is the shame for the discourtesy of youth."

Retief took out a tiny camera, flipped a copying lens in place, leafed through the drawings, clicking the shutter.

"A plague on these youths," said the oldster. "They grow more virulent day by day."

"Why don't you elders clamp down?"

"Agile are they and we are slow of foot. And this unrest is new; unknown in my youth was such insolence."

"The police—"

"Bah," the ancient rumbled. "None have we worthy of the name, nor have we needed them before now."

"What's behind it?"

"They have found leaders. The spiv, Slock, is one. And I fear they plot mischief." He pointed to the window. "They come, and a soft-one with them."

Retief, pocketing the camera, glanced out the window. A pale-featured Groacian with an ornately decorated crest stood with the youths, who eyed the hut, then started toward it.

"That's the military attaché of the Groaci Embassy," Retief said. "I wonder what he and the boys are cooking up together?"

"Naught that augers well for the dignity of Fust," the

oldster rumbled. "Flee, agile one, while I engage their attentions."

"I was just leaving," Retief said. "Which way out?"

"The rear door," the Fustian gestured with a stubby member. "Rest well, stranger on these shores," he said, moving to the entrance.

"Same to you, pop," said Retief. "And thanks."

He eased through the narrow back entrance, waited until voices were raised at the front of the shed, then strolled off toward the gate.

It was an hour along in the second dark of the third cycle when Retief left the Embassy technical library and crossed the corridor to his office. He flipped on a light and found a note tucked under a paperweight:

"Retief: I shall expect your attendance at the IAS dinner at first dark of the fourth cycle. There will be a brief but, I hope, impressive sponsorship ceremony for the SCARS group, with full press coverage, arrangements for which I have managed to complete in spite of your intransigence."

Retief snorted and glanced at his watch: less than three hours. Just time to creep home by flat-car, dress in ceremonial uniform, and creep back.

Outside he flagged a lumbering bus, stationed himself in a corner of it, and watched the yellow sun, Beta, rise above the low skyline. The nearby sea was at high tide now, under the pull of the major sun and the three moons, and the stiff breeze carried a mist of salt spray. Retief turned up his collar against the dampness. In half an hour he would be perspiring under the vertical rays of a first-noon sun, but the thought failed to keep the chill off.

Two youths clambered up on the moving platform and walked purposefully toward Retief. He moved off the rail, watching them, his weight balanced.

"That's close enough, kids," he said. "Plenty of room on this scow; no need to crowd up."

"There are certain films," the lead Fustian muttered. His voice was unusually deep for a Youth. He was wrapped in a heavy cloak and moved awkwardly. His adolescence was nearly at an end, Retief guessed.

"I told you once," Retief said. "Don't crowd me."

The two stepped close, their slit mouths snapping in anger. Retief put out a foot, hooked it behind the scaly leg of the over-age juvenile, and threw his weight against the cloaked chest. The clumsy Fustian tottered, then fell heavily. Retief was past him and off the flat-car before the other youth had completed his vain lunge toward the spot Retief had occupied. The Terrestrial waved cheerfully at the pair, hopped aboard another vehicle, and watched his would-be assailants lumber down off their car and move heavily off, their tiny heads twisted to follow his retreating figure.

So they wanted the film? Retief reflected, thumbing a cigar alight. They were a little late. He had already filed it in the Embassy vault, after running a copy for the reference files. And a comparison of the drawings with those of the obsolete Mark XXXV battle cruiser used two hundred years earlier by the Concordiat Naval Arm showed them to be almost identical—gun emplacements and all. And the term obsolete was a relative one. A ship which had been out-moded in the armories of the Galactic Powers could still be king of the walk in the Eastern Arm.

But how had these two known of the film? There had been no one present but himself and the old-timer—and Retief was willing to bet the elderly Fustian hadn't told them anything.

At least not willingly . . .

Retief frowned, dropped the cigar over the side, waited until the flat-car negotiated a mud-wallow, then swung down and headed for the shipyard.

The door, hinges torn loose, had been propped loosely back in position. Retief looked around at the battered interior of the shed. The old fellow had put up a struggle.

There were deep drag-marks in the dust behind the building. Retief followed them across the yard. They disappeared under the steel door of a warehouse.

Retief glanced around. Now, at the mid-hour of the fourth cycle, the workmen were heaped along the edge of the refreshment pond, deep in their siesta. Taking a multi-bladed tool from his pocket, Retief tried various fittings in the lock; it snicked open and he eased the door aside far enough to enter.

Heaped bales loomed before him. Snapping on the tiny lamp in the handle of the combination tool, Retief looked over the pile. One stack seemed out of alignment—and the dust had been scraped from the floor before it. He pocketed the light, climbed up on the bales, and looked over into a ring of bundles. The aged Fustian lay inside the ring, a heavy sack tied over his head. Retief dropped down beside him, sawed at the tough twine, and pulled the sack free.

"It's me, old fellow," he said, "the nosy stranger. Sorry I got you into this."

The oldster threshed his gnarled legs, rocked slightly, then fell back. "A curse on the cradle that rocked their infant slumbers," he rumbled. "But place me back on my feet and I hunt down the youth Slock though he flee to the bottom-most muck of the Sea of Torments."

"How am I going to get you out of here? Maybe I'd better get some help."

"Nay. The perfidious youths abound here," said the old Fustian. "It would be your life."

"I doubt if they'd go that far."

"Would they not?" The Fustian stretched his neck. "Cast your light here. But for the toughness of my hide . . ."

Retief put the beam of the light on the leathery neck. A great smear of thick purplish blood welled from a ragged cut. The oldster chuckled: a sound like a seal coughing.

"Traitor they called me. For long they sawed at me—in vain. Then they trussed me and dumped me here. They think to return with weapons to complete the task."

"Weapons? I thought it was illegal—"

"Their evil genius, the Soft One," the Fustian said, "he would provide fuel to the Fire-Devil."

"The Groaci again," Retief said. "I wonder what their angle is."

"And I must confess: I told them of you, ere I knew their full intentions. Much can I tell you of their doings. But first, I pray: the block and tackle."

Retief found the hoist where the Fustian directed him,

maneuvered it into position, hooked onto the edge of the carapace, and hauled away. The immense Fustian rose slowly, teetered . . . then flopped on his chest. Slowly he got to his feet.

"My name is Whonk, fleet one," he said. "My cows are yours."

"Thanks. I'm Retief. I'd like to meet the girls some time. But right now, let's get out of here."

Whonk leaned his bulk against the ponderous stacks of baled kelp, bull-dozing them aside. "Slow am I to anger," he said, "but implacable in my wrath. Slock, beware . . ."

"Hold it," said Retief suddenly. He sniffed. "What's that odor?" He flashed the light around, playing it over a dry stain on the floor. He knelt and sniffed at the spot.

"What kind of cargo was stacked here, Whonk? And where is it now?"

Whonk considered. "There were drums," he said. "Four of them, quite small, painted an evil green—the property of the Soft Ones, the Groaci. They lay here a day and a night. At full dark of the first period they came with stevedores and loaded them aboard the barge *Moss Rock*."

"The VIP boat. Who's scheduled to use it?"

"I know not. But what matters this? Let us discuss cargo movements after I have settled a score with certain youths."

"We'd better follow this up first, Whonk. There's only one substance I know of that's transported in drums and smells like that blot on the floor. That's titanite: the hottest explosive this side of a uranium pile."

Beta was setting as Retief, with Whonk puffing at his heels, came up to the sentry box beside the gangway leading to the plush interior of the Official Barge *Moss Rock*.

"A sign of the times," Whonk said, glancing inside the empty shelter. "A guard should stand here, but I see him not. Doubtless he crept away to sleep."

"Let's go aboard, and take a look around."

They entered the ship. Soft lights glowed in utter silence. A rough box stood on the floor, rollers and pry-bars beside it—a discordant note in the muted luxury of the setting. Whonk rummaged through its contents.

"Curious," he said. "What means this?" He held up a

stained Fustian cloak of orange and green, a metal bracelet, and a stack of papers.

"Orange and green," Retief muttered. "Whose colors are those?"

"I know not . . ." Whonk glanced at the arm-band. "But this is lettered." He passed the metal band to Retief.

"SCARS," Retief read. He looked at Whonk. "It seems to met I've heard the name before," he murmured. "Let's get back to the Embassy—fast."

Back on the ramp Retief heard a sound . . . and turned in time to duck the charge of a hulking Fustian youth who thundered past him, and fetched up against the broad chest of Whonk, who locked him in a warm embrace.

"Nice catch, Whonk. Where'd he sneak out of?"

"The lout hid there by the storage bin," Whonk rumbled. The captive youth thumped his fists and toes futilely against the oldster's carapace.

"Hang on to him," Retief said. "He looks like the biting kind."

"No fear. Clumsy I am, yet I am not without strength."

"Ask him where the titanite is tucked away."

"Speak, witless grub," Whonk growled, "lest I tweak you in two."

The youth gurgled.

"Better let up before you make a mess of him," Retief said.

Whonk lifted the youth clear of the floor, then flung him down with a thump that made the ground quiver. The younger Fustian glared up at the elder, his mouth snapping.

"This one was among those who trussed me and hid me away for the killing," said Whonk. "In his repentance he will tell all to his elder."

"He's the same one that tried to strike up an acquaintance with me on the bus," Retief said. "He gets around."

The youth, scrambling to his hands and knees, scuttled for freedom. Retief planted a foot on the dragging cloak; it ripped free. He stared at the bare back of the Fustian.

"By the Great Egg!" Whonk exclaimed, tripping the captive as he tried to rise. "This is no youth! His carapace has been taken from him."

Retief looked at the scarred back. "I thought he looked a little old. But I thought—"

"This is not possible," Whonk said wonderingly. "The great nerve trunks are deeply involved; not even the cleverest surgeon could excise the carapace and leave the patient living."

"It looks like somebody did the trick. But let's take this boy with us and get out of here. His folks may come home."

"Too late," said Whonk. Retief turned. Three youths came from behind the sheds.

"Well," Retief said. "It looks like the SCARS are out in force tonight. Where's your pal?" he said to the advancing trio, "the sticky little bird with the eye-stalks? Back at his Embassy, leaving you suckers holding the bag, I'll bet."

"Shelter behind me, Retief," said Whonk.

"Go get 'em, old-timer." Retief stooped and picked up one of the pry-bars. "I'll jump around and distract them."

Whonk let out a whistling roar and charged for the immature Fustians. They fanned out . . . one tripped, sprawling on his face. Retief, whirling the metal bar that he had thrust between the Fustian's legs, slammed it against the skull of another, who shook his head, then turned on Retief . . . and bounced off the steel hull of the *Moss Rock* as Whonk took him in full charge.

Retief used the bar on another head; his third blow laid the Fustian on the pavement, oozing purple. The other two club members departed hastily, dented but still mobile.

Retief leaned on his club, breathing hard. "Tough heads those kids have got. I'm tempted to chase those two lads down, but I've got another errand to run. I don't know who the Groaci intended to blast, but I have a suspicion somebody of importance was scheduled for a boatride in the next few hours, and three drums of titanite is enough to vaporize this tub and everyone aboard her."

"The plot is foiled," said Whonk. "But what reason did they have?"

"The Groaci are behind it. I have an idea the SCARS didn't know about this gambit."

"Which of these is the leader?" asked Whonk. He prodded a fallen youth. "Arise, dreaming one."

"Never mind him, Whonk. We'll tie these two up and leave them here. I know where to find the boss."

A stolid-looking crowd filled the low-ceilinged banquet hall. Retief scanned the tables for the pale blobs of Terrestrial faces, dwarfed by the giant armored bodies of the Fustians. Across the room Magnan fluttered a hand. Retief headed toward him. A low-pitched vibration filled the air, the rumble of sub-sonic Fustian music.

Retief slid into his place beside Magnan. "Sorry to be late, Mr. Ambassador."

"I'm honored that you chose to appear at all," Magnan said coldly. He turned back to the Fustian on his left.

"Ah, yes, Mr. Minister," he said. "Charming, most charming. So joyous."

The Fustian looked at him, beady-eyed. "It is the Lament of Hatching," he said, "our National Dirge."

"Oh," said Magnan. "How interesting. Such a pleasing balance of instruments."

"It is a droon solo," said the Fustian, eyeing the Terrestrial Ambassador suspiciously.

"Why don't you just admit you can't hear it," Retief whispered loudly. "And if I may interrupt a moment—"

Magnan cleared his throat. "Now that our Mr. Retief has arrived, perhaps we could rush right along to the sponsorship ceremonies . . ."

"This group," said Retief, leaning across Magnan to speak to the Fustian, "the SCARS . . . how much do you know about them, Mr. Minister?"

"Nothing at all," the huge Fustian elder rumbled. "For my taste, all youths should be kept penned with the livestock until they grow a carapace to tame their irresponsibility."

"We mustn't lose sight of the importance of channeling youthful energies," said Magnan.

"Labor gangs," said the minister. "In my youth we were indentured to the dredge-masters. I myself drew a muck-sledge."

"But in these modern times," put in Retief, "surely it's incumbent on us to make happy these golden hours."

The minister snorted. "Last week I had a golden

hour: they set upon me and pelted me with over-ripe dung-fruit."

"But this was merely a manifestation of normal youthful frustrations," cried Magnan. "Their essential tenderness—"

"You'd not find a tender spot on that lout yonder," the minister said, pointing with a fork at a newly arrived youth, "if you drilled boreholes and blasted."

"Why, that's our guest of honor," said Magnan, "a fine young fellow, Slop I believe his name is—"

"Slock," said Retief. "Nine feet of armor-plated orneriness. And—"

Magnan rose, tapping on his glass. The Fustians winced at the, to them, supersonic vibrations, and looked at each other muttering. Magnan tapped louder. The minister drew in his head, his eyes closed. Some of the Fustians rose and tottered for the doors; the noise level rose. Magnan redoubled his efforts. The glass broke with a clatter, and green wine gushed on the tablecloth.

"What in the name of the Great Egg," the minister muttered. He blinked, breathing deeply.

"Oh, forgive me," Magnan blurted, dabbing at the wine.

"Too bad the glass gave out," Retief said. "In another minute you'd have cleared the hall—and then maybe I could have gotten a word in. You see, Mr. Minister," he said, turning to the Fustian, "there is a matter you should know about . . ."

"Your attention, please," Magnan said, rising. "I see that our fine young guest of honor has arrived, and I hope that the remainder of his committee will be along in a moment. It is my pleasure to announce that our Mr. Retief has had the good fortune to win out in the keen bidding for the pleasure of sponsoring this lovely group, and—"

Retief tugged at Magnan's sleeve. "Don't introduce me yet," he said. "I want to appear suddenly—more dramatic, you know."

"Well," Magnan murmured, glancing down at Retief, "I'm gratified to see you entering into the spirit of the event at last." He turned his attention back to the assembled guests. "If our honored guest will join me on the rostrum . . ." he said. "The gentlemen of the press may want to catch a few shots of the presentation."

Magnan moved from his place, made his way forward, stepped up on the low platform at the center of the wide room, took his place beside the robed Fustian youth, and beamed at the cameras.

"How gratifying it is to take this opportunity to express once more the great pleasure we have in sponsoring SCARS," Magnan said, talking slowly for the benefit of the scribbling reporters. "We'd like to think that in our modest way we're to be a part of all that the SCARS achieve during the years ahead . . ."

Magnan paused as a huge Fustian elder heaved his bulk up the two low steps to the rostrum and approached the guest of honor. He watched as the newcomer paused behind Slock, who was busy returning the stares of the spectators and did not notice the new arrival.

Retief pushed through the crowd and stepped up to face the Fustian youth. Slock stared at him, drawing back.

"You know me, Slock," Retief said loudly. "An old fellow named Whonk told you about me, just before you tried to saw off his head, remember? It was when I came out to take a look at that battle cruiser you're building."

With a bellow Slock reached for Retief—and choked off in mid-cry as Whonk pinioned him from behind, lifting the youth clear of the floor.

"Glad you reporters happened along," Retief said to the gaping newsmen. "Slock here had a deal with a sharp operator from the Groaci Embassy. The Groaci were to supply the necessary hardware and Slock, as foreman at the shipyards, was to see that everything was properly installed. The next step, I assume, would have been a local take-over, followed by a little interplanetary war on Flamenco or one of the other nearby worlds . . . for which the Groaci would be glad to supply plenty of ammo."

Magnan found his tongue. "Are you mad, Retief?" he screeched. "This group was vouched for by the Ministry of Youth."

"That Ministry's overdue for a purge," Retief said. He turned back to Slock. "I wonder if you were in on the little diversion that was planned for today. When the *Moss Rock* blew, a variety of clues were to be planted where they'd be easy to find . . . with SCARS written all over them. The Groaci would thus have neatly laid the whole affair squarely at the door of the Terrestrial Embassy . . . whose sponsorship of the SCARS had received plenty of publicity."

"The *Moss Rock*?" Magnan said. "But that was—Retief! This is idiotic. The SCARS themselves were scheduled to go on a cruise tomorrow."

Slock roared suddenly, twisting violently. Whonk teetered, his grip loosened . . . and Slock pulled free and was off the platform, butting his way through the milling oldsters on the dining room floor. Magnan watched, openmouthed.

"The Groaci were playing a double game, as usual," Retief said. "They intended to dispose of these lads after they got things under way."

"Well, don't stand there," Magnan yelped. "Do something! If Slop is the ringleader of a delinquent gang—" He moved to give chase himself.

Retief grabbed his arm. "Don't jump down there," he called above the babble of talk. "You'd have as much chance of getting through there as a jack rabbit through a threshing contest. Where's a phone?"

Ten minutes later the crowd had thinned slightly. "We can get through now," Whonk called. "This way." He lowered himself to the floor and bulled through to the exit. Flash bulbs popped. Retief and Magnan followed in Whonk's wake.

In the lounge Retief grabbed the phone, waited for the operator, and gave a code letter. No reply. He tried another.

"No good," he said after a full minute had passed. He slammed the phone back in its niche. "Let's grab a cab."

In the street the blue sun, Alpha, peered like an arc light under a low cloud layer. Flat shadows lay across the mud of the avenue. The three mounted a passing flat-car. Whonk squatted, resting the weight of his immense shell on the heavy plank flooring.

"Would that I, too, could lose this burden, as has the false youth we bludgeoned aboard the *Moss Rock*," he sighed. "Soon will I be forced into retirement; and a mere keeper of a place of papers such as I will rate no more

than a slab on the public strand, with once-daily feedings.
Even for a man of high position retirement is no pleasure.
A slab in the Park of Monuments is little better. A dismal outlook for one's next thousand years."

"You two continue on to the police station," Retief said.
"I want to play a hunch. But don't take too long. I may
be painfully right."

"What—?" Magnan started.

"As you wish, Retief," Whonk said.

The flat-car trundled past the gate to the shipyard and
Retief jumped down and headed at a run for the VIP boat.
The guard post still stood vacant. The two youths whom
he and Whonk had left trussed were gone.

"That's the trouble with a peaceful world," Retief muttered. "No police protection." Stepping down from the
lighted entry, he took up a position behind the sentry box.
Alpha rose higher, shedding a glaring white light without
heat. Retief shivered.

There was a sound in the near entrance, like two elephants
colliding. Retief looked toward the gate. His giant acquaintance, Whonk, had reappeared and was grappling with a
hardly less massive opponent. A small figure became visible
in the melee, scuttled for the gate, was headed off by the
battling titans, turned and made for the opposite side of
the shipyard. Retief waited, jumped out and gathered in the
fleeing Groacian.

"Well, Yith," he said, "how's tricks . . . ? You should
pardon the expression."

"Release me, Retief!" the pale-featured creature lisped,
his throat bladder pulsating in agitation. "The behemoths
vie for the privilege of dismembering me."

"I know how they feel. I'll see what I can do . . . for a
price."

"I appeal to you," Yith whispered hoarsely, "as a fellow
diplomat, a fellow alien, a fellow soft-back."

"Why don't you appeal to Slock, as a fellow conspirator?" Retief said. "Now keep quiet . . . and you may get out
of this alive."

The heavier of the two struggling Fustians threw the
other to the ground. The smaller Fustian lay on its back,
helpless.

"That's Whonk, still on his feet," Retief said. "I wonder who he's caught—and why."

Whonk came toward the *Moss Rock* dragging the supine Fustian. Retief thrust Yith down well out of sight behind the sentry box. "Better sit tight, Yith. Don't try to sneak off; I can outrun you. Stay here and I'll see what I can do." Stepping out, he hailed Whonk.

Puffing like a steam engine, Whonk pulled up before him. "Hail, Retief!" he panted. "You followed a hunch; I did the same. I saw something strange in this one when we passed him on the avenue. I watched, followed him here. Look! It is Slock, strapped into a dead carapace! Now many things become clear."

Retief whistled. "So the youths aren't all as young as they look. Somebody's been holding out on the rest of you Fustians."

"The soft one," Whonk said. "You laid him by the heels, Retief. I saw. Produce him now."

"Hold on a minute, Whonk. It won't do you any good to—"

Whonk winked broadly. "I must take my revenge!" he roared. "I shall test the texture of the Soft One! His pulped remains will be scoured up by the ramp-washers and mailed home in bottles."

Retief whirled at a sound, caught up with the scuttling Yith fifty feet away, and hauled him back to Whonk.

"It's up to you, Whonk," he said. "I know how important ceremonial revenge is to you Fustians."

"Mercy!" Yith hissed, his eye-stalks whipping in distress. "I claim diplomatic immunity."

"No diplomat am I," Whonk rumbled. "Let me see; suppose I start with one of those obscenely active eyes." He reached . . .

"I have an idea," Retief said brightly. "Do you suppose— just this once—you could forego the ceremonial revenge if Yith promised to arrange for a Groacian Surgical Mission to de-carapace you elders?"

"But," Whonk protested, "those eyes; what a pleasure to pluck them, one by one—"

"Yess," Yith hissed, "I swear it; our most expert surgeons . . . platoons of them, with the finest of equipment."

"I have dreamed of how it would be to sit on this one, to feel him squash beneath my bulk . . ."

"Light as a whissle feather shall you dance," Yith whispered. "Shell-less shall you spring in the joy of renewed youth . . ."

"Maybe just one eye," Whonk said. "That would leave him four . . ."

"Be a sport," said Retief.

"Well."

"It's a deal then," Retief said. "Yith, on your word as a diplomat, an alien, and a soft-back, you'll set up the mission. Groaci surgical skill is an export that will net you more than armaments. It will be a whissle feather in your cap—if you bring it off. And in return, Whonk won't sit on you. In addition, I won't prefer charges against you of interference in the internal affairs of a free world."

Behind Whonk there was a movement. Slock, wriggling free of the borrowed carapace, struggled to his feet . . . in time for Whonk to seize him, lift him high, and head for the entry to the *Moss Rock*.

"Hey," Retief called. "Where are you going?"

"I would not deny this one his reward," Whonk called. "He hoped to cruise in luxury; so be it."

"Hold on," Retief said. "That tub is loaded with titanite!"

"Stand not in my way, Retief. For this one in truth owes me a vengeance."

Retief watched as the immense Fustian bore his giant burden up the ramp and disappeared within the ship.

"I guess Whonk means business," he said to Yith, who hung in his grasp, all five eyes goggling. "And he's a little too big for me to stop, once he sets his mind on something. But maybe he's just throwing a scare into him."

Whonk reappeared, alone, and climbed down.

"What did you do with him?" Retief said.

"We had best withdraw," Whonk said. "The killing radius of the drive is fifty yards."

"You mean—"

"The controls are set for Groac. Long may he sleep."

"It was quite a bang," Retief said, "but I guess you saw it too."

"No, confound it," Magnan said. "When I remonstrated with Hulk, or Whelk—"

"Whonk."

"—the ruffian thrust me into an alley, bound in my own cloak. I'll most certainly mention the indignity in a note to the Minister." He jotted on a pad.

"How about the surgical mission?"

"A most generous offer," Magnan said. "Frankly, I was astonished. I think perhaps we've judged the Groaci too harshly."

"I hear the Ministry of Youth has had a rough morning of it," Retief said. "And a lot of rumors are flying to the effect that Youth Groups are on the way out."

Magnan cleared this throat and shuffled papers. "I—ah—have explained to the press that last night's ah . . ."

"Fiasco."

"—affair was necessary in order to place the culprits in an untenable position. Of course, as to the destruction of the VIP vessel and the presumed death of the fellow, Slop—"

"The Fustians understand," Retief said. "Whonk wasn't kidding about ceremonial vengeance. Yith was lucky: he hadn't actually drawn blood. Then no amount of dickering would have saved him."

"The Groaci have been guilty of gross misuse of diplomatic privilege," Magnan said. "I think that a note—or perhaps an *aide memoire*: less formal . . ."

"The *Moss Rock* was bound for Groac," Retief said. "She was already in her transit orbit when she blew. The major fragments should arrive on schedule in a month or so. It should provide quite a meteorite display. I think that should be all the aid the Groaci's *memoires* will need to keep their tentacles off Fust."

"But diplomatic usage—"

"Then, too, the less that's put in writing, the less they can blame you for, if anything goes wrong."

"There's that, of course," Magnan said, his lips pursed. "Now you're thinking constructively, Retief. We may make a diplomat of you yet." He smiled expansively.

"Maybe. But I refuse to let it depress me." Retief stood up. "I'm taking a few weeks off . . . if you have no objections, Mr. Ambassador. My pal Whonk wants to show me an island down south where the fishing is good."

"But there are some extremely important matters coming up," Magnan said. "We're planning to sponsor Senior Citizen Groups."

"Count me out. Groups give me an itch."

"Why, what an astonishing remark, Retief. After all, we diplomats are ourselves a group."

"Uh, huh," Retief said. "That's what I mean."

Magnan sat quietly, his mouth open, and watched as Retief stepped into the hall and closed the door gently behind him.